LIBRARY OF SOULS

THE THIRD NOVEL OF

MISS PEREGRINE'S

PECULIAR CHILDREN

BY RANSOM RIGGS

QUIRK BOOKS
PHILADELPHIA

First paperback edition, Quirk Books, 2017.
Originally published by Quirk Books in 2015.

Library of Congress Cataloging in Publication Number: 2015939051 (hardcover edition)

ISBN: 978-1-59474-931-5

Printed in the United States of America
Typeset in Sabon, Belwe, and Dear Sarah

Cover design by Doogie Horner
Cover photograph courtesy of John Van Noate
Full image credits on page 461
Production management by John J. McGurk

Quirk Books
215 Church Street
Philadelphia, PA 19106
quirkbooks.com

10 9 8 7 6 5

FOR MY MOTHER

The ends of the earth, the depths of
the sea, the darkness of time,
you have chosen all three.

—E. M. Forster

GLOSSARY OF
PECULIAR TERMS

PECULIARS   The hidden branch of any species, human or animal, that is blessed—and cursed—with supernormal traits. Respected in ancient times, feared and persecuted more recently, peculiars are outcasts who live in the shadows.

LOOP   A limited area in which a single day is repeated endlessly. Created and maintained by ymbrynes to shelter their peculiar wards from danger, loops delay indefinitely the aging of their inhabitants. But loop dwellers are by no means immortal: each day they "skip" is a debt that's banked away, to be repaid in gruesome rapid aging should they linger too long outside their loop.

YMBRYNES   The shape-shifting matriarchs of peculiardom. They can change into birds at will, manipulate time, and are charged with the protection of peculiar children. In the Old Peculiar language, the word *ymbryne* (pronounced *imm-brinn*) means "revolution" or "circuit."

HOLLOWGAST Monstrous ex-peculiars who hunger for the souls of their former brethren. Corpselike and withered except for their muscular jaws, within which they harbor powerful, tentacle-like tongues. Especially dangerous because they're invisible to all but a few peculiars, of whom Jacob Portman is the only one known alive. (His late grandfather was another.) Until a recent innovation enhanced their abilities, hollows could not enter loops, which is why loops have been the preferred home of peculiars.

WIGHTS A hollowgast that consumes enough peculiar souls becomes a wight, which are visible to all and resemble normals in every way but one: their pupil-less, perfectly white eyes. Brilliant, manipulative, and skilled at blending in, wights have spent years infiltrating both normal and peculiar society. They could be anyone: your grocer, your bus driver, your psychiatrist. They've waged a long campaign of murder, fear, and kidnapping against peculiars, using hollowgast as their monstrous assassins. Their ultimate goal is to exact revenge upon, and take control of, peculiardom.

CHAPTER ONE

*T*he monster stood not a tongue's length away, eyes fixed on our throats, shriveled brain crowded with fantasies of murder. Its hunger for us charged the air. Hollows are born lusting after the souls of peculiars, and here we were arrayed before it like a buffet: bite-sized Addison bravely standing his ground at my feet, tail at attention; Emma moored against me for support, still too dazed from the impact to make more than a match flame; our backs laddered against the wrecked phone booth. Beyond our grim circle, the underground station looked like the aftermath of a nightclub bombing. Steam from burst pipes shrieked forth in ghostly curtains. Splintered monitors swung brokennecked from the ceiling. A sea of shattered glass spread all the way to the tracks, flashing in the hysterical strobe of red emergency lights like an acre-wide disco ball. We were boxed in, a wall hard to one side and glass shin-deep on the other, two strides from a creature whose only natural instinct was to disassemble us—and yet it made no move to close the gap. It seemed rooted to the floor, swaying on its heels like a drunk or a sleepwalker, death's head drooping, its tongues a nest of snakes I'd charmed to sleep.

Me. I'd done that. Jacob Portman, boy nothing from Nowhere, Florida. It was not currently murdering us—this horror made of gathered dark and nightmares harvested from sleeping children— because I had asked it not to. Told it in no uncertain terms to unwrap its tongue from around my neck. *Back off*, I'd said. *Stand*, I'd said— in a language made of sounds I hadn't known a human mouth could make—and miraculously it had, eyes challenging me while its body obeyed. Somehow I had tamed the nightmare, cast a spell over it. But sleeping things wake and spells wear off, especially those cast by accident, and beneath its placid surface I could feel the hollow boiling.

Addison nudged my calf with his nose. "More wights will be coming. Will the beast let us pass?"

"Talk to it again," Emma said, her voice woozy and vague. "Tell it to sod off."

I searched for the words, but they'd gotten shy. "I don't know how."

"You did a minute ago," Addison said. "It sounded like there was a demon inside you."

A minute ago, before I'd known I could do it, the words had been right there on my tongue, just waiting to be spoken. Now that I wanted them back, it was like trying to catch fish with bare hands. Every time I touched one, it slipped out of my grasp.

Go away! I shouted.

The words came in English. The hollow didn't move. I stiffened my back, glared into its inkpot eyes, and tried again.

Get out of here! Leave us alone!

English again. The hollow tilted its head like a curious dog but was otherwise a statue.

"Is he gone?" Addison asked.

The others couldn't tell for sure; only I could see it. "Still there," I said. "I don't know what's wrong."

I felt silly and deflated. Had my gift vanished so quickly?

"Never mind," Emma said. "Hollows aren't meant to be reasoned with, anyway." She stuck out a hand and tried to light a flame, but it fizzled. The effort seemed to sap her. I tightened my grip around her waist lest she topple over.

"Save your strength, matchstick," said Addison. "I'm sure we'll need it."

"I'll fight it with cold hands if I have to," said Emma. "All that matters is we find the others before it's too late."

The others. I could see them still, their afterimage fading by the tracks: Horace's fine clothes a mess; Bronwyn's strength no match for the wights' guns; Enoch dizzy from the blast; Hugh using the chaos to pull off Olive's heavy shoes and float her away; Olive caught by the heel and yanked down before she could rise out of reach. All of them weeping in terror, kicked onto the train at gunpoint, gone. Gone with the ymbryne we'd nearly killed ourselves to find, hurtling now through London's guts toward a fate worse than death. *It's already too late*, I thought. It was too late the moment Caul's soldiers stormed Miss Wren's frozen hideout. It was too late the night we mistook Miss Peregrine's wicked brother for our beloved ymbryne. But I swore to myself that we'd find our friends and our ymbryne, no matter the cost, even if there were only bodies to recover—even if it meant adding our own to the pile.

So, then: somewhere in the flashing dark was an escape to the street. A door, a staircase, an escalator, way off against the far wall. But how to reach them?

Get the hell out of our way! I shouted at the hollow, giving it one last try.

English, naturally. The hollow grunted like a cow but didn't move. It was no use. The words were gone.

"Plan B," I said. "It won't listen to me, so we go around it, hope it stays put."

"Go around it where?" said Emma.

To give it a wide berth, we'd have to wade through heaps of glass—but the shards would slice Emma's bare calves and Addison's paws to ribbons. I considered alternatives: I could carry the dog, but that still left Emma. I could find a swordlike piece of glass and stab the thing in the eyes—a technique that had served me well in the past—but if I didn't manage to kill it with the first strike, it would surely snap awake and kill us instead. The only other way around it was through a small, glass-free gap between the hollow and the wall.

It was narrow, though—a foot, maybe a foot and a half wide. A tight squeeze even if we flattened our backs to the wall. I worried that getting so close to the hollow, or worse, touching it by accident, would break the fragile trance holding it in check. Short of growing wings and flying over its head, though, it seemed like our only option.

"Can you walk a little?" I asked Emma. "Or at least hobble?"

She locked her knees and loosened her grip on my waist, testing her weight. "I can limp."

"Then here's what we're going to do: slide past it, backs to the wall, through that gap there. It's not a lot of space, but if we're careful . . . "

Addison saw what I meant and shrank back into the phone booth. "Do you think we should get so close to it?"

"Probably not."

"What if it wakes up while we're . . . ?"

"It won't," I said, faking confidence. "Just don't make any sudden moves—and whatever you do, don't touch it."

"You're our eyes now," Addison said. "Bird preserve us."

I chose a nice long shard from the floor and slid it into my pocket. Shuffling two steps to the wall, we pressed our backs to the cold tiles and began inching toward the hollow. Its eyes moved as we did, locked on me. A few creeping sidesteps later and we were enveloped by a pocket of hollow-stink so foul, it made my eyes water. Addison coughed and Emma cupped a hand over her nose.

"Just a little farther," I said, my voice reedy with forced calm. I took the glass from my pocket, gripping it with the pointed end out, then took another step, and another. We were close enough now that I could've touched the hollow with an outstretched arm. I heard its heart knocking inside its ribs, the beat quickening with each step we took. It was straining against me, fighting with every neuron to wrest my clumsy hands from its controls. *Don't move*, I said, mouthing the words in English. *You're mine. I control you. Don't move.*

I sucked in my chest, lined up and laddered each vertebra

against the wall, then crab-walked into the tight gap between the wall and the hollow.

Don't move, don't move.

Slide, shuffle, slide. I held my breath while the hollow's quickened, wet and wheezing, a vile black mist blooming from its nostrils. The urge to devour us must've been excruciating. So was my urge to run, but I ignored it; that would've been acting like prey, not master.

Don't move. Do not move.

Another few steps, a few more feet, and we'd be past it. Its shoulder a hairsbreadth from my chest.

Don't—

—and then it did. In one swift motion the hollow swiveled its head and pivoted its body to face me.

I went rigid. "Don't move," I said, this time aloud, to the others. Addison buried his face between his paws and Emma froze, her arm squeezing mine like a vise. I steeled myself for what was to come—its tongues, its teeth, the end.

Get back, get back, get back.

English, English, English.

Seconds passed during which, astonishingly, we weren't killed. But for the rising and falling of its chest, the creature seemingly had turned once again to stone.

Experimentally, moving by millimeters, I slid along the wall. The hollow followed me with slight turns of its head—locked onto me like a compass needle, its body in perfect sympathy with mine—but it didn't follow, didn't open its jaws. If whatever spell I'd cast had been broken, we'd already be dead.

The hollow was only watching me. Awaiting instructions I didn't know how to give. "False alarm," I said, and Emma breathed an audible sigh of relief.

We slid out of the gap, peeled ourselves from the wall, and hurried away as fast as Emma could limp. When we'd put a little distance between us and the hollow, I looked back. It had turned all the way around to face me.

Stay, I muttered in English. *Good.*

* * *

We passed through a veil of steam and the escalator came into view, frozen into stairs, its power cut. Around it glowed a halo of weak daylight, a tantalizing envoy from the world above. World of the living, world of now. A world where I had parents. They were here, both of them, in London, breathing this air. A stroll away.

Oh, hi there!

Unthinkable. Still more unthinkable: not five minutes ago, I'd told my father everything. The Cliff's Notes version, anyway: *I'm like Grandpa Portman was. I'm peculiar.* They wouldn't understand, but at least now they knew. It would make my absence feel less like a betrayal. I could still hear my father's voice, begging me to come home, and as we limped toward the light I had to fight a sudden, shameful urge to shake off Emma's arm and run for it—to escape this suffocating dark, to find my parents and beg forgiveness, and then to crawl into their posh hotel bed and sleep.

That was most unthinkable of all. I could never: I loved Emma, and I'd told her so, and I wouldn't leave her behind for anything. And not because I was noble or brave or chivalrous. I'm not any of those things. I was afraid that leaving her behind would rip me in half.

And the others, the others. Our poor, doomed friends. We had to go after them—but how? A train hadn't entered the station since the one that spirited them away, and after the blast and gunshots that had rocked the place, I was sure there'd be no more coming. That left us two options, each one terrible: go after them on foot through the tunnels and hope we didn't meet any more hollows, or climb the escalator and face whatever was waiting for us up there— most likely a wight mop-up crew—then regroup, reassess.

I knew which option I preferred. I'd had enough of the dark, and more than enough of hollows.

"Let's go up," I said, urging Emma toward the stalled escalator. "We'll find somewhere safe to plan our next move while you get your strength back."

"Absolutely not!" she said. "We can't just abandon the others. Never mind how I feel."

"We aren't. But we need to be realistic. We're hurt and defenseless, and the others are probably miles away by now, out of the underground and halfway to somewhere else. How will we even find them?"

"The same way I found you," said Addison. "With my nose. Peculiar folk have an aroma all their own, you see—one which only dogs of my persuasion can sniff out. And you happen to be one powerfully odoriferous group of peculiars. Fear enhances it, I think, and skipping baths . . . "

"Then we go after them!" Emma said.

She pulled me toward the tracks with a surprising burst of strength. I resisted, tug-of-warring our linked arms. "No, no—there's no way the trains are still running, and if we go in there on foot . . . "

"I don't care if it's dangerous. I won't leave them."

"It isn't just dangerous, it's pointless. They're already gone, Emma."

She took back her arm and started hobbling toward the tracks. Stumbled, caught herself. *Say something*, I mouthed to Addison, and he circled around to block her.

"I'm afraid he's right. If we follow on foot, our friends' scent trail will have dissipated long before we're able to find them. Even my profound abilities have limits."

Emma gazed into the tunnel, then back at me, her expression tortured. I held out my hand. "Please, let's go. It doesn't mean we're giving up."

"All right," she said heavily. "All right."

But just as we were starting toward the escalator, someone called out from the dark, back along the tracks.

"Over here!"

The voice was weak but familiar, the accent Russian. It was the folding man. Peering into the dark, I could just make out his crumpled form by the tracks, one arm raised. He'd been shot during the melee, and I assumed the wights had shoved him onto the train with the others. But there he lay, waving to us.

"Sergei!" cried Emma.

"You know him?" Addison said suspiciously.

"He was one of Miss Wren's peculiar refugees," I said, my ears pricking at the wail of distant sirens echoing down from the surface. Trouble was coming—maybe trouble disguised as help—and I worried that our best chance at a clean exit was slipping away. Then again, we couldn't just leave him.

Addison scuttled toward the man, dodging the deepest reefs of glass. Emma let me take her arm again and we shuffled after. Sergei was lying on his side, covered in glass and streaked with blood. The bullet had hit him somewhere vital. His wire-framed spectacles were cracked and he was adjusting them, trying to get a good look at me. "Is miracle, is miracle," he rasped, his voice thin as twice-strained tea. "I heard you speak with monster's tongue. Is miracle."

"It's not," I said, kneeling beside him. "It's gone, I've already lost it."

"If gift inside you, is forever."

Footsteps and voices echoed from the escalator passage. I cleared away glass so I could get my hands under the folding man. "We're taking you with us," I said.

"Leave me," he croaked. "I'll be gone soon enough . . ."

Ignoring him, I slipped my hands beneath his body and lifted. He was ladder-long but light as a feather, and I held him in my arms like a big baby, his skinny legs dangling over my elbow while his head lolled against my shoulder.

Two figures banged down the last few escalator steps and then stood at the bottom, rimmed by pale daylight and peering into the new dark. Emma pointed at the floor and we sank quietly to our knees, hoping they'd miss us—hoping they were just civilians come to catch a train—but then I heard the squelch of a walkie-talkie and they each fired up a flashlight, the beams shining against their bright reflective jackets.

They might've been emergency responders, or wights disguised as such. I wasn't sure until, in synchrony, they peeled off wraparound sunglasses.

Of course.

Our options had just narrowed by half. Now there were only the tracks, the tunnels. We could never outrun them, damaged as we were, but escape was still possible if they didn't see us—and they hadn't yet, amidst the chaos of the ruined station. Their searchlights dueled across the floor. Emma and I backed toward the tracks. If we could just slip into the tunnels unnoticed . . . but Addison, damn him, wasn't moving.

"Come on," I hissed.

"They are ambulance drivers and this man needs help," he said too loudly, and right away the beams of light bounced up from the floor and whipped toward us.

"Stay where you are!" one of the men boomed, unholstering a gun while the other fumbled for his walkie-talkie.

Then two unexpected things happened in quick succession. The first was that, just as I was about to drop the folding man onto the tracks and dive after him with Emma, a thunderous horn blew from inside the tunnel and a single brilliant headlight flashed into view. The rush of stale wind belonged, of course, to a train—running again, somehow, despite the blast. The second thing, announced by a painful twinge in my gut, was that the hollow had come unstuck and was loping in our direction. The instant after I felt it, I saw it, too, plowing at us through a billow of steam, black lips peeled wide, tongues thrashing the air.

We were trapped. If we ran for the stairs we'd be shot and mauled. If we jumped onto the tracks we'd be crushed by the train. And we couldn't escape onto the train because it would be ten seconds at least before it stopped and twelve before the doors opened and ten more before they shut again, and by then we'd be dead three ways. And so I did as I often do when I'm out of ideas—I looked to Emma. I could read in the desperation on her face that she understood the hopelessness of our situation and in the stony set of her jaw that she meant to act anyway. I remembered only as she began to stagger forward, palms out, that she couldn't see the hollow, and I tried to tell her, reach for her, stop her, but I couldn't get the words out and couldn't grab her without dropping the folding man, and then Addison was alongside her, barking at the wight while Emma tried uselessly to make a flame—spark, spark, nothing, like a lighter low on juice.

The wight broke out laughing, pulled back the hammer of his gun, and aimed it at her. The hollowgast ran at me, howling in counterpoint to the squeal of train brakes behind me. That's when I knew the end had come and there was nothing I could do to stop it. At that moment something inside me relaxed, and as it did, the pain I felt whenever a hollow was near faded, too. That pain was like a high-pitched whine, and as it hushed, I discovered hidden beneath it another sound, a murmur at the edge of consciousness.

A *word*.

I dove for it. Wrapped both arms around it. Wound up and shouted it with all the force of a major league pitcher. *Him*, I said, in a language not my own. It was only one syllable but held volumes of meaning, and the moment it rattled from my throat, the result was instant. The hollow stopped running at me—stopped dead, skidding on its feet—then turned sharply to one side and lashed out a tongue that whipped across the platform and wrapped three times around the wight's leg. Knocked off balance, he fired a shot that caromed off the ceiling, and then he was flipped upside down and hauled thrashing and screaming into the air.

It took my friends a moment to realize what had happened. While they stood gaping and the other wight shouted into his walkie-talkie, I heard train doors whoosh open behind me.

Here was our moment.

"COME ON!" I shouted, and they did, Emma stumble-running and Addison tangling her feet and me trying to wedge the gangly and blood-slick folding man through the narrow doors until we all crashed together across the threshold into the train car.

More gunshots rang out, the wight firing blindly at the hollow.

The doors closed halfway, then popped back open. "Clear the doors, please," came a cheerful prerecorded announcement.

"His feet!" Emma said, pointing at the shoes at the end of the folding man's long legs, the toes of which were poking through the doors. I scrambled to kick his feet clear, and in the interminable seconds before the doors closed again, the dangling wight fired more wild shots until the hollow grew tired of him and flung him against the wall, where he slid to the floor in an unmoving heap.

The other wight scurried for the exit. *Him, too*, I tried to say, but it was too little too late. The doors were closing, and with an awkward jolt the train began to move.

I looked around, grateful that the car we'd tumbled into was empty. What would regular people make of us?

"Are you okay?" I asked Emma. She was sitting up, breathing hard, studying me intensely.

"Thanks to you," she said. "Did you really make the hollow do all that?"

"I think so," I said, not quite believing it myself.

"That's amazing," she said quietly. I couldn't tell if she was frightened or impressed, or both.

"We owe you our lives," said Addison, nuzzling his head sweetly against my arm. "You're a very special boy."

The folding man laughed, and I looked down to see him grinning at me through a mask of pain. "You see?" he said. "I told you. Is miracle." Then his face turned serious. He grabbed my hand and pressed a small square of paper into it. A photograph. "My wife, my child," he said. "Taken by our enemy long ago. If you find others, perhaps . . . "

I glanced at the photo and got a shock. It was a wallet-sized portrait of a woman holding a baby. Sergei had clearly been carrying it with him a long time. Though the people in the photo were pleasant enough, the photo itself—or the negative—had been seriously damaged, perhaps narrowly survived a fire, exposed to such heat that the faces were warped and fragmented. Sergei had never mentioned his family before now; all he'd talked about since we met him was raising an army of peculiars—going loop to loop to recruit able-bodied survivors of the raids and purges. He never told us what he wanted an army *for*: to get them back.

"We'll find them, too," I said.

We both knew this was far-fetched, but it was what he needed to hear.

"Thank you," he said, and relaxed into a spreading pool of blood.

"He doesn't have long," Addison said, moving to lick Sergei's face.

"I might have enough heat to cauterize the wound," said Emma. Scooting toward him, she began rubbing her hands together.

Addison nosed the folding man's shirt near his abdomen. "Here. He's hurt here." Emma put her hands on either side of the spot, and at the sizzle of flesh I stood up, feeling faint.

I looked out the window. We were still pulling out of the station, slowed perhaps by debris on the tracks. The emergency lights' SOS flicker picked details from the dark at random. The body of a dead wight half buried in glass. The crumpled phone booth, scene of my breakthrough. The hollow—I registered its form with a shock—trotting on the platform alongside us, a few cars back, casual as a jogger.

Stop. Stay away, I spat at the window, in English. My head wasn't clear, the hurt and the whine getting in the way again.

We picked up speed and passed into the tunnel. I pressed my face to the glass, angling backward for another glimpse. It was dark, dark—and then, in a burst of light like a camera flash, I saw the hollow as a momentary still image—flying, its feet lifting from the platform, tongues lassoing the rail of the last car.

Miracle. Curse. I hadn't quite worked out the difference.

*   *   *

I took his legs and Emma his arms and gently we lifted Sergei onto a long bench seat, where beneath an advertisement for bake-at-home pizza he lay blacked out and rocking with the motion of the train. If he was going to die, it seemed wrong that he should have to do so on the floor.

Emma pulled up his thin shirt. "The bleeding's stopped," she reported, "but he'll die if he doesn't see the inside of a hospital soon."

"He may die anyway," said Addison. "Especially in a hospital here in the present. Imagine: he wakes up in three days' time, side healed but everything else failing, aged two hundred and bird-knows-what."

"That may be," Emma replied. "Then again, I'll be surprised if in three days' time any of us are alive, in any condition whatsoever. I'm not sure what more we can do for him."

I'd heard them mention this deadline before: two or three days was the longest any peculiar who'd lived in a loop could stay in the present without aging forward. It was long enough for them to visit the present but never to stay; long enough to travel between loops but short enough that they were never tempted to linger. Only dare-devils and ymbrynes made excursions into the present longer than a few hours; the consequences of a delay were too grave.

Emma rose, looking sickly in the pale yellow light, then tot-tered on her feet and grabbed for one of the train's stanchions. I took her hand and made her sit next to me, and she slumped against my side, exhausted beyond measure. We both were. I hadn't slept properly in days. Hadn't eaten properly, either, aside from the few opportunities we'd had to gorge ourselves like pigs. I'd been running and terrified and wearing these damned blister-making shoes since I couldn't remember when, but more than that, every time I spoke Hollow it seemed to carve something out of me that I didn't know how to put back. It made me feel tired to a degree that was wholly new, absolutely subterranean. I'd discovered a fresh vein inside me, a new source of power to mine, but it was depletable and finite, and I wondered if by using it up I was using myself up, too.

I'd worry about that another time. For now I tried to savor a rare moment of peace, my arm around Emma and her head on my shoulder, just breathing. Selfishly, perhaps, I didn't mention the hol-low that had chased our train. What could any of us do about it? It would either catch us or not. Kill us or not. The next time it found us—and I was sure there would be a next time—I would either find the words to stay its tongues or I wouldn't.

I watched Addison hop onto the seat across from us, unlock a window with his paw, and crack it open. The angry sound of the train and a warm funk of tunnel air came rushing in, and he sat reading it with his nose, eyes bright and snout twitching. The air smelled like stale sweat and dry rot to me, but he seemed to catch something subtler, something that required careful interpretation.

"Can you smell them?" I asked.

The dog heard me but took a long moment to reply, his eyes aimed at the ceiling as if finishing a thought. "I can," he said. "Their trail is nice and crisp, too."

Even at this high speed, he could pick up the minutes-old traces of peculiars who'd been enclosed in an earlier train car. I was impressed, and told him so.

"Thank you, but I can't take all the credit," he said. "Someone must've pushed open a window in their car, too, otherwise the trail would be much fainter. Perhaps Miss Wren did it, knowing I would try to follow."

"She knew you were here?" I asked.

"How did you find us?" Emma said.

"Just a moment," Addison said sharply. The train was slowing into a station, the windows flashing from tunnel black to tile white. He stuck his nose out the window and closed his eyes, lost in concentration. "I don't think they got off here, but be ready in any case."

Emma and I stood, doing our best to shield the folding man from view. I saw with some relief that there weren't many people waiting on the platform. Funny there were any at all, or that trains were still running. It was as if nothing had happened. The wights had made sure of it, I suspected, in hopes we'd take the bait, jump onto a train, and make it simple for them to round us up. We certainly wouldn't be hard to spot amongst modern London's workday commuters.

"Look casual," I said. "Like you belong here."

This seemed to strike Emma as funny, and she stifled a laugh. It was funny, I guess, inasmuch as we belonged nowhere in particular, least of all here.

The train stopped and the doors slid open. Addison sniffed the air deeply as a bookish woman in a pea coat stepped into our car. Seeing us, her mouth fell open, and then she turned smartly and walked out again. *Nope. No thanks.* I couldn't blame her. We were filthy, freakish-looking in bizarre old clothes, and splashed with blood. We probably looked like we'd just killed the poor man beside us.

"Look casual," Emma said, and snorted.

Addison withdrew his nose from the window. "We're on the right track," he said. "Miss Wren and the others definitely passed this way."

"They didn't get off here?" I asked.

"I don't think so. But if I don't smell them in the next station, we'll know we've gone too far."

The doors smacked closed and with an electric whine we were off again. I was about to suggest we find a change of clothes when Emma jolted beside me, as if she'd just remembered something.

"Addison?" she said. "What happened to Fiona and Claire?"

At the mention of their names, a nauseating new wave of worry shot through me. We'd last seen them at Miss Wren's menagerie, where the elder girl had stayed behind with Claire, who was too ill to travel. Caul told us he'd raided the menagerie and captured the girls, but he also told us Addison was dead, so clearly his information couldn't be trusted.

"Ah," said Addison, nodding gravely. "It's bad news, I'm afraid. Part of me, I admit, was hoping you wouldn't ask."

Emma's face drained of color. "Tell us."

"Of course," he said. "Shortly after your party left, we were raided by a gang of wights. We threw armageddon eggs at them, then scattered and hid. The larger girl, with the unkempt hair—"

"Fiona," I said, heart thudding.

"She used her facility with plants to hide us—in trees and under new-grown brush. We were so well camouflaged that it would've taken days for the wights to root us all out, but they gassed us and drove us into the open."

"Gas!" Emma cried. "The bastards swore they'd never use it again!"

"It appears they lied," said Addison.

I had seen a photo once, in one of Miss Peregrine's albums, of such an attack: wights in ghostly masks with breathing canisters, standing around casually as they launched clouds of poison gas into the air. Although the stuff wasn't fatal, it made your lungs and throat burn, caused terrible pain, and was rumored to trap ymbrynes in their bird form.

"When they'd rounded us up," Addison went on, "we were interrogated as to the whereabouts of Miss Wren. They turned her tower inside out—searching for maps, diaries, I don't know what—and when poor Deirdre tried to stop them, they shot her."

The emu-raffe's long face flashed before me, gawky, gap-toothed, and sweet, and my stomach lurched. What kind of person could kill such a creature? "God, that's awful," I said.

"Awful," Emma agreed perfunctorily. "And the girls?"

"The small one was captured by the wights," Addison said. "And the other . . . well, there was a scuffle with some of the soldiers, and they were near the cliff's edge, and she fell."

I blinked at him. "What?" For a moment the world blurred, then snapped back into focus.

Emma stiffened but her face betrayed nothing. "What do you mean, fell? Fell how far?"

"It was a sheer drop. A thousand feet at least." His fleshy jowls drooped. "I'm so sorry."

I sat down heavily. Emma kept standing, her hands white-knuckling the rail. "No," she said firmly. "No, that can't be. Perhaps she grabbed onto something on the way down. A branch or a ledge . . ."

Addison studied the gum-spackled floor. "It's possible."

"Or the trees below cushioned her fall and caught her like a net! She can speak to them, you know."

"Yes," he said. "One can always hope."

I tried to imagine being cushioned by a spiky pine tree after such a fall. It didn't seem possible. I saw the small hope Emma had kindled wink out, and then her legs began to tremble and she let go of the rail and thumped down onto the seat beside me.

She looked at Addison with wet eyes. "I'm sorry about your friend."

He nodded. "Same to you."

"None of this ever would've happened if Miss Peregrine were

here," she whispered. And then, quietly, she bowed her head and began to cry.

I wanted to put my arms around her, but somehow it felt like I'd be intruding on a private moment, claiming it for myself when really it was hers alone, so instead I sat and looked at my hands and let her mourn her lost friend. Addison turned away, out of respect, I think, and because the train was slowing into another station.

The doors opened. Addison stuck his head out the window, sniffed the air on the platform, growled at someone who tried to enter our car, then came back inside. By the time the doors closed again, Emma had lifted her head and wiped away her tears.

I squeezed her hand. "Are you all right?" I said, wishing I could think of something more or better to say than that.

"I have to be, don't I?" she said. "For the ones who are still alive."

To some it might've seemed callous, the way she boxed up her pain and set it aside, but I knew her well enough now to understand. She had a heart the size of France, and the lucky few whom she loved with it were loved with every square inch—but its size made it dangerous, too. If she let it feel everything, she'd be wrecked. So she had to tame it, shush it, shut it up. Float the worst pains off to an island that was quickly filling with them, where she would go to live one day.

"Go on," she said to Addison. "What happened to Claire?"

"The wights marched off with her. Gagged her two mouths and tossed her into a sack."

"But she was alive?" I said.

"And biting, as of noon yesterday. Then we buried Deirdre in our little cemetery and I hightailed it for London to find Miss Wren and warn all of you. One of Miss Wren's pigeons led me to her hideaway, and while I was pleased to see that you had arrived before me, unfortunately so had the wights. Their siege had already begun, and I was forced to watch helplessly as they stormed the building, and—well, you know the rest. I followed as you were led away to the underground. When that blast went off, I saw an opportunity to aid you and took it."

"Thank you for that," I said, realizing we hadn't yet acknowledged the debt we owed him. "If you hadn't dragged us away when you did . . . "

"Yes, well . . . no need to dwell on hypothetical unpleasantries," he said. "But in return for my gallantry, I was rather hoping you would assist me in rescuing Miss Wren from the wights. As unlikely as that sounds. She means everything to me, you see."

It was Miss Wren he'd wanted to snatch away from the wights, not us—but we were the realistic save, farther from the train, and he'd made a snap decision and taken what he could get.

"Of course we'll help," I said. "Isn't that what we're doing now?"

"Yes, yes," he said. "But you must realize, as an ymbryne, Miss Wren is more valuable to the wights than peculiar children, and thus she may prove more difficult to free. I worry that, if by some miracle we are lucky enough to rescue your friends . . . "

"Now *wait* a second," I snapped. "Who says she's more—"

"No, it's true," Emma said. "She'll be under heavier lock and key, no question. But we won't leave her behind. We're not leaving anyone else behind, ever again. You have our word as peculiars."

The dog seemed satisfied with that. "Thank you," he said, and then his ears flattened. He hopped up onto a seat to look out the window as we pulled into the next station. "Hide yourselves," he said, ducking down. "There are enemies near."

* * *

The wights were expecting us. I glimpsed two of them waiting on the platform, dressed as police officers among a scattering of commuters. They were scanning the cars as our train pulled into the station.

We dropped down below the windows, hoping they'd miss us—but I knew they wouldn't. The one with the walkie-talkie had radioed ahead; they must've known we were on this train. Now all they had to do was search it.

It came to a stop and people began filing on board, though not into our car. I risked a peek through the open doors and saw one of the wights down the platform, speed walking in our direction as he eyeballed each car.

"One's coming this way," I muttered. "How's your fire, Em?"

"Running on empty," she replied.

He was getting close. Four cars away. Three.

"Then get ready to run."

Two cars away. Then a soft, recorded voice: "Mind the closing doors, please."

"Hold the train!" the wight shouted. But the doors were already closing.

He stuck an arm through. The doors bounced open again. He got on board—into the car next to ours.

My eyes went to the door that connected our cars. It was locked with a chain—thank God for small mercies. The doors snicked shut and the train began to move. We shifted the folding man onto the floor and huddled with him in a spot where we couldn't be seen from the wight's car.

"What can we do?" said Emma. "The moment this train stops again, he'll come straight in here and find us."

"Are we absolutely certain he's a wight?" asked Addison.

"Do cats grow on trees?" Emma replied.

"Not in this part of the world."

"Then of course we aren't. But when it comes to wights, there's an old saying: if you're not sure, assume."

"Okay, then," I said. "The second those doors open, we run for the exit."

Addison sighed. "All this *fleeing*," he said disdainfully, as if he were a gourmand and someone had offered him a limp square of American cheese. "There's no imagination in it. Mightn't we try *sneaking*? Blending in? There's artistry in that. Then we could simply walk away, gracefully, unnoticed."

"I hate fleeing as much as anyone," I said, "but Emma and I look like nineteenth-century axe murderers, and you're a dog who wears glasses. We're bound to be noticed."

"Until they start manufacturing canine contact lenses, I'm stuck with these," Addison grumbled.

"Where's that hollowgast when you need him?" said Emma offhandedly.

"Run over by a train, if we're lucky," I said. "And what do you mean by that?"

"Only that he came in quite handy earlier."

"And before that he nearly killed us—twice! No, three times! Whatever it is I've been doing to control it has been half by accident, and the moment I'm *not* able to? We're dead."

Emma didn't respond right away, but studied me for a moment and then took my hand, all caked in grime, and kissed it gently, once, twice.

"What was that for?" I said, surprised.

"You have no idea, do you?"

"Of what?"

"How completely miraculous you are."

Addison groaned.

"You have an amazing talent," Emma whispered. "I'm certain all you need is a little practice."

"Maybe. But practicing something usually means failing at it for a while, and failing at this means people get killed."

Emma squeezed my hand. "Well, there's nothing like a little pressure to help you hone a new skill."

I tried to smile but couldn't muster one. My heart hurt too much at the thought of all the damage I could cause. This thing I could do felt like a loaded weapon I didn't know how to use. Hell, I didn't even know which end to point away from me. Better to set it down than have it blow up in my hands.

We heard a noise at the other end of the car and looked up to see the door opening. That one wasn't chained, and now a pair of leather-clad teenagers stumbled into our car, a boy and a girl, laughing and passing a lit cigarette between them.

"We'll get in trouble!" the girl said, kissing his neck.

The boy brushed a foppish wave of hair from his eyes—"I do this all the time, sweetheart"—then saw us and froze, his eyebrows parabolic. The door they'd come through banged closed behind them.

"Hey," I said casually, as if we weren't crouched on the floor with a dying man, covered in blood. "What's up?"

Don't freak out. Don't give us away.

The boy wrinkled his brow. "Are you . . . ?"

"In costume," I replied. "Got carried away with the fake blood."

"Oh," said the boy, clearly not believing me.

The girl stared at the folding man. "Is he . . . ?"

"Drunk," said Emma. "Soused out of his brain. Which is how he came to spill all our fake blood on the floor. And himself."

"And us," said Addison. The teens' heads snapped toward him, their eyes going wider still.

"You goon," Emma muttered. "Keep quiet."

The boy raised a trembling hand and pointed at the dog. "Did he just . . . ?"

Addison had said only two words. We might've played it off as a trick of echoes, something other than what it seemed, but he was too proud to play dumb.

"Of course I didn't," he said, raising his nose in the air. "Dogs can't speak English. Nor any human language—save, in one notable exception, Luxembourgish, which is only comprehensible to bankers and Luxembourgers, and therefore hardly of any use at all. No, you've eaten something disagreeable and are having a nightmare, that's all. Now, if you wouldn't mind terribly, my friends need to borrow your clothes. Please disrobe at once."

Pallid and shaking, the boy started to remove his leather jacket, but he'd only wriggled one arm free when his knees gave out and he fainted to the floor. And then the girl began to scream, and she didn't stop.

In an instant the wight was banging at the chained door, his blank eyes flashing murder.

"So much for sneaking away," I said.

Addison turned to look at him. "Definitely a wight," he said, nodding sagely.

"I'm so glad we put that mystery to rest," said Emma.

There was a jolt and a squeal of brakes. We were coming into a station. I pulled Emma to her feet and prepared to run.

"What about Sergei?" Emma said, whipping around to look back at him.

It would be hard enough to outrun a pair of wights with Emma still recovering her strength; with the folding man in my arms, it would be impossible.

"We'll have to leave him," I said. "He'll be found and brought to a doctor. It's his best chance—and ours."

Surprisingly, she agreed. "I think it's what he'd want." She went quickly to his side. "Sorry we can't take you with us. But I'm certain we'll meet again."

"In the next world," he croaked, his eyes slitting open. "In Abaton."

With those mysterious words and the girl's screams ringing in our ears, the train came to a stop and the doors opened.

*　　*　　*

We weren't clever. We weren't graceful. The moment the train doors slid open, we just ran as fast as we could.

The wight leapt out of his car and into ours, by which time we had dashed past the screaming girl, over the fainted boy, and onto the platform, where we struggled against a crowd that was streaming onto the train like a school of spawning fish. This station, unlike all the others, was heaving at the seams.

"There!" I shouted, pulling Emma toward a WAY OUT sign that glowed in the distance. I hoped Addison was somewhere at our feet, but so many people were flooding around us that I could hardly see the floor. Luckily, Emma's strength was returning—or a rush of adrenaline was kicking in—because I don't think I could've supported her weight and threaded the human stampede, too.

We'd put about twenty feet and fifty people between us and the train when the wight burst out of it, shoving commuters and yelling *I am an officer of the law!* and *Get out of my way!* and *Stop those children!* Either no one could hear him over the echoing din of the station or no one was paying attention. I looked back to see him gaining, and that's when Emma started tripping people, sweeping her legs left and right as we ran. People shouted and fell into tangles behind us, and when I looked back again the wight was struggling, stepping on legs and backs and getting swats with umbrellas and briefcases in return. Then he stopped, red-faced and frustrated, to unsnap his gun holster. But the gulf of people between us had yawned too wide now, and though I was sure he'd be heartless enough to fire into a crowd, he wasn't stupid enough to. The ensuing panic would've made us even more difficult to catch.

The third time I looked back he was so far behind and swallowed by the crowd that I could hardly see him. Maybe he didn't really care whether he caught us. After all, we were neither a great threat nor much of a prize. Maybe the dog had been right: compared to an ymbryne, we were hardly worth the trouble.

Halfway to the exits the crowd thinned enough for us to break into an open run—but we'd taken only a few strides when Emma caught me by the sleeve and stopped me. "Addison!" she cried, spinning to look around. "Where's Addison?"

A moment later he came scampering out of the thickest part of the crowd, a long piece of white fabric trailing from a spike on his collar. "You waited for me!" he said. "I became entangled in a lady's stocking . . . "

Heads turned at the sound of his voice.

"Come on, we can't stop now!" I said.

Emma plucked the stocking from Addison's collar, and we were off and running again. Before us were an escalator and an elevator. The escalator was working but very crowded, so I steered us toward the elevator instead. We ran past a lady painted blue from head to toe, and I had to turn and stare even as my legs carried me onward. Her hair was dyed blue, her face caked with blue makeup, and she wore a skin-tight jumpsuit, also blue.

She'd only just passed out of sight when I saw someone even more freakish: a man whose head was divided vertically into halves, one bald and burned to a crisp, the other untouched, hair moussed into a dapper wave. If Emma noticed him, she didn't turn to look. Maybe she was so used to meeting genuine peculiars that peculiar-looking normals hardly registered. *But what if they aren't normal?* I thought. *What if they're peculiars, and instead of the present we've ended up in some new loop? What if—*

Then I saw two boys with glowing swords battling by a wall of vending machines, each sabre clash sounding with a thin plasticky *thwack*, and reality came into sharp focus. These strange-looking people weren't peculiars. They were nerds. We were very much in the present.

Twenty feet away, the elevator doors opened. We poured on the speed and hurled ourselves inside, bouncing off the back wall with our hands while Addison tumbled in on tripping legs. I turned just in time to glimpse two things through the closing doors: the wight breaking out of the crowd and coming at us in a full run, and back by the tracks where the train was pulling away, the hollowgast leaping from the roof of the last car to the station ceiling, swinging like a spider from a light fixture by its tongues, its black eyes burning at me.

And then the doors closed and we were gliding gently upward, and someone was saying, "Where's the fire, mate?"

A middle-aged man stood in the rear corner of the elevator, costumed and sneering. His shirt was torn, his face was crosshatched with fake cuts, and strapped to the end of one arm, Captain Hook–style, was a bloodstained chainsaw.

Emma saw him and took a quick step back. "Who are you?"

He looked mildly offended. "Oh, come on."

"If you really want to know where the fire is, don't answer." She began to raise her hands, but I reached over and stopped her.

"He's no one," I said.

"I thought I was making such an obvious choice this year," the man muttered. He arched an eyebrow and raised his chainsaw a little. "Name's Ash. You know . . . *Army of Darkness*?"

"Never heard of either," said Emma. "Who's your ymbryne?"

"My what?"

"He's just doing a character," I tried to explain, but she wasn't hearing me.

"Never mind who you are," she said. "We could use an army, and beggars can't be choosers. Where are the rest of your men?"

The man rolled his eyes. "L-O-L. You guys are funny. Everyone's in the convention center, obviously."

"He's wearing a *costume*," I whispered to Emma. Then, to the guy: "She doesn't see a lot of movies."

"A costume?" Emma scrunched her brow. "But he's a grown man."

"So what?" the man said, looking us up and down. "And who are *you* supposed to be? Walking Dorks? League of Extraordinary

Dingleberries?"

"Peculiar children," said Addison, whose ego wouldn't allow him to be silent any longer. "And I am the seventh pup of the seventh pup in a long and illustrious line of—"

The man fainted before Addison could finish, his head knocking against the floor with a *clonk* that made me wince.

"You've *got* to stop doing that," Emma said, then grinned despite herself.

"Serves him right," said Addison. "What a rude person. Now quick, nick his wallet."

"No way!" I said. "We're not thieves."

Addison snorted. "I daresay we need it more than he does."

"Why on earth is he dressed like that?" said Emma.

The elevator dinged and the doors began to slide open.

"I think you're about to find out," I said.

*   *   *

The elevator doors split open and like magic the day-lit world spread before us, so bright we had to shield our eyes. I drew a welcome lungful of fresh air as we stepped out onto a swarming sidewalk. There were costumed people everywhere: superheroes in spandex, zombies shambling in heavy makeup, raccoon-eyed anime girls wielding battleaxes. They congregated in unlikely bunches and spilled into a street blocked off to traffic, drawn like moths to a large gray building where a banner proclaimed: COMIC CONVENTION TODAY!

Emma recoiled toward the elevator. "What *is* all this?"

Addison peered over his glasses at a green-haired Joker touching up his face paint. "Judging by their attire, it appears to be some sort of religious holiday."

"Something like that," I said, coaxing Emma back onto the sidewalk, "but don't be scared—they're only dressed-up normals, and that's what we look like to them, too. We only need to worry about that wight." I failed to mention the hollow, hoping we'd baffled it by vanishing into the elevator. "We should find a place to hide until he's gone, then sneak back into the Underground . . . "

"No need for that," Addison said, and he trotted into the crowded street, nose twitching.

"Hey!" Emma called after him. "Where are you going?"

But he was already circling back.

"Huzzah for fortune!" he said, wagging his stubby tail. "My nose tells me our friends were brought out of the underground here, via that escalator. We've gone the right way after all!"

"Thank the birds!" Emma said.

"Do you think you can follow their trail?" I asked.

"Do I *think* I can? They don't call me Addison the Astounding for nothing! Why, there isn't an aroma, a redolence, a peculiar eau de toilette I couldn't nose from a hundred meters—"

Addison was easily distracted by the topic of his own greatness, even when pressing matters were at hand, and his proud, booming voice had a tendency to carry.

"Okay, we get it," I said, but he steamrolled on, walking now, following his nose.

" . . . I could find a peculiar in a hollow-stack, an ymbryne in an aviary . . . "

We chased him into the costumed crowd, between the legs of a dwarf on stilts, around a pack of undead princesses, and on a near-collision course with a Pikachu and an Edward Scissorhands, who were waltzing in the street. *Of course our friends were brought this way,* I thought. It was perfect camouflage—not only for us, who amidst all this looked downright normal, but also for wights abducting a herd of peculiar children. Even if some of them had dared cry out for help, who would've taken them seriously enough to intervene? People were play-acting all around us, improvising staged fights, growling in monstrous costumes, moaning like zombies. Some strange kids yelling about being kidnapped by people who wanted to steal their souls? Wouldn't raise an eyebrow.

Addison walked a circle sniffing the ground, then sat down, perplexed. Subtly, because even in this crowd a talking dog would be shocking, I bent down and asked him what was the matter.

"It's just . . . err," he stammered, "that I seem to have—"

"Lost the trail?" Emma said. "I thought your nose was infallible."

"I've merely *mislaid* the trail. But I don't understand how . . . it leads quite clearly to this spot, then vanishes."

"Tie your shoes," Emma said suddenly. "Now."

I looked down at them. "But they're not—"

She grabbed my forearm and yanked me down. "Tie. Your. Shoes," she repeated, then mouthed, *wight!*

We knelt there, hidden below the heads of the loose-knit crowd. Then came a burst of loud static and a strained voice through a walkie-talkie. "Code 141! All crews report to the acre immediately!"

The wight was close. We heard him reply in a gruff, oddly accented voice: "This is M. I'm tracking the escapees. Request permission to continue searching. Over."

I exchanged a tense look with Emma.

"Denied, M. Cleaners will sweep the area later. Over."

"The boy seems to have some influence over the cleaners. Sweep may not be effective."

Cleaners. He must've been talking about the hollows. And he was *definitely* talking about me.

"Denied!" said the crackling voice. "Report back immediately or you'll spend tonight in the pit, over!"

The wight muttered "Acknowledged" into his walkie-talkie and stalked away.

"We've got to follow him," Emma said. "He could lead us to the others!"

"And straight into the lion's den," Addison said. "Though I suppose that can't be helped."

I was still reeling. "They know who I am," I said faintly. "They must've seen what I did."

"That's right," Emma said. "And it scared the stuffing out of them!"

I unbent myself to watch the wight go. He marched through the crowd, hopped a traffic barricade, and jogged away toward a parked police car.

We followed him as far as the traffic barrier. I looked around, trying to imagine the kidnappers' next move. Behind us was the crowd, and in front, beyond the traffic barrier, cars prowled the block for parking. "Maybe our friends came this far on foot," I said, "then were put into a car."

Brightening, Addison stood on hind legs to peek over the traffic barrier. "Yes! That must be it. Bright boy!"

"What are you so cheerful for?" said Emma. "If they were taken away in a car, they could be anywhere by now!"

"Then we'll *follow* them anywhere," Addison said pointedly. "Though I doubt they're terribly far. My old master had a town-house not far from here, and I know this part of the city well. There are no major ports nor obvious points of exit from London nearby— but there *are* a few loop entrances. It's much more likely that they've been taken to one of those. Now lift me up!"

I did, and with my help he scrambled over the barrier and began to sniff around the other side. Within seconds he'd found our friends' scent trail again. "This way!" he said, pointing down the street after the wight, who'd gotten into the police car and was driving away.

"Looks like we're in for a walk," I said to Emma. "Think you can make it?"

"I'll manage," she said, "so as long as we find another loop within a few hours. Otherwise I may start sprouting gray hairs and crow's feet." She smiled, as if this were something to joke about.

"I won't let that happen," I said.

We jumped the barricade. I took one last look at the Underground station behind us.

"Do you see the hollow?" said Emma.

"No. I don't know where it is. And that worries me."

"Let's worry about one thing at a time," she said.

*   *   *

We walked as fast as Emma could manage, keeping to the side of the street still sunk in morning shadow, watching for police and following Addison's nose. We passed into an industrial area near the docks, the River Thames revealing itself darkly between the gaps in warehouses, then into a fancy shopping district where glittering stores were crowned with glassy townhouses. Over their roofs I caught glimpses of the dome of St. Paul's Cathedral, whole again, the sky around it clear and blue. The bombs had all been dropped and the bombers were long gone—shot down, scrapped, retired into museums where they gathered dust behind ropes, to be gawked at by schoolchildren for whom that war seemed as distant as the Crusades. To me it was, quite literally, yesterday. Hard to believe these were the same cratered, blacked-out streets through which we'd run for our lives only last night. They were unrecognizable now, shopping malls seemingly conjured from the ashes—and so were the people who walked them, heads down, glued to phones, clothed in logos. The present seemed suddenly strange to me, so trivial and distracted. I felt like one of those mythical heroes who fights his way back from the underworld only to realize that the world above is every bit as damned as the one below.

And then it hit me—*I was back*. I was in the present again, and I'd crossed into it without the intervention of Miss Peregrine . . . which was supposed to be impossible.

"Emma?" I said. "How did I get here?"

She kept her eyes trained on the street ahead, always scanning for trouble. "Where, London? On a train, silly."

"No." I lowered my voice. "I mean to *now*. You said Miss Peregrine was the only one who could send me back."

She turned to glance at me, eyes narrowing. "Yes," she said slowly. "She was."

"Or so you thought."

"No—she was, I'm sure of it. That's how it works."

"Then how did I get here?"

She looked lost. "I don't know, Jacob. Maybe . . . "

"There!" Addison said excitedly, and we broke off wondering to look. His body was rigid, pointing down the street we'd just turned onto. "I'm picking up dozens of peculiar scent trails now—dozens upon dozens—and they're fresh!"

"Which means what?" I said.

"Other kidnapped peculiars were brought this way, not just our friends," said Emma. "The wights' hideout must be close by."

"Close by *here*?" I said. The block was lined with fast food joints and tacky souvenir shops, and we stood framed in the neon-lit window of a greasy diner. "I guess I'd been imagining someplace . . . *eviller.*"

"Like a dungeon in some dank castle," Emma said, nodding.

"Or a concentration camp surrounded by guards and barbed-wire fences," I said.

"In the snow. Like Horace's drawing."

"We may find such a place yet," said Addison. "Remember, this is likely just the entrance to a loop."

Across the street, tourists were taking pictures of themselves in front of one of the city's iconic red phone boxes. Then they noticed us and snapped a picture in our direction.

"Hey!" Emma said. "No photos!"

People were beginning to stare. No longer surrounded by comic conventioneers, we stuck out like sore, bloody thumbs.

"Follow me," Addison hissed. "All the trails lead this way."

We hurried after him down the block.

"If only Millard were here," I said, "he could scout this place without being noticed."

"Or if Horace were here, he might remember a dream that would help us," Emma said.

"Or find us new clothes," I added.

"If we don't stop, I'll cry," Emma said.

We came to a jetty bustling with activity. Sun glinted off the water, a narrow inlet of the murky Thames, and clumps of tourists in visors and fanny packs waddled onto and off of several large boats, each offering more or less identical sightseeing tours of London.

Addison stopped. "They were brought here," he said. "It would appear they were put onto a boat."

We followed his nose through the crowd to an empty boat slip. The wights had indeed loaded our friends onto a boat, and now we needed to follow them—but in what? We walked around the jetty looking for a ride.

"This will never do," Emma grumbled. "These boats are too large and crowded. We need a small one—something we can pilot ourselves."

"Wait a moment," said Addison, his snout twitching. He trotted away, nose to the wooden boards. We followed him across the jetty and down a little unmarked ramp that was ignored by the tourists. It led to a lower dock, below the street, just at water level. There was no one around; it was deserted.

Here Addison stopped, wearing a look of deep concentration. "Peculiars have come this way."

"*Our* peculiars?" Emma said.

He sniffed the dock again and shook his head. "Not ours. But there are many trails here, new and old, strong and faded, all mixed together. This is an oft-used pathway."

Ahead of us, the dock narrowed and disappeared beneath the main jetty, where it was swallowed in shadows.

"Oft used by whom?" Emma said, peering anxiously into the dark. "I've never heard of any loop entrance underneath a dock in Wapping."

Addison had no answer. There was nothing to do but forge on and explore, so we did, passing nervously into the shadows. As our eyes adjusted, another jetty resolved into view—one altogether different from the sunny, pleasant one above us. The boards down here were green and rotting, broken in places. A scrum of squeaking rats scampered through a mound of discarded cans, then leapt a short distance from the dock into an ancient-looking skiff, bobbing in the dark water between wooden pylons slimed with moss.

"Well," Emma said, "I guess that would do in a pinch . . . "

"But it's filled with rats!" said Addison, aghast.

"It won't be for long," Emma said, igniting a small flame in her hand. "Rats don't much care for my company."

Since there didn't seem to be anyone to stop us, we crossed to the boat, hopscotching around the weakest-looking boards, and began to untie it from the dock.

"STOP!" came a booming voice from inside the boat.

Emma squealed, Addison yelped, and I nearly leapt out of my skin. A man who'd been sitting in the boat—how had we not seen him until now?!—rose slowly to his feet, straightening himself inch by inch until he towered over us. He was seven feet tall at least, his massive frame draped in a cloak and his face hidden beneath a dark hood.

"I'm—I'm so sorry!" Emma stammered. "It's—we thought this boat was—"

"Many have tried to steal from Sharon!" the man thundered. "Now their skulls make homes for sea creatures!"

"I swear we weren't trying to—"

"We'll just be going," squeaked Addison, backing away, "so sorry to bother you, milord."

"SILENCE!" the boatman roared, stepping onto the creaking

dock with one enormous stride. "Anyone who comes for my boat must PAY THE PRICE!"

I was completely terrified, and when Emma shouted "RUN!" I was already turning to go. We'd only gotten a few paces, though, when my foot crashed through a rotting board and I pitched face-first onto the dock. I tried to scramble up but my leg was thigh deep in the hole. I was stuck, and by the time Emma and Addison circled back to help me, it was too late. The boatman was upon us, looming overhead and laughing, his cavernous guffaws booming around us. It might have been a trick of the darkness, but I could've sworn I saw a rat tumble from the hood of his cloak, and another slip from his sleeve as he slowly raised his arm toward us.

"Get away from us, you maniac!" Emma shouted, clapping her hands to light a flame. Though the light she made did nothing to chase away the dark inside the boatman's hood—I suspected not even the sun could do that—it showed us what he held in his out-stretched hand, which wasn't a knife, nor any weapon. It was a piece of paper, pinched between his thumb and a long, white forefinger.

He was offering it to me, bending low so I could reach it.

"Please," he said calmly. "Read it."

I hesitated. "What is it?"

"The price. And some other information regarding my services."

Quaking with fear, I reached up and took the paper. We all leaned in to read by the light of Emma's flame.

"IT'S THE DESTINATION, NOT THE JOURNEY"

SHARON'S RIVER TOURS,

OFFERING DAY TRIPS AND ROMANTIC
SUNSET CRUISES SINCE 1693

❖ PRICE. ❖

ONE GOLD
PIECE.

DISCRETION
GUARANTEED.

ASK ABOUT
OUR SPECIALS!

I looked up at the giant boatman. "So this is you?" I said uncertainly. "You're . . . Sharon?"

"In the flesh," he replied, his voice an oily slither that made my neck hairs stand on end.

"Good bird, man, you scared us half to death!" said Addison. "Was all that bluster and cackling really necessary?"

"My apologies. I was napping and you startled me."

"We startled *you*?"

"For a moment I thought you really were trying to steal my boat," he chuckled.

"Ha-ha!" Emma said, forcing a laugh. "No, we were just . . . making sure it was moored properly."

Sharon turned to examine the skiff, which was simply roped to one of the wooden pylons.

"And how do you find it?" he asked, the dull white crescent of a grin spreading beneath his hood.

"Totally . . . ship-shape," I said, finally jimmying my leg free from the hole. "Really good, um, mooring."

"Couldn't have tied a better knot myself," said Emma, helping me to my feet.

"By the way," said Addison. "The ones who *did* try . . . are they really all . . . ?" He glanced at the dark water and swallowed audibly.

"Never mind that," the boatman said. "Now you've woken me, and I am at your service. What can I do for you?"

"We need to hire your boat," Emma said firmly. "By ourselves."

"I can't allow that," Sharon said. "I always captain the boat."

"Ah, too bad then!" Addison said, turning eagerly to leave.

Emma caught him by the collar. "Wait!" she hissed. "We're not done here." She smiled pleasantly at the boatman. "So, we happen to know that a lot of peculiars come through this . . . "

She looked around, searching for the right word.

" . . . place. Is that because there's a loop entrance nearby?"

"I don't know what you mean," Sharon said flatly.

"Okay, yes, of course you can't just *admit* it. I completely understand. But you're in safe company with us. Obviously, *we're*—"

I elbowed her. "Emma, don't!"

"Why not? He's already seen the dog talk and me make fire. If we can't speak honestly . . . "

"But we don't know if *he* is," I said.

"Of course he is," she said, then turned to Sharon. "You are, aren't you?"

The boatman stared at us impassively.

"He is, isn't he?" Emma asked Addison. "Can't you smell it on him?"

"No, not clearly."

"Well, I suppose it doesn't matter, so long as he's not a wight." She gave Sharon a beady-eyed glare. "You're not, are you?"

"I am a businessman," he said evenly.

"Who's well accustomed to meeting talking dogs and girls who make fire with their hands," said Addison.

"In my line of work, one meets a wide variety of people."

"I'll cut to the chase," I said, shaking water off one foot, then the other. "We're looking for some friends of ours. We think they might've come this way within the last hour or so. Mostly kids, some adults. One was invisible, one could float . . . "

"They'd be hard to miss," Emma said. "They were being held at gunpoint by a gang of wights."

Sharon crossed his arms into a wide, black X. "As I said, all manner of people hire my boat, and each relies on my absolute discretion. I won't discuss my clientele."

"Is that so?" Emma said. "Excuse us just a moment."

She took me aside to whisper in my ear.

"If he doesn't start talking, I'm going to get really angry."

"Don't do anything reckless," I whispered back.

"Why? You believe that humbug about skulls and sea creatures?"

"Yes, actually. I know he's a slimebag, but—"

"Slimebag? He's practically admitted to doing business with wights! He might even *be* one!"

"—but he's a *useful* slimebag. I have a feeling he knows exactly where our friends were taken. It's just a matter of asking the right questions."

"Then have at it," she said crossly.

I turned to Sharon and said with a smile, "What can you tell me about your tours?"

He brightened immediately. "Finally, a subject I can speak freely about. I just happen to have some information right here . . . " He turned snappily and went to a nearby pylon. A shelf had been nailed onto it, and upon the shelf was displayed a skull dressed in old-time aviator garb—leather cap, goggles, a jaunty scarf. Gripped between its teeth were several pamphlets, and Sharon pulled one out and handed it to me. It was a cheesy tourist brochure that looked like it had been printed when my grandfather was a boy. I leafed through its pages as Sharon cleared his throat and spoke.

"Let's see now. Families enjoy the Famine 'n' Flames package . . . in the morning we go upriver to watch Viking siege engines catapult diseased sheep over the city walls, then have a nice boxed lunch and return in the evening via the Great Fire of 1666, which is a real treat after dark, with the flames reflecting on the water, very nice. Or if you've only a few hours to spare, we have a lovely gibbetting 'round Execution Dock—right at sunset, popular with honeymooners—in which some excellently foul-tongued pirates give colorful speeches before being put to the rope. For a small fee you can even have your photo taken with them!"

Inside the brochure were illustrations of smiling tourists enjoying the sights he'd described. The final page was a photo of one of Sharon's guests posing with a gang of surly pirates wielding knives and guns.

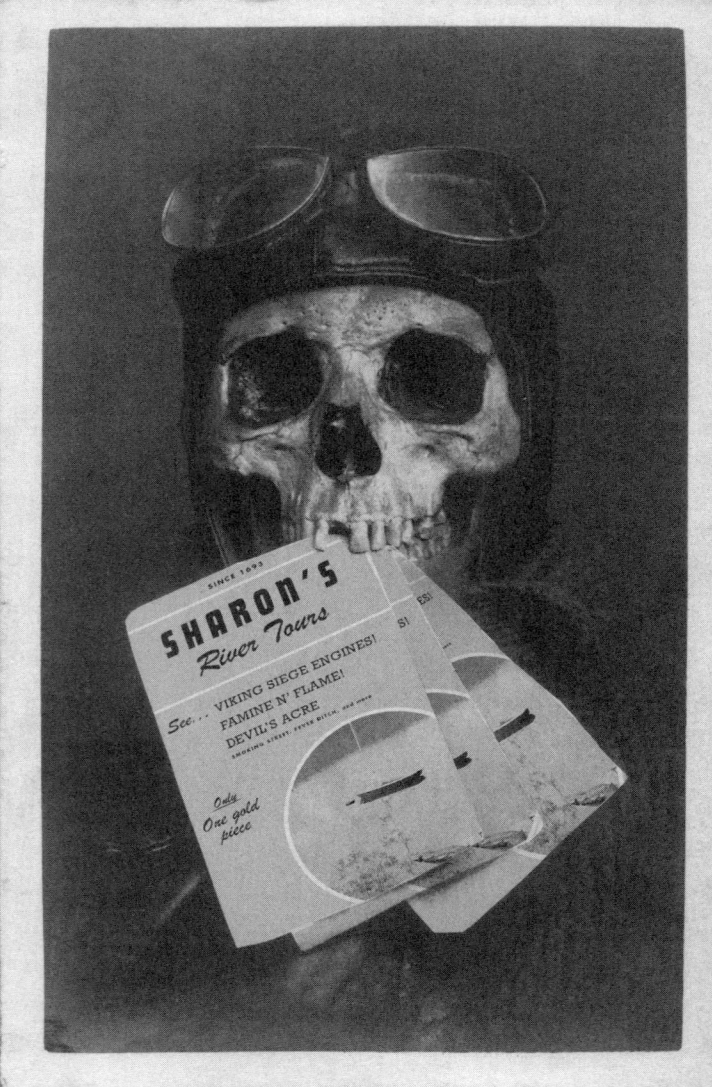

Another satisfied customer!

"Peculiars do this stuff for *fun*?" I marveled.

"This is a waste of time," Emma whispered, checking behind us anxiously. "I'll bet he's just running out the clock until the next patrol of wights arrives."

"I don't think so," I said. "Just wait . . . "

Sharon was plowing on as if he hadn't heard us. " . . . and you can see all the lunatics' heads arranged on pikes as we float beneath London Bridge! Lastly, there's our most requested excursion, which is a personal favorite of mine. But oh—never mind," he said coyly, waving his hand, "come to think of it, I doubt you'd be interested in Devil's Acre."

"Why not?" Emma said. "Too nice and pleasant?"

"Actually, it's rather a rough spot. Certainly no place for children . . . "

Emma stamped her foot and shook the whole rotting dock. "That's where our friends were taken, isn't it?" she shouted. "Isn't it!"

"Don't lose your temper, miss. Your safety is my highest concern."

"Quit winding us up and tell us what's there!"

"Well, if you insist . . . " Sharon made a sound like he was slipping into a warm bath and began rubbing his leathery hands together, as if just thinking about it brought him pleasure. "Nasty things," he said. "Dreadful things. Vile things. Anything you like, so long as what you like is nasty, dreadful, and vile. I've often dreamed of hanging up my oar pole and retiring there one day, perhaps to run the little abattoir on Oozing Street . . . "

"What name did you call it again?" said Addison.

"Devil's Acre," the boatman said wistfully.

Addison shuddered from tip to tail. "I know it," he said gravely. "It's a terrible place—the most depraved and dangerous slum in the whole long history of London. I've heard stories of peculiar animals brought there in cages and made to fight in blood-sport games.

Grimbears pitted against emu-raffes, chimpnoceri against flamin-goats . . . parents against their own children! Forced to maim and kill one another for the entertainment of a few sick peculiars."

"Disgusting," Emma said. "What peculiar would participate in such a thing?"

Addison shook his head ruefully. "Outlaws . . . mercenaries . . . exiles . . . "

"But there *are* no outlaws in peculiardom!" said Emma. "Any peculiar convicted of a crime is brought by the home guard to a punishment loop!"

"How little you know of your own world," the boatman said.

"Criminals can't be jailed if they're never caught," Addison explained. "Not if they escape to a loop like that first—lawless, un-governable."

"It sounds like Hell," I said. "Why would anyone go there voluntarily?"

"What's Hell for some," said the boatman, "is paradise for others. It's the last truly free place. Somewhere you can buy any-thing, sell anything . . . " He leaned toward me and lowered his voice. "Or *hide* anything."

"Like kidnapped ymbrynes and peculiar children?" I said. "Is that what you're getting at?"

"I said nothing of the sort," shrugged the boatman, busying himself with a rat plucked from the hem of his cloak. "Shoo there, Percy, Daddy's working."

While he placed the rat gently aside, I gathered Emma and Ad-dison in a tight huddle. "What do you think?" I whispered. "Could this . . . *devil* place . . . really be where our friends were taken?"

"Well, they have to be keeping their prisoners inside a loop, and a pretty old one," said Emma. "Otherwise most of us would age forward and die after a day or two . . . "

"But what do the wights care if we die?" I said. "They just want to steal our souls."

"Maybe, but they can't let the ymbrynes die. They need them to re-create the 1908 event. Remember the wights' crazy plan?"

"All that stuff Golan was raving about. Immortality and ruling the world . . . "

"Yeah. So they've been kidnapping ymbrynes for months and need a place to hold them where they won't turn into dried fruit leather, right? Which means a pretty old loop. Eighty, a hundred years at least. And if Devil's Acre is really a lawless jungle of depravity . . . "

"It is," said Addison.

" . . . then it sounds like a perfect spot for wights to secret away their captives."

"Right in the heart of peculiar London, too," said Addison. "Right under everyone's noses. Clever little blighters . . . "

"Guess that settles it," I said.

Emma stepped smartly toward Sharon. "We'll take three tickets to that disgusting, horrible place you described, please."

"Be very, very certain that's what you want," said the boatman. "Innocent lambs like yourselves don't always return from Devil's Acre."

"We're sure," I said.

"Very good, then. But don't say I didn't warn you."

"Only thing is, we don't have three gold pieces," said Emma.

"Is that right?" Sharon tented his long fingers and let out a sigh that smelled like an opened tomb. "Normally I insist on payment up front, but I'm feeling generous this morning. I find your plucky optimism charming. You can owe me." And then he laughed, as if he knew we'd never live to repay him, and stepping aside he raised a cloaked arm toward his boat.

"Welcome aboard, children."

CHAPTER TWO

*S*haron made a big show of plucking six wriggling rats from his boat before we boarded—as if a pestilence-free journey were a luxury afforded only to Very Important Peculiars—and then he offered Emma his arm and helped her step from the dock. We were seated three abreast on a simple wooden bench. While Sharon was busy untying the mooring rope, I wondered whether trusting him was merely unwise or if it crossed the line into recklessness, like lying down for a nap in the middle of a road.

The trouble with the merely unwise/deeply stupid line is that you often don't know which side you're on until it's too late. By the time things have settled down enough for you to reflect, the button's been pushed, the plane's left the hangar, or in our case, the boat's left the dock—and as I watched Sharon shove us away from it with his foot, which was bare, and I noticed that his bare foot was not quite human-looking, with toes as long as mini hotdogs and thick yellow nails that curled like claws, I realized with sinking certainty which side of the line we were on, and also that it was too late to do much about it.

Sharon yanked the ignition cord on a dinky outboard motor and it coughed awake in a cloud of blue fumes. Tucking his considerable legs beneath him, he lowered into the puddle of black fabric his cloak made in the boat. He revved the puttering engine, then steered us out of the underjetty, through a forest of looming wood pylons and into warm sunlight. Then we were in a canal, a man-made tributary of the Thames walled on both sides by glassy buildings and bobbing with more boats than a toddler's tub at bath time—candy-red tugs and wide, flat barges and tour boats whose upper decks teemed with sightseers taking the air. Strangely, none of them trained their cameras at, nor seemed to even notice, the unusual craft that burbled past them, with an angel of death at the tiller, two blood-spattered children in the seat, and a dog in glasses peering over the side. Which was just as well. Had Sharon charmed his boat somehow so that only peculiars could see it? I decided to believe it was so, because there was nowhere to hide in it anyway, should we have needed to.

Looking it over in the full light of day, I noticed that the boat was extremely simple but for an intricately carved figurehead rising from its bow. The carving was shaped like a fat, scaly snake that curved upward in a gentle S, but where a head should've been was a giant eyeball, lidless and large as a melon, staring forever out before us.

"What is it?" I asked, running my hand over its polished surface.

"Yew wood," Sharon called over the motor's growl.

"I would what?"

"That's what it's made from."

"But what's it *for*?"

"To see with!" he replied testily.

Sharon pushed the motor harder—possibly just to drown out my questions—and as we picked up speed the bow lifted gently from the water. I took a deep breath, enjoying the sun and wind on my face, and Addison let his tongue hang out as he leaned over the side with his paws, looking as happy as I'd ever seen him.

What a beautiful day to go to Hell.

"So I've been thinking about how you got here," Emma said. "How you got back to the present."

"Okay," I said. "What do you think?"

"There's only one explanation that makes any sense—though not bloody much. When we were in the underground tunnels with all those wights, and we crossed back into the present, the reason you came with us instead of continuing on in eighteen-whatever-it-was, suddenly alone, was that Miss Peregrine was there somehow, nearby, and helped you cross without anyone knowing it."

"I don't know, Emma, that seems . . . " I hesitated, not wanting to be harsh. "You think she was hiding in the tunnel?"

"I'm saying it's possible. We've no idea where she was."

"The wights have her. Caul admitted it!"

"Since when do you believe anything the wights say?"

"You've got me there," I said. "But since Caul was boasting about having her, I figured he was probably telling the truth."

"Maybe . . . or he said it to crush our spirits and make us want to give up. He was trying to convince us to surrender to his soldiers, remember?"

"True," I said, frowning. My brain was starting to kink from all the possibilities. "Okay. Let's say for the sake of argument that Miss P was with us in the tunnel. Why would she have gone to the trouble of sending me back to the present as a captive of the wights? We were on our way to have our second souls sucked out. I would've been better off stuck in that loop."

For a moment Emma looked genuinely stumped. Then her face lit up and she said, "Unless you and I are *supposed* to rescue everyone else. Maybe it was all part of her plan."

"But how could she have known we would escape the wights?"

Emma cast a sidelong glance at Addison. "Maybe she had help," she whispered.

"Em, this hypothetical chain of events is getting *really* unlikely." I took a breath, choosing my words carefully. "I know you want to believe Miss Peregrine is out there somewhere, free, watching over us. I do, too . . . "

"I want that so badly, it hurts," she said.

"But if she were free, wouldn't she have contacted us somehow? And if *he* were involved," I said quietly, nodding toward

Addison, "wouldn't he have mentioned it by now?"

"Not if he's sworn to secrecy. Perhaps it's too dangerous to tell anyone, even us. If we knew Miss Peregrine's whereabouts, and someone *knew* we knew, we might break under torture . . . "

"And he wouldn't?" I said a little too loudly, and the dog looked up at us, his cheeks ballooning and tongue flapping ridiculously as the wind caught them. "Ho, there!" he cried. "I've counted fifty-six fish already, though one or two might've been bits of half-submerged rubbish. What are you two whispering about?"

"Oh, nothing," said Emma.

"Somehow I doubt that," he muttered, but his suspicion was quickly overwhelmed by his instincts, and a second later he yelped, "Fish!" and his attention lasered back to the water. "Fish . . . fish . . . rubbish . . . fish . . . "

Emma laughed darkly. "It's a completely mad idea, I know. But my brain is a hope-making engine."

"I'm so glad," I said. "Mine is a worst-case-scenario generator."

"We need each other, then."

"Yes. But we already knew that, I think."

The boat's steady heaving pushed us together and apart, together and apart.

"Sure you wouldn't rather go on the romantic cruise?" Sharon said. "It isn't too late."

"Very sure," I said. "We're on a mission."

"Then I suggest you open the box you're sitting on. You're going to need what's inside when we cross over."

We opened the bench's hinged top to find a large canvas tarp.

"What's this for?" I said.

"Cowering beneath," Sharon replied, and he turned the boat down an even narrower canal lined with new, expensive-looking condos. "I've been able to keep you hidden from view thus far, but the protection I can offer doesn't work inside the Acre—and unsavory characters tend to keep watch for easy prey 'round the entrance. And you are most certainly easy prey."

"I *knew* you were up to something," I said. "Not a single tourist so much as glanced at us."

"It's safer to watch historical atrocities being committed when the participants aren't able to watch you back," he said. "Can't have my customers being carried off by Viking raiders, can I? Imagine the user reviews!"

We were fast approaching a sort of tunnel—a bridged-over stretch of canal, perhaps a hundred feet long, atop which hulked a building like a warehouse or an old mill. From the far end shone a half circle of blue sky and sparkling water. Between here and there was only darkness. It looked as much like a loop entrance as anyplace I'd seen.

We heaved out the enormous tarp, which filled half the boat. Emma lay down beside me and we wriggled beneath it, drawing the edge up to our chins like bedsheets. As the boat glided beneath the bridge into shadow, Sharon cut the motor and hid it beneath another, smaller tarp. Then he stood and extended a collapsible staff, plunged it into the water until it touched bottom, and began poling us forward in long, silent strokes.

"By the way," Emma said, "what sort of 'unsavory characters' are we hiding from? Wights?"

"There's more evil in peculiardom than merely your hated wights," Sharon said, his voice echoing through the stone tunnel. "An opportunist disguised as a friend can be every bit as dangerous as an outright enemy."

Emma sighed. "Must you always be so vague?"

"Your heads!" he snapped. "You too, dog."

Addison snuffled beneath the tarp, and we pulled the edge over our faces. It was black and hot under the fabric, and it smelled overpoweringly of motor oil.

"Are you frightened?" Addison whispered in the dark.

"Not particularly," said Emma. "Are you, Jacob?"

"So much I might throw up. Addison?"

"Of course not," the dog said. "Fearfulness isn't a characteristic of my breed."

But then he snuggled right between Emma and me, and I could feel his whole body trembling.

*   *   *

Some changeovers are as fast and smooth as superhighways, but this one felt like slamming down a washboard road full of potholes, lurching around a hairpin turn, and then careening off a cliff—all in complete darkness. When it was finally over, my head was dizzy and pounding. I wondered what invisible mechanism made some changeovers harder than others. Maybe the journey was only as rough as the destination, and this one had felt like off-roading into a savage wilderness because that's precisely what we had done.

"We have arrived," Sharon announced.

"Is everyone okay?" I said, fumbling for Emma's hand.

"We must go back," Addison groaned. "I've left my kidneys on the other side."

"Do keep quiet until I find somewhere discreet to deposit you," Sharon said.

It's amazing how much more acute your hearing becomes the moment you can't use your eyes. As I lay quietly beneath the tarp, I was hypnotized by the sounds of a bygone world blooming around us. At first there was only the splash of Sharon's pole in the water, but soon it was complemented by other noises, all stirring together to paint an elaborate scene in my mind. That steady slap of wood against water belonged, I imagined, to the oars of a passing boat piled high with fish. I pictured the ladies I could hear shouting to one another as leaning from the windows of opposite-facing houses, trading gossip across the canal while tending lines of laundry. Ahead of us, children whooped with laughter as a dog barked, and distantly I could make out voices singing in time to the rhythm of hammers: "Hark to the clinking of hammers, hark to the driving of nails!" Before long I was imagining plucky chimneysweeps in top hats skipping down streets full of rough charm and people banding together to overcome their lot in life with a wink and a song.

I couldn't help it. All I knew about Victorian slums I'd learned from the campy musical version of *Oliver Twist*. When I was twelve I'd been in a community theater production of it; I was Orphan Number Five, if you must know, and had suffered such terrible stage fright on the night of the show that I faked a stomach flu and watched the whole thing from the wings, in costume, with a barf bucket between my legs.

Anyway, such was the scene in my head when I noticed a small hole in the tarp near my shoulder—chewed by rats, no doubt—and, shifting a little, I found I could peek through it. Within seconds, the happy, musical-inspired landscape I'd imagined melted away like a Salvador Dalí painting. The first horror to greet me were the houses that lined the canal, though calling them houses was generous. Nowhere in their sagging and rotted architecture could be found a single straight line. They slouched like a row of exhausted soldiers who'd fallen asleep at attention; it seemed the only thing keeping them from tipping straight into the water was the tightness with which they were packed—that and the mortar of black-and-green filth that smeared their lower thirds in thick, sludgy strata. On each of their rickety porches a coffinlike box stood on end, but only when I heard a loud grunt issue from one and saw something tumble into the water from beneath it did I realize what they were or that the slapping sounds I'd heard earlier hadn't come from oars but from outhouses, which were contributing to the very filth that held them up.

The women calling to one another from across the canal were leaning from opposite windows, just as I'd imagined, but they weren't hanging laundry and they certainly weren't trading gossip—at least, not anymore; now they were trading insults and issuing threats. One waved a broken bottle and laughed drunkenly while the other shouted epithets I could barely understand ("Yore nuffink but a stinkin' dollymop 'ood lay wi' the devil 'imself for a farthing!")—which was ironic, if I took her meaning correctly, because she was herself stripped to the waist and didn't seem to mind who noticed. Both stopped to whistle down at Sharon as we passed, but he ignored them.

Eager to wipe that image from my head, I managed to replace it with something even worse: ahead of us was a gang of kids swinging their feet from a rickety footbridge that spanned the canal. They were dangling a dog above the water by a rope tied around its hind legs, dipping the poor creature underwater and cackling when its desperate barks turned to bubbles. I resisted an urge to kick the tarp away and scream at them. At least Addison couldn't see; if he had, no amount of reasoning would've stopped him from going after them with teeth bared, blowing our cover.

"I see what you're up to," Sharon muttered at me. "If you want to have a look around just wait, we'll be through the worst of it in a tick."

"Are you peeking?" Emma whispered, poking me.

"Maybe," I said, still doing it.

The boatman shushed us. Drawing his pole from the water, he uncapped the handle to expose a short blade, then held it out to sever the boys' rope as we drifted by. The dog splashed into the water and paddled gratefully away, and howling with rage, the boys began to improvise projectiles to throw at us. Sharon pushed on, ignoring them as he had the ladies until a flying apple core missed his head by inches. Then he sighed, turned, and calmly pulled back the hood of his cloak—just enough so that the boys could see him, but I couldn't.

Whatever they saw must've scared them half to death, because all ran screaming from the bridge, one so fast he tripped and fell into the fetid water. Chuckling to himself, Sharon readjusted his hood before facing forward again.

"What's happened?" Emma said, alarmed. "What was that?"

"A Devil's Acre welcome," replied Sharon. "Now, if you care to see where we are, you may uncover your faces a bit, and I'll attempt to give you your gold coin's worth of tour-guiding with the time we have left."

We pulled the edge of the tarp down to our chins, and both Emma and Addison gasped—Emma, I think, at the sight, and Addison, judging from his wrinkled nose, at the smell. It was unreal, like a stew of raw sewage simmering all around us.

"You get used to it," Sharon said, reading my puckered face.

Emma gripped my hand and moaned, "Oh, it's *awful* . . . "

And it was. Now that I could see it with both eyes, the place looked even more hellish. The foundations of every house were decomposing into mush. Crazy wooden footbridges, some no wider than a board, crisscrossed the canal like a cat's cradle, and its stinking banks were heaped with trash and crawling with spectral forms at work sifting through it. The only colors were shades of black, yellow, and green, the flag of filth and decay, but black most of all. Black stained every surface, smeared every face, and striped the air in columns that rose from chimneys all around us—and, more ominously, from the smokestacks of factories in the distance, which announced themselves on the minute with industrial booms, deep and primal like war drums, so powerful they shook every window yet unbroken.

"This, friends, is Devil's Acre," Sharon began, his slithering voice just loud enough for us to hear. "Actual population seven thousand two hundred and six, official population zero. The city fathers, in their wisdom, refuse even to acknowledge its existence. The charming body of water in whose current we're currently drifting is called Fever Ditch, and the factory waste, night soil, and animal carcasses which flow perpetually into it are the source not only of its bewitching odor but also of disease outbreaks so regular you could set your watch to them and so spectacular that this entire area has been dubbed 'the Capital of Cholera.'

"And yet . . . " He raised a black-draped arm toward a young girl lowering a bucket into the water. "For many of these unfortunate souls, it serves as both sewer and spring."

"She isn't going to *drink* that!" Emma said, horrified.

"In a few days, once the heavy particles settle, she'll skim the clearest liquid from the top."

Emma recoiled. "No . . . "

"Yes. Terrible shame," Sharon said casually, then continued rattling off facts as if reciting from a book. "The citizenry's primary occupations are rubbish picking and luring strangers into the Acre to cosh them on the head and rob them. For amusement, they ingest whatever flammable liquids are at hand and sing badly at the top of their lungs. The area's main exports are smelted iron slag, bone meal, and misery. Notable landmarks include—"

"It isn't funny," Emma interrupted.

"Pardon me?"

"I said, it isn't funny! These people are suffering, and you're making jokes about it!"

"I am not making jokes," Sharon replied imperiously. "I'm providing you with valuable information that may save your life. But if you'd rather plunge into this jungle cocooned in ignorance . . . "

"We wouldn't," I said. "She's very sorry. Please keep going."

Emma shot me a disapproving look, and I disapproved right back at her. This was no time to take a stand on political correctness, even if Sharon sounded a bit heartless.

"Keep your voices down, for Hades' sake," Sharon said irritably. "Now, as I was saying. Notable landmarks include St. Rutledge's Foundlings' Prison, a forward-thinking institution which jails orphans before they've had the opportunity to commit any crimes, thereby saving society enormous cost and trouble; St. Barnabus's Asylum for Lunatics, Mountebanks, and the Criminally Mischievous, which operates on a voluntary, outpatient basis and is nearly always empty; and Smoking Street, which has been in flames for eighty-seven years due to an underground fire no one's bothered to extinguish. Ah," he said, pointing to a blackened clearing between houses on the bank. "Here's one end of it, which, as you can see, is burnt to a crisp."

Several men were at work in the clearing, hammering on a wooden frame—rebuilding one of the houses, I assumed—and when they saw us passing they stopped to shout hello to Sharon, who gave just a token wave back, as if slightly embarrassed.

"Friends of yours?" I asked.

"Distant relations," he muttered. "Gallows rigging is our family trade . . . "

"*What* rigging?" said Emma.

Before he could answer, the men had resumed work, singing loudly as they swung their hammers: "Hark to the clinking of hammers! Hark to the driving of nails! What fun to build a gallows, the cure for all that ails!"

If I hadn't been so horrified, I might've broken out laughing.

*　　*　　*

We coursed steadily down Fever Ditch. Like hands closing around us, it seemed to narrow with every stroke of Sharon's staff, sometimes so dramatically that the footbridges crossing it became unnecessary; you could practically leap across the water from roof to roof, the gray sky but a crack between them, suffocating all below in gloom. All the while, Sharon nattered on like a textbook come to life. In just a few minutes he'd managed to cover fashion trends in Devil's Acre (stolen wigs hung from belt loops were popular), its gross domestic product (firmly in the negative), and the history of its settlement (by enterprising maggot farmers in the early twelfth century). He was just launching into the highlights of its architecture when Addison, who'd been squirming next to me through it all, finally interrupted him.

"You seem to know every last fact about this hellhole with the exception of anything that would be remotely useful to us."

"Such as?" Sharon said, his patience thinning.

"Whom can we trust here?"

"Absolutely no one."

"How can we find the peculiars who live in this loop?" said Emma.

"You don't want to."

"Where are the wights holding our friends?" I asked.

"It's bad for business to know things like that," Sharon replied evenly.

"Then let us off this accursed boat and we'll set about finding them ourselves!" said Addison. "We're wasting precious time, and your endless monologuing is putting me to sleep. We hired a boatman, not a schoolmarm!"

Sharon harrumphed. "I should dump you into the Ditch for being so rude, but if I did, I'd never get the gold coins you owe me."

"Gold coins!" said Emma, fairly spitting with disgust. "What about the well-being of your fellow peculiars? What about *loyalty*?"

Sharon chuckled. "If I cared about things like that, I'd have been dead long ago."

"And wouldn't we all be better off," Emma muttered, and looked away.

As we were talking, tendrils of fog had begun to curl around us. It was nothing like the gray mists of Cairnholm—this was greasy and yellow-brown, the color and consistency of squash soup. Its sudden appearance seemed to make Sharon uneasy, and as the view ahead dimmed, his head turned quickly from side to side, as if he were on the lookout for trouble—or searching for a spot to dump us.

"Drat, drat, *drat*," he muttered. "This is a bad sign."

"It's only fog," said Emma. "We're not afraid of fog."

"Neither am I," said Sharon, "but this isn't fog. It's *murk*, and it's man-made. Nasty things happen in the murk, and we must get out of it as quickly as we can."

He hissed at us to cover ourselves, and we did. I retreated to my peeking hole. Moments later a boat emerged from the murk and passed close-by going the opposite direction. A man was at the oars and a woman sat in the seat, and though Sharon said good morning they only stared back—and continued staring until they were well past us, and the murk had swallowed them up again. Grumbling under his breath, Sharon maneuvered us toward the left bank and a small dock I could just barely make out. But when we heard footsteps on the wooden planks and a low murmur of voices, Sharon leaned on his pole to turn us sharply away.

We zigzagged from bank to bank, looking for a place to land, but each time we got close, Sharon would see something he didn't like and turn away again. "Vultures," he muttered. "Vultures everywhere . . . "

I didn't see any myself until we passed beneath a sagging footbridge and a man crossing above us. As we drifted under him, the man stopped and looked down. He opened his mouth and drew a deep breath—about to yell for help, I thought—but rather than a voice, what came out of his mouth was a jet of heavy yellow smoke that shot toward us like water from a firehose.

I panicked and held my breath. What if it was poison gas? But Sharon wasn't covering his face or reaching for a mask—he was just muttering "Drat, drat, *drat*" while the man's breath swirled around us, merging with the murk and reducing our visibility to nothing. Within a few seconds the man, the bridge he stood on, and the banks on either side of us had all been blotted out.

I uncovered my head (no one could see us now anyway) and said quietly, "When you said this stuff was man-made, I thought you meant by smokestacks, not literally—"

"Oh, wow," Emma said, uncovering herself. "What's it for?"

"The vultures will murk an area to cloak their activities," Sharon said, "and to blind their prey. Fortunately for you, I am not easily preyed upon." And he drew his long staff from the water, passed it over our heads, and used it to tap the wooden eyeball at the bow of his boat. The eyeball began to glow like a fog lamp, piercing the murk before us. Then he returned his staff to the water and, leaning heavily on it, spun the boat in a slow circle, sweeping the water around us with his light.

"But if they're making this," said Emma, "then they're peculiar, aren't they? And if they're peculiar, perhaps they're friendly."

"The pure of heart don't end up as ditch pirates," said Sharon, and then he stopped the turning boat as our light fixed upon another approaching vessel. "Speak of the devil."

We could see them clearly enough, but for now all they would see of us was a glary bloom of light. It wasn't much of an advantage, but at least it allowed us to size them up before we had to retreat beneath the tarp. They were two men in a boat about twice the size of our own. The first man was operating a nearly silent outboard motor, and the second held a club.

"If they're so dangerous," I whispered, "why are we just waiting for them?"

"We're too deep inside the Acre to escape them now, and I can most likely talk us out of this."

"And if you can't?" said Emma.

"You may have to swim for it."

Emma glanced at the oily black water and said, "I'd rather die."

"That's your choice. Now, I recommend you disappear, children, and don't move a muscle under there."

We drew the tarp over our heads again. A moment later, a hearty voice called out, "Ho, there, boatman!"

"Ho, there," replied Sharon.

I heard oars drag the water, and then felt a jolt as the other boat knocked against ours.

"What's your business here?"

"Merely out for a pleasure cruise," Sharon said lightly.

"And a fine day for it!" the man replied, laughing.

The second man wasn't in the mood for jokes. "Wot's undah the rag?" he growled, his accent nearly impenetrable.

"What I carry on my boat is my own business."

"Innithin passes through Fever Ditch s'*our* business."

"Old ropes and bric-a-brac, if you must know," said Sharon. "Nothing of interest."

"Then you won't mind us having a look," said the first man.

"What about our arrangement? Haven't I paid you this month?"

"Hen't no arrangement nummore," said the second. "Wights are payin' five times the goin' rate fer nice plump feeders. Any as lets a feeder slip away . . . it's the pit, or worse."

"What could be worse than the pit?" said the first.

"I dun inten' t'fineout."

"Now gentlemen, be reasonable," said Sharon. "Perhaps it's time to renegotiate. I can offer terms competitive with anyone . . . "

Feeders. I shivered despite a clammy warmth building under the tarp from Emma's quickly heating hands. I hoped she wouldn't need to use them, but the men weren't budging, and I feared the boatman's blabber would stall them only so long. A fight would mean disaster, though. Even if we could take out the men in the boat, the vultures, as Sharon had said, were everywhere. I imagined a mob forming—coming after us in boats, firing on us from the banks, jumping onto us from the footbridges—and I began to freeze up with fear. I really, really did not want to find out what *feeders* meant.

But then I heard a hopeful sound—the clink of coins being exchanged, and the second man was saying, "Wy, 'ees *loaded*! I could retire to Spain wi' dis . . . "

But just as my hopes were rising, my stomach began to sink. A familiar old feeling crept into my belly, and I realized it had been building, slowly and gradually, for some time. It started as an itch, then become a dull ache, and now that ache was sharpening—the telltale tug of a nearby hollowgast.

But not just any hollow. *My* hollow.

The word popped into my head without warning or precedent. *Mine.* Or maybe I had it backward. Maybe *I* belonged to *it.*

Neither arrangement was any guarantee of safety. I expected it wanted to kill me just as badly as any hollow would, only something had temporarily plugged the urge. It was the same mysterious thing that had magnetized the hollow to me and tuned the compass needle inside me to it—and it was this needle that told me the hollow was close now and getting closer.

Just in time to get us caught, or killed, or kill us itself. I resolved then that should we make it safely to shore, my first order of business would be to get rid of it once and for all.

But where was it? If it was as close as it seemed to be, it would've been swimming toward us in the Ditch, and I definitely would've heard a creature with seven limbs doing the breaststroke. Then the needle shifted and dipped, and I knew—could see, almost—that it was *under* the water. Hollows did not, apparently, need to breathe often. A moment later there came a gentle *thunk* as it attached itself to the bottom of our boat. We all jumped at the sound, but only I knew what it was. I wished I could warn my friends, but I had to lie motionless, its body just inches away on the other side of the wooden boards we lay upon.

"What was that?" I heard the first man say.

"I didn't hear anything," Sharon lied.

Let go, I mouthed silently, hoping the hollow could hear. *Go away and leave us alone.* Instead, it began to make a grinding sound against the wood; I pictured it gnawing at the bottom of the boat with its long teeth.

"I heard'at plain as day," said the second man. "Boatman's tryin' to make us look like fools, Reg!"

"I think he is at that," said the first.

"I assure you, nothing could be further from the truth," said Sharon. "It's this damned defective boat of mine. Past due for a tune-up."

"Forget it, deal's off. Show us what you got."

"Or you could allow me to increase my offer," said Sharon. "We'll consider it a gratuity for all your kind understanding."

The men conferred in an undertone.

"If we let 'im go an' someone else catches 'im wi' feeders, it's the pit for us."

"Or worse."

Go away, go away, go AWAY, I begged the hollow in English.

Thud, thud, THUD, it answered, knocking against the hull.

"Pull back that rag!" demanded the first man.

"Sir, if you would wait just a moment—"

But the men were determined. Our boat rocked like someone was boarding it. There were shouts, then footfalls near our heads as a scuffle broke out.

There's no point hiding now, I thought, and the others seemed to agree. I saw Emma's glowing-hot fingers reach for the edge of the tarp.

"On three," she whispered. "Ready?"

"As a racehorse," Addison growled.

"Wait," I said, "first, you should know—under the boat, there's—"

And then the tarp was ripped away, and I never did finish that sentence.

*   *   *

What happened next happened fast. Addison bit the arm that had torn away the tarp and Emma made a swipe at its surprised owner, grazing the man's face with scalding fingers. He stumbled back howling and fell into the water. Sharon had been knocked down in the scuffle, and the second man was standing above him with his club raised. Addison leapt at him and grabbed hold of his leg. The man turned to shake off the dog, giving Sharon time to regain his feet and hit him in the stomach. The man doubled over and Sharon disarmed him with a tricky whirl of his staff.

The man decided to quit while he could and leapt back into his boat. Sharon tore away the canvas covering the outboard motor, yanked its ignition cord, and our boat sputtered to life just as a third came speeding out of the murk alongside us. Inside were three more men, one armed with an old-fashioned pistol that was leveled right at Emma.

I shouted at her to get down and tackled her just as it cracked and sent up a puff of white smoke. Then the man pointed it at Sharon, who let go of the throttle and put his hands up. And that would've been it for us, I think, had not a throat-full of strange words come gushing up and pouring out of me, loud and sure and foreign to my ears.

Sink their boat! Use your tongues to sink their boat!

In the half second it took everyone to turn and stare at me, the hollow had pushed off from our hull and flung its tongues at the other boat. They fired out of the water, whipped around the lip of its stern, and flipped the boat up and backward in a reverse somersault that launched all three men out.

The boat crashed upside down on two of them.

Sharon might've taken the opportunity to hit the throttle and get us out of there, but he stood frozen in shock, his hands still raised.

Which was fine. I wasn't done yet, anyhow.

That one, I said, looking at the gunman flailing in the water.

It seemed the hollow could hear me underwater because moments after I'd said it the man screamed, looked down, and was sucked under—gone, just like that—and immediately the water where he'd been bloomed red.

"I didn't say *eat* him!" I said in English.

"What are you waiting for?" Emma shouted at Sharon. "Go!"

"Right, right," the boatman stammered. Shaking off his stupor, he lowered his hands and leaned on the throttle. The motor whined and Sharon turned the rudder and spun us in a tight circle, tripping Emma, Addison, and me into a pile. The boat bucked and shot forward, and then we were speeding through whorls of murk, heading back the way we'd come.

Emma looked at me and I looked back, and though it was too loud to hear anything over the motor and the rush of blood in our ears, I thought I could read in her face both fear and exhilaration—a look that said, *You, Jacob Portman, are amazing and terrifying.* But when she finally spoke, I could make out only one word: *Where?*

Where, indeed. I'd hoped we could get away from the hollow while it was finishing off the Ditch pirate, but reading my gut now I knew it was still close, trailing behind us, most likely using one of its tongues as a towline.

Close, I mouthed back.

Her eyes brightened and she nodded once, sharply: *Good.*

I shook my head. Why wasn't she afraid? Why couldn't she see how dangerous it was? The hollow had tasted blood, and just left a meal half-finished behind us. Who knew what meanness still boiled inside it? But the way she looked at me. Just that crooked bit of smile gave me a surge, and I felt I could do anything.

We were coming up fast on the bridge and the murk-making peculiar. He was waiting for us, crouching and sighting us down the length of a rifle he'd rested on the bridge's handrail.

We ducked. I heard two shots. Looking up again, I saw that no one had been hit.

We were going under the bridge. In a moment we'd be out the other side and he'd have another shot at us. I couldn't let him take it.

I turned and shouted *Bridge!* in hollowspeak, and the creature seemed to know just what I meant. The two tongues that weren't holding on to our boat whipped upward, and with a wet slap each one wrapped around the bridge's flimsy supports. All three tongues unreeled triangularly until they were pulled taut, like elastic stretched to the limit. The hollow was forced up out of the water, tethered between boat and bridge like a starfish.

The boat slowed so quickly, it was like someone had thrown the emergency brake; we were all tossed forward onto the floor. The bridge groaned and rocked, and the peculiar taking aim at us stumbled and dropped his gun. I thought that surely either the bridge would give or the hollow would—it was squealing like a stuck pig, as if it might rip down the middle—but as the peculiar bent to snatch his gun, it seemed the bridge would hold, which meant I'd traded all our momentum and speed for nothing. Now we weren't even moving targets.

Let go! I screamed at the hollow, this time in its language.

It didn't—the thing would never leave me of its own accord. So I rushed to the back of the boat and bellied over the stern. There was one of its tongues, knotted around the rudder. Remembering how Emma's touch had once made a hollow's tongue release her ankle, I pulled her over and told her to burn the rudder. She did—nearly falling over the side to make the reach—and the hollow squealed and let go.

It was like releasing a slingshot. The hollow flew away and slammed into the bridge with a splintering crash; the whole tottering contraption buckled and went tumbling into the water. At the same time, the back of our boat dropped, and the motor, once again submerged, flung us forward. The sudden acceleration toppled us like bowling pins. Sharon managed to hold on to the rudder, and righting himself, he steered us sharply away from a collision course with the canal wall. We flew down the spine of the Ditch, a black V of water shooting out behind us.

We hunched low should any more bullets fly. We seemed to be out of immediate danger. The vultures were somewhere behind us, and I couldn't imagine how they'd catch us now.

Panting, Addison said, "That was the same creature we met in the Underground, wasn't it?"

I realized I'd been holding my breath and so let it out, then nodded. Emma looked at me, waiting for more, but I was still processing, every nerve jangling with the strangeness of what had just happened. This much I knew: this time I'd nearly had him. It was as if, with each encounter, I dove a little deeper into the hollowgast's nerve center. The words came easier, felt less foreign to my tongue, met less resistance from the hollow. Still, it was like a tiger onto which I'd managed to clap a dog leash. At any moment it might decide to turn and take a bite out of me, or any of us. And yet, for reasons beyond my understanding, it hadn't.

Maybe, I thought, with another attempt or two, I could really get my hands around it. And then—and then. My God, what a thought.

Then we'd be unstoppable.

I gazed back at the ghost of a bridge, dust and wood pulp spiraling in the air where the structure had stood only moments ago. In the wreckage below, I watched for a limb to break the surface, but there was only a lifeless swirl of trash. I tried to feel for it, but my gut was useless now, wrung out and empty. Then the mud-colored mist closed behind us and painted away the view.

Just when I needed a monster, it had gotten itself killed.

* * *

The boat nodded as Sharon eased the throttle and banked right, through the slowly clearing murk, toward a block of ghastly tenements.

They stood at the edge of the water in a vast unbroken wall, resembling not so much houses as the outermost boundary of a maze, scowling and fortresslike, with few points of entry. We drifted along at a crawl, searching for a way in. It was Emma who finally spotted one, though I had to squint to recognize it as more than just a trick of shadows.

To call it an alley would've been exaggerating. It was a slot canyon, narrow as a knife's edge, a shoulder's width from wall to wall and fifty times as high, its entrance marked by a moss-shagged ladder screwed flat to the bankside. I could see only a little distance in before the passage hid itself, curving away into sunless dark.

"Where does it go?" I asked.

"Where angels fear to tread," Sharon replied. "This wasn't the landing I'd have chosen for you, but our choices are limited now. Are you certain you wouldn't rather leave the Acre altogether? There's still time."

"*Quite* certain," Emma and Addison said simultaneously.

Me, I would've been happy to debate the matter—but it was too late to turn back now. *Get them back or die trying* was something I'd said in the past few days. Time to dive in.

"In that case, land ho," Sharon said dryly. He retrieved the mooring rope from under his seat, tossed it over the ladder, and pulled us toward the bank. "Everyone out, please. Do watch your step. Wait, allow me."

Sharon climbed the slippery, half-runged ladder with the nimbleness of someone who'd done it many times. Once at the top, he knelt on the bank and reached down to help each of us up in turn. Emma went first, then I handed up a nervous and wiggling Addison, and then, because I was proud and dumb, I climbed the ladder without taking Sharon's hand and nearly slipped off.

The moment we were all safely on land, Sharon was climbing back down the ladder. He'd left the motor idling.

"Just a minute," said Emma. "Where are you going?"

"Away from here!" Sharon replied, hopping from the ladder into his boat. "Would you mind tossing down that rope?"

"I will not! You must show us where to go first. We've no idea where we are!"

"I don't do land tours. I'm strictly a boat guide."

We exchanged looks of disbelief.

"Give us directions, at least!" I implored him.

"Or better yet, a map," said Addison.

"A map!" Sharon exclaimed, as if this were the silliest thing he'd ever heard. "There are more thief passageways, murder tunnels, and illegal dens in Devil's Acre than anywhere in the world. The place is unmappable! Now stop being childish and hand me down my rope."

"Not until you tell us something useful!" Emma said. "The name of someone we can ask for help—who won't try to sell us to the wights!"

Sharon broke out laughing.

Emma struck a defiant pose. "There must be *one*."

Sharon bowed—"You're speaking to him!"—then climbed the ladder halfway and plucked his rope from Emma's hands. "Enough of this. Goodbye, children. I'm quite sure I'll never see you again."

And with that he stepped into his boat—and right into a puddle of ankle-deep water. He let out a girlish squeal and bent down to look. It seemed the gunshots that missed our heads had drilled a few holes in his hull, and the boat had sprung leaks.

"Look what you've done! My boat's shot all to pieces!"

Emma's eyes flashed. "What *we've* done?"

Sharon made a quick inspection and concluded the wounds were grave. "I am marooned!" he announced dramatically, then cut the motor, collapsed his long staff to the size of a baton, and climbed the ladder again. "I'm going find a craftsman qualified to repair my dinghy," he said, breezing past us, "and I won't have you following me."

We trailed him single file into the narrow passageway.

"And why not?" Emma shrilled.

"Because you're cursed! Bad luck!" Sharon waved his arm behind him as if shooing flies. "Begone!"

"What do you mean, *begone*?" She jogged a few paces and grabbed Sharon by his cloaked elbow. He spun around fast and yanked it away, and I thought for a moment his raised hand was about to strike her. I tensed, ready to leap at him, but his hand just hung there, a warning.

"I've run this route more times than I can count, and not once have I been attacked by Ditch pirates. Never have I been forced to abandon cover and use my petrol engine. And never, *ever* has my boat been damaged. You're more trouble than you're worth, plain and simple, and I want nothing more to do with you."

While he spoke, I glanced past him down the passage. My eyes were still adjusting to the dark, but what I could see was terrifying: winding and mazelike, it was lined with doorless doorways that gaped like missing teeth, and it was alive with sinister sounds—murmurs, scrapes, scurrying steps. Even now I could feel hungry eyes watching us, knives being drawn.

We couldn't be left here alone. The only thing to do was beg.

"We'll pay double what we promised," I said.

"And fix your boat," Addison chimed in.

"Never mind your bloody pocket change!" Sharon said. "Can't you see I'm ruined? How can I return to Devil's Acre? Do you think the vultures will ever let me be, now that my clients have killed two of them?"

"What did you want us to do?" Emma said. "We had to fight back!"

"Don't be facile. They would never have forced the issue if it wasn't for . . . for that . . . " Sharon looked at me, his voice falling to a whisper. "You might've mentioned earlier you were in league with *creatures of the night*!"

"Umm," I said awkwardly, "I wouldn't say 'in league with,' exactly . . . "

"There isn't much in this world I fear, but as a rule I keep my distance from soul-sucking monsters—and apparently you've got one following you like a bloodhound! I suppose it'll be along any minute?"

"Not likely," Addison said. "Don't you recall, some moments ago, when a bridge fell on its head?"

"Only a small one," Sharon said. "Now if you'll excuse me, I have to see a man about a boat." And with that he hurried away.

Before we could catch up to him he'd rounded a corner, and by the time we reached it he'd disappeared—vanished, perhaps, into one of those tunnels he'd mentioned. We stood turning circles, confounded and afraid.

"I can't believe he'd just abandon us like this!" I said.

"Neither can I," Addison replied coolly. "In fact, I don't think he has—I think he's negotiating." The dog cleared his throat, sat up on his hind legs, and addressed the rooftops in a booming voice. "Good sir! We mean to rescue our friends and our ymbrynes, and mark me, we will—and when we do, and they learn how you've aided us, they'll be *most* grateful."

He let that ring out for a moment, then went on.

"Never mind compassion! Fie on loyalty! If you're as intelligent and ambitious a fellow as I think you are, then you'll recognize an extraordinary opportunity for advancement when you see one. We are indebted to you already, but scrounging coins from children and animals is an awfully modest living compared to what having several ymbrynes in your debt could mean. Perhaps you'd enjoy having a loop all to yourself, your own personal playground with no other peculiars to spoil it! Anytime and anyplace you like: a lush summer isle in an age of abiding peace; some lowly pit in a time of plague. As you prefer."

"Could they really do that?" I whispered to Emma.

Emma shrugged.

"Imagine the possibilities!" Addison gushed.

His voice echoed away. We waited, listening.

Somewhere two people were arguing.

A hacking cough.

Something heavy was dragged down steps.

"Well, it was a nice speech," Emma sighed.

"Forget him, then," I said, peering into the passages that branched away left, right, and straight ahead. "Which way?"

We chose a passage at random—straight on—and started down it. We'd gone only ten paces when we heard a voice say, "I wouldn't go that way, if I were you. That's Cannibals' Alley, and it isn't just a cute nickname."

There was Sharon behind us, hands on his hips like a fitness coach. "My heart must be getting soft in my old age," he said. "Either that or my head."

"Does that mean you'll help us?" said Emma.

A light rain had begun to fall. Sharon looked up, letting a little splash his hidden face. "I know a lawyer here. First I want you to sign a contract laying out what you owe me."

"Fine, fine," said Emma. "But you'll help us?"

"Then I've got to see about getting my boat fixed."

"And *then*?"

"Then I'll help you, yes. Though I can't promise any results, and I want to state at the outset that I think you're all fools."

We couldn't quite bring ourselves to thank him, given what he'd put us through.

"Now stay close, and follow every instruction I give you to the letter. You killed two vultures today, and they'll be hunting you, mark my words."

We readily agreed.

"If they catch you, you don't know me. Never saw me."

We nodded like bobbleheads.

"And whatever you do, never, *never* touch so much as a drop of ambrosia, or on my eyes, you'll never leave this place."

"I don't know what that is," I said, and from their expressions I saw that Emma and Addison were likewise in the dark.

"You'll find out," Sharon said ominously, and with a swish of his cloak he turned and plunged into the maze.

CHAPTER THREE

*J*ust before a cow is put to the hammer in a modern slaughterhouse, it is prodded through a winding maze. The tight curves and blind corners prevent the animal from seeing more than a short distance ahead, so it doesn't realize until the last few steps, when the maze abruptly narrows and a metal collar clamps tight around its neck, where the journey has taken it. But as the three of us hurried after Sharon into the heart of Devil's Acre, I felt sure I knew what was coming, if not when nor how. With each step and each turn, we threaded deeper inside a knot, one I feared we'd never work apart.

The fetid air did not move, its only outlet an uneven crack of sky high above our heads. The bulged and slumping walls were so narrow that we had to go shoulder-first in places, the tight spots greased black by the clothes of those who'd gone before. There was nothing natural here, nothing green, nothing living at all save scurrying vermin and the bloodshot-eyed revenants who lurked behind doorways and under grates in the street, and who surely would've jumped at us if not for our towering, black-clad guide. We were chasing Death himself into the pit of Hell.

We turned and turned again. Every passage looked just like the one before it. There were no signs, no markers. Either Sharon was navigating by some brilliant feat of memory, or completely at random, trying to throw off any Ditch pirates who might've been pursuing us.

"Do you really know where we're going?" Emma asked him.

"Of course I do!" Sharon barked, bombing around a corner

without looking back. Then he stopped, doubled back, and stepped down through a doorway sunk half below street level. Inside was a dank cellar, just five feet high and lit by the merest breath of sallow gray light. We ran hunched along a subterranean corridor, discarded animal bones underfoot, the ceiling brushing our heads, past things I tried not to see—a slumped figure in a corner, sleepers shivering on miserable mats of straw, a boy in rags lying on the ground with a beggar's pail bangled around one arm. At its far end the passage widened into a room, and in the light of a few grimed windows there knelt a pair of miserable washerwomen, scrubbing laundry in a stinking pool of Ditch water.

Then we mounted more steps and went out, thank God, into a walled courtyard common to the backs of several buildings. In some other reality it might've contained a happy patch of grass or a little gazebo, but this was Devil's Acre, and it was a dump and a pigsty. Waves of fly-blown trash tossed from windows crested against the walls, and in the center, staked crookedly in the mud, was a wooden pen in which a skinny boy stood guarding an even skinnier pig—just one. By a mud-brick wall a woman sat smoking and reading a newspaper while a young girl stood behind her, picking nits from her hair. The woman and girl took no notice as we trooped past, but the boy leaned the tines of a pitchfork at us. When it was clear we had no designs on his pig, he sank into an exhausted squat.

Emma stopped in the middle of the yard to look up at lines of laundry strung between roof gutters. She pointed out again that our bloodstained clothes made us look like participants in a murder, and suggested we should change. Sharon replied that murderers were hardly outlandish here and urged her on, but she hung back, arguing that a wight in the Underground had seen our bloodstained clothes and radioed his comrades about us; they made us too easy to pick out of a crowd. Really, I think it was more that she felt uncomfortable in a blouse now stiff with another person's blood. I did, too—and if we found our friends again, I didn't want them to see us like this.

Sharon grudgingly assented. He'd been leading us toward a fence at the edge of the yard but now pivoted and took us into one of the buildings. We climbed two, three, four flights of stairs, until even Addison was wheezing, then followed Sharon through an open door into a small, squalid room. A gash in the ceiling had let in rain and warped the landing like ripples in a pond. Black mold veined the walls. At a table by a smoky window, two women and a girl were sweating over foot-powered sewing machines.

"We need some clothes," Sharon said, addressing the women in a stentorian basso that shook the thin walls.

Their pale faces looked up. One of the women picked up a sewing needle and gripped it like a weapon. "Please," she said.

Sharon reached up and pulled back the hood of his cloak a little, so that only the seamstresses could see his face. They gasped, then whimpered and fainted forward onto the table.

"Was that really necessary?" I said.

"Not strictly," Sharon replied, replacing his hood. "But it was expedient."

The seamstresses had been assembling simple shirts and dresses from scraps of cloth. The rags they worked with were heaped around the floor, and the results, which had more patches and seams than Frankenstein's monster, were hung on a line out the window.

As Emma reeled them in, my gaze crawled around the room. It was clearly more than just a workspace: the women lived here, too. There was a bed nailed together from scrap wood. I peered into a dented pot that hung in the hearth and saw the makings of starvation soup, fish skin and withered cabbage leaves. Their half-hearted attempts at decorating—a sprig of dried flowers, a horseshoe nailed to the mantel, a framed portrait of Queen Victoria—were somehow sadder than nothing at all.

Despair was tangible here, weighting down everything, the very air. I'd never been confronted with such pure misery. Could peculiars really be living these discarded lives? As Sharon pulled in an armful of shirts through the window, I asked him. He seemed almost offended by the idea. "Peculiars would never allow themselves to be so reduced. These are common slum dwellers, trapped in an endless repetition of the day this loop was made. Normals occupy the Acre's festering edges—but its heart belongs to us."

They were normals. Not only that, but loop-trapped normals, like the ones on Cairnholm whom the crueler kids would torment during games of Raid the Village. As much a part of the background scenery as the sea or the cliffs, I told myself. But somehow, looking at the women's weathered faces buried in rags, I felt no less terrible about stealing from them.

"I'm sure we'll know the peculiars when we see them," Emma said, sorting through a pile of dirty blouses.

"One always does," said Addison. "Subtlety has never been our kind's strength."

I slipped out of my bloody shirt and traded it for the least filthy alternative I could find, the kind of garment you'd be issued at a prison camp: collarless and striped, its sleeves of unequal length, patched together from cloth rougher than sandpaper. But it fit me, and with the addition of a simple black coat I found tossed over a chair back, I now looked like someone who might plausibly be from this place.

We turned our backs while Emma changed into a sacklike dress that pooled around her feet. "It'll be impossible to run in this," she grumbled. Plucking a pair of scissors from the seamstresses' table, she began to alter it with all the care of a butcher, ripping and jabbing until she'd sliced off the bottom at the knee.

"There." She admired her rough handiwork in a mirror. "A bit raggedy, but . . . "

Without thinking I said, "Horace can make you one better." Somehow I'd forgotten that our friends weren't just waiting for us in the next room. "I mean . . . if we see them again . . . "

"Don't," Emma said. For an instant she looked so sad, absolutely lost in it—and then she turned away, put down the scissors, and moved purposefully toward the door. When she turned to face us again, her expression had gone hard. "Come on. We've wasted enough time here as it is."

She had this amazing capacity to turn sadness into anger and anger into action, which meant nothing ever kept her down for long. And then Addison and I—and Sharon, who I suspect hadn't quite known whom he was dealing with until now—were following her out the door and down the stairs.

*   *   *

The whole of Devil's Acre—the peculiar heart of it, anyway—was only ten or twenty blocks square. After coming down from the workhouse we pried loose a board from a fence and squeezed into a suffocating passageway. It led to another that was slightly less suffocating, and that led to one a bit wider still, and that to one wide enough that Emma and I could walk side by side. On they widened, like arteries relaxing after a heart attack, until we came to something that might properly have been called a street, with red bricks running down the middle and sidewalks paving the edges.

"Fall back," Emma muttered. We shrank behind a corner and

peeked out like commandos, our heads stacked.

"What do you think you're doing?" Sharon said. He was still in the street and seemed more worried about being embarrassed by us than being killed.

"Looking for ambush points and escape routes," Emma said.

"No one's ambushing anyone," Sharon replied. "The pirates only operate in no man's land. They won't come after us here—this is Louche Lane."

There was, in fact, a street sign to that effect—the first I'd seen in all of Devil's Acre. *Louche Lane*, it read in fancy handwritten script. *Piracy discouraged.*

"Discouraged?" I said. "Then what's murder? Frowned upon?"

"I believe murder is 'tolerated with reservations.'"

"Is *anything* illegal here?" Addison asked.

"Library late fines are stiff. Ten lashes a day, and that's just for paperbacks."

"There's a library?"

"Two. Though one won't lend because all the books are bound in human skin and quite valuable."

We shuffled out from behind the wall and cast a somewhat baffled look around. In no man's land I'd anticipated death at every turn, but Louche Lane, from all appearances, was a haven of civic order. The street was lined with neat little shops, and the shops had signs and display windows and apartments on the upper floors. There was not a caved roof or a broken pane of glass in sight. There were people on the street, too, and they lingered, ambling along in singles and pairs, pausing now and then to duck into a shop or look in a window. Their clothes weren't rags. Their faces were clean. Maybe everything here wasn't new and sparkling, but the weathered surfaces and patched paint gave it all a handmade, worn-around-the-edges look that was quaint, even charming. My mother, if she'd seen Louche Lane in one of those thumbed-through-but-never-read travel magazines that papered our coffee table at home, would've crooned about its cuteness and complained that she and my dad had never taken a real European vacation—*Oh, Frank, let's go.*

Emma seemed palpably disappointed. "I was expecting something more sinister."

"Me too," I said. "Where are all the murder dens and bloodsport arenas?"

"I don't know what sort of business you think people get up to around here," Sharon said, "but I've never heard of a murder den. As for bloodsport arenas, there's only the one—Derek's, down Oozing Street. Good chap, Derek. Owes me a fiver . . . "

"And the wights?" said Emma. "What about our kidnapped friends?"

"Keep your voice down," Sharon hissed. "As soon as I take care of my own business, we'll find someone who can help you. Until then, don't repeat that to anyone."

Emma got in Sharon's face. "Then don't make me repeat *this*. While we appreciate your help and expertise, our friends' lives have been given an expiration date. I won't stall and dawdle about simply to avoid ruffling some feathers."

Sharon looked down at her, quiet for a moment. Then he said, "We all have an expiration date. If I were you, I wouldn't be in such a hurry to find out what it is."

We set off to find Sharon's lawyer. He quickly became frustrated. "I could've sworn his office was along this street," he said, turning on his heel. "Though it's been years since I've been to see him. Perhaps he's moved."

Sharon decided to go looking on his own and told us to stay put. "I'll be back in a few minutes. Don't speak to anyone."

He strode away, leaving us alone. We clustered awkwardly on the sidewalk, unsure what to do with ourselves. People stared as they passed by.

"He really had us going, didn't he?" said Emma. "He made this place sound like a hotbed of criminality, but it looks like any other loop to me. In fact, the people here look more normal than any peculiars I've ever seen. It's as if they've had every distinguishing characteristic vacuumed out of them. It's downright boring."

"You must be joking," said Addison. "I've never seen anyplace so vile or disgusting."

We both looked at him in surprise.

"How's that?" said Emma. "All that's here are little shops."

"Yes, but look what they're selling."

We hadn't until now. Just behind us was a display window, and in it stood a well-dressed man with mournful eyes and a cascading beard. When he saw that he had our attention, he nodded slightly, held up a pocketwatch, and touched a button on its side. The moment he pressed it he froze, and his image seemed to blur. A few seconds later, he moved without moving—disappearing and then reappearing instantaneously in the opposite corner of the window.

"Wow," I said. "That's quite a trick!"

He did it a second time, teleporting back to the other corner. While I stood mesmerized, Emma and Addison moved on to the next shop's window. I joined them and found a similar display, only standing behind the glass here was a woman in a black dress, a long string of beads dangling from one hand.

When she saw that we were looking, she closed her eyes and stretched her arms like a sleepwalker. She began to pass the beads slowly through her fingers, turning each one. My eyes were so locked on the beads that it took me a few seconds to realize something was happening to her face: it was changing, subtly, with each bead she turned. At the turn of one bead, I watched the pallor of her skin lighten. At the next, her lips thinned. Then her hair reddened ever so slightly. The cumulative effect, over the course of several dozen beads, was that her face became entirely different, morphing from that of a dark, round-featured grandmother to a young, sharp-nosed redhead. It was both enthralling and unsettling.

When the show was over, I turned to Addison. "I don't understand," I said. "What are they selling?"

Before he could answer, a preteen boy came hustling up to us and forced a pair of cards into my hand. "Two for one, today only!" he crowed. "No reasonable offer refused!"

I turned the cards over in my hand. One had the stopwatch man's photo on it, and on the back it read *J. Edwin Bragg, bilocationalist*. The other was a photo of the bead lady in a trance, and it read *G. Fünke, woman of a thousand faces*.

"Shoo, we're not buying," Emma said, and the boy scowled at her and scurried off.

"Now do you see what they're selling?" said Addison.

I cast my eyes down the street. There were people like the stopwatch man and bead lady in almost every shop window along Louche Lane—peculiars, ready to put on a show if you so much as glanced in their direction.

I hazarded a guess. "They're selling . . . themselves?"

"Like a dim bulb flickering to life," said Addison.

"And that's bad?" I said, guessing again.

"Yes," Addison said sharply. "It's outlawed throughout peculiardom, and for good reason."

"One's peculiarity is a sacred gift," Emma said. "To sell it cheapens what is most special about us."

It sounded like she was parroting a platitude that had been drilled into her from an early age.

"Huh," I said. "Okay."

"You aren't convinced," said Addison.

"I guess I don't see what the harm would be. If I need the services of an invisible person, and that invisible person needs money, why shouldn't we trade?"

"But you have strong morals, and that sets you apart from ninety-nine percent of humanity," said Emma. "What if a bad person—or even a below-averagely-moraled person—wanted to buy the services of the invisible peculiar?"

"The invisible peculiar should say no."

"But it isn't always so black and white," Emma said, "and selling yourself erodes your moral compass. Pretty soon you're dipping into the wrong side of that gray area without knowing it, doing things you'd never do if you weren't being paid to do them. And if someone were desperate enough, they might sell themselves to anyone, no matter what the other's intentions."

"To a wight, for instance," Addison added pointedly.

"Okay, yeah, that would be bad," I said. "But do you really think a peculiar would do that?"

"Don't be daft!" said Addison. "Just look at the state of this place. Probably the only loop in Europe that hasn't been laid waste to by the wights! And why do you think that is? Because it's been extremely useful, I am sure, to have an entire population of perfectly willing turncoats and informants waiting to do your bidding."

"Maybe you should keep your voice down," I said.

"It makes sense," Emma said. "They must have infiltrated our loops with peculiar informants. How else could they have known so much? Loop entrances, defenses, weak spots . . . only with help from people like this." She cast a venomous look around, her expression that of someone who'd just drunk curdled milk.

"No reasonable offer refused, indeed," Addison snarled. "Traitors, every one of them. Ought to be hanged!"

"What's the matter, hon? Having a bad day?"

We turned to find a woman standing behind us. (How long had she been there? What had she heard?) She was dressed in sharp and businesslike 1950s style—knee-length skirt and short black pumps—and puffed lazily at a cigarette. Her hair was teased up in a beehive and her accent was as flat and American as the Midwestern plains.

"I'm Lorraine," she said, "and you're new in town."

"We're waiting for someone," said Emma. "We're . . . on holiday."

"Say no more!" said Lorraine. "I'm on vacation myself. Have been for the last fifty years." She laughed, showing lipstick-stained teeth. "You just let me know if I can help you with anything. Lorraine's got the best selection on Louche Lane, and that's an actual fact."

"No, thanks," I said.

"Don't worry, hon. They won't bite."

"We're not interested."

Lorraine shrugged. "I was just being friendly. You looked a

little lost, is all."

She started to leave, but something she'd said had piqued Emma's interest.

"Selection of what?"

Lorraine turned back and flashed a greasy smile. "Old ones, young ones. All sorts of talents. Some of my customers just want a show, and that's fine, but others have specific needs. We make sure everyone leaves satisfied."

"The boy said no thank you," Addison said gruffly, and he seemed about to tell the woman off when Emma stepped in front of him and said, "I'd like to see."

"You what?" I said.

"I want to see," Emma said, an edge creeping into her voice. "Show me."

"Serious inquiries only," said Lorraine.

"Oh, I'm very serious."

I didn't know what Emma was up to, but I trusted her enough to go with it.

"What about them?" Lorraine said, casting an uncertain gaze at Addison and me. "They always so rude?"

"Yes. But they're all right."

Lorraine squinted at us as if imagining what it might take to forcibly eject us from her place, should the need arise.

"What can you do?" she said to me. "Anything?"

Emma cleared her throat, then bugged her eyes at me. I knew right away what she was telegraphing: *Lie!*

"I used to be able to levitate pencils and things," I said, "but now I can't even get one to stand on end. I think I'm . . . out of order, or something."

"Happens to the best of 'em." She looked to Addison. "And you?"

Addison rolled his eyes. "I'm a talking dog?"

"And that's all you do, talk?"

"Sometimes it seems that way," I couldn't resist saying.

"I don't know whom to feel more insulted by," said Addison.

Lorraine took a final puff of her cigarette and flicked it away. "All right, sugars. Follow me."

She started to walk away. We hung behind a moment and conferred in a whisper.

"What about Sharon?" I said. "He told us to wait here."

"This will only take a minute," Emma said. "And I have a hunch she knows a lot more about where the wights are hiding than Sharon does."

"And you think she's just going to volunteer such information?" said Addison.

"We'll see," Emma said, and she turned to follow Lorraine.

*   *   *

Lorraine's place had no window and no sign, just a blank door with a silver bell on a pull chain. Lorraine rang the bell. We waited while a series of deadbolts were slid from the inside, and then the door opened a crack. An eye glinted at us from the shadows.

"Fresh meat?" said a man's voice.

"Customers," Lorraine replied. "Let us in."

The eye disappeared and the door opened the rest of the way. We came into a formal entrance hall, where the doorman waited to look us over. He wore a massive overcoat with a high collar and a wide-brimmed fedora, the hat tilted so low that all we could see of his face were two pinprick eyes and the tip of his nose. He stood blocking our way, staring us down.

"Well?" said Lorraine.

The man seemed to decide we weren't a threat. "Okay," he said, stepping aside. He closed and locked the door behind us, then trailed after as Lorraine showed us down a long hallway.

We came into a dim parlor flickering with oil lamps. It was a sleazy place with delusions of grandeur: the walls were trimmed with gold scrollwork and velvet drapes, the domed ceiling was painted with tanned and tunicked Greek gods, and marble columns framed the entrance to the hall.

Lorraine nodded to the doorman. "Thank you, Carlos."

Carlos glided away to the back of the room. Lorraine walked to a curtained wall and pulled a cord, and the fabric slid aside to reveal a wide panel of sturdy glass. We stepped forward to look, and through it saw another room. It was very much like the one we were standing in, but smaller, and people were lazing about on chairs and sofas, some reading while others napped.

I counted eight of them. A few were older, graying at the temples. Two, a boy and a girl, were under the age of ten. They were all, I realized, prisoners.

Addison started to ask a question, but Lorraine gestured impatiently. "Questions after, please." She strode to the glass, picked up a tube connected umbilically to the wall below it, and spoke into one end. "Number thirteen!"

On the other side of the glass, the youngest boy stood and shuffled forward. His hands and legs were chained, and he was the only peculiar wearing anything resembling prisoner's garb: a striped suit and cap with the number 13 stitched boldly onto them. Though he couldn't have been older than ten, he had a man's facial hair: a bushy, triangular goatee and eyebrows like jungle caterpillars, the eyes below them cold and appraising.

"Why is he chained like that?" I said. "Is he dangerous?"

"You'll see," Lorraine said.

The boy closed his eyes. He seemed to be concentrating. A moment later, hair began to emerge from the brim of his cap, creeping down his forehead. His goatee grew, too, twisting into a clump, then rising and swaying like a charmed snake.

"Heavenly herons," said Addison. "How marvelously strange."

"Watch closely now," said Lorraine, grinning.

Number thirteen raised his shackled hands. The pointed end of his charmed goatee aimed itself at the lock, sniffed around the keyhole, and wriggled inside. The boy opened his eyes and stared ahead, expressionless. After ten or so seconds, the twisted goatee stiffened and began to vibrate, making a high musical note we could hear through the glass.

The padlock opened and the chains fell away from his wrists.

He bowed slightly. I stifled an urge to applaud.

"He can open any lock in the world," Lorraine said with a hint of pride.

The boy returned to his chair and magazine.

Lorraine covered the tube with her hand. "He's one of a kind, and so are the rest. One's a thought reader, very adept. Another can reach through walls up to her shoulder. That's more useful than it sounds, believe me. The little girl here flies if she's had enough grape soda."

"Is that right," Addison said thickly.

"She'd be happy to demonstrate," said Lorraine, and speaking into the tube, she summoned the girl to the window.

"It's not necessary," Emma said through clenched teeth.

"It's their job," said Lorraine. "Five, come forward!"

The little girl went to a table stocked with bottles, selected one filled with purple liquid, and took a long drink. When she'd drained it, she set down the bottle, let out a dainty hiccup, and went to stand by a cane-backed chair. A moment later she hiccupped again and her feet began to lift off the ground, pivoting upward while her head remained level. By the third hiccup, her feet had risen ninety degrees and she lay flat on her back in the air, her only support the top of the chair beneath her neck.

I think Lorraine expected more of a reaction from us, but—though impressed—we were a study in silence. "Tough crowd," she said and dismissed the girl.

"Now," Lorraine said, hanging up the tube and turning to face us. "If none of that was your cup of tea, I have lending agreements with other stables. By no means are your choices limited to what you see here."

"Stables," Emma said. Her voice was flat, but I could tell she was boiling just below the surface. "So you admit you treat them like animals?"

Lorraine studied Emma for a moment. Her eyes flitted to the man in the overcoat standing guard in the back. "Course not," she said. "These are high-performance assets. They're well fed, well rested, trained to perform under pressure, and pure as the driven snow. Most have never touched so much as a drop of ambro—and I've got the papers to prove it in my office. Or you could just ask them. Numbers thirteen and six!" she shouted into the speaking tube. "Come tell these people how you like it here."

The little boy and girl got up and shuffled to the window. The boy picked up the speaking tube. "We like it here very much," he said robotically. "Mam treats us real nice."

He handed the tube to the girl. "We like to do our work. We . . . " She paused, trying to recall something learned and forgotten. "We like our work," she mumbled.

Lorraine dismissed them irritably. "And there you have it. Now, I can let you test drive one or two more, but beyond that I'll need some kind of down payment."

"I'd like to see those papers," Emma said, glancing back at the overcoat man. "The ones in your office." Her hands, clenched at her sides, were starting to go red. I could see we needed to leave before things turned ugly. Whatever information this woman might've had wasn't worth the fight, and rescuing all these kids . . . well, as callous as it sounded, we had our own kids to rescue first.

"Actually, that won't be necessary," I said, then leaned in to Emma and whispered, "we'll come back to help them. We have to prioritize."

"The papers," she said, ignoring me.

"No problem," Lorraine replied. "Step into my office and let's talk turkey."

And then Emma was going and there was no unsuspicious way to stop her.

Lorraine's office was a desk and chair crammed into a walk-in closet. She had only just closed the door behind us when Emma sprang at her, pushing her hard against it. Lorraine swore and shouted for Carlos but went quiet when Emma held a hand to her face that glowed hot as an oven coil. On Lorraine's blouse, two blackened handprints smoked where Emma had pushed her.

There was a thump on the door and a grunt from the other side.

"Tell him you're fine," Emma said, her voice low and flinty.

"I'm fine!" Lorraine said stiffly.

The door rattled against her back.

"Tell him again."

Lorraine, more convincing now: "Get lost! I'm doing business!"

Another grunt, then receding footsteps.

"You're being very stupid," Lorraine said. "No one's ever stolen from me and lived."

"We don't want money," Emma said. "You're going to answer some questions."

"About what?"

"Those people out there. You think you own them?"

Lorraine's brow furrowed. "What's this about?"

"Those people. Those children. You bought them—do you think you own them?"

"I never bought anyone."

"You bought them and now you're selling them. You're a slaver."

"That isn't how it works. They came to me willingly. I'm their agent."

"You're their pimp," Emma spat.

"Without me they'd have starved. Or been taken."

"Taken by who?"

"You know who."

"I want to hear you say it."

The woman laughed. "That's not a good idea."

"Yeah?" I said, taking a step forward. "Why not?"

"They have ears everywhere, and they don't like being talked about."

"I've killed wights," I said. "I'm not scared of them."

"Then you're an idiot."

"Shall I bite her?" said Addison. "I'd really like to. Just a little."

"What happens when they take people?" I said, ignoring him.

"No one knows," she said. "I've tried to find out, but . . . "

"I'll bet you tried *very* hard," Emma said.

"They come in here sometimes," Lorraine said. "To shop."

"Shop," Addison said. "That's a nice word for it."

"To use my people." She looked around. Her voice dropped to a whisper. "I hate it. You never know how many they're going to want or for how long. But you give them what they ask for. I'd complain, but . . . you don't complain."

"Bet you don't complain about what they pay," Emma said contemptuously.

"It's not hardly enough for what they put 'em through. I try to hide the little ones when I hear they're coming. They bring 'em back roughed up, memories blanked out. I say, 'Where'd you go? What'd they make you do?' But the kids don't remember zip." She shook her head. "They get these nightmares, though. Nasty ones. It's hard to sell 'em after that."

"I oughta sell *you*," Emma said, livid, trembling. "Not that anyone would pay half a farthing."

I stuffed my fists into my pockets to stop them from flying at

Lorraine. There was more to be gotten from her. "What about the peculiars they kidnap from other loops?" I asked.

"They bring them through in trucks. Used to be a rare thing. Lately it's been all the time."

"Did one come through earlier today?" I said.

"A couple of hours ago," she said. "They had guards with guns all over the place, blocking the street. Made a big production of it."

"They don't usually?"

"Not usually. Guess they feel safe here. This delivery must've been important."

It was them, I thought. A trill of excitement shot through me—but was immediately stifled by Addison lunging at Lorraine. "I'm sure they feel *quite* safe here," he snarled, "among such perfect traitors!"

I snatched his collar and held him back. "Calm down!"

Addison struggled against me, and I thought for a moment he might snap at my hand, but then he relaxed.

"We do what we have to to survive," Lorraine hissed.

"So do we," said Emma. "Now tell us where those trucks go, and if you lie, or it turns out to be a trap, I'll come back and melt your nostrils shut." She held one burning finger just beyond the tip of Lorraine's nose. "Agreed?"

I could almost imagine Emma doing it. She was tapping into a deep well of hatred I'd never seen fully revealed before, and as useful as it was in situations like this, it was a little scary, too. I didn't like to think what she might be capable of, given the proper motivation.

"They go to their part of the Acre," Lorraine said, turning her head away from Emma's hot finger. "Over the bridge."

"What bridge?" said Emma, holding it closer.

"At the top end of Smoking Street. Don't bother trying to cross, though, unless you want your head to end up on a pike."

I reckoned that was all we were going to get out of Lorraine. Now we had to figure out what to do with her. Addison wanted to bite her. Emma wanted to trace an *S* on her forehead with her white-hot finger, branding her for life as a slaver. I talked them out of doing either, and instead we gagged her with a sash cord from the curtains and tied her to a leg of the desk. We were about to leave her like that when I thought of one last thing I wanted to know.

"The peculiars they kidnap. What happens to them?"

"Mrrrf!"

I pulled down her gag.

"None have escaped to tell," she said. "But there are rumors."

"About?"

"Something worse than death." She gave us a smile dripping with slime. "I guess you'll just have to find out, won't you?"

*   *   *

The moment we opened the office door, the man in the overcoat charged at us from across the parlor, something heavy raised in his hand. Before he could reach us, a muffled shout of alarm sounded from the office and he stopped, changing course to see about Lorraine. When he'd crossed the office threshold, Emma slammed the door behind him and melted the handle into useless slag.

That bought us a minute or two.

Addison and I bolted for the exit. Halfway there, I realized Emma hadn't followed. She was banging on the window of the enslaved peculiars' quarters.

"We can help you escape! Show me where the door is!"

They turned sluggishly to stare, splayed on their chaises and daybeds.

"Throw something to break the glass!" Emma said. "Be quick!"

None moved. They seemed confused. Perhaps they didn't believe rescue was really possible—or perhaps they didn't want to be rescued.

"Emma, we can't wait," I said, tugging at her arm.

She wouldn't give up. "Please!" she cried into the tube. "At least send out the children!"

Full-throated shouts from inside the office. The door shook on its hinges. Frustrated, Emma slammed the glass with her fist.

"What's the matter with them?"

Rattled stares. The little boy and girl began to cry.

Addison tugged the hem of Emma's dress with his teeth. "We must go!"

Emma let the speaking tube fall and turned away bitterly.

We hit the door running and burst out onto the sidewalk. A thick yellow murk had blown in, bundling everything in gauze and hiding one side of the street from the other. By the time we'd sprinted to the end of the block we could hear Lorraine bellowing behind us but couldn't see her; we turned one corner and then another until it seemed we'd lost her. On a deserted street by a boarded-up storefront, we stopped to catch our breaths.

"It's called Stockholm syndrome," I said. "When people start to sympathize with their captors."

"I think they were just scared," said Addison. "Where would they have run to? This whole place is a prison."

"You're both wrong," Emma said. "They were drugged."

"You sound pretty sure," I said.

She pushed back hair that had fallen over her eyes. "When I was working in the circus, after I'd run away from home, a woman approached me after one of my fire-eating shows. She said she knew what I was—knew others like me—and that I could make a lot more money if I went and worked for her." Emma gazed out at the street, her cheeks flushed from the sprint. "I told her I didn't want to go. She kept insisting. When she finally left she was angry. That night I woke up in the back of a wagon with my mouth gagged and hands cuffed. I couldn't move, couldn't think straight. It was Miss Peregrine who rescued me. If she hadn't found me when they stopped to reshoe their horse the next day"—Emma nodded behind us, to where we'd come from—"I might have ended up like them."

"You never told me that," I said quietly.

"It's not something I like to talk about."

"I'm very sorry that happened to you," said Addison. "Was that woman back there—was she the one who kidnapped you?"

Emma thought for a moment.

"It happened such a long time ago. I've blocked out the worst of it, including my abductor's face. But I know this. If you'd left me alone with that woman, I'm not sure I could've stopped myself from taking her life."

"We've all got demons to slay," I said.

I leaned against a boarded window, a sudden wave of exhaustion breaking over me. How long had we been awake? How many hours since Caul had revealed himself? It seemed like days ago, though it couldn't have been more than ten or twelve hours. Every moment since had been a war, a nightmare of struggle and terror without end. I could feel my body inching toward collapse. Panic was the only thing keeping me upright, and whenever it began to fade, I did, too.

For the merest fraction of a second, I allowed my eyes to close. Even in that slim black parenthesis, horrors awaited me. A specter of eternal death, crouched and feeding upon the body of my grandfather, its eyes weeping oil. Those same eyes planted with the twin stalks of garden shears, howling as it sank into a boggy grave. Its master's face contorted in pain, tumbling backward into a void, gutshot, screaming. I had slain my demons already, but the victories were fleeting; others had risen up quickly to replace them.

My eyes flew open at the sound of footsteps behind me, on the other side of the boarded-up window. I hopped away and turned. Though the store looked abandoned, someone was inside, and they were coming out.

There it was: panic. I was awake again. The others had heard the noise, too. Acting on collective instinct, we ducked behind a stack of firewood nearby. Through the logs I peeked at the storefront, reading the faded sign that hung above the door.

Munday, Dyson and Strype, attnys at law. Hated and feared since 1666.

A bolt slid and slowly the door opened. A familiar black hood appeared: Sharon. He looked around, judged the coast clear, then slipped out and locked the door behind him. As he hurried away in the direction of Louche Lane, we consulted in whispers about whether to go after him. Did we need him anymore? Could he be trusted? Maybe and maybe. What had he been doing in that shuttered storefront? Was this the lawyer he'd talked about seeing? Why the sneaking?

Too many questions, too many uncertainties about him. We decided we could make it on our own. We stayed put and watched as he turned ghostly in the murk and was gone.

* * *

We set out to find Smoking Street and the wights' bridge. Not wanting to risk another unpredictable encounter, we resolved to search without asking for directions. That became easier once we discovered the Acre's street signs, which were concealed in the most inconvenient places—behind public benches at knee height, dangling from the tops of lampposts, inscribed into worn cobblestones underfoot—but even with their help, we took as many wrong turns as right. It seemed the Acre had been designed to drive those trapped inside it mad. There were streets that ended at blank walls only to begin again elsewhere. Streets that curved so sharply they spiraled back on themselves. Streets with no name—or two or three. None were as tidy or tended to as Louche Lane, where it was clear a special effort had been made to create a pleasing environment for shoppers in the market for peculiar flesh—the idea of which, now that I'd seen Lorraine's wares and heard Emma's story, turned my stomach.

As we wandered, I began to get a handle on the Acre's unique geography, learning the blocks less by their names than by their character. Each street was distinct, the shops along them grouped according to type. Doleful Street boasted two undertakers, a medium, a carpenter who worked exclusively with "repurposed coffinwood," a troupe of professional funeral-wailers who did weekend duty as a barbershop quartet, and a tax accountant. Oozing Street was oddly cheerful, with flower boxes hanging from windowsills and houses painted bright colors; even the slaughterhouse that anchored it was an inviting robin's-egg blue, and I resisted an odd impulse to go inside and ask for a tour. Periwinkle Street, on the other hand, was a cesspit. There was an open sewer running down its center, a thriving population of aggressive flies, and sidewalks that overflowed with putrefying vegetables, the property of a cut-rate greengrocer whose sign claimed he could turn them fresh again with a kiss.

Attenuated Avenue was just fifty feet long and had only one business: two men selling snacks from a basket on a sled. Children crowded around, clamoring for handouts, and Addison veered off to snuffle around their feet for droppings. I was about to call after him when one of the men shouted, "Cat's meat! Boiled cat's meat here!" He came scurrying back on his own, tail tucked between his legs, whimpering, "I shall never eat again, never, never again . . . "

We approached Smoking Street from Upper Smudge. The closer we got, the more the block seemed to wither, its storefronts abandoned, its sidewalks emptying, the pavement blackening with currents of ash that blew around our feet, as if the street itself had been infected by some creeping death. At the end it curved sharply to the right, and just before the bend was an old wooden house with an equally old man guarding its stoop. He swept at the ash with a stubbly broom, but it piled up faster than he could ever hope to collect it.

I asked him why he bothered. He looked up suddenly, hugging the broom to his chest as if afraid I'd steal it. His feet were bare and black and his pants were sooty to the knee. "Someone's got to," he said. "Can't let the place go to hell."

As we passed he returned grimly to his task, though his arthritic hands could hardly close around the stick. There was something almost regal about him, I thought; a defiance I admired. He was a holdout who refused to give up his post. The last watchman at the end of the world.

Turning with the road, we moved through a zone of buildings that shed their skins as we walked: first the paint was singed away, and farther along the windows had blackened and burst; next, the roofs were caving and the walls coming down, and finally, as we came to the junction with Smoking Street, only their bones were left—a chaos of timbers charred and leaning, embers glowing in the ash like tiny hearts beating their last. We stood and looked around, thunderstruck. Sulfurous smoke rose from deep cracks that fissured the pavement. Fire-stripped trees loomed like scarecrows over the ruins. Drifts of ash flowed down the street, a foot deep in places. It was as close to Hell as I ever intend to find myself.

"So this is the wights' front driveway," said Addison. "How fitting."

"It's unreal," I said, unbuttoning my coat. Sauna-like warmth rose all around, radiating through the soles of my shoes. "What did Sharon say happened here?"

"Underground fire," Emma said. "They can burn for years. Notoriously difficult to extinguish."

There was a sound like a giant can of soda being opened, and a tall prong of orange flame shot up from a seam in the pavement not ten feet away. We started and jumped and then had to collect ourselves.

"Let's not spend one minute longer here than we need to," said Emma. "Which way?"

There was only left and right to choose from. We knew that Smoking Street terminated at the Ditch on one end and at the wights' bridge on the other, but we didn't know which way was which, and between the smoke, the fog, and the wind-blown ash, we couldn't see far in either direction. Choosing at random could mean a dangerous detour and a waste of time.

We were getting desperate when we heard a warbling tune drifting toward us through the fog. We scuttled off the road to hide among the carbonized ribs of a house. As the singers approached, their voices growing louder, we could make out the words to their strange song:

> The night before the thief was stretched,
>   the hangman came around
> I've come, he said, before you're dead,
>   a warning to expound
> I'll strangle your neck and send you to heck
>   and cut off your arm and do you some harm
>   and flay your hide and give you a riiiiiiiide . . .

Here they all paused for breath, then finished with: "SIX FEET UNDER THE GROUND!"

Long before they emerged from the fog, I knew whose voices they were. The figures took form in black overalls and sturdy black boots, tool bags swinging gaily at their sides. Even after a hard day's work, the indomitable gallows riggers were still singing at the top of their lungs.

"Bless their tuneless souls," Emma said, laughing softly.

Earlier we'd seen them working at the Ditch end of Smoking Street, so it seemed reasonable to assume that's where they were coming from—which meant they were walking in the direction of the bridge. We waited for the men to pass and disappear again into the fog before venturing back onto the road to follow.

We shuffled through reefs of ash that blackened everything—the cuffs of my pants, Emma's shoes and bare ankles, the full height of Addison's legs. Somewhere in the distance the riggers took up another song, their voices echoing weirdly through the burned landscape. Nothing around us but ruin. Now and then we heard a sharp *whoosh*, quickly followed by a spout of flame bursting from the ground. None erupted as close as the first one. We were lucky—getting roasted alive here would've been easy.

Out of nowhere a wind kicked up, sending ash and hot cinders skyward in a black blizzard. We turned and covered our faces in an effort to breathe. I pulled my shirt collar over my mouth, but it didn't help much and I started to cough. Emma took Addison into her arms, but then she started to choke. I tore off my coat and threw it over their heads. Emma's coughing quieted and I heard Addison's muffled voice say "Thank you!" beneath the fabric.

It was all we could do to huddle there and wait for the ash storm to end. I had my eyes closed when I heard something move nearby, and peeking through slit fingers I saw something that even here, amidst all I'd witnessed in Devil's Acre, startled me: a man strolling casual as could be, a handkerchief pressed to his mouth but otherwise unperturbed. He had no trouble navigating the dark because beams of strong white light were shooting from each of his eye sockets.

"Evening!" he called out, swinging his sight-beams toward me and tipping his hat. I tried to reply but my mouth filled with ash and then so did my eyes, and when I reopened them he was gone.

As the wind began to die, we coughed and spat and rubbed our eyes until we could function again. Emma set Addison on the ground. "If we're not careful, this loop will kill us before the wights do," he said. Emma handed me back my coat and hugged me hard until the air cleared. She had a way of wrapping her arms around me and nudging her head into the hollow of my chest so that no gaps were left between us, and I wanted badly to kiss her, even here, covered in soot from head to toe.

Addison cleared his throat. "I hate to interrupt, but we really should be getting on."

We unhooked our limbs, slightly embarrassed, and continued walking. Soon pale figures appeared in the fog ahead. They were milling in the street, crossing between shacks that encrusted the roadside. We hesitated, nervous about who they might be, but there was no other way forward.

"Chin up, back straight," Emma said. "Try to look scary."

We closed ranks and walked into their midst. They were shifty eyed and wild looking. Soot-stained all over. Dressed in scavenged castoffs. I scowled, doing my best impression of a dangerous person. They shied away like beaten dogs.

Here was a kind of shantytown. Low-slung huts made from fire-proof scrap metal, tin roofs weighed down with boulders and tree stumps, canvas flaps for doors if they had doors at all. A fungal smear of life overgrowing the bones of a burned civilization; hardly there at all.

Chickens ran in the street. A man knelt by a smoking hole in the road, cooking eggs in its blistering heat.

"Don't get too close," Addison muttered. "They look ill."

I thought so, too. It was the limping way they carried themselves, their glassy stares. Several wore crude masks or sacks over their heads with only slits for eyes, as if to hide faces chewed by disease, or to slow a disease's transmission.

"Who are they?" I asked.

"No idea," said Emma, "and I'm not about to ask."

"My guess is they're welcome nowhere else," Addison said. "Untouchables, plague carriers, criminals whose offenses are considered unforgivable even in Devil's Acre. Those who escaped the noose settled here, at the very bottom, the absolute edge of peculiar society. Exiled from the outcasts of outcasts."

"If this is the edge," said Emma, "then the wights can't be far away."

"Are we sure these people are peculiar?" I asked. There seemed to be nothing unique about them, aside from their wretchedness. Maybe it was pride, but I didn't believe a community of peculiars, however degraded, would allow themselves to live in such medieval squalor.

"Don't know, don't care," Emma replied. "Just walk."

We kept our heads down and our eyes forward, feigning disinterest in hopes that these people would return the favor. Most stayed away, but a few trailed us, begging.

"Anything, anything. A dropper, a vial," said one, gesturing to his eyes.

"Please," implored another. "We haven't had a kick in days."

Their cheeks were pocked and scarred, like they'd been crying tears of acid. I could hardly look at them.

"Whatever you want, we haven't got it," said Emma, shooing them away.

The beggars dropped back and stood in the road, watching us darkly. Another called out in a high, fraying voice. "You there! Boy!"

"Ignore him," Emma muttered.

I side-eyed him without turning my head. He was squatting against a wall, in rags, pointing at me with a trembling hand.

"You him? Boy! You're him, aincha?" He wore an eyepatch over glasses and flipped it up to study me. "Yeahhhhh." He whistled low, then flashed a black-gummed smile. "They been *waitin'* for you."

"Who has?"

I couldn't take it anymore. I stopped in front of him. Emma sighed impatiently.

The beggar's smile grew wider, crazier. "The dust-mothers and knot-blowers! The damned librarians and blessed cartographers! Anyone who's everyone!" He raised his arms and bowed in mocking worship, and I got a whiff of ripe funk. "Waitin' a *lonnnnnng* time."

"For what?"

"Come on," said Emma, "he's obviously a lunatic."

"The big show, the big show," said the beggar, his voice rising and falling like a carnival barker's. "The biggest and best and most and last! It's *allllllll*most here . . . "

A weird chill rattled through me. "I don't know you, and you sure as hell don't know me." I turned and walked away.

"Sure I do," I heard him say. "You're the boy who talks to hollows."

I froze. Emma and Addison turned to gape at me.

I ran back, confronting him. "Who are you?" I shouted in his face. "Who told you that?"

But he just laughed and laughed, and I could get nothing more out of him.

We slipped away just as a crowd began to gather.

"Don't look back," Addison warned.

"Forget him," said Emma. "He's a madman."

I think we all knew he was more than that—but that's all we knew. We walked fast in paranoid silence, our brains humming with unanswerable questions. No one mentioned the beggar's bizarre pronouncements, for which I was grateful. I had no clue what they meant and was too exhausted to speculate, and I could tell from their dragging feet that Emma and Addison were flagging, too. We didn't talk about that, either. Exhaustion was our new enemy, and to name it would only have empowered it more.

We strained to see any sign of the wights' bridge as the road ahead sloped downward into an obscuring bowl of fog. It occurred to me that Lorraine might've lied to us. Maybe there was no bridge. Maybe she'd sent us into this pit hoping its denizens would eat us alive. If only we had brought her with us, then we could've have forced her to—

"There it is!" Addison cried, his body forming an arrow that pointed straight ahead.

We struggled to see what he saw—even with his glasses, Addison's vision was sharper than ours—and after a dozen paces we could make out, just dimly, how the road narrowed and then arched over some sort of chasm.

"The bridge!" Emma cried.

We broke into a run, exhaustion momentarily forgotten, our feet sending up puffs of black dust. A minute later when we stopped for breath, the view had cleared. A shroud of greenish mist hung over the chasm. Looming faintly beyond was a long wall of white stone, and beyond that, a high pale tower, the top of which was lost among low clouds.

That was it: the wights' fortress. There was an unsettling

blankness about it, like a face with its features wiped clean. There was a wrongness about its placement, too—its great white edifice and clean lines contrasting bizarrely with the burned-over waste of Smoking Street, like a suburban shopping center plopped in the midst of the Battle of Agincourt. Just looking at it charged me with dread and purpose, as if I could feel all the disparate strands of my silly and scattered life converging toward a single point, unseen behind those walls. That's where it was: the thing I was supposed to do—or die trying. The debt I had to pay. The thing for which all the joys and terrors of my life thus far had been a prelude. If everything happens for a reason, my reason was on the other side.

Beside me, Emma was laughing. I gave her a baffled look and she composed herself.

"*That's* where they've been hiding?" she said by way of explanation.

"It would seem so," Addison said. "Do you find that humorous?"

"Nearly all my life I've hated and feared the wights. Across all those years, I can't tell you how many times I've imagined the moment we'd finally find their lair, their den. I'd expected at the very least a foreboding castle. Walls dripping with blood. A lake of boiling oil. But no."

"So you're disappointed?" I said.

"I am, a bit." She pointed accusingly at the fortress. "Is that the best they can do?"

"I'm disappointed, too," said Addison. "I hoped at least we'd have an army alongside us. But from the looks of it, perhaps we won't need one."

"I doubt that," I said. "Anything could be waiting for us on the other side of that wall."

"Then we'll be *ready* for anything," Emma said. "What could they throw at us that we haven't faced already? We've survived bullets, bombing, hollow attacks. . . . The point is, we're finally here, and after all these years of them ambushing *us*, we're finally bringing some fight to *them*."

"I'm sure they're quaking in their boots," I said.

"I'm going to find Caul," Emma went on. "I'm going to find him and make him weep for his mother. I'm going to make him beg for his worthless life, and then I'm going to put both hands around his neck and squeeze until his head melts off . . . "

"Let's not get ahead of ourselves," I said. "I'm sure there's a lot standing between us and him. There'll be wights everywhere. And armed guards probably."

"Maybe even hollows," Addison said.

"Definitely hollows," said Emma. She sounded vaguely excited by the idea.

"Point being," I said, "I don't think we should storm the gates without knowing more about what's waiting for us on the other side. We may only have one chance at this, and I don't want to throw it away."

"Okay," said Emma. "What do you suggest?"

"That we find a way to sneak Addison inside. He's the least likely to be noticed, small enough to hide almost anywhere, and he's got the best nose. He could do recon, then sneak out again and tell us what he found. That is, if he's up for it."

"And if I don't return?" said Addison.

"Then we'll come after you," I said.

The dog took a moment to consider—but only a moment. "I accept, on one condition."

"Name it," I said.

"In the tales that are told about us after our victory, I should like to be known as Addison the Intrepid."

"And so you shall," said Emma.

"Make that Extremely Intrepid," Addison said. "And handsome."

"Done," I said.

"Excellent," said Addison. "Time to have at it, then. Nearly everyone we care about in the world is on the other side of that bridge. Every minute I spend on this side is a minute wasted."

We would accompany Addison as far as the bridge, then wait nearby for his return. We began to jog downhill, the going easy, the shantytown around us growing denser as we advanced. The gaps between shacks closed until none remained, the whole of it blurring past in an unbroken patchwork of rust-eaten metal. Then abruptly the shacks and lean-tos came to an end, and for a hundred yards Smoking Street returned to a wilderness of caved walls and blackened timbers—a buffer zone of sorts, perhaps enforced by the wights. At last we came to the bridge, the mouth of it bearded by a scrum of people, a few dozen in all. While we were still too far away to register the state of their clothes, Addison said, "Look, an encamped army laying siege to the fortress! I knew we wouldn't be the only ones to take up the fight . . . "

Upon closer inspection, however, these were anything but soldiers. With a disappointed *humph* Addison's bright little hope winked out.

"They're not laying siege," I said. "They're just . . . laying."

The wretchedest shantytowners we'd seen yet, they were slumped in the ashes, arranged in postures of such listless torpor that for a moment I mistook even the ones who were sitting upright for dead. Their hair and bodies were blacked with ash and grease, and their faces so afflicted with pits and scars that I wondered if they were lepers. As we picked our way between them a few looked up weakly, but if they were waiting for something, it wasn't us, and their heads slumped down again. The only one standing was a boy in a flap-eared hunting cap who prowled between the sleepers, rifling their pockets. Those he woke swatted at him but didn't bother giving chase. They had nothing worth stealing anyway.

We were nearly past when one called out: "You'll die!"

Emma stopped and turned, defiant. "What was that?"

"You'll die."

The man who spoke lounged on a sheet of cardboard, his yellow eyes peeping through a burrow of black hair. "No one crosses their bridge without permission."

"We mean to cross it anyway. So if you know something we should beware of, speak now!"

The lounger stifled a laugh. The rest were silent.

Emma looked them over. "None of you will help us?"

One man started to say, "Be careful to—" but as soon as he'd begun, another man hushed him.

"Let them go, and in a few days we'll have their drippings!"

A moan of agonized desire went up among the shantytowners.

"Oh, what I wouldn't give for a vial of that," said a woman by my feet.

"For just a drop, a drop!" sang a man, bouncing on his haunches. "A drop o' their drippings!"

"Stop, it's torture!" another whimpered. "Don't even mention it!"

"To hell with all of you!" Emma shouted. "Let's get you across, Addison the Intrepid."

And we turned away in disgust.

*   *   *

The bridge was narrow, arched in the middle, and built from marble so clean that even ash from the street seemed wary of trespassing on it. Addison stopped us just shy of the edge. "Wait, there's something here," he said, and we stood by nervously while he closed his eyes and sniffed the air like a clairvoyant reading a crystal ball.

"We need to cross *now*—we're exposed out here," Emma muttered, but Addison was elsewhere; besides, it really didn't seem like we were in much danger. No one was on the bridge, nor was anyone guarding the barred gate on the other side. The top of the long white wall, where you might expect to see men posted with rifles and binoculars, was similarly empty. Other than its walls, the fortress's sole defense seemed to be the chasm that curved around it like a moat, at the bottom of which churned a boiling river that released the sulfurous green steam which hung all around us. The bridge was the only way across that I could see.

"Still disappointed?" I asked Emma.

"Downright insulted," she replied. "It's like they're not even trying to keep us out."

"Yeah, that's what worries me."

Addison gasped and his eyes sprang open. They shone, electric.

"What is it?" Emma said, breathless.

"It's only the faintest of traces, but I'd know Balenciaga Wren's scent anywhere."

"And the others?"

Addison sniffed again. "There were more of our kind with her. I can't say who, precisely, or how many. The trail goes quite muddy. Many peculiars have come this way recently—and I don't mean them," he said, looking banefully at the squatters behind us. "Their peculiar essence is weak, almost nonexistent."

"Then that woman we interrogated was telling the truth," I said. "This is where the wights bring their captives. Our friends were here."

Ever since they'd been taken, an awful suffocating hopelessness had been tightening around my heart, but its grip loosened now, slightly. For the first time in hours, we were running on more than just hope and guesswork. We had tracked our friends across hostile territory all the way to the wights' doorstep. That in itself was a small victory, and it made me feel, if only for a moment, like anything was possible.

"Then it's even stranger that no one's guarding this place," Emma said darkly. "I don't like this at all."

"I don't either," I said. "But I don't see any other way across."

"I might as well get it over with," said Addison.

"We'll come with you as far as we can," said Emma.

"I appreciate that," Addison replied, sounding somewhat less than extremely intrepid.

The bridge could be sprinted across in under a minute, I guessed, but why run? *Because*, I thought, a line from Tolkien materializing in my head, *one does not simply walk into Mordor.*

We started across at a brisk pace, murmurs and muted laughs following us. I glanced back at the squatters. Certain we were about to meet some grisly end, they were shifting around, angling for good views. All they needed was popcorn. I wanted to go back and pitch every last one into the boiling river.

In a few days we'll have their drippings. I didn't know what that meant and hoped I never would.

The bridge steepened. An encroaching paranoia was making my heart beat double time. I felt sure something was about to swoop down and we'd have nowhere to run. I felt like a mouse scurrying toward a trap.

In whispers we reviewed our plan: get Addison through the gate, then fall back to the shantytown and find somewhere unobtrusive to wait. If he hadn't returned within three hours, Emma and I would find a way in.

We were coming to the crest of the bridge, beyond which I'd be able to see a small section of the downslope that till now had been hidden. And then the lampposts shouted:

"Stop!"

"Who goes there!"

"None shall pass!"

We stopped and gaped at them, stunned to realize they weren't lampposts at all but desiccated heads impaled on long pikes. They were horrible, skin drawn and gray, tongues lolling—and yet, despite not being attached to throats, three of the heads had spoken to us. There were eight altogether, mounted in pairs on either side of the bridge.

Only Addison seemed unsurprised. "Don't tell me you've never seen a bridge head," he said.

"Go no further!" said the head on our left. "Almost certain death awaits those who cross without permission!"

"Perhaps you should say *certain* death," said the head on our right. "*Almost* sounds wishy-washy."

"We have permission," I said, improvising a lie. "I'm a wight, and I'm delivering these two captured peculiars to Caul."

"No one told *us*," the head on the left said irritably.

"Do they look captured to you, Richard?" said the one on the right.

"I couldn't tell you," said the left. "Ravens pecked out my eyes weeks ago."

"Yours, too?" said the right. "Pity."

"He don't sound like any wight *I* know," said the left. "What's your name, sirrah?"

"Smith," I said.

"Ha! We don't have a Smith!" said the right.

"I just joined up."

"Nice try. No, I don't think we'll let you through."

"And who's going to stop us?" I said.

"Obviously not us," said the left. "We're just here to forebode."

"And to inform," said the right. "Did you know I took a degree in museum studies? I never wanted to be a bridge head . . . "

"No one *wants* to be a bridge head," snapped the left. "No child grows up dreaming of becoming a bloody bridge head, foreboding at people all day and having your eyes pecked out by ravens. But life doesn't always scatter roses at your feet, does it?"

"Let's go," muttered Emma. "All they can do is natter at us."

We ignored them and continued up the bridge, each head warning us in turn as we passed.

"Step no further!" shouted the fourth.

"Continue at your peril!" wailed the fifth.

"I don't think they're listening," said the sixth.

"Oh, well," said the seventh airily. "Don't say we didn't warn you."

The eighth only stuck out his fat green tongue at us. Then we were beyond them and cresting the bridge, and there it came to a sudden end—a yawning, twenty-foot gap in the place where stone should've been, and I nearly stepped into it. Emma caught me as I reeled backward, arms pinwheeling.

"They didn't finish the damned bridge!" I said, my cheeks flushing with adrenaline and embarrassment. I could hear the heads laughing at me, and behind them, the road squatters.

If we'd been going at a run, we wouldn't have stopped in time and would've pitched right over the edge.

"Are you all right?" Emma asked me.

"I'm fine," I said, "but *we're* not. How are we supposed to get Addison across now?"

"This *is* vexing," said Addison, pacing along the edge. "I don't suppose we could jump?"

"No chance," I said. "It'd be way too far, even at a full run. Even with a pole vault."

"Huh," said Emma. She looked behind us. "You just gave me an idea. I'll be right back."

Addison and I watched as she marched down the bridge. At the first head she came to, she stopped, wrapped her hands around the pike it was impaled on, and pulled.

The pike came out with ease. As the head protested loudly, she laid it on the ground, planted her foot on its face, and gave a mighty yank. The pike slid free of the head, which went rolling off down the bridge, howling with rage. Emma returned triumphant, stood the pike at the edge of the gap, and let it fall across with a loud metallic clang.

Emma looked at it and frowned. "Well, it isn't London Bridge."
Twenty feet long by one inch wide and slightly bowed in the middle,
it looked like something a circus acrobat might balance on.

"Let's get a few more," I suggested.

We ran back and forth, prying up pikes and laying them across
the gap. The heads spat and swore and issued empty threats. When
the last of them had been pried off and rolled away, we'd made a
small metal bridge, roughly a foot wide, slippery with head goo and
rattling in the ashy breeze.

"For England!" Addison said, and he shimmied haltingly onto
the pikes.

"For Miss Peregrine," I said, following him.

"For the love of birds, just go," said Emma, and she stepped
on behind me.

Addison slowed us down badly. His little legs kept slipping
between the pikes, which made the pikes roll like axles and gave me
awful stomach flutters. I tried focusing on where to place my feet
without seeing past them into the chasm, but it was impossible; the
boiling river attracted my eyes like a magnet, and I found myself
wondering whether we were high enough for the fall alone to kill me
or whether I'd survive long enough to feel myself cooking to death.
Addison, meanwhile, had given up trying to walk altogether and
instead laid down, whereupon he began to push himself along the
pikes like a slug. In this way we proceeded, inch by undignified inch,
to just beyond the halfway point—and then my flutters sharpened
and gave way to something else: a knot in my stomach that I'd come
to know all too well.

Hollow. I tried to say it aloud but my mouth had gone dry; by
the time I'd swallowed and got the word out, the feeling had multiplied tenfold.

"What dreadful luck," Addison said. "Is it ahead of us or behind?"

I couldn't tell right away and had to poke around the feeling for a moment before I could pin it down.

"Jacob! Ahead or behind?" Emma shouted in my ear.

Ahead. My gut-compass was certain, but it made no sense: the downward slope of the bridge was now visible all the way to the gate, and the whole length was deserted. There was nothing there.

"I don't know!" I said.

"Then keep going!" Emma replied.

We were closer to the far side of the gap than the near; we'd be off the pikes faster if we continued forward. I shoved down my fear, bent and scooped up Addison, and started to run, slipping and wobbling on the unsteady pikes. The hollow felt close enough to touch, and I could hear it now, grunting toward us from some unseen place ahead. My eyes followed the sound to a spot in front of us but below our feet—on the cut-away face of the bridge, where several tall, narrow apertures had been carved into the stone.

There. The bridge was hollow, and a hollow was inside the bridge. Though its body would never fit through the openings in the stone, its tongues easily could.

I'd made it across the pikes and onto solid bridge when I heard Emma cry out. I dropped Addison and spun to see her behind me, one of the hollow's tongues wrapped around her waist and whisking her into the air.

She screamed my name and I screamed hers. The tongue flipped her upside down and shook her. She screamed again. There was no worse sound.

Another of its tongues slapped the underside of the pikes and our makeshift bridge went flying, clattering apart and plunging like matchsticks into the chasm below. Then the second tongue went for Addison, and the third punched me in the chest.

I fell to the ground, the wind knocked out of me. While I struggled for a breath, the tongue slithered around my waist and scooped me into the air. The other had Addison by his hind legs. In a moment, all three of us were dangling upside down.

Blood rushed to my head, darkening my vision. I could hear Addison barking and nipping at the tongue.

"Don't, it'll drop you!" I shouted, but he kept on.

Emma was helpless, too; if she burned the tongue around her waist, the hollow would drop her.

"Talk to it, Jacob!" she shouted. "Make it stop!"

I twisted to see the narrow openings through which its tongues had squeezed. Its teeth gnawed at the stone slats. Its black eyes bulged hungrily. We hung like fruit on thick black vines, the chasm yawning below.

I tried to speak its language. "SET US DOWN!" I shouted—but what came out was English.

"Again!" Addison said.

I shut my eyes and imagined the hollow doing as I asked, then tried again.

"Put us down on the bridge!"

More English. This wasn't the hollow I'd come to know, the one I'd communed with for hours while it was frozen in ice. This was a new one, a stranger, and my connection with it was thin and weak. It seemed to sense that I was fumbling for a key to its brain, and it hauled us suddenly upward, as if winding up to fling us into the chasm. I had to connect, somehow, *now*—

"STOP!" I screamed, my throat raw—and this time, out came the guttural scratch of hollowspeak.

We jolted to a stop in midair. For a moment we just hung there, swinging like laundry in a breeze. My words had done something but not enough. I'd merely confused it.

"Can't breathe," Emma croaked. The tongue around her was squeezing too hard, and her face was turning purple.

"Put us down on the bridge," I said—in Hollow again!—the words clawing at my throat as they came. Every burst of hollow-speak felt like I was coughing up staples.

The hollow made an uncertain rattle. For an optimistic

moment I thought it might actually do as I'd asked. Then it snapped me up and down as fast and hard as you'd shake out a towel.

Everything blurred and briefly went black. When I came to, my tongue was numb and I tasted blood.

"Tell it to put us down!" Addison was shouting. But now I could hardly speak at all.

"Ahm twying," I mumbled. I coughed, spitting out a mouthful of blood. "Puhh uff dow," I said, in broken-tongued English. "Puhh uff—"

I stopped, reoriented my brain. Took a deep breath.

"Put us down on the bridge," I said in crisp hollowspeak.

I repeated it three more times, hoping it might slip into some furrow of the hollow's reptilian brain. "Put us down on the bridge. Put us down on the bridge. Put us down on the—"

It gave a sudden bone-rattling roar of frustration, pulled me to the openings in the bridge where it was imprisoned, and roared again, flecks of black spittle spraying my face. Then it hauled all three of us up and hurled us back the way we'd come.

We tumbled through the air for what felt like too long—we were falling now, I was sure of it, arcing downward to our doom—and then my shoulder connected with the hard stone of the bridge, and we slid and skidded all the way down its slope to the bottom.

＊　　＊　　＊

We were, miraculously, alive—banged up but conscious, our limbs still connected to our bodies. We'd tumbled down the smooth marble bridge, scattering the pile of heads at the bottom as we rolled to a stop. They were all around now, taunting us as we collected ourselves.

"Welcome back!" said the one nearest me. "We quite enjoyed your screams of terror. What powerful lungs you have!"

"Why didn't you tell us a hollow was hiding in the damned

bridge?" I said, rocking myself up to a sitting position. Pains flared all over my body, from scraped hands, scuffed knees, and a throbbing shoulder that was likely dislocated.

"Where's the fun in that? Surprises are much better."

"Tickles must've taken a fancy to you," said another. "He chewed the legs off his last visitor!"

"That's nothing," said a head with a shiny hoop earring like a pirate. "Once I saw him tie a rope around a peculiar, lower him into the river for five minutes, then reel him up and eat him."

"Peculiar al dente," the third said, impressed. "Our Tickles is a gourmand."

Not quite ready to stand, I scooted over a few feet to Emma and Addison. While she sat rubbing her head, he tested his weight on an injured paw.

"You okay?" I asked.

"I knocked my head pretty good," Emma replied, wincing as I parted her hair to examine a trickle of blood.

Addison held up a limp paw. "I fear it's broken. I don't suppose you could've asked the beast to set us down gently."

"Very funny," I said. "Come to think of it, why didn't I just tell it kill to all the wights and rescue our friends, too?"

"Actually, I was wondering the same thing," said Emma.

"I'm *joking*."

"Well, I'm not," she said. I dabbed at her wound with my shirt cuff. She drew a sharp breath and pushed my hand away. "What happened back there?"

"I think the hollow understood me, but I couldn't make it obey. I don't have a connection with that hollow like I do—did—with the other one."

That beast was dead, crushed under a bridge and probably drowned, and now I was a little sorry about it.

"How did you connect with the first one?" asked Addison.

I quickly recounted how I'd found it frozen in ice up to its eyeballs, and after a night spent in strangely intimate, hand-atop-head communion I had, apparently, managed to safe-crack some vital part of its neurology.

"If you had no connection with the bridge hollow," said Addison, "why did it spare our lives?"

"Maybe I confused it?"

"You need to get better at this," Emma said bluntly. "We have to get Addison across."

"Better? What am I supposed to do, take lessons? That thing will kill us the next time we get near it. We'll have to find another way across."

"Jacob, there *is* no other way." Emma raked a veil of mussed hair away from her face and held me with her eyes. "*You're* the way."

I was launching into a creaky rebuttal when I felt a sharp pain in my backside and leapt yelping to my feet. One of the heads had bitten me on the ass.

"Hey!" I shouted, rubbing the spot.

"Stick us back on our pikes like you found us, vandal!" it said.

I punted it as hard as I could and it tumbled away into the crowd of squatters. All the heads began to shout and curse us, rolling about grotesquely with the action of their jaws. I cursed back and kicked ash in their horrible leathery faces until they were all spitting and choking. And then something small and round came sailing through the air and hit me wetly in the back.

A rotten apple. I spun to face the squatters. "Who threw that?"

They laughed like stoners, low and snickering.

"Go back where you came from!" one of them yelled.

I was starting to think that wasn't a bad idea.

"How dare they," Addison snarled.

"Forget it," I said to him, my anger already fading. "Let's just—"

"How *dare* you!" Addison shouted, livid, rising up to address them on hind legs. "Are you not peculiar? Have you no shame? We're trying to help you!"

"Give us a vial or get stuffed!" said a ragged woman.

Addison trembled with outrage. "We're trying to help you," he said again, "and here you are—*here you are!*—while our people are being murdered, our loops torn out root and branch, sleeping before the enemy's gate! You should be flinging yourselves at it!" He pointed his wounded paw at them. "You are all traitors, and I swear one day I shall see you dragged before the Council of Ymbrynes and punished!"

"Okay, okay, don't waste all your energy on them," Emma said, wobbling to her feet. Then a rotten head of cabbage bounced off her shoulder and fell *splat* to the ground.

She lost it.

"All right, someone's gonna get their face melted!" she yelled, waving a flaming hand at the squatters.

During Addison's speech, a group had been muttering in a conspiratorial huddle, and now they came forward holding blunt weapons. A sawed branch. A length of pipe. The scene was turning ugly fast.

"We're tired of you," a bruised man said in a lazy drawl. "We're puttin' you in the river."

"I'd like to see that," Emma said.

"I wouldn't," I said. "I think we should go."

There were six of them, three of us, and we were in rough shape: Addison was limping, Emma had blood running down her face, and thanks to my injured shoulder I could hardly lift my right arm. Meanwhile, the men were spreading apart and closing in. They meant to drive us into the chasm.

Emma looked back at the bridge and then at me. "Come on. I know you can get us across. One more try."

"I can't, Em. I *can't*. I'm not messing around."

And I wasn't. I didn't have it in me to control that hollow—not yet, at least—and I knew it.

"If the boy says he can't do it, I'm not inclined to disbelieve him," Addison said. "We must find another way out of this."

Emma huffed. "Like what?" She looked at Addison. "Can you run?" She looked at me. "Can you fight?"

The answer to both was no. I took her point: our options were winnowing fast.

"At times like this," Addison said imperiously, "my kind don't fight. We orate!" Facing the men, he called out in a booming voice, "Fellow peculiars, be reasonable! Allow me a few words!"

They paid him no attention. As they continued closing off our escape routes, we backed toward the bridge, Emma crafting the largest fireball she could muster while Addison yammered about how the animals of the forest live in harmony, so why can't we? "Consider the simple hedgehog, and his neighbor, the opossum . . . do they waste their energy trying to throw one another into chasms when they face a common enemy, the winter? No!"

"He's gone completely crackers," Emma said. "Shut your gob and bite one of them!"

I looked around for something to fight with. The only hard objects within reach were the heads. I picked one up by the last wisps of its hair.

"Is there another way across?" I shouted into its face. "Quick, or I'm throwing you into the river!"

"Go to Hell!" it spat, then snapped at me with its teeth.

I flung it at the men—awkwardly, with my left arm. It fell short. I rooted around for another head, picked it up, and repeated my question.

"Sure there is," the head sneered. "In the back of a prizzo van! Though if I were you I'd take my chances with the bridge hollow . . . "

"What's a prizzo van? Tell me or I'll fling you, too!"

"You're about to get hit by one," it replied, and then three gunshots rang out in the distance—*bam, bam, bam*, slow and measured, like a warning. Immediately the men who'd been coming at us stopped, and everyone turned to look down the road.

Half drawn through a cloud of swirling ash, something large and boxy was rumbling toward us. Then came the growl of a big engine downshifting, and out of the black appeared a truck. It was a modern machine of military issue, all rivets and reinforcements and tires half a man high. The back was a windowless cube, and two flak-jacketed, machine-gun-armed wights stood guard along its running boards.

The moment it appeared, the squatters went into a kind of frenzy, laughing and gasping for joy, waving their arms and clasping their hands like marooned shipwreck survivors flagging down a passing plane—and just like that, we were forgotten. A golden opportunity had smacked into us, and we weren't about to waste it. I tossed aside the head, scooped Addison into the crook of my left arm, and scrambled out of the road after Emma. We could've kept going—cut away from Smoking Street and retreated to some safer quarter of Devil's Acre—but here, finally, was our enemy in the flesh, and whatever was happening or about to happen was clearly of importance. We stopped not far off the roadside, barely hidden behind a knot of charred trees, and watched.

The truck slowed and the crowd swarmed it, groveling and begging—for *vials*, for *suulie* and *ambro* and *just a taste, just a little, please sir*, disgusting in their worship of these butchers, pawing at the soldiers' clothes and shoes and getting steel-toed kicks in return. I thought surely the wights would start shooting, or gun the engine and crush those foolish enough to stand between them and the bridge. Instead the truck stopped and the wights began to shout instructions. *Form a line, right over here, keep orderly or you'll get nothing!* The crowd fell into formation like destitutes in a bread line, cowed and fidgeting in anticipation of what they were about to receive.

Without warning, Addison began to struggle to be set down. I asked him what was the matter, but he only whimpered and struggled harder, a desperate look on his face like he'd just caught a major scent trail. Emma pinched him and he snapped out of it long enough to say, "It's her, it's her—it's Miss Wren," and I realized that *prizzo van* was short for prison van, and that the cargo in the back of the wights' enormous vehicle was almost certainly human.

Then Addison bit me. I yelped and let him go, and in an instant he was scrambling away. Emma swore and I said, "Addison, don't!" But it was useless; he was operating on instinct, the irrepressible reflex of a loyal dog trying to protect his master. I dove for him and missed—he was surprisingly speedy for a creature with just three working legs—and then Emma hauled me up and together we were after him, out of our hiding place and into the road.

There was a moment, a fleeting instant, when I thought we could catch him, that the soldiers were too mobbed and the crowd too preoccupied to notice us. And it might've happened but for the shift that came over Emma halfway across the road, when she spied the doors at the back of the truck. *Doors with locks that could be melted. Doors that could be flung open*, she must've thought—I could read it in the hope dawning on her face—and she passed Addison without even reaching for him and clambered onto the truck's bumper.

Shouts from the guards. I grabbed for Addison but he slid away, under the truck. Emma was starting to melt the handle of one door when the first guard swung his gun like a baseball bat. It hit her in the side and she tumbled to the ground. I ran at the guard, ready to do to him whatever I could with my one good arm, but my legs were kicked out from under me and I crashed down onto my hurt shoulder, a thunderbolt of pain surging through me.

Hearing the guard scream I looked up, saw him unarmed and waving an injured hand, and then he was tripping away into the mad swim of churning bodies. The squatters swarmed him, not just begging but demanding, threatening, crazed—and now, somewhere, one of them had his weapon. Looking panicked, he waved to the other wight with a two-hands-over-the-head *get me out of here!*

I struggled to my feet and ran for Emma. The other guard dove into the crowd, firing into the air until he could pull out his comrade and get back to the truck. The moment their feet hit the running boards, they slapped the side of the truck and the engine roared. I reached Emma just as it took off for the bridge, its monster tires spitting gravel and ash.

I clasped her arm to reassure myself she was still whole. "You're bleeding," I said, "a lot," which was a clunky statement of fact but also the best I could articulate how awful it felt to see her hurt— limping, a gash on her scalp leaking blood into her hair.

"Where's Addison?" she said. But before "I don't know" had left my lips, she interrupted—"We've got to go after it. This may be our only chance!"

We looked up as the truck was reaching the bridge and saw the guard gun down two squatters chasing after it. As they fell writhing to the dirt, I knew she was wrong: there was no chasing down the truck, no getting across the bridge. It was hopeless—and now the squatters knew it. As their comrades fell, I could feel their desperation turn to rage, and in what seemed an instant that rage turned on us.

We tried to run but found ourselves blocked on all sides. The mob was shouting that we'd "ruined it," that "they'd cut us off now," that we deserved to die. Blows started raining down on us—slaps, punches, hands tearing at our hair and clothes. I tried to protect Emma but she ended up protecting me, for a few moments at least, swinging her hands around, burning whomever she could. Even her fire wasn't enough to get them away from us, and the hits kept coming until we were on our knees, then balled up on the ground, arms protecting our faces, pain coming from every direction.

I was almost sure I was dying, or dreaming, because I heard at that moment singing—a loud, peppy chorus of "Hark to the driving of hammers, hark to the driving of nails!"—but with each line came a smattering of fleshy thuds and corresponding yelps: "What *(SMACK!)* to build a gallows, the *(THWACK!)* for all that ails!"

After a few lines and a few thwacks, the blows stopped raining down and the mob backed away, wary and grumbling. I saw dimly, through a haze of blood and grit, five brawny gallows riggers, tool belts hung from their waists and hammers raised in their hands. They'd cut a wedge through the crowd, and now they circled us, looking down doubtfully as if we were some strange species of fish they hadn't been expecting to find in their nets.

"Is this them?" I heard one of them say. "They don't look so good, cousin."

"Of course it's them!" said another, his voice like a foghorn, deep and familiar.

"It's Sharon!" Emma cried.

I could move my hand just enough to wipe one eye clear of blood. There he stood, all seven black-cloaked feet of him. I felt myself laugh, or try to; I'd never been so glad to see someone so ugly. He was digging something out of his pocket—little glass vials— and raised them above his head shouting, "I'VE GOT WHAT YOU WANT RIGHT HERE, YOU SICK MONKEYS! GO TAKE THEM AND LEAVE THESE CHILDREN BE!"

He turned and threw the vials down the road. The mob flooded after them, gasping and shouting, ready to tear one another apart to get them. And then it was just the riggers, slightly rumpled from the melee but unscathed, tucking their hammers back into their belts. Sharon, striding toward us with one snow-white hand outstretched, was saying, "What were you thinking, wandering off like that? I was worried sick!"

"It's true," said one of the riggers. "He was beside himself. Had us looking everywhere for you."

I tried sitting up but couldn't. Sharon was right over top of us, peering down like he was examining roadkill.

"Are you whole? Can you walk? What in the devil's name have these reprobates done to you?" His tone was somewhere between angry drill sergeant and concerned father.

"Jacob's hurt," I heard Emma say, her voice cracking. "So are you," I tried to say but couldn't get my tongue straight. It seemed she was right: my head felt heavy as stone, and my vision was a failing satellite signal, good one moment, gone the next. I was being lifted, carried in Sharon's arms—he was much stronger than he looked— and I had a sudden flashing thought, which I tried to say aloud:

Where's Addison?

I was all mush-mouthed but somehow he understood me, and turning my head toward the bridge, he said, "There."

In the distance, the truck seemed to be floating in midair. Was my concussed brain playing tricks?

No. I could see it now: the truck was being lifted across the gap by the hollow's tongues.

But where's Addison?

"There," Sharon repeated. "Underneath."

Two hind legs and a small brown body dangled from the truck's underside. Addison had clamped onto some part of its undercarriage with his teeth and caught a ride, the clever devil. And as the tongues deposited the truck on the far side of the bridge, I thought, *Godspeed, intrepid little dog. You may be the best hope we've got.*

And then I was fading, fading, the world irising toward night.

CHAPTER FOUR

*T*urbulent dreams, dreams in strange languages, dreams of home, of death. Odd bits of nonsense that spooled out in flickers of consciousness, swimmy and unreliable, inventions of my concussed brain. A faceless woman blowing dust into my eyes. A sensation of being immersed in warm water. Emma's voice assuring me everything would be okay, they're friends, we're safe. Then deep and dreamless dark for unknown hours.

The next time I woke, I wasn't dreaming and I knew it. I was tucked into a bed in a small room. Weak light spilled from behind a drawn window shade. So, daytime. But what day?

I was in a nightgown, not my old, blood-stained clothes, and my eyes were clear of grit. Someone had been taking care of me. Also: though I was bone-tired, I felt little pain. My shoulder had stopped aching, and so had my head. I wasn't sure what that meant.

I tried sitting up. I had to stop halfway and rest on my elbows. A glass pitcher of water stood on a night table by the bedside. In one corner of the room was a hulking wooden wardrobe. In the other— I blinked and rubbed my eyes, making sure—yes, there was a man sleeping in a chair. My mind was moving so sluggishly that I wasn't even startled; I merely thought, *that's odd*. And he was: so odd-looking, in fact, that I struggled briefly to understand what I was seeing. He seemed a man composed of halves: half his hair was slicked down while the other half was cowlicked all over the place; half his face was scraggly beard and the other half clean-shaven. Even his clothes (pants, rumpled sweater, ruffled Elizabethan collar) were half modern, half archaic.

"Hello?" I said uncertainly.

The man shouted, startling so badly that he fell out of his chair and landed on the floor in a clatter. "Oh, my! Oh, goodness!" He climbed back into the chair, eyes wide and hands aflutter. "You're awake!"

"Sorry, I didn't mean to scare you . . . "

"Ah, no, it was my fault entirely," he said, smoothing his clothes and straightening his ruffled collar. "Please don't tell anyone I fell asleep watching you!"

"Who are you?" I asked. "Where am I?" My mind was clearing fast, and as it did it filled with questions. "And where's Emma?"

"Right, yes!" the man said, looking flustered. "I might not be the best-equipped member of the household to answer . . . *questions* . . . "

He whispered the word, eyebrows raised, as if questions were forbidden. "But!" He pointed at me. "*You're* Jacob." He pointed at himself. "*I'm* Nim." He made a whirling motion with his hand. "And *this* is Mr. Bentham's house. He's very eager to meet you. In fact, I'm to notify him as soon as you're awake."

I squirmed up from my elbows to sit fully upright, the effort of which nearly exhausted me. "I don't care about any of that. I want to see Emma."

"Of course! Your friend . . . "

He flapped his hands like little wings while his eyes darted from side to side, as if he might find Emma in a corner of the room.

"I want to see her. Now!"

"My name's Nim!" he squeaked. "And I'm to notify—yes, under *strict* instructions . . . "

A panicky thought flew into my head—that Sharon, mercenary that he was, had rescued us from the mob only to sell us for spare parts.

"EMMA!" I managed to shout. "WHERE ARE YOU?"

Nim went blank and plopped into the chair—I'd scared him silly, I think.

A moment later feet came pounding down the hall. A man in a white coat burst into the room. "You're awake!" he exclaimed. I could only assume he was a doctor.

"I want to see Emma!" I said. I tried to swing my legs out of the bed, but they felt heavy as logs.

The doctor rushed to my side and pushed me back toward the sheets. "Don't exert yourself, you're still recovering!"

The doctor ordered Nim to go find Mr. Bentham. Nim ran out, bouncing off the doorjamb and flopping into the hall. And then Emma was at the door, out of breath and beaming, her hair spilling down a clean white dress.

"Jacob?"

At the sight of her, a burst of strength coursed through me and I sat up, pushing the doctor aside.

"Emma!"

"You're awake!" she said, running to me.

"Careful with him, he's delicate!" the doctor warned.

Checking herself, Emma gave me the gentlest of hugs, then sat

on the edge of the bed next to me. "I'm sorry I wasn't here when you woke up. They said you'd be out for hours more . . . "

"It's okay," I said. "But where are we? How long have we been here?"

Emma glanced at the doctor. He was writing in a small note-book but obviously listening. Emma turned her back to him and lowered her voice. "We're at a rich man's house in Devil's Acre. Someplace hidden. Sharon brought us here a day, day and a half ago."

"Is that all?" I said, studying Emma's face. Her skin was per-fectly smooth, her cuts faded to thin white lines. "You look almost healed!"

"I only had a few nicks and bumps . . . "

"No way," I said. "I remember what happened out there."

"You had a broken rib and a torn shoulder," the doctor inter-jected.

"They have a woman here," Emma said. "A healer. Her body produces a powerful dust . . . "

"And a double concussion," said the doctor. "Nothing we couldn't handle in the end. But you, boy—you were nearly dead when you arrived."

I patted my chest, my stomach, all the places I'd been pum-meled. No pain. I lifted my right arm and rotated the shoulder. No problem. "It feels like I've got a new arm," I said, marveling.

"You're lucky you didn't need a new head," came another voice—Sharon, ducking to fit his full height through the doorway. "In fact, it's a shame they *didn't* give you one, because apparently the one you've got now is full of sawdust. Disappearing like that, running off without a clue where you were going—and after all my warnings about the Acre! What were you *thinking*?" He towered over Emma and me, wagging his long white finger.

I grinned at him. "Hello, Sharon. Nice to see you again."

"Yes, ha-ha, it's all smiles now that everything's rosy, but you nearly got yourselves killed out there!"

"We were lucky," Emma said.

"Yes—lucky *I* was there! Lucky my gallows-rigging cousins were available that evening and I was able to catch them before they'd had too much Ditch lager at the Cradle and Coffin! They don't work for free, by the way. I'm adding their services to your tab, along with my damaged boat!"

"Fine, fine!" I said. "Settle down, okay?"

"What were you thinking?" he said again, his awful breath settling over us like a cloud.

And then it came back to me, what I'd been thinking, and I kind of lost it. "That you were an untrustworthy lout!" I fired back. "That it's only about money with you, and you probably would have sold us into slavery the first chance you got! Yeah," I said, "we looked into it. We know all about the shady things you peculiars get up to around here, and if you think for a minute we believe that *you*"—I pointed at Sharon—"or *any* of you"—I pointed at the doctor—"are helping us purely out of kindness, you're nuts! So either tell us what you want with us or let us go, because we've . . . we've got . . . "

A sudden, crashing wave of exhaustion. My vision unfocused.

"Got better things to . . . "

I shook my head, tried standing up, but the room had begun to spin. Emma held my arms and the doctor pushed me back gently onto my pillow. "We're helping you because Mr. Bentham asked us to," he said tersely. "What he wants with you, well, you'll have to ask him yourself."

"Like I keep saying, Mister whoever can kiss my *mmmff*—"

Emma clapped a hand over my mouth. "Jacob's not feeling himself at the moment," she said. "I'm sure what he meant to say was, thanks for saving us. We're in your debt."

"That, too," I mumbled through her fingers.

I was angry and scared, but also genuinely happy to be alive—

and to see Emma whole and healed. When I thought about that, all the fight leaked out of me and I was filled with simple gratitude. I closed my eyes to stop the room from spinning and listened to them whisper about me.

"He's a problem," said the doctor. "He can't be allowed to meet Mr. Bentham like this."

"His brain is addled," Sharon said. "If the girl and I could just talk with him in private, I'm sure he could be brought around. Might we have the room to ourselves?"

Reluctantly, the doctor left. When he was gone, I opened my eyes again and focused on Emma, looking down at me.

"Where's Addison?" I asked.

"He got across," she said.

"Right," I said, remembering. "Have you heard from him? Has he come back yet?"

"No," she said quietly. "Not yet."

I considered what that might mean—what might have happened to him—but I couldn't bear the thought. "We promised to go after him," I said. "If he can get across, so can we."

"That bridge hollow might not have cared about a dog getting across," Sharon butted in, "but you he'd peel off and toss right into the boil."

"Go away," I said to him. "I want to talk to Emma in private."

"Why? So you can climb out the window and run away again?"

"We're not going anywhere," Emma said. "Jacob can't even get out of bed."

Sharon wasn't swayed. "I'll go to the corner and mind my own business," he said. "That's my best offer." He went and perched himself on Nim's one-armed chair and began to whistle and clean his fingernails.

Emma helped me sit up, and we pressed our foreheads together and spoke in whispers. For a moment I was so overwhelmed by her closeness that all the questions flooding my brain vanished, and there was only her hand touching my face, brushing my cheek, my jaw.

"You had me so frightened," Emma said. "I really thought I'd lost you."

"I'm fine," I said. I knew I hadn't been, but it embarrassed me to be worried over.

"You weren't. Not at all. You should apologize to the doctor."

"I know. I was just freaked out. And I'm sorry if I scared you."

She nodded and then looked away. Her eyes drifted briefly to the wall, and when they returned, a new hardness glittered in them.

"I like to think I'm strong," she said. "That the reason I'm free right now instead of Bronwyn or Millard or Enoch is that I'm strong enough to be depended upon. That's always been me—the one who could take anything. Like there's a pain sensor inside me that's not switched on. I can block out awful things and get on with it, do what needs doing." Her hand found mine atop the sheets. Our fingers knotted together, automatic. "But when I think about you—how you looked when they pulled you off the ground, after those people . . . "

She let out a shaky breath and shook her head, as if chasing away the memory. "I just break."

"Me, too," I said, remembering the pain I felt whenever I saw Emma hurt, the terror that gripped me every time she was in danger. "Me, too." I squeezed her hand and searched for something more to say, but she spoke first.

"I need you to promise me something."

"Anything," I said.

"I need you not to die."

I cracked a smile. Emma didn't. "You can't," she said. "If I lose you, the rest isn't worth a damn."

I slid my arms around her, pulled her tight against me. "I'll do my best."

"That's not good enough," she whispered. "Promise me."

"Okay. I won't die."

"Say, 'I promise.'"

"I promise. You say it, too."

"I promise," she said.

"Ahh," Sharon said airily from the corner, "the sweet lies lovers tell . . . "

We broke apart. "You're not supposed to be listening!" I said.

"That was long enough," he said, dragging his chair loudly across the floor and planting it next to the bed. "We have important things to discuss. Namely, the apology you owe me."

"For what?" I said, irritated.

"Impugning my character and reputation."

"Every word was true," I said. "This loop *is* full of scumbags and creeps, and you *are* a money-driven lout."

"With not an ounce of sympathy for the plight of his own people," Emma added. "Though, again, thank you for saving us."

"Around here you learn to look out for number one," Sharon said. "Everyone's got a story. A plight. Everyone wants something from you, and they're almost always lying. So yes, I remain unapologetically self-directed and profit motivated. But I deeply resent your suggestion that I would have dealings of any kind with someone who trades in peculiar flesh. Just because I'm a capitalist doesn't mean I'm a black-hearted bastard."

"And how could we have known that?" I said. "We had to beg and bribe you not to abandon us at the dock, remember?"

He shrugged. "That was before I realized who you are."

I glanced at Emma, then pointed to my chest. "Who *I* am?"

"You, my boy. Mr. Bentham's been waiting a long time to speak to you. Since the day I first hung my shingle as a boatman—forty-odd years ago. Bentham ensured me safe passage in and out of the Acre if I promised to keep an eye out for you while I did it. I was to bring you to see him. And now, finally, I've kept my end of the bargain."

"You must have me confused with someone else," I said. "I'm nobody."

"He said you'd be able to speak to hollowgast. How many peculiars do you know who can do that?"

"But he's only sixteen," Emma said. "*Really* sixteen. So how can—"

"That's why it took me a while to put it all together," said Sharon. "I had to go see Mr. Bentham about it personally, which is where I was when you two ran away. You don't fit the description, see. All these years I've been keeping watch for an old man."

"An old man," I said.

"Right."

"Who can talk to hollows."

"As I said."

Emma tightened her grip on my hand and we exchanged a look—*no, it couldn't be*—and then I swung my legs out of bed, charged with new energy. "I want to talk to this Bentham guy. Right now."

"He'll see you when he's ready," Sharon said.

"No," I said. "*Now*."

As it happened, at that very moment there was a knock at the door. Sharon opened it to find Nim. "Mr. Bentham will meet our guests for tea in one hour," he said, "in the library."

"We can't wait an hour," I said. "We've wasted too much time here already."

At this, Nim went a bit red and puffed out his cheeks. "Wasted?"

"What Jacob meant," Emma said, "is that we have another pressing engagement elsewhere in the Acre that we're already late for."

"Mr. Bentham insists upon meeting you properly," Nim said. "As he always says, the day there's no time for manners, the world's lost to us anyway. Speaking of which, I'm to make sure you're dressed appropriately." He went to the wardrobe and swung open its heavy doors. Inside were several racks of clothes. "You may choose what you like."

Emma pulled out a frilly dress and curled her lip. "This feels so wrong. Playing dress-up and having tea while our friends and ymbrynes are forced to endure bird knows what."

"We're doing it for them," I said. "We only have to play along till Bentham tells us what he knows. It could be important."

"Or he could just be a lonely old man."

"Don't talk about Mr. Bentham that way," Nim said, his face puckering. "Mr. Bentham is a saint, a giant among men!"

"Oh calm down," Sharon said. He went to the window and pulled open the blinds, allowing a weak, pea-soup daylight to dribble into the room. "Up and at 'em!" he said to us. "You two have a date."

I threw back my covers and Emma helped me out of bed. To my surprise, my legs took my weight. I glanced out the window at an empty street enveloped in yellow murk, and then, with Emma holding my arm, went to the wardrobe to pick out a change of clothes. I found an outfit on a hanger tagged with my name.

"Can we have some privacy to change, please?" I said.

Sharon looked at Nim and shrugged. Nim's hands flapped. "It wouldn't be proper!"

"Ahh, they're fine," Sharon said, waving his hand. "No monkey business, all right?"

Emma turned beet red. "I wouldn't have any idea what you mean."

"Sure you wouldn't." He shooed Nim out of the room, then paused at the doorway. "I can trust you not to run away again?"

"Why would we?" I said. "We want to meet Mr. Bentham."

"We're not going anywhere," Emma said. "But why are *you* still here?"

"Mr. Bentham asked me to keep an eye on you."

I wondered if that meant Sharon would stop us if we tried to leave.

"Must be a pretty big favor you owed him," I said.

"Massive," he replied. "I owe the man my life." And bending himself nearly in half, he squeezed out into the hallway.

*   *   *

"You change clothes in there," Emma said, nodding toward a small connecting bathroom. "I'll change in here. And no peeking until I knock!"

"Ok*ayyy*," I said, exaggerating my disappointment in order to hide it. While seeing Emma in her underwear was an undeniably appealing prospect, all the life-threatening peril we'd endured lately had put that part of my teenage brain into a kind of deep freeze. A few more serious kisses, though, and my baser instincts might start to reassert themselves.

But anyway.

I shut myself in the bathroom, all gleaming white tile and heavy iron fixtures, and leaned over the sink to examine myself in a silvered mirror.

I was a mess.

My face was puffy and crosshatched with angry pink lines, which were healing quickly but still there, reminders of every blow I'd suffered. My torso was a geography of bruises, painless but ugly. Blood was caked into the hard-to-clean folds of my ears. The sight of it made me dizzy, and I had to grip the sink to stay upright. I had a sudden nasty flashback: fists and feet thrashing at me, the ground rushing up.

No one had ever tried to kill me with bare hands before. That was something new, much different than being hunted by hollows, which ran on instinct. Different, too, than being shot at: bullets were a quick, impersonal way to kill. Using your hands, though—that took work. It required hate. It was a strange and sour thing to know that such hatred had been directed at me. That peculiars who didn't even know my name had, in a moment of collective madness, hated me enough to try to beat out my life with their fists. I felt shamed by it, dehumanized somehow, though I couldn't exactly understand why. It was something I'd have to reckon with, if one day I ever had the luxury of time to reckon with such things.

I turned on the tap to wash my face. The pipes shuddered and groaned, but after a big orchestral flourish, they produced only a hiccup of brown water. This Bentham fellow might've been rich, but no amount of luxury could cocoon him from the reality of the hellish place where he lived.

How had he ended up here?

More intriguing still: how did the man know, or know about, my grandfather? Surely that's who Sharon had been referring to when he said Bentham was looking for an old man who could speak to hollows. Perhaps my grandfather had met Bentham during his war years, after he'd left Miss Peregrine's house but before he'd come to America. It was a defining period of his life which he'd spoken about only rarely, and never in detail. Despite all I'd learned about my grandfather in the past few months, in many respects he remained a mystery to me. Now that he was gone, I thought sadly, perhaps it would always be so.

I put on the clothes Bentham had given me, a preppy-looking blue shirt and gray wool sweater combo with simple black pants. It all fit perfectly, as if they'd known I was coming. As I was slipping into a pair of brown leather oxford shoes, Emma knocked on the door.

"How're you faring in there?"

I opened the door to a blast of yellow. Emma looked miserable in an enormous canary-colored dress with poufy sleeves and a hem that swam around her feet.

She sighed. "It was the lesser of many sartorial evils, I assure you."

"You look like Big Bird," I said, following her out of the bathroom, "and I look like Mr. Rogers. This Bentham is a cruel man."

Both references were lost on her. Ignoring me, she crossed to the window and looked out.

"Yes. Good."

"What's good?" I said.

"This ledge. It's the size of Cornwall, and there are handholds everywhere. Safer than a jungle gym."

"And why would we care about the safety of the ledge?" I asked, joining her at the window.

"Because Sharon's watching the hall, so obviously we can't go out that way."

Sometimes it seemed like Emma had whole conversations with me inside her head—ones I wasn't privy to—and then she'd get frustrated that I was confused when she finally let me in on them. Her brain worked so quickly that once in a while it got ahead of itself.

"We can't go anywhere," I said. "We've got to meet Bentham."

"And we will, but I'll be hanged if I'm spending the next hour twiddling my thumbs in this room. Saintly Mr. Bentham is an exile living in Devil's Acre, which means he's likely a dangerous lowlife with a sordid past. I want to have a look 'round his house and see what we can find out. We'll be back before anyone notices we're gone. Word of honor."

"Ah, good, a stealth operation. We're dressed perfectly, then."

"Very funny."

I was in hard-soled shoes that made every footstep sound like a hammer blow, she was in a dress yellower than a hazard sign, and I'd only recently found the energy to stand on my own two feet—and yet I agreed. She was often right about these things, and I had come to depend on her instincts.

"If someone spots us, so be it," she said. "The man's waited eons to meet you, apparently. He's not going to kick us out now for giving ourselves a little tour."

She opened the window and climbed onto the ledge. I stuck my head out cautiously. We were two stories above an empty street in the "good" section of Devil's Acre. I recognized a stack of firewood: it was where we'd been hiding when Sharon exited the abandoned-looking storefront. Directly below us was the law office of Munday, Dyson, and Strype. There was no such firm, of course. It was a front, a secret entrance to Bentham's house.

Emma offered her hand to me. "I know you're not a great fan of heights, but I won't let you fall."

After being dangled above a boiling river by a hollow, this little drop didn't seem so frightening. And Emma was right—the ledge was wide, and decorative knobs and gargoyle faces protruded everywhere from the masonry, making natural handholds. I climbed out, grabbed on, and shimmied along after her.

When the ledge turned a corner, and we felt fairly certain that we were paralleling a hallway out of Sharon's view, we tried opening a window.

It was locked. We shimmied on and tried the next one, but it, too, was locked—as were the third, fourth, and fifth windows.

"We're running out of building," I said. "What if none of them open?"

"This next one will," Emma said.

"How do you know?"

"I'm clairvoyant." And with that she kicked it, sending shattered glass into the room and tinkling down the front of the building.

"No, you're a hoodlum," I said.

Emma grinned at me and then knocked the last few shards from the frame with the flat of her hand.

She stepped through the opening. I followed, somewhat reluctantly, into a dark and cavernous room. It took a moment for our eyes to adjust. The only light came from the window shade we'd just broken, its puny glow revealing the edge of a packrat's paradise.

Wooden crates and boxes climbed to the ceiling in teetering stacks, leaving only a small aisle between them.

"I get the feeling Bentham doesn't like to throw things away," Emma said.

In reply, I released a rapid-fire triple sneeze. The air was swimming with dust. Emma blessed me and lit a flame in her hand, which she held up to the nearest crate. It was labeled *Rm. AM-157*.

"What do you think is in them?" I said.

"We'd need a crowbar to find out," said Emma. "These are sturdy."

"I thought you were clairvoyant."

She made a face at me.

Lacking a crowbar, we ventured farther into the room, Emma enlarging her flame as we left the petering window light behind. The narrow path between the boxes led through an arched door and into another room, which was equally dark and nearly as cluttered. Instead of crates, it was crammed with bulky objects hidden beneath white dust covers. Emma was about to pull one away, but before she could I caught her arm.

"What's wrong?" she said, annoyed.

"There might be something awful under there."

"Yes, exactly," she said, and tore away the cover, which scared up a cyclone of dust.

When the air cleared, we saw ourselves reflected dimly in a glass-topped case of the sort you find in museums, waist high and about four feet square. Inside, neatly arranged and labeled, were a carved coconut husk, a whale vertebra fashioned into a comb, a small stone axe, and a few other items, the usefulness of which wasn't immediately obvious. A placard on the glass read *Housewares Used by Peculiars on the Island of Espiritu Santo, New Hebrides, South Pacific Region, circa 1750.*

"Huh," Emma said.

"Weird," I replied.

She replaced the dust cover, even though there was little use in covering our tracks—it wasn't as if we could unbreak the window—and we moved slowly through the room, uncovering other objects at random. All were museum displays of one type or another. The contents bore little relation to one another save that they had once been owned or used by peculiars. One contained a selection of brightly colored silks worn by peculiars in the Far East, circa 1800. Another displayed what appeared at first glance to be a wide cross-section of tree trunk but upon closer inspection was in fact a door with iron hinges and a knob made from a tree knot. Its placard read *Entrance to a Peculiar Home in the Great Hibernian Wilderness, circa 1530.*

"Wow," Emma said, leaning in for a closer look. "I never knew there were so many of us in the world."

"Or used to be," I said. "I wonder if they're still out there."

The last display we looked at was labeled *Weaponry of the Hittite Peculiars, Kaymakli Underground City, no date.* Bafflingly, all we could see inside were dead beetles and butterflies.

Emma swung her flame around to look at me. "I think we've established that Bentham's a history buff. Ready to move on?"

We hurried through two more rooms filled with dust-covered display cases, then arrived at a utilitarian staircase, which we climbed to the next floor. The landing door opened onto a long and lushly carpeted hallway. It seemed to go on forever, its regularly spaced doors and repeating wallpaper creating a dizzying impression of endlessness.

We walked along peeking into rooms. They were furnished identically, laid out identically, wallpapered identically: each had a bed, a night table, and a wardrobe, just like the room I'd recuperated in. A pattern of red poppy vines curled across the wallpaper and continued through the carpeting in hypnotic waves, making the whole place seem like it was being slowly reclaimed by nature. In fact, the rooms would've been entirely indistinguishable had it not been for the small brass plaques nailed to the doors, which gave each a unique name. All were exotic sounding: *The Alps Room*, *The Gobi Room*, *The Amazon Room*.

Perhaps fifty rooms lined the hallway, and we were halfway down its length—hurrying now, certain there was nothing of use to be discovered here—when a blast of air rolled over us that was so cold it prickled my skin.

"Whoo!" I said, hugging myself. "Where'd that come from?"

"Could be someone left a window open?" Emma said.

"But it's not cold outside," I said, and she shrugged.

We continued down the hall, the air chilling more the farther we went. Finally, we turned a corner and came to a section of hall where icicles had formed on the ceiling and frost glistened on the carpet. The cold seemed to be emanating from one room in particular, and we stood before it watching flakes of snow waft, one by one, from the crack beneath its door.

"That is very strange," I said, shivering.

"Definitely unusual," Emma agreed, "even by my standards."

I stepped forward, my feet crunching on the snowy carpet, to examine the plaque on the door. It read: *The Siberia Room*.

I looked at Emma. She looked at me.

"It's probably just a hyperactive air conditioner," she said.

"Let's open it and find out," I said. I reached for the knob and tried it, but it wouldn't turn. "It's locked."

Emma put her hand on the knob and kept it there for several seconds. It began to drip water as ice melted from inside it.

"Not locked," she said. "Frozen."

She twisted the knob and pushed the door, but it opened only an inch; snow was piled up on the other side. We put our shoulders to its surface and, on the count of three, shoved. The door flung open and a gust of arctic air slapped us. Snow flurried everywhere, into our eyes, into the hall behind us.

Shielding our faces, we peered inside. It was furnished like the other rooms—bed, wardrobe, night table—but here were indistinct humps of white buried under deep-piled snow.

"What *is* this?" I said, shouting to be heard above the wind's howl. "Another loop?"

"It can't be!" Emma shouted back. "We're already in one!"

Leaning into the wind, we stepped inside for a closer look. I'd thought that the snow and ice were coming through an open window, but then the flurry abated and I saw there was no window at all, not even a wall at the far end of the room. Ice-coated walls stood on either side of us, a ceiling above us, and probably a carpet was somewhere below our feet, but where a fourth wall should've been the room gave way to an ice cave, and beyond that to open air, open ground, and an endless vista of white snow and black rocks.

This was, as near as I could tell, Siberia.

A single track of shoveled snow led through the room and into the whiteness beyond. We shuffled down the path, out of the room and into the cave, marveling at everything around us. Giant spikes of ice rose from the floor and hung from the ceiling like a forest of white trees.

Emma was hard to impress—she was nearly a hundred years old and had seen a lifetime's worth of peculiar things—but this place seemed to fill her with genuine wonder.

"This is astonishing!" she said, bending to scoop up a handful of snow. She tossed it at me, laughing. "Isn't it astonishing?"

"It is," I said through chattering teeth, "but what's it doing here?"

We threaded between the giant icicles and emerged into the open. Looking back, I could no longer see the room at all; it was perfectly camouflaged inside the cave.

Emma hurried ahead, then turned back and said, "Over here!" in an urgent voice.

I shuffled through deepening snow to her side. The landscape was bizarre. Before us was a white, flat field, past which the ground fell away in deep, undulating folds, like crevasses.

"We're not alone," said Emma, and pointed to a detail I'd missed. A man was standing at the edge of a crevasse, peering down into it.

"What's he doing?" I said, more or less rhetorically.

"Looking for something, it would seem."

We watched him walk slowly along the crevasse, always staring down. After about a minute, I realized I was so cold that I could no longer feel my face. A gust of snowy wind blew up and blanked the scene.

When it died down a moment later, the man was staring right at us.

Emma stiffened. "Uh-oh."

"Do you think he sees us?"

Emma looked down at her bright yellow dress. "Yes."

We stood there for a moment, our eyes locked on the man as he stared at us across the white wasteland—and then he took off running in our direction. He was hundreds of yards away through deep snow and a landscape of undulating fissures. It was unclear whether he meant us harm, but we were in a place we weren't supposed to be and it seemed like the best thing to do was leave—a decision that was soundly reinforced by a howl, the likes of which I'd heard only once before, in the Gypsies' camp.

A bear.

A quick look over our shoulders confirmed it: a giant black bear had clawed its way up from one of the crevasses to join the man on the snow, and *they were both coming after us*, the bear clearing ground much more quickly than the man.

"BEAR!" I shouted, redundantly.

I tried to run but my frozen feet refused to cooperate. Seemingly impervious to the cold, Emma grabbed my arm and swept me along. We lurched back into the cave, stumbled through the room, and tripped out the door, around which a penumbra of blowing snow was filling the hallway. I pulled the door shut behind us—as if that would stop a bear—and we retraced our steps down the long hall, down the stairs, and back into Bentham's dead museum to hide ourselves among his white-draped phantoms.

*   *   *

We hid between a wall and a hulking dust-sheeted monolith in the farthest corner we could find, straitjacketing ourselves into a space so narrow that we could not turn to face each other, the cold we'd run from settling firmly into our bones. We stood silent and shivering, stiff as mannequins, the snow on our clothes melting into puddles at our feet. Emma's left hand took my right—it was all the warmth and meaning we could trade. We were developing a language that was entirely untranslatable into words, a special vocabulary of gestures and glances and touches and increasingly deep kisses that was grow-ing richer, more intense, more complex by the hour. It was fascinat-ing and essential and in moments like this, made me just a little less cold and a little less scared than I might've been otherwise.

When, after a few minutes, no bears showed up to eat us, we dared to exchange whispers.

"Was that a loop we were in?" I asked. "A loop within a loop?"

"I don't know what that was," Emma replied.

"Siberia. That's what the door said."

"If that was Siberia, then the room it was in was some kind of portal, not a loop. And portals don't exist, of course."

"Of course," I replied, though it wouldn't have been so strange to believe, in a world where time loops existed, that portals did, too.

"What if it was just a really old loop?" I suggested. "Like ice-age old, ten or fifteen thousand years? Devil's Acre might've looked like that back then."

"I don't think there are any loops that ancient," Emma said.

My teeth chattered. "I can't stop shaking." I said.

Emma pressed her side to mine and rubbed my back with her warm hand.

"If I could make a portal to anywhere," I said, "Siberia would not be high on my list of choices."

"Where would you go, then?"

"Hm. Hawaii, maybe? Though I guess that's boring. Everyone would say Hawaii."

"Not me."

"Where would you go?"

"The place you're from," Emma said. "In Florida."

"Why on earth would you want to go there?"

"I think it'd be interesting to see where you grew up."

"That's sweet," I said. "There's not much to it, though. It's really quiet."

She leaned her head on my shoulder and exhaled a warm breath

down my arm. "Sounds like heaven."

"You've got snow in your hair," I said, but it melted when I tried to brush it out. I shook the cold water from my hand onto the floor—and that's when I noticed our footprints. We'd left a trail of melting snow that probably led right to our hiding spot.

"What dimwits we are," I said, pointing out the tracks. "We should've left our shoes behind!"

"It's okay," said Emma. "If they haven't tracked us by now, they probably—"

Loud, clonking footsteps echoed from across the room, accompanied by the sound of a large animal breathing.

"Back to the window, quick as you can," Emma hissed, and we wormed out of our hiding spot.

I tried to run but slipped in a puddle. I grabbed the closest thing at hand, which happened to be the sheet covering the large object we'd been hiding behind. The sheet came ripping away, uncovering another display case with a resounding *zzzzzwit!* and landing me on the floor in a pile of rumpled canvas.

When I looked up, the first thing I saw was a girl—not Emma, who was standing above me, but past her, inside the case, behind the glass. She had a perfectly angelic face and a ruffled dress and a bow in her hair, and she stared glassily at nothing in what seemed the permanent rictus of a taxidermied human being.

I freaked. Emma turned to see what I was freaking out about, and then *she* freaked.

She dragged me to my feet and we ran.

* * *

I'd forgotten all about the guy chasing us, the bear, Siberia. I just wanted to get out of that room, away from the stuffed girl, and far away from any possibility that Emma and I might end up like her, dead and encased behind glass. Now I knew all I needed to know about this Bentham guy—he was some kind of twisted collector, and I was sure that if we looked under more dust covers, we'd find more specimens like the girl.

We sped around a corner only to find, towering before us, a terrifying ten-foot mountain of fur and claws. We screamed, tried too late to stop running, and slid into a pile at the bear's feet. There we cowered, waiting to die. Hot, stinking breath rolled over us. Something wet and rough mopped the side of my face.

I'd been licked by a bear. I'd been licked by a bear, and someone was *laughing*.

"Calm yourself, he won't bite!" the someone said, and I uncovered my face to see a long furry nose and big brown eyes staring down at me.

Had the bear spoken? Do bears talk about themselves in the third person?

"His name's PT," the someone continued, "and he's my bodyguard. He's quite friendly, provided you stay on my good side. PT, sit!"

PT sat, then began licking his paw instead of my face. I flipped myself right side up, wiped the slobber from my cheek, and finally saw the owner of the voice. He was an older man—a gentleman—and he wore a subtle smirk that complemented his killer outfit: top hat, cane, gloves, and a high white collar that rose from the top of his dark jacket.

He bowed slightly and tipped his hat. "Myron Bentham, at your service."

"Back away slowly," Emma whispered in my ear, and we stood up together and side-stepped out of the bear's reach. "We don't want any trouble, mister. Just let us go and no one gets hurt."

Bentham spread his arms and smiled. "You're free to leave anytime you like. But that would be such a disappointment. You've only just arrived, and we have so much to talk about."

"Yeah?" I said. "Maybe you can start by explaining that girl in the case over there!"

"And the Siberia Room!" said Emma.

"You're upset, you're cold, and you're wet. Wouldn't you rather discuss all this over a pot of hot tea?"

Yes, but I wasn't going to say so.

"We're not going anywhere with you until we know what's happening here," said Emma.

"Very well," Bentham replied, not losing an ounce of his good humor. "That was my assistant you surprised in the Siberia Room—which, as you likely gathered, leads to a time loop in Siberia."

"But that's impossible," said Emma. "Siberia is thousands of miles away."

"Three thousand four hundred and eighty-nine," he replied. "But making interloop travel possible has been my life's work." He turned to me. "As for the case you uncovered, that's Sophronia Winstead. She was the first peculiar child born to the royal family of England. Fascinating life she led, if a bit tragic in the end. I have all sorts of notable peculiars here in my *peculiarium*—well known and unknown, famous and infamous—any or all of which I'm happy to show you. I have nothing to hide."

"He's a psycho," I muttered to Emma. "He just wants to stuff us and add us to his collection!"

Bentham laughed. (His hearing, apparently, was very sharp.) "They're only wax models, my boy. I am a collector and a preservationist, yes—but not of humans. Do you really think I waited so long to meet you, only to pull out your insides and lock you in a cabinet?"

"I've heard of stranger hobbies," I said, thinking of Enoch and his army of homunculi. "What is it you want with us?"

"All in good time," he said. "Let's get you warm and dry first. Then, tea. Then—"

"I don't mean to be rude," Emma cut in, "but we've spent too much time here already. Our friends—"

"Are all right, for the moment," Bentham said. "I've looked into the matter, and it isn't as close to midnight for them as you might imagine."

"How do you know?" Emma said quickly. "What do you mean, it isn't close—"

"What do you mean, looked into it?" I said, talking over her.

"All in good time," Bentham repeated. "I know it's difficult, but you must be patient. There's too much to tell all at once, and in such a sorry state." He stretched out an arm toward us. "Look. You're shivering."

"Fine, then," I said. "Let's have tea."

"Excellent!" said Bentham. He rapped his cane twice on the floor. "PT, come!"

The bear grunted in an agreeable sort of way, stood on its hind legs, and walked—waddling like a stubby-legged fat person—to where Bentham stood. Upon reaching him, the animal bent down and scooped him into the air, carrying him like a baby, one paw supporting his back and the other his legs.

"I know it's an unconventional way to travel," Bentham said over PT's bushy shoulder, "but I tire easily." He pointed ahead of them with his cane and said, "PT, library!"

Emma and I watched in amazement as PT began to walk away with Mr. Bentham.

You don't see that every day, I thought. Which was true of nearly everything I'd seen that day.

"PT, stop!" Bentham commanded.

The bear stopped. Bentham waved to us.

"Are you coming?"

We'd been staring.

"Sorry," Emma said, and we ran to catch up.

*　　*　　*

We wended our way through the maze after Bentham and his bear.

"Is your bear peculiar?" I asked.

"Yes, he's a grimbear," said Bentham, rubbing PT's shoulder affectionately. "They are the preferred companion of ymbrynes in Russia and Finland, and grimbear-taming is an old and respected art among peculiars there. They're strong enough to fight off a hollowgast yet gentle enough to care for a child, they're warmer than electric blankets on winter nights, and they make fearsome protectors, as you'll see here . . . PT, left!"

As Bentham extolled the virtues of grimbears, we came into a small anteroom. Under a glass canopy in the middle of the room were three ladies and, towering over them, a giant, vicious-looking bear. My breath caught for a moment before I realized they were motionless, another of Bentham's displays.

"That's Miss Waxwing, Miss Troupial, and Miss Grebe," Bentham said, "and their grim, Alexi."

The grimbear, on second look, appeared to be protecting the wax ymbrynes. The ladies were posed calmly around it while the bear was raised on its hind legs, frozen in midroar while swiping its paw at an enemy. Its other paw rested almost sweetly on one of the ymbrynes' shoulders, and her fingers were hooked around one of its long nails, as if to demonstrate her casual mastery over such a fearsome creature.

"Alexi was PT's great-uncle," Bentham said. "Say hello to your uncle, PT!"

PT grunted.

"If only you could do that with hollows," Emma whispered to me.

"How long does it take to train a grimbear?" I asked Bentham.

"Years," he replied. "Grims are naturally very independent."

"Years," I whispered to Emma.

Emma rolled her eyes. "And is Alexi made of wax, too?" she said to Bentham.

"Oh no, he's taxidermy."

Apparently Bentham's aversion to stuffing peculiar folk did not extend to peculiar animals. If Addison were here, I thought, there'd be fireworks.

I shivered. Emma ran a warm hand up my back. Bentham noticed, too, and said, "Forgive me! I so seldom have visitors that I can't help showing off my collection when they come. Now, I keep promising tea, and tea there shall be!"

Bentham pointed his cane and PT resumed walking. We followed them out of the dust-sheeted artifact storerooms through other parts of the house. It was in many ways the home of an average rich man—there was a marble-columned entry hall, a formal dining room with tapestried walls and seating for dozens, wings whose sole purpose seemed to be the display of tastefully arranged furnishings. But in each room, alongside everything else, were always a few objects from Bentham's peculiar collection.

"Fifteenth-century Spain," he said, indicating a gleaming suit of armor standing in a hall. "Had it made new. Fits me like a glove!"

At last we came to the library—the most beautiful I'd ever seen. Bentham told PT to set him down, brushed fur from his jacket, and showed us in. The room was three stories high at least, with shelves rising to dizzying heights above us. An array of staircases, catwalks, and rolling ladders had been constructed to reach them.

"I confess I haven't read them all," Bentham said, "but I'm working on it."

He ushered us toward a battalion of couches surrounding a flaming hearth whose warmth filled the room. Waiting by the fire were Sharon and Nim. "Call *me* an untrustworthy lout!" Sharon hissed, but before he berated me further Bentham shooed him away to fetch us blankets. We were under the protection of the master's good graces, and Sharon's tongue-lashing would have to wait.

Within a minute we were seated on a couch and wrapped in blankets. Nim fluttered around preparing tea on gilded trays, and PT, curled before the flames, was fast settling into a state of hibernation. I tried to resist the feeling of cozy contentedness that was beginning to settle over me and focus on our unfinished business—the big questions and seemingly intractable problems. Our friends and ymbrynes. The absurd and hopeless task we had assigned ourselves. It was enough to crush me if I thought about it all at once. So I asked Nim for three lumps of sugar and enough cream to turn the tea white, then downed it in three gulps and asked for more.

Sharon had retreated to a corner, where he could sulk but still overhear our conversation.

Emma was eager to dispense with the formalities. "So," she said. "Can we talk now?"

Bentham ignored her. He was sitting across from us but staring at me, the oddest little grin on his face.

"What?" I said, wiping a dribble of tea from my chin.

"It's uncanny," he replied. "You're the spitting image."

"Of who?"

"Of your grandfather, of course."

I lowered my teacup. "You knew him?"

"I did. He was a friend to me, long ago, when I badly needed one."

I glanced at Emma. She'd gone a bit pale and was clenching her teacup.

"He died a few months ago," I said.

"Yes. I was very sorry to hear it," Bentham said. "And surprised, to be honest, that he held out as long as he did. I assumed he'd been killed years ago. He had so many enemies—but he was exceedingly talented, your grandfather."

"What was the nature of your friendship, exactly?" said Emma, her tone like a police interrogator's.

"And you must be Emma Bloom," Bentham said, finally looking at her. "I've heard a great deal about you."

She seemed surprised. "You have?"

"Oh, yes. Abraham was very fond of you."

"That's news to me," she said, blushing.

"You're even prettier than he said you were."

She clenched her jaw. "Thank you," she said flatly. "How did you know him?"

Bentham's smile wilted. "Down to business, then."

"If you wouldn't mind."

"Not at all," he said, though his demeanor had cooled by a few degrees. "Now, you asked me before about the Siberia Room, and I know, Miss Bloom, that you were unsatisfied with the answer I gave."

"Yes, but I'm—we are—more interested in Jacob's grandfather, and why you brought us here."

"They are related, I promise. That room, and this house generally, is the place to begin."

"Okay," I said. "Tell us about the house."

Bentham took a breath and steepled his fingers against his lips for a moment, thinking. Then he said, "This house is filled with priceless artifacts I've brought back over a lifetime of expeditions, but none are more valuable than the house itself. It is a machine, a device of my own invention. I call it the Panloopticon."

"Mr. Bentham's a genius," Nim said, laying a plate of sandwiches before us. "Sandwich, Mr. Bentham?"

Bentham waved him away. "But even that is not quite bedrock," he continued. "My story begins long before this house was built, when I was a lad about your age, Jacob. My brother and I fancied ourselves explorers. We pored over the maps of Perplexus Anomalous and dreamed of visiting all the loops he'd discovered. Of finding new ones, and visiting them not just once, but again and again. In this way we hoped to make peculiardom great again." He leaned forward. "Do you understand what I mean?"

I frowned. "Make it great . . . with maps?"

"No, not just with maps. Ask yourself: what makes us weak, as a people?"

"Wights?" Emma guessed.

"Hollows?" I said.

"Before either of them existed," Bentham prodded.

Emma said, "Persecution by normals?"

"No. That is just a symptom of our weakness. What makes us weak is *geography*. There are, by my rough estimate, some ten thousand peculiars in the world today. We know there must be, just as we know there must be other planets in the universe that harbor intelligent life. It is mathematically mandatory." He smiled and sipped his tea. "Now just imagine ten thousand peculiars, all with astounding talents, all in one place and united by a common cause. They'd be a power to be reckoned with, no?"

"I suppose so," Emma said.

"Most definitely so," Bentham said. "But we are splintered by geography into hundreds of weak subunits—ten peculiars here, twelve there—because it is extraordinarily difficult to travel from a loop in the Australian outback, for example, to a loop in the horn of Africa. There are not only the inherent dangers of normals and the natural world to consider, but the dangers of aging forward during a long journey. The tyranny of geography precludes all but the most cursory visits between distant loops, even in this modern era of air travel."

He paused for a moment before continuing, his eyes scanning the room.

"Now then. Imagine there was a link between that loop in Australia and the one in Africa. Suddenly those two populations could develop a relationship. Trade with each other. Learn from each other. Band together to defend each other in times of crisis. All sorts of exciting possibilities arise which were previously impossible. And gradually, as more and more such connections are made, the peculiar world is transformed from a collection of far-flung tribes hiding in isolated loops to a mighty nation, united and strong!"

Bentham had grown increasingly animated as he spoke, and at this last bit he'd raised his hands and spread his fingers like he was grasping for an invisible pull-up bar.

"Hence the machine?" I ventured.

"Hence the machine," he said, lowering his hands. "We'd been searching, my brother and I, for an easier way to explore the peculiar world, and instead we hit upon a way to unite it. The Panloopticon was to be the savior of our people, an invention that would change the nature of peculiar society forever. It works like this: you begin here, in the house, with a small piece of the machine called a shuttle. It fits in your hand," he said, opening his palm. "You take it with you, out of the house, out of the loop, and then across the present to another loop, which could be on the other side of the world or the next village over. And when you return here, the shuttle will have collected and brought back the DNA-like signature of that other loop, which can be used to grow a second entrance to it—here, inside this house."

"In that hallway upstairs," Emma guessed. "With all the doors and little plaques."

"Exactly," said Bentham. "Every one of those rooms is a loop entrance that my brother and I, over the course of many years, harvested and brought back. With the Panloopticon, the initial, arduous trek of first contact has to be made only once, and every return trip thereafter is instantaneous."

"Like laying telegraph lines," Emma said.

"Just so," said Bentham. "And in that way, theoretically, the house becomes a central repository for all loops everywhere."

I thought about that. About how hard it had been to reach Miss Peregrine's loop the first time. What if instead of having to go all the way to a little island off the coast of Wales, I could've entered Miss Peregrine's loop from my closet in Englewood? I could have lived both lives—at home with my parents, and here, with my friends and Emma.

Except. If that had existed, Grandpa Portman and Emma never would've had to break up. Which was a sentence so strange it gave me the tailbone-tingling willies.

Bentham stopped and sipped his tea. "Cold," he said, and set it down.

Emma peeled off her blanket, got up, crossed the floor to Bentham's couch, and dipped the tip of her index finger in his tea. In a moment it was boiling again.

He grinned at her. "Fantastic," he said.

She removed her finger. "One question."

"I'll bet I know what it is," Bentham said.

"Okay. What is it?"

"If such a wonderful thing really exists, why haven't you heard about it before now?"

"That's it," she said, and returned to sit next to me.

"You never heard about it—no one did—because of the unfortunate trouble with my brother." Bentham's expression darkened. "The machine was born with his help, but ultimately he was its downfall as well. Ultimately, the Panloopticon was never used as a tool to unite our people, as it was intended, but for quite the opposite purpose. The trouble began when we realized that the task of visiting every loop in the world so that we might re-create their entrances here was laughable at best—so far beyond our abilities that it bordered on delusional. We needed help, and a great deal of it. Luckily, my brother was such a charismatic and convincing fellow that recruiting all the help we needed proved easy. Before long we had a small army of young, idealistic peculiars willing to risk life and limb to help us achieve our dream. What I didn't realize at the time was that my brother had a different dream than I did—a hidden agenda."

With some effort, Bentham stood up. "There is a legend," he said. "You might know it, Miss Bloom." Tapping with his cane, he moved across the floor to the shelves and pulled down a small book. "It's the tale of a lost loop. A kind of afterworld where our peculiar souls are stored after we die."

"Abaton," Emma said. "Sure, I've heard of it. But it's just a legend."

"Perhaps you can tell the tale," he said, "for the benefit of our neophyte friend."

Bentham hobbled back to the couches and handed me the book. It was slim and green and so old it crumbled around the edges. On the front was printed *Tales of the Peculiar*.

"I've read this!" I said. "Part of it, at least."

"This edition is nearly six hundred years old," said Bentham. "It was the last to contain the story Miss Bloom is about to recount, because it was regarded as dangerous. For a time it was a criminal act simply to tell it, and thus the book you hold is the only volume in the history of peculiardom ever to have been banned."

I opened the book. Every page was handwritten in ornate, superhumanly neat script, and every margin was crowded with illustrations.

"It's been a long time since I heard it," Emma said tentatively.

"I'll help you along," Bentham said, lowering himself gently onto the couch. "Go on."

"Well," Emma began, "the legend goes that back in the old days—the really, really, thousands-of-years-ago old days—there was a special loop peculiars went to when they died."

"Peculiar Heaven," I said.

"Not quite. We didn't stay there for all eternity or anything. It was more like a . . . library." She seemed uncertain of her word choice, and looked to Bentham. "Right?"

"Yes," he said, nodding. "It was thought that peculiar souls were a precious thing in limited supply, and it would be a waste to take them with us to the grave. Instead, at the end of our lives we were to make a pilgrimage to the library, where our souls would be deposited for future use by others. Even in spiritual matters, we peculiars have always been frugal-minded."

"The first law of thermodynamics," I said.

He looked at me blankly.

"Matter can neither be created nor destroyed. Or souls, in this case." (Sometimes I surprise myself with the things I remember from school.)

"The principle is similar, I suppose," said Bentham. "The ancients believed that only a certain number of peculiar souls were available to humanity, and that when a peculiar was born, he or she checked one out, as you or I might borrow a book from a library." He gestured at the stacks around us. "But when your life—your borrowing term—was over, the soul had to be returned."

Bentham gestured to Emma. "Please go on."

"So," Emma said, "there was this library. I always imagined it filled with beautiful, glowing books, each containing a peculiar soul. For thousands of years people checked out souls and returned them just before they died, and everything was rosy. Then one day someone figured out that you could break in to the library, even if you weren't about to die. And he did break in—and then robbed the place. He stole the most powerful souls he could find and used them to wreak havoc." Emma looked at Bentham. "Right?"

"Factually correct, if a bit artless in the telling," Bentham said.

"Used them?" I said. "How?"

"By combining their powers with his own," Bentham explained. "Eventually the library's guardians killed the rogue, took back the stolen souls, and set things aright. But the genie was out of the bottle, so to speak. The knowledge that the library could be breached became a poison that spread throughout our society. Whoever controlled the library could dominate all peculiardom, and before long more souls were stolen. There dawned a dark time, in which the power-mad waged epic battles against one another for control of Abaton and the Library of Souls. Many lives were lost. The land was scorched. Famine and pestilence reigned while peculiars with power beyond imagination murdered one another with floods and lightning bolts. This is where normals got their tales of gods fighting for supremacy in the sky. Their *Clash of the Titans* was our battle for the Library of Souls."

"I thought you said this story wasn't real," I said.

"I'm getting to that," Bentham said, then turned to Nim, who was hovering nearby. "You can go, Nim. We don't need any more tea."

"Sorry, sir, didn't mean to eavesdrop, sir, but this is my favorite part."

"Then sit!"

Nim dropped cross-legged to the floor and propped his chin on his hands.

"As I was saying. For a short but terrible time, destruction and misery befell our people. Control of the library changed hands often, accompanied by immense bloodletting. Then one day it stopped. The self-declared king of Abaton had been killed in battle, and the one who killed him was on his way to claim the library for himself—but he never found it. Overnight, the loop had disappeared."

"Disappeared?" I said.

"There one day, gone the next," said Emma.

"Poof," said Nim.

"According to legend, the Library of Souls was located in the hills of the ancient city of Abaton. But when the would-be king arrived to claim his prize, the library was gone. So was the town. Gone as if they'd never been there at all, a smooth green meadow in their place."

"That's crazy," I said.

"There's nothing to it, though," Emma said. "It's just an old tale."

"*The Legend of the Lost Loop*," I said, reading the page that the book in my hands was open to.

"We may never know for certain if Abaton is a real place," Bentham said, his lips spreading into a sphinx's smile. "That's what makes it a legend. But like rumors of buried treasure, the legendariness of the story has not stopped people, over the centuries, from searching for it. It is said that Perplexus Anomalous himself committed years to the hunt for the lost loop of Abaton—which is how he began to discover so many of the loops that appear on his famous maps."

"I didn't know that," said Emma. "I suppose something good came of it, then."

"And something very bad," Bentham added. "My brother, too, believed the story. Foolishly, I forgave him this frailty—and I ignored it, realizing too late how completely it drove him. By then, my charismatic brother had convinced our small army of young recruits that it was true. Abaton was real. The Library of Souls was discoverable. Perplexus had gotten so close, he told them, and all that was left to do was to complete his work. Then the vast and dangerous power contained in the library could belong to us. To them.

"I waited too long, and this idea became a cancer. They searched and searched for the lost loop, mounting expedition after expedition, each failure only fueling their zeal. The goal of uniting peculiardom was forgotten. All along, my brother had cared only about ruling it, like the would-be peculiar gods of old. And when I tried to challenge him and regain control of the machine I'd built, he smeared me as a traitor, turned the others against me, and locked me in a cell."

Bentham had been squeezing the crook of his cane like a neck he wished he could wring, but now he looked up, his face gaunt as a death mask. "Perhaps by now you've guessed his name."

My eyes snapped to Emma. Hers were wide as moons. We said it together:

"Caul."

Bentham nodded. "His real name is Jack."

Emma leaned forward. "Then your sister is . . . "

"My sister is Alma Peregrine," he said.

*   *   *

We gaped at Bentham, thunderstruck. Could the man before us really be Miss Peregrine's brother? I'd known she had two—she'd mentioned them once or twice, even shown me a picture of them as boys. She told me the story, too, of how their quest for immortality led to the disaster in 1908 that turned them and their followers into hollowgast and, later, the wights we knew and feared. But she'd never mentioned either brother by name, and her story bore little resemblance to the one Bentham had just laid out.

"If what you say is true," I said, "then you must be a wight."

Nim's mouth fell open. "Mr. Bentham is *not*." He was ready to stand and defend his master's honor when Bentham waved him off.

"It's all right, Nim. They've only heard Alma's version of things. But there are gaps in her knowledge."

"I don't hear you denying it," said Emma.

"I'm not a wight," Bentham said sharply. He was also not accustomed to being questioned by the likes of us, and his pride was beginning to poke through his genteel veneer.

"Then would you mind if we checked," I said, "just so we can be sure . . . "

"Not at all," Bentham said. He pushed himself up with his

cane and hobbled into the no-man's-land between our couches. PT raised his head, idly curious, while Nim turned his back, angry that his master should have to endure such humiliations.

We met Bentham on the carpet. He bent down a little so we wouldn't have to stand on our tiptoes—he was surprisingly tall—and waited while we searched the whites of his eyes for signs of contact lenses or other fakery. His pupils were terribly bloodshot, as if he hadn't slept in days, but otherwise unsuspicious.

We stepped back. "Okay, you're not a wight," I said. "But that means you can't be Caul's brother."

"I'm afraid the set of assumptions you are working from is erroneous," he said. "I was responsible for my brother and his followers becoming hollowgast, but I never became one myself."

"*You* made the hollows?" Emma said. "Why?!"

Bentham turned and gazed into the fire. "It was a terrible mistake. An accident." We waited for him to explain. It seemed to cost him real effort to drag up the story from wherever he'd hidden it away. "It was my fault for letting things go on as long as they did," he said heavily. "I kept telling myself that my brother wasn't as dangerous as he seemed. It was only after he imprisoned me, and it was too late to act, that I realized how wrong I'd been."

He stepped closer to the warmth of the fire and knelt down to stroke the bear's wide belly, letting his fingers get lost in PT's fur. "I knew Jack had to be stopped, and not simply for my own sake—nor because there was any danger he'd ever find the Library of Souls. No, it was clear his ambitions had grown beyond that. For months he'd been molding our recruits into the foot soldiers of a dangerous political movement. He cast himself as an underdog fighting to wrest control of our society from what he called 'the infantilizing influence of ymbrynes.'"

"Ymbrynes are the reason our society still exists," Emma said bitterly.

"Yes," Bentham said, "but you see, my brother was terribly

jealous. From the time we were boys, Jack envied our sister's power and status. Our inborn abilities were puny compared to hers. By her third birthday the elder ymbrynes who cared for us knew Alma was a great talent. People made such a fuss over her, and it drove Jack mad. When she was a baby he would pinch her just to see her cry. When she practiced turning into a bird, he would chase her and pluck her feathers."

I saw an angry flame curl up from one of Emma's fingers, which she extinguished in her tea.

"That ugliness only deepened over time," Bentham said. "Jack was able to harness and exploit the same poisonous envy latent in some of our fellow peculiars. He held meetings and made speeches, rallying malcontents to his cause. Devil's Acre was fertile ground, since many of the peculiars here were exiles, alienated from and hostile to the ymbrynic matriarchy."

"The Claywings," Emma said. "Before the wights became wights, that's what they called themselves. Miss Peregrine taught us a little about them."

"'We don't need their wings!' Jack used to preach. 'We'll grow wings of our own!' He meant this metaphorically, of course, but they used to march around wearing fake wings as a symbol of their movement." Bentham stood up and motioned us toward the bookshelves. "Look here. I still have a photo or two from those days. A few he wasn't able to destroy." He pulled down an album from a shelf and turned to a picture of a large crowd listening to a man speak. "Ah, here's Jack giving one of his hateful speeches."

The crowd, almost exclusively male, wore big sturdy hats and were packed thirty deep, balancing on boxes and clinging to fence tops to hear what Caul had to say.

Bentham turned the page and showed us another photo, this one of two hale young men in suits and hats, one grinning earnestly, the other expressionless. "That's me on the left, Jack on the right," Bentham said. "Jack smiled only when he was trying to get something out of you."

Lastly, he turned to a photo of a boy with a pair of large owlish wings that spread from behind his shoulders. He was slouched on a pedestal and regarded the camera with quiet contempt, one eye hidden behind his cocked hat. Printed across the bottom were the words *We don't need their wings.*

"One of Jack's recruiting posters," Bentham explained.

WE DON'T NEED THEIR WINGS

Bentham held the second photo closer, studying his brother's face. "There had always been a darkness in him," he said, "but I refused to see it. Alma's vision was sharper—she pushed Jack away early. But Jack and I were close in age and in mentality, or so I thought. We were chums, thick as thieves. But he hid his true self from me. I didn't see him for what he was until the day I said, 'Jack, you have stop this,' and he had me beaten and thrown into a lightless hole to die. By then it was too late."

Bentham looked up, his eyes reflecting the fire's glow. "It's quite something to realize you mean less than nothing to your own brother." He was quiet for a moment, tangled in an awful memory.

"But you didn't die," said Emma. "You turned them into hollows."

"Yes."

"How?"

"I tricked them."

"Into becoming horrible monsters?" I said.

"I never meant to turn them into monsters. I meant only to get rid of them." He returned stiffly to the couch and lowered himself onto the cushions. "I was starving, near death when it came to me: the perfect story with which to ensnare my brother. A lie as old as humanity itself. The fountain of youth. With my finger I scratched it into the dirt of my cell floor: the steps of an obscure loop manipulation technique that could reverse, and forever eliminate, the dangers of aging forward. Or so it seemed. In reality, that was just a side effect of what the steps truly described, which was an arcane and largely forgotten procedure to collapse loops, quickly and permanently, in an emergency."

I pictured the "autodestruct" button of sci-fi cliché. A supernova in miniature; stars winking out.

"I never expected my trick to work so well," Bentham said. "A member of the movement whose sympathy I had earned circulated my technique as his own, and Jack believed it. He led his followers to a distant loop to enact the procedure—and there, I hoped, they would slam the door behind themselves forever."

"But that's not what happened," said Emma.

"Is that when half of Siberia got blown up?" I asked.

"The reaction was so strong, it lasted a day and a night," said Bentham. "There are photos of it, and of the aftermath . . . "

He nodded at the album on the floor, then waited while we found the pictures. One, taken at night in some indistinct wilderness, was striped by a jet of vertical flame, a massive but distant release of white-hot energy that lit the night like a skyscraper-sized Roman candle. The other was a ruined village made up of rubble and cracked houses and trees raked clean of bark. Just looking at it, I could almost hear a lonely wind blowing; the palpable silence of a place robbed suddenly of life.

Bentham shook his head. "Never in my wildest dreams did I imagine what would crawl out of that collapsed loop," he said. "For a brief time afterward, things were quiet. Released from confinement, I began to recover. I regained control of my machine. It seemed my brother's dark age had drawn to a close—but it was only beginning."

"That was the start of the Hollow Wars," Emma said.

"Soon we began to hear stories about creatures made of shadow. They were emerging from the ruined forests to feed on peculiars—and normals, and animals, and anything that would fit between their jaws."

"Once I saw one eat a car," Nim said.

I said, "A car?"

"I was inside it," he replied.

We waited for him to elaborate.

"And?" said Emma.

"I got away," he said, shrugging. "The steering column got stuck in its throat."

"May I continue?" said Bentham.

"Of course, sir. My apologies."

"As I was saying, there wasn't much that would stop these new abominations, save the odd steering column—and loop entrances. Luckily, we had plenty of those. So most of us dealt with the hollowgast problem by staying put in our loops, venturing out only when we had no choice. The hollows didn't end our lives, but they made them vastly more difficult, isolated, and dangerous."

"What about the wights?" I asked.

"I imagine he's coming to that," said Emma.

"I am," said Bentham. "Five years after encountering my first hollowgast, I met my first wight. There was a knock at my door after midnight. I was in my house, safe inside my loop—or so I thought. But when I opened the door, there stood my brother Jack, a bit worse for wear but looking like his old self—save his dead eyes, which were blank as unmarked paper."

Emma and I had folded ourselves into cross-legged positions and were now leaning toward Bentham, hanging on his every word. Bentham stared over our heads with haunted eyes.

"He'd consumed enough peculiars to fill his hollow soul and turn himself into something that resembled my brother—but wasn't, quite. What little humanity he'd clung to through the years was gone completely, leaked away with the color in his eyes. A wight is to the peculiar he once was as a thing copied many times is to its original. Detail is lost, and color . . . "

"What about memory?" I asked.

"Jack retained his. A pity: otherwise he might've forgotten all about Abaton and the Library of Souls. And what I'd done to him."

"How did he find out it was you?" Emma asked.

"Chalk it up to brotherly intuition. And then one day, when he had nothing better to do, he tortured me until I confessed to it." Bentham nodded at his legs. "Never quite healed properly, as you can see."

"But he didn't kill you," I said.

"Wights are pragmatic creatures, and revenge is not a great motivator," Bentham said. "Jack was more obsessed than ever with finding Abaton, but to do it he needed my machine—and me to operate it. I became his prisoner and his slave, and Devil's Acre the secret headquarters for a small but influential contingent of wights bent on finding and cracking open the Library of Souls. Which is, you'll have guessed by now, their ultimate goal."

"I thought they wanted to re-create the reaction that turned them into hollows," I said, "only bigger and better. '*Do it right this time*,'" I said, making air quotes.

Bentham frowned. "Where did you hear that?"

"A wight told us just before he died," Emma said. "He said that's why they needed all the ymbrynes. To make the reaction more powerful."

"Utter nonsense," Bentham said. "Probably just a cover story to throw you off the scent. Though it's possible the wight who told you this lie believed it. Only Jack's innermost circle knew about the search for Abaton."

"But if they didn't need the ymbrynes for their reaction," I said, "then why'd they go to all the trouble of kidnapping them?"

"Because the lost loop of Abaton isn't just lost," said Bentham. "According to legend, before it was lost it was also locked—and it was ymbrynes who locked it. Twelve of them, to be exact, who came together from twelve far-flung corners of peculiardom. To open Abaton again, if you can manage to find it, would require those same twelve ymbrynes, or their successors. So it's no surprise that my brother has kidnapped precisely twelve ymbrynes, whom he spent many years hunting and tracking."

"I knew it," I said. "It had to be something more than just re-creating the reaction that turned them into hollows."

"Then he's found it," Emma said. "Caul wouldn't have pulled the trigger and kidnapped the ymbrynes if he didn't know where Abaton was."

"I thought you said it was legendary," I said. "Now you're talking like it's a real. Which is it?"

"The official position of the Council of Ymbrynes is that the Library of Souls is nothing but a story," Bentham said.

"I don't care what the council says," said Emma. "What do *you* say?"

"My opinions are my own," he said evasively. "But if the library is real, and Jack manages to find and open it, he still won't be able to steal its souls. He doesn't know it, but there's a third element he needs, a third key."

"And what's that?" I said.

"No one can take the soul jars. To most everyone they would be invisible and intangible. Even ymbrynes can't touch them. In the stories, only special adepts called librarians can see and handle them—and a librarian hasn't been born for a thousand years. If the library exists, all Jack would find there are empty shelves."

"Well, that's a relief," I said.

"Yes and no," said Emma. "What's he going to do when he figures out the ymbrynes he spent so long hunting are useless to him? He'll go mad!"

"That's what I worry about most," Bentham said. "Jack has a bad temper, and when the dream he's nurtured for so long dies . . . "

I tried to imagine what that could mean—all the tortures a man like Caul might be capable of—but my mind recoiled from the idea. It seemed the same horrors had broadcast themselves to Emma, because what she said next was sharp and charged with anger.

"We're going to get them back."

"We share a common goal," Bentham said. "To destroy my brother and his kind, and to save my sister and hers. Together, I believe we can do both."

He looked so small in that moment, sunk into the massive couch, cane leaning against his rickety legs, that I nearly laughed.

"How?" I said. "We'd need an army."

"Incorrect," he replied. "The wights could easily repel an army. Luckily, we have something even better." He looked at Emma and me, his lips curling into a smile. "We have the both of you. And luckily for you, you have me." Bentham leaned on his cane and rose slowly to his feet. "We have to get you inside their fortress."

"It seems pretty impenetrable," I said.

"That's because it is, conventionally speaking," Bentham replied. "In the years when Devil's Acre was a prison loop, it was designed to hold the worst of the worst. After the wights returned here, they adopted it as their home—and what had been an inescapable prison became their impenetrable fortress."

"But you have a way in," Emma guessed.

"I might, if you can help me," Bentham said. "When Jack and his wights came, they stole the heart of my Panloopticon. They forced me to break my own machine, to copy its loops and re-create them inside their fortress so that they could continue their work in a more protected location."

"So there's . . . *another* one?" I said.

Bentham nodded. "Mine is the original and theirs is the copy," he said. "The two are linked, and there are doorways in each that lead to the other."

Emma sat up straight. "You mean, we can use your machine to get inside theirs?"

"Correct."

"Then why haven't you?" I said. "Why didn't you do it years ago?"

"Jack broke my machine so irrevocably that I thought it could never be fixed," Bentham said. "For years, only one room has remained functional: the one that leads to Siberia. But though we've searched and searched, we haven't found a way through it into Jack's machine."

I remembered the man we'd seen peering into the crevasse—looking for a door, it seemed, deep in the snow.

"We need to open other doors, other rooms," Bentham said, "but to do that I need an adequate replacement for the part Jack stole—the dynamo at the heart of my Panloopticon. I've long suspected there's something that might work—a very powerful, very dangerous item—but though it exists right here in Devil's Acre, getting one has never been possible for me. Until now."

He turned to me.

"My boy, I need you to bring me a hollowgast."

*   *   *

I agreed to, of course. I would've said yes to almost anything then if I thought it might help free our friends. It occurred to me only after I'd said it, though, and Bentham had clapped his hands around mine and shook them, that I had no idea where to *get* a hollowgast. I was sure there were plenty inside the wights' fortress, but we'd already established that there was no getting inside. That's when Sharon stepped out of the shadows that had been growing at the edges of the room to give us a bit of good news.

"Remember your friend who got smashed by a falling bridge?" he said. "Turns out he's not quite dead. They pulled him out of the Ditch a few hours ago."

"They?" I said.

"The pirates. They've got him chained and caged down the end of Oozing Street. He's causing quite a stir, I hear."

"That's it, then," Emma said, tensing with excitement. "We'll steal the hollow and bring him back here, restart Mr. Bentham's machine, open a door to the wights' fortress, and get our friends back."

"Simple!" Sharon said, and he let out a barking laugh. "Except for that last part."

"And the first," I said.

Emma stepped close to me. "Sorry, love. I volunteered your services without asking. Think you can handle that hollow?"

I wasn't sure. True, I'd been able to make it perform a few spectacular moves in Fever Ditch, but bringing it to heel like a puppy and leading it all the way back to Bentham's house was asking a great deal of my rudimentary hollow-taming skills. My confidence, too, was at an all-time low after my last disastrous encounter. But everything hinged on me being able to do it.

"Of course I can handle it," I took too long to say. "When can we go?"

Bentham clapped his hands. "That's the spirit!"

Emma's gaze lingered on my face. She could tell I was faking.

"You can leave as soon as you're ready," Bentham said. "Sharon will be your guide."

"We shouldn't wait," Sharon said. "Once the locals have had their fun with that hollow, I reckon they'll kill it."

Emma picked at the front of her poufy dress. "In that case, I think we should change."

"Naturally," said Bentham, and he sent Nim to find us clothes more befitting our errand. He returned a minute later with thick-soled boots and modern work pants and jackets: black, waterproof, and with a bit of stretch to them.

We retreated to separate rooms to change and then met in a hallway, just Emma and me dressed in our adventure clothes. Rough and shapeless, they made Emma look slightly mannish (though not in a bad way), but she didn't grumble—she just tied back her hair, snapped her head to attention, and saluted me. "Sergeant Bloom, reporting for duty."

"Purdiest soldier I ever did see," I said, drawling out a terrible John Wayne impression.

There was a direct correlation between how nervous I was and how many dumb jokes I made. And right now I was practically quaking, my stomach a leaky faucet dripping acid all over my insides. "You really think we can do this?" I said.

"I do," she said.

"You never doubt, ever?"

Emma shook her head. "Doubt is the pinprick in the life raft."

She stepped close and we hugged. I could feel her trembling ever so slightly. She wasn't bulletproof. I knew then that my shaky faith in myself was starting to dig a hole in hers, and Emma's confidence was what held everything together. It was the life raft.

I'd come to regard her faith in me as somewhat reckless. She seemed to think that I should be able to snap my fingers and make hollowgast dance at will. That I was allowing some inner weakness to block my ability. Part of me resented that, and part of me wondered if maybe she was right. The only way to find out for sure was to approach the next hollow with an unshakable belief that I could master it.

"I wish I could see myself the way you do," I whispered.

She hugged me harder, and I resolved to try.

Sharon and Bentham came into the hall. "Ready?" Sharon asked.

We let go of each other. "Ready," I said.

Bentham shook my hand, then Emma's. "I'm so happy you're here," he said. "It's proof, I think, that the stars are beginning to align for us."

"I hope you're right," Emma said.

We were about to go when a question came to me that I'd been meaning to ask the whole time—and it occurred to me that, in a worst-case scenario, this could be my last chance to ask it.

"Mr. Bentham," I said, "we never did talk about my grandfather. How did you know him? Why were you looking for him?"

Bentham's eyebrows shot up and then he smiled quickly, as if to cover his moment of surprise. "I missed him, that's all," he said. "We were old friends, and I hoped I might see him again one day."

I knew that wasn't the whole truth, and I could see in Emma's narrowed eyes that she knew it, too, but there was no time to dig any further. Right now the future was of much greater concern than the past.

Bentham raised his hand goodbye. "Be careful out there," he said. "I'll be here, preparing my Panloopticon for its triumphant return to service." And then he hobbled back into his library, and we could hear him shouting at his bear. "PT, up! We have work to do!"

Sharon led us down a long hall, his wooden staff swinging and his massive bare feet slapping the stone floor. When we came to the door that led outside, he stopped, bent down to match our height, and laid out his ground rules.

"It's dangerous where we're going. There are very few un-owned peculiar children left in Devil's Acre, so people will notice you. Don't speak unless spoken to. Don't look anyone in the eye. Follow me at a slight distance, but never lose sight of me. We'll pretend you're my slaves."

"What?" said Emma. "We will *not*."

"It's the safest thing," said Sharon.

"It's demeaning!"

"Yes, but it will raise the fewest questions."

"How do we do it?" I said.

"Just do whatever I say, immediately and without question. And keep a slightly glazed expression."

"Yesss, master," I said robotically.

"Not like that," Emma said. "He means like the kids in that awful place on Louche Lane."

I let my face slacken and said in a flat voice: "Hello, we're all very happy here."

Emma shuddered and turned away.

"Very good," said Sharon, and then he looked at Emma. "Now you try."

"If we must do this," she said, "I'll pretend to be mute."

That was good enough for Sharon. He opened the door and swept us out into the dying day.

CHAPTER FIVE

*T*he air outside was a toxic-looking yellowish soup, such that I couldn't tell the position of the sun in the sky except to say it must've been getting toward evening, the light slowly leaking away. We walked a few paces behind Sharon, struggling to keep up whenever he saw someone he knew on the street and sped up to avoid conversation. People seemed to know him; he had a reputation, and I think he was concerned that we might do something to ruin it.

We made our way down oddly cheerful Oozing Street, with its window-box flowers and brightly painted houses, then turned onto Periwinkle Street, where the pavement gave way to mud and the houses to shabby, sagging flats. Men with hats pulled low over their eyes were congregating around the end of a seedy cul-de-sac. They appeared to be guarding the door to a house with its windows blacked out. Sharon told us to stay put, and we waited while he went to talk with them.

The air smelled faintly of gasoline. In the distance loud, laughing voices swelled and fell away, swelled and fell away. It was the sound of men in a sports bar watching a game—only it couldn't have been; that was strictly a modern sound, and there were no televisions here.

A man in mud-splashed pants came out of the house. As the door swung open, the voices grew louder and then faded when it slammed shut. He walked across the street carrying a bucket. We turned, watching as he walked toward something I hadn't noticed: a pair of bear cubs chained to a sawed-off lamppost at the edge of the street. They were terribly sad looking, with only a few feet of slack on their chains, and they sat on the muddy ground watching the man approach with something like dread, their furry ears flattened back. The man dumped some putrid table scraps before them and left without a word. The whole scene made me unutterably depressed.

"Those there are training grims," Sharon said, and we turned to find him standing behind us. "Blood sport is big business here, and fighting a grimbear is considered the ultimate challenge. Young fighters have to train somehow, so they start out fighting the cubs."

"That's awful," I said.

"The bears have the day off, though, thanks to your beastie." Sharon pointed at the little house. "He's in there, out through the back. But before we go in, I should warn you: this is an ambrosia den, and there'll be peculiars in there who are lit out of their minds. Don't talk to them, and whatever you do, don't look them in the eye. I know people who've been blinded that way."

"What do you mean, blinded?" I said.

"Just what it sounds like. Now follow me and don't ask any more questions. Slaves don't question their masters."

I saw Emma grit her teeth. We fell in behind Sharon as he crossed to the men clustered around the door of the house.

Sharon talked with the men. I struggled to overhear while maintaining a slavelike distance and averting my eyes. One of them told Sharon there was an "admission fee," and he dug a coin from his cloak and paid it. Another asked about us.

"I haven't given them names yet," Sharon said. "Just got 'em yesterday. They're still so green, I don't dare let them out of my sight."

"Is that right?" the man said, approaching us. "Don't have names?"

I shook my head no, playing mute along with Emma. The man looked us up and down. I wanted to squirm out of my skin. "Haven't I seen you somewhere?" he said, leaning closer.

I said nothing.

"Maybe in the window at Lorraine's," Sharon offered.

"Nah," the man said, then waved his hand. "Ah, I'm sure it'll come to me."

I only risked a direct look at him once he'd turned away. If he was a Ditch pirate, he wasn't one of those we'd tangled with. He had a bandage over his chin and another over his forehead. Several of the other men were similarly bandaged, and one sported an eyepatch. I wondered if they'd been injured fighting grims.

The man with the eyepatch opened the door for us. "Enjoy yourselves," he said, "but I wouldn't send them into the cage today, unless you're ready to scrape them off the ground."

"We're just here to watch and learn," said Sharon.

"Smart man."

We were waved in and hurried close at Sharon's heels, anxious to escape the door lurkers' stares. Seven-foot Sharon had to duck to pass through the doorway, and he stayed ducked the entire time we were inside, so low were the ceilings. The room we entered was dark and reeked of smoke, and until my eyes adjusted all I could see were pinpricks of orange light glowing here and there. Slowly the room came into view, lit by oil lamps trimmed so low they gave no more light than matches. It was long and narrow, with bunk beds built into the walls like you might find in the lightless bowels of an ocean-going ship.

I tripped over something and nearly lost my balance.

"Why is it so dark in here?" I muttered, already breaking my promise not to ask questions.

"The eyes get sensitive as the effects of ambro wear off," Sharon explained. "Even weak daylight is nearly unbearable."

That's when I noticed the people in the bunks, some sprawled and sleeping, others sitting up in nests of rumpled sheets. They watched us, smoking listlessly and speaking in murmurs. A few talked to themselves, reeling out incomprehensible monologues. Several had bandaged faces, like the doormen, or wore masks. I wanted to ask about the masks, but I wanted to get that hollow and get out of there even more.

We pushed through a curtain of hanging beads and entered a room that was somewhat brighter and considerably more crowded than the first. A burly man stood on a chair at the opposite wall, directing people to one of two doors. "Fighters to the left, spectators to the right!" he shouted. "Place your bets in the parlor!"

I could hear voices yelling a few rooms away, and a moment later the crowd parted to allow three men to pass, two of whom were dragging the third, who was unconscious and bleeding. Whistles and catcalls followed them.

"That's what losers look like!" the man on the chair bellowed. "And that," he said, pointing into a side room, "is what cowards look like!"

I peeked into the room, where two men under guard stood miserably for all to see. They were covered in tar and feathers.

"Let them be a reminder," said the man. "All fighters must spend two minutes in the cage, minimum!"

"So which are you?" Sharon asked me. "A fighter or a spectator?"

I felt my chest tighten as I tried to imagine what was about to happen: I wasn't just going to tame this hollow, but do it in front of a rowdy and potentially hostile audience—and then try and get out. I found myself hoping that it wasn't too injured, because I had a feeling I'd need its strength to clear us an exit. These peculiars weren't going to give up their new toy without a fight.

"A fighter," I said. "To really control it, I'm going to have to get close."

Emma met my eyes and smiled. *You can do this*, her smile said, and I knew, in that moment, that I could. I strode through the door meant for fighters, buoyed with new confidence, Sharon and Emma following behind me.

That confidence lasted approximately four seconds, which was the length of time it took me to walk into the room and notice the blood that was puddled and smeared all over the floors and walls. A river of it led down a light-filled hall and out an open door, through which I could see another crowd and, just beyond them, the bars of a large cage.

A shrill call came from outside. The next combatant was being summoned.

A man emerged from a darkened room to our right. He was stripped to the waist and wore a plain white mask. He stood at the top of the hall for a moment as if gathering his courage. Then he tipped back his head and raised his hand above it. In his hand he held a small glass vial.

"Don't look," Sharon said, backing us against a wall. But I couldn't help myself.

Slowly the man poured black liquid from the vial into each of his mask's eye holes. Then he dropped the empty vial, lowered his head, and began to groan. For a few seconds he seemed paralyzed, but then his body shuddered and two cones of white light shot from the eye holes of his mask. Even in the bright room they were distinct.

Emma gasped. The man, who had thought he was alone, turned toward us in surprise. His eye-beams arced over our heads and the wall above us sizzled.

"Just passing through!" Sharon said, the tone of which managed to say, *Howdy, friend!* and *Please don't kill us with those things!* at the same time.

"Pass through, then," the man snarled.

By then his eye beams were starting to fade, and just as he turned away they flickered and winked out. He walked down the hall and went out the door, leaving two wisps of smoke curling in his wake. When he'd gone I ventured a look at the wallpaper above our heads. A pair of caramel singe marks traced the path his eyes had made across the wall. Thank God he hadn't looked me in the eye.

"Before we go a step farther," I said to Sharon, "I think you'd better explain."

"Ambrosia," Sharon said. "Fighters take it to give themselves enhanced abilities. Trouble is, it doesn't last long, and when it wears off you're left weaker than before. If you make a habit of it, your ability wears down to almost nothing—until you take more ambro.

Pretty soon you're taking it not just to fight, but to function as a peculiar. You become dependent on whoever's selling it." He nodded to the room on our right, where murmuring voices created an odd counterpoint to the full-throated shouts outside. "It was the greatest trick the wights ever pulled, making that stuff. No one here will ever betray them, so long as they're addicted to ambrosia."

I peeked into the side room to see what a peculiar drug dealer looked like, and I caught a glimpse of someone in a bizarre bearded mask flanked by two men holding guns.

"What happened with that man's eyes?" Emma asked.

"The burst of light is a side effect," Sharon said. "Another is that, over a period of years, the ambro melts your face. That's how you know the hard-core users—they wear masks to hide the damage."

As Emma and I shared a look of disgust, a voice inside the room summoned us. "Hello out there," the dealer called. "Come in here, please!"

"Sorry," I said, "We have to go—"

Sharon poked my shoulder and hissed, "You're a slave, remember?"

"Uh, yes sir," I said, and went as far as the door.

The masked man was sitting in a little chair in a room with frescoed walls. He held himself with unsettling stillness, one arm resting on a side table and his legs crossed delicately at the knee. His gunmen occupied two corners of the room, and in another stood a wooden chest on wheels.

"Don't be afraid," the dealer said, beckoning me in. "Your friends can come, too."

I took another few steps into the room, Sharon and Emma just behind me.

"I haven't seen you around before," the dealer said.

"I just bought him," Sharon said. "He doesn't even have a—"

"Was I speaking to you?" the dealer said sharply.

Sharon went quiet.

"No, I wasn't," the dealer said. He stroked his fake beard and seemed to study me through the hollowed eyes of his mask. I wondered what he looked like underneath, and just how much ambrosia you'd have to pour into your face before you melted it. Then I shuddered and wished I hadn't.

"You're here to fight," he said.

I told him that I was.

"Well, you're in luck. I just got a prime batch of ambro, so your chances of survival have shot up dramatically!"

"I don't need any, thank you."

He looked at his gunmen for a reaction—they remained stone-faced—and then he laughed. "That's a hollowgast out there, you know. You've heard of them?"

They were all I could think about, especially the one outside. I was desperate to be on my way, but this creepy guy clearly ran the place, and making him angry was more trouble than we needed.

"I've heard of them," I said.

"And how do you think you'll do against one?"

"I think I'll do okay."

"Just okay?" The man crossed his arms. "What I want to know is: should I put money on you? Are you going to win?"

I told him what he wanted to hear. "Yes."

"Well, if I'm going to put money on you, you're going to need some help." He stood up, went to the medicine cabinet, and opened its doors. The interior glittered with glass vials—rows of them, all brimming with dark liquid, the tops plugged with tiny corks. He plucked one out and brought it to me. "Take this," he said, holding out the vial. "It takes all your best attributes and magnifies them times ten."

"No thank you," I said. "I don't need it."

"That's what they all say at first. Then, after they get beaten—if they survive—everyone takes it." He turned the vial in his hand and held it to the weak light. The ambrosia inside swam with spar-kling, silvery particles. I stared, despite myself.

"What's it made of?" I asked.

He laughed. "Snips and snails and puppy dog's tails." He held it toward me again. "No charge," he said.

"He said he doesn't want any," Sharon said sharply.

I thought the dealer would lash out at him, but instead he cocked his head at Sharon and said, "Don't I know you?"

"I don't think so," Sharon said.

"Sure I do," the dealer said, nodding. "You were one of my best customers. What happened to you?"

"I kicked the habit."

The dealer stepped toward him. "Looks like you waited too long," he said, and pulled teasingly on Sharon's hood.

Sharon snatched the dealer's hand. The guards raised their guns.

"Careful," the dealer said.

Sharon held him a moment longer, then let go.

"Now," the dealer said, turning toward me. "You're not going to refuse a free sample, are you?"

I had no intention of ever uncorking the stuff, but it seemed like the best way to end this was to take it. So I did.

"Good boy," the dealer said, and he shooed us from the room.

"You were an addict?" Emma hissed at Sharon. "Why didn't you tell us?"

"What difference would it have made?" Sharon said. "Yes, I had some bad years. Then Bentham took me in and weaned me off the stuff."

I turned to look at him, trying to imagine. "Bentham did?"

"Like I said, I owe the man my life."

Emma took the vial and held it up. In the stronger light, the silvery bits inside the black liquid shone like tiny flakes of sun. It was mesmerizing, and despite the side effects, I couldn't help but wonder how a few drops might enhance my abilities. "He wouldn't say what was in it," Emma said.

"We are," Sharon said. "Little bits of our stolen souls, crushed up and fed back to us by the wights. A piece of every peculiar they kidnap winds up in a vial like that one."

Emma thrust the vial away in horror, and Sharon took it and

tucked it into his cloak. "Never know when one of these might come in handy," he said.

"Knowing what it's made of," I said, "I can't believe you'd ever take that stuff."

"I never said I was proud of myself," Sharon said.

The whole diabolical scheme was perfect in its evilness. The wights had turned the peculiars of Devil's Acre into cannibals, hungry for their own souls. Addicting them to ambrosia ensured their control and kept the population in check. If we didn't free them soon, our friends' souls would be the next to fill those vials.

I heard the hollow roar—it sounded like a cry of victory—and the man we'd watched take ambro a minute earlier was dragged through door and past us down the hall, bleeding and unconscious.

My turn, I thought, and a thrill of adrenaline shot through me.

*   *   *

Out back of the ambro den was a walled courtyard, the centerpiece of which was a freestanding cage about forty feet square, its sturdy bars easily capable, it seemed to me, of containing a hollowgast. A line had been painted in the dirt approximately as far from the cage bars as a hollow's tongues could reach, and the crowd, made up of forty or so rough-looking peculiars, had wisely planted themselves behind it. The courtyard's walls were ringed with smaller cages, and inside a tiger, a wolf, and what looked like a full-grown grimbear— animals of lesser interest, at least compared to a hollowgast—were being held to fight another day.

The main attraction could be seen pacing inside the big cage, tethered to a heavy iron post by a chain around its neck. It was in such a sorry state that I was tempted to feel bad for it. The hollowgast had been splashed with white paint and daubed here and there with mud, which made it visible to everyone but also a bit ridiculous looking, like a Dalmatian or a mime. It was limping badly and leaving trails of black blood, and its muscular tongues, which in anticipation of a fight would normally have been whipping around in the air, were dragging limply behind it. Hurt and humiliated, it was far from the nightmare vision I had become accustomed to, but the crowd, having never seen a hollow, seemed impressed nevertheless. Which was just as well: even in this much-reduced state, the hollow had managed to knock out several fighters in a row. It was still plenty dangerous, and very unpredictable. Which is why, I assumed, men armed with rifles were stationed around the courtyard. Better safe than sorry.

I huddled with Sharon and Emma to strategize. The problem, we agreed, wasn't getting me into the cage with the hollow. It wasn't even controlling the hollow—we were working under the assumption that I could do it. The problem would be getting the hollow out, and away from these people.

"Think you could melt through that chain around its neck?" I asked Emma.

"If I had two days to do it," she said. "I don't suppose we could just explain to everyone that we really need the hollow and we'll bring it back when we're finished?"

"You wouldn't even get that whole sentence out," said Sharon, eyeing the rowdy crowd. "This is more fun than these blighters have had in years. No chance."

"Next fighter!" shouted a woman standing watch from a second-story window.

Away from the crowd, a small clutch of men argued about which of them would fight next. There was already plenty of blood soaking the ground inside the cage, and none seemed in a hurry to contribute more. They'd been drawing straws, and a well-built man who was stripped to the waist had just picked the short one.

"No mask," Sharon said, noting the man's bushy mustache and relatively unscarred face. "He must be just starting out."

The man gathered his courage and strutted toward the crowd.

In a loud, Spanish-accented voice, he told them he'd never been beaten in a fight, that he was going to kill the hollow and keep its head for a trophy, and that his peculiar ability—ultraquick healing—would make it impossible for the hollow to inflict a mortal wound.

"See these beauty marks?" he said, turning to show off a collection of nasty, claw-shaped scars on his back. "A grim gave them to me last week. They were an inch deep," he claimed, "and healed the same day!" He pointed at the hollow in the cage. "That wrinkled old thing doesn't stand a chance!"

"Now it's *definitely* going to kill him," Emma said.

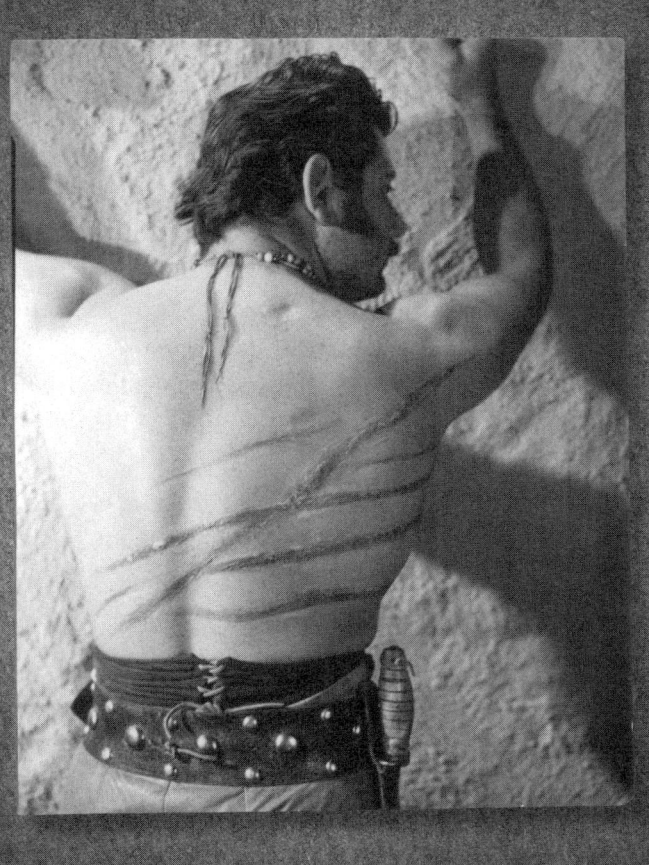

The man poured a vial of ambro into his eyes. His body stiffened and light beams shot from his pupils, leaving a cataract of burn marks on the ground. A moment later they winked out. Thus fortified, he strode confidently to the cage door, where a man with a large key ring met him to unlock it.

"Keep an eye on the guy with the keys," I said. "We might need those."

Sharon reached into his pocket and drew out a wriggling rat by its tail. "Did you hear that, Xavier?" he said to the rat. "Go get the keys." He dropped the rodent on the ground and it scurried away.

The boastful fighter entered the cage and began to face off with the hollow. He'd taken a small knife from his belt and assumed a bent-kneed stance, but other than that he showed little appetite for a fight. Instead, he seemed to be running out the clock by running his mouth, giving a speech with all the blowhard bluster of a professional wrestler. "Come at me, you animal! I am not afraid! I'll slice out your tongues and make a belt to hold up my pants! I'll pick my teeth with your toenails and mount your head on my wall!"

The hollow watched him boredly.

The fighter made a show of drawing his knife across his forearm, and as blood began to well he held up the wound. It healed and closed before a single drop could reach the ground. "I am invincible!" he cried. "I am not afraid!"

Suddenly the hollow faked toward the man and roared, which so startled him that he dropped his knife and threw his arms across his face. It seemed the hollow had grown tired of him.

The crowd burst into riotous laughter—and so did we—and the man, red-faced with embarrassment, bent to pick up his knife. Now the hollow was moving toward him, chains clinking as it went, tongues extended and curled like clenched fists.

The man realized he'd have to engage the monster if he was to salvage his dignity, so he took a few tentative steps forward while brandishing the knife. The hollow flicked one of its painted tongues at him. The man swiped at it with his knife—and connected. Cut, the hollow squealed and retracted the tongue, then hissed at the man like an angry cat.

"That'll teach you to attack Don Fernando!" the man shouted.

"This guy never learns," I said. "Taunting hollows is a bad idea."

He seemed to have the hollow on the run. It backed away while the man approached, still hissing and waving his knife. When the hollow could retreat no farther, its back against the bars of the cage, the man raised his knife. "Prepare to die, demon spawn!" he shouted, and charged.

For a moment I wondered if I'd have to step in and save the hollow, but soon it became clear that it had set a trap. Snaking beneath the man was all the slack of the hollow's chain, which the hollow grabbed and swept violently to one side, sending Don Fernando flying head-first into a metal post. *Clonk*—and he was out, limp on the ground. Another KO.

He'd been such a shameless braggart that the crowd couldn't help cheering.

A team of men with torches and electric-tipped taser poles ran into the cage and kept the hollow at bay while the unconscious fighter was dragged out.

"Who's next?" the referee woman shouted.

The remaining fighters traded looks of apprehension, then resumed arguing. Now no one wanted to enter the cage.

Except me.

The man's ridiculous performance and the hollow's trick had given me an idea. It wasn't a sure-fire plan, or even a good one, but it was something, and that was better than nothing. We—meaning the hollow and I—were going to fake its death.

*   *   *

I screwed up my courage and, as tends to happen while I'm doing something either slightly brave or very foolish, my brain disengaged from my body. I seemed to watch myself from afar as I waved an arm at the referee and shouted, "I'll go next!"

Before then I'd been invisible; now the crowd and the fighters all turned to stare.

"What's your plan?" Emma whispered to me.

I had one but had been so caught up with working it out that I'd failed to share it with Emma or Sharon, and now I had no time to lay it out for them. Which was probably for the best. If spoken aloud, I feared it might sound ridiculous or, worse yet, impossible, and then I'd lose my nerve.

"I think it's better if I just show you," I said. "But it definitely won't work unless we get those keys."

"Don't worry, Xavier's on the job," said Sharon. We heard a squeak and looked down to see the rat in question with a piece of cheese in its mouth. Sharon picked him up and scolded him. "*Keys,* I said, not cheese!"

"I'll get them," Emma assured me. "Just promise you'll come back in one piece."

I promised. She wished me luck and kissed me on the lips. Then I looked at Sharon, who tilted his head at me as if to say, *I hope you're not expecting a kiss from me, too,* and I just laughed and walked toward the fighters.

They were looking me up and down. I was sure they thought I was crazy, and yet none of them tried to stop me. After all, if this ill-prepared kid, who wasn't even going to take a vial of ambro before his fight, wanted to throw himself at the beast and wear it down a little, that was a gift they were willing to accept. And if I died trying, I was just a slave anyway. Which made me hate them and put me in mind of the poor kidnapped peculiars whose extracted souls were swimming around in the vials they all clutched—which made me even angrier. I did my best to channel all that rage into unwavering determination and focus, but it was mostly just distracting.

And yet. While the man with the keys was working to open the cage, I looked inward and found, to my surprise and delight, that I was not racked with doubt, nor haunted by visions of my impending death, nor battling waves of terror. I had met and exerted control over this hollow twice before; this would be the third time. Despite my anger, I was calm and quiet, and within this quiet I found that the words I needed were waiting for me, ready to be spoken.

The man opened the door and I stepped into the cage. He'd only just closed it when the hollow started toward me, rattling its chain like an angry ghost.

Tongue, don't fail me now.

I raised a hand to hide my mouth and said, in guttural Hollow: *Stop.*

The hollow stopped.

Sit, I said.

It sat.

A wave of relief washed over me. I'd had nothing to worry about; reestablishing the connection was as easy as picking up the reins of an old compliant mare. Controlling the monster was a bit like wrestling someone much smaller than I: it was pinned and wriggling to get free, but so outmatched by my strength that it posed little danger. But then the ease with which I controlled the hollow was its own sort of problem. There was no simple way to get it out of the cage unless everyone believed it was dead and no longer a threat, and there was no way anyone would believe it was dead if my victory came too easily. I was a scrawny, un-ambro-enhanced kid; I couldn't just slap it and have it keel over. For this ruse to be properly convincing, I needed to put on a show.

How was I going to "kill" it? Definitely not with my bare hands. Searching the cage for inspiration, my eyes fell upon the previous fighter's knife, which he'd dropped by the metal post. The hollow was sitting next to the post, which was a problem—so I picked up a handful of gravel, ran toward it suddenly, and threw it.

Corner, I said, again covering my mouth. The hollow turned and darted into the corner, which made it seem as though the handful of rocks had startled it. Then I dashed to the post, snatched the knife from the ground, and retreated, a bit of bravery that earned me a whistle from someone in the crowd.

Angry, I said, and the hollow roared and waved its tongues as if infuriated by my bold move. I glanced behind me to find Emma in the crowd, and I saw her moving furtively toward the man with the keys.

Good.

I needed to make things tough for myself. *Come at me*, I ordered, and once the hollow had lurched a few paces in my direction, I told it to lash out a tongue and grab me by the leg.

It did, the tongue connecting with a sting and wrapping twice around my calf. Then I made the hollow pull me off my feet and drag me toward it through the dirt while I pretended to grasp for a handhold.

As I passed the metal post, I threw my arms around it.

Pull up, I said—*not hard.*

Though my words weren't very descriptive, the hollow seemed to understand exactly what I meant, as if just by picturing an action in my head and speaking a word or two aloud I could convey a paragraph's worth of information. So when the hollow pulled upward as I clung to the post, raising my body into the air, it was precisely as I'd imagined it.

I'm getting good at this, I thought with some satisfaction.

I struggled and groaned for a few seconds in what I hoped sounded like authentic pain, then released the post. The crowd, expecting that I was about to be killed in what was probably the shortest match yet, began to jeer and call me names.

It was time for me to get in a hit.

Leg, I said. The hollow again lashed a tongue around my leg.

Pull.

It began to drag me toward it as I kicked and flailed.

Mouth.

It opened its mouth as if to swallow me whole. I quickly turned my body and slashed at the tongue around my ankle. I hadn't really cut the hollow, but I told it to quickly let go and scream so that it would look like I had. The hollow complied, screeching and then reeling its tongues back into its mouth. It felt like bad pantomime to me—there'd been a second of lag between my command and the hollow's response—but apparently the crowd bought it. The jeers turned to cheers for a match that was getting interesting, with an underdog who maybe had a fighting chance after all.

In what I hoped didn't seem like a fight scene from a low-budget movie, the hollow and I squared off and traded a few blows. I ran at it and it knocked me down. I slashed at it and it backed off. It howled and waved its tongues in the air as we circled each other. I even had it pick me up with a tongue and (gently) shake me, until I (pretended to) stab the tongue and it (probably too gently) dropped me again.

I risked another glance at Emma. She was standing in the middle of the group of fighters near the man with the keys. She made a line-across-the-throat gesture at me.

Quit messing around.

Right. Time to end this. I took a deep breath, gathered my courage, and went for the big finish.

I ran at the hollow with my knife raised. It swung a tongue at my legs, which I jumped over, then another at my head, which I ducked.

All as planned.

What was supposed to happen next was that I would jump over another tongue at my feet, then pretend to stab the hollow in the heart—but instead the tongue hit me directly in the chest. It connected with the force of a heavyweight boxer, flinging me onto my back and knocking the wind out of me. I lay there stunned, unable to breathe as the crowd booed.

Back, I tried to say, but I didn't have the breath.

And then it was on top of me, jaws wide and bellowing with anger. The hollow had thrown off my yoke, if only for a moment, and it was not happy. I had to regain control, and fast, but its tongues had pinned my arms and one leg, and its arsenal of gleaming teeth was closing in on my face. I was only just drawing breath—a gagging lungful of the hollow's stink—and instead of speaking I choked.

That might've been the end of me but for the strange anatomy of hollows: fortunately, it couldn't close its jaws around my head with its tongues extended. It had to release my limbs before it could bite off my head, and the moment I felt its tongue release my arm—the arm with the hand that still held the knife—I did the only thing I could think of to preserve myself. I thrust the knife upward.

The blade plunged deep into the hollow's throat. It screeched and rolled away, tongues flipping and grasping at the knife.

The crowd went crazy with excitement.

I was finally able to draw a full, clean breath, and I sat up to see the hollow writhing on the ground a few yards away, black blood spurting from its wounded neck. I realized, with none of the satisfaction I might've felt under different circumstances, that I had probably just killed the thing. *Really* killed it, which was not even remotely the plan. From the corner of my eye I saw Sharon shaking his open hands at me, the universal sign for *you just ruined everything*.

I stood up, determined to salvage what I could. Reexerting my control over the hollow, I told it to relax. That it felt no pain. Gradually it quit struggling, its tongues sinking toward the ground. Then I walked over to it, pulled my bloody knife from its neck, and held it up to show the crowd. They screamed and cheered, and I did my best to look triumphant when really I felt like a giant failure. I was deathly afraid I'd just botched our friends' rescue.

The man with the keys opened the cage door, and two men ran

over to check the hollow.

Don't move, I murmured as they examined it, one of them aiming a shotgun at its head while the other poked it with a stick and then held a hand below its nostrils.

Don't breathe, either.

It didn't. In fact, the hollow did such a great job pretending to be dead that I, too, would've been convinced if not for the ongoing connection between us.

The men bought it. The examiner tossed away his stick, held up my arm like the victor in a boxing match, and declared me the winner. The crowd cheered again, and I could see money changing hands, the disappointed people who'd bet against me grumbling as they shelled out bills.

Soon spectators were entering the cage to get a better look at the supposedly dead hollow, Emma and Sharon among them.

Emma threw her arms around me. "It's okay," she said. "You had no choice."

"It's not dead," I whispered to her. "But it's hurt. I don't know how long it has. We've got to get it out of here."

"Then it's a good thing I managed to get these," she said, slipping a ring of keys into my pocket.

"Ha," I said, "you're a genius!"

But when I turned to unlock the hollow's chain, I found myself blocked by a swarm of people all clamoring to get close to it. Everyone wanted to get a good look at the thing, to touch it, to take a wisp of its hair or a clod of blood-soaked dirt as a memento. I started to shove my way through, but people kept stopping me to shake my hand and slap me on the back.

"That was unbelievable!"

"You got lucky, kid."

"You *sure* you didn't take ambro?"

All the while I was chanting under my breath for the hollow to stay down and stay dead, because I could feel it beginning to squirm, like a little kid who'd sat still for too long. It was antsy and hurt, and it required every spare ounce of my concentration to keep it from leaping up and filling its jaws with all the tempting peculiar flesh that surrounded it.

I'd finally reached the hollow's chain and was looking for the padlock when the ambro dealer accosted me. I turned to see his creepy bearded mask just inches from my face.

"You think I don't know what you're doing?" he said. He was flanked by his two armed guards. "You think I'm blind?"

"I don't know what you're talking about," I said. For a queasy second I thought he was on to me and knew the hollow wasn't really dead. But his men weren't even looking at it.

He grabbed me by my jacket collar. "No one hustles me!" he said. "This is *my* place!"

People were starting to back away. This guy clearly had a bad reputation.

"No one's hustling anyone," I heard Sharon say behind me. "Just calm down."

"You can't trick a trickster," the dealer said. "You come in here claiming he's fresh meat, never fought so much as a grim cub before, and then this?" He swept his arm toward the fallen hollow. "Not in a million years!"

"He's dead," I said. "Check for yourself if you want to."

The dealer let go of my jacket and put his hands around my throat instead.

"HEY!" I heard Emma say.

The guards pointed their guns at her.

"My only question," said the dealer, "is what are you selling?"

He began to squeeze.

"Selling?" I croaked.

He sighed, irritated at being forced to explain. "You come into *my* place, kill *my* hollow, and convince *my* customers they don't need to buy my product?"

He thought I was a rival drug dealer, there to steal his business. Madness.

He squeezed harder.

"Let the boy go," Sharon pleaded.

"If you're not on ambro, then what is it? What are you selling?"

I tried to respond but couldn't. I looked down at his hands. He took my hint and loosened his grip slightly.

"Speak," he said magnanimously.

What I said next probably sounded to him like a choked cough. *The one on the left*, I said in hollowspeak. And then the hollow sat up stiff and straight like Frankenstein's monster come to life, and the few peculiars still nearby screamed and ran. The dealer turned to look and I punched him in the mask; the guards didn't know who to shoot first, me or the hollow.

That split second of indecision was their undoing. In the time it took for them to turn their heads, the hollow had flung all three of its tongues at the closest guard. One disarmed him while the remaining two grabbed him by the waist, picked him up, and used him like a battering ram to knock down the other.

Then it was just the dealer and me. It seemed to dawn on him that I was the one controlling the hollow. He dropped to his knees and began to beg.

"This might be your place," I said to him, "but that's *my* hollow."

I made it wrap a tongue around the dealer's neck. I told him we would be leaving with the hollowgast, and the only way he would survive is if we were allowed to go in peace.

"Yes, yes," he agreed, his voice shaking. "Yes, of course . . . "

I unlocked the padlock and unchained the hollow. With the crowd looking on, Emma, Sharon, and I led the limping hollow toward the open cage door, the dealer in front of us saying, "Don't shoot! No one shoot!" as best he could with a hollowgast's tongue collared around his neck.

We locked the cage behind us with most of the spectators still inside, then walked out through the ambro den, back the way we'd come, and onto the street. I was tempted to make a pit stop to destroy the dealer's ambro supply but decided it wasn't worth the risk. Let them choke on it. Besides, maybe it was better not to waste the stuff, if there was even a tiny chance that those stolen souls could one day be reunited with their owners.

We left the dealer on his hands and knees in the gutter, gasping for air, his mask dangling from one ear. We were about to put the whole filthy scene behind us when I heard a tiny growl and remembered the grimcubs.

I looked back at them, torn. They were at the end of their chains, straining to come with us.

"We can't," Sharon said, urging me on.

I might've left them if Emma hadn't caught my eye. *Do it*, she mouthed.

"It'll just take a second," I said.

It took fifteen, in the end, to make the hollow uproot the post the cubs were chained to, and by then a gang of angry addicts had gathered outside the ambro den. It seemed worth it, though, when we left with those cubs trailing after, chains and post dragging behind them—slow and encumbered until my hollow, in a gesture all its own, scooped them into its arms and whisked them along.

*   *   *

It quickly became obvious that we had a problem. We'd walked only a few blocks, but already people on the street had noticed the hollow. To anyone but me it was just a half-visible collection of paint splotches, but it still attracted attention. And because we didn't want anyone to see where we were going, we had to figure out a subtler way to get it back to Bentham's.

We ducked into a back street. The moment I stopped forcing it to walk, the hollow sank into an exhausted squat. It looked so frail there on the ground, bleeding, its body curled into itself, tongues tucked away in its mouth. Sensing its distress, the cubs it had rescued snuffled against it with their wet wiggling snouts, and the hollow reacted with a quiet snarl that seemed almost tender. I couldn't help feeling a pulse of affection for all three—estranged siblings of a sort.

"I hate to say it, but that's almost cute," Emma said.

Sharon snorted. "Dress it up in a pink tutu if you like. It's still a killing machine."

We brainstormed ways to get it to Bentham's without it dying en route. "I could close that wound in its neck," Emma said, offering a hand that was just starting to glow.

"Too risky," I said. "The pain could snap it out of my control."

"Bentham's healer might be able to help it," Sharon said. "We'll just have to get to her quickly."

My first thought was to run across the rooftops. If only the hollow had the strength, it could've carried us up the side of a building and bounded to Bentham's out of sight. But right now I wasn't even sure walking was an option. Instead I suggested we wash off the hollow's white paint so that no one could see it but me.

"Absolutely not, no way, no sir," said Sharon, shaking his head vigorously. "I don't trust that thing. I want to keep an eye on it."

"I've got it under control," I said, slightly offended.

"So far," Sharon shot back.

"I agree with Sharon," said Emma. "You're doing marvelously, but what happens when you're in another room, or fall asleep?"

"Why would I leave the room?"

"To relieve yourself?" said Sharon. "Are you planning on taking your pet hollowgast into the water closet?"

"Um," I said, "I guess I'll cross that bridge when I come to it?"

"The paint stays on," said Sharon.

"Fine," I said irritably. "So what do we do?"

A door banged open down the alley and a cloud of steam came billowing out. A man emerged pushing a wheeled cart, which he parked in the alley before going back inside.

I ran to take a look. The door belonged to a laundry, and the cart was filled with dirty linens. It was just large enough to fit a small person—or a curled-up hollowgast.

I'll admit it: I stole the cart. I wheeled it back to the others, emptied it, and made the hollow climb in. Then we piled the dirty laundry on top, lifted the bear cubs in, and wheeled the whole thing down the street.

No one gave us a second look.

CHAPTER SIX

*W*hen we reached the house it was nearly dark. Nim rushed us into the entrance hall, where Bentham waited anxiously. He didn't even bother to greet us. "Why have you brought these grims?" he said, his eyes darting to the laundry cart. "Where's the creature?"

"It's here," I said. Lifting out the cubs, I began to pull back the linens.

Bentham looked but kept his distance. The sheets on top were white but grew bloodier as I dug, becoming a black cocoon as I reached the bottom. I pulled back the last and there it was, a small, withered thing in a fetal curl. It was hard to believe this pathetic creature was the same one that had given me such nightmares.

Bentham stepped closer. "My God," he said, looking at the bloody sheets. "What did they do to him?"

"Actually, I did that," I said. "I didn't really have a choice."

"It was about to swallow Jacob's head," Emma explained.

"You didn't kill it, did you?" Bentham said. "It's no use to us dead."

I said, "I don't think so," and then told the hollow to open its eyes, and very slowly, it did. It was still alive, but weak. "I don't know how much longer it'll last, though."

"In that case, we've not a moment to waste," said Bentham. "We must send for my healer right away and hope to heaven her dust works on hollows."

Nim was sent running to fetch the healer. While we waited, Bentham led us into his kitchen and offered us biscuits and canned fruit. Either because of nerves or all the squeamish things we'd seen, neither Emma nor I had an appetite. We picked at the food out of politeness while Bentham filled us in on what had happened while we were gone. He'd made all necessary preparations to his machine, he said, and everything was ready—all he needed was to plug in the hollowgast.

"Are you sure it'll work?" Emma said.

"Sure as I can be without ever having tried it," he replied.

"Will it hurt him?" I asked, feeling oddly protective of the hollow, if only because I'd gone to such trouble to rescue it.

"Of course not," Bentham said with a dismissive wave.

The healer arrived, and upon seeing her I nearly shouted in surprise. Not because she was so unusual looking—though she was—but because I was absolutely certain I had seen her before, though I couldn't say where or how I'd managed to forget an encounter with someone so strange.

Her only visible body parts were her left eye and left hand. The rest was hidden beneath acres of fabric: shawls, scarves, a dress, and a bell-shaped hoop skirt. She seemed to be missing her right hand, and the left was in the grip of a young man with brown skin and wide, bright eyes. He wore a jaunty silk shirt and a wide-brimmed hat, and he was leading the healer as if she were blind or otherwise disabled.

"I'm Reynaldo," said the young man in a crisp French accent, "and this is Mother Dust. I speak for her."

Mother Dust leaned toward Reynaldo and whispered something in his ear. Reynaldo looked at me and said, "She hopes you are feeling better."

That's when I realized where I'd seen her: in my dreams—or what I thought had been dreams—while recovering from my attack.

"Yes, much better," I said, unnerved.

Bentham skipped the formalities. "Can you heal one of these?" he said, leading Reynaldo and Mother Dust to the laundry cart. "It's a hollowgast, visible to us only where it's been painted."

"She can heal anything with a beating heart," said Reynaldo.

"Then, please," Bentham said. "It's very important that we save this creature's life."

Via Reynaldo, Mother Dust issued orders. Take the beast out of the cart, they said, so Emma and I tipped the hollowgast onto the floor. Put it in the sink, they said, so Emma and Sharon helped me lift it and place it in the basin of the long, deep sink. We cleaned its wounds with water from the tap, careful not to wash away too much of the white paint. Next, Mother Dust examined the hollowgast as Reynaldo asked me to identify all the places it was hurt.

"Now, Marion," Bentham said, addressing Mother Dust informally, "you needn't heal every last cut and bruise. We don't want the creature in top health; we only want to keep it alive. You see?"

"Yes, yes," Reynaldo said dismissively. "We know what we are doing."

Bentham harrumphed and turned his back, making a show of his unhappiness.

"Now she will make the dust," Reynaldo said. "Stand back, and be careful not to breathe it in. It will put you to sleep instantly."

We backed away. Reynaldo strapped a dust mask over his nose and mouth and then untied the shawl that wrapped what was left of Mother Dust's right arm. The stump beneath was only a few inches long, and it came to an end well above what would have been her elbow.

With her left hand Mother Dust began to rub the stump, which released a fine white powder that hung in the air. Holding his breath, Reynaldo combed the air with one hand and collected the dust. We watched, fascinated and slightly repulsed, until he'd gathered about an ounce of the stuff and the size of Mother Dust's stump had been reduced by the same amount.

Reynaldo transferred the dust into his mistress's hand. She leaned over the hollow and blew some of it in its face—as I remembered her doing to me. The hollow inhaled and then jerked suddenly. Everyone but Mother Dust leapt back.

Stay down, stay still, I said, but I needn't have—it was an automatic reaction to the powder, Reynaldo explained: the body downshifting into lower gear. As Mother Dust sprinkled more into the gash on the hollow's neck, Reynaldo told us that the powder could heal wounds and induce sleep, depending on how much was used. As he spoke, a white foam developed around the hollow's wound and began to glow. Mother Dust's dust, Reynaldo said, was *her*, and of inherently limited quantity. She wore herself away a little every time she healed someone.

"I hope this doesn't seem like a rude question," Emma said, "but why do you do it if it hurts you?"

Mother Dust stopped work on the hollow for a moment, turned so that her good eye could see Emma, and spoke as loudly as we'd ever heard her—in the mushy garble of someone who had no tongue.

Reynaldo translated. "I do it," he said, "because this is how I was chosen to serve."

"Then . . . thank you," Emma said humbly.

Mother Dust nodded and turned back to her task.

*   *   *

The hollow's recovery would not be instantaneous. It was deeply sedated and would wake only after the direst of its wounds had healed, a process that would likely take all night. Because the hollow had to be awake when Bentham "plugged it in" to his machine, phase two of our rescue plan would have to wait several hours. Until then, most of us were stuck in the kitchen: Reynaldo and Mother Dust, who had to reapply her powder to the hollow's wounds every so often, and Emma and me, because I didn't feel comfortable leaving the hollow alone, even though it was deeply asleep. The hollow was my responsibility now, the way an unhousebroken pet was the responsibility of whoever brought it home. Emma stayed close, too, because I had in some sense become *her* responsibility (and she mine), and if I fell asleep she would tickle me awake or tell me stories about the good old days in Miss Peregrine's house. Bentham checked in occasionally but was mostly off doing security sweeps of the house with Sharon and Nim, paranoid that his brother's foot soldiers might attack at any time.

As the night wore on, Emma and I talked about what the coming day might hold. Assuming Bentham could get his machine working again, it was possible that in a matter of hours we would find ourselves inside the wights' fortress. We might see our friends again, and Miss Peregrine.

"If we're very sneaky, and very, very lucky," Emma said. "And if . . . "

She hesitated. We were sitting side by side on a long wooden bench against a wall, and now she shifted so that I couldn't see her face.

"What?" I said.

She looked back at me, her face pained. "If they're still alive."

"They are."

"No, I'm tired of pretending. By now the wights could've harvested their souls for ambrosia. Or realized the ymbrynes are useless and decided to torture them instead, or milk their souls, or made an example of someone for trying to escape . . . "

"Stop it," I said. "It hasn't been *that* long."

"By the time we get there it'll have been forty-eight hours, at least. And a lot of awful things can happen in forty-eight hours."

"We don't have to imagine every single one of them. You sound like Horace with all these worst-case scenarios. There's no use tormenting ourselves until we know for sure what's happened."

"Yes, there is," she insisted. "There's a perfectly good reason to torment ourselves. If we've considered all the worst possibilities and one turns out to be true, we won't be completely unprepared for it."

"I don't think I could ever prepare myself for those kinds of things."

She put her head in her hands and let out a shaky sigh. It was all too much to think about.

I wanted to tell her then that I loved her. I thought that might help, by grounding us in something we were sure about rather than everything we weren't—but we hadn't said the words to each other many times, and I couldn't bring myself to say them now in front of two perfect strangers.

The more I thought about loving Emma, the shakier and sicker it made me feel, precisely because our future was so uncertain. I needed to imagine a future for myself with Emma in it, but it was impossible to picture our lives even a day from now. It was a constant struggle for me, having no idea what tomorrow held. I'm cautious by nature, a planner—someone who likes to know what's around the next corner and the corner after that—and this entire experience, from the moment I ventured into the abandoned shell of Miss Peregrine's house to now, had been one long free-fall into the void. To survive it I'd had to become a new person, someone flexible and sure footed and brave. Someone my grandfather would've been proud of. But my transformation had not been total. This new Jacob was grafted onto the old one, and I still had moments—plenty of them—of abject terror and wishing I'd never heard of any damned Miss Peregrine and needing very badly for the world to stop spinning so I could just hang on to something for a few minutes. I wondered, with a sinking ache, which Jacob loved Emma. Was it the new one, who was ready for anything, or the old one, who just needed something to hang on to?

I decided that I didn't want to think about it right now—a distinctly old-Jacob way of handling things—and focused instead on the distraction nearest at hand: the hollow, and what would happen when it woke. I would have to give him up, it seemed.

"I wish I could take him with us," I said. "He would make it so easy to smash anyone who got in our way. But I guess he has to stay behind to keep the machine running."

"So it's a *him* now." She raised an eyebrow. "Don't get too attached. Remember, if you gave that thing half a chance, it would eat you alive."

"I know, I know," I said, sighing.

"And maybe it wouldn't be so easy to smash everything. I'm sure the wights know how to handle hollows. After all, they used to *be* hollows."

"It's a unique gift you have," said Reynaldo, speaking to us for the first time in over an hour. He had taken a break from monitoring the hollow's wound to rummage through Bentham's cabinets for food, and now he and Mother Dust were seated at a small table, sharing a block of blue-veined cheese.

"It's a strange gift, though," I said. I'd been thinking about how strange it was for a while but hadn't quite been able to articulate it until now. "In an ideal world, there wouldn't be any hollows. And if there weren't any hollows, my special sight would have nothing to see, and no one would understand the weird language I can speak. You wouldn't even know I had a peculiar ability."

"Then it's a good thing you're here now," Emma said.

"Yeah, but . . . doesn't it seem almost too random? I could've been born anytime. My grandfather, too. Hollows have existed for only the last hundred years or so, but it just so happens that we were both born now, right when we were needed. Why?"

"I guess it was meant to be," Emma said. "Or maybe there have always been people who can do what you do, only they never knew it. Maybe lots of people go through life never knowing they're peculiar."

Mother Dust leaned toward Reynaldo and whispered.

"She says it's neither," said Reynaldo. "Your true gift probably isn't manipulating hollowgast—that's just its most obvious application."

"What do you mean?" I said. "What else could it be?"

Mother Dust whispered again.

"It's simpler than that," said Reynaldo. "Just as someone who's a gifted cellist wasn't born with an aptitude for only that instrument but for music in general, you weren't born only to manipulate hollows. Nor you," he said to Emma, "to make fire."

Emma frowned. "I'm over a hundred years old. I think I know my own peculiar ability by now—and I definitely can't manipulate water, or air, or dirt. Believe me, I've tried."

"That doesn't mean you can't," Reynaldo said. "Early in life we recognize certain talents in ourselves, and we focus on those to the exclusion of others. It's not that nothing else is possible, but that nothing else was nurtured."

"It's an interesting theory," I said.

"The point is, it's not so impossibly random that you have a talent for hollowgast manipulation. Your gift developed in that direction because that's what was needed."

"If that's true, then why can't all of us control hollows?" Emma said. "Every peculiar could use some of what Jacob's got."

"Because only *his* basic talent was capable of developing that way. In the times before hollows, the talents of peculiars with souls akin to his probably manifested some other way. It's said that the Library of Souls was staffed by people who could read peculiar souls like they were books. If those librarians were alive today, perhaps they'd be like him."

"Why do you say that?" I said. "Is there something about seeing hollows that's like reading souls?"

Reynaldo conferred with Mother Dust. "You seem to be a reader of hearts," he said. "You saw some good in Bentham's, after all. You chose to forgive him."

"Forgive him?" I said. "What would I have to forgive him for?"

Mother Dust knew she'd said too much, but it was too late to hold back. She whispered to Reynaldo.

"For what he did to your grandfather," he said.

I turned to Emma, but she seemed just as confused as I was.

"And what did he do to my grandfather?"

"I'll tell them," said a voice from the doorway, and then Bentham hobbled in by himself. "It's my shame, and I should be the one to confess it."

He shuffled past the sink, pulled a chair away from the table, and sat down facing us.

"During the war, your grandfather was highly valued for his special facility with hollows. We had a secret project, some technologists and I—we thought we could replicate his ability and give it to other peculiars. Inoculate them against hollows, like a vaccine. If we could all see and sense them, they would cease to be a threat, and the war against their kind would be won. Your grandfather made many noble sacrifices, but none so great as this: he agreed to participate."

Emma's face was tense as she listened. I could see she'd never heard any of this before.

"We took just a little bit," Bentham said. "Just a piece of his second soul. We thought it could be spared, or would be replenished, like when someone gives blood."

"You took his soul," Emma said, her voice wavering.

Bentham held his finger and thumb a centimeter apart. "*This* much. We split it up and administered it to several test subjects. Although it had the desired effect, it didn't last long, and repeated exposure began to rob them of their native abilities. It was a failure."

"And what about Abe?" Emma said. In her tone was the special malice she reserved for those who hurt people she loved. "What did you do to him?"

"He was weakened, and his talent diluted," said Bentham. "Before the procedure, he was much like young Jacob. His ability to control hollows was a deciding factor in our war with the wights.

After the procedure, however, he found he couldn't control them any longer, and his second sight became blurred. I'm told that soon afterward he left peculiardom altogether. He worried he would be a danger to his fellow peculiars, rather than a help. He felt he could no longer protect them."

I looked at Emma. She was staring at the floor, her face unreadable.

"A failed experiment is nothing to be sorry for," Bentham said. "It's how scientific progress is made. But what happened to your grandfather is one of the great regrets of my life."

"That's why he left," Emma said, her face tilting upward. "It's why he went to America." She turned to me. She didn't look angry, but wore an expression of dawning relief. "He was ashamed. He said so in a letter once and I never understood why. That he felt ashamed, and unpeculiar."

"It was taken from him," I said. Now I had an answer to another question: how a hollowgast could've bested my grandfather in his own backyard. He wasn't senile, or even particularly frail. But his defenses against hollows were mostly gone, and had been for a long time.

"That's not what you should be sorry for," said Sharon, standing in the doorway with his arms crossed. "One man wasn't going to win that war. The real shame is what the wights did with your technology. You created the precursor to ambrosia."

"I've tried to repay my debt," Bentham said. "Didn't I help you? And you?" He looked at Sharon and then Mother Dust. Like Sharon, it seemed she, too, had been an ambro addict. "For years I've wanted to apologize," he said, turning to me. "To make it up to your grandfather. That's why I've been looking for him all this time. I hoped he would come back to see me, and I might figure out a way to restore his talent."

Emma laughed bitterly. "After what you did to him, you thought he'd come back for more?"

"I didn't consider it likely, but I hoped. Fortunately, redemption comes in many forms. In this case, in the guise of a grandson."

"I'm not here to redeem you," I said.

"Nevertheless, I am your servant. If I can do anything, it is yours for the asking."

"Just help us get our friends back, and your sister."

"Gladly," he said, seeming relieved I hadn't demanded more or stood up and screamed in his face. I still might've—my head was spinning, and I hadn't quite sorted out how to react. "Now," he said, "as for how to proceed from here . . . "

"Can we have a moment?" Emma said. "Just Jacob and me?"

We exited into the hall to talk in private—out of sight of the hollow, but only just.

"Let's make a list of all the terrible things this man is responsible for," Emma said.

"Okay," I said. "One: he created hollows. Without meaning to, though."

"But he did. And he created ambrosia, and he took away Abe's power, or most of it."

Without meaning to, I nearly said again. But Bentham's intentions were beside the point. I knew what she was getting at: after all these revelations, I wasn't so confident about putting our fates and those of our friends in Bentham's hands—or his plans. He may have been well-meaning, but he had a dismal track record.

"Can we trust him?" Emma said.

"Do we have a choice?"

"That wasn't my question."

I thought for a moment. "I think we can," I said. "I just hope he's used up all his bad luck."

*   *   *

"COME QUICKLY! IT'S WAKING UP!"

Shouts echoed from the kitchen. Emma and I dashed through the doorway to find everyone cowering in a corner, terrified of a groggy hollowgast that was struggling to sit up but had managed only to droop its upper body over the edge of the sink. Only I could see its open mouth, its tongues lolling limply across the floor.

Close your mouth, I said in Hollow. Making a sound like it was slurping spaghetti, it sucked them back into its jaws.

Sit up.

The hollow couldn't quite do it, so I took it by the shoulders and guided it into a seated position. It was recovering with remarkable speed, though, and after another few minutes it had regained enough motor skill to be coaxed out of the sink and onto its feet. It no longer limped. All that was left of the gash in its neck was a faint white line, not unlike the ones fast disappearing from my own face. As I relayed this, Bentham couldn't hide his irritation that Mother Dust had healed the hollow so thoroughly.

"Can I help it if my dust is potent?" Mother Dust said via Reynaldo.

Exhausted, they went off to find beds. Emma and I were tired, too—it was nearing dawn and we hadn't slept—but the progress we were making was exciting and hope had given us a second wind.

Bentham turned to us, eyes alight. "Moment of truth, friends. Shall we see if we can get the old girl running again?"

By that he meant his machine, and there was no need to ask.

"Let's not waste another second," Emma said.

Bentham summoned his bear and I rallied my hollowgast. PT appeared in the doorway, scooped his master into his arms, and together they led us through the house. What a strange sight we would've made, had anyone been watching: a dapper gentleman cradled in the arms of a bear, Sharon in his billowing black cloak, Emma stifling yawns with a hand that kept smoking, and plain old me muttering at my white-daubed hollowgast, who even in perfect health shuffled as he walked, as if his bones didn't quite fit his body.

Through the halls and down the stairs we went, into the bowels of the house: rooms crowded with clanking machinery, each smaller than the last, until finally we came to a door that the bear couldn't fit through. We stopped. PT set his master down.

"Here it is," Bentham said, beaming like a proud father. "The heart of my Panloopticon."

Bentham opened the door. PT waited outside while the rest of us followed him in.

The small room was dominated by a fearsome machine made of iron and steel. Its guts stretched from wall to wall, a baffling array of flywheels and pistons and valves glistening with oil. It looked like a machine capable of making unholy noise, but for now it sat cold and silent. A greasy man stood between two giant gears, tightening something with a wrench.

"This is my assistant, Kim," said Bentham.

I recognized him: he was the man who'd chased us out of the Siberia Room.

"I'm Jacob," I said. "We surprised you in the snow yesterday."

"What were you doing out there?" Emma asked him.

"Freezing half to death," the man said bitterly, and he went on wrenching.

"Kim's been helping me search for a way into my brother's Panloopticon," said Bentham. "If such a door exists in the Siberia Room, it's likely at the bottom of a deep crevasse. I'm certain Kim will be grateful if your hollowgast succeeds in bringing some of our other rooms online, where there are sure to be doors in more accessible places."

Kim grunted, his face skeptical as he looked us up and down. I wondered how many years he'd spent battling frostbite and combing the crevasses.

Bentham got down to business. He issued clipped orders to his assistant, who twisted a few dials and pulled a long lever. The gears of the machine gave a hiss and sputter, then turned a degree.

"Bring in the creature," Bentham said in a low voice.

The hollow had been waiting outside, and I called him in. He shuffled through the doorway and let out a low gravelly growl, as if he knew something unpleasant was about to happen to him.

The assistant dropped his wrench but quickly retrieved it.

"Here is the battery chamber," Bentham said, drawing our attention to a large box in the corner. "You must guide the creature inside, where he'll be restrained."

The chamber resembled a windowless phone booth made of cast iron. A nest of tubes sprouted from its top and connected to pipes that ran along the ceiling. Bentham grasped the heavy door's handle and pulled it open with a grating rasp. I peered inside. The walls were smooth gray metal perforated with small holes, like the interior of an oven. Along the back hung a collection of thick leather straps.

"Will it hurt him?" I asked.

I surprised myself with the question, and Bentham, too.

"Does that matter?" he replied.

"I'd rather it didn't. If we have a choice."

"We don't," Bentham said, "but it won't feel any pain. The chamber fills with anesthetic sleeping gas before anything else happens."

"And then what?" I said.

He smiled and patted my arm. "It's very technical. Suffice to say, your creature will leave the chamber alive, in more or less the condition he entered it. Now, if you would kindly have it step inside."

I wasn't sure I believed him, nor why it mattered to me. The hollows had put us through hell and seemed so lacking in feeling that inflicting pain on them should have been a pleasure. But it wasn't.

I didn't want to kill the hollow any more than I wanted to kill a strange animal. In the course of leading this creature around by the nose, I had gotten close enough to understand that there was more than just void inside it. There was a tiny spark, a little marble of soul at the bottom of a deep pool. It wasn't hollow—not really.

Come, I said to it, and the hollow, which had been lurking shyly in the corner, stepped around Bentham to stand before the booth. *Inside*.

I felt it waver. It was healed now, and strong, and if my hold on it faltered for even a moment, I knew what it might do. But I was stronger, and a battle of wills between us would've been no contest. It wavered, I think, because I had.

I'm sorry, I said to it.

The hollow didn't move; *sorry* was input it didn't know what to do with. I just needed to say it.

Inside, I said again, and this time the hollow complied and stepped into the chamber. Since no one else would touch it, from that point Bentham told me what to do. Per his instructions, I pushed the hollow against the back wall and crossed the leather straps over its legs, arms, and chest, buckling them tight. They were clearly designed to restrain a human being, which raised questions to which I didn't want the answers right now. All that mattered was moving forward with the plan.

I stepped out, feeling stifled and panicky from the few moments I'd spent inside.

"Close the door," Bentham said.

When I hesitated the assistant moved to do it, but I blocked his way. "It's my hollow," I said. "I'll do it."

I planted my feet and grabbed the handle and then—though I tried not to—looked into the hollow's face. Its great black eyes were wide and frightened, all out of proportion with its body, small and shriveled like a cluster of figs. It was still and would always be a disgusting creature, but it looked so pathetic that I felt unaccountably terrible, like I was about to put to sleep a dog who didn't understand why it was being punished.

All hollowgast need to die, I told myself. I knew I was right, but it didn't make me feel any better.

I pulled on the door and it screamed shut. Bentham's assistant hooked a giant padlock through its handles, then went back to the machine's controls and began twiddling dials.

"You did the right thing," Emma whispered in my ear.

Gears began to turn, pistons to pump, the machine itself to thrum with a rhythm that shook the entire room. Bentham clapped his hands and grinned, happy as a schoolkid. Then from inside the chamber came a scream the likes of which I'd never heard.

"You said it wouldn't hurt him!" I shouted at Bentham.

He turned to shout at his assistant. "The gas! You forgot the anesthesia!"

The assistant scrambled to pull another lever. There was a loud hiss of compressed air. A wisp of white smoke curled from a crack in the chamber door. The hollow's screams gradually faded.

"There," said Bentham. "Now it feels nothing."

I wished for a moment that Bentham was in that chamber instead of my hollow.

Other pieces of the machine came alive. There was the sound of liquid sloshing through the pipes above our heads. Several small valves near the ceiling rang like bells. Black fluid began dripping down through the machine's guts. It wasn't oil, but something even darker and more pungent—the fluid that the hollowgast produced almost constantly, that wept from its eyes and dripped from its teeth. Its blood.

I'd seen enough and walked out of the room feeling sick to my stomach. Emma followed me.

"Are you okay?"

I couldn't expect her to understand my reaction. I hardly understood it myself. "I'll be fine," I said. "This is the right thing."

"It's the only thing," she said. "We're so close."

Bentham hobbled out of the room. "PT, upstairs!" he said, and he tipped himself into the bear's waiting arms.

"Is it working now?" Emma said.

"We're going to find out," Bentham replied.

With my hollow restrained, sedated, and locked inside an iron chamber, there was little danger in leaving him behind—and yet I lingered by the door.

Sleep, I said. *Sleep, and don't wake up until this is over.*

I followed the others out through the machine rooms and up several flights of stairs. We came to the long, carpeted hallway that was lined with exotically named rooms. The walls hummed with energy; the house seemed alive.

PT set Bentham on the carpet. "Moment of truth!" he said.

He marched to the nearest door and flung it open.

A humid breeze blew into the hall.

I stepped forward to look inside. What I saw gave me goosebumps. Like the Siberia Room, it was portal to another time and place. The room's simple furniture—bed, wardrobe, side table—was caked with sand. The rear wall was missing. Beyond it was a curving palm-fringed beach.

"I give you Rarotonga, 1752!" Bentham declared proudly. "Hello, Sammy! Long time!"

Squatting in the near distance was a small man cleaning a fish. He regarded us with mild surprise, then raised the fish and waved to us with it. "Long time," he agreed.

"This is good, then?" Emma said to Bentham. "This is what you wanted?"

"What I wanted, what I've been dreaming of . . . " Bentham laughed as he hurried off to throw open another door. Inside was a yawning, tree-filled canyon, a narrow bridge suspended across it. "British Columbia, 1929!" he crowed.

He pirouetted down the hall to open a third door—by now we

were chasing him—inside which I could see hulking stone pillars, the dusty ruins of an ancient city.

"Palymra!" he shouted, slapping his hand against the wall. "Huzzah! The damned thing works!"

Bentham could hardly contain himself. "My beloved Panloopticon," he cried, throwing his arms wide. "How I missed you!"

"Congratulations," Sharon said. "I'm glad I could be here to witness this."

Bentham's excitement was infectious. It was an astounding thing, his machine: a universe contained in a single hallway. Looking down it, I could see hints of other worlds peeking out—wind moaning behind one door, grains of sand blowing into the hall from beneath another. At any other time, under any other circumstances, I would've run and thrown them open. But right now there was only one door I cared about opening.

"Which of these leads inside the wights' fortress?" I asked.

"Yes, yes, to business," Bentham said, reining himself in. "My apologies if I got a bit carried away. I've put my life into this machine, and it's good to see it up and running again."

He leaned against a wall, suddenly sapped of energy. "Getting you into the fortress should be a simple enough proposition. Behind these doors are at least a half dozen crossover points. The question is, what will you do once you get there?"

"That depends," Emma said. "What are we going to find when we get there?"

"It's been a long time since I was inside," Bentham said, "so my knowledge is dated. My brother's Panloopticon doesn't look like mine—it is arranged vertically, in a high tower. The prisoners are kept elsewhere. They'll be in separate cells under heavy guard."

"The guards will be our biggest problem," I said.

"I may be able help with them," said Sharon.

"You're coming with us?" Emma said.

"Absolutely not!" Sharon said. "But I'd like to do my bit somehow—with minimal risk to myself, of course. I'll create a disturbance outside the fortress walls that will draw the guards' attention.

That should make it easier for you to skulk about unnoticed."

"What kind of disturbance?" I asked.

"The wights' least favorite kind: a civil one. I'll get those lay-abouts on Smoking Street to catapult nasty, flaming things at the walls until we've got the whole guard force after us."

"And why would they help you?" Emma said.

"Because there's lots more where this came from." He reached into his cloak and pulled out the vial of ambro he'd snatched from Emma. "Promise them enough of it and they'll do just about any-thing."

"Put it away, sir!" Bentham snapped. "You know I don't allow that in my house."

Sharon apologized and stuffed the vial back into his cloak.

Bentham consulted his pocket watch. "Now, it's just after four-thirty in the morning. Sharon, I imagine your disturbers of the peace are asleep. Could you have them riled and ready by six?"

"Absolutely," Sharon said.

"Then see to it."

"Happy to be of service." And with a swoosh of his cloak, Sharon turned and hurried away down the hall.

"That gives you an hour and a half to prepare," Bentham said—though it wasn't immediately clear what preparations could be made. "Anything I have is at your disposal."

"Think," Emma said. "What would be useful in a raid?"

"Do you have any guns?" I asked.

Bentham shook his head. "PT here is all the protection I need."

"Explosives?" Emma said.

"I'm afraid not."

"I don't suppose you have an Armageddon chicken," I said, only half kidding.

"A stuffed one, among my displays."

I imagined throwing a stuffed chicken at a gun-toting wight and wasn't sure whether to laugh or cry.

"Perhaps I'm confused," Bentham said. "Why would you need guns and explosives when you can control hollows? There are many inside the fortress. Tame them and the battle is won."

"It's not that easy," I said, weary of explaining. "It takes a long time to take control of even one . . . "

My grandfather could've done it, I wanted to say. *Before you broke him.*

"Well, that's your business," Bentham said, sensing he'd stepped on my toes. "However you accomplish it, the ymbrynes must be your priority. Bring them back first—as many as you can, starting with my sister. They're the most wanted, the biggest prize, and they're in the worst danger."

"I agree with that," Emma said. "Ymbrynes first, then our friends."

"And then what?" I said. "Once they notice we're stealing back our peculiars, they're going to come after us. Where do we go from here?" It was like robbing a bank: getting the money was only half the job. Then you had to get *away* with the money.

"Go anywhere you like," Bentham said, gesturing down the length of the hall. "Pick any door, any loop. You have eighty-seven potential escape routes in this hallway alone."

"He's right," Emma said. "How would they ever find us?"

"I'm sure they'd find a way," I said. "This will only slow them down."

Bentham held up a finger to stop me. "Which is why I'll lay a trap for them, and make it look as if we've hidden ourselves in the Siberia Room. PT has a large extended family there, and they'll be waiting just inside the door, good and hungry."

"And if the bears can't finish them off?" Emma said.

"Then I suppose we'll have to," said Bentham.

"And Bob's your uncle," Emma said, a Britishism that would've been incomprehensible if not for her sarcastic tone of voice. Translation: *your nonchalant attitude strikes me as insane.* Bentham spoke as if the whole thing were no more complicated than a trip to the grocery store: storm in, rescue everyone, hide, finish off the bad guys, and Bob's your uncle. Which was, of course, insane.

"You realize we're just two people," I said. "Two kids."

"Yes, exactly," Bentham said, nodding sagely. "That's to your advantage. If the wights are expecting resistance of any kind, it's an army at their gates, not a couple of children in their midst."

His optimism was beginning to wear me down. Maybe, I thought, we did have a chance.

"Hullo, there!"

We turned to see Nim running down the hall toward us, panting for breath. "Bird for Mr. Jacob!" he called. "Messenger bird . . . for Mr. Jacob . . . just winged in . . . waiting downstairs!" Upon reaching us, he doubled over and launched into a coughing fit.

"How could I have a message?" I said. "Who even knows I'm here?"

"We'd better find out," said Bentham. "Nim, lead the way."

Nim fell over in a heap.

"Oh, lord," said Bentham. "We're getting you a calisthenics trainer, Nim. PT, give the poor man a lift!"

*　　*　　*

The messenger was waiting in a foyer downstairs. It was a large green parrot. It had flown into the house through an open window several minutes before and begun squawking my name, at which point Nim had caught it and put it in a cage.

It was still squawking my name.

"JAYY-cob! JAYY-cob!"

Its voice sounded like a rusty hinge.

"He won't talk to anyone but you," Nim explained, hurrying me toward the cage. "Here he is, you silly bird! Give him the message!"

"Hello, Jacob," the parrot said. "This is Miss Peregrine speaking."

"What!" I said, shocked. "She's a parrot now?"

"No," Emma said, "the message is *from* Miss Peregrine. Go ahead, parrot, what does she say?"

"I'm alive and well in my brother's tower," said the bird, speaking now in an eerily human-sounding voice. "The others are here, too: Millard, Olive, Horace, Bruntley, Enoch, and the rest."

Emma and I glanced at one another. *Bruntley?*

Like a living answering machine, the bird went on: "Miss Wren's dog told me where I might find you—you and Miss Bloom. I want to dissuade you from any rescue attempts. We are in no danger here, and there's no need to risk your life with silly stunts. Instead, my brother has made this offer: give yourselves up to his guards at the Smoking Street bridge and you won't be harmed. I urge you to comply. This is our only option. We will be reunited, and under my brother's care and protection, we'll all be part of the new peculiardom."

The parrot whistled, indicating the message was over.

Emma was shaking her head. "That didn't sound like Miss Peregrine. Unless she's been brainwashed."

"And she never calls the kids by only their first or last names," I said. "That would've been *Miss* Bruntley."

"You don't believe the message is authentic?" Bentham said.

"I don't know *what* that was," Emma replied.

Bentham leaned toward the cage and said, "Authenticate!"

The bird said nothing. Bentham repeated his command, wary, and cocked his ear toward the bird. Then, suddenly, he straightened.

"Oh, hell."

And then I heard it, too: ticking.

"BOMB!" Emma screamed.

PT knocked the cage into a corner, swept us into a protective embrace, and turned his back to the bird. There was a blinding flash and a deafening bang, but I felt no pain; the bear had taken the brunt of the blast. Other than a pressure wave that popped my ears and blew off Bentham's hat, followed by a searing but mercifully brief sensation of heat, we'd been spared.

It was raining paint flakes and parrot feathers as we stumbled out of the room. We were all unscathed but the bear, who sank onto all fours and showed us his back with a trembling whimper. It was seared black and stripped of fur, and when Bentham saw it he cried out in anger and hugged the animal by its neck.

Nim ran off to wake Mother Dust.

"Do you know what this means?" Emma said. She was shaking, eyes wide. I'm sure I looked the same; surviving a bomb attack will do that to a person.

"I'm pretty sure it wasn't Miss Peregrine who sent that parrot," I said.

"Obviously . . ."

"And Caul knows where we are."

"If he didn't before, he does now. Messenger birds are trained to find people even if the sender doesn't have their exact address."

"It definitely means he caught Addison," I said, my heart sinking at the thought.

"Yes—but it means something else, too. Caul's scared of us. He wouldn't have bothered trying to kill us otherwise."

"Maybe," I said.

"Definitely. And if he's scared of us, Jacob . . . " She narrowed her eyes at me. "That means there's something to be scared of."

"He isn't frightened," said Bentham, lifting his head from the folds of PT's neck. "He should be, but he isn't. That parrot wasn't meant to kill you, only to incapacitate. It seems my brother wants young Jacob alive."

"Me?" I said. "What for?"

"I can think of only one reason. Word of your performance with the hollowgast reached him, and it convinced him you're quite special."

"Special how?" I said.

"My hunch is this: he believes you may be the last key to the Library of Souls. One who can see and manipulate the soul jars."

"Like Mother Dust said," whispered Emma.

"That's crazy," I said. "Could it be true?"

"All that matters is that he believes it," said Bentham. "But it changes nothing. You'll execute the rescue as planned, and then we'll get you, your friends, and our ymbrynes as far from my brother and his mad schemes as possible. But we must hurry: Jack's foot soldiers will trace the exploded parrot to this house. They'll be coming for you shortly, and you must be gone before they arrive." He consulted his pocket watch. "Speaking of which, it's nearly six o'clock."

We were about to go when Mother Dust and Reynaldo rushed in.

"Mother Dust would like to give you something," he said, and Mother Dust held out a small object wrapped in cloth.

Bentham told them we had no time for gifts, but Reynaldo insisted. "In case you run into trouble," he said, pressing the item into

Emma's hand. "Open it."

Emma peeled back the rough cloth. The small thing inside looked at first like a stub of chalk, until Emma rolled it in her palm.

It had two knuckles and a small, painted nail.

It was a pinky finger.

"You shouldn't have," I said.

Reynaldo could see we didn't understand. "It's Mother's finger," he said. "Crush it up and use it as you will."

Emma's eyes widened and her hand dropped a little, as if the finger had just tripled in weight. "I can't accept this," she said. "It's too much."

Mother Dust reached out with her good hand—it was smaller than before, a bandage covering the knuckle where her pinky used to be—and closed Emma's hand around the gift. She mumbled and Reynaldo translated: "You and he might be our last hope. I'd give you my whole arm if I could spare it."

"I don't know what to say," I said. "Thank you."

"Use it sparingly," Reynaldo said. "A little goes a long way. Oh, and you'll want these." He pulled two dust masks from his back pocket and dangled them. "Otherwise you'll put yourselves to sleep along with your enemies."

I thanked him again and accepted the masks. Mother Dust gave us a little bow, her enormous skirt dusting the floor.

"And now we really must be going," Bentham said, and we left PT in the company of the healers and the two bear cubs, who had come in to snuggle their ailing elder.

We returned upstairs to the hall of loops. When we came off the landing I felt a brief whirl of vertigo, a sudden cliff's-edge dizziness in recognition of where I was standing, eighty-seven worlds behind eighty-seven doors all stretching out before us, all those infinities connecting back here like nerves to a brain stem. We were about to go into one and maybe never come out again. I could feel old Jacob and new Jacob wrestling over that, terror and exhilaration coming at me in successive waves.

Bentham was talking, walking quickly with his cane. Telling us which door to use and where to find the door inside that door that would cross over to Caul's side of the loop and how to get out again into the Panloopticon machine inside Caul's stronghold. It was all very complicated, but Bentham promised that the route was short and marked with signs. To make doubly sure we didn't get lost, he'd send along his assistant to guide us. The assistant was summoned from tending the machine's gears and stood grim and silent while we said goodbye.

Bentham shook our hands. "Goodbye, good luck, and thank you," he said.

"Don't thank us yet," Emma replied.

The assistant opened one of the doors and waited beside it.

"Bring back my sister," Bentham said. "And when you find the ones who have her . . . " He raised his gloved hand and made a fist with it, the leather creaking as it tightened. "Don't spare their feelings."

"We won't," I said, and walked through the doorway.

CHAPTER SEVEN

*W*e followed Bentham's assistant into the room, past the usual furnishings, through the missing fourth wall, and out into a thick grove of evergreens. It was midday, late fall or early spring, the air chill and tinged with wood smoke. Our feet crunched along a well-worn path, the only other sounds a songbird's whistle and the low but rising roar of falling water. Bentham's assistant said little and that was fine by us; Emma and I were filled with a high, buzzing tension and had no interest in idle conversation.

We passed through the trees and out onto a track that curved around a mountainside. A desaturated landscape of gray rocks and patches of snow. Distant pines like rows of bristling brushes. We jogged at a moderate pace, careful not to exhaust ourselves too soon. After a few minutes we rounded a bend and found ourselves standing before a thundering waterfall.

Here was one of the signs Bentham had promised. THIS WAY, it read, plain as day.

"Where are we?" Emma asked.

"Argentina," the assistant replied.

Obeying the sign, we followed a path that became gradually overgrown with trees and thickets. We pushed aside the brambles and trudged on, the waterfall quieting behind us. The path ended at a small stream. We followed the stream a few hundred yards until it, too, ended, the water flowing into a low opening in a hillside, the entrance to which was hidden by ferns and moss. The assistant knelt on the stream bank and pulled back a curtain of weeds—then froze.

"What is it?" I whispered.

He pulled a pistol from his belt and fired three shots into the opening. A chilling cry came back, and then a creature rolled out into the stream, dead.

"What is it?" I asked again, staring at the creature. It was all fur and claws.

"Dunno," said the assistant. "But it was waiting for you."

It was nothing I could identify—it had a lumpy body, fanged teeth, and giant bulbous eyes, and even they seemed to be covered with fur. I wondered if Caul put it there—if maybe he'd anticipated his brother's plan and booby-trapped all the shortcuts into his Pan-loopticon.

The stream carried the body away.

"Bentham said he didn't have any guns," Emma said.

"He doesn't," the assistant said. "This one's mine."

Emma looked at him expectantly. "Well, could we *borrow* it?"

"No." He put it away. Pointed to the cave. "Go through there. Retrace your steps backward to the place we came from. Then you'll be with the wights."

"Where will you be?"

He sat down in the snow. "Here."

I looked at Emma and she looked back, both of us trying to hide how vulnerable we felt. Trying to grow a sheath of steel around our hearts. For what we might see. Might do. Might be done to us.

I descended into the stream and helped Emma in. The water was numbingly cold. Bending to peer into the cave, I saw daylight glinting dimly at the other end. Another changeover, darkness into light, pseudo-birth.

There appeared to be no more toothy creatures waiting inside, so I lowered myself into the water. The stream rushed up over my legs and waist in a freezing swirl that took away my breath. I heard Emma gasp behind me as she did the same, and then I grabbed the lip of the cave and slid inside.

Being immersed in cold, rushing water hurts like being stabbed with needles all over your body. All pain is motivating, and this type especially so; I scrabbled and pushed myself through the stone tunnel with a quickness, over slick sharp rocks and low under-hangs, half choking as water flowed over my face. Then I was out, and turned to help Emma.

We jumped out of the freezing stream and looked around. The place was identical to the other side of the cave except there was no assistant, no bullet casings in the snow, no footprints. As if we'd stepped through a mirror and into the world it reflected, minus a few details.

"You're blue," Emma said, and she pulled me up onto the bank and held me. Her warmth coursed through me, bringing feeling back to numbed limbs.

We walked, retracing every step of the route we'd taken. We found our way back through the brambles, up the hill, past the waterfall—all the scenery just the same except for the THIS WAY sign Bentham had set out for us. It was not here. This loop did not belong to him.

We arrived again at the small forest. Darted from tree to tree, using each one as cover until we reached the place where the path ended and became a floor and then a room, framed and hidden by a pair of crossed firs. But this room was different from Bentham's. It was spartan—no furnishings, no poppy-laced wallpaper—and the floor and walls were smooth concrete. We stepped inside and searched the darkness for a door, running our hands along the walls until I happened to hook a small recessed handle.

We pressed our ears to the door, listening for voices or footsteps. I heard only vague echoes.

Slowly, carefully, I slid the door open a crack. Inched my head through the gap to peek out. Here was a wide curving hall of stone, hospital clean and blindingly bright, its smooth walls toothed with tall, black, tomblike doors, dozens of them curving away sharply.

This was it: the wights' tower. We had made it inside the lion's den.

I heard footsteps approaching. Pulled my head back inside the door. There was no time to close it.

Through the crack I glimpsed a flash of white as a man walked by. He was moving quickly, dressed in a lab coat, head down to read a paper in his hand.

He didn't see me.

I waited for his footsteps to recede and then squeezed into the hall. Emma followed, pulling the door shut behind us.

Left or right? The floor ran uphill to the left, downhill to the right. According to Bentham we were in Caul's tower, but his prisoners were not. We needed to get out. Down, then. Down and right.

We turned right, hugging the inner wall as the hallway spiraled downward. The rubber soles of my shoes squeaked. I hadn't noticed the noise until now, and in the amplified quiet of the hard-walled hallway, each step was cringe-inducing.

We went on for a short while, and then Emma tensed and threw her arm across my chest to stop me.

We listened. With our footsteps silenced, we could hear others. They were ahead of us, and close. We rushed to the closest door. It slid open easily. We dove inside, closed it, threw our backs against it.

The room we'd entered was round, walls and ceiling both. We were inside a huge drainage pipe, thirty feet wide and still under construction—and we weren't alone. Where the pipe ended and broke into rainy daylight, a dozen men sat on a pipe-shaped scaffold, staring at us, dumbfounded. We'd interrupted them during their lunch break.

"Hey! How'd you get in there?" one shouted.

"They're kids," said another. "Hey, this ain't a playground!"

They were American, and they didn't seem to know what to make of us. We didn't dare respond for fear that the wights in the hall might hear us, and I worried that the workers' shouting would attract their attention, too.

"Have you got that finger?" I whispered to Emma. "Now seems like a good time to test it out."

So we gave them the finger. By which I mean we put on the dust masks (wet from the stream but still serviceable), Emma crushed a tiny bit of Mother Dust's pinky, and we walked down the pipe toward the men and attempted to launch the powder at them. First Emma tried blowing it out of her cupped hand, but it just swirled into a cloud around our heads, which made my face tingle and go a bit numb. Next I tried throwing it, which didn't work at all. The dust, it seemed, wasn't much good as an offensive weapon. By now the pipe builders were growing impatient, and one had jumped down from the scaffold to remove us by force. Emma tucked the finger away and made a flame with her hand—there was a *poof!* as Emma's flame ignited the dust hanging in the air, turning it instantly to smoke.

"Woah!" the man said. He began coughing and soon slumped to the floor, fast asleep. When a few of his friends ran to help him, they too fell victim to the cloud of anesthetizing smoke and fell to the ground beside him.

Now the remaining workmen were afraid, angry, and shouting at us. We ran back to the door before the situation could devolve further. I checked that the coast was clear and we slipped into the hall.

When I closed the door behind us, the sound of the men's voices was muted completely, as if it hadn't just shut them inside but had somehow turned them off.

We ran a short way, then stopped and listened for footsteps, then ran, then stopped and listened, spiraling down the tower in stuttering bursts of action and silence. Twice more we heard people coming and ran to hide behind doors. Inside one was a steaming jungle echoing with the screams of monkeys, and another opened into an adobe room, beyond which lay hard-packed ground and looming mountains.

The floor leveled and the hallway straightened. Around the last bend was a pair of double doors with daylight gleaming beneath them.

"Shouldn't there be more guards around?" I said nervously.

Emma shrugged and nodded toward the doors, which appeared to be the only way out of the tower. I was about to push them open when I heard voices on the other side. A man telling a joke. I could hear only the burble of his voice, not the words, but it was definitely a joke, because when he finished there was an eruption of laughter.

"Your guards," Emma said, like a waiter presenting a fancy meal.

We could either wait and hope they went away, or open the door and deal with them. The latter option was braver and faster, so I summoned New Jacob and told him we were going to throw open the door and fight, and to please not discuss the matter with Old Jacob, who inevitably would whine and resist. But by the time I'd gotten it all settled, Emma was already doing it.

Silently and quickly, she pulled open one of the swinging doors. Arrayed before us were the backs of five wights in mismatched uniforms, all wearing modern police-issue-type pistols at their waists. They were standing casually, facing away from us. None had seen the door open. Beyond them was a courtyard surrounded by low barracks-like buildings, and rising in the farther distance was the fortress wall. I jabbed my finger toward the finger hidden in Emma's pocket—*sleep*, I mouthed, by which I meant that rendering these wights unconscious and then dragging them inside the tower seemed the most expedient course of action. She understood, pulled the door halfway closed, and began to dig out the finger. I reached for the dust masks, which were stuffed into my waistband.

And then a flaming mass of something flew over the fortress wall in the distance, sailed toward us through the air in a graceful arc, and fell *splat* in the middle of the courtyard, spraying dribbly blobs of fire everywhere and sending the guards into a state of excitement. Two ventured to see what had landed, and as they bent over to examine the flaming muck, another hunk came sailing over the wall and hit one of them. He was sent sprawling, his body aflame. (From the smell of it, which was pungent and traveled fast, it was a mixture of gasoline and excrement.)

The remaining guards ran to extinguish him. A loud alarm began to sound. Within seconds, wights were flying out of the buildings around the courtyard and rushing toward the wall. Sharon's assault had begun, bless him, and not a moment too soon. With any luck, it would give us enough cover to search unimpeded—at least for a few minutes. I couldn't imagine it would take longer than that for the wights to repel a few ambro addicts armed with catapults.

We scanned the courtyard. It was surrounded on three sides by low-slung buildings, each more or less identical to the next. There were no flashing arrows or neon signs advertising the presence of ymbrynes. We would have to search, as fast as we could, and hope we got lucky.

Three of the wights had run off to the wall, leaving two behind to extinguish the one covered in flaming excrement. They were rolling him in the dirt, their backs to us.

We chose a building at random—the one on the left—and ran to its door. Inside was a large room suffocatingly packed with what looked and smelled like secondhand clothes. We ran down an aisle lined with racks of clothes of every description, from all different time periods and cultures, all labeled and organized. A wardrobe, perhaps, for every loop the wights had infiltrated. I wondered if the cardigan Dr. Golan always wore to our meetings had hung in this room.

But our friends weren't here and the ymbrynes weren't either, so we tore through the aisles looking for a way into the next building that didn't lead back through the exposed courtyard.

There were none. We'd have to risk another dash outside.

We went to the door and watched through the crack, waiting as a straggler ran through the courtyard, pulling on his guard's uniform as he went. Once the coast was clear, we ran out into the open.

Catapulted objects landed all around us. Having run out of excrement, Sharon's improvised army had begun to launch other things—bricks, garbage, small dead animals. I heard one such projectile utter a string of profanities as it smacked into the ground and recognized the shriveled form of a bridge head spinning across the ground. If my heart hadn't been thrumming so tremendously I might've laughed out loud.

We made it across the courtyard to the building opposite. Its door seemed promising: heavy and metal, it would surely have been guarded had the guard not abandoned his post to go to the wall. Surely there was something important inside.

We opened it and slipped into a small white-tiled laboratory that smelled strongly of chemicals. My eyes were drawn to a cabinet filled with terrifying surgical tools, all steely and shining. There was a deep hum coming through the walls, the dissonant heartbeat of machines, and something else, too—

"Do you hear that?" Emma said, tense, listening.

I did. It was sustained and chattering, but distinctly human. Someone was laughing.

We traded a baffled look. Emma gave Mother Dust's finger to me and lit a flame in her hand, and we each put on our masks. Ready for anything, we thought, though in retrospect we were not at all prepared for the house of horrors that lay waiting for us.

We moved through rooms I struggle to describe now because

I've tried to erase them from my memory. Each was more nightmarish than the last. The first was a small operating theater, the table armed with straps and restraints. Porcelain tubs along the walls stood ready to collect drained fluids. Next was a research area where tiny skulls and other bones were connected to electrical equipment and gauges. The walls were papered in Polaroids documenting experiments conducted on animals. By then we were shuddering, shielding our eyes.

The worst was yet to come.

In the next room was an actual, ongoing experiment. We surprised two nurses and a doctor as they were performing some ghastly procedure on a child. They had a young boy stretched between two tables, newspapers spread below him to catch drips. A nurse held his feet while a doctor gripped his head and peered coldly into his eyes.

They turned and saw us with our dust masks and flaming hands and shouted for help, but no one was there to hear them. The doctor dashed for a table full of cutting tools but Emma beat him to it, and after a brief scramble he gave up and raised his hands. We pinned the adults in the corner and demanded they tell us where the prisoners were kept. They refused to say a word, so I blew dust in their faces until they slumped into a pile on the floor.

The child was dazed but unhurt. He couldn't seem to generate more than a whimper in response to our hurried questions—*Are you okay? Are there more like you? Where?*—so we thought it best to hide him for now. Wrapping him in a sheet for warmth, we stowed him in a small closet, with promises to return that I hoped we could keep.

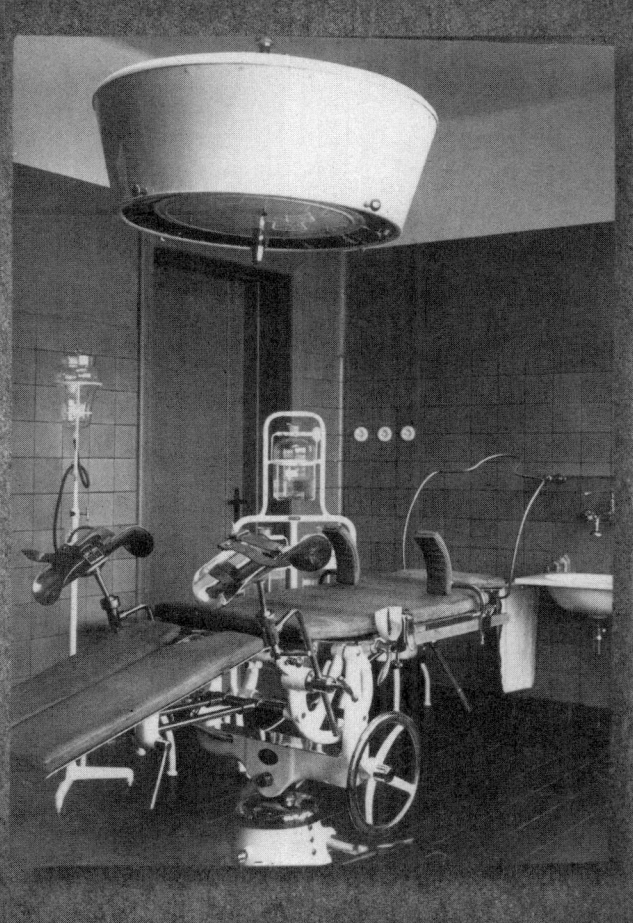

The next room was wide and open like a hospital ward. Twenty or more beds were chained to the walls, and peculiars, adults and children alike, were strapped into the beds. None appeared conscious. Needles and tubes snaked from the soles of their feet to bags that were filling slowly with black liquid.

"They're being drained," Emma said, her voice shaking. "Their souls drawn out."

I didn't want to look at their faces, but we had to. "Who's here, who's here, who are you," I muttered as we raced from bed to bed.

I hoped, shamefully, that none of these poor wretches were our friends. There were several we recognized: the telekinetic girl, Melina. The pale brothers, Joel-and-Peter, separated so there was no chance of another destructive blast. Their faces were twisted, their muscles tense and fists clenched even in sleep, as if both were in the grip of terrible dreams.

"My God," Emma said. "They're trying to fight it."

"Then let's help them," I said, and stepping to the end of Melina's bed I drew the needle carefully from her foot. A tiny drop of black liquid leaked from the wound. After a moment her face relaxed.

"Hello," said a voice from elsewhere in the room.

We spun around. In the corner sat a man in leg shackles. He was curled in a ball and rocking, and he laughed without smiling, his eyes like shards of black ice.

It was his cold laugh we'd heard echoing through the rooms.

"Where are the others being held?" Emma said, dropping to her knees in front of him.

"Why, they're all right here!" the man said.

"No, the others," I said. "There have to be more."

He laughed again, his breath coming out in a little puff of frost—which was strange, because it wasn't cold in the room. "You're standing on top of them," the man said.

"Make sense!" I shouted, losing my temper. "We don't have time for this!"

"Please," Emma begged. "We're peculiars. We're here to help you, but first we have to find our ymbrynes. Which building are they in?"

He repeated himself very slowly. "You're. Standing. On top of them." His words blew a steady stream of icy air in our faces.

Just as I was about to grab him and shake him, the man raised an arm and pointed to something behind us. I turned around and noticed, camouflaged in the tile floor, a handle—and the square outline of a hatch door.

On top of them. Literally.

We ran to the handle, turned it, and pulled up a door in the floor. A set of metal stairs spiraled into darkness.

"How do we know you're telling the truth?" Emma asked.

"You don't," the man said, which was true enough.

"Let's give it a try," I said. There was, after all, nowhere else to go but back the way we'd come.

Emma looked torn, her gaze traveling from the stairs below to the beds around us. I knew what she was thinking, but she didn't even ask—there was no time to go bed to bed, unhooking everyone. We'd have to come back for them. I just hoped that when we did, there would be something to come back to.

*   *   *

Emma lowered herself onto the metal stairs and descended into the dark hole in the floor. Before I followed, I locked eyes with the madman and raised a finger to my lips. He grinned and copied my gesture. I hoped he meant it. Guards would be there soon, and if he kept his mouth shut, maybe they wouldn't follow us into the hatch. I started down the stairs and pulled the door shut after me.

Emma and I huddled near the top of a narrow cylinder of spiraling stairs and peered down. It took a moment for our eyes to transition from the bright room above to this mostly lightless dungeon walled in rough rock.

She gripped my arm and whispered in my ear.

"Cells."

She pointed. Dimly it came into view: the bars of a prison cell.

We crept down the stairs. The space began to reveal itself: we were at the end of a long, subterranean hallway lined with cells, and though we couldn't see yet who was in them, I had a soaring moment of hope. This was it. This was the place we'd hoped to find.

Then came a sudden slap of boots in the hall. Adrenaline surged through me. A guard was patrolling, rifle over his shoulder, pistol at his hip. He hadn't seen us yet, but he would, any moment now. We were too far from the hatch to escape the way we'd come, and too far from the ground to easily leap down and fight him, so we hunkered and shrank back, hoping the stairs' spindly railing would be enough to hide us.

But it couldn't be. We were nearly at his eye level. He was twenty steps away, then fifteen. We had to do something.

So I did.

I stood up and walked down the stairs. He noticed me right away, of course, but before he could get a good look I started talking. Loud and bossy, I said: "Didn't you hear the alarm? Why aren't you outside defending the walls?"

By the time he realized that I was not someone he took orders from I had reached the floor, and by the time he'd started to grab for his gun I had already closed half the distance between us, barreling toward him like a quarterback. I hit him with my shoulder just as he pulled the trigger. The gun roared, the shot ricocheting behind me. We sprawled to the ground. I made the mistake of trying to stop him from squeezing off another shot while trying to give him the finger—I had it now—which was stuffed deep in my right pocket. I didn't have enough limbs to do both, and he threw me off him and stood up. I'm sure that would've been the end of me if he hadn't seen Emma running toward him, hands aflame, and turned to shoot her instead.

He squeezed off a round but it was wild, too high, and that gave me just the opportunity I needed to scramble to my feet and charge him again. I tackled him and we fell across the hallway, his back slamming into the bars of one of the cells. He hit me—hard, in the face, with his elbow—and I spun and fell. And then he was raising the gun to shoot me, and neither Emma nor I were close enough to stop him.

Suddenly, a pair of meaty hands reached out of the darkness, through the bars, and grabbed the guard by his hair. His head snapped back hard and rung the bars like a bell.

The guard went limp and slid to the ground. And then Bronwyn came forward inside the cell, pressed her face to the bars, and smiled.

"Mr. Jacob! Miss Emma!"

I had never been so glad to see anyone. Her large, kind eyes, her strong chin, her lank brown hair—it was Bronwyn! We stuck our arms through the bars and hugged her as best we could, so excited and relieved that we started babbling—"Bronwyn, Bronwyn," Emma gasped, "is it really you?"

"Is that *you*, miss?" said Bronwyn. "We've been praying and hoping and, oh, I was so worried the wights had got you—"

Bronwyn was squeezing us against the bars so hard I thought I might pop. The bars were thick as bricks and made of something stronger than iron, which I realized was the only reason Bronwyn hadn't broken out of her cell.

"Can't . . . breathe," Emma groaned, and Bronwyn apologized and let us go.

Now that I could get a proper look at her, I noticed a bruise on Bronwyn's cheek and a dark stain that might've been blood spotting one side of her blouse. "What did they do to you?" I said.

"Nothing serious," she replied, "though there's been threats."

"And the others?" Emma said, panicked again. "Where are the others?"

"Here!" came a voice from down the hallway. "Over here!" came another.

And then we turned and saw, pressed against the bars of the cells lining the hall, the faces of our friends. There they were: Horace and Enoch, Hugh and Claire, Olive, gasping through the bars at us from the top of her cell, her back against the ceiling—all there, all of them breathing and alive, except poor Fiona—lost when she fell from the cliff at Miss Wren's menagerie. But mourning her was a luxury we didn't have right then.

"Oh, thank the birds, the miraculous bloody birds!" Emma cried, running to take Olive's hand. "You can't imagine how worried we've been!"

"Not half as worried as we've been!" Hugh said from down the hall.

"I told them you'd come for us!" Olive said, near tears. "I told them and told them, but Enoch kept saying I was a loony for thinking so . . ."

"Never mind, they're here now!" said Enoch. "What took you so bloody long?"

"How in Perplexus's name did you find us?" said Millard. He was the only one the wights had bothered to dress in prisoners' garb—a striped jumpsuit that made him easy to see.

"We'll tell you the whole story," said Emma, "but first we need to find the ymbrynes and get you all out of here!"

"They're down the hall!" said Hugh. "Through the big door!"

At the end of the hall was a huge metal door. It looked heavy enough to secure a bank vault—or hold back a hollowgast.

"You'll need the key," said Bronwyn, and she pointed out a ring on the unconscious guard's belt. "It's the big gold one. I've been watching him!"

I scrambled to the guard and tore the keys from his belt. Then I stood frozen with them in my hand, my eyes darting between the cell doors and Emma.

"Hurry up and let us out!" Enoch said.

"With which key?" I said. The ring held dozens, all identical save the big gold one.

Emma's face fell. "Oh, no."

More guards would be coming soon, and unlocking every cell would cost precious minutes. So we ran to the end of the hall, unlocked the door, and gave the keys to Hugh, whose cell was closest. "Free yourself and then the others!" I said.

"Then stay here until we come back to get you," Emma added.

"No chance!" Hugh said. "We're coming after you!"

There was no time to argue—and I was secretly relieved to hear it. After all this time struggling on our own, I was looking forward to having some backup.

Emma and I heaved open the big bunker-like door, took a last look at our friends, and slipped away.

*   *   *

On the other side of the door was a long rectangular room cluttered with utilitarian furniture and lit from above by greenish fluorescent bulbs. It was doing its best impression of an office, but I wasn't fooled. The wall was spongy with foam soundproofing. The door was thick enough to withstand a nuclear blast. This was no office.

We could hear someone moving around at the far end of the room, but our view was blocked by a bulky filing cabinet. I touched Emma's arm and nodded my head—*let's go*—and we began to advance quietly, hoping to sneak up on whoever was in here with us.

I caught a glimpse of a white coat and a man's balding head. Definitely not an ymbryne. Had they not heard the door opening? No, they hadn't, and then I realized why: they were listening to music. A woman's voice sang a soft, slinky rock song—an old one I'd heard before but couldn't name. So strange, so dislocating, to hear it here, now.

We slid forward, the song just loud enough to mask our footsteps, passing desks crowded with papers and maps. A rack mounted to a wall held hundreds of glass beakers, silver-flecked black liquid spinning inside. Lingering, I saw that each was labeled, the names of the victims whose souls they contained printed in small type.

Peeking around the filing cabinet, we saw a lab-coated man seated at a desk shuffling papers, his back to us. All around him was a horror-show of random anatomy. A skinned arm with musculature exposed. A spine hung like a trophy on the wall. A few bloodless organs scattered like lost puzzle pieces on the desk. The man was writing something, nodding his head, humming along with the song—something about love, something about miracles.

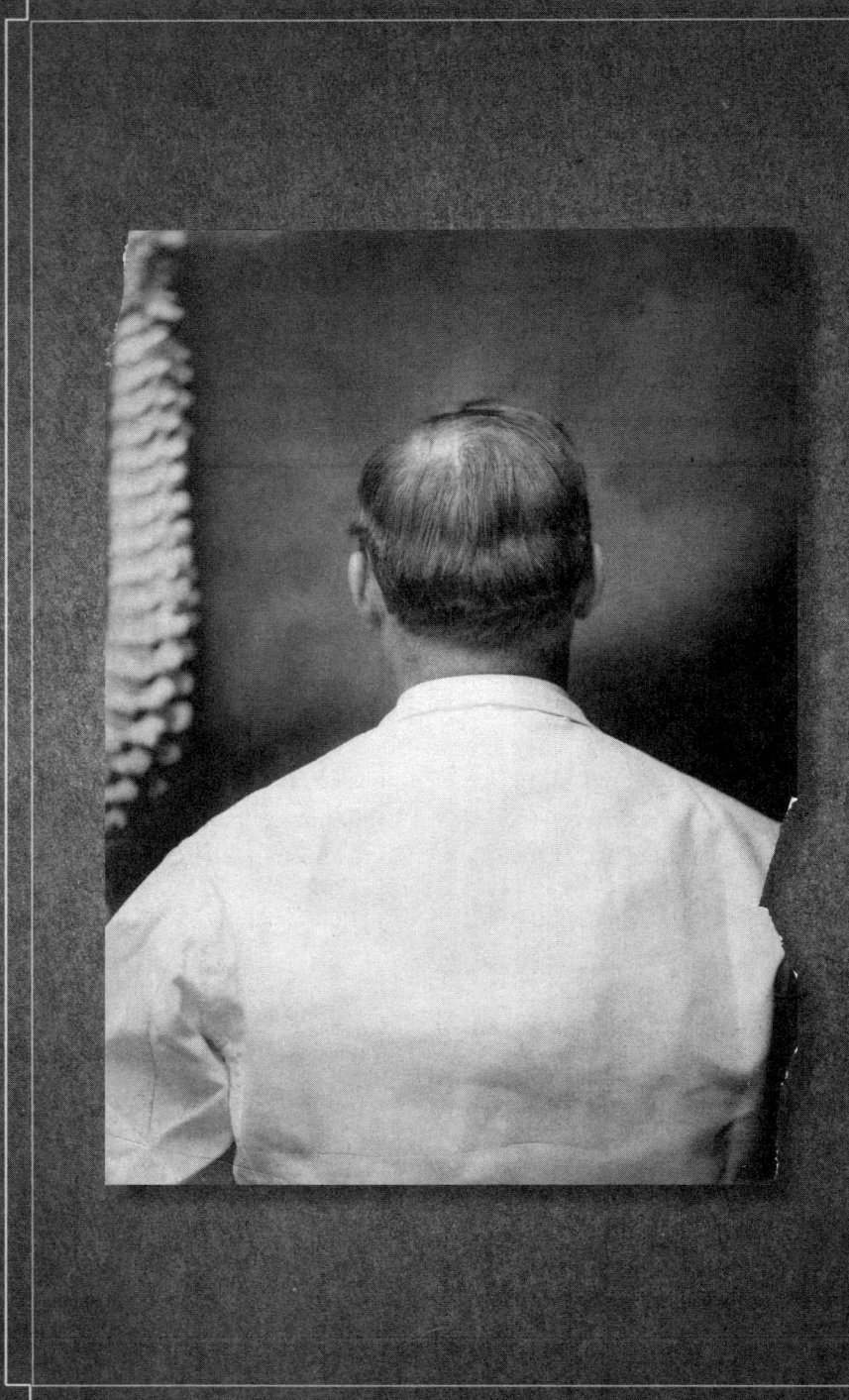

We stepped into the open and moved toward him across the floor. I remembered where I'd last heard the song: at the dentist, while a metal pick stabbed at the soft, pink flesh of my gums.

"You Make Loving Fun."

Now we were only a few yards away. Emma held out a hand, ready to light it. But just before we got within reach of the man, he spoke to us.

"Hello, there. I've been expecting you."

It was a slimy-smooth voice I would never forget. Caul.

Emma summoned flames that shot from her palms with the sound of a whip-crack. "Tell us where the ymbrynes are, and I might spare your life!"

Startled, the man spun around in his chair. What we saw startled us, too: below his wide eyes, his face was a ruin of melted flesh. This man was not Caul—he wasn't even a wight—and it couldn't have been him who'd spoken. The man's lips were fused together. In his two hands he held a mechanical pencil and a small remote control. Pinned to his coat was a name tag.

Warren.

"Gee, you wouldn't hurt old Warren, would you?" Caul's voice again, coming from the same place as the music: a speaker in the wall. "Though it wouldn't matter much if you did. He's only my intern."

Warren sank low into his swivel chair, looking fearfully at the flame in Emma's hand.

"Where are you?" Emma shouted, looking around.

"Never mind that!" Caul said through the speaker. "What matters is that you've come to see me. I'm delighted! It's so much easier than hunting you down."

"We've got a whole army of peculiars on their way!" Emma bluffed. "The crowd at your gates is just the tip of the spear. Tell us where the ymbrynes are and maybe we can settle this peacefully!"

"Army!" Caul said, laughing. "There aren't enough fight-ready peculiars left in London to form a fire brigade, much less an army. As for your pathetic ymbrynes, save your empty threats—I'll gladly show you where they are. Warren, would you do the honors?"

Warren pushed a button on the remote in his hand, and with a loud *whoosh* a panel slid aside in the wall to one side of us. Behind it was a second wall made of thick glass, which looked into an expansive room engulfed in shadow.

We pressed against the glass, cupping our hands around our faces to see. Gradually, there came into view a space like a neglected basement, jumbled with furnishings and heavy drapes and human forms frozen in strange postures, many of which appeared, like the spare parts on Warren's desk, to have been stripped of their skin.

Oh God what's he done to them—

My eyes darted around the dark, my heart racing.

"That's Miss Glassbill!" Emma cried, and then I saw her, too. She sat in a chair off to one side, mannish and flat-faced, perfectly symmetrical braids falling down either side of her head. We pounded on the glass and called to her, but she merely stared, in a daze, unresponsive to our shouts.

"What have you done to her?" I shouted. "Why won't she answer?"

"She's had bit of her soul removed," Caul said. "Tends to numb the brain."

"You bastard!" Emma shouted, and punched the glass. Warren backed his rolling chair into the corner. "You black-hearted, despicable, cowardly . . . "

"Oh, calm down," Caul said. "I only took a *little* of her soul, and the rest of your nursemaids are in top health, if not spirits."

A harsh overhead light flicked on in the jumbled room, and it became suddenly clear that most of the figures were just dummies—no, obviously not real—mannequins or anatomical models of some kind, posed like statues with their tendons and muscles all flexed and popping. But in among them, gagged, bound to chairs and wooden posts, flinching and squeezing their eyes shut against the sudden light, were real, living people. Women. Eight, ten—I hadn't time to count them all—most of them older, disheveled but distinguished-looking.

Our ymbrynes.

"Jacob, it's them!" Emma cried. "Can you see Miss—"

The light flicked off before we could find Miss Peregrine, and now my eyes, ruined for the dark, could see nothing through the glass.

"She's there, too," Caul said with a bored sigh. "Your pious bird, your wet-nurse . . . "

"Your *sister*," I said, hoping that might inject some humanity into him.

"I would hate to kill her," he said, "and I suppose I won't—provided you give me what I want."

"And what's that?" I said, pulling away from the glass.

"Nothing much," he said casually. "Just a little bit of your soul."

"What!" Emma barked.

I laughed out loud.

"Now, now, hear me out!" Caul said. "I don't even want the entire thing. Merely an eyedropper's worth. Less even than I took from Miss Glassbill. Yes, it'll make you a bit dopey for a while, but in a few days you will have fully recovered your faculties."

"You want my soul because you think it'll help you use the library," I said. "And take all that power."

"I see you've been talking to my brother," Caul replied. "You might as well know: I've nearly accomplished it now. After a life-time of searching, I've finally found Abaton, and the ymbrynes—this perfect combination of ymbrynes—have unlocked the door for me. Alas, it was only then that I learned I needed still another component. A peculiar with a very specific talent, not often seen in the world these days. I had nearly despaired of ever finding such a person when I realized that a certain peculiar's grandson might fit the bill, and that these ymbrynes, otherwise useless to me now, could act as a lure. And so they have! I do believe it's fate, my boy. You and I, we'll go down in peculiar history together."

"We're not going anywhere together," I said. "If you get that kind of power, you'll make the world a living hell."

"You misunderstand me," he continued. "That's not surpris-ing; most people do. Yes, I've had to make the world a hell for those who've stood in my way, but now that I've nearly achieved my goal, I am prepared to be generous. Magnanimous. Forgiving."

The music, still warbling below Caul's voice, had faded into a calm instrumental number, so at odds with the panic and terror I was feeling that it gave me a chill.

"We'll finally live in peace and harmony," he said, his voice smooth and reassuring, "with me as your king, your god. This is peculiardom's natural hierarchy. We were never meant to live like this, decentralized and powerless. Ruled by women. There will be no more hiding when I'm in charge. No more pathetic cowering be-neath the skirts of ymbrynes. Our rightful place as peculiars is at the head of the human table. We'll rule the earth and all its people. We'll finally inherit what's ours!"

"If you think we're going to play any role in that," said Emma, "you're out of your gourd."

"I expected as much from you, girl," said Caul. "You're so typical of ymbryne-raised peculiars: no ambition, and no sense at all but one of entitlement. Quiet yourself, I am speaking to the male."

Emma's face went as red as the flame in her hand.

"Get on with it," I said tersely, thinking of the guards that were probably on their way, and our friends, still fumbling with keys in the hallway.

"Here's my offer," said Caul. "Allow my specialists to perform their procedure on you, and when I've got what I want, I'll let you and your friends go free—and your ymbrynes, too. They'll pose me no threat then, anyhow."

"And if I refuse?"

"If you won't let me remove your soul the easy and painless way, then my hollows would be more than happy to do it. They aren't known for their bedside manner, though, and once they're through with you, I'm afraid I'll be powerless to stop them from moving on to your ymbrynes. So you see, I'll get what I want either way."

"That won't work," Emma said.

"Are you referring to the boy's little trick? I've heard he's been able to control one hollow, but how about two at once? Or three, or five?"

"As many as I want," I said, trying to sound confident, unflappable.

"That I would very much like to see," said Caul. "Shall I take that as your answer, then?"

"Take it however you like," I said. "I'm not helping you."

"Oh, goody," Caul said. "This will be loads more fun!"

We could hear Caul laughing over the PA, and then I startled at the sound of a loud buzzer.

"What've you done now?" Emma said.

I felt a sharp pulse in my gut, and without Caul having to explain anything, I could picture exactly what was happening: in a tunnel below the ymbrynes' room, a hollow had been released from deep within the bowels of the complex. It was coming closer, climbing toward a grate in the floor that was scraping open. It would be among the ymbrynes soon.

"He's sending up a hollow!" I said. "It's coming into that room!"

"We'll start with just one hollowgast," said Caul. "If you can manage him, I'll introduce you to his friends."

I banged on the glass. "Let us in!"

"With pleasure," said Caul. "Warren?"

Warren pushed another button on the remote. A door-sized section of the glass wall slid open.

"I'm going!" I said to Emma. "You stay here and guard him!"

"If Miss Peregrine's in there, I'm coming, too."

It was clear there was no talking her out of it.

"Then we're bringing him with us," I said.

Warren tried to dart away, but Emma caught him by the back of his coat.

I ran through the door, into the dark and jumbled room, and Emma was behind me with the squirming, mouthless intern collared in one hand.

I heard the glass door bang shut behind us.

Emma swore.

I turned to look.

On the other side of the door, on the floor, lay the remote. We were locked in.

* * *

We'd only been inside the room a few seconds when the intern managed to wriggle from Emma's grasp and tumble off into the darkness. Emma started to chase him, but I held her back—he didn't matter. What mattered was the hollow, which was nearly out of its hole now and into the room.

It was starving. I could feel its gnawing hunger as if it were my own. In moments it would start feasting on ymbrynes, unless we could stop it. Unless *I* could stop it. First, though, I would have to find it, and the room was so crowded with junk and shadows that my ability to see hollows wasn't of great advantage.

I asked Emma for more light. She strengthened the flames in her hands as much as she could, but it seemed to only lengthen the shadows.

To keep her safe, I asked her to stay by the door. She refused. "We stick together," she said.

"Stick together behind me, then. Way behind me."

That, at least, she granted me. As I moved past catatonic Miss Glassbill and deeper into the room, Emma hung back several paces, holding one hand high above her head to light our way. What we could see of the room looked like a bloodless battlefield hospital, deconstructed human forms scattered everywhere.

My foot kicked an arm. It rung dully and spun away—plaster. Here was a torso on a table. There a head in a liquid-filled jar, its eyes and mouth agape, almost certainly real but not of recent vintage. This seemed to be Caul's lab, torture chamber, and storage closet all in one. He was a hoarder, like his brother, of strange and ghastly things—only where Bentham was organized to a tee, Caul badly needed a maid.

"Welcome to the hollows' play space," Caul said, his amplified voice echoing through the room. "We conduct experiments on them here, feed them, watch them disassemble their food. I wonder what part of you they'll eat first? Some hollows start with the eyes . . . a little amuse-bouche . . . "

I tripped over a body, which yelped as my foot dug into it. Looking down, I saw the scared-to-death face of a middle-aged woman peeping back at me, wild-eyed—an ymbryne I didn't know. Without stopping I bent down and whispered, "Don't worry, we'll get you out of here," but no, I thought, we would not; this chaos of forms and mad shadows would be the scene of our death—Old Jacob ascending, doom-saying, un-shut-uppable.

I heard something shift deeper in the room, followed by the wet draw of a hollowgast's mouth opening. It was here among us. I aimed myself toward it and ran—tripping, catching myself, Emma running too, saying, "Jacob, hurry!"

Caul, over the PA, mocking us: "Jacob, hurry!"

He had turned up the music: driving, upbeat, deranged.

We passed three, four more ymbrynes, all tied and struggling, before I finally saw it.

I stopped, breathless, my mind reeling at its sheer size. The hollow was a giant—several heads taller than the one I'd tamed, its skull nearly scraping the ceiling despite its hunched frame. It was twenty feet away, its jaws wide and tongues raking the air. Emma stumbled a few feet ahead of me and stuck out her hand, pointing at something and lighting it at the same time.

"There! Look!"

It wasn't the hollow she'd seen, of course, but what it was moving toward: a woman, upside down and twisting, hung up like a side of beef, her black skirts blooming about her head. Even like that, even in the dark, I knew her—it was Miss Wren.

Addison was hanging right next to her. They were struggling, gagged, and mere feet from a hollowgast whose tongues were now stretching toward them, slipping around Miss Wren's shoulders, drawing her into its jaws.

"STOP!" I screamed, first in English, then in the rasping language the hollow could understand. I shouted again, then again, until it did stop—though not because it was under my control, but because I had suddenly become more interesting prey.

It released the ymbryne and she swung away like a pendulum. The hollow turned its tongues toward me.

"Cut down Miss Wren while I draw the hollow away," I said.

I moved away from Miss Wren while talking to the hollow in a constant stream, hoping to draw it away from her and keep its attention on me.

Close your mouth. Sit down. Lie down.

It turned away from Miss Wren as I moved—*good, good*—and then as I backed away, it came forward.

Yes. Okay. Now what?

My hands went to my pockets. In one I had what remained of Mother Dust's finger. In the other, a secret—a vial of ambro I'd swiped from the previous room while Emma wasn't looking. I'd taken it during a momentary lapse of confidence. What if I couldn't do this on my own? What if I needed a boost?

Sit down, I said. *Stop.*

The hollow whipped one of its tongues at me. I ducked behind a mannequin and the tongue lassoed that instead, lifted it up and flung it against a wall, where it shattered.

I dove away from a second tongue. Banged my shins on a tipped-over chair. The tongue slapped the empty floor where I'd just been. The hollow was toying with me now, but soon it would go in for the kill. I had to do something, and there were two somethings I could do.

The vial or the finger.

There was no way I'd be able to control this hollow without the boost in my abilities a vial of ambro could give. Mother Dust's crushed finger, on the other hand, wasn't something I could launch away from me, and I'd lost my mask. If I tried to use it, I'd only put myself to sleep; it was worse than useless.

As another tongue smashed into the ground beside me, I slid beneath a table and pulled the vial from my pocket. I fumbled to uncork it, my hands shaking. Would it make a hero of me, or a slave? Could one vial really addict me for life? And what would be the worse outcome, being an addict and a slave, or being dead in this hollow's stomach?

The table was ripped away, leaving me exposed. I leapt to my feet. *Stop, stop*, I shouted, taking small hops backward as the hollow's tongues lashed at me, missing by mere inches.

My back hit the wall. There was nowhere left to go.

I took a blow to the stomach, and then the tongue that had hit me uncurled and moved to wrap around my neck. I needed to run but I was stunned, doubled over, breath knocked out of me. Then I heard an angry snarl—one that hadn't come from the hollow—and a stout, echoing bark.

Addison.

Suddenly the tongue that was reaching for my neck stiffened, as if in pain, and retracted across the room. The dog, that brave little boxer, had bitten it. I heard him growling and yelping as he began to do battle with an invisible creature twenty times his size.

I slid to the floor, back against the wall, breath filling my lungs again. I held up the vial, determined now. Convinced I had no chance without it. I pulled the cork, raised the bottle above my eyes, and tilted back my head.

And then I heard my name. "Jacob," softly spoken in the dark, a few feet away.

I turned to look, and there on the floor, lying amidst a pile of parts, was Miss Peregrine. Bruised, tied, struggling to speak through a haze of pain or drugs, but there nonetheless and gazing at me with those piercing green eyes.

"Don't," she said softly. "Don't do that." Her voice barely audible, barely there.

"Miss Peregrine!"

I lowered the vial, corked it, scrambled on my hands to where she lay. This second mother of mine, this peculiar saint. Fallen, hurt.

Dying, perhaps.

"Tell me you're okay," I said.

"Put that down," she said. "You don't need it."

"Yes, I do. I'm not like he was."

We both knew who I meant: my grandfather.

"Yes, you are," she said. "Everything you need is inside you already. Put it down and take that instead." She nodded at something lying between us: a jagged stake of wood from a broken chair.

"I can't. It's not enough."

"It is," she assured me. "Just aim for the eyes."

"I can't," I said, but I did. I put down the vial and took the stake.

"Good lad," she whispered. "Now, go and do something gruesome with it."

"I will," I said, and she smiled, her head sinking back to the floor.

I stood up, determined now, the wooden stake gripped in my hand. Across the room, Addison had his teeth clamped deep into one of the hollow's tongues and was riding it like a rodeo cowboy, clinging valiantly and snarling as the hollow whipped him back and forth. Emma had cut down Miss Wren from the rope where she'd been hanging and was standing guard over her, swinging her flaming hands blindly.

The hollow smacked Addison into a pole, and the dog was flung loose.

I started toward the hollow, running as fast as I could through an obstacle course of scattered limbs. But like a moth to flame, the creature seemed more interested in Emma. It was starting to close in on her, and so I shouted at it, first in English—"Hey! Over here!"— and then in Hollow: *Come and get me, you bastard!*

I picked up the closest thing at hand—which happened to be a hand—and threw it. It bounced off the hollow's back, and the thing turned around to face me.

Come and get me come and get me

For a moment the hollow was confused, which was just enough time for me to get close to it without getting caught up in its tongues. I stabbed it with the stake, once, twice in the chest. It reacted as if it'd been stung by a bee—no worse than that—and then knocked me to the ground with a tongue.

Stop, stop, stop, I shouted in Hollow, desperate for something to get through, but the beast seemed bulletproof, totally inoculated against my suggestions. And then I remembered the finger, the little chalk-stub of dust in my pocket. As I reached for it, a tongue wrapped around me and hoisted me into the air. I could hear Emma shouting at it to put me down—and Caul, too. "Don't you eat him!" he screeched over the PA. "He's mine!"

As I drew Mother Dust's finger from my pocket, the hollow dropped me into its open jaws.

I was trapped in its mouth from knees to chest, its teeth pinning me in place, starting to cut into my flesh, its jaws quickly expanding to swallow me.

This would be my last act. My last moment. I crushed the finger in my hand and shoved it down what I hoped was the hollow's throat. Emma was beating it, burning it—and then, just before it could close its jaws and saw me in half with its teeth, the creature began to choke. It stumbled away from Emma, burned and gagging, retreating toward the grate in the floor from which it had crawled. Bounding back to its nest, where it would have all the time it wanted to devour me.

I tried to stop it, to shout (*Let me go!*) but it was biting down and the pain was so blacking that I couldn't think—and then we were there, at the grate, slipping down into it. Its mouth so full of me that it couldn't catch hold of the rungs on the wall and it was falling, falling and choking, and I was still, somehow, alive.

When we hit bottom, it was with a great, bone-breaking crack that flattened our lungs and sent all the sedative dust I'd shoved down the hollow's gullet blowing into the air around us. As it snowed down I could feel it working, numbing my pain and dulling my brain, and it must've been doing the same to the hollow because it was hardly biting me at all now, its jaws slackening.

As we lay in a stunned and tranquilized pile, racing toward sleep, I could see forming before me, through all those billowing white particles, a dank and lightless tunnel heaped with bones. The last thing I saw before the dust took me was a throng of hollows, hunched and curious, shuffling forward.

CHAPTER EIGHT

woke up. That in itself is worthy of note, I think, given the circumstances.

I was in the hollows' burrow, and piled around me were the bodies of many hollowgast. They might've been dead, but it was likelier they'd breathed what remained of Mother Dust's pinky finger, and the result was tangled in a spaghetti of stinking, snoring, mostly unconscious hollowflesh.

I gave a silent prayer of thanks for Mother Dust and then wondered, with rising alarm, how long I'd been down here. An hour? A day? What had happened to everyone above?

I had to go. A few of the hollows were beginning to stir from sleep, like me, but they were still woozy. With great effort, I stood. Apparently my wounds were not so grave, my bones not so broken. I swayed, dizzy, then caught my balance and began to move through the enmeshed hollows.

I kicked one in the head by accident. With a grunt it came awake and opened its eyes. I froze, thinking that if I ran it would only chase me down. It seemed to register me—but as neither a threat nor a potential meal—then closed its eyes again.

I continued on, placing each foot with care until I had passed the carpet of hollows and reached a wall. Here the tunnel ended. The way out was above me: a chute leading upward a hundred feet or so to an open grate and that cluttered room. There were holds along the chute, but they were spaced too far apart, built for hollows' acrobatic tongues, not human hands and feet. I stood peering up at a ring of dim light far overhead, hoping a friendly face might appear there, but I dared not shout for help.

In desperation I jumped, scrabbling at the hard wall and grasping for the first hold. Somehow I reached it. Pulled myself up. Suddenly I was more than ten feet off the ground. (*How had I done that?*) I jumped again and reached the next hold—and the next one. I was climbing the chute, my legs launching me higher and my arms reaching farther than I knew was possible—*this is insane*—and then I was at the top, poking my head out, pushing myself up into the room.

I wasn't even breathing hard.

I looked around, saw Emma's firelight, and ran toward it across the cluttered floor. I tried calling out but couldn't seem to make the words. No matter—there she was, on the other side of the open glass door, in the office. Warren was on this side, tied to the chair Miss Glassbill had sat in, and when I came close he groaned fearfully and knocked himself over. Then their faces were at the door, suspicious and peering—Emma and Miss Peregrine and Horace, and behind them other ymbrynes and friends, too. All there, alive, beautiful. They had been freed from their cells only to be imprisoned once more in here, locked behind Caul's bomb-proof bunker door, safe from wights (for now) but trapped.

Their expressions were fearful, and the closer I got to the glass door, the more terrified they became. *It's me,* I tried to say, but the words didn't come out right, and my friends jumped back.

It's me, it's Jacob!

What came out instead of English was a husky snarl and three long, fat tongues, waving in the air before me, spat from my own mouth in my attempt to speak. And then I heard one of my friends—Enoch, it was Enoch—say aloud the terrible thing that had just occurred to me:

"It's a hollow!"

I'm not, I tried to say, *I'm not*—but all evidence was to the contrary. I had somehow *become one of them*, been bitten and turned, like a vampire, or been killed, eaten, recycled, reincarnated—*oh god oh god oh god it can't be . . .*

I tried to reach out with my hands, to make some sign that might be recognized as human now that my mouth had failed me, but it was my tongues that reached out.

I'm sorry, I'm sorry, I don't know how to drive this thing

Emma swiped blindly at me with her hand—and connected. Sudden, searing pain flashed through me.

And then I woke up.

Again.

Or rather, jolted by sudden pain, I woke back into my body— my hurt, human body, still lying in the dark in the slack jaws of a sleeping hollow. And yet I was still the hollow above, too, snatching my hurt tongue back into my mouth and stumbling away from the door. I was somehow dually present in both my mind and the hollow's, and I found now that I could control both—could lift my own arm and the hollow's, turn my own head and the hollow's, and do it all without saying a word aloud, but merely by thinking.

Without realizing it—without consciously trying—I had mastered the hollow to such a degree (seeing through its eyes, feeling through its skin) that it had felt, for a time, like I *was* the hollow. But now a distinction was becoming clear. I was this fallible and broken-bodied boy, deep in a hole surrounded by groggy monsters. They were waking, all but the one who had brought me down here in its jaws (it had so much dust in its system that it might sleep for years), and they were sitting up now, shaking the numbness from their limbs.

But they didn't seem interested in killing me. They were watching me, quiet and attentive. Semicircled around like well-behaved children at storytime. Waiting for input.

I rolled myself out of the hollow's jaws and onto the floor. I could sit up but was too hurt to stand. But *they* could stand.

Stand.

I didn't say it, didn't even think it, really. It felt like *doing*, only it wasn't me who did it. They did it, eleven hollowgast all rising to their feet before me in perfect synchrony. This was astounding, of course, and yet I felt a profound sense of calm spreading through me. I was relaxing into the purest depths of my ability. Something about shutting down all our minds at once, then bringing them back online together—a collective reboot—had brought us into a kind of harmony, allowing me to tap into the unconscious heart of my power, as well as into the hollows' minds at just the moment their defenses were down.

And now they were mine. Marionettes I could control with invisible strings. But how much could I do? What were the limits? How many could I control at once, discretely?

To find out, I began to play.

In the room above, I lay the hollow down.

He lay down.

(They were all *he*s, I had decided.)

I made the ones in front of me jump.

They jumped.

They were two distinct groups now, the loner above and the ones before me. I tried controlling each individually, making one raise a hand without the rest doing it. It was a bit like asking just one toe on your foot to wiggle—difficult, not impossible—but before long I'd gotten the hang of it. The less conscious I was of trying, the easier it became. The control came most naturally when I simply imagined an action being performed.

I sent them away into the bone-piles farther down the tunnel, then had them pick up bones with their tongues and toss them to one another: first one at a time, then two, then three and four, piling action upon action until I'd gotten up to six. It was only when I made the hollow upstairs stand and do jumping jacks that the bone-tossers began to miss catches.

I don't think it would be bragging to say I was very good at this.

A natural, even. I could tell that with more time to practice, I had the capacity to become masterful. I could've played both sides of an all-hollow basketball game. I could've made them dance every role in *Swan Lake*. But there was no more time to practice; this would have to do. And so I gathered them around me, had the strongest one pick me up and saddle me to its back with a wrapped-around tongue, and one by one my monstrous little army bounded up the chute and into the room above.

* * *

The overhead lights had been turned on in the cluttered room, and in their harsh glow I could see that the only bodies remaining were mannequins and models—the ymbrynes had all been taken out. The glass door to Caul's observation room was closed. I made the hollows hang back while I approached it alone, save the hollow I was riding, then called out to my friends—this time with my own voice, in English.

"It's me! It's Jacob!"

They rushed to the door, Emma's face circled by the others'.

"Jacob!" Her voice was muffled behind the glass. "You're alive!" But as she studied me her face turned strange, as if she couldn't understand what she was seeing. Because I was on the hollow's back, I realized, it looked to Emma like I was floating above the ground.

"It's all right," I said, "I'm riding a hollowgast!" I slapped its shoulder to prove there was something solid and fleshy beneath me. "He's completely under my control—and so are these."

I brought the eleven hollows forward, stamping their feet to announce themselves. My friends' mouths went oval-shaped with wonder.

"Is that really you, Jacob?" Olive asked.

"What do you mean you're controlling them?" Enoch said.

"You've got blood on your shirt!" said Bronwyn.

They opened the glass door just wide enough to talk through. I explained how I fell into the hollows' pit, was nearly bitten in half, was numbed and put to sleep, and woke up with a dozen of them under my control. As further demonstration I had the hollows pick up Warren, the chair he was tied to and all, and toss him back and forth a few times, the chair flipping end over end until the kids were cheering and Warren was groaning as if he was going to be sick. Finally I had them set him down.

"If I hadn't seen it with my own eyes, I'd never have believed it," Enoch said. "Not in a million years!"

"You're fantastic!" I heard a little voice say, and there was Claire.

"Let me get a look at you!" I said, but when I approached the open door she shrank away. Impressed with my skills though they were, overcoming a peculiar's natural fear of hollowgast is no easy thing—and the smell probably didn't help, either.

"It's safe," I said, "I promise."

Olive came right to the door. "*I'm* not scared."

"Me, neither," said Emma, "and me first."

She stepped through the door and came to meet me. I made the hollow kneel, leaned away from it, and managed somewhat awkwardly to put my arms around Emma. "Sorry, I can't quite stand up on my own," I said, my face against her cheek, my closed eyes brushing her soft hair. It wasn't enough, but for now it would have to be.

"You're hurt." She pulled away to look me over. "You've got cuts everywhere—and they're deep."

"I can't feel them. I got dust all over me . . . "

"That could mean you're only numb, not healed."

"I'll worry about it later. How long was I down there?"

"Hours," she whispered. "We thought you were dead."

I nudged her forehead with mine. "I made you a promise, remember?"

"I need you to make me a new promise. Quit scaring the hell out of me."

"I'll do my best."

"No. *Promise.*"

"Once this is over, I'll make any promise you like."

"I'm going to remember that," she said.

Miss Peregrine appeared at the door. "You two had better come in here. And leave that beast outside, please!"

"Miss P," I said, "you're on your feet!"

"Yes, I'm recovering," she replied. "I was spared by my late arrival here, and by some nepotistic favoritism on my brother's part. Not all my fellow ymbrynes were so lucky."

"I wasn't sparing you, sister," said a booming voice from above—Caul again, through the PA system. "I was merely saving the tastiest dish for last!"

"You shut up!" Emma shouted. "When we find you, Jacob's hollows will eat you for breakfast!"

Caul laughed. "I doubt that," he said. "You're more powerful than I imagined, boy, but don't be fooled. You're surrounded with no way out. You've only delayed the inevitable. But if you give up now, I might consider sparing some of you . . . "

With a quick flick of their tongues, I made the hollows rip the speakers from the ceiling and smash them on the ground. As wires and parts sprang everywhere, Caul's voice went dead.

"When we find him," Enoch said, "I'd like to pull out his fingernails before we kill him. Anyone have a problem with that?"

"As long as I can send a squadron of bees up his nose first," said Hugh.

"That's not our way," Miss Peregrine said. "When this is all over, he'll be sentenced by ymbrynic law to rot in a punishment loop for the rest of his unnatural life."

"Where's the fun in that?" said Enoch.

Miss Peregrine gave him a withering look.

I made the hollow let me go, and with Emma's help I limped through the door and into the observation room. My friends were all there—all but Fiona. Ranged along the walls and resting on office chairs, I could see pale, frightened faces watching me. The ymbrynes.

But before I could go to them, my friends blocked my way. They threw their arms around me, holding up my tottering body with their embraces. I gave in to it. I hadn't felt anything so sweet in a long time. Then Addison came trotting up as nobly as he could with two hurt paws, and I broke away to greet him.

"That's twice now you've saved me," I said, putting a hand on his furry head. "I don't know how I'll ever repay you."

"You can start by getting us out of this bloody loop," he growled. "I'm sorry I ever crossed that bridge!"

Those who heard him laughed. Maybe it was his canine nature, but Addison had no filter; he always said just what he meant.

"That stunt you pulled with the truck was one of the bravest things I ever saw," I said.

"I was captured the minute I got inside the compound. I'm afraid I let you all down."

There was a sudden, loud boom from outside the heavy door. The room shook. Small items tumbled off shelves.

"The wights are trying to blow in the door," Miss Peregrine explained. "They've been at it for some time."

"We'll deal with them," I said. "But first I want to know who's unaccounted for. Things will get out of hand when we open that door, so if there are peculiars elsewhere in this compound who need rescuing, I want to keep them in mind as we go into battle."

It was so dark and crowded that we resorted to a roll call. I called our friends' names twice, just to make doubly sure they were all here. Then I asked after the peculiars who'd been snatched from Miss Wren's ice house alongside us: the clown (thrown into the chasm, Olive told us through hitching sobs, for refusing orders from the wights), the folding man (left on the Underground in grave condition), telekinetic Melina (upstairs and unconscious, having had some of her soul drained), and the pale brothers (same). Then there were the kids Miss Wren had rescued: the plain-looking boy in the floppy hat and the frizzy-haired snake-charmer girl. Bronwyn said she'd seen them being led off to another part of the compound, where other peculiars were being held.

Lastly, we counted the ymbrynes. There was Miss Peregrine, of course, whose side the kids had not left since they were reunited. There was so much I wanted to talk with her about. All that had happened to us since we last saw her. All that had happened to her. Though there was no time to say any of it, something did pass between us, in the brief moments our eyes would meet in passing. She regarded Emma and me with a certain pride and wonder. *I trust you*, her eyes said.

But Miss Peregrine, as deeply glad as we were to see her, wasn't the only ymbryne we had to be concerned about. There were twelve in all. She introduced her friends: Miss Wren, whom Emma had cut down from the ceiling, was wounded but coherent. Miss Glassbill was still staring in her vague and mindless way. The eldest, Miss Avocet, who hadn't been seen since she and Miss Peregrine were kidnapped together on Cairnholm, occupied a chair near the door. Miss Bunting, Miss Treecreeper, and several others fussed over her, adjusting blankets around her shoulders.

Nearly all of them looked frightened, which seemed distinctly unymbrynelike. They were supposed to be our elders and our leaders, but they'd been in captivity here for weeks, and they had seen things and had things done to them that had left them shell-shocked. (They also didn't share my friends' confidence in my ability to control a dozen hollowgast and were keeping as far away from my creatures as the dimensions of the room would allow.)

At the end of it, there was still one person among us who hadn't been named: a bearded, small-statured man who stood silently by the ymbrynes, watching us through dark glasses.

"And who's this?" I said. "A wight?"

The man became incensed. "*No!*" He tore off the glasses to show us his eyes, which were severely crossed. "I am *heem!*" he said, his accent thick and Italian. There was a large, leather-bound book on a table next to him, and he pointed to it, as if this somehow explained his identity.

I felt a hand on my arm. It was Millard, invisible now, his suit of stripes removed. "Allow me to introduce history's foremost temporal cartographer," he said grandly. "Jacob, this is Perplexus Anomalous."

"*Buongiorno*," said Perplexus. "How do you do."

"It's an honor to meet you," I said.

"Yes," he said, nose rising in the air. "It is."

"What's he doing here?" I whispered to Millard. "And how is he still alive?"

"Caul found him living in some fourteenth-century loop in Venice that no one knew existed. He's been here two days, though, which means he could age forward very soon."

As I had come to understand such things, Perplexus was in danger of aging forward because the loop he'd been living in was considerably older than the one we were in now, and the difference between those times would eventually catch up with him.

"I'm your biggest fan!" Millard said to Perplexus. "I have all your maps . . . "

"Yes, you tell me already," Perplexus said. "*Grazie.*"

"None of that explains what he's doing here," said Emma.

"Perplexus wrote about finding the Library of Souls in his journals," said Millard, "so Caul tracked him down, kidnapped him, and made him tell where it was."

"I made oath of blood to never say nothing," Perplexus said miserably. "Now I am cursed forever!"

"I want to get Perplexus back to his loop before he ages," said Millard. "I won't be responsible for the loss of peculiardom's greatest living treasure!"

From outside the door came another boom, this one even bigger and louder than before. The room trembled and pebbly bits of rock rained from the ceiling.

"We'll do our best, dear," Miss Peregrine said. "But we've got other things to see about first."

*   *   *

We quickly hatched a plan of action, such as it was: throw open the big door and use my hollows to clear the way. They were expendable, seemed in good working order, and my connection with them was only growing stronger. As for what could go wrong, I dared not even wonder. We would find Caul if we could, but our priority was escaping the compound alive.

I brought my hollows into the little room. Everyone gave them a wide berth, pressing their backs to the walls and their hands over their noses as the creatures shuffled past and gathered round the heavy door. The largest hollow knelt down and I saddled myself to him once more, which made me so tall I had to hunch forward to keep my head from scraping the ceiling.

We could hear the voices of wights outside in the corridor. No doubt they were planting another bomb. We decided to wait until they set it off before going out, so we stood by, waiting, a taut silence filling the room.

Finally, Bronwyn broke the tension. "I think Mr. Jacob should say something to all of us."

"Like what?" I said, making my hollow turn so I was facing everyone.

"Well, you're about to lead us into battle," said Bronwyn. "Something leader-ly."

"Something inspiring," said Hugh.

"Something that'll make us less terrified," said Horace.

"That's a lot of pressure," I said, feeling a bit self-conscious. "I don't know if this will make anyone less terrified, but it's something I've been thinking about. I've only known you for a few weeks, but it feels like so much longer than that. You're the best friends I've ever had. And it's weird to think that just a couple of months ago I was back at home, and I didn't even know you were real. And I still had my grandfather."

There were noises outside in the hall, muffled voices, the thud of something metal being dropped on the ground.

I continued, louder. "I miss my grandfather every day, but a very smart friend once told me that everything happens for a reason. If I hadn't lost him, well, I never would've found you. So I guess I had to lose one part of my family to find another. Anyway, that's how you make me feel. Like family. Like one of you."

"You *are* one of us," Emma said. "You're our family."

"We love you, Jacob," said Olive.

"It's been quite something knowing you, Mr. Portman," Miss Peregrine said. "You would've made your grandfather very proud."

"Thanks," I said, getting emotional and a bit embarrassed.

"Jacob?" said Horace. "May I give you something?"

"Of course," I said.

The others, sensing that something private was unfolding between us, began to murmur amongst themselves.

Horace came as close to the hollow as he could bear and, trembling slightly, held out a folded square of cloth. I took it, reaching down from my high place on the hollow's back.

"It's a scarf," said Horace. "Miss P was able to smuggle me a pair of needles, and I knitted it while I was in my cell. I reckon that making it kept me from going mad in there."

I thanked him and unfolded it. The scarf was simple and gray with knotted tassels on the ends, but it was well made and even had my initials monogrammed in one corner. *JP.*

"Wow, Horace, it's . . . "

"It's no great work of art. If I'd had my book of patterns I could've done better."

"It's amazing," I said. "But how did you know you'd even see me again?"

"I had a dream," he said, smiling coyly. "Will you wear it? I know it isn't cold, but . . . for luck?"

"Of course," I said, and wrapped it clumsily around my neck.

"No, that'll never stay on. Like this." He showed me how to fold it in half lengthwise, then loop it around my neck and back through itself so that it knotted perfectly at my throat and the loose ends hung neatly down my shirt. Not exactly battle-wear, but I didn't see the harm.

Emma sidled up to us. "Did you dream about anything besides men's fashion?" she said to Horace. "Like where Caul might be hiding?"

Horace shook his head and started to answer—"No, but I did have a fascinating dream about postage stamps"—but before he could tell us more, there was a noise from the corridor like a dump truck crashing into a wall, a sonic thud that shook us to the marrow. The big bunker door in the end of the room blew open, flinging hinges and bits of shrapnel into the opposite walls. (Thankfully, everyone had been standing clear of it.) There followed a blank moment while the smoke cleared and everyone slowly uncrouched themselves. Then, through the ringing of my ears, I heard an amplified voice say, "Send the boy out alone and no one gets hurt!"

"Somehow I don't believe them," said Emma.

"Definitely not," said Horace.

"Don't even think about it, Mr. Portman," said Miss Peregrine.

"I wasn't," I replied. "Is everyone ready?"

Murmurs of assent. I moved the hollows to either side of the door, their great jaws hinging open, tongues at the ready. I was about to launch my surprise attack when I heard Caul's voice through a PA in the hallway: "They have control of the hollows! Fall back, men! Defensive positions!"

"Damn him!" Emma cried.

The sound of retreating boots filled the corridor. Our surprise attack had been spoiled.

"It doesn't matter!" I said. "When you've got twelve hollows, you don't need surprise."

It was time to use my secret weapon. Rather than a welling-up of tension before the strike, I felt the opposite, a loosening of my full and present self as my awareness relaxed and split among the hollows. And then, while my friends and I hung back, the creatures began hurling themselves through the jagged, blasted door into the hall, running, snarling, jaws gaping, their invisible bodies carving tunnels in the curling bomb smoke. The wights fired at them, their gun barrels flashing, then fell back. Bullets whizzed through the open doorway and into the room where I and the others were taking cover, cracking into the wall behind us.

"Tell us when!" Emma shouted. "We'll go at your word!"

My mind in a dozen places at once, I could muster hardly a word of English in reply. I was them, those hollows in the hall, my own flesh stinging in sympathy with every shot that tore theirs.

Our tongues reached them first: the wights who had not run fast enough and the brave-but-foolish ones who'd lingered to fight. We pummeled them, smacked their heads into the walls, and a small number of us stopped to—here I tried to disconnect my own senses—to sink our teeth into them, swallowing their guns, silencing their screams, leaving them gashed and gaping.

Bottlenecked at the stairs at the end of the corridor, the guards fired again. A second curtain of bullets passed through us, deep and painful, but we ran on, tongues flailing.

Some of the wights escaped through the hatch. Others weren't so lucky, and when they'd stopped screaming we tossed their bodies clear of the stairs. I felt two of my hollows die, their signals blanking from my mind, the connection lost. And then the corridor was clear.

"Now!" I said to Emma, which at the moment was the most complex speech I could manage.

"Now!" Emma shouted, turning to the rest of our group. "This way!"

I drove my hollow into the corridor, clutching at its neck to keep from being thrown off its back. Emma fell in behind me with the others, using her flaming hands as signals in the smoke. Together we charged down the hall, my battalion of monsters before me, my army of peculiars behind. First among them were the strongest and the bravest: Emma, Bronwyn, and Hugh, then the ymbrynes and grumbling Perplexus, who insisted on bringing his heavy Map of Days. Last came the youngest children, the timid, the injured.

The corridor smelled of gunpowder and blood.

"Don't look!" I heard Bronwyn say as we began to pass the bodies of dead wights.

I counted them as we ran: there were five, six, seven of them to my two fallen hollows. Those were encouraging numbers, but how many wights were there in total? Forty, fifty? I worried that there were too many of them to kill and too many of us to protect, and that aboveground we'd be easily overwhelmed, surrounded, and confused. I had to kill as many wights as I could before they broke into the open and this fight turned into something we couldn't win.

My awareness slid to the hollows again. Bounding up the spiral steps, the first one was up through the hatch—then searing pain, blankness.

It had been ambushed as it came out.

I made the next one out of the hatch pick up the dead one's body to use as a shield. It soaked up a volley of gunfire, pushing forward into the room as other hollows leapt from the hatch behind it. I had to push the wights out fast, to get them away from the peculiars who lay everywhere in hospital beds. With a few lashes of our tongues, the closest ones were struck down, and the rest ran.

I sent my hollows after them as we peculiars emerged from the hatch. There were so many of us now, so many hands, that unhooking our bedridden brethren from their soul-drains would be easy. We spread out and made quick work of it. As for the chained madman and the boy we'd stashed in a closet, they were safer here than with us. We'd be back.

Meanwhile, my remaining hollows chased the wights toward the building's exit. The wights fired wildly behind them as they fled. Snatching at their heels with our tongues, we were able to trip two or three, who met a quick but gruesome end once my hollows caught up with them. One wight had hidden himself behind a counter, where he was arming a bomb. A hollow rooted him out, then bundled both the wight and his bomb into a side room. The bomb went off moments later. Another hollow winked out of my consciousness.

The wights had scattered and more than half had escaped, diving through windows and out side doors. We were losing them; the fight was shifting. We'd finished unhooking the bedridden peculiars and had nearly caught up to my hollows, which now numbered seven, plus the one I was riding. We were near the exit, in the room of horrible tools, and we had a choice. I posed the question to those closest to me—Emma, Miss Peregrine, Enoch, Bronwyn.

"Do we use the hollows as cover and run for the tower?" I said, my language coming back as the hollows I had to keep track of dwindled. "Or do we keep fighting?"

Surprisingly, they all agreed. "We can't stop now," Enoch said, wiping blood from his hands.

"If we do, they'll just keep chasing us forever," Bronwyn said.

"No, we won't!" said an injured wight, who was cowering on the floor nearby. "We'll sign a peace treaty!"

"We tried that in 1945," said Miss Peregrine. "It wasn't worth the lavatory paper it was written on. We must keep fighting, children. We may not have such an opportunity again."

Emma raised a flaming hand. "Let's burn this place to the ground."

*   *   *

I sent my hollows racing out of the lab building, into the courtyard, after the remaining wights. The hollows were ambushed again and another was killed, going dark from my mind as it died. Save the one I was riding, by now all my hollows had taken at least a bullet apiece, but despite their wounds most were still going strong. Hollows, as I had learned several times the hard way, are tough little buggers. The wights, on the other hand, seemed to be running scared, but that didn't mean I could count them out. Not knowing precisely where they were only made them more dangerous.

I tried to keep my friends inside the building while I sent the hollows to do reconnaissance, but the peculiars were angry and charged up, itching to get into the fight.

"Out of my way!" said Hugh, trying to push past Emma and me, who were blocking the door.

"It ain't fair for Jacob to do everything!" Olive said. "You've killed near half the wights now, but I hate 'em just as much as you do! If anything I've hated 'em longer—near a hundred years! So come *on*!"

It was true: these kids had a century of wight hatred to work out of their systems, and I was hogging all the glory. This was their fight, too, and it wasn't my place to keep them from it. "If you really want to help," I said to Olive, "here's what you can do . . . "

Thirty seconds later we were out in the open courtyard, and Horace and Hugh were reeling Olive up into the air by a rope around her waist. Right away she became our invaluable eye in the sky, shouting back intel that my ground-bound hollows could never have gathered.

"There's a couple to the right, past the little white shed! And another on the roof! And some running toward the big wall!"

They hadn't scattered to the winds but were mostly out beyond the courtyard. With any luck they could still be caught. I called my six remaining hollows back to us. Spread four of them into a phalanx that would march before us and two behind us as a guard against rear attacks. That left my friends and me to sweep the space between and deal with any wights that might breach our wall of hollows.

We began marching toward the edge of the courtyard. Astride my personal hollow, I felt like a general commanding his troops from horseback. Emma was at my side, and the other peculiars were just behind: Bronwyn collecting loose bricks to hurl, Horace and Hugh hanging on to Olive's rope, Millard attaching himself to Perplexus, who was unleashing a constant stream of Italian profanities while shielding himself with his Map of Days. At the back, the ymbrynes whistled and made loud bird calls in attempt to recruit winged friends to our cause, but Devil's Acre was such a dead zone that there were few wild birds to be found. Miss Peregrine had taken charge of old Miss Avocet and the few shell-shocked ymbrynes. There was nowhere to leave them; they'd have to accompany us into battle.

We came to the edge of the courtyard, beyond which was a run of open ground about fifty meters long. In all that space was just one small building, all that stood between us and the outer wall. It was a curious structure with a pagoda roof and tall, ornate doors, into which I saw a number of wights flee. According to Olive, nearly all the remaining wights had taken up positions inside the little building. One way or another, we were going to have to flush them out.

A quiet had settled over the compound. There were no wights visible anywhere. We lingered behind a protective wall to discuss our next move.

"What are they doing in there?" I said.

"Trying to lure us out into the open," Emma said.

"No problem. I'll send the hollows."

"Won't that leave us unguarded?"

"I don't know that we have a choice. Olive counted twenty wights going in there at least. I need to send enough hollows to overwhelm them or they'll just get slaughtered."

I took a breath. Scanned the tense, waiting faces around me. I sent the hollows out one by one, sliding across the open yard on tiptoe, hoping light footsteps might allow them to surround the building unnoticed.

It seemed to work: the building had three doors, and I managed to place two hollows at each one without a single wight showing his face. The hollows stood guard outside the doors while I listened through their ears. Inside, I could hear someone with a high voice speaking, though I couldn't make out the words. Then a bird whistled. My blood went cold.

There were ymbrynes inside. More that we hadn't known were here.

Hostages.

But if that was true, why weren't the wights trying to negotiate?

My original plan had been to break down all the doors at once and charge inside. But if there were hostages—especially ymbryne hostages—I couldn't risk such rash action.

I decided to have one of the hollows risk a look inside. All the windows were shuttered, though, which meant I'd have to send it through a door.

I chose the smallest hollow. Reeled out its dominant tongue. It licked the knob, gripped it.

"I'm sending one inside," I said. "Just one, to look around."

Slowly, the hollow turned the knob. On my silent count of three, the hollow pushed open the door.

It leaned forward and pressed its black eye to the crack.

"I'm looking inside."

Through its eye I could see a slice of wall lined with cages. Heavy, black birdcages of various shapes and sizes.

The hollow pressed the door open farther. I saw more cages, and now birds, too, in the cages and out of them, chained to perches.

But no wights.

"What do you see?" Emma said.

There wasn't time to explain, only to act. I made all my hollows throw open the doors at once, and they burst inside.

There were birds everywhere, startled and squawking.

"Birds!" I said. "The room's full of ymbrynes!"

"What?" Emma said. "Where are the wights?"

"I don't know."

The hollows were turning, smelling the air, searching every nook and cranny.

"That can't be!" Miss Peregrine said. "All the kidnapped ymbrynes are right here."

"Then what are these birds?" I said.

Then, in a scratchy parrot voice, I heard one sing, "Run, rabbit, run! Run, rabbit, run!" And I realized: these were not ymbrynes. These were parrots. And they were *ticking*.

"HIT THE DIRT!" I shouted, and we all dove to the ground behind the courtyard wall, the hollow pitching backward and taking me with it.

I flung my hollows at the doors but the parrot-bombs went off before they could get through them, ten at once, obliterating the building and the hollows in a terrible clap of thunder. As dirt and brick and bits of building flew through the courtyard and rained down on us, I felt the hollows' signals go dead together, all but one blacking from my mind.

A cloud of smoke and feathers blew over the wall. The peculiars and ymbrynes were streaked with dirt, coughing, checking one another for holes. I was in shock, or something like it, my eyes locked on a splattered patch of ground where a bit of pulped and quivering hollowgast had been flung. For an hour my mind had been stretching to accommodate twelve of them, and their sudden death had created a disorienting vacuum that left me feeling dizzy and strangely bereft. But crisis has a way of focusing the mind, and what happened next had my last remaining hollow and me sitting bolt upright.

From beyond the wall came the sound of many voices shouting together—a great and rising battle cry—and beneath it a thunder of stampeding boots. Everyone froze and looked at me, dread furrowing their faces.

"What is *that*?" said Emma.

"Let me see," I said, and crawled away from my hollow to peer around the edge of the wall.

A horde of wights was charging toward us across the smoking ground. Twenty of them in a cluster, running with rifles and pistols raised, their white eyes and white teeth shining. They were unscathed by the explosion, having escaped, I assumed, into some underground shelter. We'd been lured into a trap, of which the parrot bombs were only the first component. Now that our best weapon had been stripped from us, the wights were making their final assault.

There was a panicked scramble as others looked around the wall to see the charging horde for themselves.

"What do we do?" cried Horace.

"We fight!" said Bronwyn. "Give 'em everything we've got!"

"No, we must run while we can!" said Miss Avocet, whose bent back and deeply lined face made it hard to imagine her running from anything. "We can't afford to lose another peculiar life!"

"Excuse me, but I was asking Jacob," said Horace. "He got us this far, after all . . ."

Instinctively I looked to Miss Peregrine, whom I considered the final authority on matters of authority. She returned my gaze and nodded. "Yes," she said, "I think Mr. Portman should decide. Quickly, though, or the wights will make the decision for you."

I nearly protested. My hollows were all dead but one—but I suppose this was Miss Peregrine's way of saying she believed in me, hollows or no. Anyway, what we should do seemed obvious. In a hundred years, the peculiars had never been so close to destroying the wight menace, and if we ran away now, I knew that chance may never come again. My friends' faces were scared but determined—ready, I thought, to risk their lives for a chance to finally eradicate the wight scourge.

"We fight," I said. "We've come too far to give up now."

If there was someone among us who would rather have fled, they stayed quiet. Even the ymbrynes, who had sworn oaths to keep us safe, didn't argue. They knew what sort of fate awaited any of us who were recaptured.

"You give the word," said Emma.

I craned my neck around the wall. The wights were closing fast, no more than a hundred feet away now. But I wanted them closer still—close enough that we might easily knock the guns from their hands.

Shots rang out. A piercing scream came from above.

"Olive!" Emma shouted. "They're shooting at Olive!"

We'd left the poor girl hanging up there. The wights were taking potshots at her while she squealed and waved her limbs like a starfish. There was no time to reel her in, but we couldn't just leave her for target practice.

"Let's give them something better to shoot at," I said. "Ready?"

Their answer was resounding and affirmative. I shimmied onto the back of my crouched hollow. "LET'S GO!" I shouted.

The hollow leapt to its feet, nearly bucking me off, then launched forward like a racehorse at the starting gun. We burst from behind the wall, the hollow and I leading the charge, my friends and our ymbrynes close behind. I let out a screaming war cry, not so much to scare the wights as to tear down the fear that was clawing at me, and my friends did the same. The wights balked, and for a moment they couldn't seem to decide whether to keep charging or stop and shoot at us. That bought the hollow and me enough time to clear much of the open ground that separated us.

It didn't take long for the wights to make up their minds. They stopped, leveled their guns at us like a firing squad, and let loose a volley of bullets. They whizzed around me, pocking the ground, lighting up my pain receptors as they slammed into the hollow. Praying it hadn't been hit anywhere vital, I sank low to shield myself behind its body and urged it forward, faster, using its tongues like extra legs to speed us on.

The hollow and I closed the remaining gap in just a few seconds, my friends close behind. Then we were among them, fighting hand-to-hand, and the advantage was ours. While I concentrated on knocking the guns out of the wights' hands, my friends put their peculiar talents to good use. Emma swung her hands like flaming clubs, cutting through a line of wights. Bronwyn hurled the bricks she'd gathered, then punched and pummeled the wights with her bare hands. Hugh's lone bee had recently made some friends, and as he cheered them on ("Go for the eyes, fellows!") they swirled around and dive-bombed our enemy wherever they could. So did the ymbrynes, who'd turned themselves into birds after the first gunshots. Miss Peregrine was most fearsome, her huge beak and talons sending wights running, but even small, colorful Miss Bunting made herself useful, ripping one wight's hair and pecking his head hard enough to make him miss the shot he was taking—which allowed Claire to leap up and bite him on the shoulder with her wide, sharp-toothed backmouth. Enoch did his part, too, revealing from under his shirt three clay men with forks for legs and knives for arms, which he sent hacking after the wights' ankles. All the while, Olive shouted advice to us from her bird's-eye view. "Behind you, Emma! He's going for his gun, Hugh!"

Despite all our peculiar ingenuity, however, we were outnumbered, and the wights were fighting as if their lives depended on it—which likely they did.

Something hard crashed into my head—the butt of a gun—and I hung limp from the hollow's back for a moment, the world spinning around me. Miss Bunting was caught and thrown to the ground. It was chaos, awful bloody chaos, and the wights were beginning to take the momentum, forcing us back.

And then, from behind me, I heard a familiar roar. My senses returning, I looked and saw Bentham, galloping toward the fight astride the back of his grimbear. Both were soaking wet, having come through the Panloopticon the same way Emma and I had.

"Hullo, young man!" he called, riding up next to me. "In need of some assistance?"

Before I could reply, my hollow was shot again, the bullet passing through the side of its neck and grazing my thigh, painting a bloody line through my torn pants.

"Yes, please!" I shouted.

"PT, you heard the boy!" Bentham said. "KILL!"

The bear dove into the fight, swinging his giant paws and knocking wights aside like they were bowling pins. One ran up and shot PT point-blank in the chest with a small handgun. The bear seemed merely annoyed, then picked up the wight and sent him flying. Soon, with my hollow and Bentham's grim working together, we had the wights on the defensive. When we'd picked off enough of them that it became clear they were outnumbered, their ranks whittled to no more than ten, they took off and ran.

"Don't let them escape!" Emma cried.

We tore after the wights on foot, on wing, on bearback and hollowback. We chased them through the smoking ruins of the parrot house, across ground stippled with catapulted rodents from Sharon's insurrection, toward an arched gate built into the looming outer wall.

Miss Peregrine screamed overhead, dive-bombing fleeing wights. She pulled one off his feet by the back of his neck, but this, and more attacks from Hugh's bees, only made the nine that were left run even faster. Their lead was growing and my hollow was beginning to fail, leaking black fluid from a half dozen wounds.

The wights crashed on blindly, the gate's iron portcullis rising as they neared it.

"Stop them!" I shouted, hoping that beyond the gate, Sharon and his unruly crowd might hear.

And then I realized: the bridge! There was still another hollow-gast left—the one inside the bridge. If I could get control of him in time, maybe I could stop the wights from escaping.

But no. They were already through the gate, running up the bridge, and I was hopelessly behind. By the time I passed through the gate, the bridge hollow had already picked up and tossed five of them across to Smoking Street, where only a thin crowd of ambro addicts was lingering—not enough to stop them. The four wights who hadn't yet crossed were stuck at the bridge gap, waiting their turn to be flung.

As my hollow and I started running up the bridge, I felt the bridge hollow come online inside me. It was picking up three of the four wights and lifting them across.

Stop, I said aloud in Hollow.

Or at least that's what I thought I said, though maybe something got lost in translation, and maybe *stop* sounds a lot like *drop* in hollowspeak. Because rather than stopping midair and then bringing the three kicking and terrified wights back to our side of the bridge, the hollow simply let them go. (How strange!)

All the peculiars on our side of the chasm and the addicts on the other side came to the edge to watch them fall, howling and flailing all the way down through layers of sulfurous green mist until—*ploop!*—they plunged into the boiling river and disappeared.

A cheer went up on both sides, and a grating voice I recognized said, "Serves 'em right. They were lousy tippers, anyway!"

It was one of two bridge heads that were still on their pikes. "Didn't your mum ever tell you not to swim on a full stomach?" said the other. "WAIT TWENTY MINUTES!"

The lone wight remaining on our side threw down his gun and

raised his hands in surrender, while the five who'd made it across were quickly vanishing into a cloud of ash the wind had kicked up.

We stood watching them go. There was no way we'd catch them now.

"Curse our luck," Bentham said. "Even that small number of wights could wreak havoc for years to come."

"Agreed, brother, though honestly I didn't realize you gave a titmouse what happened to the rest of us." We turned to see Miss Peregrine walking toward us, returned to human form, a shawl clasped modestly around her shoulders. Her eyes were locked on Bentham, her expression sour and unwelcoming.

"Hello, Alma! Fantastic to see you!" he said with overeager cheerfulness. "And of course I give a . . . " He cleared his throat awkwardly. "Why, I'm the reason you're not still in a prison cell! Go on, children, tell them!"

"Mr. Bentham helped us a lot," I admitted, though I didn't really want to insert myself into a sibling spat.

"In that case, all due thanks," Miss Peregrine said coldly. "I'll ensure the Council of Ymbrynes is made aware of the role you played here. Perhaps they'll see fit to lighten your sentence."

"Sentence?" Emma said, looking sharply at Bentham. "What sentence?"

His lip twisted. "Banishment. You don't think I'd live in this pit if I was welcome anywhere else, do you? I was framed, unjustly accused of—"

"Collusion." Miss Peregrine said. "Collaboration with the enemy. Betrayal after betrayal."

"I was acting as a double agent, Alma, mining our brother for information. I explained this to you!" He was whining, his palms out like a beggar's. "You know I have every reason to hate Jack!"

Miss Peregrine raised her hand to stop him. She'd heard this story before and didn't want to again. "When he betrayed your grandfather," she said to me, "that was the last straw."

"That was an *accident*," Bentham said, drawing back in offense.

"Then what became of the suul you drew from him?" said Miss Peregrine.

"It was injected into the test subjects!"

Miss Peregrine shook her head. "We reverse-engineered your experiment. They were given suul from barnyard animals, which can only mean that you kept Abe's for yourself."

"What an absurd allegation!" he cried. "Is that what you told the council? That's why I'm still rotting in here, isn't it?" I couldn't tell if he was genuinely surprised or just acting. "I knew you felt threatened by my intellect and superior leadership capabilities. But that you'd stoop to such lies to keep me out of your way . . . do you know how many years I've spent fighting to eradicate the scourge of ambrosia use? What on earth would I want with that poor man's suul?"

"The same thing our brother wants with young Mr. Portman," Miss Peregrine said.

"I won't even honor that accusation with a denial. I only wish this haze of bias would clear so that you could see the truth: I'm on your side, Alma, and I've always been."

"You're on whatever side fits your interests at the moment."

Bentham sighed and aimed a hangdog look at Emma and me. "Goodbye, children. It's been a distinct pleasure knowing you. I'll go back home now; saving all your lives has taken quite a toll on this old man's body. But I hope one day, when your headmistress comes to her senses, we'll meet again."

He tipped his hat, and he and his bear began to walk away through the crowd, back through the compound toward the tower.

"What a drama queen," I muttered, though I did feel a little bad for him.

"Ymbrynes!" Miss Peregrine called. "Watch him!"

"Did he really steal Abe's soul?" Emma asked.

"Without proof we can't be certain," replied Miss Peregrine. "But the rest of his crimes taken together would earn him more than a lifetime's banishment." Watching him go, her hard expression gradually melted away. "My brothers taught me a hard lesson. No one can hurt you as badly as the people you love."

*   *   *

The wind shifted, sending the ash cloud that had aided the wights' escape in our direction. It came faster than we could react, the air around us howling and stinging, the daylight dimming away. There was a sharp flutter of wings as the ymbrynes changed form and flew up above the storm. My hollow sank to its knees, bowed its head, and shielded its face with its two free tongues. It was accustomed to ash storms, but our friends were not. I could hear them panicking in the dark.

"Stay where you are!" I shouted. "It'll pass!"

"Everyone breathe through your shirts!" said Emma.

When the storm began to subside a little, I heard something from across the bridge that made the hairs on my neck stand up. It was three baritone voices united in a song, the lines of which were punctuated by thuds and groans.

"Hark to the clinking of hammers . . . "

Thwack!

"Hark to the driving of nails!"

"Gahh, my legs!"

"What fun to build a gallows . . . "

"Let me go, let me go!"

" . . . the cure for all that ails!"

"Please, no more! I give up!"

And then, as the ash began to clear, Sharon and his three burly cousins appeared, each of them dragging a subdued wight. "Morning, all!" Sharon called. "Did you lose something?"

Wiping ash from their eyes, our friends saw what they'd done and began to cheer.

"Sharon, you brilliant man!" shouted Emma.

All around us the ymbrynes were landing and resuming human form. As they slipped quickly into the clothes they'd dropped, we respectfully kept our eyes on the wights.

Suddenly, one of them broke away from his captor and ran. Rather than chasing him, the rigger calmly selected a small hammer from his tool belt, planted his feet, and threw it. It tumbled end over end straight toward the wight's head, but what would've been a perfect takedown was spoiled when the wight ducked. He darted toward the chaos of scrap at the road's edge. Just as the wight was about to disappear between two shanty houses, a crack in the road erupted and the wight was engulfed in a belch of yellow flame.

Though it was a grisly sight, everyone whooped and cheered.

"You see!" said Sharon. "The Acre itself wants to be rid of them."

"That's wonderful," I said, "but what about Caul?"

"I agree," said Emma. "None of these victories will matter if we can't catch him. Right, Miss P?"

I glanced around but didn't see her. Emma looked, too, her eyes scanning the crowd.

"Miss Peregrine?" she said, panic creeping into her voice.

I made my hollow stand tall so I could get a better view. "Does anyone see Miss Peregrine?" I shouted. Now everyone was looking, checking the sky in case she was still airborne, the ground in case she'd landed but not yet turned human.

Then from behind us, a high, gleeful shout cut through our chatter.

"Look no further, children!" For a moment I couldn't pinpoint the voice. It came again: "Do as I say and no harm will come to her!"

Then I saw emerge, from beneath the branches of a small, ash-blackened tree just inside the wights' gate, a familiar figure.

Caul. A twig of a man with no weapons in his hand nor guards by his side. His face pale and contorted into an unnatural grin, his eyes capped by bulging sunglasses, insectine. He was dandied up in a cloak, a cape, loops of gold jewelry, and a bouffant silk tie. He looked flamboyantly insane, like some mad doctor from gothic fiction who'd performed too many experiments on himself. And it was his evident madness, I think—and that we all knew him to be capable of true evil—that stopped us from rushing to tear him apart. A man like Caul was never as defenseless as he seemed.

"Where's Miss Peregrine?" I shouted, inspiring a chorus of similar demands from the ymbrynes and peculiars behind me.

"Right where she belongs," Caul said. "With her family."

The last of the ash cloud gusted out of the compound behind him, revealing Bentham and Miss Peregrine, the latter in human form, held captive in the arms of Bentham's bear. Though her eyes flashed with rage, she knew better than to struggle against a sharp-clawed, short-tempered grimbear.

It seemed a recurring nightmare we were doomed to dream again and again: Miss Peregrine kidnapped, this time by Bentham. He stood slightly behind the bear with eyes downcast, as if ashamed to meet our looks.

Cries of shock and anger rippled through the peculiars and ymbrynes.

"Bentham!" I shouted. "Let her go!"

"You traitorous bastard!" cried Emma.

Bentham raised his head to look at us. "As recently as ten minutes ago," he said in a high and imperious tone, "you had my loyalty. I could have betrayed you to my brother days ago, but I didn't." He narrowed his eyes at Miss Peregrine. "I chose *you*, Alma, because I believed—naively, it seems—that if I helped you and your wards, you might see how unfairly you'd judged me, might finally rise above past differences and let bygones be bygones."

"You'll be sent to the Pitiless Waste for this!" Miss Peregrine shouted.

"I'm not frightened of your little council anymore!" Bentham said. "You won't keep me down any longer!" He stamped his cane. "PT, muzzle!"

The bear clamped its paw over Miss Peregrine's face.

Caul strode toward his brother and sister, his arms and smile spreading. "Benny's made a choice to stand up for himself, and I, for one, congratulate him! There's nothing like a family reunion!"

Suddenly, Bentham was pulled backward by an unseen force. A

knife flashed at his throat. "Make the bear release Miss Peregrine or else!" a familiar voice shouted.

"Millard!" someone gasped, one of many that rippled through our crowd.

It was Millard, disrobed and invisible. Bentham looked terrified, but Caul seemed merely annoyed. He drew an antique pepperbox pistol from one of the deep pockets in his cloak and pointed it at Bentham's head. "Let her go and *I'll* kill you, brother."

"We made a pact!" Bentham protested.

"And you caving to the demands of a nude boy with a dull knife would be breaking that pact." Caul cocked the gun, walked it forward until it was pressed against Bentham's temple, and addressed Millard. "If you make me kill my only brother, consider your ymbryne dead, too."

Millard hesitated for a moment, then dropped the knife and ran. Caul made a grab for him but missed, and Millard's footsteps curved away in a trail of divots.

Bentham composed himself and straightened his mussed shirt. Caul, his good humor gone, turned the gun on Miss Peregrine.

"Now listen to me!" he barked. "You there, across the bridge! Let those guards go!"

They had little choice but to do as he asked. Sharon and his cousins released their collared wights and backed away, and the wight who'd been standing on our side of the bridge lowered his hands and picked his gun up off the ground. Within seconds the balance of power had been reversed completely, and there were four guns aimed at the crowd and one at Miss Peregrine. Caul could do what he wanted.

"Boy!" he said, pointing at me. "Pitch that hollow into the chasm!" His shrill voice a needle in my eardrum.

I walked my hollow to the edge of the chasm.

"Now make him leap!"

It seemed I didn't have a choice. It was an awful waste, but perhaps just as well: the hollow was suffering badly now, its wounds leaking black blood that flowed around its feet. It wouldn't have survived.

I unwrapped its tongue from my waist, unsaddled myself, and stepped down. My strength had returned enough for me to stand on my own, but the hollow's was going fast. As soon as I was off its back it bellowed softly, sucked its tongues back into its mouth, and sank to its knees, a willing sacrifice.

"Thank you, whoever you were," I said. "I'm sure that if you'd ever become a wight, you wouldn't have been a completely evil one."

I put my foot on its back and pushed. The hollow tumbled forward and dropped silently into the misty void. After a few seconds, I felt its consciousness disappear from my mind.

The wights across the bridge rode over to our side on the hollow's tongues, Miss Peregrine's life threatened again if I interfered. Olive was yanked out of the sky. The guards set about herding us into a tight and easily controllable cluster. Then Caul shouted for me, and one of the guards reached into the crowd and dragged me out.

"He's the only one we really need alive," Caul said to his guards. "If you must shoot him, shoot him in the knees. As for the rest of them . . . " Caul swung his gun toward the tightly packed crowd and fired. There were screams as the crowd surged. "Shoot them anywhere you please!"

He laughed and twirled with his arms poised like a squat ballerina. I was about to run at him, ready to dig out his eyes with my bare hands and damn the consequences, when a long-barreled revolver appeared front and center in my field of view.

"Don't," grunted my monosyllabic guard, a wight with broad shoulders and a shiny bald head.

Caul fired his own gun into the air and shouted for quiet, and every voice fell away but the whimpers of whomever he'd shot.

"Don't cry, I have a treat for you people!" he said, addressing the crowd. "This is a historic day. My brother and I are about to culminate a lifetime's worth of innovation and struggle by crowning ourselves the twin kings of peculiardom. And what would a coronation be without witnesses? So we're bringing you along. Provided you behave yourselves, you'll see something no one has witnessed for a thousand years: the domination and expropriation of the Library of Souls!"

"You have to promise one thing, or I won't help you," I said to Caul. I didn't have much negotiating power, but he believed he needed me, and that was something. "Once you get what you want, let Miss Peregrine go."

"I'm afraid that won't do," Caul said, "but I'll let her live. Peculiardom will be more fun to rule with my sister in it. Once I clip your wings I'll keep you as my personal slave, Alma, how would you like that?"

She tried to respond, but her words were lost beneath the bear's meaty paw.

Caul cupped a hand behind his ear and laughed. "What's that? I can't hear you!" Then he turned and began walking toward the tower.

"Let's go!" the guards shouted, and soon we were all stumbling after him.

CHAPTER NINE

*W*e were herded toward the pale tower at a brutal pace, the wights encouraging stragglers with shoves and kicks. Without my hollow I was a limping, hobbling mess: I had nasty bite wounds across my torso and the dust that had kept me from feeling them was beginning to wear off. I forced myself forward anyway, my mind spinning out ways we might save ourselves, each more implausible than the last. Without my hollows, all our peculiar powers were outmatched by the wights and their guns.

We stumbled past the wrecked building where my hollows had died, over bricks misted with the blood of parrots and wights. Marched through the walled courtyard, into the tower door and then up and up its winding hallway past a blur of identical black doors. Caul paraded before us like a deranged bandleader, high-stepping and swinging his arms one moment and turning to hurl profane insults at us the next. Behind him, the bear waddled along with Bentham riding in the crook of one arm and Miss Peregrine slung over its shoulder.

She pled with her brothers to reconsider their course of action.

"Remember the old stories of Abaton, and the ignominious end that came to every peculiar who stole the library's souls! Its power is cursed!"

"I'm not a child anymore, Alma, and I'm no longer frightened by old ymbrynes' tales," Caul scoffed. "Now hold your tongue. That is, if you want to keep it!"

She soon gave up trying to convince them and stared silently at us over the bear's shoulder, her face projecting strength. *Don't be afraid*, she seemed to telegraph. *We'll survive this, too.*

I worried not all of us would survive even the trip to the top of the tower. Turning around, I tried to see who it was that had been shot. Amidst the tight-packed group behind me, Bronwyn was carrying someone limp in her arms—Miss Avocet, I think—and then a meaty hand smacked me in the head.

"Face forward or lose a kneecap," growled my guard.

Finally we came to the top of the tower and its very last door. In the hallway beyond, pale daylight shone on the curving wall. There was an open deck above us, a fact I filed away for future reference.

Caul stood beaming before the door. "Perplexus!" he called. "*Signor* Anomalous—yes, there in the back! Since I owe this discovery in part to your expeditions and hard work—credit where credit is due!—I think you should do the honors and open the door."

"Come now, we've no time for ceremony," said Bentham. "We've left your compound unguarded . . . "

"Don't be such a ninny-willow," Caul said. "This won't take but a moment."

One of the guards dragged Perplexus out of the crowd and up to the door. Since I'd last seen him, his hair and beard had turned alabaster white, his spine had curved, and deep wrinkles grooved his face. He'd spent too long away from his loop, and now his true age was beginning to catch up to him. Perplexus seemed about to open the door when he was struck by a fit of coughing. Once he'd regained his breath, he faced Caul, drew in a snorting lungful of air, and spat a glistening wad of phlegm onto his cloak.

"You are an ignorant pig!" Perplexus cried.

Caul raised his pistol to Perplexus's head and pulled the trigger. There were screams—"Jack, don't!" Bentham shouted—and Perplexus threw up his hands and spun away, but the only sound the gun made was a dry click.

Caul opened the gun and peered into its chamber, then shrugged. "It's an antique, like yourself," he said to Perplexus, then used its barrel to flick the spittle from his jacket. "I suppose fate has intervened on your behalf. Just as well—I'd rather watch you turn to dust than bleed to death."

He motioned for the guards to take him away. Perplexus, muttering oaths at Caul in Italian, was dragged back to the group.

Caul turned to the door. "Oh, to hell with it," he muttered, and opened it. "Get in there, all of you!"

Inside was the same familiar gray-walled room, only this time its missing fourth wall extended into a long, dark corridor. With a few shoves from the guards, we were hurrying along it. The smooth walls became rough and uneven, then widened into a primitive, day-lit room. The room was made from rock and clay, and I might've called it a cave but for its approximately rectangular door and two windows. Someone had carved them, and this room, using tools to dig it out of soft rock.

We were herded outside into a hot, dry day. The view opened dizzyingly. We were high in a landscape that could've been an alien world: everywhere around us, towering on one side and rolling away into valleys on the other, were humps and spires of strange, reddish rock, all honeycombed with crude doors and windows. A constant wind blew through them, producing a human-sounding moan that seemed to emanate from the earth itself. Though the sun was no-where near setting, the sky glowed orange, as if the end of the world were brewing just beyond the horizon. And despite evidence here of a civilization, other than ourselves there was no one in sight. I had a heavy, watched feeling, like we were trespassing someplace we were not meant to be.

Bentham climbed down from his bear and removed his hat in awe. "So this is the place," he said, gazing across the hills.

Caul threw a big-brotherly arm across his shoulders. "I told you this day would come. We certainly put each other through hell getting here, didn't we?"

"We did," Bentham agreed.

"But I say all's well that ends well, because now I get to do this." Caul turned to face us. "Friends! Ymbrynes! Peculiar children!" He let his voice echo away into the strange, moaning canyons. "Today will go down in history. Welcome to Abaton!"

He paused, waiting for applause that didn't come.

"You're standing now in the ancient city that once protected the Library of Souls. Until recently, it hadn't been seen in over four hundred years, nor conquered in a thousand—until I rediscovered it! Now, with you as my witnesses . . . "

He stopped, looked down for a moment, then laughed. "Why am I wasting my breath? You philistines will never appreciate the gravity of my achievement. Look at you—like donkeys contemplating the Sistine Chapel!" He patted Bentham on the arm. "Come on, brother. Let's go and take what's ours."

"And ours as well!" said a voice behind me. One of the guards. "You won't forget us, will you, sir?"

"Of course I won't," Caul said, attempting a smile and failing. He couldn't disguise his irritation at having been challenged in front of everyone. "Your loyalty will be repaid tenfold."

He turned with Bentham and started down a footpath, the guards pushing us after them.

* * *

The sunbaked path split and split again, sending branches and feeders into the spiked hills. Following a route he'd no doubt forced Perplexus to reveal and had trod many times in recent days, Caul led us down obscure and bramble-choked lanes with certainty, his every step oozing the arrogance of a colonizer. The watched feeling I had only grew. As if the rough openings bored into the rock were a colony of half-closed eyes, some ancient intelligence encased in stone, waking slowly from a thousand-year sleep.

I was fevered with anxiety, my thoughts tripping over one another. What happened next would be up to me. The wights needed me, after all. What if I refused to handle the souls for them? What if I found a way to trick them?

I knew what would happen. Caul would kill Miss Peregrine. Then he'd start killing the other ymbrynes, one after another until I gave him what he wanted. And if I didn't, he'd kill Emma.

I wasn't strong enough. I knew I'd do anything to stop them from hurting her—even hand Caul the keys to untold power.

Then I had a thought that scared the bejesus out of me: what if I *couldn't* do it? What if Caul was wrong and I couldn't see the soul jars, or I could see them but not handle them? He wouldn't believe me. He'd think I was lying. He'd start murdering my friends. And even if I somehow convinced him it was true—that I couldn't—he might get so livid that he'd kill everyone anyway.

I said a silent prayer to my grandfather—can you pray to dead people? Well, I did—and I asked, if he was watching me, to see me through this, and to make me as strong and as powerful as he once was. *Grandpa Portman*, I prayed, *I know this sounds crazy, but Emma and my friends mean the world to me, the whole damned world, and I would gladly give every bit of it to Caul in exchange for their lives. Does that make me evil? I don't know, but I thought you might understand. So please.*

Looking up, I was surprised to see Miss Peregrine watching me from over the bear's shoulder. As soon as she met my eyes she looked away, and I could see tears tracking through the grime on her pale cheeks. As if somehow she'd heard me.

Our route wound through an ancient maze of twisting paths

and stairways cut into the hills, their steps worn into crescent moons. In some places the path all but disappeared, swallowed by weeds. I heard Perplexus complain that it had taken him years to puzzle out the way to the Library of Souls, and to have this ungrateful thief tromping along it now with no regard—a terrible insult!

And then I heard Olive say, "Why did no one ever tell us the library was real?"

"Because, my dear," replied an ymbryne, "it wasn't allowed. It was safer to say . . . "

The ymbryne paused to catch her breath.

" . . . that it was just a story."

Just a story. It had become one of the defining truths of my life that, no matter how I tried to keep them flattened, two-dimensional, jailed in paper and ink, there would always be stories that refused to stay bound inside books. It was never just a story. I would know: a story had swallowed my whole life.

We'd been walking for several minutes along a plain-looking wall, the wind's eerie moan rising and falling, when Caul raised a hand and shouted for everyone to stop.

"Have we gone too far?" he said. "I could've sworn the grotto was along here somewhere. Where's the cartographer?"

Perplexus was hauled forth from the crowd.

"Aren't you glad you didn't shoot him?" Bentham muttered.

Caul ignored him. "Where's the grotto?" he demanded, getting in Perplexus's face.

"Ahh, perhaps it's hidden itself from you," Perplexus teased.

"Don't test me," Caul replied. "I'll burn every copy of your Map of Days. Your name will be forgotten by next year."

Perplexus knotted his fingers together and sighed. "There," he said, pointing behind us.

We had passed it.

Caul stomped down to a vine-choked patch of wall—an opening so humble and well-hidden that anyone might've missed it; not so much a door as a hole. He pushed aside the vines and poked his head through. "Yes!" I heard him say, and then he pulled out his head again and began giving orders.

"Essential persons only are allowed past this point. Brother, sister." He pointed at Bentham and Miss Peregrine. "Boy." He pointed at me. "Two guards. And . . . " He searched the crowd. "It's dark in there, we'll need a flashlight. You, girl." He pointed at Emma.

As my stomach turned knots, Emma was pulled out of the group.

"If the others give you trouble," Caul said to the guards, "you know what to do." Caul raised his pistol at the crowd. They all screamed and ducked their heads. Caul howled with laughter.

Emma's guard pushed her through the hole. Bentham's bear would never fit through, so Miss Peregrine was set down and my wight given double duty guarding both her and me.

The youngest children began to weep. Who knew if they would ever see her again? "Be brave, children!" Miss Peregrine called to them. "I'll be back!"

"That's right, children!" Caul sang mockingly. "Listen to your headmistress! Ymbryne knows best!"

Miss Peregrine and I were pushed through the opening together, and there was a moment, tangled in the vines, when I was able to whisper to her unnoticed.

"What should I do when we get inside?"

"Anything he asks," she whispered back. "If we don't anger him, we may yet survive."

Survive, yes—but at what cost?

And then we were parting the vines and stumbling into a strange new space: a stone room open to the sky. For an instant my breath abandoned me, so shocked was I by the giant, misshapen face staring back at us from opposite wall. A wall—that's all it was—but one with a gaping mouth for a door, two warped eyes for windows, a pair of holes for nostrils, and grown over with long grass that resembled hair and an unruly beard. The moaning wind was louder than ever here, as if the mouth-shaped door were trying to warn us away in some ancient language made of vowels a week long.

Caul indicated the door. "The library awaits."

Bentham removed his hat. "Extraordinary," he said, hushed and reverent. "It almost seems to be singing to us. Like all the resting souls here are coming awake to welcome us."

"Welcoming," said Emma. "I doubt that."

The guards pushed us toward the door. We ducked through the low opening and into another cavelike room. Like the others we'd seen in Abaton, it had been dug by hand from soft rock, untold ages ago. It was low-ceilinged and bare, empty but for some scattered straw and broken shards of pottery. Its most unique feature was the walls, into which had been dug many dozens of small coves. They were oval-topped and flat on the bottom, large enough to hold a bottle or a candle. At the back of the room, several doors forked away into darkness.

"Well, boy?" said Caul. "Can you see any?"

I looked around. "Any what?"

"Don't trifle with me. Soul jars." He stepped to a wall and swept his hand inside one of the coves. "Go and pick one up."

I turned slowly, scanning the walls. Every cove appeared to be empty. "I don't see anything," I said. "Maybe there aren't any."

"You're lying."

Caul nodded to my guard. The guard punched me in the stomach.

Emma and Miss Peregrine shouted as I fell to my knees, groaning. Looking down at myself, I saw blood trickling through my shirt—not from the punch, but from my hollow bite.

"Please, Jack!" cried Miss Peregrine. "He's just a boy!"

"Just a boy, just a boy!" Caul said mockingly. "That's the very heart of the problem! You've got to punish them like men, water them with a bit of blood, and then the shoot begins to spring up, the plant to grow." He strode toward me while spinning the barrel of his odd, antique pistol. "Straighten his leg. I want a clean shot at the knee."

The guard shoved me to the ground and grabbed ahold of my calf. My cheek ground into the dirt, my face aimed at the wall.

I heard the gun's hammer pull back. And then, as the women begged Caul for mercy, I saw something in one the coves in the wall. A shape I hadn't noticed before—

"Wait!" I shouted. "I see something!"

The guard flipped me over.

"Come to your senses, have you?" Caul was standing over me, looking down. "What do you see?"

I looked again, blinking. Forced myself to be calm, my vision to focus.

There in the wall, coming gradually into view like a Polaroid photo, was the faint image of a stone jar. It was a simple, unadorned thing, cylindrical in shape with a tapered neck and a cork plugging its top, its stone the same reddish color as the strange hills of Abaton.

"It's a jar," I said. "Just one. It was tipped over, that's why I didn't notice it at first."

"Stand," Caul said. "I want to see you pick it up."

I drew my knees to my chest, rocked forward onto my feet, and stood, pain rioting through my midsection. I shuffled across the room and reached slowly into the cove. I slid my fingers around the jar, then got a shock and pulled my hand away.

"What is it?" Caul said.

"It's *freezing*," I replied. "I wasn't expecting it."

"Fascinating," murmured Bentham. He'd been lingering near the door, as if reconsidering this whole endeavor, but now he took a step closer.

I reached into the cove again, ready for the cold this time, and removed the jar.

"This is wrong," Miss Peregrine said. "There's a peculiar soul in there, and it should be treated with respect."

"To be eaten by me would be the greatest respect a soul could be paid," Caul said. He came and stood next to me. "Describe the jar."

"It's very simple. Made of stone." It was starting to freeze my right hand, so I passed it to my left, and then I saw, written across the back in tall, spidery letters, a word.

Aswindan.

I wasn't going to mention it, but Caul was watching me like a hawk and had seen me notice something. "What is it?" he demanded. "I warn you, hold nothing back!"

"It's a word," I said. "Aswindan."

"Spell it."

"A-s-w-i-n-d-a-n."

"Aswindan," Caul said, his brow furrowing. "That's Old Peculiar, isn't it?"

"Obviously," Bentham said. "Don't you remember your lessons?"

"Of course I do! I was a quicker study than you, remember? Aswindan. The root is *wind*. Which doesn't refer to the weather but denotes quickness, as in quickening—as in strengthening, invigoration!"

"I'm not so sure about that, brother."

"Oh you're *not*," Caul said sarcastically. "I think you want it for yourself!"

Caul reached out and tried to snatch the jar from me. He managed to get his fingers around it, but as soon as the jar left my hand his fingers closed on themselves, as if there were suddenly nothing between them, and the jar dropped to the floor and smashed.

Caul swore and looked down, dumbfounded, as blue and brightly glowing liquid puddled at our feet.

"I can see it now!" he said excitedly, pointing at the blue puddle. "That, I can see!"

"Yes—yes, me too," said Bentham, and the guards concurred. They could all see the liquid, but not the jars that contained and protected it.

One of the guards bent down to graze the blue liquid with his finger. The moment he touched it he cried out and jumped back, flapping his hand to shake the stuff off. If the jar was freezing, I could only imagine how cold the blue stuff was.

"What a waste," Caul said. "I would have liked to combine that with a few other choice souls."

"Aswindan," Bentham recited. "Root word *swind*. Meaning *shrink*. Be glad you didn't take that one, brother."

Caul frowned. "No. No, I'm certain I was right."

"You're not," said Miss Peregrine.

His gaze darted between them, paranoid, as if he were weighing the possibility they might somehow be in league against him. Then he seemed to let it go. "This is just the first room," he said. "The better souls are deeper in, I'm sure."

"I agree," said Bentham. "The farther we go, the older the

souls will be, and the older the soul, the more powerful."

"Then we shall plumb the very heart of this mountain," said Caul, "and eat it."

*　　*　　*

We were prodded through one of the black doors, pistols at our ribs. The next room was much like the first, with coves combing its walls and doors leading into the dark. There were no windows, though, and just a single blade of afternoon sun slicing down the dusty floor. We were leaving daylight behind us.

Caul ordered Emma to make a flame. He ordered me to inventory the contents of the walls. I duly reported three jars, but my word wasn't enough; he made me tap each one with my fingernail to prove it was there, and pass my hand through dozens of empty coves to prove they were vacant.

Next he made me read them. *Heolstor. Unge-sewen. Meagan-wundor.* The words were meaningless to me, unsatisfactory to him. "The souls of piddling slaves," he complained to Bentham. "If we're to be kings, we need the souls of kings."

"Onward, then," said Bentham.

We plunged into a baffling and seemingly endless maze of caverns, daylight a memory, the floor sloping ever downward. The air grew colder. Passageways branched off into the dark like veins. Caul seemed to navigate by some sixth sense, confidently bounding left or right. He was insane, manifestly insane, and I was sure he was getting us so lost that even if we managed to escape him, we could expect to spend eternity trapped in these caves.

I tried to imagine the battles that had been waged over these souls—ancient, titanic peculiars clashing among the spires and valleys of Abaton—but it was too mind-boggling. All I could think of was how terrifying it would be to be trapped down here without a light.

The farther we went, the more jars were in the walls, as if plunderers had long ago raided the outermost rooms but something had stopped them from getting too far—a healthy sense of self-preservation, maybe. Caul barked at me for updates, but he'd stopped demanding proof of which coves were occupied and which were vacant, and only occasionally made me read a jar's label aloud. He was hunting bigger game and seemed to have decided there was little worth bothering with in this part of the library.

We went on in silence. The rooms grew larger and grander, in their crude way, the ceilings rising and walls widening. The jars were everywhere now: filling every cove, stacked in totemic pillars in the corners, wedged into cracks and crevices, the cold that seeped from them refrigerating the air. Shivering, I pulled my arms close to my body, my breath pluming before me, the watched feeling that had haunted me earlier creeping back. This library, so-called, was a vast underworld, a catacomb and hiding place for the second soul of every peculiar who had ever lived, prior to the last millennium— hundreds of thousands of them. That great accretion of souls had begun to exert a strange pressure on me, compressing the air spaces in my head and lungs as if I were sinking gradually into deep water.

I wasn't the only one feeling out of sorts. Even the guards were skittish, startling at small noises and checking constantly over their shoulders.

"Did you hear that?" mine said.

"The voices?" said the other one.

"No, more like water, rushing water . . . "

While they talked I stole a quick glance at Miss Peregrine. Was she frightened? No—she seemed to be biding her time, waiting and watching. I took some comfort in that, and in the fact that she could have taken bird form and escaped her captors long ago, but hadn't. So long as Emma and I were prisoners, she would be. Maybe that was more than just her protective instinct at work. Maybe she had a plan.

The air grew colder still, a thin sweat on my neck turning steadily to ice water. We trudged through a chamber so littered with jars I had to hopscotch around them to keep from kicking them over—though everyone else's feet passed right through them. I felt suffocated by the dead. It was standing-room only here, the platform of a rush hour train station, Times Square on New Year's Eve, all the revelers slack-faced and staring, unhappy to see us. (I could *feel* this, if not quite see it.) Finally, even Bentham lost his nerve.

"Brother, wait," he said, breathless, holding Caul back. "Don't you suppose we've gone far enough?"

Caul turned slowly to look at him, his face split evenly by shadow and fire-glow. "No, I do not," he said.

"But I'm sure the souls here are sufficiently—"

"We haven't found it yet." His voice sharp, brittle.

"Found what, sir?" my guard ventured.

"I'll know it when I see it!" Caul snapped.

Then he tensed, excited, and ran away into the dark.

"Sir! Wait!" the guards shouted, shoving us after him.

Caul vanished briefly before reappearing at the end of the chamber, illuminated by a shaft of faint blue light. He stood half-rimmed in it, transfixed by something. When we caught up to him and rounded a corner, we saw what it was: a long tunnel shining with azure light. A square opening at the other end was ablaze with it. I could hear something, too, a vague white noise like rushing water.

Caul clapped his hands and whooped. "We're close, by God!"

He skipped down the corridor, manic, and we were forced after him at a stumbling run. When we came to the end, the light that enveloped us was so dazzling that we all staggered to a stop, too blinded to see where we were going.

Emma let her flames die. They weren't needed here. Squinting through my fingers, the space came slowly into view. Bathed in undulating curtains of gauzy blue light, it was the largest cavern we'd seen—a huge, circular space like a beehive, a hundred feet across at the bottom but tapering to a single point at its top, several stories above. Ice crystals gleamed on every surface, in every cove and on every jar—of which there were thousands. They climbed to impossible heights, festooning the walls.

Despite the freeze, there was free-flowing water here: it sprung from a tap shaped like a falcon's head, tumbled into a small channel that circled the room at the base of the walls, and flowed into a shallow pool at the edge of the room. This water was the source of the cavern's heavenly light. Like the stuff inside soul-jars, it glowed a ghostly blue, and it pulsed dimmer and brighter in regular cycles, as if breathing. It might've been oddly soothing, all this, like some Nordic spa experience, if it weren't for the distinct and human sound moaning at us beneath the water's pleasant burble. It was exactly like the moan we'd heard outside—the one I'd dismissed as wind whistling through doors—but there was no wind here, nor any possibility of hearing wind. This was something else.

Bentham hobbled into the cavern behind us, winded and shielding his eyes, while Caul strode to the middle of the room. "VICTORY!" he cried, seeming to enjoy the way his voice ricocheted between the towering walls. "This is it! Our treasure house! Our throne room!"

"It's magnificent," Bentham said weakly, shuffling to join his brother. "I see now why so many were willing to give their lives fighting for it . . . "

"You're making a terrible mistake," Miss Peregrine said. "You mustn't desecrate this sacred place."

Caul sighed dramatically. "Must you spoil every moment with your schoolmarmish moralizing? Or are you simply jealous and mourning the end of your reign as the more-gifted sister? *Look at me, I can fly, I can make time loops!* A generation from now, no one will remember there was ever such a silly creature as an ymbryne!"

"You're wrong!" Emma shouted, no longer able to hold her

tongue. "It's you two who will be forgotten!"

Emma's guard moved to strike her, but Caul told him to leave her be. "Let her speak," he said. "It may be her last opportunity."

"Actually, you won't be forgotten," said Emma. "We'll write a new chapter in the *Tales* about you. The Greedy Brothers, we'll call it. Or the Horrible Awful Traitors Who Got What They Deserved."

"Hmm, a bit flat," Caul said. "I think we'll call it How the Magnificent Brothers Overcame Prejudice to Become the Rightful God-Kings of Peculiardom, or something to that effect. And you're fortunate that I'm in such excellent humor right now, girl."

His attention turned to me. "Boy! Tell me about the jars here, and skip no detail, however small." He demanded an exhaustive description, which I gave, reading aloud many dozens of their spidery, hand-scripted labels. If only I spoke Old Peculiar, I thought, I could've lied about what was written on them, maybe tricked Caul into taking a soul that was weak and silly. But I was the perfect automaton: blessed with ability but cursed with ignorance. The only thing I could do was try to divert his attention from the most obviously promising jars.

Though most of them were small and plain, a few were large, ornate, and heavy, with hourglass shapes and double handles and gem-toned wings painted on their surfaces; it seemed clear they contained the souls of powerful and important (or self-important) peculiars. The larger size of their coves was a giveaway, though, and when Caul made me rap on them with my knuckle, they rang deep and loud.

I had no tricks left. Caul would get what he wanted, and there was nothing I could do about it. But then he did something that surprised everyone. Something that seemed, at first, bizarrely generous. He turned to his guards and said, "Now! Who would like first crack at this?"

The guards looked at each other, confused.

"What do you mean?" said Bentham, hobbling toward him in

alarm. "Shouldn't it be you and I? We've worked so long . . . "

"Don't be greedy, brother. Didn't I tell them their loyalty would be repaid?" He looked again to the guards, grinning like a game show host. "So which of you will it be?"

Both of their hands shot up.

"Me, sir, me!"

"I'd like to!"

Caul pointed to the wight who'd been guarding me. "You!" he said. "I like your spirit. Get over here!"

"Thank you, sir, thank you!"

Caul pointed his gun at me, thus relieving my guard of his duty. "Now, which of those souls sounds like your cup of tea?" He remembered where I'd identified certain jars and began to point them out. "*Yeth-Faru*. Something to do with water, flooding. Good one if you've ever fancied a life under the sea. *Wolsenwyrsend*. I believe that's a sort of centaurish half-horse, half-man creature who controls clouds? Ben, sound familiar?"

Bentham mumbled something in reply, but Caul was hardly listening.

"*Styl-hyde*, that was a good one. Metal skin. Could be useful in a fight, though I wonder if you'd have to oil yourself . . . "

"Sir, I hope you don't mind my asking," the guard said meekly, "but what about one of the larger urns?"

Caul wagged his finger. "I like a man with ambition, but those are for my brother and me."

"Of course, sir, of course," the guard said. "Then . . . um . . . were there any others?"

"I gave you the best options," said Caul, his tone edging toward warning. "Now *choose*."

"Yes, yes, sorry, sir . . . " The guard looked anguished. "I choose *Yeth-faru*."

"Excellent!" Caul boomed. "Boy, retrieve the jar."

I reached into the cove Caul indicated and removed the jar. It was so cold, I pulled the cuff of my jacket over my hand like a glove, but even through the fabric it felt like the jar was stealing all the warmth left in my body.

The guard stared at my hand. "What do I do with it?" he said. "Take it like ambrosia?"

"I'm not certain," Caul said. "What do you think, brother?"

"I'm not sure, either," said Bentham. "It's not mentioned in any of the old texts."

Caul scratched his chin. "I think . . . yes, I think you should take it like ambrosia." He nodded, suddenly sure of himself. "Yes, that's the ticket. Just like ambro."

"Are you sure?" asked the guard.

"Absolutely one hundred percent sure," said Caul. "Don't be nervous. You'll go down in history for this. A pioneer!"

The guard locked eyes on me. "No tricks," he said.

"No tricks," I said.

I uncorked the jar. Blue light shone out of it. The guard put his hand around mine, guided it and the jar above his head, and tilted back his face.

He took a long, shuddering breath. "Here goes nothing," he muttered, and tipped my hand.

The liquid poured from the jar in a viscous stream. The instant it reached his eyes, his hand clenched so tight around mine that I thought my fingers would break. I wrenched free and leapt backward, and the jar fell to the ground and smashed.

The guard's face was smoking and turning blue. He screamed and fell to his knees, his body shuddering, and then he pitched forward. When his head smacked the ground, it shattered like glass. Bits of frozen skull shot out around my feet. And then he was silent—and very, very dead.

"Oh, my God!" cried Bentham.

Caul clucked his tongue as if someone had spilled a glass of expensive wine. "Well, drat," he said. "I guess it's not like taking ambrosia after all." His gaze roved around the room. "Well, now someone else has got to try it . . . "

"I'm quite busy, milord!" cried the other guard, who had his gun trained on both Emma and Miss Peregrine.

"Yes, I can see you've got your hands full there, Jones. Perhaps one of our guests, then?" He looked at Emma. "Girl, do this for me and I'll make you my court jester!"

"Go to hell," Emma snarled.

"That can be arranged," he snarled back.

Then there was a loud hiss and a brightening of light at one edge of the room, and everyone turned to look. The liquid from the broken jar was dripping into the channel by the wall, and where the water and blue liquid had mixed, a reaction was taking place. The water bubbled and churned, glowing brighter than ever.

Caul was gleeful. "Look at this!" he exclaimed, bobbing on the balls of his feet.

The quickly flowing channel pushed the bright, bubbling water around the edges of the room. We turned, watching it go, until it reached the shallow, stone-rimmed pool at the far end of the room—and then the pool itself began to churn and glow, a column of strong blue light rising from it all the way to the ceiling.

"I know what this is!" Bentham said, his voice trembling. "It's called a spirit pool. An ancient means of summoning and communicating with the dead."

Hovering above the pool's surface in the column of light was a ghostly white vapor, and it was coalescing, slowly, into the form of a man.

"But if a living person enters the pool during the summoning . . . "

"He absorbs the spirit being summoned," Caul said. "I do believe we've found our answer!"

The spirit hovered, motionless. It was dressed in a simple tunic that revealed scaly skin and a dorsal fin that jutted from his back.

This was the soul of the *Yeth-faru*, the merman chosen by the guard. The column of light seemed a sort of prison from which it could not escape.

"Well?" Bentham said, gesturing at the pool. "Are you going?"

"I'm not interested in another man's leftovers," Caul said. "I want *that* one." He pointed to the jar I'd rung for him earlier, the largest of them all. "Tip it into the water, boy." He pointed his gun at my head. *"Now."*

I did as I was told. Reaching into the oversized cove, I took the urn by both handles and tipped it toward me—carefully, lest it splatter and ruin my face.

Bright blue liquid ran down the wall into the channel. The water went crazy, hissing and bubbling, the light it produced so bright that I had to squint. As the urn's liquid flowed around the room toward the spirit pool, my eyes darted to Miss Peregrine and Emma. This was our last chance to stop Caul, and there was only one guard left—but he wasn't taking his eyes or his gun off the women, and Caul still had his pistol aimed squarely at my head. It seemed we were still at their mercy.

The great urn's liquid reached the spirit pool. The pool frothed and heaved as if a sea creature was about to break the surface. The column of light rising from it grew brighter still, and *Yeth-faru* evaporated into nothing.

A new vapor began to coalesce, much larger than the one it replaced. If this was taking the shape of a man, it was a giant one, twice as tall as any of us, its chest twice as broad. Its hands were claws, and they were raised, palms upturned, in a way that implied great and terrible power.

Caul looked at the thing and smiled. "And that, as they say, is my cue." He reached into his cloak with his free hand, pulled out a folded piece of paper, and shook it open. "I just have a word or two I'd like to say first, before I officially change stations in life."

Bentham hobbled toward him. "Brother, I think we'd better

not dally any longer . . . "

"I don't believe it!" Caul shouted. "Will no one allow me a moment to glory in all this?"

"*Listen!*" Bentham hissed.

We listened. For a moment I heard nothing, but then, distantly, there came a high, sharp sound. I saw Emma tense and her eyes widen.

Caul scowled. "Is that . . . a *dog*?"

Yes! A dog! It was the bark of a dog, far away and lost in echoes.

"The peculiars had a dog with them," Bentham said. "If it's following our scent, I doubt it's alone."

Which could mean only one thing: our friends had overpowered their guards, and led by Addison, they were coming after us. Yes—the damned *cavalry* was coming! But Caul was moments from taking power, and who knew how far echoes traveled in these caverns. They could still be minutes away, and by then it would be too late.

"Well, then," Caul said, "I suppose my remarks will have to wait." He tucked the paper back into his pocket. He seemed in no particular hurry, and it was driving Bentham mad.

"Go, Jack! Take your spirit and then I'll take mine!"

Caul sighed. "About that. You know, I've been thinking: I'm not sure you could handle all this power. You're weak-minded, see. By which I don't mean unintelligent. On the contrary, you're more intelligent than I am! But you *think* like a weak person. Your *will* is weak. It isn't enough to be smart, you know. You've got to be vicious!"

"No, brother! Don't do this!" Bentham begged. "I'll be your number two, your loyal confidant . . . anything you need me to be . . . "

Serves you right, I thought. *Keep talking . . .*

"This groveling is precisely what I mean," said Caul, shaking his head. "It's the sort of thing that could only change the mind of a weak-willed person, like yourself. But I am not susceptible to emotional entreaties."

"No, this is about revenge," Bentham said bitterly. "As if breaking my legs and enslaving me for years wasn't enough."

"Oh, it was, though," Caul said. "True, I was cross with you for turning us all into hollowgast, but having an army of monsters at my disposal turned out to be quite useful. But if I'm being honest, it's not even about your weak character. It's just . . . it's my own failing as a brother, I suppose. Alma can speak to this. I don't like to share."

"Then do it!" Bentham spat. "Get it over with and shoot me!"

"I could do that," Caul said. "But I think it would be more effective if I shot . . . him."

And he aimed the gun at my chest and pulled the trigger.

* * *

I felt the impact of the bullet almost before I heard the gun roar. It was like being walloped by giant, invisible fists. I was knocked off my feet and thrown backward, and then everything became abstract. I was looking up at the ceiling, my vision tunneled to a pinhole. Someone was screaming my name. Another gun fired, then fired again.

More screams.

I was dimly aware that my body was experiencing a great deal of pain. That I was dying.

Then Emma and Miss Peregrine were kneeling over me, anguished, shouting, the guard out of the picture. I couldn't understand their words, as if my ears were underwater. They were trying to move me, to drag me by the shoulders toward the door, but my body was limp and heavy. Then came a howl like hurricane winds from the direction of the spirit pool, and despite unbearable pain, I managed to turn my head and look.

Caul was standing calf-deep in the pool, his arms outstretched and head tilted back, in a state of paralysis as the vapor gripped him, merged with him. It poured into every opening in his face—tendrils of it sliding down his throat, ropes of it reeling up his nose, clouds of it settling into his eyes and ears. Then, in a matter of seconds, it was gone, the blue light that had shone throughout the cavern dimming to half strength, as if Caul had soaked up its power.

I could hear Miss Peregrine shouting. Emma picked up one of the guards' guns and emptied it at Caul. He wasn't far and she was a good shot. She must have hit him, but Caul didn't so much as flinch. Rather than falling, he seemed to be doing the opposite—he was *growing*. He was growing very quickly, doubling in height and breadth in just a few seconds. He let out an animal scream as his skin split open and healed, split open and healed. Soon he was a tower of raw pink flesh and tattered clothes, his giant eyes electric blue, a stolen soul having finally filled the old blankness he'd nurtured so long. Worst of all were his hands. They had become huge, gnarled things, thick and twisted like tree roots, ten fingers each.

Emma and Miss Peregrine tried again to drag me toward the door, but now Caul was coming after us. He stomped out of the spirit pool and bellowed in a bone-rattling voice: *"ALMA, COME BACK HERE!"*

Caul raised his awful hands. Some unseen force ripped Miss Peregrine and Emma away from me. They were pulled into the air and hovered there, flailing, ten feet off the ground, until Caul flipped his palms down again. Quick as a bounced ball, they slammed back to earth.

"I'LL GRIND YOU BETWEEN MY TEETH!" Caul howled, starting across the cavern toward them, his every footfall an earthquake.

Adrenaline, it seemed, had begun to focus my vision and hearing. I could imagine no crueler death sentence than this: to spend my last moments watching the women I loved be torn apart. And then

I heard a dog bark, and something worse occurred to me: watching my friends die, too.

Emma and Miss Peregrine ran. They had no choice. To come back for me now was impossible.

The others began pouring out of the corridor. Kids and ymbrynes, all mixed up. Sharon and the gallows riggers, too. Addison must have led them here, as he led all of them now, a lantern dangling from his mouth.

They had no idea what they were up against. I wished I could warn them—*don't bother fighting it, just run*—but they wouldn't have listened to me. They saw the towering beast and threw all they had at it. The gallows men pitched their hammers. Bronwyn hurled a chunk of wall she'd carried in, winding back and letting it go like a shot-put. Some of the kids had guns they'd taken from the wights, which they fired at Caul. The ymbrynes transformed into birds and swarmed his head, pecking him wherever they could.

None of it had the slightest effect on him. The bullets bounced off. He batted away the chunk of wall. He caught the hammers between his giant teeth and spat them out. Like a swarm of gnats, the ymbrynes seemed merely to irritate him. And then he spread his arms and his knotty fingers, the little feeder roots that dangled from them dancing like live wires, and slowly brought his palms together. As he did, all the ymbrynes circling his head were pushed away, and all the peculiars were smashed together in a clump.

He brought his palms together and folded them over and over as if crumpling a piece of paper. The ymbrynes and the peculiars rose from the ground in a spherical crush of limbs and wings. I was the only one left alone (except Bentham—where was Bentham?) and I tried to get up, to stand and do something, but I could only lift my head. My God, they were being pulverized, their terrified screams echoing off the walls—and I thought that was it, that in a moment blood would pour from them like juice from a squeezed fruit, but then one of Caul's hands flew up and began to flap in front of his face, waving something away.

It was bees. A stream of Hugh's bees had flown out of the crush and now they were in Caul's eyes, stinging him as he let out a shattering howl. The ymbrynes and peculiars fell to the ground, the ball they'd formed collapsing, bodies spilling out everywhere. They hadn't been crushed, thank God.

Miss Peregrine, screeching and flapping in bird form, pulled people to their feet and propelled them toward the corridor. *Run. Run. Go!*

Then she winged off for Caul. He had dealt with the bees and was again spreading his arms, ready to scoop everyone up and splatter them against a wall. Before he could, Miss Peregrine dive-bombed him with her talons and raked deep cuts across his face. He spun to take a lumbering swipe at her, smacking her so hard she flew across the room, bounced off the wall, and fell to the ground, where she lay motionless.

By the time he turned back to deal with the others, they had nearly disappeared into the corridor. Caul extended his palm toward them, closed his hand and scooped it back—but they were farther away, apparently, than his powers of telekinesis would reach. Bellowing in frustration, he ran after them, then flopped onto his belly and tried to wriggle into the corridor after them. He could just fit inside, though it was a tight squeeze.

That's when, finally, I saw Bentham. He had rolled into the channel of water to hide, and now he was climbing out again, soaking wet but otherwise unaffected. He was bent over, his back to me, working at something—I couldn't see what.

I felt like I was coming back to life. The pain in my chest was receding. I tried to move my arms—an experiment—and found that I could. I slid them up my body and over my chest, expecting to find a couple of holes and a lot of blood. But I was dry. Instead of holes, my hands found a piece of metal flattened like a coin. I closed my hands around it, picked it up to look.

It was a bullet. It had not pierced my body. I was not dying. The bullet had embedded itself in my scarf.

The scarf Horace had knit for me.

He had known, somehow, that this would happen and had made me this scarf from the wool of peculiar sheep. Thank God for Horace . . .

I saw something flash across the room and lifted my head—I could just do it—to see Bentham standing with his eyes ablaze, cones of hot white light beaming from his sockets. He dropped something and I heard a tinkle of glass.

He'd taken a vial of ambro.

I used all my strength to turn onto my side, then curled and began to sit up. Bentham hurried along the walls, looking up at the jars. He was studying each one carefully.

As if he could see them.

And then I realized what he'd done, what he'd taken. He'd been saving my grandfather's stolen soul all these years, and now he'd consumed it.

He *could* see the jars. He could do what I did.

I was on my knees. Palms to the ground. Pulled one foot under me, then pushed myself up to standing. I was back, risen from the dead.

By then Caul had wriggled into the corridor and was halfway down it. I could hear my friends' voices echoing from the other end. They hadn't escaped yet. Perhaps they refused to leave Miss Peregrine behind (or me, possibly). They were still fighting.

Bentham was running now, as best he could. He'd spied the other large urn and was heading right for it. I took a few limping steps toward him. He reached the urn and tipped it over. Its blue liquid hissed into the channel and began circulating toward the spirit pool.

He turned and saw me.

He limped for the pool and I limped for him. The urn's liquid reached the pool. Its water began to rage and a column of blinding light shot up toward the ceiling.

"WHO IS TAKING MY SOULS!" Caul bellowed from the corridor. He began to worm his way back into the chamber.

I tackled Bentham—or fell on him, whichever you prefer. I was weak and dizzy, and he was old and brittle, and we were just about a match for each other. We struggled briefly, and when it was clear I had him pinned, he gave up.

"Listen to me," he said. "I've got to do this. I'm the only hope you have."

"Shut up!" I said, grabbing at his hands, which were still flailing. "I won't listen to your lies."

"He'll kill us all if you don't let me go!"

"Are you insane? If I let you go, you'll just help him!" I grabbed his wrists, finally. He'd been trying to get something from his pocket.

"No, I won't!" he cried. "I've made so many mistakes . . . but I can put them right if you let me help you."

"*Help* me?"

"Look in my pocket!"

Caul was backing slowly out of corridor, roaring about his souls.

"My vest pocket!" Bentham shouted. "There's a paper in it. One I carry with me always, just in case."

I let go of one of his hands and reached into his pocket. I found a small piece of folded paper, which I tore open.

"What is this?" I said. It was written in Old Peculiar; I couldn't read it.

"It's a recipe. Show it to the ymrbynes. They'll know what to do."

A hand reached over my shoulder and snatched the paper from me. I spun around to see Miss Peregrine, battered but human.

She read the paper. Her eyes flashed at Bentham. "You're certain this will work?"

"It worked once," he said. "I don't see why it shouldn't again. And with even more ymbrynes . . . "

"Let him go," she said to me.

I was shocked. "What? But he's going to—"

She put a hand on my shoulder. "I know."

"He stole my grandfather's soul! He's taken it . . . it's in him, right now!"

"I know, Jacob." She looked down at me, her face kind but firm. "That's all true and worse. And it was a good thing you caught him. But now you must let him go."

So I released his hand. Stood up, with help from Miss Peregrine. And then Bentham stood, too, a sad, bent-backed old man with the starry black drippings of my grandfather's soul running down his cheeks. For a moment I thought I could see a flash of Abe in his eyes—a little of his spirit there, sparking back at me.

Bentham turned and ran for the column of light and the spirit pool. The vapor was gathering into the shape of a giant almost as large as Caul, but with wings. If Bentham reached the pool in time, Caul would have a worthy challenger.

Caul was nearly out of the corridor now, and he was raging mad. "WHAT HAVE YOU DONE!" he cried. "I'LL KILL YOU!"

Miss Peregrine pushed me flat to the ground and lay beside me. "There's no time to hide," she said. "Play dead."

Bentham stumbled into the pool, and immediately the vapor began funneling into him. Caul had finally wriggled out of the corridor and lurched heavily to his feet, then ran toward Bentham. We were nearly crushed as one of his enormous feet crashed down not far from our heads, but Caul arrived at the pool too late to stop Bentham from merging with whatever old, great soul had been in that urn. Miss Peregrine's younger, weaker brother was already rocketing up to twice his original height.

Miss Peregrine and I helped each other up. Behind us, Caul and Bentham began to clash, the sound erupting like bombs. No one had to tell me to run.

We were halfway to the corridor when Emma and Bronwyn sped out of it to meet us. They caught us by the arms and whisked us toward safety faster than our weak and battered bodies could've managed alone. We didn't speak—there was no time to do anything but run, no way to shout loud enough to be heard—but Emma's face, electrified with wonder and relief at the simple fact that I was alive, said it all.

The black tunnel enveloped us. We'd made it. I looked back just once, to catch a glimpse of the riot exploding behind us. Through clouds of dust and vapor I saw two creatures, taller than houses, trying to murder each other: Caul choking Bentham with one spiky hand, gouging his eyes with the other. Bentham, insect-headed, thousands of eyes to spare, feeding on Caul's neck with long, flexible mandibles and battering him with great leathery wings. They danced, a tangle of limbs, slamming together into walls, the room coming down around them, the contents of countless shattered soul jars flying, a luminous rain.

With that preview of my nightmares thus cemented in my brain, I let Emma pull me into the dark.

*　　*　　*

We found our friends in the next chamber, swallowed by the dark, their only light a fading gleam from the lantern in Addison's mouth. When Emma fired a flame and they saw us loping toward them, worse for wear but alive, they let out a great whooping cheer. I saw them in her light and winced. They were in rough shape themselves, bloodied and bruised from being slammed around by Caul, a few limping on sprained or broken legs.

There was a momentary lull in the blasting noises coming from the cavern, and Emma was finally able to hug me. "I saw him shoot you! By what miracle are you alive?"

"By the miracle of peculiar sheep's wool and Horace's dreams!" I said, and then I kissed Emma and broke away to find Horace in the crowd. When I did, I hugged him so hard his patent leather shoes lifted off the ground. "I hope one day I'll be able to repay you for this," I said, tugging on my scarf.

"I'm so glad it helped!" he said, beaming at me.

The destruction resumed, the sound immense, unbelievable. Rocky debris rolled out of the corridor at us. Even if Caul and Bentham couldn't reach us from where they were, they could still bring the whole place crashing down on our heads. We had to get out of the library—and then out of this *loop*.

We ran, scraping and hobbling back the way we'd come, half of us a limping mess, the others acting as human crutches. Addison guided us with his nose, back through the maze and out the way we'd come. The sound of Caul and Bentham's battle seemed to pursue us, growing louder even as we got farther away, as if they were growing. How big could they get, and how strong? Perhaps the souls from all the jars they'd broken were raining into the pool, feeding them, making them even more monstrous.

Would the Library of Souls bury them? Would it be their grave, their prison? Or would it crack open like an eggshell and birth these horrors into the world?

We reached the grotto exit and dashed once again into the orange daylight. The rumble behind us had become constant, a quake that reverberated through the hills.

"We must keep going!" Miss Peregrine shouted. "To the loop exit!"

We were halfway there, stumbling through a clearing, when the ground beneath us shook so violently that we were all thrown off our feet. I'd never heard a volcano erupt in person, but it couldn't have sounded much scarier than the thunderous boom that echoed from the low hills behind us. We turned in shock to see acres of pulverized rock flying into the air—and then we heard, clear as day, the screams of Bentham and Caul.

They were free of the library now. They had torn through the cavern ceiling, and untold depths of stone, to daylight.

"We can't wait any longer!" Miss Peregrine cried. She picked herself up and held aloft Bentham's crumple of paper. "Sisters, it's time to close this loop!"

That's when I realized what it was he'd given us, and why Miss Peregrine had let him go. *A recipe*, he'd called it. *It worked once . . .*

It was the procedure he'd tricked Caul and his followers into enacting, all those years ago in 1908. The one that had collapsed the loop they were in, rather than resetting their internal clocks as they'd hoped. This time the collapse would be intentional. There was only one problem . . .

"Won't that turn them into hollows?" asked Miss Wren.

"A hollow's no problem," I said, "but last time someone collapsed a loop this way, didn't it make an explosion big enough to flatten half of Siberia?"

"The ymbrynes my brother coerced into helping him were young and inexperienced," Miss Peregrine said. "We'll do a better job."

"We'd better," said Miss Wren.

Over the hill, a giant face rose like a second sun peeking over the horizon. It was Caul, large as ten houses now. In a terrible voice that trumpeted across the hills, he bellowed, "*ALMAAAAAAAAA!*"

"He's coming for you, miss!" Olive cried. "We must get to safety!"

"In a moment, dear."

Miss Peregrine shooed all of us peculiar children (and Sharon and his cousins) a good distance away, then gathered the ymbrynes around her. They looked like some mystical secret society about to enact an ancient ritual. Which, I suppose, they were. Reading from the paper, Miss Peregrine said, "According to this, once we start the reaction, we'll have only a minute to escape the loop."

"Will that be enough time?" said Miss Avocet.

"It'll have to be," said Miss Wren grimly.

"Perhaps we should get closer to the exit before we try," suggested Miss Glassbill, who had just recently come to her senses.

"There isn't time," said Miss Peregrine. "We have to—"

The rest of her sentence was drowned out by a distant-but-thunderous shout from Caul, his words gibberish now, his mind likely melting from the extraordinary stress of rapid growth. His breath reached us a few seconds after his voice, a foul yellow wind that curdled the air.

Bentham hadn't been heard from in a few minutes. I wondered if he'd been killed.

"Wish your elders luck!" Miss Peregrine shouted to us.

"Good luck!" we all cried.

"Don't blow us up!" Enoch added.

Miss Peregrine turned to her sisters. The twelve ymbrynes formed a tight circle and joined hands. Miss Peregrine spoke in Old Peculiar. The others replied in unison, all their voices rising in an eerie, lilting song. This went on for thirty seconds or more, during which time Caul started to climb out of the cavern, rubble tumbling down the hills where his massive hands grasped for purchase.

"Well, this is fascinating," Sharon said, "and you're all free to stay and watch, but I think my cousins and I will be going." He began to walk away, then saw that the path ahead split five ways, and the hard ground had captured none of our footprints. "Um," he said, turning back, "does anyone happen to remember the way?"

"You'll have to wait," Addison growled. "No one leaves until the ymbrynes do."

Finally they unclasped their hands and broke their circle.

"That's it?" Emma said.

"That's it!" Miss Peregrine replied, hurrying toward us. "Let's be on our way. We don't want to be here fifty-four seconds from now!"

Where the ymbrynes had been standing a crack was splitting open in the ground, the clay falling away into a quickly widening sinkhole from which a loud, almost mechanical buzz issued forth. The collapse had begun.

In spite of exhaustion and broken bodies and faltering steps, we ran, pushed faster by terror and awful, apocalyptic noises—and by the giant, lumbering shadow that fell across our path. We ran over ground that was splitting open, down ancient stairways that crumbled beneath our feet, back into the first house we'd exited from, choked with red dust from pulverizing walls, and finally into the passageway that led back to Caul's tower.

Miss Peregrine herded us through, the passageway disintegrating around us, and then out the other side, into the tower. I looked back to see the passage cave in behind us, a giant fist smashing down through its roof.

Miss Peregrine, frantic: "Where's the door gone? We must close it, or the collapse may spread beyond this loop!"

"Bronwyn kicked it in!" Enoch tattled. "It's broken!"

She'd been the first to reach it and, for Brownyn, kicking down the door had been faster than turning its knob. "I'm sorry!" she cried. "Have I doomed us all?"

The loop's shaking had begun to spread to the tower. It swayed, spilling us from one side of the hall to the other.

"Not if we can escape the tower," Miss Peregrine said.

"We're too high!" cried Miss Wren. "We'll never make it to the bottom in time!"

"There's an open deck just above us," I said. Though I wasn't sure why I said it, because leaping to our deaths seemed no better than being crushed in a collapsing tower.

"Yes!" cried Olive. "We'll jump!"

"Absolutely not!" Miss Wren said. "We ymbrynes would be just fine, but you children . . . "

"I can float us!" Olive said. "I'm strong enough!"

"No way!" Enoch said. "You're tiny, and there are too many of us!"

The tower rocked sickeningly. Ceiling tiles crashed down around us and cracks spidered through the floor.

"Fine, then!" Olive said. "Stay behind!"

She started upstairs. It took the rest of us only a moment, and one more wobble of the tower, to decide that Olive was our only hope.

Our lives were now in the dainty hands of our smallest member. Bird help us.

We ran up the sloping hallway, then out into open air and what remained of the day. Below us spread a commanding view of Devil's Acre: the compound and its pale walls, the misty chasm and its hollow-gapped bridge, the black tinders of Smoking Street and the packed tenements beyond—and then the Ditch, snaking along the loop's edge like a ring of scum. Whatever happened next, whether we lived or died, I'd be happy at least to see the last of this place.

We bellied up to the circular railing. Emma gripped my hand. "Don't look down, eh?"

One by one the ymbrynes turned to birds and perched on the rail, ready to help however they could. Olive took hold of the railing with both hands and slipped out of her shoes. Her feet bobbed upward until she was doing a weightless headstand on the rail, her heels aimed at the sky.

"Bronwyn, take my feet!" she said. "We'll make a chain. Emma grabs Bronwyn's legs, and Jacob Emma's legs, and Horace Emma's, and Horace Hugh's . . . "

"My left leg's hurt!" Hugh said.

"Then Horace will grab your right one!" Olive said.

"This is madness!" said Sharon. "We'll be much too heavy!"

Olive started to argue, but a sudden tremor shook the tower so hard that we had to cling to the rail or be shaken off.

It was Olive's way or nothing.

"You get the idea!" Miss Peregrine shouted. "Do as Olive says and, most importantly, don't let go until we reach the ground!"

Little Olive bent her knees, kicked one foot down toward Bronwyn, and offered it to her. Bronwyn took Olive's foot, then reached up and grabbed the other one. Olive let go of the rail and stood up in Bronwyn's hands, pushing toward the sky like a swimmer kicking off the wall of a pool.

Bronwyn was lifted off her feet. Emma quickly grabbed hold of Bronwyn's legs, and then she was lifted, too, as Olive strained upward, gritting her teeth, willing herself higher. Then it was my turn—but Olive, it seemed, was running out of lift power. She struggled and groaned, dog-paddling toward the sky, but she was out of juice. That's when Miss Peregrine turned into a bird, flapped into the air, hooked her talons through the back of Olive's dress, and lifted.

My feet came off the ground. Hugh grabbed onto my legs and Horace onto his legs and Enoch onto his and so on, until even Perplexus and Addison and Sharon and his cousins had caught a ride. We strung out into the air like a strange, wiggling kite, Millard its invisible tail. The other, smaller ymbrynes hooked into our clothes here and there and flapped furiously, adding what lift they could.

The last of us had only just left the tower when the whole thing began to crumble. I looked down in time to see it fall. It happened quickly, tumbling in on itself, the top section seeming to implode as if it had been sucked into the collapsing loop. After that the rest just went, tipping over in one section before breaking in the middle and slumping into a huge cloud of dust and debris, the sound like a million bricks being poured into a quarry. By then Miss Peregrine's strength was flagging and we were falling slowly toward the ground, the ymbrynes pulling us hard to one side for a soft landing away from the wreckage.

We touched down in the courtyard, Millard first and then finally Olive, who was so spent that she landed on her back and stayed there, breathing like she'd just run a marathon. We gathered around, cheering and applauding her.

Her eyes got big and she pointed up. "Look!"

In the air behind us, where the top of the tower had been just moments before, there spun a small vortex of shimmering silver, like a miniature hurricane. It was the last of the collapsing loop. We watched hypnotized as it shrank, spinning faster and faster. When it became too small to see, there issued from it a sound like the crack of a sonic boom:

"ALMAAAAAAAAAA . . . "

And then the whirlwind winked out, sucking Caul's voice away with it.

CHAPTER TEN

After the loop collapsed and the tower fell, we weren't allowed to stand shell-shocked and gaping—at least not for long. Though it seemed the worst dangers were behind us and most of our enemies had been felled or captured, there was chaos all around and work to be done. Despite our exhaustion and bruises and sprains, the ymbrynes set about doing what ymbrynes do best, which was to create order. They changed into human form and took charge. The compound was searched for hidden wights. Two surrendered outright, and Addison discovered another—a miserable-looking woman hiding in a hole in the ground.

She came out with her arms raised, begging for mercy. Sharon's cousins were employed constructing a makeshift jail to hold our small but growing number of prisoners, and they set happily to work, singing while they hammered. Sharon was interrogated by Miss Peregrine and Miss Avocet, but after just a few minutes of questioning, they were satisfied that he was merely a mercenary, not a secret operative or a traitor. Sharon had seemed as shocked by Bentham's betrayal as the rest of us.

In short order the wights' prisons and laboratories were emptied and their machines of terror smashed. The subjects of their horrible experiments were brought out into the open and attended to. Dozens more were freed from another block of cells. They emerged from the underground building where they'd been held looking thin and ragged. Some wandered in a daze and had to be corralled and watched, lest they walk away and get lost. Others were so over-

whelmed by gratitude that they couldn't stop thanking us. One small girl spent half an hour going from one peculiar to another, surprising us with hugs. "You don't know what you did for us," she kept saying. "You don't know what you did."

It was impossible not to be affected by it, and as we gave them what comfort we could, we were beset by sniffles and sighs. I could not begin to imagine what my friends had been through, much less those who'd spent weeks or months in Caul's keeping. Compared to that, my bruises and traumas were inconsequential.

The rescued peculiars I'll remember most were three brothers. They seemed in fair health but were so shocked by what they'd experienced that they would not speak. At the first opportunity they retreated from the crowd, found a bit of rubble to hunker on, and stared hollowly around them, the oldest with his arms stretched around the younger two. As if they could not quite square the scene before them with the hell they had accepted as reality.

Emma and I crossed to where they were sitting. "You're safe now," she said gently.

They looked at her as if they didn't know the meaning of the word.

Enoch saw us talking to them and came over with Bronwyn. She was dragging a barely conscious wight behind her, a white-coated lab worker with his hands tied. The boys recoiled.

"He can't hurt you anymore," Bronwyn said. "None of them can."

"Maybe we should leave him here with you awhile," said Enoch with a devilish grin. "I'll bet you'd have a lot to talk about."

The wight lifted his head. When he saw the boys, his blackened eyes widened.

"Stop it," I said. "Don't torment them."

The youngest boy's hands curled into fists and he started to get up, but the oldest boy held him back and whispered something in his ear. The younger boy closed his eyes and nodded, as if putting something away, then tucked his fists tightly under his arms.

"No thank'y," he said in a polite Southern drawl.

"Come on," I said, and we let them be, Bronwyn dragging the wight along behind her.

We milled about the compound, awaiting instructions from the ym-brynes. It was a relief, for once, not to be the ones who decided everything. We felt spent but energized, exhausted beyond belief but charged with the crazy knowledge that we had survived.

There were spontaneous bursts of cheering, laughter, songs. Millard and Bronwyn danced across the scarred ground. Olive and Claire clung to Miss Peregrine, who carried them in her arms as she buzzed around, checking on things. Horace kept pinching himself, suspicious that this was just one of his dreams, some beautiful future that hadn't yet come to be. Hugh wandered off by himself, no doubt missing Fiona, whose absence had left a hole in us all. Millard was busy fretting over his hero, Perplexus, whose rapid aging had stopped when we entered Abaton and, strangely, not yet resumed. But it would, Millard assured us, and now that Caul's tower was destroyed, it was unclear how Perplexus would reach his old loop. (There was Bentham's Panloopticon, of course, but which of its hundred doors was the right one?)

Then there was the matter of Emma and me. We were attached at the hip and yet hardly exchanged a word. We were afraid to talk to each other, I think, because of what we had to talk about.

What would happen next? What would become of us? I knew Emma couldn't leave peculiardom. She would have to live inside a loop for the rest of her life, be it Devil's Acre or some other, better place. But I was free to go. I had family and a home waiting for me. A life, or the pale approximation of one. But I had a family here, too. And I had Emma. And there was this new Jacob I had become, was still becoming. Would he survive back in Florida?

I needed all of it. Both families, both Jacobs—all of Emma. I knew I would have to choose, and I was afraid it would split me in half.

It was all too much, more than I could face so soon after the trials we'd just endured. I needed a few more hours, a day, to pretend. So Emma and I stood shoulder to shoulder and looked outward, throwing ourselves into whatever the ymbrynes needed of us.

The ymbrynes, overly protective by nature, decided we'd been through enough. We needed rest, and besides, there were tasks, they said, that peculiar children had no business taking part in. When the tower fell it had crushed a smaller building beneath it, but they didn't want us combing the wreckage for survivors. Elsewhere in the compound there were ambro vials to be recovered, which they didn't want us going near. I wondered what they'd do with them, or if those stolen souls could ever be reunited with their rightful owners.

I thought about the vial made from my grandfather's soul. I'd felt so violated when Bentham used it—and yet, if he hadn't, we never would have escaped the Library of Souls. So in the end, really, it was my grandfather's soul that had saved us. It was gratifying to know that at least it had not gone to waste.

There was work to be done outside the wights' compound, as well. Along Louche Lane and elsewhere in Devil's Acre, enslaved peculiar children needed to be freed, but the ymbrynes insisted they should be the ones to do it, along with some peculiar adults. As it happened, they would face no resistance: the slavers and other turncoats had fled the Acre the moment the wights fell. The children would be collected and brought to a safe house. The traitors hunted down and brought before tribunals. None of this was our concern, we were told. Right now we needed a place to recuperate, as well as a base of operations from which the reconstruction of peculiardom could begin—and none of us wanted to stay in the wights' fear-haunted fortress any longer than we had to.

I suggested Bentham's house. It had tons of space, beds, facilities, a live-in doctor, and a Panloopticon (which, you never know, might come in handy for something). We moved as dark was falling, loading one of the wights' transport trucks with those of us who couldn't walk, the rest marching behind it. We crossed out of the fortress with a little help from the bridge hollow, which lifted the truck across the gap first and the rest of us in groups of three. Some of the kids were frightened of the hollow and needed coaxing. Others couldn't wait and clamored for another ride once they'd crossed. I indulged them. My control over hollows had become second nature, which was satisfying if slightly bittersweet. Now that hollows were nearly extinct, my peculiar ability seemed obsolete—this manifestation of it, anyway. But I was okay with that. I didn't care about having a showy power; it was just a party trick now. I'd have been much happier if hollows had never existed.

We traveled through Devil's Acre in a slow procession, those of us on foot surrounding the vehicle like a float in a parade, others riding its bumpers and roof. It felt like a victory lap, and the Acre's peculiars flooded out of their homes and hovels to watch us pass by. They had seen the tower fall. They knew things had changed. Many applauded. Some gave salutes. Others lurked in the shadows, ashamed of the role they'd played.

When we arrived at Bentham's house, Mother Dust and Reynaldo met us at the door. We were welcomed warmly and told the house was ours to use as we needed. Mother Dust immediately began treating the injured, showing them to beds, making them comfortable, anointing them with dust. She offered to heal my bruises and the bite wounds across my stomach first, but I told her I could wait. Others were worse off.

I told her how I'd used her finger. How it had saved my life, and the lives of others. She shrugged it off and turned back to her work.

I insisted. "You deserve a medal," I said. "I don't know if peculiars give medals, but if they do I'll make sure you get one."

She seemed taken aback by this somehow, and let out a choking sob before hurrying away.

"Did I say something wrong?" I asked Reynaldo.

"I don't know," he said, concerned, and went after her.

Nim meandered about the house in a daze, unable to believe

what Bentham had done. "There must be some mistake," he kept repeating. "Mr. Bentham would *never* betray us like that."

"Snap out of it!" Emma said to him. "Your boss was a slime-ball."

The truth was a bit more nuanced, I thought, but making an argument for the complexity of Bentham's moral character wasn't going to make me terribly popular. Bentham didn't have to give up that recipe or take on his monstrous brother. He made a choice. In the end he'd damned himself in order to save the rest of us.

"He just needs time," Sharon said of Nim. "It's a lot to process. Bentham had a lot of us fooled."

"Even you?" I said.

"Me especially." He shrugged and shook his head. He seemed conflicted and sad. "He weaned me off ambrosia, pulled me out of addiction, saved my life. There was good in him. I suppose I let that blind me to the bad."

"He must've had *one* confidant," Emma said. "You know, a henchman. An Igor."

"His assistant!" I said. "Has anyone seen him?"

No one had. We searched the house for him, but Bentham's stone-faced right-hand man had disappeared. Miss Peregrine gathered everyone together and asked Emma and me to describe him in detail, in case he returned. "He should be considered dangerous," she said. "If you see him, do not engage. Run and tell an ymbryne."

"Tell an ymbryne," Enoch muttered. "Doesn't she realize that *we* saved *them*?"

Miss Peregrine overheard him. "Yes, Enoch. You were brilliant, all of you. And you've grown up remarkably. But even grown-ups have elders who know better."

"Yes, miss," he said, chastened.

Afterward I asked Miss Peregrine if she thought Bentham had planned to betray us from the beginning.

"My brother was an opportunist above all else," she said. "I think part of him did want to do the right thing, and when he helped you and Miss Bloom, he did so genuinely. But all along he'd been making preparations to betray us, in case that turned out to be advantageous for him. And when I told him where to stuff it, he decided that it was."

"It wasn't your fault, Miss P," said Emma. "After what he did to Abe, I wouldn't have forgiven him, either."

"Still, I could have been kinder." She frowned, her eyes wandering. "Sibling relationships can be complex. I wonder, sometimes, if my own actions had some bearing upon the paths my brothers chose. Could I have been a better sister to them? Perhaps, as a young ymbryne, I was too focused on myself."

I said, "Miss Peregrine, that's"—and then stopped myself from using the word *ridiculous*, because I'd never had a brother or sister, and maybe it wasn't.

*　　*　　*

Later we took Miss Peregrine and some of the ymbrynes down to the basement to show them the heart of Bentham's Panloopticon machine. I could feel my hollow inside the battery chamber, weak but alive. I felt awful for it and asked if I could take it out, but Miss Peregrine said that for now they needed the machine working. Having so many loops accessible under one roof would allow them to spread news of our victory quickly throughout peculiardom, to assess the damage done by the wights and to begin rebuilding.

"I hope you understand, Mr. Portman," said Miss Peregrine.

"I do . . . "

"Jacob has a soft spot for that hollow," Emma said.

"Well," I said, a little embarrassed. "He was my first."

Miss Peregrine looked at me strangely but promised she'd do what she could.

The bite wound across my stomach was becoming too unbearable to ignore, so Emma and I joined the line to see Mother Dust, which snaked out of her makeshift clinic in the kitchen and down the hall. It was amazing to watch person after person hobble in, battered and bruised, nursing a broken toe or a mild concussion—or in Miss Avocet's case, a bullet from Caul's antique pistol lodged in her shoulder—only to stride out a few minutes later looking better than new. In fact, they were looking so good that Miss Peregrine pulled Reynaldo aside and asked him to remind Mother Dust that she was not a renewable resource, and not to waste herself on minor wounds that would heal just fine on their own.

"I tried to tell her myself," he replied, "but she's a perfectionist. She won't listen to me."

So Miss Peregrine went into the kitchen to have a word with Mother Dust in person. She came out again five minutes later looking sheepish, several cuts on her face having disappeared and her arm, which hadn't hung straight since Caul had slammed her into that cavern wall, swinging freely at her side. "What a stubborn woman!" she exclaimed.

When it was my turn to go in and see her, I almost refused treatment—she only had a thumb and forefinger left on her good hand. But she took one look at the zagging, blood-encrusted cuts across my belly and practically shoved me onto the cot they'd set up by the sink. The bite was becoming infected, she told me through Reynaldo. Hollow teeth were crawling with nasty bacteria, and left untreated I would get very sick. So I relented. Mother Dust sprinkled her powder across my torso, and in a few minutes I was feeling much improved.

Before I left, I tried to tell her again how much her sacrifice had meant, and how the piece of herself she'd given to me had saved us. "Really, without that finger, I never would've been able to—"

But she turned away as soon as I started talking, as if the words *thank you* burned her ears.

Reynaldo hurried me out. "I'm sorry, Mother Dust has many

other patients to see."

Emma met me in the hall. "You look marvelous!" she said. "Thank the birds, I was really starting to worry about that bite . . . "

"Be sure and tell her about your ears," I said.

"What?"

"Your *ears*," I said louder, pointing to them. Emma's ears hadn't stopped ringing since the library. Because she'd had to keep her hands aflame to light our way as we escaped, she hadn't been able to block out the terrific noise—which, I worried, had literally been deafening. "Just don't mention the finger!"

"The what?"

"The finger!" I said, holding up my finger. "She's very touchy about it. No pun intended . . . "

"Why?"

I shrugged. "No idea."

Emma went in. Three minutes later she came out snapping her fingers by her ears. "Amazing!" she said. "Clear as a bell."

"Thank goodness," I said. "Shouting is no fun."

"Ha. I mentioned the finger, by the way."

"What! Why?"

"I was curious."

"And?"

"Her hands started shaking. Then she mumbled something Reynaldo wouldn't translate, and he practically chased me out."

We might've pursued it further, I think, if we hadn't been so tired and hungry, and if at that moment the smell of food had not wafted its way past our noses.

"Come and get it!" Miss Wren shouted from down the hall, and the conversation was tabled.

*   *   *

As night fell we gathered to eat in Bentham's library, the only room big enough to hold all of us comfortably. The fire was stoked and a feast donated by grateful locals brought in, roast chicken and potatoes and wild game and fish (which I avoided, on the off chance they might have been caught in the Ditch). We ate and talked and rehashed the adventures of the past few days. Miss Peregrine had heard only a little about our journey from Cairnholm to London, and then across bombed-out London to reach Miss Wren, and wanted to know every last detail. She was a great listener, always laughing at the funny parts and reacting with satisfying gasps to our dramatic flourishes.

"And then the bomb fell right on the hollow and blew it to *smithereens*!" Olive cried, leaping out of her chair as she reenacted the moment. "But we had Miss Wren's peculiar sweaters on, so the shrapnel didn't kill us!"

"Oh my heavens!" Miss Peregrine said. "That was very lucky!"

When our stories had finished, Miss Peregrine sat quietly for a time, studying us with a mixture of sadness and awe. "I'm so very, very proud of you," she said, "and so sorry for all that happened. I can't tell you how much I wish it had been me by your side, and not my deceitful brother."

We observed a moment of silence for Fiona. She wasn't dead, Hugh insisted, but merely lost. The trees had cushioned her fall, he said, and she was probably wandering in the forest somewhere near Miss Wren's menagerie. Or had knocked her head on the way down and forgotten where she came from. Or was hiding . . .

He looked around hopefully at us, but we avoided his eyes.

"I'm sure she'll turn up," Bronwyn assured him.

"Don't give him false hope," Enoch said. "It's cruel."

"You would know about cruel," Bronwyn replied scornfully.

"Let's change the subject," Horace said. "I want to know how the dog rescued Jacob and Emma in the Underground."

Addison hopped gamely onto the table and began to narrate

the story, but he embellished it with so many asides about his own heroism that Emma was forced to take over. Together, she and I told them how we'd found our way to Devil's Acre, and how with Bentham's help we'd mounted our mini-invasion of the wights' compound. Then everyone had questions for me—they wanted to know about the hollows.

"How did you teach yourself their language?" Millard asked.

"What's it like to control one?" asked Hugh. "Do you imagine you're one of them, like I do my bees?"

"Does it tickle?" asked Bronwyn.

"Do you ever wish you could keep one as a pet?" asked Olive.

I answered as best I could but was feeling tongue-tied because it was a hard thing to describe, my connection with the hollows, like piecing together a dream the morning after. I was distracted, too, by the talk Emma and I had been putting off. When I'd finished, I caught Emma's eye and nodded to the door, and we excused ourselves. As we walked away from the table, I could feel the eyes of the room on our backs.

We ducked into a lantern-lit cloakroom cramped with coats, hats, and umbrellas. It was not a spacious or comfortable place, but it was at least private; somewhere we wouldn't be walked in on or overheard. I felt suddenly and irrationally terrified. I had a difficult choice to make, one I had not fully grappled with until now.

We were silent for a moment, facing each other, the room so deadened by fabric that I thought I could hear the beating of our hearts.

"So," Emma said, because of course she would start first. Emma, always direct, never afraid of an awkward moment. "Will you stay?"

I did not know what I would say until the words left my mouth. I was running on autopilot, no filter. "I have to see my parents."

That was unquestionably true. They were hurting and frightened and didn't deserve to be, and I had left them dangling too long.

"Of course," Emma said. "I understand. Of course you do."

A question hung in the air, unasked. *See my parents* had been a half-measure, a non-answer. *See* them, sure. And then what? What would I say to them?

I tried to imagine telling my parents the truth. In that regard, the phone conversation I'd had with my father in the Underground had been a preview of coming attractions. *He's lost it. Our son is insane. Or on drugs. Or maybe not on enough drugs.*

No, the truth wouldn't work. So, what? I would see them, assure them I was alive and well, make up a story about sightseeing in London, then tell them to go home without me? Ha. They would chase me. They'd have cops hiding in the bushes at our meeting place. Men in white coats with Jacob-sized nets. I'd have to run. Telling them the truth would only make things worse. Seeing them only to run away again would torture them more. But the idea of not seeing my parents at all, of never going home again—I couldn't get my mind around it. Because, if I was really being honest with myself, as much as it hurt to think about leaving Emma and my friends and this world, part of me wanted to go home. My parents and their world represented a return to sanity and predictability, something I was longing for after all this madness. I needed to be normal for a while. To catch my breath. Just for a while.

I had repaid my debt to the peculiars and Miss Peregrine. I had become one of them. But I wasn't *only* one of them. I was also my parents' son, and as imperfect as they were, I missed them. I missed home. I even sort of missed my dumb, ordinary life. Of course, I would probably miss Emma more than any of those things. The problem was, I wanted too much. I wanted both lives. Dual citizenship. To be peculiar, and learn everything there was to learn about the peculiar world, and to be with Emma, and explore all the loops Bentham had catalogued in his Panloopticon. But also to do the stupid, ordinary things normal teenagers do, while I could still pass for one. Get my driver's license. Make a friend my own age. Finish high school. Then I'd be eighteen, and I could go anywhere I wanted—or any*when*. I could come back.

Here was the truth, the root and bone of it: I couldn't live the rest of my life in a time loop. I didn't want to be a peculiar child forever. But one day, maybe, I could be a peculiar adult.

Maybe, if I was very careful, there was a way to have it all.

"I don't want to go," I said, "but I think I might need to, for a while."

Emma's expression flattened. "Then go," she said.

I was stung. She hadn't even asked what "a while" meant.

"I'll come visit," I said quickly. "I can come back anytime."

Theoretically, this was true: now that the wight menace had been crushed, there would—bird willing—always be something to come back to. But it was hard to imagine my parents signing off on more trips to the U.K. anytime soon. I was lying to myself—to both of us—and Emma knew it.

"No," she said. "I don't want that."

My heart dropped. "What?" I said quietly. "Why not?"

"Because that's what Abe did. Every few years he'd come back. And every time he was older and I was the same. And then he met someone and got married . . . "

"I wouldn't do that," I said. "I love you."

"I know," she said, turning away. "So did he."

"But we're not . . . it won't be like that with us . . . " I grasped blindly for the right words, but my thoughts were a muddle.

"It would, though. You know I'd go with you if I could, but I can't—I would age forward. So I'd just be waiting for you. Frozen in amber. I can't do that again."

"It wouldn't be long! Just a couple of years. And then I could do what I wanted. I could go to college somewhere. Maybe here in London!"

"Maybe," she said. "Maybe. But now you're making promises you might not be able to keep, and that's how people in love get very badly hurt."

My heart was racing. I felt desperate and pathetic. Screw it, I'd never see my parents again. Fine. But I couldn't lose Emma.

"I wasn't thinking straight," I said. "I didn't mean it. I'll stay."

"No, I think you were being honest," she said. "I think if you stay you won't be happy. And eventually you'll come to resent me for it. And that would be worse."

"No. No, I would never . . . "

But I'd shown my hand, and now it was too late to take it back.

"You should go," she said. "You have a life and a family. This was never supposed to be forever."

I sat down on the floor, then leaned back into the wall of coats and let them swallow me up. For a few long seconds I pretended none of this was happening, that I wasn't here, that my entire world was woolen and black and smelled of mothballs. When I surfaced again to breathe, Emma was sitting cross-legged on the floor beside me.

"I don't want this either," she said. "But I think I understand why it has to be. You have your world to rebuild, and I have mine."

"But it's mine too, now," I said.

"That's true." She thought for a moment, kneading her chin. "That's true, and I very much hope you do come back, because you've become a part of us, and our family won't feel whole without you. But when you do, I think you and I should just be friends."

I thought about that for a moment. Friends. It sounded so pale and lifeless.

"I guess it's better than never talking again."

"I agree," she said. "I don't think I could bear that."

I scooted next to her and put my arm around her waist. I thought she might pull away, but she didn't. After a while, her head tipped onto my shoulder.

We sat like that for a long time.

*   *   *

When Emma and I finally emerged from the cloakroom, most everyone was asleep. The hearth in the library was burned down to embers, the platters overflowing with food reduced to scraps, the room's high ceilings echoing with contented snores and murmurs. Kids and ymbrynes lay draped across couches and curled upon the rug, even though there were plenty of comfortable bedrooms upstairs. Having nearly lost one another, they weren't about to let go again so soon, even if just for the night.

I would leave in the morning. Now that I knew what had to happen between Emma and me, a longer delay would only torment us. Right now, though, we needed sleep. How long had it been since we'd closed our eyes for more than a minute or two? I couldn't remember feeling more exhausted.

We piled some cushions in a corner and fell asleep holding each other. It was our last night together, and I clung tight, my arms locked around her, as if by squeezing hard enough I could lock her into my sense memory. How she felt, how she smelled. The sound of her breathing as it slowed and evened. But sleep pulled me down hard, and it seemed I'd only just closed my eyes when suddenly I was squinting against glaring yellow daylight pouring in from a bank of high windows.

Everyone was awake and milling around the room, talking in whispers so as not to disturb us. We untangled ourselves in a hurry, self-conscious without the privacy of the dark. Before we'd had a chance to compose ourselves, in breezed Miss Peregrine with a pot of coffee and Nim with a tray of mugs. "Good morning, all! I trust you're well-rested, because we've got lots of—"

Miss Peregrine saw us and stopped midsentence, her eyebrows rising.

Emma hid her face. "Oh, *no*."

In the exhaustion and emotion of last night, it hadn't occurred to me that sleeping in the same bed as Emma (even if sleeping is all we did) might offend Miss Peregrine's Victorian sensibilities.

"Mr. Portman, a word." Miss Peregrine set down the coffeepot and crooked a finger at me.

Guess I was taking the rap for this one. I stood up and smoothed my rumpled clothes, color rising in my cheeks. I wasn't ashamed in the least, but it was hard not to feel a little embarrassed.

"Wish me luck," I whispered to Emma.

"Admit nothing!" she whispered back.

I heard giggles as I crossed the room, and someone chanting, "Jacob and Emma, sittin' in a tree . . . y-m-b-r-y-n-e!"

"Oh, grow up, Enoch," said Bronwyn. "You're just jealous."

I followed Miss Peregrine into the hall.

"Nothing happened," I said, "just so you know."

"I'm sure I'm not interested," she said. "You're leaving us to-day, correct?"

"How did you know?"

"I may, strictly speaking, be an elderly woman, but I've still got my wits about me. I know you feel torn between your parents and us, your old home and your new one . . . or what's left of it. You want to strike a balance without choosing sides, and without hurting any of the people you love. But it isn't easy. Or even, necessarily, possible. Is that about the size of it?"

"It's . . . yeah. That's pretty much it."

"And where have you left things with Miss Bloom?"

"We're friends," I said, testing the word uneasily.

"And you're unhappy about it."

"Well, yeah. But I understand . . . I think."

She cocked her head. "Do you?"

"She's protecting herself."

"And you," Miss Peregrine added.

"That I don't get."

"You're very young, Jacob. There are many things you're not

likely to 'get.'"

"I don't see what my age has to do with it."

"Everything!" She laughed, quick and sharp. And then she saw that I really didn't understand, and she softened a bit. "Miss Bloom was born near the turn of the last century," she said. "Her heart is old and steady. Perhaps you worry she'll soon replace you—that some peculiar Romeo will turn her head. I wouldn't count it likely. She's fixed on you. I've never seen her as happy with anyone. Even Abe."

"Really?" I said, a surge of warmth building in my chest.

"Really. But as we've established, you're young. Only sixteen—sixteen for the first time. Your heart is just waking up, and Miss Bloom is your first love. Is she not?"

I nodded sheepishly. But yes, undoubtedly. Anyone could see it.

"You may have other loves," Miss Peregrine said. "Young hearts, like young brains, can have short attention spans."

"I don't," I said. "I'm not like that."

I knew it sounded like something an impulsive teenager would say, but at that moment, I was as sure about Emma as I'd ever been about anything.

Miss Peregrine nodded slowly. "I'm glad to hear that," she said. "Miss Bloom may have given you permission to break her heart, but I have not. She's very important to me, and not half as tough as she lets on. I can't have her mooning about and setting things on fire should you find yourself distracted by the feeble charms of some normal girl. I've been through that already, and we simply haven't the furniture to spare. Do you understand?"

"Um," I said, caught off guard, "I think so . . . "

She stepped closer and said it again, her voice dropping low and stony. "Do you understand?"

"Yes, Miss Peregrine."

She nodded sharply, then smiled and patted my shoulder. "Okay, then. Good talk." And before I could respond she was marching back into the library and calling out, "Breakfast!"

*   *   *

I left an hour later, accompanied to the dock by Emma and Miss Peregrine and a full complement of our friends and ymbrynes. Sharon was waiting with a new boat left behind by fleeing Ditch pirates. There was a long exchange of hugs and tearful goodbyes, which ended with me promising I would come and see everyone again—even though I didn't know how I'd manage that anytime soon, what with international flights to pay for and parents to convince.

"We'll never forget you, Jacob!" Olive said, sniffling.

"I shall record your story for posterity," Millard promised. "That will be my new project. And I'll see that it's included in a new edition of the *Tales of the Peculiar*. You'll be famous!"

Addison approached with the two grimbear cubs trailing him. I couldn't tell if he had adopted them or they him. "You're the fourth-bravest human I've ever known," he said. "I hope we'll meet again."

"I hope so, too," I said, and meant it.

"Oh, Jacob, may we come and visit you?" begged Claire. "I've always wanted to see America."

I didn't have the heart to explain why it wasn't possible. "Of course you can," I said. "I'd love that."

Sharon rapped his staff on the side of the boat. "All aboard!"

Reluctantly I climbed in, and then Emma and Miss Peregrine boarded, too. They had insisted on staying with me until I met my parents, and I hadn't put up a fight. It would be easier to say goodbye in stages.

Sharon unmoored the boat and we pushed off. Our friends waved and called to us as we floated away. I waved back, but it hurt too much to watch them recede, so I half closed my eyes until the current had taken us around a bend in the Ditch, and they were gone.

None of us felt like talking. In silence we watched the sagging buildings and rickety bridges pass. After a while we came to the crossover, were sucked rudely through the same underpass by which we'd entered, and spat out the other side into a muggy, modern afternoon. The crumbling tenements of Devil's Acre were gone, glass-fronted condos and shining office towers risen up in their place. A motorboat buzzed past.

The sounds of a busy, preoccupied present-day filtered in. A car alarm. A cell phone ringing. Jangly pop music. We passed a fancy canal-side restaurant, but thanks to Sharon's enchantment, the diners on the patio didn't see us as we floated by. If they had, I wondered what they would've thought of us: two teenagers in black, a woman in Victorian formalwear, and Sharon in his Grim Reaper cloak, poling us out of the underworld. Who knows—maybe the modern world was so jaded that no one would have batted an eye.

My parents were another story, though—and now that we were back in the present, just what that story would be was starting to concern me. They already thought I'd lost my mind, or gotten into hard drugs. I'd be lucky if they didn't ship me off to a mental hospital. Even if they didn't, I'd be doing damage control for years. They would never trust me again.

But it was my struggle, and I would find a way to deal with it. The easiest thing for *me* would be to tell them the truth—but again, I couldn't. My parents would never understand this part of my life, and to try and force them to could land *them* in a mental hospital.

My dad already knew more about the peculiar children than was good for him. He'd met them all on Cairnholm, though he'd thought he was dreaming. Then Emma had left him that letter and a photo of herself with my grandfather. As if that weren't bad enough, over the phone I'd actually *told* my dad I was peculiar. That had been a mistake, I realized, and selfish. And now here I was heading to meet them with Emma and Miss Peregrine at my side.

"On second thought," I said, turning to them in the boat, "Maybe you shouldn't come with me."

"Why not?" Emma said. "We won't age forward *that* quickly . . ."

"I don't think my parents should see me with you. This is all going to be hard enough to explain as it is."

"I've given some thought to this," said Miss Peregrine.

"To what? My parents?"

"Yes. I can help you with them, if you like."

"How?"

"One of an ymbryne's myriad duties is dealing with normals who become problematically curious about us, or otherwise troublesome. We have ways of making them uncurious, of making them forget they've seen certain things."

"Did you know about this?" I asked Emma.

"Sure. If it wasn't for the wipe, peculiars would be in the news every other day."

"So it . . . wipes people's memories?"

"It's more a selective cherry-picking of certain inconvenient recollections," said Miss Peregrine. "It's quite painless and has no side effects. Still, it may strike you as extreme. I leave it to your discretion."

"Okay," I said.

"Okay what?" said Emma.

"Okay, please do the memory wipe thing to my parents. That sounds amazing. And while you're at it, there was this time when I was twelve that I crashed my mom's car into the garage door . . . "

"Let's not get carried away, Mr. Portman."

"Just kidding," I said, though I'd only sort of been. Either way, I was hugely relieved. Now I wouldn't have to spend the rest of my adolescence apologizing for the time I ran away, made my parents think I was dead, and nearly ruined their lives forever. Which was nice.

CHAPTER ELEVEN

*S*haron dropped us off at the same dark, rat-infested under-jetty where we'd first met him. Stepping off his boat there gave me a twinge of bittersweet nostalgia. I may have been terrified and filthy and in various exotic forms of pain every second of the last several days, but I would probably never have an adventure like this again. I would miss it—not so much the trials I'd endured as the person I'd been while I endured them. There was an iron will inside me, I knew that now, and I hoped I could hang on to it even as my life grew softer.

"So long," Sharon said. "I'm glad I met you, despite all the endless trouble you caused me."

"Yeah, me too." We shook hands. "It's been interesting."

"Wait here for us," Miss Peregrine said to him. "Miss Bloom and I will be back within an hour or two."

Finding my parents turned out to be easy. It would've been even easier if I'd still had my phone, but as it was, all we had to do was report to a police station. I was a known missing person, and within half an hour of giving an officer my name and sitting down on a bench to wait, my mother and father arrived. They were wearing rumpled clothes that had clearly been slept in, my mother's normally perfect makeup was a mess, my dad had a three-day beard, and they were both holding stacks of MISSING posters with my face on them. I felt instantly and comprehensively awful for what I'd put them through. But as I tried to apologize, they dropped the posters and wrapped me in a two-way hug, and my words were lost in the folds of my dad's sweater.

"Jake, Jake, ohmygod, my little Jake," my mother cried.

"It's him, it's really him," my father said. "We were so worried, we were *so* worried . . . "

How long had I been gone? A week? Something like that, though it seemed like an eternity.

"Where *were* you?" my mother said. "What were you *doing*?"

The hug broke but still I couldn't get a word in.

"Why did you run away like that?" my father demanded. "What were you thinking, Jacob?"

"You gave me gray hairs!" my mother said, then threw her arms around me a second time.

My dad looked me over. "Where are your clothes? What's this you're wearing?"

I was still in my black adventure clothes. Oops. They'd be easier to explain than nineteenth-century clothes, though, and thankfully Mother Dust had healed all the cuts on my face . . .

"Jacob, say something!" my father demanded.

"I'm really, really sorry," I said. "I would never have put you through this if I could've helped it, but everything's okay now. Things are going to be fine. You won't understand, and that's okay, too. I love you guys."

"You're right about one thing," my dad said. "We don't understand. At all."

"But it's not okay," said my mom. "You *will* give us an explanation."

"We'll need one, too," said a police officer who'd been standing by. "And a drug test."

Things were slipping beyond my control. It was time to pull the rip cord.

"I'll tell you everything," I said, "but first I'd like you to meet a friend of mine. Mom, Dad, this is Miss Peregrine."

I saw my dad's eyes go to Miss P, then to Emma. He must've recognized her, because he looked like he'd seen a ghost. But it was okay—he would forget soon enough.

"Pleased to make your acquaintance," said Miss Peregrine, shaking both my parents' hands. "You have a terrific son, just a top-notch boy. Not only is Jacob a perfect gentleman, he's even more talented than his grandfather."

"His grandfather?" said my dad. "How do you . . . "

"Who is this bizarre woman?" my mother said. "How do you know our son?"

Miss Peregrine gripped their hands and stared deeply into their eyes. "Alma Peregrine, Alma LeFay Peregrine. Now, I understand you've had a dreadful time here in the British Isles. Just an awful trip. I think it would be best for everyone involved if you just forgot it ever happened. Don't you agree?"

"Yes," my mother said, a faraway look in her eyes.

"I agree," said my father, sounding slightly hypnotized.

Miss Peregrine had paused their brains.

"Fantastic, wonderful," she said. "Now cast your eyes upon this, please." She let go of their hands and drew a long, blue-spotted falcon feather from her pocket. And then a hot wave of guilt flashed through me, and I stopped her.

"Wait," I said. "I don't think I want you to do it, after all."

"Are you sure?" She looked a bit disappointed. "It could get very complicated for you."

"It feels like cheating," I said.

"Then what will you tell them?" Emma asked.

"I don't know yet. But it doesn't seem right to just . . . wipe their brains."

If telling them the truth was selfish, it seemed doubly so to simply erase the need for an explanation. And what about the police? My extended family? My parents' friends? Surely they all knew I'd been missing, and for my parents to forget what had happened . . . it would've been a mess.

"That's up to you," said Miss Peregrine. "But I think it would be wise to at least let me wipe the past two or three minutes, so they'll forget Miss Bloom and me."

"Well . . . okay," I said. "So long as they don't lose the English language along with it."

"I'm very precise," said Miss Peregrine.

"What's all this about wiping brains?" said the police officer. "Who are you?"

"Alma Peregrine," said Miss Peregrine, rushing over to shake his hand. "Alma Peregrine, Alma LeFay Peregrine."

The officer's head dropped, and he was suddenly fascinated by a spot on the floor.

"I can think of a few wights you might've done that to," said Emma.

"Unfortunately, it only works on the pliable minds of normals," Miss Peregrine said. "Speaking of which." She held up the feather.

"Wait," I said. "Before you do." I put out my hand for her to shake. "Thank you for everything. I'm really going to miss you, Miss Peregrine."

Miss Peregrine ignored my hand and hugged me. "The feeling is mutual, Mr. Portman. And I'm the one who should be thanking you. If it hadn't been for your and Miss Bloom's heroism . . . "

"Well," I said, "if it hadn't been for you saving my grandfather all those years ago . . . "

She smiled. "Let's call it even."

There was one goodbye left. The hardest one. I put my arms around Emma, and she squeezed back ferociously.

"Can we write to each other?" she said.

"Are you sure you want to?"

"Of course. Friends keep in touch."

"Okay," I said, relieved. At least we could—

And then she kissed me. A big, full-on-the-lips kiss that left my head spinning.

"I thought we were just friends!" I said, pulling back in surprise.

"Um, yes," she said sheepishly. "*Now* we are. I just needed one to remember us by."

We were both laughing, our hearts soaring and breaking at once.

"Children, stop that!" Miss Peregrine hissed.

"Frank," my mother said faintly, "who is that girl Jake's kissing?"

"I haven't the slightest idea," my father mumbled. "Jacob, who is that girl, and why are you kissing her?"

My cheeks flushed. "Um, this is my . . . friend. Emma. We're just saying goodbye."

Emma waved bashfully. "You won't remember me, but . . . hello!"

"Well, stop kissing strange girls and come along," said my mother.

"Okay," I said to Miss Peregrine. "I'd guess we'd better get on with it."

"Don't think this is goodbye," Miss Peregrine said. "You're one of us now. You won't get rid of us that easily."

"I sure hope not," I said, grinning despite a heavy heart.

"I'll write you," Emma said, trying to smile, her voice cracking. "Good luck with . . . whatever it is normal people do."

"Goodbye, Emma. I'll miss you." It seemed so inadequate a thing to say, but at times like this, words themselves were inadequate.

Miss Peregrine turned to finish her work. She raised the falcon feather and tickled my parents under their noses.

"Excuse me!" my mother said, "what do you think you're doooo-AAAAAA-*CHOO*!"

And then both she and my father had a sneezing fit, and while they were sneezing, Miss Peregrine tickled the police officer, and he had a sneezing fit, too. By the time they were all finished, noses running and red in the face, Miss Peregrine and Emma had whisked out the door and were gone.

"As I was saying," my dad said, picking up as if the last few minutes hadn't happened. "Wait . . . what *was* I saying?"

"That we could just go home and talk about all this later?" I said hopefully.

"Not before you answer some questions," the officer said.

We spent a few minutes talking to the police. I kept my answers vague, laced every sentence with an apology, and swore up and down that I hadn't been abducted, abused, or drugged. (Thanks to Miss Peregrine's memory wipe, the officer had forgotten about making me take that drug test.) When my parents explained about my grandfather's death and the "troubles" I'd suffered following it, the police seemed satisfied that I was just a garden-variety runaway who'd forgotten to take his meds. They made us sign a few forms and sent us on our way.

"Yes, yes, let's please go home," my mother said. "But we *will* talk about this, young man. In *depth*."

Home. The word had become foreign to me. Some distant land I could hardly imagine.

"If we hurry," said my dad, "we might be able to catch an evening flight . . . "

He had cemented his arm around my shoulder, as if afraid I'd run away the moment he let go. My mom couldn't stop staring at me, her eyes wide and grateful, blinking back tears.

"I'm okay," I said, "I promise."

I knew they didn't believe me, and wouldn't for a long while.

We went outside to hail a black cab. As one was pulling up, I saw two familiar faces watching me from a park across the street. Occupying the dappled shade of an oak were Emma and Miss Peregrine. I raised a hand goodbye, my chest aching.

"Jake?" My dad was holding the cab door open for me.

"What's the matter?"

I turned my wave into a head scratch. "Nothing, Dad."

I got into the cab. My dad turned to stare into the park. When I looked out the window, all I saw under the oak were a bird and some blowing leaves.

*　　*　　*

My return home was neither triumphant nor easy. I had shattered my parents' trust, and piecing it back together would be slow, painstaking work. Considered a flight risk, I was watched all the time. I went nowhere unsupervised, not even for walks around the block. A complicated security system was installed in the house, less to stop thieves from getting in than me sneaking out. I was rushed back into therapy, subjected to countless psychological evaluations, and prescribed new, stronger drugs (which I hid under my tongue and later spat out). But I'd endured far worse deprivations that summer, and if a temporary loss of freedom was the price I had to pay for the friends I'd made, the experiences I'd had, and the extraordinary life I now knew to be mine, it seemed a bargain. It was worth every awkward conversation with my parents, every lonely night spent dreaming about Emma and my peculiar friends, every visit to my new psychiatrist.

She was an unflappable older lady named Dr. Spanger, and I spent four mornings a week in the glow of her face-lifted permasmile. She questioned me incessantly about why I'd run away from the island and how I'd spent the days after, that smile never wavering. (Her eyes, for the record, were dishwater brown, pupils normal, no contacts.) The story I concocted was a temporary insanity plea sprinkled with a dash of memory loss, every bit of which was totally unverifiable. It went like this: frightened by what appeared to be a sheep-murdering maniac loose on Cairnholm, I cracked, stowed away on a boat to Wales, briefly forgot who I was, and hitchhiked to

London. I slept in parks, spoke to no one, made no acquaintances, consumed no mood- or mind-altering substances, and wandered the city for several days in a disoriented fugue state. As for the phone call with my father in which I'd admitted to being "peculiar"—um, what phone call? I couldn't remember any phone call . . .

Eventually Dr. Spanger chalked the whole thing up to a manic episode, characterized by delusions, triggered by stress, grief, and unresolved grandpa issues. In other words: I'd gone a little nuts, but it was probably a one-time thing and I was feeling much better now, thank you. Still, my parents were on pins and needles. They were waiting for me to crack, do something crazy, run away again—but I was on my best behavior. I played the role of good kid and penitent son like I was out to win an Oscar. I volunteered my help around the house. I rose long before noon and hung out in plain view of my watchful parents. I watched TV with them and ran errands and lingered at the table after meals to participate in the inane discussions they liked to have—about bathroom remodeling, homeowners' association politics, fad diets, birds. (There was never more than a glancing allusion to my grandfather, the island, or my "episode.") I was pleasant, kind, patient, and in a hundred ways not quite the son they remembered. They must've thought I'd been abducted by aliens and replaced with a clone or something—but they weren't complaining. And after a few weeks, it was deemed safe to bring the family around, and this uncle or that aunt would drop by for a little coffee and stilted conversation, and so I could demonstrate in person how sane I was.

Weirdly, my dad never mentioned the letter Emma had left for him back on the island, nor the photo of her and Abe tucked inside it. Maybe it was more than he could deal with, or maybe he worried that talking about it with me might trigger a relapse. Whatever the reason, it was like it never happened. As for having actually met Emma and Millard and Olive, I'm sure he'd long ago dismissed that as a bizarre dream.

After a few weeks my parents began to relax. They'd bought my story and Dr. Spanger's explanations for my behavior. They could've probed deeper, probably—asked more questions, gotten a second or third opinion from other psychiatrists—but they really wanted to believe I was doing better. That whatever drugs Dr. Spanger had put me on were working their magic. More than anything, they wanted our lives to return to normal, and the longer I was home, the more that seemed to be happening.

Privately, though, I was struggling to adjust. I was bored and lonely. The days dragged. I had thought, after the hardships of the past few weeks, that the comforts of home would be sweeter, but pretty soon even laundered sheets and Chinese takeout lost their luster. My bed was too soft. My food too rich. There was too *much* of everything, and it made me feel guilty and decadent. Sometimes, wandering mall aisles on an errand with my parents, I would think about the people I'd seen living on the margins of Devil's Acre and get angry. Why did we have more than we knew what to do with, while they had less than they needed to stay alive?

I had trouble sleeping. I woke at odd hours, my mind looping scenes from my time with the peculiars. Though I'd given Emma my address and checked the mailbox several times a day, no letters had arrived from her or the others. The longer I went without hearing from them—two weeks, then three—the more abstract and unreal the whole experience began to seem. Had it really happened? Had it all been a delusion? In dark moments, I wondered. What if I *was* crazy?

So it was much to my relief when, a month after returning home, a letter finally arrived from Emma. It was short and breezy, just filling me in on the rebuilding process and asking me how things were going. The return address was a post office box in London, which Emma explained was close enough to the Devil's Acre loop entrance that she could sneak into the present fairly often and check it. I wrote back the same day, and pretty soon we were exchanging two or three letters a week. As home grew more suffocating, those letters became a lifeline.

I couldn't risk my parents finding one, so every day I stalked the mailman and dashed out to meet him as soon as he appeared at the end of our driveway. I suggested to Emma that we trade e-mails instead, which would have been safer and faster, and I filled several pages attempting to explain what the Internet was and how she might find a public Internet café and create an e-mail address—but it was hopeless; she'd never even used a keyboard. The letters were worth the risk, though, and I came to enjoy communicating by hand. There was something sweet about holding a tangible thing that had been touched and marked upon by someone I loved.

In one letter she included a few snapshots. She wrote:

> *Dear Jacob, things are finally getting interesting around here again. Remember the people on display in the basement, the ones Bentham said were wax models? Well, he was lying. He kidnapped them from different loops and was using Mother Dust's powder to keep them in suspended animation. We think he'd been trying to power his machine using different types of peculiars as batteries—but nothing worked until your hollowgast. Anyway, Mother Dust confessed to having known about it, which explains why she was acting so strangely. I think Bentham was blackmailing her somehow, or threatening to hurt Reynaldo if she didn't help him. Anyway, she's been helping us wake everyone up and return them to their rightful loops. Isn't that just pure madness?*
>
> *We've also been using the Panloopticon to explore all sorts of places and meet new people. Miss Peregrine says it's good for us to see how other peculiars live around the world. I found a camera in the house and brought it along on our last excursion, and I've included a few of the photos I took. Bronwyn says I'm already getting good!*

*I miss you like mad. I know I shouldn't talk like that . . .
it only makes this harder. But sometimes I can't help it. Maybe
you could come visit soon? I'd like that so much. ~~Or maybe~~*

She'd scratched out *or maybe* and written: *Uh-oh, I hear Sharon calling my name. He's leaving now and I want to make sure this
letter gets into the post today. Write soon! Love, Emma.*

What was that "or maybe," I wondered?

I looked over the photos she'd included. A few lines of description had been penned on the back of each. The first was a snapshot
of two Victorian ladies standing in front of a striped tent beneath a
sign that read CURIOS. On the back Emma had written: *Miss Bob-
olink and Miss Loon started a traveling exhibit using some of Bentham's old artefacts. Now that peculiars are freer to travel, they've
been doing quite a business. Many of us don't know much about our
history . . .*

The next was a photo of several adults descending a set of narrow steps to a beach and a rowboat. *There's a very nice loop on the
shore of the Caspian Sea*, Emma had written, *and last week Nim
and some of the ymbrynes went on a boating trip there. Hugh and
Horace and I tagged along but stayed on the shore. We've all had
enough of rowboats, thank you.*

The last picture was of conjoined twin girls wearing giant white
bows in their raven-black hair. They were seated next to each other,
their hands pulling aside a bit of their shirts to reveal a section of
shared torso. *Carlotta and Carlita are conjoined*, the back read, *but
that isn't what's most peculiar about them. Their bodies produce an
adhesive glue that's stronger than concrete when it dries. Enoch sat
in some and attached his bottom to a chair for two whole days! He
was so mad I thought his head would pop off. I wish you could've
been there . . .*

I replied right away. *What did you mean by "or maybe"?*

Ten days passed and I didn't hear from her. I worried that she felt she'd gone too far in her letter; had violated our just-friends agreement and was stepping back. I wondered if she'd even sign her next letter *Love, Emma*, two little words I had come to depend on. After two weeks, I began to wonder if there would even *be* another letter.

Then the mail stopped coming altogether. I watched obsessively for the mailman, and when he didn't show for four days, I knew something was up. My parents always got tons of catalogs and bills. I mentioned, casually as I could, that it seemed strange we hadn't gotten any mail recently. My father mumbled something about a national holiday and changed the subject. Then I really started to worry.

The mystery was solved during the next morning's session with Dr. Spanger, which, unusually, my parents had been invited to attend. They were tense and ashen-faced, struggling even to make small talk as we sat down. Spanger began with the usual softball questions. How had I been feeling? Any interesting dreams? I knew she was leading up to something big, and finally I couldn't take the suspense.

"Why are my parents here?" I asked. "And why do they look like they just got back from a funeral?"

For the first time ever, Dr. Spanger's permasmile faded. She reached into a folder on her desk and pulled out three envelopes.

They were letters from Emma. All had been opened. "We need to talk about these," she said.

"We agreed there wouldn't be any secrets," my dad said. "This is bad, Jake. Very bad."

My hands started to shake. "Those are private," I said, struggling to control my voice. "They're addressed to me. You shouldn't have read them."

What was in those letters? What had my parents seen? It was a disaster, an utter disaster.

"Who is Emma?" said Dr. Spanger. "Who is Miss Peregrine?"

"This isn't fair!" I shouted. "You stole my private letters, and now you're using them to ambush me!"

"Lower your voice!" my dad said. "It's out in the open now, so just be honest, and this will be easier for all of us."

Dr. Spanger held up a photograph, one Emma must have included in the letters. "Who are these people?"

I leaned forward to look at it. It was a picture of two older ladies in a rocking chair, one cradling the other in her lap like a baby.

"I have no idea," I said curtly.

"There's writing on the back," she said. It says: 'We're finding new ways to help those who've had parts of their soul removed. Close contact seems to work miracles. After just a few hours, Miss Hornbill was like a new ymbryne.'"

Eyem-brine, she pronounced it.

"It's *imm-brinn*," I corrected her, unable to help myself. "The 'i' sounds are flat."

"I see." Dr. Spanger set the photo down and steepled her fingers beneath her chin. "And what *is* an . . . *imm-brinn*?"

In retrospect maybe it was foolish, but at the time I felt cornered, like I had no choice but to tell the truth. They had letters, they had photos, and all my flimsy stories had blown away in the wind.

"They protect us," I said.

Dr. Spanger glanced at my parents. "All of us?"

"No. Just peculiar children."

"Peculiar children," Dr. Spanger repeated slowly. "And you believe you're one of them."

I stuck out my hand. "I'd like to have my letters now."

"You'll get them. But first we need to talk, okay?"

I retracted my hand and folded my arms. She was talking to me like I had an IQ of seventy.

"Now, what makes you think you're peculiar?".

"I can see things other people can't."

From the corner of my eye, I saw my parents going increasingly pale. They were not taking this well.

"In the letters you mention something called a . . . Pan . . . loopticon? What can you tell me about that?"

"*I* didn't write the letters," I said. "Emma did."

"Sure. Let's switch gears, then. Tell me about Emma."

"Doctor," my mother interrupted, "I don't think it's a good idea to encourage—"

"Please, Mrs. Portman." Dr. Spanger held up a hand. "Jake, tell me about Emma. Is she your girlfriend?"

I saw my dad's eyebrows rise. I'd never had a girlfriend before. Never so much as been on a date.

"She was, I guess. But now we're sort of . . . taking a break."

Dr. Spanger wrote something down, then tapped her pen against her chin. "And when you imagine her, what does she look like?"

I shrank back in my chair. "What do you mean, imagine her?"

"Oh." Dr. Spanger pursed her lips. She knew she'd messed up. "What I mean is . . . "

"Okay, this has gone on long enough," my father said. "We know you wrote those letters, Jake."

I nearly jumped out of the chair. "You think I *what*? That's not even my handwriting!"

My dad took a letter out of his pocket—the one Emma had left for him. "You wrote *this*, didn't you? It's the same writing."

"That was Emma, too! Look, her name's right there!" I grabbed for the letter. My dad whipped it out of reach.

"Sometimes we want things so badly, we imagine they're real," Dr. Spanger said.

"You think I'm crazy!" I shouted.

"We don't use that word in this office," Dr. Spanger said. "Please calm down, Jake."

"What about the postmark on the envelopes?" I said, pointing at the letters on Spanger's desk. "They came all the way from London!"

My father sighed. "You took Photoshop last semester at school, Jakey. I might be old, but I know how easy that sort of thing is to fake."

"And the photos? Did I fake those, too?"

"They're your grandpa's. I'm sure I've seen them before."

By now my head was spinning. I felt exposed and betrayed and horribly embarrassed. And then I stopped talking, because everything I said seemed only to further convince them I had lost my mind.

I sat fuming while they talked about me like I wasn't in the room. Dr. Spanger's new diagnosis was that I'd suffered a "radical break with reality," and that these "peculiars" were part of an elaborate universe of delusions I'd constructed for myself, complete with fantasy girlfriend. Because I was very intelligent, for weeks I'd managed to fool everyone into thinking I was sane, but the letters proved I was far from cured, and could even be a danger to myself. She recommended I be sent to an "in-patient clinic" for "rehabilitation and monitoring" with all due haste—which I understood to be psychiatrist talk for "looney-bin."

They'd had it all planned out. "It'll just be for a week or two," my father said. "It's a really nice place, super expensive. Think of it as a little vacation."

"I want my letters."

Dr. Spanger tucked them back into her folder. "Sorry, Jake," she said. "We think it's best if I hold on to them."

"You lied to me!" I said. Leaping at her desk, I swiped at them, but Spanger was quick and jumped back with the folder in her hand. My dad shouted and grabbed me, and a second later two of my uncles burst through the door. They'd been waiting in the hall the whole time. Bodyguards, in case I made a break for it.

They escorted me out to the parking lot and into the car. My uncles would be living with us for a few days, my mom explained nervously, until a room opened up for me at the clinic.

They were scared to be alone with me. My own parents. Then they'd send me off to a place where I'd be someone else's problem. The *clinic*. Like I was going in to have a hurt elbow bandaged. Call a spade a spade: it was an asylum, expensive though it may be. Not a place I could fake swallowing my meds and spit them out later. Not somewhere I could dupe doctors into believing my stories about fugue states and memory loss. They would dope me with antipsychotics and truth serums until I told them every last thing about peculiardom, and with that as proof that I was irredeemably insane, they'd have no choice but to lock me in a padded cell and flush the key down a toilet.

I was well and truly screwed.

*   *   *

For the next several days I was watched like a criminal, a parent or uncle never more than a room-length away. Everyone was waiting for a call from the clinic. It was a popular place, I guess, but the minute there was an open room—any day now—I would be bundled off.

"We'll visit every day," my mom assured me. "It's just for a few weeks, Jakey, promise."

Just a few weeks. Yeah, right.

I tried reasoning with them. Begging. I implored them to hire a handwriting expert, so I could prove the letters weren't mine. When that failed, I reversed myself completely. I admitted to writing the letters (when of course I hadn't), saying I realized now that I'd invented it all—there were no peculiar children, no ymbrynes, no Emma. This pleased them, but it didn't change their minds. Later I overheard them whispering to each other and learned that in order to secure me a spot on the waiting list, they'd had to pay for the first week of the clinic—the very expensive clinic—in advance. So there was no backing out.

I considered running away. Snatching the car keys and making a break for it. But inevitably I'd be caught, and then things would be even worse for me.

I fantasized about Emma coming to my rescue. I even wrote a letter telling her what had happened, but I had no way to send it. Even if I could've snuck out to the mailbox without being seen, the mailman didn't come to our house anymore. And if I'd reached her, what would it have mattered? I was stuck in the present, far from a loop. She couldn't have come anyway.

On the third night, in desperation, I swiped my dad's phone (I wasn't allowed one anymore) and used it to send Emma an email. Before I'd realized how hopeless she was with computers, I'd set up an address for her—*firegirl1901@gmail.com*—but she was so firmly disinterested that I'd never written her there, nor even, I realized, bothered to tell her the password. A message in a bottle thrown into the sea would've had a better chance of reaching her, but it was the only chance I had.

The call came the following evening: a room had opened up for me. My bags had been packed and waiting for days. It didn't matter that it was nine o'clock at night, or that it was a two-hour drive to the clinic—we would go right away.

We piled into the station wagon. My parents sat in front, and I was squashed between my uncles in the back, as if they thought I might try leaping from a moving car. In truth, I might've. But as the garage door rumbled open and my dad started the car, what little hope I'd been nurturing began to shrivel. There really was no escaping this. I couldn't argue my way out of it, nor run from it—unless I managed to run all the way to London, which would've required passports and money and all sorts of impossible things. No, I would have to endure this. But peculiars had endured far worse.

We backed out of the garage. My father flipped on the headlights, then the radio. The smooth chatter of a DJ filled the car. The moon was rising behind the palm trees that edged the yard. I lowered my head and shut my eyes, trying to swallow back the dread that was filling me. Maybe I could wish myself elsewhere. Maybe I could disappear.

We began to move, the broken shells that paved our driveway crunching beneath the wheels. My uncles talked across me, something about sports, in an attempt to lighten the mood. I shut out their voices.

I'm not here.

We hadn't yet left the driveway when the car jerked to a stop.

"What the heck is this?" I heard my father say.

He honked the horn and my eyes flew open, but what I saw convinced me that I'd succeeded in willing myself into a dream. Standing there before of our car, lined up across the driveway and shining in the glare our headlights, were all my peculiar friends. Emma, Horace, Enoch, Olive, Claire, Hugh, even Millard—and out in front of them, a traveling coat across her shoulders and a carpet-bag in her hand, Miss Peregrine.

"What the hell's going on?" said one of my uncles.

"Yeah, Frank, what the hell is this?" said the other.

"I don't know," said my father, and he rolled down his window. "Get out of my driveway!" he shouted.

Miss Peregrine marched to his door. "We will not. Exit the vehicle, please."

"Who the hell are you?" my dad said.

"Alma LeFay Peregrine, Ymbryne Council leader pro tem and headmistress to these peculiar children. We've met before, though I don't expect you'd remember. Children, say hello."

As my father's jaw dropped and my mother began hyperventilating, the children waved, Olive levitated, Claire opened her back-mouth, Millard twirled, a suit of clothes without a body, and Emma lit a flame in her hand while walking toward my dad's open window. "Hello, Frank!" she said. "My name's Emma. I'm a good friend of your son's."

"See?" I said. "I *told* you they were real!"

"Frank, get us out of here!" my mother screeched, and slapped him on the shoulder.

He'd seemed frozen until then, but now he laid on the horn and jammed his foot on the accelerator, and as shells spit from the back tires, the car lurched forward.

"STOP!" I screamed as we sped toward my friends. They jumped out of the way—all but Bronwyn, who simply planted her feet, stuck out her arms, and caught the front of our car in her hands.

We slammed to a stop, the wheels spinning uselessly while my mother and uncles howled in terror.

The car stalled. The headlights died and the engine went quiet. As my friends surrounded the car, I tried to reassure my family. "It's okay, they're my friends, they're not going to hurt you."

My uncles passed out, their heads slumping onto my shoulders, and my mother's screams gradually faded to whimpers. My dad was jumpy and wide-eyed. "This is nuts this is nuts this is totally *nuts,*" he kept muttering.

"Stay in the car," I said, and reaching over an unconscious uncle I opened the door, crawled over him, and slid out.

Emma and I slammed together in a dizzy, twirling embrace. I could hardly speak. "What are you—how did you—"

I was tingling all over, certain I was still dreaming.

"I got your electrical letter!" she said.

"My . . . e-mail?"

"Yes, whatever you call it! When I didn't hear from you I got worried, and then I remembered the machinated postbox you said you'd made for me. Horace was able to guess your password, and—"

"We came as soon as we heard," said Miss Peregrine, shaking her head at my parents. "Very disappointing, but not entirely surprising."

"We're here to save you!" Olive crowed. "Like you saved us!"

"And I'm so glad to see you!" I said. "But don't you have to go? You'll start aging forward!"

"Didn't you read my last few letters?" Emma said. "I explained everything . . . "

"My parents took them. That's why they freaked out."

"What? How awful!" She glared at my parents. "That's stealing, you know! In any case, there's nothing to worry about. We made an exciting discovery!"

"You mean *I* made an exciting discovery," I heard Millard say. "All thanks to Perplexus. It took me days to figure out how to get him back to his loop using Bentham's convoluted machine—during which time Perplexus should have aged forward. But he didn't. What's more, his gray hair even turned black again! That's when I realized something had happened to him while he was in Abaton with us: his true age had been reset. When the ymbrynes collapsed the loop, it wound back his clock, so to speak, so that his body was exactly as old as it looked, rather than his actual age of five hundred and seventy-one."

"And it wasn't just Perplexus's clock that got wound back," Emma said excitedly, "but all of ours! Everyone who was in Abaton that day!"

"Apparently it's a side effect of loop collapse," Miss Peregrine said. "An extremely dangerous Fountain of Youth."

"So this means . . . you won't age forward? Ever?"

"Well, no faster than you!" Emma said, and laughed. "One day at a time!"

"That's . . . amazing!" I said, overjoyed but struggling to take it all in. "Are you sure I'm not dreaming?"

"Quite sure," said Miss Peregrine.

"Can we stay a while, Jacob?" said Claire, bouncing up to me. "You said we could come anytime!"

"I figured we'd make a holiday of it," Miss Peregrine said before I could reply. "The children know almost nothing of the twenty-first century, and besides, this house looks *much* more comfortable than Bentham's drafty old rat-trap. How many bedrooms?"

"Um . . . we have five, I think?"

"Yes, that'll do. That'll do just fine."

"But what about my parents? And my uncles?"

She glanced at the car and waved a hand. "Your uncles can be memory-wiped with ease. As for your parents, I believe the cat's out of the bag, as they say. They'll have to be watched closely for a time, kept on a short leash. But if any two normals can be brought 'round to our way of seeing things, it's the parents of the great Jacob

Portman."

"And the son and daughter-in-law of the great Abraham Portman!" said Emma.

"You . . . you knew my father?" my dad said timidly, peeping at us from the car window.

"I loved him like a son," said Miss Peregrine. "As I do Jacob."

Dad blinked, then slowly nodded, but I don't think he understood.

"They're going to stay with us for a while," I said. "Okay?"

His eyes widened and he shrank away. "It's . . . uh . . . I think you'd better ask your mother . . . "

She was curled in the passenger seat with her hands blocking her eyes.

I said, "Mom?"

"Go away," she said. "Just go away, all of you!"

Miss Peregrine leaned down. "Mrs. Portman, look at me, please."

Mom peeked through her fingers. "You aren't really there. I had too much wine at dinner, that's all."

"We're quite real, I assure you. And this may be hard to believe now, but we're all going to be friends."

My mom turned away. "Frank, change the channel. I don't like this show."

"Okay, honey," my dad said. "Son, I think I'd better, um . . . um . . . " and then he shut his eyes, shook his head, and rolled up the window.

"Are you sure this isn't going to melt their brains?" I asked Miss Peregrine.

"They'll come around," she replied. "Some take longer than others."

* * *

We walked back toward my house in a group, the moon bright and rising, the hot night alive with wind and cicadas. Bronwyn pushed the dead car along behind us, my family still in it. I walked hand in hand with Emma, my mind reeling from all that had happened.

"One thing I don't understand," I said. "How did you get here? And so quickly?"

I tried to picture a girl with a mouth in the back of her head and a boy with bees buzzing around him getting through airport security. And Millard: had they snuck him onto an airplane? How did they even get passports?

"We got lucky," Emma said. "One of Bentham's rooms led to a loop just a hundred miles from here."

"Some appalling swamp," Miss Peregrine said. "Crocodiles and knee-deep muck. No idea what my brother wanted with the place. Anyhow, from there I managed to effect our exit into the present, and then it was just a matter of catching two buses and walking three and one-half miles. The whole trip took less than a day. Needless to say, we're tired and parched from our journey."

We had arrived on my front porch. Miss Peregrine looked at me expectantly.

"Right! There are sodas in the fridge, I think . . . "

I fumbled the key into door and opened it.

"Hospitality, Mr. Portman, hospitality!" Miss Peregrine said, breezing past me into the house. "Leave your shoes outside, children, we're not in Devil's Acre anymore!"

I stood holding the door as they tramped inside, muddy shoes and all.

"Yes, this will do nicely!" I heard Miss Peregrine say. "Where's the kitchen?"

"What should I do with the car?" Bronwyn said, still standing at its rear bumper. "And, uh . . . the normals?"

"Could you put them in the garage?" I said. "And maybe keep an eye on them for a minute or two?"

She looked at Emma and me, then smiled. "Sure thing."

I found the garage door opener and hit the button. Bronwyn rolled the car and my dazed parents inside, and then Emma and I were left alone on the front porch.

"You're sure it's okay that we stay?" Emma said.

"It'll be tricky with my family," I said. "But Miss P seems to think we can make it work."

"I meant, is it okay with *you*. The way we left things was . . . "

"Are you kidding? I'm so happy you're here, I can hardly speak."

"Okay. You're smiling, so I suppose I believe you."

Smiling? I was grinning like a fool.

Emma took a step toward me. I slipped my arms around her. We held each other, my cheek pressed to her forehead.

"I never wanted to lose you," she whispered. "But I didn't see a way around it. A clean break seemed easier than losing you in slow motion."

"You don't have to explain. I understand."

"Anyway, maybe we don't have to, now. Be just friends. If you don't want to."

"Maybe it's a good idea, though," I said. "Just for a while."

"Oh," she said quickly, disappointed. "Sure . . . "

"No, what I mean is . . . " I pulled away gently, looking at her. "Now that we have time, we can go slow. I could ask you out to the movies . . . we could go for walks . . . you know, like normal people do."

She shrugged. "I don't know too much about what normal people do."

"It's not complicated," I said. "You taught me how to be peculiar. Maybe now I can teach you how to be normal. Well, as normal as I know how to be."

She was quiet for a moment. Then she laughed. "Sure, Jacob. I think that sounds nice." She took my hand, leaned toward me, and kissed me on the cheek. "Now that we have time."

And it occurred to me, standing there, just breathing with her, quiet settling around us, that those might be the three most beautiful words in the English language.

We have time.

About the Photography

The images that appear in this book are authentic, vintage found photographs, and with the exception of a handful that have undergone digital processing, they are unaltered. They were painstakingly collected over the course of several years: discovered at flea markets, vintage paper shows, and in the archives of photo collectors more accomplished than I, who were kind enough to part with some of their most peculiar treasures to help create this book.

The following photos were graciously lent for use by their owners:

PAGE	TITLE	FROM THE COLLECTION OF
32	Wights testing gas	Erin Waters
57	Man with pirates	John Van Noate
113	Floating girl	Jack Mord/The Thanatos Archive
179	Taxidermied girl	Adriana Müller
181	Myron Bentham	John Van Noate
185	Ymbrynes and their grim	Jack Mord/The Thanatos Archive
202	Boy with wings	John Van Noate
225	Bloody hallway	Jack Mord/The Thanatos Archive
264	Bowels of the machine	John Van Noate
278	Parrot in cage	John Van Noate
290	Inside the tower	Peter J. Cohen
293	Drainage pipe	John Van Noate
301	Doctor and nurses	John Van Noate
310	Man with thinning hair	John Van Noate
336	Man in dark glasses	John Van Noate
461	Boy and girl	John Van Noate

ENTER THE WORLD OF THE
PECULIARS

COLLECT ALL THREE BOOKS IN
THE ORIGINAL MISS PEREGRINE TRILOGY
WITH THIS HANDSOME BOXED SET

| Miss Peregrine's Home for Peculiar Children | Hollow City | Library of Souls |

CHRONICLE
YOUR OWN
EXTRAORDINARY
ADVENTURES
WITH
MISS PEREGRINE'S
JOURNAL FOR
PECULIAR CHILDREN

LIBRARY
OF
SOULS

"Riggs deftly moves between fantasy and reality, prose and photography to create an enchanting and at times positively terrifying story."

—Associated Press

"It's an enjoyable, eccentric read, distinguished by well-developed characters, a believable Welsh setting, and some very creepy monsters."

—Publishers Weekly

"An original work that defies categorization, this first novel should appeal to readers who like quirky fantasies. Riggs includes many vintage photographs that add a critical touch of the peculiar to his unusual tale."

—Library Journal

"Somewhat reminiscent of Jack Finney's *Time and Again*, Riggs's first novel is enchanting. . . . Highly recommended."

—Ellery Queen Mystery Magazine

"In a time when so much summer entertainment seems to be more of the same, *Miss Peregrine's Home for Peculiar Children* is a pleasant surprise—a story that is fresh and new, engrosses and grips, and provides enough clues so that the ending makes sense and seems thoughtful."

—Popmatters.com

"Brace yourself for the last 70 pages of relentless, squirm-in-your-chair action. I loved every minute of it."

—Cleveland Plain Dealer

"An unforgettable novel that mixes fiction and photography in a thrilling reading experience." —Savannah Morning News

"This is a Book of the Year candidate and right now I'm calling it the front runner. Absolutely magical in every sense of the word, *Miss Peregrine* has a peerless combination of witty, intelligent dialogue and prose, combined with an absolutely beautiful design. . . . *Miss Peregrine's Home for Peculiar Children* is the sharpest thing you'll read all year." —Shelf Unbound

HOLLOW
CITY

HOLLOW CITY

THE SECOND NOVEL OF

MISS PEREGRINE'S

PECULIAR CHILDREN

BY RANSOM RIGGS

QUIRK BOOKS

PHILADELPHIA

First paperback edition, Quirk Books, 2015.
Originally published by Quirk Books in 2014.

Library of Congress Cataloging in Publication Number: 2013914959
(hardcover edition)

ISBN: 978-1-59474-735-9

Printed in the United States of America
Typeset in Sabon, Belwe, and Dear Sarah

Designed by Doogie Horner
Cover photograph courtesy of John Van Noate, Rex USA, and the Everett Collection
Production management by John J. McGurk

Quirk Books
215 Church St.
Philadelphia, PA 19106
quirkbooks.com

20

FOR TAHEREH

And lo! towards us coming in a boat

    An old man, grizzled with the hair of eld,

    Moaning: "Woe unto you, debased souls!

Hope nevermore to look upon the heavens.

    I come to lead you to the other shore;

    Into eternal darkness; into fire and frost.

And thou, that yonder standest, living soul,

    Withdraw from these people, who are dead!"

    But he saw that I did not withdraw . . .

—Dante's *Inferno*, Canto III

✦ PECULIAR PERSONAE ✦

JACOB PORTMAN
Our hero, who can see and sense hollowgast

EMMA BLOOM
A girl who can make fire with her hands, formerly involved with Jacob's grandfather

ABRAHAM PORTMAN (DECEASED)
Jacob's grandfather, killed by a hollowgast

BRONWYN BRUNTLEY
An unusually strong girl

PECULIAR PERSONAE

MILLARD NULLINGS

An invisible boy, scholar of all
things peculiar

OLIVE
ABROHOLOS ELEPHANTA

A girl who is lighter than air

HORACE SOMNUSSON

A boy who suffers from pre-
monitory visions and dreams

ENOCH O'CONNOR

A boy who can animate the
dead for brief periods of time

PECULIAR PERSONAE

HUGH APISTON

A boy who commands and
protects the many bees that
live in his stomach

CLAIRE DENSMORE

A girl with an extra mouth
in the back of her head; the
youngest of Miss Peregrine's
peculiar children

FIONA FRAUENFELD

A silent girl with a peculiar
talent for making plants grow

ALMA LEFAY PEREGRINE

Ymbryne, shape-shifter,
manipulator of time;
headmistress of Cairnholm's
loop; arrested in bird form

ESMERELDA AVOCET

An ymbryne whose loop was
raided by the corrupted;
kidnapped by wights

FRANKLIN PORTMAN

Jacob's father; bird hobbyist,
wannabe writer

MARYANN PORTMAN

Jacob's mother; heiress to
Florida's second-largest
drugstore chain

RICKY PICKERING

Jacob's only normal friend

DOCTOR GOLAN (DECEASED)

A wight who posed as a psychiatrist to deceive Jacob and
his family; later killed by Jacob

RALPH WALDO EMERSON (DECEASED)

Essayist, lecturer, poet

PART

ONE

CHAPTER ONE

We rowed out through the harbor, past bobbing boats weeping rust from their seams, past juries of silent seabirds roosting atop the barnacled remains of sunken docks, past fishermen who lowered their nets to stare frozenly as we slipped by, uncertain whether we were real or imagined; a procession of waterborne ghosts, or ghosts soon to be. We were ten children and one bird in three small and unsteady boats, rowing with quiet intensity straight out to sea, the only safe harbor for miles receding quickly behind us, craggy and magical in the blue-gold light of dawn. Our goal, the rutted coast of mainland Wales, was somewhere before us but only dimly visible, an inky smudge squatting along the far horizon.

We rowed past the old lighthouse, tranquil in the distance, which only last night had been the scene of so many traumas. It was there that, with bombs exploding around us, we had nearly drowned, nearly been torn apart by bullets; that I had taken a gun and pulled its trigger and killed a man, an act still incomprehensible to me; that we had lost Miss Peregrine and got her back again—snatched from the steel jaws of a submarine—though the Miss Peregrine who was returned to us was damaged, in need of help we didn't know how to give. She perched now on the stern of our boat, watching the sanctuary she'd created slip away, more lost with every oar stroke.

Finally we rowed past the breakwater and into the great blank open, and the glassy surface of the harbor gave way to little waves that chopped at the sides of our boats. I heard a plane threading the clouds high above us and let my oars drag, neck craning up, arrested by a vision of our little armada from such a height: this world I had chosen, and everything I had in it, and all our precious, peculiar lives, contained in three splinters of wood adrift upon the vast, unblinking eye of the sea.

Mercy.

*   *   *

Our boats slid easily through the waves, three abreast, a friendly current bearing us coastward. We rowed in shifts, taking turns at the oars to stave off exhaustion, though I felt so strong that for nearly an hour I refused to give them up. I lost myself in the rhythm of the strokes, my arms tracing long ellipses in the air as if pulling something toward me that refused to come. Hugh manned the oars opposite me, and behind him, at the bow, sat Emma, her eyes hidden beneath the brim of a sun hat, head bent toward a map spread across her knees. Every so often she'd look up from her map to consult the horizon, and just the sight of her face in the sun gave me energy I didn't know I had.

I felt like I could row forever—until Horace shouted from one of the other boats to ask how much ocean was left between us and the mainland, and Emma squinted back toward the island and then down at her map, measuring with spread fingers, and said, somewhat doubtfully, "Four miles?" But then Millard, who was also in our boat, muttered something in her ear and she frowned and turned the map sideways, and frowned again, then said, "I mean, five." As the words left her mouth, I felt myself—and saw everyone else—wilt a little.

Five miles: a journey that would've taken an hour in the stomach-churning ferry that had brought me to Cairnholm weeks ago. A distance easily covered by an engine-powered boat of any size. Roughly one mile less than my out-of-shape uncles ran on odd weekends for charity, and only a bit more than my mother boasted she could manage during rowing-machine classes at her fancy gym. But the ferry between the island and the mainland wouldn't start running for another thirty years, and rowing machines weren't loaded down with passengers and luggage, nor did they require constant course corrections just to stay pointed in the right direction. Worse still, the ditch of water we were crossing was treacherous, a notorious ship-swallower: five miles of moody, changeable sea, its floor fanned with greening wrecks and sailors' bones and, lurking somewhere in the fathoms-deep darkness, our enemies.

Those of us who worried about such things assumed the wights were nearby, somewhere below us in that German submarine, waiting. If they didn't already know we'd fled the island, they'd find out soon enough. They hadn't gone to such lengths to kidnap Miss Peregrine only to give up after one failed attempt. The warships that inched along like centipedes in the distance and the British planes that kept watch overhead made it too dangerous for the submarine to surface in broad daylight, but come nightfall, we'd be easy prey. They would come for us, and take Miss Peregrine, and sink the rest. So we rowed, our only hope that we could reach the mainland before nightfall reached us.

*   *   *

We rowed until our arms ached and our shoulders knotted. We rowed until the morning breeze stilled and the sun blazed down as through a magnifying glass and sweat pooled around our collars, and I realized no one had thought to bring fresh water, and that sunblock in 1940 meant standing in the shade. We rowed until the skin wore away from the ridges of our palms and we were certain we absolutely couldn't row another stroke, but then did, and then another, and another.

"You're sweating buckets," Emma said. "Let me have a go at the oars before you melt away."

Her voice startled me out of a daze. I nodded gratefully and let her switch into the oar seat, but twenty minutes later I asked for it back again. I didn't like the thoughts that crept into my head while my body was at rest: imagined scenes of my father waking to find me gone from our rooms on Cairnholm, Emma's baffling letter in my place; the panic that would ensue. Memory-flashes of terrible things I'd witnessed recently: a monster pulling me into its jaws; my former psychiatrist falling to his death; a man buried in a coffin of ice, torn momentarily from the next world to croak into my ear with half a throat. So I rowed despite my exhaustion and a spine that felt like it might never bend straight again and hands rubbed raw from friction, and tried to think of exactly nothing, those leaden oars both a life sentence and a life raft.

Bronwyn, seemingly inexhaustible, rowed one of the boats all by herself. Olive sat opposite but was no help; the tiny girl couldn't pull the oars without pushing herself up into the air, where a stray gust of wind might send her flying away like a kite. So Olive shouted encouragement while Bronwyn did the work of two—or three or four, if you took into account all the suitcases and boxes weighing down their boat, stuffed with clothes and food and maps and books and a lot of less practical things, too, like several jars of pickled reptile hearts sloshing in Enoch's duffel bag; or the blown-off front doorknob to Miss Peregrine's house, a memento Hugh had found in the grass on our way to the boats and decided he couldn't live without; or the bulky pillow Horace had rescued from the house's flaming shell—it was his lucky pillow, he said, and the only thing that kept his paralyzing nightmares at bay.

Other items were so precious that the children clung to them even as they rowed. Fiona kept a pot of wormy garden dirt pressed between her knees. Millard had striped his face with a handful of bomb-pulverized brick dust, an odd gesture that seemed part mourning ritual. If what they kept and clung to seemed strange, part of me sympathized: it was all they had left of their home. Just because they knew it was lost didn't mean they knew how to let it go.

After three hours of rowing like galley slaves, distance had shrunk the island to the size of an open hand. It looked nothing like the foreboding, cliff-ringed fortress I had first laid eyes upon a few weeks ago; now it seemed fragile, a shard of rock in danger of being washed away by the waves.

"Look!" Enoch shouted, standing up in the boat next to ours. "It's disappearing!" A spectral fog enshrouded the island, blanking it from view, and we broke from rowing to watch it fade.

"Say goodbye to our island," Emma said, standing and removing her big hat. "We may never see it again."

"Farewell, island," said Hugh. "You were so good to us."

Horace set his oar down and waved. "Goodbye, house. I shall miss all your rooms and gardens, but most of all I shall miss my bed."

"So long, loop," Olive sniffled. "Thank you for keeping us safe all these years."

"Good years," said Bronwyn. "The best I've known."

I, too, said a silent goodbye, to a place that had changed me forever—and the place that, more than any graveyard, would forever contain the memory, and the mystery, of my grandfather. They were linked inextricably, he and that island, and I wondered, now that both were gone, if I would ever really understand what had happened to me: what I had become; was becoming. I had come to the island to solve my grandfather's mystery, and in doing so I had discovered my own. Watching Cairnholm disappear felt like watching the only remaining key to that mystery sink beneath the dark waves.

And then the island was simply gone, swallowed up by a mountain of fog.

As if it had never existed.

*   *   *

Before long the fog caught up to us. By increments we were blinded, the mainland dimming and the sun fading to a pale white bloom, and we turned circles in the eddying tide until we'd lost all sense of direction. Finally we stopped and put our oars down and waited in the doldrummy quiet, hoping it would pass; there was no use going any farther until it did.

"I don't like this," Bronwyn said. "If we wait too long it'll be night, and we'll have worse things to reckon with than bad weather."

Then, as if the weather had heard Bronwyn and decided to put us in our place, it turned *really* bad. A strong wind blew up, and within moments our world was transformed. The sea around us whipped into white-capped waves that slapped at our hulls and broke into our boats, sloshing cold water around our feet. Next came rain, hard as little bullets on our skin. Soon we were being tossed around like rubber toys in a bathtub.

"Turn into the waves!" Bronwyn shouted, slicing at the water with her oars. "If they broadside us we'll flip for sure!" But most of us were too spent to row in calm water, let alone a boiling sea, and the rest were too scared even to reach for the oars, so instead we grabbed for the gunwales and held on for dear life.

A wall of water plowed straight toward us. We climbed the massive wave, our boats turning nearly vertical beneath us. Emma clung to me and I clung to the oarlock; behind us Hugh held on to the seat with his arms. We crested the wave like a roller coaster, my stomach dropping into my legs, and as we raced down the far side, everything in our boat that wasn't nailed down—Emma's map, Hugh's bag, the red roller suitcase I'd lugged with me since Florida— went flying out over our heads and into the water.

There was no time to worry about what had been lost, because initially we couldn't even see the other boats. When we'd resumed an even keel, we squinted into the maelstrom and screamed our friends' names. There was a terrible moment of silence before we heard voices call back to us, and Enoch's boat appeared out of the mist, all four passengers aboard, waving their arms at us.

"Are you all right?" I shouted.

"Over there!" they called back. "Look over there!"

I saw that they weren't waving hello, but directing our attention to something in the water, some thirty yards away—the hull of an overturned boat.

"That's Bronwyn and Olive's boat!" Emma said.

It was upside down, its rusty bottom to the sky. There was no sign of either girl around it.

"We have to get closer!" Hugh shouted, and forgetting our exhaustion we grabbed the oars and paddled toward it, calling their names into the wind.

We rowed through a tide of clothes ejected from split-open suitcases, every swirling dress we passed resembling a drowning girl. My heart hammered in my chest, and though I was soaked and shivering I hardly felt the cold. We met Enoch's boat at the overturned hull of Bronwyn's and searched the water together.

"Where are they?" Horace moaned. "Oh, if we've lost them . . ."

"Underneath!" Emma said, pointing at the hull. "Maybe they're trapped underneath it!"

I pulled one of my oars from its lock and banged it against the overturned hull. "If you're in there, swim out!" I shouted. "We'll rescue you!"

For a terrible moment there was no response, and I could feel any hope of recovering them slipping away. But then, from the underside of the overturned boat, there was a knock in reply—and then a fist smashed through the hull, wood chips flying, and we all jumped in surprise.

"It's Bronwyn!" Emma cried. "They're alive!"

With a few more strikes Bronwyn was able to knock a person-sized hole in the hull. I extended my oar to her and she grabbed it, and with Hugh and Emma and me all pulling, we managed to drag her through the churning water and into our boat just as hers sank, vanishing beneath the waves. She was panicked, hysterical, shouting with breath she didn't have to spare. Shouting for Olive, who hadn't been under the hull with her. She was still missing.

"Olive—got to get Olive," Bronwyn sputtered once she'd tumbled into the boat. She was shivering, coughing up seawater. She stood up in the pitching boat and pointed into the storm. "There!" she cried. "See it?"

I shielded my eyes from the stinging rain and looked, but all I could see were waves and fog. "I don't see anything!"

"She's there!" Bronwyn insisted. "The rope!"

Then I saw what she was pointing at: not a flailing girl in the water but a fat thread of woven hemp trailing up from it, barely visible in all the chaos. A strand of taut brown rope extended up from the water and disappeared into the fog. Olive must've been attached to the other end, unseen.

We paddled to the rope and Bronwyn reeled it down, and after a minute Olive appeared from the fog above our heads, one end of the rope knotted around her waist. Her shoes had fallen off when her boat flipped, but Bronwyn had already tied Olive to the anchor line, the other end of which was resting on the seafloor. If not for that, she surely would've been lost in the clouds by now.

Olive threw her arms around Bronwyn's neck and crowed, "You saved me, you saved me!"

They embraced. The sight of them put a lump in my throat.

"We ain't out of danger yet," said Bronwyn. "We still got to reach shore before nightfall, or our troubles have only just begun."

*   *   *

The storm had weakened some and the sea's violent chop died down, but the idea of rowing another stroke, even in a perfectly calm sea, was unimaginable now. We hadn't made it even halfway to the mainland and already I was hopelessly exhausted. My hands throbbed. My arms felt heavy as tree trunks. Not only that, but the endless diagonal rocking of the boat was having an undeniable effect on my stomach—and judging from the greenish color of the faces around me, I wasn't alone.

"We'll rest awhile," Emma said, trying to sound encouraging.

"We'll rest and bail out the boats until the fog clears . . ."

"Fog like this has a mind of its own," said Enoch. "It can go days without breaking. It'll be dark in a few hours, and then we'll have to hope we can last until morning without the wights finding us. We'll be utterly defenseless."

"And without water," said Hugh.

"Or food," added Millard.

Olive raised both hands in the air and said, "*I* know where it is!"

"Where what is?" said Emma.

"Land. I saw it when I was up at the end of that rope." Olive had risen above the fog, she explained, and briefly caught a clear view of the mainland.

"Fat lot of good that does," grumbled Enoch. "We've circled back on ourselves a half-dozen times since you were dangling up there."

"Then let me up again."

"Are you certain?" Emma asked her. "It's dangerous. What if a wind catches you, or the rope snaps?"

Olive's face went steely. "Reel me up," she repeated.

"When she gets like this, there's no arguing," said Emma. "Fetch the rope, Bronwyn."

"You're the bravest little girl I ever knew," Bronwyn said, then set to working. She pulled the anchor out of the water and up into our boat, and with the extra length of rope it gave us we lashed together our two remaining boats so they couldn't be separated again, then reeled Olive back up through the fog and into the sky.

There was an odd quiet moment when we were all staring at a rope in the clouds, heads thrown back—waiting for a sign from heaven.

Enoch broke the silence. "Well?" he called, impatient.

"I can see it!" came the reply, Olive's voice barely a squeak over the white noise of waves. "Straight ahead!"

"Good enough for me!" Bronwyn said, and while the rest of us clutched our stomachs and slumped uselessly in our seats, she clambered into the lead boat and took the oars and began to row, guided only by Olive's tiny voice, an unseen angel in the sky.

"Left . . . more left . . . not that much!"

And like that we slowly made our way toward land, the fog pursuing us always, its long, gray tendrils like the ghostly fingers of some phantom hand, ever trying to draw us back.

As if the island couldn't quite let us go, either.

CHAPTER TWO

*O*ur twin hulls ground to a halt in the rocky shallows. We hove up onto shore just as the sun was dimming behind acres of gray clouds, perhaps an hour left until full dark. The beach was a stony spit clogged with low-tide sea wrack, but it was beautiful to me, more beautiful than any champagne-white tourist beach back home. It meant we had made it. What it meant to the others I could hardly imagine; most of them hadn't been off Cairnholm in a lifetime, and now they gazed around in wonder, bewildered to still be alive and wondering what on earth to do about it.

We staggered from our boats with legs made of rubber. Fiona scooped a handful of slimy pebbles into her mouth and rolled them over her tongue, as if she needed all five senses to convince herself she wasn't dreaming—which was just how I'd felt about being in Miss Peregrine's loop, at first. I had never, in all my life, so distrusted my own eyes. Bronwyn groaned and sank to the ground, exhausted beyond words. She was surrounded and fussed over and showered with thanks for all she'd done, but it was awkward; our debt was too great and the words *thank you* too small, and she tried to wave us away but was so tired she could barely raise her hand. Meanwhile, Emma and the boys reeled Olive down from the clouds.

"You're positively *blue*!" Emma exclaimed when Olive appeared through the fog, and she leapt up to pull the little girl into her arms. Olive was soaked and frozen, her teeth chattering. There were no blankets, nor even a stitch of dry clothing to give her, so Emma ran her ever-hot hands around Olive's body until the worst of her shudders subsided, then sent Fiona and Horace away to gather driftwood for a fire. While waiting for their return, we gathered round the boats to take stock of all we'd lost at sea. It was a grim tally. Nearly everything we'd brought now littered the seafloor.

What we had left were the clothes on our backs, a small amount of food in rusty tins, and Bronwyn's tank-sized steamer trunk, indestructible and apparently unsinkable—and so absurdly heavy that only Bronwyn herself could ever hope to carry it. We tore open its metal latches, eager to find something useful, or better yet, edible, but all it held was a three-volume collection of stories called *Tales of the Peculiar*, the pages spongy with seawater, and a fancy bath mat embroidered with the letters *ALP*, Miss Peregrine's initials.

"Oh, thank heavens! Someone remembered the bath mat," Enoch deadpanned. "We are saved."

Everything else was gone, including both our maps—the small one Emma had used to navigate us across the channel and the massive leather-bound loop atlas that had been Millard's prized possession, the Map of Days. When Millard realized it was gone he began to hyperventilate. "That was one of only five extant copies!" he moaned. "It was of incalculable value! Not to mention it contained years of my personal notes and annotations!"

"At least we still have the *Tales of the Peculiar*," said Claire, wringing seawater from her blonde curls. "I can't get to sleep at night without hearing one."

"What good are fairy tales if we can't even find our way?" Millard asked.

I wondered: *Find our way to where?* It occurred to me that, in our rush to escape the island, I had only ever heard the children talk about reaching the mainland, but we'd never discussed what to do once we got there—as if the idea of actually surviving the journey in those tiny boats was so far-fetched, so comically optimistic, that planning for it was a waste of time. I looked to Emma for reassurance, as I often did. She gazed darkly down the beach. The stony sand backed up to low dunes swaying with saw grass. Beyond was forest: an impenetrable-looking barrier of green that continued in both directions as far as I could see. Emma with her now-lost map had been aiming for a certain port town, but after the storm hit, just making it to dry land had become our goal. There was no telling how far we'd strayed off course. There were no roads I could see, or signposts, or even footpaths. Only wilderness.

Of course, we didn't really need a map, or a signpost, or anything else. We needed Miss Peregrine—a whole, healed one—the Miss Peregrine who would know just where to go and how to get us there safely. The one perched before us now, fanning her feathers dry on a boulder, was as broken as her maimed wing, which hooked downward in an alarming V. I could tell it pained the children to see her like this. She was supposed to be their mother, their protector. She'd been queen of their little island world, but now she couldn't speak, couldn't loop time, couldn't even fly. They saw her and winced and looked away.

Miss Peregrine kept her eyes trained on the slate-gray sea. They were hard and black and contained unutterable sorrow.

They seemed to say: *I failed you.*

*   *   *

Horace and Fiona arced toward us through the rocky sand, the wind poofing Fiona's wild hair like a storm cloud, Horace bouncing with his hands pressed against the sides of his top hat to keep it secure on his head. Somehow he had kept hold of it throughout our near disaster at sea, but now it was stove in on one side like a bent muffler pipe. Still, he refused to let it go; it was the only thing, he said, that matched his muddy, sopping, finely tailored suit.

Their arms were empty. "There's no wood anywhere!" Horace said as they reached us.

"Did you look in the *woods*?" said Emma, pointing at the dark line of trees behind the dunes.

"Too scary," Horace replied. "We heard an owl."

"Since when are you afraid of birds?"

Horace shrugged and looked at the sand. Then Fiona elbowed him, and he seemed to remember himself, and said: "We found something else, though."

"Shelter?" asked Emma.

"A road?" asked Millard.

"A goose to cook for supper?" asked Claire.

"No," Horace replied. "Balloons."

There was a brief, puzzled silence.

"What do you mean, balloons?" said Emma.

"Big ones in the sky, with men inside."

Emma's face darkened. "Show us."

We followed them back the way they'd come, curving around a bend in the beach and climbing a small embankment. I wondered how we could have possibly missed something as obvious as hot air balloons, until we crested a hill and I saw them—not the big, colorful teardrop-shaped things you see in wall calendars and motivational posters ("*The sky's the limit!*"), but a pair of miniature zeppelins: black egg-shaped sacs of gas with skeletal cages hung below them, each containing a single pilot. The craft were small and flew low, banking back and forth in lazy zigzags, and the noise of the surf had covered the subtle whine of their propellers. Emma herded us into the tall saw grass and we dropped down out of sight.

"They're submarine hunters," Enoch said, answering the question before anyone had asked it. Millard might've been the authority when it came to maps and books, but Enoch was an expert in all things military. "The best way to spot enemy subs is from the sky," he explained.

"Then why are they flying so close to the ground?" I asked. "And why aren't they farther out to sea?"

"That I don't know."

"Do you think they could be looking for . . . us?" Horace

ventured.

"If you mean could they be wights," said Hugh, "don't be daft. The wights are with the Germans. They're on that German sub."

"The wights are allied with whomever it suits their interests to be allied with," Millard said. "There's no reason to think they haven't infiltrated organizations on both sides of the war."

I couldn't take my eyes off the strange contraptions in the sky. They looked unnatural, like mechanical insects bloated with tumorous eggs.

"I don't like the way they're flying," Enoch said, calculating behind his sharp eyes. "They're searching the coastline, not the sea."

"Searching for what?" asked Bronwyn, but the answer was obvious and frightening and no one wanted to say it aloud.

They were searching for us.

We were all squeezed together in the grass, and I felt Emma's body tense next to mine. "Run when I say run," she hissed. "We'll hide the boats, then ourselves."

We waited for the balloons to zag away, then tumbled out of the grass, praying we were too far away to be spotted. As we ran I found myself wishing that the fog which had plagued us at sea would return again to hide us. It occurred to me that it had very likely saved us once already; without the fog those balloons would've spotted us hours ago, in our boats, when we'd had nowhere to run. And in that way, it was one last thing that the island had done to save its peculiar children.

We dragged our boats across the beach toward a sea cave, its entrance a black fissure in a hill of rocks. Bronwyn had spent her strength completely and could hardly manage to carry herself, much less the boats, so the rest of us struggled to pick up the slack, groaning and straining against hulls that kept trying to bury their noses in the wet sand. Halfway across the beach, Miss Peregrine let out a warning cry, and the two zeppelins bobbed up over the dunes and into our line of sight. We broke into an adrenaline-fueled sprint, flying those boats into the cave like they were on rails, while Miss Peregrine hopped lamely alongside us, her broken wing dragging in the sand.

When we were finally out of sight we dropped the boats and flopped onto their overturned keels, our wheezing breaths echoing in the damp and dripping dark. "Please, please let them not have seen us," Emma prayed aloud.

"Ah, birds! Our tracks!" Millard yelped, and then he stripped off the overcoat he'd been wearing and scrambled back outside to cover the drag marks our boats had made; from the sky they'd look like arrows pointing right to our hiding place. We could only watch his footsteps trail away. If anyone but Millard had ventured out, they'd have been seen for sure.

A minute later he came back, shivering, caked in sand, a red stain outlining his chest. "They're getting close now," he panted. "I did the best I could."

"You're bleeding again!" Bronwyn fretted. Millard had been grazed by a bullet during our melee at the lighthouse the previous night, and though his recovery so far was remarkable, it was far from complete. "What have you done with your wound dressing?"

"I threw it away. It was tied in such a complicated manner that I couldn't remove it quickly. An invisible must always be able to disrobe in an instant, or his power is useless!"

"He's even more useless dead, you stubborn mule," said Emma. "Now hold still and don't bite your tongue. This is going to hurt." She squeezed two fingers in the palm of her opposite hand, concentrated for a moment, and when she took them out again they glowed, red hot.

Millard balked. "Now then, Emma, I'd rather you didn't—"

Emma pressed her fingers to his wounded shoulder. Millard gasped. There was the sound of singeing meat, and a curl of smoke rose up from his skin. In a moment the bleeding stopped.

"I'll have a scar!" Millard whined.

"Yes? And who'll see it?"

He sulked and said nothing.

The balloons' engines grew louder, then louder still, amplified by the cave's stone walls. I pictured them hovering above the cave, studying our footprints, preparing their assault. Emma leaned her shoulder into mine. The little ones ran to Bronwyn and buried their faces in her lap, and she hugged them. Despite our peculiar powers, we felt utterly powerless: it was all we could do to sit hunched and blinking at one another in the pale half-light, noses running from the cold, hoping our enemies would pass us by.

Finally the engines' whine began to dwindle, and when we could hear our own voices again, Claire mumbled into Bronwyn's lap, "Tell us a story, Wyn. I'm scared and I don't like this at all and I think I'd like to hear a story instead."

"Yes, would you tell one?" Olive pleaded. "A story from the *Tales*, please. They're my favorite."

The most maternal of the peculiars, Bronwyn was more like a mother to the young ones than even Miss Peregrine. It was Bronwyn who tucked them into bed at night, Bronwyn who read them stories and kissed their foreheads. Her strong arms seemed made to gather them in warm embraces, her broad shoulders to carry them. But this was no time for stories—and she said as much.

"Why, certainly it is!" Enoch said with singsongy sarcasm. "But skip the *Tales* for once and tell us the story of how Miss Peregrine's wards found their way to safety without a map or any food and weren't eaten by hollowgast along the way! I'm ever so keen to hear how *that* story ends."

"If only Miss Peregrine could tell us," Claire sniffled. She disentangled herself from Bronwyn and went to the bird, who'd been watching us from her perch on one of the boats' overturned keels. "What are we to do, headmistress?" said Claire. "Please turn human again. Please wake up!"

Miss Peregrine cooed and stroked Claire's hair with her wing. Then Olive joined in, her face streaking with tears: "We need you, Miss Peregrine! We're lost and in danger and increasingly peckish and we've got no home anymore nor any friends but one another and we *need* you!"

Miss Peregrine's black eyes shimmered. She turned away, unreachable.

Bronwyn knelt down beside the girls. "She can't turn back right now, sweetheart. But we'll get her fixed up, I promise."

"But *how*?" Olive demanded. Her question reflected off the stone walls, each echo asking it again.

Emma stood up. "*I'll* tell you how," she said, and all eyes went to her. "We'll *walk*." She said it with such conviction that I got a chill. "We'll walk and walk until we come to a town."

"What if there's no town for fifty miles?" said Enoch.

"Then we'll walk for fifty-one miles. But I know we weren't blown *that* far off course."

"And if the wights should spot us from the air?" said Hugh.

"They won't. We'll be careful."

"And if they're waiting for us in the town?" said Horace.

"We'll pretend to be normal. We'll pass."

"I was never much good at that," Millard said with a laugh.

"You won't be seen at all, Mill. You'll be our advance scout, and our secret procurer of necessary items."

"I *am* quite a talented thief," he said with a touch of pride. "A veritable master of the five-fingered arts."

"And then?" Enoch muttered sourly. "Maybe we'll have food in our bellies and a warm place to sleep, but we'll still be out in the open, exposed, vulnerable, loopless . . . and Miss Peregrine is . . . is still . . ."

"We'll find a loop somehow," said Emma. "There are landmarks and signposts for those who know what to look for. And if there aren't, we'll find someone like us, a fellow peculiar who can show us where the nearest loop is. And in that loop there will be an ymbryne, and that ymbryne will be able to give Miss Peregrine the help she needs."

I'd never met anyone with Emma's brash confidence. Everything about her exuded it: the way she carried herself, with shoulders thrown back; the hard set of her teeth when she made up her mind about something; the way she ended every sentence with a declarative period, never a question mark. It was infectious and I loved it, and I had to fight a sudden urge to kiss her, right there in front of everyone.

Hugh coughed, and bees tumbled out of his mouth to form a question mark that shivered in the air. "How can you be so bloody *sure*?" he asked.

"Because I am, that's all." And she brushed her hands as if that were that.

"You make a nice rousing speech," said Millard, "and I hate to spoil it, but for all we know, Miss Peregrine is the only ymbryne left uncaptured. Recall what Miss Avocet told us: the wights have been raiding loops and abducting ymbrynes for *weeks* now. Which means that even if we *could* find a loop, there'd be no way of knowing whether it still had its ymbryne—or was occupied instead by our enemies. We can't simply go knocking on loop doors and hoping they aren't full of wights."

"Or surrounded by half-starved hollows," Enoch said.

"We won't *have* to hope," Emma said, then smiled in my direction. "Jacob will tell us."

My entire body went cold. "*Me?*"

"You can sense hollows from a distance, can't you?" said Emma. "In addition to seeing them?"

"When they're close, it kind of feels like I'm going to puke," I admitted.

"How close do they have to be?" asked Millard. "If it's only a few meters, that still puts us within devouring range. We'd need you to sense them from much farther away."

"I haven't exactly tested it," I said. "This is all so new to me."

I'd only ever been exposed to Dr. Golan's hollow, Malthus—the creature who'd killed my grandfather, then nearly drowned me in Cairnholm's bog. How far away had he been when I'd first felt him stalking me, lurking outside my house in Englewood? It was impossible to know.

"Regardless, your talent can be developed," said Millard. "Peculiarities are a bit like muscles—the more you exercise them, the bigger they grow."

"This is madness!" Enoch said. "Are you all really so desperate that you'd stake everything on *him*? Why, he's just a boy—a soft-bellied normal who knows next to nothing of our world!"

"He isn't *normal*," Emma said, grimacing as if this were the direst insult. "He's one of us!"

"Stuff and rubbish!" yelled Enoch. "Just because there's a dash of peculiar blood in his veins doesn't make him my brother. And it certainly doesn't make him my protector! We don't know what he's capable of—he probably wouldn't know the difference between a hollow at fifty meters and gas pains!"

"He *killed* one of them, didn't he?" said Bronwyn. "Stabbed it through the eyes with a pair of sheep shears! When's the last time you heard of a peculiar so young doing anything like that?"

"Not since Abe," Hugh said, and at the mention of his name a reverent hush fell over the children.

"I heard he once killed one with his bare hands," said Bronwyn.

"*I* heard he killed one with a knitting needle and a length of twine," said Horace. "In fact, I dreamed it, so I'm certain he did."

"Half of those stories are just tall tales, and they get taller with every year that passes," said Enoch. "The Abraham Portman I knew never did a single thing to help us."

"He was a great peculiar!" said Bronwyn. "He fought bravely and killed scores of hollows for our cause!"

"And then he ran off and left us to hide in that house like refugees while he galavanted around America, playing hero!"

"You don't know what you're talking about," Emma said, flushing with anger. "There was a lot more to it than that."

Enoch shrugged. "Anyway, that's all beside the point," he said. "Whatever you thought of Abe, this boy isn't him."

In that moment I hated Enoch, and yet I couldn't blame him for his doubts about me. How could the others, so sure and seasoned in their abilities, put so much faith in mine—in something I was only beginning to understand and had known I was capable of for only a few days? Whose grandson I was seemed irrelevant. I simply didn't know what I was doing.

"You're right, I'm not my grandfather," I said. "I'm just a kid from Florida. I probably got lucky when I killed that hollow."

"Nonsense," said Emma. "You'll be every bit the hollow-slayer Abe was, one day."

"One day soon, let's hope," said Hugh.

"It's your destiny," said Horace, and the way he said it made me think he knew something I didn't.

"And even if it ain't," said Hugh, clapping his hand on my back, "you're all we've got, mate."

"If that's true, bird help us all," said Enoch.

My head was spinning. The weight of their expectations threatened to crush me. I stood, unsteady, and moved toward the cave exit. "I need some air," I said, pushing past Enoch.

"Jacob, wait!" cried Emma. "The balloons!"

But they were long gone.

"Let him go," Enoch grumbled. "If we're lucky, he'll swim back to America."

Walking down to the water's edge, I tried to picture myself the way my new friends saw me, or wanted to: not as Jacob, the kid who once broke his ankle running after an ice cream truck, or who reluctantly and at the behest of his dad tried and failed three times to get onto his school's noncompetitive track team, but as Jacob, inspector of shadows, miraculous interpreter of squirmy gut feelings, seer and slayer of real and actual monsters—and all that might stand between life and death for our merry band of peculiars.

How could I ever live up to my grandfather's legacy?

I climbed a stack of rocks at the water's edge and stood there, hoping the steady breeze would dry my damp clothes, and in the dying light I watched the sea, a canvas of shifting grays, melded and darkening. In the distance a light glinted every so often. It was Cairnholm's lighthouse, flashing its hello and last goodbye.

My mind drifted. I lapsed into a waking dream.

I see a man. He is of middle age, cloaked in excremental mud, crabbing slowly along the knife tip of a cliff, his thin hair uncombed and hanging wet across his face. Wind whips his thin jacket like a sail. He stops, drops to his elbows. Slips them into divots he'd made weeks before, when he was scouting these coves for mating terns and shearwaters' nests. He raises a pair of binoculars to his eyes but aims them low, below the nests, at a thin crescent of beach where the swelling tide collects things and heaves them up: driftwood and seaweed, shards of smashed boats—and sometimes, the locals say, bodies.

The man is my father. He is looking for something that he desperately does not want to find.

He is looking for the body of his son.

I felt a touch on my shoe and opened my eyes, startled out of my half-dream. It was nearly dark, and I was sitting on the rocks with my knees drawn into my chest, and suddenly there was Emma, breeze tossing her hair, standing on the sand below me.

"How are you?" she asked.

It was a question that would've required some college-level math and about an hour of discussion to answer. I felt a hundred conflicting things, the great bulk of which canceled out to equal cold and tired and not particularly interested in talking. So I said, "I'm fine, just trying to dry off," and flapped the front of my soggy sweater to demonstrate.

"I can help you with that." She clambered up the stack of rocks and sat next to me. "Gimme an arm."

I offered one up and Emma laid it across her knees. Cupping her hands over her mouth, she bent her head toward my wrist. Then, taking a deep breath, she exhaled slowly through her palms and an incredible, soothing heat bloomed along my forearm, just on the edge of painful.

"Is it too much?" she said.

I tensed, a shudder going through me, and shook my head.

"Good." She moved farther up my arm to exhale again. Another pulse of sweet warmth. Between breaths, she said, "I hope you're not letting what Enoch said bother you. The rest of us believe in you, Jacob. Enoch can be a wrinkle-hearted old titmouse, especially when he's feeling jealous."

"I think he's right," I said.

"You don't really. Do you?"

It all came pouring out. "I have no idea what I'm doing," I said. "How can any of you depend on me? If I'm really peculiar then it's just a little bit, I think. Like I'm a quarter peculiar and the rest of you guys are full-blooded."

"It doesn't work that way," she said, laughing.

"But my grandfather was more peculiar than me. He had to be. He was so strong . . ."

"No, Jacob," she said, narrowing her eyes at me. "It's astounding. In so many ways, you're just like him. You're different, too, of course—you're gentler and sweeter—but everything you're saying . . . you sound like Abe, when he first came to stay with us."

"I do?"

"Yes. He was confused, too. He'd never met another peculiar. He didn't understand his power or how it worked or what he was capable of. Neither did we, to tell the truth. It's very rare, what you can do. Very rare. But your grandfather learned."

"How?" I asked. "Where?"

"In the war. He was part of a secret all-peculiar cell of the British army. Fought hollowgast and Germans at the same time. The sorts of things they did you don't win medals for—but they were heroes to us, and none more than your grandfather. The sacrifices they made set the corrupted back decades and saved the lives of countless peculiars."

And yet, I thought, *he couldn't save his own parents. How strangely tragic.*

"And I can tell you this," Emma went on. "You're every bit as peculiar as he was—and as brave, too."

"Ha. Now you're just trying to make me feel better."

"No," she said, looking me in the eye. "I'm not. You'll learn, Jacob. One day you'll be an even greater hollow-slayer than he was."

"Yeah, that's what everyone keeps saying. How can you be so sure?"

"It's something I feel very deeply," she said. "You're *supposed to*, I think. Just like you were supposed to come to Cairnholm."

"I don't believe in stuff like that. Fate. The stars. Destiny."

"I didn't say destiny."

"*Supposed to* is the same thing," I said. "Destiny is for people in books about magical swords. It's a lot of crap. I'm here because my grandfather mumbled something about your island in the ten seconds before he died—and that's it. It was an accident. I'm glad he did, but he was delirious. He could just as easily have rattled off a grocery list."

"But he *didn't*," she said.

I sighed, exasperated. "And if we go off in search of loops, and you depend on me to save you from monsters and instead I get you all killed, is that destiny, too?"

She frowned, put my arm back in my lap. "I didn't say *destiny*," she said again. "What I believe is that when it comes to big things in life, there are no accidents. Everything happens for a reason. *You're* here for a reason—and it's not to fail and die."

I didn't have the heart to keep arguing. "Okay," I said. "I don't think you're right—but I do *hope* you are." I felt bad for snapping at her before, but I'd been cold and scared and feeling defensive. I had good moments and bad, terrified thoughts and confident ones—though my terror-to-confidence ratio was pretty dismal at present, like three-to-one, and in the terrified moments it felt like I was being pushed into a role I hadn't asked for; volunteered for front-line duty in a war, the full scope of which none of us yet knew. "Destiny" sounded like an obligation, and if I was to be thrust into battle against a legion of nightmare creatures, that had to be my choice.

Though in a sense the choice had been made already, when I agreed to sail into the unknown with these peculiar children. And it wasn't true, if I really searched the dusty corners of myself, that I hadn't asked for this. Really, I'd been dreaming of such adventures since I was small. Back then I'd believed in destiny, and believed in it absolutely, with every strand and fiber of my little kid heart. I'd felt it like an itch in my chest while listening to my grandfather's extraordinary stories. *One day that will be me.* What felt like obligation now had been a promise back then—that one day I would escape my little town and live an extraordinary life, as he had done; and that one day, like Grandpa Portman, I would do something that mattered. He used to say to me: "You're going to be a great man, Yakob. A very great man."

"Like you?" I would ask him.

"Better," he'd reply.

I'd believed him then, and I still wanted to. But the more I learned about him, the longer his shadow became, and the more impossible it seemed that I could ever matter the way he had. That maybe it would be suicidal even to try. And when I imagined myself trying, thoughts of my father crept in—my poor about-to-be-devastated father—and before I could push them out of my mind, I wondered how a great man could do something so terrible to someone who loved him.

I began to shiver. "You're cold," Emma said. "Let me finish what I started." She picked up my other arm and kissed with her breath the whole length of it. It was almost more than I could handle. When she reached my shoulder, instead of placing the arm in my lap, she hung it around her neck. I lifted my other arm to join it, and she put her arms around me, too, and our foreheads nodded together.

Speaking very quietly, Emma said, "I hope you don't regret the choice you made. I'm so glad you're here with us. I don't know what I'd do if you left. I fear I wouldn't be all right at all."

I thought about going back. For a moment I really tried to play it out in my head, how it would be if I could somehow row one of our boats back to the island again, and go back home.

But I couldn't do it. I couldn't imagine.

I whispered: "How could I?"

"When Miss Peregrine turns human again, she'll be able to send you back. If you want to go."

My question hadn't been about logistics. I had meant, simply: *How could I leave you?* But those words were unsayable, couldn't find their way past my lips. So I held them inside, and instead I kissed her.

This time it was Emma whose breath caught short. Her hands rose to my cheeks but stopped just shy of making contact. Heat radiated from them in waves.

"Touch me," I said.

"I don't want to burn you," she said, but a sudden shower of sparks inside my chest said *I don't care*, so I took her fingers and raked them along my cheek, and both of us gasped. It was hot but I didn't pull away. Dared not, for fear she'd stop touching me. And then our lips met again and we were kissing again, and her extraordinary warmth surged through me.

My eyes fell closed. The world faded away.

If my body was cold in the night mist, I didn't feel it. If the sea roared in my ears, I didn't hear it. If the rock I sat on was sharp and jagged, I hardly noticed. Everything outside the two of us was a distraction.

And then a great crash echoed in the dark, but I thought nothing of it—could not take myself away from Emma—until the sound doubled and was joined by an awful shriek of metal, and a blinding light swept over us, and finally I couldn't shut it out anymore.

The lighthouse, I thought. *The lighthouse is falling into the sea.* But the lighthouse was a pinpoint in the distance, not a sun-bright flash, and its light only traveled in one direction, not back and forth, searching.

It wasn't a lighthouse at all. It was a searchlight—and it was coming from the water close to shore.

It was the searchlight of a submarine.

* * *

Brief second of terror in which brain and legs were disconnected. My eyes and ears registered the submarine not far from shore: metal beast rising from the sea, water rushing from its sides, men bursting onto its deck from open hatches, shouting, training cannons of light at us. And then the stimulus reached my legs and we slid, fell, and pitched ourselves down from the rocks and ran like hell.

The spotlight threw our pistoning shadows across the beach,

ten feet tall and freakish. Bullets pocked the sand and buzzed the air.

A voice boomed from a loudspeaker. "STOP! DO NOT RUN!"

We burst into the cave—*They're coming, they're here, get up, get up*—but the children had heard the commotion and were already on their feet—all but Bronwyn, who had so exhausted herself at sea that she had fallen asleep against the cave wall and couldn't be roused. We shook her and shouted in her face, but she only moaned and brushed us away with a sweep of her arm. Finally we had to hoist her up by the waist, which was like lifting a tower of bricks, but once her feet touched the ground, her red-rimmed eyelids split open and she took her own weight.

We grabbed up our things, thankful now that they were so small and so few. Emma scooped Miss Peregrine into her arms. We tore outside. As we ran into the dunes, I saw behind us a gang of silhouetted men splashing the last few feet to shore. In their hands, held above their heads to keep them dry, were guns.

We sprinted through a stand of windblown trees and into the trackless forest. Darkness enveloped us. What moon wasn't already hidden behind clouds was blotted out now by trees, branches filtering its pale light to nil. There was no time for our eyes to adjust or to feel our way carefully or to do anything other than run in a gasping, stumbling herd with arms outstretched, dodging trunks that seemed to coalesce suddenly in the air just inches from us.

After a few minutes we stopped, chests heaving, to listen. The voices were still behind us, only now they were joined by another sound: dogs barking.

We ran on.

CHAPTER THREE

*W*e tumbled through the black woods for what seemed like hours, no moon or movement of stars by which to judge the passing time. The sound of men shouting and dogs barking wheeled around us as we ran, menacing us from everywhere and nowhere. To throw the dogs off our scent, we waded into an icy stream and followed it until our feet went numb, and when we crossed out of it again, it felt like I was stumbling along on prickling stumps.

After a time we began to fail. Someone moaned in the dark. Olive and Claire started to fall behind, so Bronwyn hefted them into her arms, but then she couldn't keep up, either. Finally, when Horace tripped over a root and fell to the ground and then lay there begging for a rest, we all stopped. "Up, you lazy sod!" Enoch hissed at him, but he was wheezing, too, and then he leaned against a tree to catch his breath and the fight seemed to go out of him.

We were reaching the limit of our endurance. We had to stop.

"It's no use running circles in the dark like this, anyway," said Emma. "We could just as easily end up right back where we started."

"We'll be able to make better sense of this forest in the light of day," said Millard.

"Provided we live that long," said Enoch.

A light rain hissed down. Fiona made a shelter for us by coaxing a ring of trees to bend their lower branches together, petting their bark and whispering to their trunks until the branches meshed to form a watertight roof of leaves just high enough for us to sit beneath. We crawled in and lay listening to the rain and the distant barking of dogs. Somewhere in the forest, men with guns were still hunting us. Alone with our thoughts, I'm sure each of us was wondering the same thing—what might happen to us if we were caught.

Claire began to cry, softly at first but then louder and louder, until both of her mouths were bawling and she could hardly catch a breath between sobs.

"Get ahold of yourself!" Enoch said. "They'll hear you—and then we'll all have something to cry about!"

"They're going to feed us to their dogs!" she said. "They're going to shoot holes in us and take Miss Peregrine away!"

Bronwyn scooted next to her and wrapped the little girl in a bear hug. "Please, Claire! You've got to think about something else!"

"I'm truh-trying!" she wailed.

"Try *harder*!"

Claire squeezed her eyes shut, drew in a deep breath, and held it until she looked like a balloon about to pop—then burst into a fit of gasping cough-sobs that were louder than ever.

Enoch clapped his hands over her mouths. "*Shhhhhhh!*"

"I'm suh-suh-sorry!" she blubbered. "Muh-maybe if I could hear a story . . . one of the tuh-*Tales* . . ."

"Not this again," said Millard. "I'm beginning to wish we'd lost those damned books at sea with the rest of our things!"

Miss Peregrine spoke up—inasmuch as she was able to—hopping atop Bronwyn's trunk and tapping it with her beak. Inside, along with the rest of our meager possessions, were the *Tales*.

"I'm with Miss P," said Enoch. "It's worth a try—anything to stop her bawling!"

"All right then, little one," Bronwyn said, "but just one tale, and you've got to promise to stop crying!"

"I pruh-promise," Claire sniffled.

Bronwyn opened the trunk and pulled out a waterlogged volume of *Tales of the Peculiar*. Emma scooted close and lit the tiniest wisp of flame on her fingertip to read by. Then Miss Peregrine, apparently impatient to pacify Claire, took one edge of the book's cover in her beak and opened it to a seemingly random chapter. In a hushed voice, Bronwyn began to read.

"Once upon a peculiar time, in a forest deep and ancient, there roamed a great many animals. There were rabbits and deer and foxes, just as there are in every forest, but there were animals of a less common sort, too, like stilt-legged grimbears and two-headed lynxes and talking emu-raffes. These peculiar animals were a favorite target of hunters, who loved to shoot them and mount them on walls and show them off to their hunter friends, but loved even more to sell them to zookeepers, who would lock them in cages and charge money to view them. Now, you might think it would be far better to be locked in a cage than to be shot and mounted upon a wall, but peculiar creatures must roam free to be happy, and after a while the spirits of caged ones wither, and they begin to envy their wall-mounted friends."

"This is a sad story," Claire groused. "Tell a different one."

"I like it," said Enoch. "Tell more about the shooting and mounting."

Bronwyn ignored them both. "Now this was an age when giants still roamed the Earth," she went on, "as they did in the long-ago *Aldinn* times, though they were few in number and diminishing. And it just so happened that one of these giants lived near the forest, and he was very kind and spoke very softly and ate only plants and his name was Cuthbert. One day Cuthbert came into the forest to gather berries, and there saw a hunter hunting an emu-raffe. Being the kindly giant that he was, Cuthbert picked up the little 'raffe by the scruff of its long neck, and by standing up to his full height, on tiptoe, which he rarely did because it made all his old bones crackle, Cuthbert was able to reach up very high and deposit the emu-raffe on a mountaintop, well out of danger. Then, just for good measure, he squashed the hunter to jelly between his toes.

"Word of Cuthbert's kindness spread throughout the forest,

and soon peculiar animals were coming to him every day, asking to be lifted up to the mountaintop and out of danger. And Cuthbert said, 'I'll protect you, little brothers and sisters. All I ask in return is that you talk to me and keep me company. There aren't many giants left in the world, and I get lonely from time to time.'

"And they said, 'Of course, Cuthbert, we will.'

"So every day Cuthbert saved more peculiar animals from the hunters, lifting them up to the mountain by the scruffs of their necks, until there was a whole peculiar menagerie up there. And the animals were happy there because they could finally live in peace, and Cuthbert was happy, too, because if he stood on his tiptoes and rested his chin on the top of the mountain he could talk to his new friends all he liked. Then one morning a witch came to see Cuthbert. He was bathing in a little lake in the shadow of the mountain when she said to him, 'I'm terribly sorry, but I've got to turn you into stone now.'

"'Why would you do something like that?' asked the giant. 'I'm very kindly. A helping sort of giant.'

"And she said, 'I was hired by the family of the hunter you squashed.'

"'Ah,' he replied. 'Forgot about him.'

"'I'm terribly sorry,' the witch said again, and then she waved a birch branch at him and poor Cuthbert turned to stone.

"All of the sudden Cuthbert became very heavy—so heavy that he began to sink into the lake. He sank and sank and didn't stop sinking until he was covered in water all the way up to his neck. His animal friends saw what was happening, and though they felt terrible about it, they decided they could do nothing to help him.

"'I know you can't save me,' Cuthbert shouted up to his friends, 'but at least come and talk to me! I'm stuck down here, and so very lonely!'

"'But if we come down there the hunters will shoot us!' they called back.

"Cuthbert knew they were right, but still he pleaded with them.

"'Talk to me!' he cried. 'Please come and talk to me!'

"The animals tried singing and shouting to poor Cuthbert from the safety of their mountaintop, but they were too distant and their voices too small, so that even to Cuthbert and his giant ears they sounded quieter than the whisper of leaves in the wind.

"'Talk to me!' he begged. 'Come and talk to me!'

"But they never did. And he was still crying when his throat turned to stone like the rest of him. The end."

Bronwyn closed the book.

Claire looked appalled. "That's *it*?"

Enoch began to laugh.

"That's it," Bronwyn said.

"That's a *terrible* story," said Claire. "Tell another one!"

"A story's a story," said Emma, "and now it's time for bed."

Claire pouted, but she had stopped crying, so the tale had served its purpose.

"Tomorrow's not likely to be any easier than today was," said Millard. "We'll need what rest we can get."

We gathered cuts of springy moss to use as pillows, Emma drying the rain from them with her hands before we tucked them under our heads. Lacking blankets, we nestled together for warmth: Bronwyn cuddling the small ones; Fiona entangled with Hugh, whose bees came and went from his open mouth as he snored, keeping watch over their sleeping master; Horace and Enoch shivering with their backs to one another, too proud to snuggle; myself with Emma. I lay on my back and she in the crook of my arm, head on my chest, her face so invitingly close to mine that I could kiss her forehead anytime I liked—and I wouldn't have stopped except that I was as tired as a dead man and she was as warm as an electric blanket and pretty soon I was asleep and dreaming pleasant, forgettable nothings.

I never remember nice dreams; only the bad ones stick.

It was a miracle that I could sleep at all, given the circumstances. Even here—running for our lives, sleeping exposed, facing death—even here, in her arms, I was able to find some measure of peace.

Watching over us all, her black eyes shining in the dark, was Miss Peregrine. Though damaged and diminished, she was still our protector.

The night turned raw, and Claire began to shake and cough. Bronwyn nudged Emma awake and said, "Miss Bloom, the little one needs you; I'm afraid she's taking ill," and with a whispered apology Emma slipped out of my arms to go and attend to Claire. I felt a twinge of jealousy, then guilt for being jealous of a sick friend. So I lay alone feeling irrationally forsaken and stared into the dark, more exhausted than I had ever been and yet unable now to sleep, listening to the others shift and moan in the grip of nightmares that could not have equalled the one we would likely wake to. And eventually the dark peeled back layer by layer, and with imperceptible gradations the sky feathered to a delicate pale blue.

*　　*　　*

At dawn we crawled from our shelter. I picked moss out of my hair and tried in vain to brush the mud from my pants, but succeeded only in smearing it, making me look like some bog creature vomited from the earth. I was hungry in a way I'd never experienced, my belly gnawing at itself from the inside, and I ached just about everywhere it was possible to ache, from rowing and running and sleeping on the ground. Still, a few mercies prevailed: overnight the rain had let up, the day was warming by degrees, and we seemed to have evaded the wights and their dogs, at least for the time being; either they'd stopped barking or were too far away to be heard.

In doing so we'd gotten ourselves hopelessly lost. The forest was no easier to navigate by day than it had been in the dark. Green-boughed firs stretched away in endless, disordered rows, each direction a mirror of the others. The ground here was a carpet of fallen leaves that hid any tracks we might've made the night before. We'd woken in the heart of a green labyrinth without a map or compass, and Miss Peregrine's broken wing meant she couldn't fly above the treeline to guide us. Enoch suggested we raise Olive above the trees, like we had in the fog, but we didn't have any rope to hold her, and if she slipped and fell into the sky, we'd never get her back again.

Claire was sick and getting sicker, and lay curled in Bronwyn's lap, sweat beading her forehead despite a chill in the air. She was so skinny I could count her ribs through her dress.

"Will she be all right?" I asked.

"She's feverish," Bronwyn said, pressing a hand to the girl's cheek. "She needs medicine."

"First we'll have to find our way out of this accursed forest," said Millard.

"First we should eat," said Enoch. "Let's eat and discuss our options."

"What options?" said Emma. "Pick a direction and we'll walk in it. Any one's as good as another."

In sullen silence we sat and ate. I've never tasted dog food but I'm sure this was worse—brownish squares of congealed meat fat from rusted tins, which, lacking utensils, we dug out with our fingers.

"I packed five salted game hens and three tins of foie gras with cornichons," Horace said bitterly, "and *this* is what survives our shipwreck." He held his nose and dropped a gelatinous nugget down his throat without chewing. "I think we're being punished."

"For what?" said Emma. "We've been perfect angels. Well, most of us."

"The sins of past lives, maybe. I don't know."

"Peculiars don't have past lives," said Millard. "We live them all at once."

We finished quickly, buried our empty tins, and prepared to go. Just as we were about to, Hugh burst through a thicket of bushes into our makeshift camp, bees circling his head in an agitated cloud. He was out of breath with excitement.

"Where have *you* been?" Enoch demanded.

"I needed some privacy to attend to my morning never-you-minds," Hugh said, "and I found—"

"Who gave you permission to be out of visual range?" Enoch said. "We nearly left without you!"

"Who says I need permission? Anyway, I saw—"

"You can't just wander away like that! What if you'd gotten lost?"

"We're *already* lost."

"You ignoramus! What if you couldn't find your way back?"

"I left a trail of bees, like I always do—"

"Would you kindly *let him finish*!" Emma shouted.

"Thank you," said Hugh, and then he turned and pointed back the way he'd come. "I saw water. Quite a lot of it, through the trees there."

Emma's face clouded. She said, "We're trying to get *away* from the sea, not back to it. We must've doubled back on ourselves in the night."

We followed Hugh back the way he'd come, Bronwyn carrying Miss Peregrine on her shoulder and poor sick Claire in her arms. After a hundred yards, a glisten of gray ripples appeared beyond the trees: some wide body of water.

"Oh, this is just *awful*," said Horace. "They've chased us right back into their arms!"

"I don't *hear* any soldiers," said Emma. "In fact, I don't hear anything at all. Not even the ocean."

Enoch said, "That's because it's *not* the ocean, you dolt," and he stood up and ran toward the water. When we caught up with him he was standing with his feet planted in wet sand, looking back at us with a self-satisfied *I-told-you-so* grin. He'd been right: this wasn't the sea. It was a misty, gray lake, wide and ringed with firs, its calm surface smooth as slate. But its most distinguishing feature was something I didn't notice right away; not until Claire pointed out a large rock formation jutting from the shallows nearby. My eyes skimmed it at first but then went back for a second glance. There was something eerie about it—and decidedly familiar.

"It's the giant from the story!" said Claire, pointing from her place in Bronwyn's arms. "It's Cuthbert!"

Bronwyn stroked her head. "Shh, honey, you've got fever."

"Don't be ridiculous," said Enoch. "It's just a rock."

But it wasn't. Though wind and rain had worn its features some, it looked just like a giant who'd sunk up to its neck in the lake. You could see clearly that it had a head and a neck and a nose and even an Adam's apple, and some scrubby trees were growing atop it like a crown of wild hair. But what was really uncanny was the position of its head—thrown back with its mouth open, as if, like the giant in the story we'd heard just last night, it had turned to stone while crying out to its friends on the mountaintop.

"And look!" said Olive, pointing at a rocky bluff rising in the distance. "That must be Cuthbert's mountain!"

"Giants are real," Claire murmured, her voice weak but full of wonder. "And so are the *Tales*!"

"Let's not jump to absurd conclusions," said Enoch. "What's more likely? That the writer of the tale we read last night was inspired by a rock that just happened to be shaped like a giant head, or that this head-shaped rock was really a giant?"

"You take the fun out of everything," said Olive. "*I* believe in giants, even if you don't!"

"The *Tales* are just tales and nothing more," Enoch grumbled.

"Funny," I said, "that's exactly what I thought all of *you* were, before I met you."

Olive laughed. "Jacob, you're silly. You really thought we were made up?"

"Of course. And even after I met you I still did, for a while. Like maybe I was losing my mind."

"Real or not, it's an incredible coincidence," said Millard. "To have been reading that story just last night, and then happen upon the very bit of geography that inspired it the next morning? What are the chances?"

"I don't think it's a coincidence," Emma said. "Miss Peregrine opened the book herself, remember? She must've chosen that story on purpose."

Bronwyn turned to look at the bird on her shoulder and said, "Is that right, Miss P? Why?"

"Because it means something," said Emma.

"Absolutely," said Enoch. "It means we should go and climb that bluff. Then maybe we'll see a way out of this forest!"

"I mean the *tale* means something," said Emma. "In the story, what was it the giant wanted? That he asked for over and over again?"

"Someone to talk to!" Olive answered like an eager student.

"Exactly," said Emma. "So if he wants to talk, let's hear what he has to say." And with that, she waded into the lake.

We watched her go, slightly perplexed.

"Where's she heading?" said Millard. He seemed to be asking me. I shook my head.

"We've got wights chasing us!" Enoch shouted after her. "We're desperately lost! What on bird's green earth are you thinking?"

"I'm thinking peculiarly!" Emma shouted back. She sloshed through the shallows to the base of the rock, then climbed up to its jaw and peered into its open mouth.

"Well?" I called. "What do you see?"

"Don't know!" she replied. "Looks like it goes down a long way, though. I'd better get a closer look!"

Emma hoisted herself into the giant's stone mouth.

"You'd better come down from there before you get hurt!" shouted Horace. "You're making everyone anxious!"

"Everything makes *you* anxious," Hugh said.

Emma tossed a rock down the giant's throat, listening for whatever sound came back. She started to say "I think it might be a . . ." but then slipped on loose gravel, and her last word was lost as she scrambled and caught herself before she could fall.

"Be careful!" I shouted, my heart racing. "Wait, I'm coming, too!"

I splashed into the lake after her.

"It might be a what?" called Enoch.

"Only one way to find out!" Emma said excitedly, and climbed farther into the giant's mouth.

"Oh, Lord," said Horace. "There she goes . . ."

"Wait!" I shouted again—but she was gone already, disappeared down the giant's throat.

*　　*　　*

The giant appeared even larger up close than it had from the shore, and peering down into its dark throat, I swore I could almost hear old Cuthbert breathing. I cupped my hands and called Emma's name. My own voice came echoing back. The others were wading into the lake now, too, but I couldn't wait for them—what if she was in trouble down there?—so I gritted my teeth, lowered my legs into the dark, and let go.

I fell for a long time. A full second. Then *splash*—a plunge into water so cold it made me gasp, all my muscles constricting at once. I had to remind myself to tread water or sink. I was in a dim, narrow chamber filled with water, with no way back up the giant's long, smooth throat; no rope, no ladder, no footholds. I shouted for Emma, but she was nowhere around.

Oh God, I thought. *She's drowned!*

But then something tickled my arms, and bubbles began breaking all around me, and a moment later Emma broke the surface, gasping for breath.

She looked okay by the pale light. "What are you waiting for?" she said slapping the water with her hand like she wanted me to dive down with her. "Come on!"

"Are you insane?" I said. "We're trapped in here!"

"Of course we're not!" she said.

Bronwyn's voice called from above. "Hellooooo, I hear you down there! What have you found?"

"I think it's a loop entrance!" Emma called back. "Tell everyone to jump in and don't be afraid—Jacob and I will meet you on the other side!"

And then she took my hand, and though I didn't quite understand what was going on, I drew a deep breath and let her pull me underwater. We flipped and scissor-kicked downward toward a person-sized hole in the rock through which a gleam of daylight was visible. She pushed me inside and then came after, and we swam through a shaft about ten feet long and then out into the lake. Above us I could see its rippling surface, and above that the blue, refracted sky, and as we rose toward it the water warmed dramatically. Then we broke into the air and gasped for breath, and instantly I could feel that the weather had changed: it was hot and muggy now, and the light had changed to that of a golden afternoon. The depth of the lake had changed, too—now it came all the way to the giant's chin.

"See?" Emma said, grinning. "We're somewhen else!"

And just like that, we'd entered a loop—abandoned a mild morning in 1940 for a hot afternoon in some other, older year, though it was difficult to tell just how much older, here in the forest, away from the easily datable cues of civilization.

One by one, the other children surfaced around us, and seeing how much things had changed, had their own realizations.

"Do you realize what this *means*?" Millard squealed. He was splashing around, turning in circles, out of breath with excitement. "It means there's secret knowledge embedded in the *Tales*!"

"Not so useless now, are they?" said Olive.

"Oh, I can't *wait* to analyze and annotate them," said Millard, rubbing his hands together.

"Don't you dare write in my book, Millard Nullings!" said Bronwyn.

"But what *is* this loop?" asked Hugh. "Who do you think lives here?"

Olive said, "Cuthbert's animal friends, of course!"

Enoch rolled his eyes but stopped short of saying what he was probably thinking—*It's just a story!*—maybe because his mind was starting to change, too.

"Every loop has an ymbryne," said Emma, "even mystery loops from storybook tales. So let's go and find her."

"All right," said Millard. "Where?"

"The only place the story made mention of aside from this lake was that mountain," Emma said, indicating the bluff beyond the trees. "Who's ready to do some climbing?"

We were tired and hungry, every one of us, but finding the loop had given us a burst of new energy. We left the stone giant behind and set off through the woods toward the foot of the bluff, our clothes drip-drying quickly in the heat. As we neared the bluff, the ground began to slope upward, and then a well-worn path appeared and we followed it up and up through clusters of brushy firs and winding rocky passages, until the path became so vertical in places that we had to go on all fours, clawing at the angled ground to pull ourselves forward.

"There'd better be something wonderful at the end of this trail," said Horace, dabbing sweat from his forehead. "A gentleman doesn't perspire!"

The path narrowed to a ribbon, the ground rising sharply on our right side and dropping away on the left, a carpet of green tree-tops spreading beyond it. "Hug the wall!" Emma warned. "It's a long way down."

Just glancing at the drop-off made me dizzy. Suddenly, it seemed, I had developed a new and stomach-clenching fear of heights, and it took all my concentration simply to put one foot in front of the other.

Emma touched my arm. "Are you all right?" she whispered. "You look pale."

I lied and said I was, and succeeded in faking allrightness for exactly three more twists in the path, at which point my heart was racing and my legs shaking so badly that I had to sit down, right there in the middle of the narrow path, blocking everyone behind me.

"Oh, dear," Hugh muttered. "Jacob's cracking up."

"I don't know what's wrong with me," I muttered. I'd never been afraid of heights before, but now I couldn't so much as look off the edge of the path without my stomach doing flips.

Then something terrible occurred to me: what if this wasn't a fear of heights I was feeling—but of hollows?

It couldn't be, though: we were inside a loop, where hollows couldn't go. And yet the more I studied the feeling churning in my gut, the more convinced I became that it wasn't the drop itself that bothered me, but something *beyond* it.

I had to see for myself.

Everyone chattered anxiously in my ear, asking what was the matter, was I okay. I shut out their voices, tipped forward onto my hands, and crawled toward the edge of path. The closer I got, the worse my stomach felt, like it was being clawed to shreds from the inside. Inches away, I pressed my chest flat to the ground and reached out to hook my fingers over the ledge, then dragged myself forward until I could peek over it.

It took my eyes a moment to spot the hollow. At first it was just a shimmer against the craggy mountainside; a quivering spot in the air like heat waves rising from a hot car. An error, barely detectable.

This was how they looked to normals, and to other peculiars— to anyone who could not do what I did.

Then I actually experienced my peculiar ability coming to life. Very quickly, the churning in my belly contracted and focused into a single point of pain; and then, in a way I can't fully explain, it became *directional*, lengthening from a point into a line, from one dimension to two. The line, like a compass needle, pointed diagonally at that faltering spot a hundred yards below and to the left on the mountainside, the waves and shimmers of which began to gather and coalesce into solid black mass, a humanoid thing made from tentacles and shadow, clinging to the rocks.

And then it saw me see it and its whole awful body drew taut. Hunkering close against the rocks, it unhinged its saw-toothed mouth and let loose an ear-splitting shriek.

My friends didn't need me to describe what I was seeing. The sound alone was enough.

"*Hollow!*" someone shouted.

"*Run!*" shouted another, belaboring the obvious.

I scrambled back from the ledge and was pulled to my feet, and then we were all running in a pack, not down the mountain but up it, farther into the unknown rather than back toward the flat ground and loop exit that lay behind us. But it was too late to turn back; I could feel the hollow leaping from boulder to crag up the cliffside—but away from us, down the path, to cut us off in case we tried to run past it down the mountain. It was trapping us.

This was new. I'd never been able to track a hollow with anything other than my eyes before, but now I felt that little compass needle inside me pointing behind us, and I could almost picture the creature scrambling toward flat ground. It was as if, upon seeing the hollow, I'd planted a sort of homing beacon in it with my eyes.

We raced around a corner—my fleeting fear of heights now apparently gone—and were confronted by a smooth wall of rock, fifty feet high at least. The path ended here; all around us the ground fell away at crazy angles. The wall had no ladders, no handholds. We searched frantically for some other way—a secret passage in the rock, a door, a tunnel—but there was none, and no way forward but up; and no way up, apparently, other than via hot air balloon or the helping hand of a probably mythical giant.

Panic took hold. Miss Peregrine began to screech and Claire to cry as Horace stood and wailed, "This is the end, we're all going to die!" The rest looked for last-ditch ways to save ourselves. Fiona dragged her hands along the wall, searching for crevices that might contain soil from which she could grow a vine or something else we could climb. Hugh ran to the edge of the path and peered over the drop-off. "We could jump, if only we had a parachute!"

"I can be a parachute!" said Olive. "Take hold of my legs!"

But it was a long way down, and at the bottom was dark and dangerous forest. It was better, Bronwyn decided, to send Olive up the rock face than down the mountain, and with limp, feverish Claire in one arm, Bronwyn led Olive by the hand to the wall. "Give me your shoes!" she said to Olive. "Take Claire and Miss P and get to the top as quick as you can!"

Olive looked terrified. "I don't know if I'm strong enough!" she cried.

"You've got to try, little magpie! You're the only one who can keep them safe!" And she knelt and set Claire down on her feet, and the sick girl tottered into Olive's arms. Olive squeezed her tight, slipped off her leaden shoes, and then, just as they began to rise, Bronwyn transferred Miss Peregrine from her shoulder to the top of Olive's head. Weighed down, Olive rose very slowly—it was only when Miss Peregrine began to flap her good wing and pull Olive up by the hair, Olive yelping and kicking her feet, that the three of them really took off.

The hollow had nearly reached level ground. I knew it as surely as if I could see it with my eyes. Meanwhile, we scoured the ground for anything that might be used as a weapon—but all we could find were pebbles. "*I* can be a weapon," said Emma, and she clapped her hands and drew them apart again, an impressive fireball roaring to life between them.

"And don't forget about my bees!" said Hugh, opening his mouth to let them out. "They can be fierce when provoked!"

Enoch, who always found a way to laugh at the most inappropriate times, let out a big guffaw. "What're you going to do," he said, "pollinate it to death?"

Hugh ignored him, turning to me instead. "You'll be our eyes, Jacob. Just tell us where the beast is and we'll sting his brains out!"

My compass needle of pain told me it was on the path now, and the way its venom was expanding to fill me meant it was closing in fast. "Any minute now," I said, pointing to the bend in the path we'd come around. "Get ready." If not for the adrenaline flooding my system, the pain would've been totally debilitating.

We assumed fight-or-flight positions, some of us crouching with fists raised like boxers, others like sprinters before the starting gun, though no one knew which way to run.

"What a depressing and inauspicious end to our adventures,"

said Horace. "Devoured by a hollow in some Welsh backwater!"

"I thought they couldn't enter loops," said Enoch. "How the hell did it get in here?"

"It would seem they have evolved," said Millard.

"Who gives a chuck how it happened!" Emma snapped. "It's here and it's hungry!"

Then from above us a small voice cried, "Look out below!" and I craned my neck to see Olive's face pull back and disappear over the top of the rock wall. A moment later something like a long rope came sailing over the ledge. It unreeled and snapped taut, and then a net unfurled at the end of it and smacked against the ground. "Hurry!" came Olive's voice again. "There's a lever up here—everyone grab hold of the net and I'll pull it!"

We ran to the net, but it was tiny, hardly large enough for two. Pinned to the rope at eye level was a photograph of a man inside the net—this very net—with his legs folded in front of him and hanging just above the ground before a sheer rock face—this very rock face. On the back of the photo a message was printed:

ONLY ACCESS TO MENAGERIE: CLIMB INSIDE!

WEIGHT LIMIT: ONE RIDER

STRICTLY ENFORCED

This contraption was some sort of primitive elevator—meant for one rider at a time, not eight. But there was no time to use it as intended, so we all dog-piled onto it, sticking our arms and legs through its holes, clinging to the rope above it, attaching ourselves any way we could.

"Take us up!" I shouted. The hollow very close now; the pain extraordinary.

For a few endless seconds, nothing happened. The hollow bolted around the bend, using its muscular tongues like legs, its atrophied human limbs hanging useless. Then a metallic squeal rang out, the rope pulled taut, and we lurched into the air.

The hollow had nearly closed the distance between us. It galloped with jaws wide open, as if to collect us between its teeth the way a whale feeds on plankton. We weren't quite halfway up the wall when it reached the ground below us, looked up, and squatted like a spring about to uncoil.

"It's going to jump!" I shouted. "Pull your legs into the net!"

The hollow drove its tongues into the ground and sprang upward. We were rising fast and it seemed like the hollow would miss us, but just as it reached the apex of its jump, one of its tongues shot out and lassoed Emma around the ankle.

Emma screamed and kicked at it with her other foot as the net came to a jolting stop, the pulley above too weak to raise all of us and the hollow, too.

"Get it off me!" Emma shouted. "Get it off get it off get it off!"

I tried kicking at it, too, but the hollow's tongue was as strong as woven steel and the tip was covered in hundreds of wriggling sucker-cups, so that anyone who tried to pry the tongue off would only get stuck to it themselves. And then the hollow was reeling itself up, its jaws inching closer until we could smell its stinking gravebreath.

Emma shouted for someone to hold her and with one hand I grabbed the back of her dress. Bronwyn let go of the net entirely, clinging to it with just her legs, then threw her arms around Emma's waist. Then Emma let go, too—Bronwyn and I being all that kept her from falling—and with her hands now free she reached down and clapped them around the tongue.

The hollow shrieked. The sucker-cups along its tongue, withered and reeking black smoke, hissed from its flesh. Emma squeezed harder and closed her eyes and howled, not a cry of pain, I thought, but a kind of war cry, until the hollow was forced to release, its injured tentacle unslithering from around her ankle. There was a surreal moment where it was no longer the hollow who was holding Emma but Emma who was holding the hollow, the thing writhing and shrieking below us, the acrid smoke of its burned flesh filling our noses, until finally we had to shout at her to *let go*, and Emma's eyes flew open again and she seemed to remember where she was and pulled her hands apart.

The hollow tumbled away from us, grasping at empty space as it fell. We rocketed up and away in the net, the tension that had been holding us down suddenly released, and soaring over the lip of the wall, we collapsed in a heap on top of it. Olive, Claire, and Miss Peregrine were waiting there for us, and as we extricated ourselves from the net and stumbled away from the cliff's edge, Olive cheered, Miss Peregrine screeched and beat her good wing, and Claire raised her head from where she'd been lying on the ground and gave a weak smile.

We were giddy—and for the second time in as many days, stunned to be alive. "That's twice you've saved our necks, little magpie," Bronwyn said to Olive. "And Miss Emma, I already knew you were brave, but that was beyond anything!"

Emma shrugged it off. "It was him or me," she said.

"I can't believe you *touched* it," said Horace.

Emma wiped her hands on her dress, held them to her nose, and made a face. "I just hope this smell comes off soon," she said. "That beast stank like a landfill!"

"How's your ankle?" I asked her. "Does it hurt?"

She knelt and pushed down her sock to reveal a fat, red welt ringing it. "Not too bad," she said, touching the ankle gingerly. But when she stood up again and put weight on it, I caught her wincing.

"A lot of help *you* were," Enoch growled at me. "'Run away!'

says the hollow-slayer's grandson!"

"If my grandfather had run from the hollow that killed him, he might still be alive," I said. "It's good advice."

I heard a thud from beyond the wall we'd just scaled, and the Feeling churned up inside me again. I went to the ledge and looked over. The hollow was alive and well at the base of the wall, and busy punching holes in the rock with its tongues.

"Bad news," I said. "The fall didn't kill it."

In a moment Emma was at my side. "What's it doing?"

I watched it twist one of its tongues into a hole it had made, then hoist itself up and begin making a second. It was creating foot-holds—or tongue-holds, rather.

"It's trying to climb the wall," I said. "Good God, it's like the freaking Terminator."

"The what?" said Emma.

I almost started to explain, then shook my head. It was a stupid comparison, anyway—hollowgast were scarier, and probably dead-lier, than any movie monster.

"We have to stop it!" said Olive.

"Or better yet, run!" said Horace.

"No more running!" said Enoch. "Can we please just kill the damn thing?"

"Sure," Emma said. "But how?"

"Anyone got a vat of boiling oil?" said Enoch.

"Will this do instead?" I heard Bronwyn say, and turned to see her lifting a boulder above her head.

"It might," I said. "How's your aim? Can you drop it where I tell you?"

"I'll certainly try," Bronwyn said, tottering toward the ledge with the rock balanced precariously on her hands.

We stood looking over the ledge. "Farther this way," I said, urging her a few steps to the left. Just as I was about to give the sig-nal for her to drop the boulder, though, the hollow leapt from one hold to the next, and now she was standing in the wrong place.

The hollow was getting faster at making the holds; now it was a moving target. To make matters worse, Bronwyn's boulder was the only one in sight. If she missed, we wouldn't get a second shot.

I forced myself to stare at the hollow despite a nearly unbearable urge to look away. For a few strange, head-swimmy seconds, the voices of my friends faded away and I could hear my own blood pumping in my ears and my heart thumping in the cavity of my chest, and my thoughts drifted to the creature that killed my grandfather; that stood over his torn and dying body before fleeing, cowardly, into the woods.

My vision rippled and my hands shook. I tried to steady myself. *You were born for this*, I thought to myself. *You were built to kill monsters like this.* I repeated it under my breath like a mantra.

"Hurry up, please, Jacob," Bronwyn said.

The creature faked left, then jumped right. I didn't want to guess, and throw away our best chance at killing it. I wanted to *know*. And somehow, for some reason, I felt that I could.

I knelt, so close to the cliff's edge now that Emma hooked two fingers through the back of my belt to keep me from falling. Focusing on the hollow, I repeated the mantra to myself—*built to kill you, built to kill*—and though the hollow was for the moment stationary, hacking away at one spot on the wall, I felt the compass needle in my gut prick ever so slightly to the right of it.

It was like a premonition.

Bronwyn was beginning to tremble under the boulder's weight. "I can't hold this much longer!" she said.

I decided to trust my instinct. Even though the spot my compass pointed to was empty, I shouted for Bronwyn to drop the boulder there. She angled toward it and, with a groan of relief, let go of the rock.

The moment after she let go, the hollow leapt to the right—into the very place my compass had pointed. The hollow looked up to see the rock sailing toward it and poised to jump again—but there wasn't time. The boulder slammed into the creature's head and swept its body off the wall. With a thunderous crash, hollow and boulder hit the ground together. Tentacle tongues shot out from beneath the rock, shivered, went limp. Black blood followed, fanning around the boulder in a great, viscous puddle.

"Direct hit!" I yelled.

The kids began to jump and cheer. "It's dead, it's dead," Olive cried, "the horrible hollow is dead!"

Bronwyn threw her arms around me. Emma kissed the top of my head. Horace shook my hand and Hugh slapped me on the back. Even Enoch congratulated me. "Good work," he said a bit reluctantly. "Now don't go getting a big head over it."

I should've been overjoyed, but I hardly felt anything, just a spreading numbness as the trembling pain of the Feeling receded. Emma could see I was drained. Very sweetly, and in a way no one else could quite detect, she took my arm and half supported me as we walked away from the ledge. "That wasn't luck," she whispered in my ear. "I was right about you, Jacob Portman."

*   *   *

The path that had dead-ended at the bottom of the wall began again here at the top, following the spine of a ridge up and over a hill.

"The sign on the rope said *Access to Menagerie*," said Horace. "Do you suppose that's what's ahead?"

"You're the one who dreams about the future," said Enoch. "Suppose you tell *us*."

"What's a menagerie?" asked Olive.

"A collection of animals," Emma explained. "Like a zoo, sort of."

Olive squeaked and clapped her hands. "It's Cuthbert's friends!

From the story! Oh, I can't wait to meet them. Do you suppose that's where the ymbryne lives, too?"

"At this juncture," Millard said, "it's best not to suppose anything."

We started walking. I was still reeling from my encounter with the hollow. My ability did seem to be developing, as Millard said it would, growing like a muscle the more I worked it. Once I'd seen a hollow I could track it, and if I focused on it in just the right way, I could anticipate its next move, in some felt-more-than-known, gut-instinctual way. I felt a certain satisfaction at having learned something new about my peculiarity, and with nothing to teach me but experience. But this wasn't a safe, controlled environment I was learning in. There were no bumper lanes to keep my ball out of the gutter. Any mistake I made would have immediate and deadly consequences, for both myself and those around me. I worried the others would start believing the hype about me—or worse yet, *I* would. And I knew that the minute I got cocky—the minute I stopped being pants-wettingly terrified of hollowgast—something terrible would happen.

Maybe it was lucky, then, that my terror-to-confidence ratio was at an all-time low. Ten-to-one, easy. I stuck my hands in my pockets as we walked, afraid the others would see them shaking.

"Look!" said Bronwyn, stopping in the middle of the path. "A house in the clouds!"

We were halfway up the ridge. Up ahead of us, high in the distance, was a house that almost seemed to be balanced on a cloudbank. As we walked farther and crested the hill, the clouds parted and the house came into full view. It was very small, and perched not atop cloud but on a very large tower constructed entirely from stacked-up railroad ties, the whole thing set smack in the middle of a grassy plateau. It was one of the strangest man-made structures I'd ever seen. Around it on the plateau were scattered a few shacks, and at the far end was a small patch of woods, but we paid no attention—our eyes were on the tower.

"What *is* it?" I whispered.

"A lookout tower?" guessed Emma.

"A place to launch airplanes from?" said Hugh.

But there were no airplanes anywhere, nor any evidence of a landing strip.

"Perhaps it's a place to launch zeppelins from," said Millard.

I remembered old footage of the ill-fated Hindenburg docking to the top of what looked like a radio tower—a structure not so different from this—and felt a cold wave of dread pass through me. What if the balloons that hunted us on the beach were based here, and we'd unwittingly stumbled into a nest of wights?

"Or maybe it's the ymbryne's house," said Olive. "Why does everyone always leap to the awfullest conclusions right away?"

"I'm sure Olive's right," said Hugh. "There's nothing to be afraid of here."

He was answered right away by a loud, inhuman growl, which seemed to come from the shadows beneath the tower.

"What was *that*?" said Emma. "Another hollow?"

"I don't think so," I said; the Feeling still fading in me.

"I don't know and I don't want to know," said Horace, backing away.

But we didn't have a choice; it wanted to meet us. The growl came again, prickling the hairs on my arms, and a moment later a furry face appeared between two of the lower railroad ties. It snarled at us like a rabid dog, reels of saliva dripping from its fang-toothed mouth.

"What in the name of the Elderfolk is *that*?" muttered Emma.

"Capital idea, coming into this loop," said Enoch. "Really working out well for us so far."

The whatever-it-was crawled out from between the ties and into the sun, where it crouched on its haunches and leered at us with an unbalanced smile, as if imagining how our brains might taste. I couldn't tell if it was human or animal; dressed in rags, it had the body of a man but carried itself like an ape, its hunched form like some long-lost ancestor of ours whose evolution had been arrested millions of years ago. Its eyes and teeth were a dull yellow, its skin pale and blotched with dark spots, its hair a long, matted nest.

"Someone make it die!" Horace said. "Or at least make it quit looking at me!"

Bronwyn set Claire down and assumed a fighting stance, while Emma held out her hands to make a flame—but she was too stunned, apparently, to summon more than a sputter of smoke. The man-thing tensed, snarled, and then took off like an Olympic sprinter—not toward us but *around* us, diving behind a pile of rocks and popping up again with a fang-bearing grin. It was toying with us, like a cat toys with its prey just before the kill.

It seemed about to make another run—*at us* this time—when a voice from behind commanded it to "Sit down and behave!" And the thing did, relaxing onto its hindquarters, tongue lolling from its mouth in a dopey grin.

We turned to see a dog trotting calmly in our direction. I looked past it to see who had spoken, but there was no one—and then the dog itself opened its mouth and said, "Don't mind Grunt, he's got no manners at all! That's just his way of saying thank you. That hollowgast was *most* bothersome."

The dog seemed to be talking to me, but I was too surprised to respond. Not only was it speaking in an almost-human voice—and a refined British one at that—but it held in its jowly mouth a pipe and on its face wore a pair of round, green-tinted glasses. "Oh dear, I hope you're not *too* offended," the dog continued, misinterpreting my silence. "Grunt means well, but you'll have to excuse him. He was, quite literally, raised in a barn. I, on the other hand, was educated on a grand estate, the seventh pup of the seventh pup in an illustrious line of hunting dogs." He bowed as well as a dog could, dipping his nose to the ground. "Addison MacHenry, at your humble service."

"That's a fancy name for a dog," said Enoch, apparently unimpressed to meet a talking animal.

Addison peered over his glasses at Enoch and said, "And by what appellation, dare I ask, are *you* denominated?"

"Enoch O'Connor," Enoch said proudly, sticking his chest out a little.

"That's a fancy name for a grimy, pudge-faced boy," Addison said, and then he stood up on his hind legs, rising nearly to Enoch's height. "I am a dog, yes, but a peculiar one. Why, then, should I be saddled with a common dog's name? My former master called me 'Boxie' and I despised it—an assault on my dignity!—so I bit him on the face and took his name. Addison: much more befitting an animal of my intellectual prowess, I think. That was just before Miss Wren discovered me and brought me here."

Faces brightened at the mention of an ymbryne's name, a pulse of hope firing through us.

"Miss Wren brought you?" said Olive. "But what about Cuthbert the giant?"

"Who?" Addison said, and then he shook his head. "Ah, right, the story. It's just that, I'm afraid—a *story*, inspired long ago by that curious rock down below and Miss Wren's peculiar menagerie."

"Told you," muttered Enoch.

"Where's Miss Wren now?" Emma said. "We've got to speak to her!"

Addison looked up at the house atop the tower and said, "That's her residence, but she isn't home at the moment. She winged off some days ago to help her ymbryne sisters in London. There's a war on, you see . . . I assume you've heard all about it? Which explains why you're traveling in the degraded style of refugees?"

"Our loop was raided," said Emma. "And then we lost our things at sea."

"And nearly ourselves," Millard added.

At the sound of Millard's voice, the dog startled. "An invisible! What a rare surprise. And an American, too," he said, nodding at me. "What a peculiar lot you are, even for peculiars." He fell back onto all fours and turned toward the tower. "Come, I'll introduce you to the others. They'll be absolutely fascinated to meet you. And you must be famished from your journey, poor creatures. Nutrifying provender shall be forthcoming!"

"We need medicine, too," said Bronwyn, kneeling to pick up Claire. "This little one is very ill!"

"We'll do all we can for her," the dog said. "We owe you that and more for solving our little hollowgast problem. *Most* bothersome, as I was saying."

"Nutrifying *what* did he say?" said Olive.

"Sustenance, comestibles, rations!" the dog replied. "You'll eat like royalty here."

"But I don't like dog food," said Olive.

Addison laughed, the timbre surprisingly human. "Neither do I, miss."

CHAPTER FOUR

*A*ddison walked on all fours with his snub nose in the air while the man-thing called Grunt scampered around us like a psychotic puppy. From behind tufts of grass and the shacks scattered here and there, I could see faces peeking out at us—furry, most of them, and of all different shapes and sizes. When we came to the middle of the plateau, Addison reared up on his hind legs and called out, "Don't be afraid, fellows! Come and meet the children who dispatched our unwelcome visitor!"

One by one, a parade of bizarre animals ventured out into the open. Addison introduced them as they came. The first creature looked like the top half of a miniature giraffe sutured onto the bottom half of a donkey. It walked awkwardly on two hind legs—its only limbs. "This is Deirdre," said Addison. "She's an emu-raffe, which is a bit like a donkey and a giraffe put together, only with fewer legs and a peevish temper. She's a terrible sore loser at cards," he added in a whisper. "*Never* play an emu-raffe at cards. Say hello, Deirdre!"

"Goodbye!" Deirdre said, her big horse lips pulling back into a bucktoothed grin. "Terrible day! Very displeased to meet you!" Then she laughed—a braying, high-pitched whinny—and said, "Only teasing!"

"Deirdre thinks she's quite funny," Addison explained.

"If you're like a donkey and a giraffe," said Olive, "then why aren't you called a donkey-raffe?"

Deirdre frowned and answered, "Because what kind of an awful name is that? Emu-raffe rolls off the tongue, don't you think?" And then she stuck out her tongue—fat, pink, and three feet long—and pushed Olive's tiara back on her head with its tip. Olive squealed and ran behind Bronwyn, giggling.

"Do all the animals here talk?" I asked.

"Just Deirdre and I," Addison said, "and a good thing, too. The chickens won't shut up as it is, and they can't say a word!" Right on cue, a flock of clucking chickens bobbled toward us from a burned and blackened coop. "Ah!" said Addison. "Here come the girls now."

"What happened to their coop?" Emma asked.

"Every time we repair it, they burn it down again," he said. "Such a bother." Addison turned and nodded in the other direction. "You might want to back away a bit. When they get excited . . ."

BANG!—a sound like a quarter-stick of dynamite going off made us all jump, and the coop's last few undamaged boards splintered and flew into the air.

". . . their eggs go off," he finished.

When the smoke cleared, we saw the chickens still coming toward us, unhurt and seemingly unsurprised by the blast, a little cloud of feathers wafting around them like fat snowflakes.

Enoch's jaw fell open. "Are you telling me these chickens lay *exploding eggs*?!" he said.

"Only when they get excited," said Addison. "Most of their eggs are quite safe—and delicious! But it was the exploding ones that earned them their rather unkind name: Armageddon chickens."

"Keep away from us!" Emma shouted as the chickens closed in. "You'll blow us all up!"

Addison laughed. "They're sweet and harmless, I assure you, and they don't lay anywhere but inside their coop." The chickens clucked happily around our feet. "You see?" the dog said. "They like you!"

"This is a madhouse!" said Horace.

Deirdre laughed. "No, doveling. It's a menagerie."

Then Addison introduced us to a few animals whose peculiarities were subtler, including an owl who watched us from a branch, silent and intense, and a cadre of mice who seemed to fade subtly in and out of view, as if they spent half their time on some other plane of reality. There was a goat, too, with very long horns and deep black eyes; an orphan from a herd of peculiar goats who once roamed the forest below.

When all the animals were assembled, Addison cried, "Three cheers for the hollow-killers!" Deirdre brayed and the goat stamped the ground and the owl hooted and the chickens clucked and Grunt grunted his appreciation. And while all this was going on, Bronwyn and Emma kept trading looks—Bronwyn glancing down at her coat, where Miss Peregrine was hiding, and then raising her eyebrows at Emma to ask, *Now?* and Emma shaking her head in reply: *Not quite yet.*

Bronwyn laid Claire in a patch of grass beneath a shade tree. She was sweating and shivering, fading in and out of consciousness.

"There's a special elixir I've seen Miss Wren prepare for treating fever," Addison said. "Foul-tasting but effective."

"My mom used to make me chicken soup," I offered.

The chickens squawked with alarm, and Addison shot me a nasty look. "He was joking!" he said. "Only joking, such an absurd joke, ha-ha! There's no such thing as chicken soup!"

With the help of Grunt and his opposable thumbs, Addison and the emu-raffe went to prepare the elixir. In a little while they returned with a bowl of what looked like dirty dishwater. Once Claire had drunk every drop and fallen back asleep, the animals laid out a modest feast for us: baskets of fresh bread and stewed apples and hard-boiled eggs—of the nonexploding variety—all served straight into our hands, as they had no plates or silverware. I didn't realize how hungry I'd been until I wolfed down three eggs and a loaf of bread in under five minutes.

When I was done I belched and wiped my mouth and looked up to see all the animals looking back, watching us eagerly, their faces so alive with intelligence that I went a little numb and had to fight an overwhelming sensation that I was dreaming.

Millard was eating next to me, and I turned to him and asked, "Before this, had you ever heard of peculiar animals?"

"Only in children's stories," he said through a mouthful of bread. "How strange, then, that it was one such story that led us to them."

Only Olive seemed unfazed by it all, perhaps because she was still so young—or part of her was, anyway—and the distance between stories and real life did not yet seem so great. "Where are the other animals?" she asked Addison. "In Cuthbert's tale there were stilt-legged grimbears and two-headed lynxes."

And just like that, the animals' jubilant mood wilted. Grunt hid his face in his big hands and Deirdre let out a neighing groan. "Don't ask, don't ask," she said, hanging her long head. But it was too late.

"These children helped us," Addison said. "They deserve to hear our sad story, if they wish."

"If you don't mind telling us," said Emma.

"I love sad stories," said Enoch. "Especially ones where princesses get eaten by dragons and everyone dies in the end."

Addison cleared his throat. "In our case, it's more that the dragon got eaten by the princess," he said. "It's been a rough few years for the likes of us, and it was a rough few centuries prior to that." The dog paced back and forth, his voice taking on a preacherly kind of grandness. "Once upon a time, this world was full of peculiar animals. In the *Aldinn* days, there were more peculiar animals on Earth than there were peculiar folk. We came in every shape and size you could imagine: whales that could fly like birds, worms as big as houses, dogs twice as intelligent as I am, if you can believe it. Some had kingdoms all their own, ruled over by animal leaders." A spark moved behind the dog's eyes, barely detectable—as if he were old enough to remember the world in such a state—and then he sighed deeply, the spark snuffed, and continued. "But our numbers are not a fraction of what they were. We have fallen into near extinction. Do any of you know what became of the peculiar animals that once roamed the world?"

We chewed silently, ashamed that we didn't.

"Right, then," he said. "Come with me and I'll show you." And he trotted out into the sun and looked back, waiting for us to follow.

"Please, Addie," said the emu-raffe. "Not now—our guests are eating!"

"They asked, and now I'm telling them," said Addison. "Their bread will still be here in a few minutes!"

Reluctantly, we put down our food and followed the dog. Fiona stayed behind to watch Claire, who was still sleeping, and with Grunt and the emu-raffe loping after us, we crossed the plateau to the little patch of woods that grew at the far edge. A gravel path wound through the trees, and we crunched along it toward a clearing. Just before we reached it, Addison said, "May I introduce you to the finest peculiar animals who ever lived!" and the trees parted to reveal a small graveyard filled with neat rows of white headstones.

"Oh, *no*," I heard Bronwyn say.

"There are probably more peculiar animals buried here than are currently alive in all of Europe," Addison said, moving through the graves to reach one in particular, which he leaned on with his forepaws. "This one's name was Pompey. She was a fine dog, and could heal wounds with a few licks of her tongue. A wonder to behold! And yet *this* is how she was treated." Addison clicked his tongue and Grunt scurried forward with a little book in his hands, which he thrust into mine. It was a photo album, opened to a picture of a dog that had been harnessed, like a mule or a horse, to a little wagon. "She was enslaved by carnival folk," Addison said, "forced to pull fat, spoiled children like some common beast of burden— whipped, even, with riding crops!" His eyes burned with anger. "By the time Miss Wren rescued her, Pompey was so depressed she was nearly dead from it. She lingered on for only a few weeks after she arrived, then was interred here."

I passed the book around. Everyone who saw the photo sighed or shook their head or muttered bitterly to themselves.

Addison crossed to another grave. "Grander still was Ca'ab Magda," he said, "an eighteen-tusked wildebeest who roamed the loops of Outer Mongolia. She was terrifying! The ground thundered under her hooves when she ran! They say she even marched over the Alps with Hannibal's army in 218 BC. Then, some years ago, a hunter shot her."

Grunt showed us a picture of an older woman who looked like she'd just gotten back from an African safari, seated in a bizarre chair made of horns.

"I don't understand," said Emma, peering at the photo. "Where's Ca'ab Magda?"

"Being sat upon," said Addison. "The hunter fashioned her horns into a chair."

Emma nearly dropped the album. "That's disgusting!"

"If that's her," said Enoch, tapping the photo, "then what's buried here?"

"The chair," said Addison. "What a pitiful waste of a peculiar life."

"This burying ground is filled with stories like Magda's," Addison said. "Miss Wren meant this menagerie to be an ark, but gradually it's become a tomb."

"Like all our loops," said Enoch. "Like peculiardom itself. A failed experiment."

"'This place is dying,' Miss Wren often said." Addison's voice rose in imitation of her. "'And I am nothing but the overseer of its long funeral!'"

Addison's eyes glistened, remembering her, but just as quickly went hard again. "She was very theatrical."

"Please don't refer to our ymbryne in the past tense," Deirdre said.

"Is," he said. "Sorry. *Is*."

"They hunted you," said Emma, her voice wavering with emotion. "Stuffed you and put you in zoos."

"Just like the hunters did in Cuthbert's story," said Olive.

"Yes," said Addison. "Some truths are expressed best in the form of myth."

"But there was no Cuthbert," said Olive, beginning to understand. "No giant. Just a bird."

"A very *special* bird," said Deirdre.

"You're worried about her," I said.

"Of course we are," said Addison. "To my knowledge, Miss Wren is the only remaining uncaptured ymbryne. When she heard that her kidnapped sisters had been spirited away to London, she flew off to render assistance without a moment's thought for her own safety."

"Nor ours," Deirdre muttered.

"London?" said Emma. "Are you sure that's where the kidnapped ymbrynes were taken?"

"Absolutely certain," the dog replied. "Miss Wren has spies in the city—a certain flock of peculiar pigeons who watch everything and report back to her. Recently, several came to us in a state of terrible distress. They had it on good information that the ymbrynes were—and still are—being held in the punishment loops."

Several of the children gasped, but I had no idea what the dog meant. "What's a punishment loop?" I asked.

"They were designed to hold captured wights, hardened criminals, and the dangerously insane," Millard explained. "They're nothing like the loops we know. Nasty, nasty places."

"And now it is the wights, and undoubtedly their hollows, who are guarding them," said Addison.

"Good God!" exclaimed Horace. "Then it's worse than we feared!"

"Are you joking?" said Enoch. "This is *precisely* the sort of thing I feared!"

"Whatever nefarious end the wights are seeking," Addison said, "it's clear that they need all the ymbrynes to accomplish it. Now only Miss Wren is left . . . brave, foolhardy Miss Wren . . . and who knows for how long!" Then he whimpered the way some dogs do during thunderstorms, tucking his ears back and lowering his head.

*   *   *

We went back to the shade tree and finished our meals, and when we were stuffed and couldn't eat another bite, Bronwyn turned to Addison and said, "You know, Mister Dog, everything's not quite as dire as you say." Then she looked at Emma and raised her eyebrows, and this time Emma nodded.

"Is that so," Addison replied.

"Yes, it is. In fact, I have something right here that may just cheer you up."

"I rather doubt that," the dog muttered, but he lifted his head from his paws to see what it was anyway.

Bronwyn opened her coat and said, "I'd like you to meet the

second-to-last uncaptured ymbryne, Miss Alma Peregrine." The bird poked her head out into the sunlight and blinked.

Now it was the animals' turn to be amazed. Deirdre gasped and Grunt squealed and clapped his hands and the chickens flapped their useless wings.

"But we heard your loop was raided!" Addison said. "Your ymbryne stolen!"

"She was," Emma said proudly, "but we stole her back!"

"In that case," said Addison, bowing to Miss Peregrine, "it is a most extraordinary pleasure, madam. I am your servant. Should you require a place to change, I'll happily show you to Miss Wren's private quarters."

"She *can't* change," said Bronwyn.

"What's that?" said Addison. "Is she shy?"

"No," said Bronwyn. "She's stuck."

The pipe dropped from Addison's mouth. "Oh, no," he said quietly. "Are you quite certain?"

"She's been like this for two days now," said Emma. "I think if she could change back, she would've done it by now."

Addison shook the glasses from his face and peered at the bird, his eyes wide with concern. "May I examine her?" he asked.

"He's a regular Doctor Dolittle," said the emu-raffe. "Addie treats us all when we're sick."

Bronwyn lifted Miss Peregrine out of her coat and set the bird on the ground. "Just be careful of her hurt wing," she said.

"Of course," said Addison. He began by making a slow circle around the bird, studying her from every angle. Then he sniffed her head and wings with his big, wet nose. "Tell me what happened to her," he said finally, "and when, and how. Tell me all of it."

Emma recounted the whole story: how Miss Peregrine was kidnapped by Golan, how she nearly drowned in her cage in the ocean, how we'd rescued her from a submarine piloted by wights. The animals listened, rapt. When we'd finished, the dog took a moment to gather his thoughts, then delivered his diagnosis: "She's been poisoned. I'm certain of it. Dosed with something that's keeping her in bird form artificially."

"Really?" said Emma. "How do you know?"

"To kidnap and transport ymbrynes is a dangerous business when they're in human form and can perform their time-stopping tricks. As birds, however, their powers are very limited. This way, your mistress is compact, easily hidden . . . much less of a threat." He looked at Miss Peregrine. "Did the wight who took you spray you with anything?" he asked her. "A liquid or a gas?"

Miss Peregrine bobbed her head in the air—what seemed to be a nod.

Bronwyn gasped. "Oh, miss, I'm so awfully sorry. We had no idea."

I felt a stab of guilt. *I* had led the wights to the island. *I* was the reason this had happened to Miss Peregrine. *I* had caused the peculiar children to lose their home, at least partly. The shame of it lodged like a stone in my throat.

I said, "She'll get better though, won't she? She'll turn back?"

"Her wing will mend," Addison replied, "but without help she won't turn human again."

"What sort of help does she need?" Emma asked. "Can you give it to her?"

"Only another ymbryne can assist her. And she's running very short on time."

I tensed. This was something new.

"What do you mean?" Emma said.

"I hate to be the bearer of bad news," said Addison, "but two days is a very long time for an ymbryne to be arrested like this. The more time she spends as a bird, the more her human self will be lost. Her memory, her words—everything that made her who she was— until, eventually, she won't be an ymbryne at all anymore. She'll just be a bird, for good and ever."

An image came to me of Miss Peregrine splayed on an emergency room table, buzzed around by doctors, her breathing stopped—every second that ticked by doing her brain some new and irreparable harm.

"How long?" asked Millard. "How much longer does she have?"

Addison squinted, shook his head. "Two days, if she's strong."

Whispers and gasps. We collectively went pale.

"Are you sure?" said Emma. "Are you absolutely, positively certain?"

"I've seen it happen before." Addison padded over to the little owl, who was perched on a branch nearby. "Olivia here was a young ymbryne who had a bad accident during her training. They brought her to us five days later. Miss Wren and I did everything we could to try to change her back, but she was beyond help. That was ten years ago; she's been this way ever since."

The owl stared mutely. There was no life in her anymore beyond that of an animal; you could see it in the dullness of her eyes.

Emma stood. She seemed about to say something—to rally us, I hoped, kick us into action with some inspiring speech—but she couldn't seem to get the words out. Choking back a sob, she stumbled away from us.

I called after her, but she didn't stop. The others just watched her go, stunned by the terrible news; stunned, too, by any sign of weakness or indecision from Emma. She had maintained her strength in the face of all this for so long that we had come to take it for granted, but she wasn't bulletproof. She might've been peculiar, but she was also human.

"You'd better fetch her, Mister Jacob," Bronwyn said to me. "We mustn't linger here too long."

*   *   *

When I caught up to Emma she was standing near the plateau's edge, gazing out at the countryside below, sloping green hills falling away to a distant plain. She heard me coming but didn't turn to look.

I shuffled up next to her and tried to think of something comforting to say. "I know you're scared, and—and three days doesn't seem like a long time, but—"

"*Two* days," she said. "Two days *maybe*." Her lip trembled. "And that's not even the worst of it."

I balked. "How could things possibly be worse?"

She'd been waging a battle against tears, but now, in a sudden break, she lost it. She sank to the ground and sobbed, a storm overtaking her. I knelt and wrapped my arms around her and hung on. "I'm so sorry," she said, repeating it three times, her voice raw, a fraying rope. "You never should've stayed. I shouldn't have let you. But I was selfish . . . so terribly selfish!"

"Don't say that," I said. "I'm here—I'm here, and I'm not going anywhere."

That only seemed to make her cry harder. I pressed my lips to her forehead and kissed it until the storm began to pass out of her, the sobs fading to whimpers. "Please talk to me," I said. "Tell me what's wrong."

After a minute she sat up, wiped her eyes, and tried to compose herself. "I had hoped I'd never have to say this," she said. "That it wouldn't matter. Do you remember when I told you, the night you decided to come with us, that you might never be able to go home again?"

"Of course I do."

"I didn't know until just now how true that really was. I'm afraid I've doomed you, Jacob, my sweet friend, to a short life trapped in a dying world." She drew a quivering breath, then continued. "You came to us through Miss Peregrine's loop, and that means only Miss Peregrine or her loop can send you back. But her loop is gone now—or if it isn't yet, it will be soon—which leaves

Miss Peregrine herself as your only way home. But if she never turns human again . . ."

I swallowed hard, my throat dry. "Then I'm stuck in the past."

"Yes. And the only way to return to the time you knew as your own would be to wait for it—day by day, year by year."

Seventy years. By then my parents, and everyone I ever knew or cared about, would be dead, and I'd be long dead to all of them. Of course, provided we survived whatever tribulations we were about to face, I could always go and find my parents in a few decades, once they were born—but what would be the point? They'd be children, and strangers to me.

I wondered when my present-day back-home parents would give up on finding me alive. What story they'd tell themselves to make sense of my disappearance. Had I run away? Gone insane? Thrown myself off a sea cliff?

Would they have a funeral for me? Buy me a coffin? Write my name on a gravestone?

I'd become a mystery they would never solve. A wound that would never heal.

"I'm so sorry," Emma said again. "If I'd known Miss Peregrine's condition was so dire, I swear to you, I never would've asked you to stay. The present means nothing to the rest of us. It'll kill us if we stay there too long! But you—you still have family, a life . . ."

"No!" I said, shouting, slapping the ground with my hand—chasing away the self-pitying thoughts that had started to cloud my head. "That's all gone now. I chose *this*."

Emma laid her hand atop mine and said gently: "If what the animals say is true, and all our ymbrynes have been kidnapped, soon even *this* won't be here." She gathered some dirt in her hand and scattered it in the breeze. "Without ymbrynes to maintain them, our loops will collapse. The wights will use the ymbrynes to re-create their damned experiment and it'll be 1908 all over again—and either they'll fail and turn all creation into a smoking crater, or they'll succeed and make themselves immortal, and we'll be ruled by those monsters. Either way, before long we'll be more extinct than the peculiar animals! And now I've dragged *you* into this hopeless mess—and for what?"

"Everything happens for a reason," I said.

I couldn't believe those words had come out of my mouth, but as soon as they were spoken I felt the truth of them, resonating in me loud as a bell.

I was here for a reason. There was something I was meant not simply to *be*, but to *do*—and it wasn't to run or hide or give up the minute things seemed terrifying and impossible.

"I thought you didn't believe in destiny," said Emma, assessing me skeptically.

I didn't—not exactly—but I wasn't quite sure how to explain what I *did* believe, either. I thought back to the stories my grandfather used to tell me. They were filled with wonder and adventure, but something deeper ran through them, as well—a sense of abiding gratitude. As a kid I'd focused on Grandpa Portman's descriptions of a magical-sounding island and peculiar children with fantastic powers, but at heart his stories were about Miss Peregrine, and how, in a time of great need, she had helped him. When he arrived in Wales, my grandfather had been a young, frightened boy who didn't speak the language, a boy hunted by two kinds of monsters: one that would eventually kill most of his family, and the other, cartoonishly grotesque and invisible to all but him, which must've seemed lifted directly from his nightmares. In the face of all this, Miss Peregrine had hidden him, given him a home, and helped him discover who he really was—she had saved his life, and in doing so had enabled my father's life, and by extension, my own. My parents had birthed and raised and loved me, and for that I owed them a debt. But I would never have been born in the first place if not for the great and selfless kindness Miss Peregrine had shown my grandfather. I was coming to believe I had been sent here to repay that debt—my own, my father's, and my grandfather's, too.

I tried my best to explain. "It's not about destiny," I said, "but I do think there's balance in the world, and sometimes forces we don't understand intervene to tip the scales the right way. Miss Peregrine saved my grandfather—and now I'm here to help save *her*."

Emma narrowed her eyes and nodded slowly. I couldn't tell if she was agreeing with me or thinking of a polite way to tell me I'd lost my mind.

Then she hugged me.

I didn't need to explain any further. She understood.

She owed Miss Peregrine her life, too.

"We've got three days," I said. "We'll go to London, free one of the ymbrynes, and fix Miss Peregrine. It's not hopeless. We'll save her, Emma—or we'll die trying." The words sounded so brave and resolute that for a moment I wondered if it was really me who'd said them.

Emma surprised me by laughing, as if this struck her as funny somehow, and then she looked away for a moment. When she looked back again her jaw was set and her eyes shone; her old confidence was returning. "Sometimes I can't decide whether you're completely mad or some sort of miracle," she said. "Though I'm starting to think it's the latter."

She put her arms around me again and we held each other for a long moment, her head on my shoulder, breath warm on my neck, and suddenly I wanted nothing more than to close all the little gaps that existed between our bodies, to collapse into one being. But then she pulled away and kissed my forehead and started back toward the others. I was too dazed to follow right away, because there was something new happening, a wheel inside my heart I'd never noticed before, and it was spinning so fast it made me dizzy. And the farther away she got, the faster it spun, like there was an invisible cord unreeling from it that stretched between us, and if she went too far it would snap—and kill me.

I wondered if this strange, sweet pain was love.

*   *   *

The others were clustered together beneath the shade tree, children and animals together. Emma and I strode toward them. I had an impulse to link arms with her, and nearly did before something caught me and I thought better of it. I was suddenly aware—as Enoch turned to look at us with that certain suspicion he always reserved for me and now, increasingly, for both of us—that Emma and I were becoming a unit apart from the others, a private alliance with its own secrets and promises.

Bronwyn stood as we approached. "Are you all right, Miss Emma?"

"Yes, yes," Emma said quickly, "had something caught in my eye, was all. Now, everyone gather your things. We must go to London at once, and see about making Miss Peregrine whole again!"

"We're thrilled you agree," Enoch said with an eye roll. "We came to the same conclusion several minutes ago, while you two were over there whispering."

Emma flushed, but she declined to take Enoch's bait. There were more important things to attend to now than petty conflicts—namely, the many exotic dangers of the journey we were about to undertake. "As I'm sure you're all aware," Emma said, "this is by most standards a very poor plan with little hope of success." She laid out some of the reasons why. London was far away—not by the standards of the present-day world, maybe, when we might've GPSed our way to the nearest train station and caught an express that would've whisked us to the city center in a few hours. In 1940, though, in a Britain convulsed by war, London was a world away: the roads and rails might be clogged by refugees, or ruined by bombs, or monopolized by military convoys, any of which would cost us time Miss Peregrine didn't have to spare. Worse, we would be hunted—

and even more intensely than we had already been, now that nearly all the other ymbrynes had been captured.

"Forget the journey!" said Addison. "That's the least of your worries! Perhaps I was not sufficiently dissuasive when we discussed this earlier. Perhaps you do not fully understand the circumstances of the ymbrynes' incarceration." He enunciated each syllable as if we were hard of hearing. "Haven't any of you read about the punishment loops in your peculiar history books?"

"Of course we have," said Emma.

"Then you'll know that attempting to breach them is tantamount to suicide. They're death traps, every one of them, containing the very bloodiest episodes from London's history—the Great Fire of 1666; the exceedingly lethal Viking Siege of 842; the pestilent height of the terrible Plague! They don't publish temporal maps of these places, for obvious reasons. So unless one of you has a working knowledge of the secretest parts of peculiardom . . ."

"I am a student of obscure and unpleasant loops," Millard spoke up. "Been a pet hobby for many years."

"Bully for you!" said Addison. "Then I suppose you have a way to get past the horde of hollows who'll be guarding their entrances as well!"

Suddenly it felt like everyone's eyes were on me. I swallowed hard, kept my chin high, and said, "Yeah, in fact, we do."

"We'd better," grumbled Enoch.

Then Bronwyn said, "I believe in you, Jacob. I haven't known you too long, but I feel I know your heart, and it's a strong, true thing—a peculiar heart—and I trust you." She leaned against me and hugged my shoulder with one arm, and I felt my throat tighten.

"Thank you," I said, feeling lame and small in the face of her big emotion.

The dog clucked his tongue. "Madness. You children have no self-preservation instincts at all. It's a wonder any of you are still breathing."

Emma stepped in front of Addison and tried to shut him down. "Yes, wonderful," she said, "thank you for illuminating us with your opinion. Now, doomsaying aside, I have to ask the rest of you: Are there any objections to what we're proposing? I don't want anyone volunteering because they feel pressured."

Slowly, timidly, Horace raised his hand. "If London is where all the wights are, won't going there be walking right into their hands? Is that a good idea?"

"It's a *genius* idea," Enoch said irritably. "The wights are convinced we peculiar children are docile and weak. Us coming after *them* is the last thing they'd expect."

"And if we fail?" said Horace. "We'll have hand-delivered Miss Peregrine right to their doorstep!"

"We don't *know* that," said Hugh. "That London is their doorstep."

Enoch snorted. "Don't sugarcoat things. If they've broken open the prison loops and they're using them to keep our ymbrynes, then you can bet your soft parts they've overrun the rest of the city, too! It'll be absolutely *crawling* with them, mark my words. If it weren't, the wights would never have bothered coming after us in little old Cairnholm. It's basic military strategy. In battle you don't aim for the enemy's pinky toe first—you stab him right through the heart!"

"Please," Horace moaned, "enough talk of smashing loops and stabbing hearts. You'll frighten the little ones!"

"I ain't scared!" said Olive.

Horace shrank into himself. Someone muttered the word *coward*.

"None of that!" Emma said sharply. "There's nothing wrong with being frightened. It means you're taking this very serious thing we're proposing very seriously. Because, yes, it *will* be dangerous. Yes, the chances of success are abysmal. And should we even make it to London, there's no guarantee we'll be able to *find* the ymbrynes, much less rescue one. It's entirely likely that we'll end our days wasting away in some wightish prison cell or dissolved in the belly of a hollowgast. Everyone got that?"

Grim nods of understanding.

"Am I sugarcoating anything, Enoch?"

Enoch shook his head.

"If we try this," Emma went on, "we may well lose Miss Per-egrine. That much is uncontroversial. But if we *don't* try, if we *don't* go, then there's no *question* we'll lose her—and the wights will likely catch us anyway! That said, anyone who doesn't feel up to it can stay behind." She meant Horace and we all knew it. Horace stared at a spot on the ground. "You can stay here where it's safe, and we'll come collect you later, when the trouble's through. There's no shame in it."

"My left ventricle!" said Horace. "If I sat this out, I'd never live it down."

Even Claire refused to be left behind. "I've just had eighty years of pleasantly boring days," she said, raising up on one elbow from the shady spot where she'd been sleeping. "Stay here while the rest of you go adventuring? Not a chance!" But when she tried to stand, she found she couldn't, and lay back again, coughing and dizzy. Though the dishwatery liquid she'd drunk had cooled her fever some, there was no way she'd be able to make the journey to London—not today, not tomorrow, and certainly not in time to help Miss Per-egrine. Someone would have to stay behind with Claire while she recuperated.

Emma asked for volunteers. Olive raised her hand, but Bron-wyn told her to forget it—she was too young. Bronwyn started to raise her own hand, then thought better of it. She was torn, she said, between wanting to protect Claire and her sense of duty to Miss Peregrine.

Enoch elbowed Horace. "What's the matter with you?" Enoch taunted. "Here's your big chance to stay behind!"

"I *want* to go adventuring, I really and truly do," Horace in-sisted. "But I should also like to see my 105th birthday, if at all possible. Promise we won't try to save the whole blasted world?"

"We just want to save Miss P," said Emma, "but I make no guarantees about anyone's birthday."

Horace seemed satisfied with this, and his hands stayed planted at his sides.

"Anyone else?" said Emma, looking around.

"It's all right," Claire said. "I can manage on my own."

"Out of the question," said Emma. "We peculiars stick together."

Fiona's hand drifted up. She'd been so quiet, I'd nearly forgotten she was sitting with us.

"Fee, you can't!" said Hugh. He looked hurt, as if by volunteering to stay behind she was rejecting him. She looked at him with big, sad eyes, but her hand stayed in the air.

"Thank you, Fiona," said Emma. "With any luck, we'll see you both again in just a few days."

"Bird willing," said Bronwyn.

"Bird willing," echoed the others.

*　　*　　*

Afternoon was slipping toward evening. In an hour the animals' loop would be dark, and finding our way down the mountain would be much more dangerous. As we made preparations to leave, the animals kindly outfitted us with stores of fresh food and sweaters spun from the wool of peculiar sheep, which Deirdre swore had some peculiar property, though what exactly it was she couldn't quite remember. "Impervious to fire, I think—or perhaps water. Yes, they never sink in water, like fluffy little lifejackets. Or maybe—oh, I don't know, they're warm in any case!"

We thanked her and folded them into Bronwyn's trunk. Then Grunt came loping forward holding a package wrapped up with paper and twine. "A gift from the chickens," Deirdre explained, winking as Grunt pressed it into my hands. "Don't drop it."

A smarter person than I might've thought twice about bringing explosives along on our trip, but we were feeling vulnerable, and both the dog and emu-raffe swore that if we were gentle with the eggs they wouldn't go off, so we nestled them carefully between the sweaters in Bronwyn's trunk. Now at least we wouldn't have to face men with guns without weapons of our own.

Then we were nearly ready, except for one thing: when we left the animals' loop, we'd be just as lost as when we'd come in. We needed directions.

"I can show you the way out of the forest," said Addison. "Meet me at the top of Miss Wren's tower."

The space up top was so small that only two of us could fit at a time, so Emma and I went, climbing its railroad ties like the rungs of a giant ladder. Grunt monkeyed his way up in half the time, delivering Addison to the top under one arm.

The view from the top was amazing. To the east, forested slopes stretched away to a vast, barren plain. To the west, you could see all the way to the ocean, where an old-looking ship rigged with giant, complicated sails glided down the coast. I'd never asked what year it was here—1492? 1750?—though to the animals I guess it hardly mattered. This was a safe place apart from the world of people, and only in the world of people did the year make any difference.

"You'll head north," Addison said, jabbing his pipe in the direction of a road, just visible, tracing through the trees below like a faint, pencil-drawn line. "Down that road is a town, and in that town—in your time, anyway—is a train station. Your medium of inter-loop travel is when—1940?"

"That's right," Emma replied.

Though I only vaguely understood what they were talking about, I'd never been afraid to ask dumb questions. "Why can't we just go out into this world?" I asked. "Travel to London through whatever year it is here?"

"The only way is by horse and carriage," said Addison, "which takes several days . . . and causes considerable chafing, in my experience. I'm afraid you don't have that much time to spare." He turned and nosed open the door to the tower's little shack. "Please," he said, "there's one more thing I'd like to show you."

We followed him inside. The shack was modest and tiny, a far cry from Miss Peregrine's queenly setup. The entirety of its furniture was a small bed, a wardrobe, and a rolltop desk. A telescope sat mounted on a tripod, aimed out the window: Miss Wren's lookout station, where she watched for trouble, and the comings and goings of her spy pigeons.

Addison went to the desk. "Should you have any difficulty locating the road," he said, "there's a map of the forest in here."

Emma opened the desk and found the map, an old, yellowed roll of paper. Underneath it was a creased snapshot. It showed a woman in a black sequined shawl with gray-streaked hair worn in a dramatic upsweep. She was standing next to a chicken. At first glance the photo looked like a discard, taken during an off moment when the woman was looking away with her eyes closed, and yet there was something just right about it, too—how the woman's hair and clothes matched the black-and-white speckle of the chicken's feathers; how she and the chicken were facing opposite directions, implying some odd connection between them, as if they were speaking without words; dreaming at one another.

This, clearly, was Miss Wren.

Addison saw the photo and seemed to wince. I could tell he was worried for her, much more than he wanted to admit. "Please don't take this as an endorsement of your suicidal plans," he said, "but if you should succeed in your mad quest . . . and should happen to encounter Miss Wren along the way . . . you might consider . . . I mean, *might* you consider . . ."

"We'll send her home," Emma said, and then scratched him on the head. It was a perfectly normal thing to do to a dog, but seemed a strange thing to do to a talking one.

"Dog bless you," Addison replied.

Then I tried petting him, but he reared up on his hind legs and said, "Do you mind? Keep your hands at bay, sir!"

"Sorry," I mumbled, and in the awkward moment that followed it became obvious that it was time to go.

We climbed down the tower to join our friends, where we exchanged tearful goodbyes with Claire and Fiona under the big shade tree. By now Claire had been given a cushion and blanket to lie on, and like a princess she received us one by one at her makeshift bedside on the ground, extracting promises as we knelt down beside her.

"Promise you'll come back," she said to me when it was my turn, "and promise you'll save Miss Peregrine."

"I'll try my best," I said.

"That isn't good enough!" she said sternly.

"I'll come back," I said. "I promise."

"And save Miss Peregrine!"

"And save Miss Peregrine," I repeated, though the words felt empty; the more confident I tried to sound, the less confident I actually felt.

"Good," she said with a nod. "It's been awfully nice knowing you, Jacob, and I'm glad you came to stay."

"Me, too," I said, and then I got up quickly because her bright, blonde-framed face was so earnest it killed me. She believed, unequivocally, everything we told her: that she and Fiona would be all right here, among these strange animals, in a loop abandoned by its ymbryne. That we'd return for them. I hoped with all my heart that it was more than just theater, staged to make this hard thing we had to do seem possible.

Hugh and Fiona stood off to one side, their hands linked and foreheads touching, saying goodbye in their own quiet way. Finally, we'd all finished with Claire and were ready to go, but no one wanted to disturb them, so we stood watching as Fiona pulled away from Hugh, shook a few seeds from her nest of wild hair, and grew a rose bush heavy with red flowers right where they stood. Hugh's bees rushed to pollinate it, and while they were occupied—as if she'd done it just so they could have a moment to themselves—Fiona embraced him and whispered something in his ear, and Hugh nodded and whispered something back. When they finally turned and saw all of us looking, Fiona blushed, and Hugh came toward us with his hands jammed in his pockets, his bees trailing behind him, and growled, "Let's go, show's over."

We began our trek down the mountain just as dusk was falling. The animals accompanied us as far as the sheer rock wall.

Olive said to them, "Won't you all come with us?"

The emu-raffe snorted. "We wouldn't last five minutes out there! *You* can at least hope to pass for normal. But one look at *me* . . ." She wiggled her forearm-less body. "I'd be shot, stuffed, and mounted in no time."

Then the dog approached Emma and said, "If I could ask one last thing of you . . ."

"You've been so kind," she replied. "Anything."

"Would you mind terribly lighting my pipe? We have no matches here; I haven't had a real smoke in years."

Emma obliged him, touching a lit finger to the bowl of his pipe. The dog took a long, satisfied puff and said, "Best of luck to you, peculiar children."

CHAPTER FIVE

*W*e clung to the swinging net like a tribe of monkeys, bumping clumsily down the rock face while the pulley squealed and the rope creaked. Coming to earth in a knotted pile, we extricated ourselves from its tangles in what could've been a lost Three Stooges bit; several times I thought I was free, only to try standing and fall flat on my face again with a cartoonish *whump!* The dead hollow lay just feet away, its tentacles splayed like starfish arms from beneath the boulder that had crushed it. I almost felt embarrassed for it: that such a fearsome creature had let itself be laid low by the likes of us. Next time—if there was a next time—I didn't think we'd be so lucky.

We tiptoed around the hollow's reeking carcass. Charged down the mountain as fast as we could, given the limits of the treacherous path and Bronwyn's volatile cargo. Once we'd reached flat land we were able to follow our own tracks back through the squishy moss of the forest floor. We found the lake again just as the sun was setting and bats were screeching out of their hidden roosts. They seemed to bear some unintelligible warning from the world of night, crying and circling overhead as we splashed through the shallows toward the stone giant. We climbed up to his mouth and pitched ourselves down his throat, then swam out the back of him into the instantly cooler water and brighter light of midday, September 1940.

The others surfaced around me, squealing and holding their ears, everyone feeling the pressure that accompanied quick temporal shifts.

"It's like an airplane taking off," I said, working my jaw to release the air.

"Never flown in an airplane," said Horace, brushing water from the brim of his hat.

"Or when you're on the highway and someone rolls down a window," I said.

"What's a highway?" asked Olive.

"Forget it."

Emma shushed us. "Listen!"

In the distance I could hear dogs barking. They seemed far away, but sound traveled strangely in deep woods, and distances could be deceiving. "We'll have to move quickly," Emma said. "Until I say different, no one make a sound—and that includes you, headmistress!"

"I'll throw an exploding egg at the first dog that gets near us," said Hugh. "That'll teach them to chase peculiars."

"Don't you dare," said Bronwyn. "Mishandle one egg and you're liable to set them all off!"

We waded out of the lake and started back through the forest, Millard navigating with Miss Wren's creased map. After half an hour we came to the dirt road Addison had pointed to from the top of the tower. We stood in the ruts of an old wagon track while Millard studied the map, turning it sideways, squinting at its microscopic markings. I reached into the pocket of my jeans for my phone, thinking I'd call up a map of my own—an old habit—then found myself tapping on a blank rectangle of glass that refused to light up. It was dead, of course: wet, chargeless, and fifty years from the nearest cell tower. My phone was the only thing I owned that had survived our disaster at sea, but it was useless here, an alien object. I tossed it into the woods. Thirty seconds later I felt a pang of regret and ran to retrieve it. For reasons that weren't entirely clear to me, I wasn't quite ready to let it go.

Millard folded his map and announced that the town was to our left—a five- or six-hour walk, at least. "If we want to arrive before dark, we'd better move quickly."

We hadn't been walking long when Bronwyn noticed a cloud of dust rising on the road behind us, way in the distance. "Someone's coming," she said. "What should we do?"

Millard removed his greatcoat and threw it into the weeds by the side of the road, making himself invisible. "I recommend you make yourselves disappear," he said, "in whatever limited way you are able."

We got off the road and crouched behind a screen of brush. The dust cloud expanded, and with it came a clatter of wooden wheels and the clip-clop of horses' hooves. It was a caravan of wagons. When they emerged clanking and rumbling from the dust and began to pass us, I saw Horace gasp and Olive break into a smile. These were not the gray, utilitarian wagons I'd gotten used to seeing on Cairnholm, but like something from a circus, painted every color of the rainbow, sporting ornately carved roofs and doors, pulled by long-maned horses, and driven by men and women whose bodies fluttered with beaded necklaces and bright scarves. Remembering Emma's stories of performing in traveling sideshows with Miss Peregrine and the others, I turned to her and asked, "Are they peculiar?"

"They're Gypsies," she replied.

"Is that good news or bad?"

She narrowed her eyes. "Dunno yet."

I could see her weighing a decision, and I was pretty sure I knew what it was. The town we were heading for was far away, and these wagons were moving a lot faster than we could ever travel on foot. With wights and dogs hunting us, the extra speed might mean the difference between getting caught and getting away. But we didn't know who these Gypsies were, or whether we could trust them.

Emma looked at me. "What do you think, should we hitch a ride?"

I looked at the wagons. Looked back at Emma. Thought about

how my feet would feel after a six-hour walk in still-wet shoes. "Absolutely," I said.

Signaling to the others, Emma pointed at the last wagon and mimed running after it. It was shaped like a miniature house, with a little window on each side and a platform that jutted from the back like a porch, probably just wide and deep enough to hold all of us if we squeezed tight together. The wagon was moving fast but not faster than we could sprint, so when it had passed us and we were out of the last driver's sight, we leapt out of the brush and scurried after it. Emma climbed on first, then held out a hand for the next person. One by one we pulled ourselves up and settled into cramped positions along the wagon's rear porch, careful to do so quietly lest the driver hear us.

We rode like that for a long time, until our ears rang with the clatter of wagon wheels and our clothes were caked with dust, until the midday sun had wheeled across the sky and dipped behind the trees, which rose up like the walls of a great green canyon on either side of us. I scanned the forest constantly, afraid that at any moment the wights and their dogs would burst out and attack us. But for hours we didn't see anyone—not a wight, not even another traveler. It was as if we'd arrived in an abandoned country.

Now and then the caravan would stop and we'd all hold our breath, ready to flee or fight, sure we were about to be discovered. We'd send Millard out to investigate, and he would creep down from the wagon only to find that the Gypsies were just stretching their legs or reshoeing a horse, and then we'd start moving again. Eventually I stopped worrying about what would happen if we were discovered. The Gypsies seemed road-weary and harmless. We'd pass as normal and appeal to their pity. *We're just orphans with no home*, we'd say. *Please, could you spare a morsel of bread?* With any luck, they'd give us dinner and escort us to the train station.

It wasn't long before my theory was put to the test. The wagons pulled abruptly off the road and shuddered to a stop in a small clearing. The dust had hardly settled when a large man came striding around back of our wagon. He wore a flat cap on his head, a caterpillar mustache below his nose, and a grim expression that pulled down the corners of his mouth.

Bronwyn hid Miss Peregrine inside her coat while Emma leapt off the wagon and did her best impression of a pathetic orphan. "Sir, we throw ourselves at your mercy! Our house was hit by a bomb, you see, and our parents are dead, and we're terribly lost . . ."

"Shut your gob!" the man boomed. "Get down from there, all of you!" It was a command, not a request, emphasized by the decorative-but-deadly-looking knife balanced in his hand.

We looked at one another, unsure what to do. Should we fight him and run, and probably give away our secret in the process—or play normal for a while longer and wait to see what he does? Then dozens more of them appeared, piling out of their wagons to range around us in a wide circle, many holding knives of their own. We were surrounded, our options dramatically narrowed.

The men were grizzled and sharp-eyed, dressed in dark, heavy-knit clothes built to hide layers of road dust. The women wore bright, flowing dresses, their long hair held back by scarves. Children gathered behind and between them. I tried to square what little I knew about Gypsies with the faces before me. Were they about to massacre us—or were they just naturally grumpy?

I looked to Emma for a cue. She stood with her hands pressed to her chest, not held out like she was about to make flame. If she wasn't going to fight them, I decided, then neither was I.

I got down from the wagon like the man had asked, hands above my head. Horace and Hugh did the same, and then the others—all but Millard, who had slipped away, unseen, presumably to lurk nearby, waiting and watching.

The man with the cap, whom I'd pegged as their leader, began to fire questions at us. "Who are you? Where do you come from? Where are your elders?"

"We come from the west," Emma said calmly. "An island off the coast. We're orphans, as I already explained. Our houses were smashed by bombs in an air raid, and we were forced to flee. We rowed all the way to the mainland and nearly drowned." She attempted to manufacture some tears. "We have nothing," she sniffled. "We've been lost in the woods for days with no food to eat and no clothes but the ones we have on. We saw your wagons passing but were too frightened to show ourselves. We only wanted to ride as far as the town . . ."

The man studied her, his frown deepening. "Why were you forced to flee your island after your house was bombed? And why did you run into the woods instead of following the coast?"

Enoch spoke up. "No choice. We were being chased."

Emma gave him a sharp look that said: *Let me do this.*

"Chased by who?" asked the leader.

"Bad men," Emma said.

"Men with guns," added Horace. "Dressed like soldiers, although they aren't, really."

A woman in a bright yellow scarf stepped forward. "If soldiers are after them, they're trouble we don't need. Send them away, Bekhir."

"Or tie them to trees and leave them!" said a rangy-looking man.

"No!" cried Olive. "We have to get to London before it's too late!"

The leader cocked an eyebrow. "Too late for what?" We hadn't aroused his pity—only his curiosity. "We'll do nothing until we find out who you are," he said, "and what you're worth."

*   *   *

Ten men holding long-bladed knives marched us toward a flatbed wagon with a big cage mounted on top of it. Even from a distance I could see that it was something meant for animals, twenty feet by ten, made of thick iron bars.

"You're not going to lock us in there, are you?" Olive said.

"Just until we sort out what to do with you," said the leader.

"No, you can't!" cried Olive. "We have to get to London, and quick!"

"And why's that?"

"One of us is ill," said Emma, shooting Hugh a meaningful look. "We need to get him a doctor!"

"You don't need to go all the way to London for no doctor," said one of the Gypsy men. "Jebbiah's a doctor. Ain't you, Jebbiah?"

A man with scabrous lesions spanning his cheeks stepped forward. "Which one of ye's ill?"

"Hugh needs a *specialist*," said Emma. "He's got a rare condition. Stinging cough."

Hugh put a hand to his throat as if it hurt him and coughed, and a bee shot out of his mouth. Some of the Gypsies gasped, and a little girl hid her face in her mother's skirt.

"It's some sort of trick!" said the so-called doctor.

"Enough," said their leader. "Get in the cage, all of you."

They shoved us toward a ramp that led to it. We clustered together at the bottom. No one wanted to go first.

"We can't let them do this!" whispered Hugh.

"What are you waiting for?" Enoch hissed at Emma. "Burn them!"

Emma shook her head and whispered, "There are too many." She led the way up the ramp and into the cage. Its barred ceiling was low, its floor piled deep with rank-smelling hay. When we were all inside, the leader slammed the door and locked it behind us, slipping the key into his pocket. "No one goes near them!" he shouted to anyone within earshot. "They could be witches, or worse."

"Yes, that's what we are!" Enoch said through the bars. "Now let us go, or we'll turn your children into warthogs!"

The leader laughed as he walked away down the ramp. Meanwhile, the other Gypsies retreated to a safe distance and began to set up camp, pitching tents and starting cookfires. We sank down into the hay, feeling defeated and depressed.

"Look out," Horace warned. "There are animal droppings everywhere!"

"Oh, what does it matter, Horace?" Emma said. "No one gives a chuck if your clothes are dirty!"

"*I* do," Horace replied.

Emma covered her face with her hands. I sat down next to her and tried to think of something encouraging to say, but came up blank.

Bronwyn opened her coat to give Miss Peregrine some fresh air, and Enoch knelt beside her and cocked his ear, as if listening for something. "Hear that?" he said.

"What?" Bronwyn replied.

"The sound of Miss Peregrine's life slipping away! Emma, you should've burned those Gypsies' faces off while you had the chance!"

"We were surrounded!" Emma said. "Some of us would've gotten hurt in a big fight. Maybe killed. I couldn't risk that."

"So you risked Miss Peregrine instead!" said Enoch.

"Enoch, leave her be," said Bronwyn. "It ain't easy, deciding for everyone. We can't take a vote every time there's a choice to be made."

"Then maybe you should let *me* decide for everyone," Enoch replied.

Hugh snorted. "We would've been killed ages ago if *you* were in charge."

"Look, it doesn't matter now," I said. "We have to get out of this cage and make it to that town. We're a lot closer now than if we hadn't hitched a ride in the first place, so there's no need to cry over milk that hasn't even spilled yet. We just need to think of a way to escape."

So we thought, and came up with lots of ideas, but none that seemed workable.

"Maybe Emma can burn through this floor," Bronwyn suggested. "It's made of wood."

Emma swept a clear patch in the hay and knocked on the floor. "It's too thick," she said miserably.

"Wyn, can you bend these bars apart?" I asked.

"Maybe," she replied, "but not with those Gypsies so close by. They'll see and come running with their knives again."

"We need to *sneak* out, not *break* out," said Emma.

Then we heard a whisper from outside the bars. "Did you forget about me?"

"Millard!" Olive exclaimed, nearly floating out of her shoes with excitement. "Where have you been?"

"Getting the lay of the land, as it were. And waiting for things to calm down."

"Think you can steal the key for us?" said Emma, rattling the cage's locked door. "I saw the head man put it in his pocket."

"Prowling and purloinment are my specialty," he assured us, and with that he slipped away.

*   *   *

The minutes crawled by. Then a half hour. Then an hour. Hugh paced the length of the cage, an agitated bee circling his head. "What's taking him so long?" he grumbled.

"If he doesn't come back soon, I'm going to start tossing eggs," said Enoch.

"Do that and you'll get us all killed," said Emma. "We're sitting ducks in here. Once the smoke clears, they'll flay us alive."

So we sat and waited more, watching the Gypsies, the Gypsies watching back. Every minute that ticked by felt like another nail in Miss Peregrine's coffin. I found myself staring at her, as if by looking closely enough I might be able to detect the changes happening to her—to see the still-human spark within her slowly winking out. But she looked the same as she always had, only calmer somehow, asleep in the hay next to Bronwyn, her small, feathered chest rising and falling softly. She seemed to have no awareness of the trouble we were in, or of the countdown that was hanging over her head. Maybe the fact that she could sleep at a time like this was evidence enough that she was changing. The old Miss Peregrine would've been having nervous fits.

Then my thoughts strayed to my parents, as they always did when I didn't keep a tight rein on them. I tried to picture their faces as I'd last seen them. Bits and pieces coalesced in my mind: the thin rim of stubble my dad had developed after a few days on the island; the way my mom, without realizing it, would fiddle with her wedding ring when my dad talked too long about something that disinterested her; my dad's darting eyes, always checking the horizon on his never-ending search for birds.

Now they'd be searching for me.

As evening settled in, the camp came alive around us. The Gypsies talked and laughed, and when a band of children with battered horns and fiddles struck up a song, they danced. Between songs one of the boys from the band snuck around back of our cage with a bottle in his hands. "It's for the sick one," he said, checking behind him nervously.

"Who?" I said, and then he nodded at Hugh, who wilted to the floor in spasms of coughing, right on cue.

The boy slipped the bottle through the bars. I twisted off the cap, gave it a sniff, and nearly fell over. It smelled like turpentine mixed with compost. "What *is* it?" I said.

"Works, that's all I know." He looked behind him again. "All right, I done something for you. Now you owes. So tell me—what crime did you do? You're thieves, aincha?" Then he lowered his voice and said, "Or didja *kill* someone?"

"What's he talking about?" said Bronwyn.

We didn't kill anyone, I came close to saying, but then an image of Golan's body tumbling through the air toward a battery of rocks flashed in my mind, and I kept quiet.

Emma said it for me instead. "We didn't kill anyone!"

"Well, you musta done *something*," the boy said. "Why else would they have a reward out for you?"

"There's a reward?" said Enoch.

"Sure as rain. They're offering a whole pile of money."

"*Who* is?"

The boy shrugged.

"Are you going to turn us in?" Olive asked.

The boy twisted his lip. "Dunno if we will or we won't. The big shots are chewing it over. Though I'll say they don't much trust the sort of people who's offerin' the reward. Then again, money's money, and they don't much like it that you won't answer their questions."

"Where we come from," Emma said haughtily, "you don't question people who come to you asking for help."

"And you don't put 'em in cages, either!" said Olive.

Just then a tremendous bang went off in the middle of the camp. The Gypsy boy lost his balance and fell off the ramp into the grass, and the rest of us ducked as pots and pans went flying through the air away from a cookfire. The Gypsy woman who'd been tending it sped off screaming bloody murder, her dress on fire, and she might've run all the way to the ocean if someone hadn't picked up a horse's drinking bucket and doused her with it.

A moment later we heard the footsteps of an invisible boy pounding up the ramp outside our cage. "That's what happens when you try and make an omelet from a peculiar chicken egg!" said Millard, out of breath and laughing.

"*You* did that?" said Horace.

"Everything was too orderly and quiet . . . bad weather for

pickpocketing! So I slipped one of our eggs in with theirs, *et voilà*!"
Millard made a key appear out of thin air. "People are much less
likely to notice my hand in their pockets when dinner's just exploded
in their faces."

"Took you long enough," said Enoch. "Now let us out of
here!"

But before Millard could get the key in the door, the Gypsy boy
stood up and shouted, "Help! They're trying to get away!"

The boy had heard everything—but in the confusion following
the blast, hardly anyone noticed his shouts.

Millard twisted the key in the lock. The door wouldn't open.
"Oh, drat," he said. "Perhaps I stole the wrong key?"

"*Ahhhh!*" the boy screamed, pointing at the space Millard's
voice emanated from. "*A ghost!*"

"Will someone *please* shut him up!" said Enoch.

Bronwyn obliged, reaching through the cage to grab the boy's
arms, then pulling him off his feet and up against the bars.

"*Haaaaalp!*" he screamed. "They've got *mmmfff*—"

She slapped a hand over his mouth, but she'd silenced him too
late. "Galbi!" a woman shouted. "Let him go, you savages!"

And suddenly, without really meaning to, we'd taken a hostage. Gypsy men rushed at us, knives flashing in the failing light.

"What are you doing?" cried Millard. "Let that boy go before
they murder us!"

"No, don't!" Emma said, and then she screamed, "Free us or
the boy dies!"

The Gypsies surrounded us, shouting threats. "If you harm him
in any way," the leader yelled, "I'll kill every last one of you with
my bare hands!"

"Stay back!" Emma said. "Just let us go and we won't hurt
anyone."

One of the men made a run at the cage, and instinctively, Emma
flicked out her hands and sparked a roaring fireball between them.

The crowd gasped and the man skidded to a stop.

"Now you've done it!" hissed Enoch. "They'll hang us for being witches!"

"I'll burn the first one that tries!" Emma shouted, widening the space between her palms to make the fireball even larger. "Come on, let's show them who they're messing with!"

It was time to put on a show. Bronwyn went first: with one hand she raised the boy even higher, his feet kicking in the air, and with the other she grabbed one of the roof bars and began to bend it. Hugh stuck his face between the bars and shot a line of bees from his open mouth, and then Millard, who'd sprinted away from the cage the moment the boy had noticed him, shouted from somewhere behind the crowd, "And if you think you can contend with them, you haven't met me!" and launched an egg into the air. It arced above their heads and landed in a nearby clearing with a huge bang, scattering dirt as high as the treetops.

As the smoke cleared, there was a breathless moment in which no one moved or spoke. I thought at first that our display had paralyzed the Gypsies with awe—but then, when the ringing in my ears had faded, I realized they were listening for something. Then I was, too.

From the darkening road came the sound of an engine. A pair of headlights flickered into view beyond the trees, along the road. Everyone, Gypsy and peculiar, watched as the lights passed the turnoff to our clearing—then slowed, then came back. A canvas-topped military vehicle rumbled toward us. From inside it, the sounds of angry voices shouting and dogs, their throats hoarse from barking but unable to stop now that they'd caught our scent again.

It was the wights who'd been hunting us—and here we were inside a cage, unable even to run.

Emma extinguished her flame with a clap of her hands. Bronwyn dropped the boy and he stumbled away. The Gypsies fled back to their wagons or into the woods. In moments we were left alone, seemingly forgotten.

Their leader strode toward us.

"Open the cage!" Emma begged him.

She was ignored. "Hide yourselves under the hay and don't make a sound!" the man said. "And no magic tricks—unless you'd rather go with them."

There was no time for more questions. The last thing we saw before everything went black were two Gypsy men running at us with a tarp in their hands. They flipped it over the top of our cage.

Instant night.

*   *   *

Boots tromped by outside the cage, heavy and thudding, as if the wights sought to punish the very ground they walked upon. We did as instructed and dug ourselves into the stinking hay.

Nearby, I heard a wight talking to the Gypsy leader. "A group of children were seen along the road this morning," the wight said, his voice clipped, accent obscure—not quite English, not quite German. "There's a reward for their capture."

"We haven't run across anyone all day, sir," the leader said.

"Don't let their innocent faces fool you. They're traitors to the war effort. Spies for Germany. The penalty for hiding them . . ."

"We aren't hiding anything," the leader said gruffly. "See for yourself."

"I'll do that," said the wight. "And if we find them here, I'll cut your tongue out and feed it to my dog."

The wight stomped away.

"*Don't. Even. Breathe,*" the leader hissed at us, and then his footsteps trailed away, too.

I wondered why he would lie for us, given the harm these wights could cause his people. Maybe it was out of pride, or some deep-rooted disdain for authority—or, I thought with a cringe, maybe the

Gypsies just wanted the satisfaction of killing us themselves.

All around us we could hear the wights spreading throughout the camp, kicking things over, throwing open caravan doors, shoving people. A child screamed and a man reacted angrily, but was cut short with the sound of wood meeting flesh. It was excruciating to lie there and listen to people suffer—even if those same people had been ready to tear us limb from limb just minutes ago.

From the corner of my eye I saw Hugh rise from the hay and crawl to Bronwyn's trunk. He slipped his fingers over the latch and began to open the lid, but Bronwyn stopped him. "What are you doing?" she mouthed.

"We've got to get them before they get us!"

Emma lifted herself out of the hay on her elbows and rolled toward them, and I got closer too, to listen.

"Don't be insane," said Emma. "If we throw the eggs now, they'll shoot us to ribbons."

"So what, then?" said Hugh. "We should just lie here until they find us?"

We clustered around the trunk, speaking in whispers.

"Wait until they unlock the door," said Enoch. "Then I'll throw an egg through the bars behind us. That'll distract the wights long enough for Bronwyn to crack the skull of whichever one comes into the cage first, which should give the rest of us time to run. Scatter to the outer edges of camp, then turn and throw your eggs back at the middle-most campfire. Everyone in a thirty-meter radius will be a memory."

"I'll be damned," said Hugh. "That just might work."

"But there are children in the camp!" said Bronwyn.

Enoch rolled his eyes. "Or we can worry about collateral damage, run into the woods, and leave the wights and their dogs to hunt us down one by one. But if we plan on reaching London—or living beyond tonight—I don't recommend it."

Hugh patted Bronwyn's hand, which was covering the trunk

latch. "Open it," he said. "Give them out."

Bronwyn hesitated. "I can't. I can't kill children who've done nothing to harm us."

"But we don't have a choice!" whispered Hugh.

"You always have a choice," said Bronwyn.

Then we heard a dog snarl very near the bottom rim of the cage, and went silent. A moment later a flashlight shone against the outside of the tarp. "Tear this sheet down!" someone said—the dog's handler, I assumed.

The dog barked, its nose snuffling to get beneath the tarp and up through the cage bars. "Over here!" shouted the handler. "We've got something!"

We all looked to Bronwyn. "Please," Hugh said. "At least let us defend ourselves."

"It's the only way," said Enoch.

Bronwyn sighed and took her hand away from the latch. Hugh nodded gratefully and opened the trunk lid. We all reached in and took an egg from between the layered sweaters—everyone but Bronwyn. Then we stood and faced the cage door, eggs in hand, and prepared for the inevitable.

More boots marched toward us. I tried to prepare myself for what was coming. *Run*, I told myself. *Run and don't look back and then throw it.*

But knowing that innocent people would die, could I really do it? Even to save my own life? What if I just dropped the egg in some grass and ran into the woods?

A hand grabbed one edge of the tarp and pulled. The tarp began to slide away.

Then, just shy of exposing us, it stopped.

"What's the matter with you?" I heard the dog's handler say.

"I'd steer well away from that cage if I was you," said another voice—a Gypsy's.

I could see half the sky above us, stars twinkling down through the branches of oaks.

"Yeah? And why is that?" said the handler.

"Old Bloodcoat ain't been fed in a few days," the Gypsy said. "He don't usually care for the taste of humans, but when he's this hungry he ain't so discriminating!"

Then came a sound that stole the breath right out of me—the roar of a giant bear. Impossibly, it seemed to be coming from among us, inside our cage. I heard the dog's handler shout in surprise and then scramble down the ramp, pulling his yelping dog along with him.

I couldn't fathom how a bear had gotten into the cage, only that I needed to get away from it, so I pressed myself hard against the bars. Next to me I saw Olive stick her little fist in her mouth to keep from crying out.

Outside, other soldiers were laughing at the handler. "Idiot!" he said, embarrassed. "Only Gypsies would keep an animal like that in the middle of their camp!"

I finally worked up the courage to turn around and look behind me. There was no bear in our cage. What had made that awful roar?

The soldiers kept searching the camp, but now they left our cage alone. After a few minutes we heard them pile back into their truck and restart the engine, and then, at last, they were gone.

The tarp slid away from our cage. The Gypsies were all gathered around us. I held my egg in one trembling hand, wondering if I'd have to use it.

The leader stood before us. "Are you all right?" he said. "I'm sorry if that frightened you."

"We're alive," Emma replied, looking around warily. "But where's this bear of yours?"

"You aren't the only ones with unusual talents," said a young man at the edge of the crowd, and then in quick succession he growled like a bear and yowled like a cat, throwing his voice from one place to another with slight turns of his head so that it sounded like we were being stalked from all directions. When we'd gotten over our shock, we broke into applause.

"I thought you said they weren't peculiar," I whispered to Emma.

"Anyone can do parlor tricks like that," she said.

"Apologies if I failed to properly introduce myself," said the Gypsy leader. "My name is Bekhir Bekhmanatov. And you are our honored guests." He bowed deeply. "Why didn't you tell us you were *syndrigasti*?"

We gaped at him. He had used the ancient name for peculiars, the one Miss Peregrine had taught us.

"Do we know you from somewhere?" Bronwyn asked.

"Where did you hear that word?" said Emma.

Bekhir smiled. "If you'll accept our hospitality, I promise to explain everything." Then he bowed again and strode forward to unlock our cage.

*　　*　　*

We sat with the Gypsies on fine, handwoven carpets, talking and eating stew by the shimmering light of twin campfires. I dropped the spoon I'd been given and slurped straight from a wooden bowl, my table manners a distant memory as greasy, delicious broth dribbled down my chin. Bekhir walked among us, making sure each peculiar child was comfortable, asking if we had enough to eat and drink, and apologizing repeatedly for the state of our clothes, now covered in filthy bits of hay from the cage. Since witnessing our peculiar display he'd changed his attitude toward us completely; in the span of a few minutes we'd graduated from being prisoners to guests of honor.

"I'm very sorry for the way you were treated," he said, lowering himself onto a cushion between the fires. "When it comes to the safety of my people, I must take every precaution. There are many strangers wandering the roads these days—people who aren't what they appear to be. If you'd only told me you were *syndrigasti* . . ."

"We were taught never, ever to tell anyone," said Emma.

"*Ever*," Olive added.

"Whoever taught you that is very wise," Bekhir said.

"How do you know about us?" Emma asked. "You speak the old tongue."

"Only a few words," Bekhir said. He gazed into the flames, a spit of darkening meat roasting there. "We have an old understanding, your people and mine. We aren't so different. Outcasts and wanderers all—souls clinging to the margins of the world." He pinched a hunk of meat from the spit and chewed it thoughtfully. "We are allies of a sort. Over the years, we Gypsies have even taken in and raised some of your children."

"And we're grateful for it," said Emma, "and for your hospitality as well. But at the risk of seeming rude, we can't possibly stay with you any longer. It's very important that we reach London quickly. We have a train to catch."

"For your sick friend?" Bekhir asked, raising an eyebrow at Hugh, who had long ago dropped his act and was now gulping down stew with abandon, bees buzzing happily around his head.

"Something like that," said Emma.

Bekhir knew we were hiding something, but he was kind enough to let us have our secrets. "There won't be any more trains tonight," he said, "but we'll rise at dawn and deliver you to the station before the first one leaves in the morning. Good enough?"

"It'll have to be," Emma said, her brow pinched with worry. Even though we'd saved time by hitching a ride instead of walking, Miss Peregrine had still lost an entire day. Now she had only two left, at most. But that was in the future; right now we were warm, well fed, and out of immediate danger. It was hard not to enjoy ourselves, if only for the moment.

We made fast friends with the Gypsies. Everyone was eager

to forget what had happened between us earlier. Bronwyn tried to apologize to the boy she'd taken hostage, but he brushed it off like it had been nothing. The Gypsies fed us relentlessly, refilling my bowl again and again—overfilling it when I tried to refuse more. When Miss Peregrine hopped out of Bronwyn's coat and announced her appetite with a screech, the Gypsies fed her, too, tossing hunks of raw meat in the air and cheering when she leapt up to snatch them. "She's hungry!" Olive laughed, clapping as the bird shredded a pig knuckle with her talons.

"Now aren't you glad we didn't blow them up?" Bronwyn whispered to Enoch.

"Oh, I *suppose*," he replied.

The Gypsy band struck up another song. We ate and danced. I convinced Emma to take a turn around the fire with me, and though I was usually shy about dancing in public, this time I let myself go. Our feet flew and our hands clapped in time to the music, and for a few shining minutes we lost ourselves in it. I was able to forget how much danger we were in, and how that very day we had nearly been captured by wights and devoured by a hollow, our meat-stripped bones spat off a mountainside. In that moment I was deeply grateful to the Gypsies, and for the simplemindedness of the animal part of my brain; that a hot meal and a song and a smile from someone I cared about could be enough to distract me from all that darkness, if only for a little while. Then the song ended and we stumbled back to our seats, and in the lull that followed I felt the mood change. Emma looked at Bekhir and said, "May I ask you something?"

"Of course," he said.

"Why did you risk your lives for us?"

He waved his hand. "You would've done the same."

"I'm not sure we would've," said Emma. "I just want to understand. Was it because we're peculiar?"

"Yes," he said simply. A moment passed. He looked away at the trees that edged our clearing, their firelit trunks and the blackness beyond. Then he said, "Would you like to meet my son?"

"Of course," Emma said.

She stood, and so did I and several others.

Bekhir raised a hand. "He's shy, I'm afraid. Just you," he said, pointing to Emma, "and you"—he pointed at me—"and the one who can be heard but not seen."

"Impressive," said Millard. "And I was trying so hard to be subtle!"

Enoch sat down again. "Why am I always being left out of things? Do I smell?"

A Gypsy woman in a flowing robe swept into the campfire circle. "While they're gone, I'll read your palms and tell your fortunes," she said. She turned to Horace. "Maybe you'll climb Kilimanjaro one day!" Then to Bronwyn—"Or marry a rich, handsome man!"

Bronwyn snorted. "My fondest dream."

"The future is *my* specialty, madam," said Horace. "Let me show you how it's done!"

Emma, Millard, and I left them and started across the camp with Bekhir. We came to a plain-looking caravan wagon, and he climbed its short ladder and knocked on the door.

"Radi?" he called gently. "Come out, please. There are people here to see you."

The door opened a crack and a woman peeked out. "He's scared. Won't leave his chair." She looked us over carefully, then opened the door wide and beckoned us in. We mounted the steps and ducked into a cramped but cozy space that appeared to be a living room, bedroom, and kitchen all in one. There was a bed under a narrow window, a table and chair, and a little stove that vented out a chimney in the roof; everything you'd need to be self-sufficient on the road for weeks or months at a time.

In the room's lone chair sat a boy. He held a trumpet in his lap. I'd seen him play earlier, I realized, as part of the Gypsy children's band. This was Bekhir's son, and the woman, I assumed, was

Bekhir's wife.

"Take off your shoes, Radi," the woman said.

The boy kept his gaze trained on the floor. "Do I have to?" he asked.

"Yes," Bekhir said.

The boy tugged off one of his boots, then the other. For a second I wasn't sure what I was seeing: there was nothing inside his shoes. He appeared to have no feet. And yet he'd had to work to get his boots off, so they had to have been attached to *something*. Then Bekhir asked him to stand, and reluctantly the boy slid forward in the chair and rose out of it. He seemed to be levitating, the cuffs of his pants hanging empty a few inches above the floor.

"He began disappearing a few months ago," the woman explained. "First just his toes. Then his heels. Finally the rest, both feet. Nothing I've given him—no tincture, no tonic—has had the slightest effect in curing him."

So he had feet, after all—invisible ones.

"We don't know what to do," said Bekhir. "But I thought, perhaps there's a healer among you . . ."

"There's no healing what he's got," said Millard, and at the sound of his voice in the empty air the boy's head jerked up. "We're alike, he and I. It was just the same for me when I was young. I wasn't born invisible; it happened a little at a time."

"Who's speaking?" the boy said.

Millard picked up a scarf that lay on the edge of the bed and wrapped it around his face, revealing the shape of his nose, his forehead, his mouth. "Here I am," he said, moving across the floor toward the boy. "Don't be frightened."

As the rest of us watched, the boy reached up his hand and touched Millard's cheek, then his forehead, then his hair—the color and style of which it had never occurred to me to imagine—and even pulled a little hank of it, gently, as if testing its realness.

"You're *there*," the boy said, his eyes sparkling with wonder.

"You're really there!"

"And you'll be, too, even after the rest of you goes," said Millard. "You'll see. It doesn't hurt."

The boy smiled, and when he did, the woman's knees wobbled and she had to steady herself against Bekhir. "Bless you," she said to Millard, near tears. "Bless you."

Millard sat down at Radi's disappeared feet. "There's nothing to be afraid of, my boy. In fact, once you adjust to invisibility, I think you'll find it has many advantages . . ."

And as he began to list them, Bekhir went to the door and nodded at Emma and me. "Let's let them be," he said. "I'm sure they have a lot to talk about."

We left Millard alone with the boy and his mother. Returning to the campfire, we found nearly everyone, peculiar and Gypsy alike, gathered around Horace. He was standing on a tree stump before the astounded fortune teller, his eyes closed and one hand atop her head, and seemed to be narrating a dream as it came to him: ". . . and your grandson's grandson will pilot a giant ship that shuttles between the Earth and the moon like an omnibus, and on the moon he'll have a very small house, and he'll fall behind on the mortgage and have to take in lodgers, and one of those lodgers will be a beautiful woman with whom he'll fall very deeply in moon-love, which isn't quite the same as Earth-love because of the difference in gravity there . . ."

We watched from the edge of the crowd. "Is he for real?" I asked Emma.

"Might be," she replied. "Or he might just be having a bit of fun with her."

"Why can't he tell *our* futures like that?"

Emma shrugged. "Horace's ability can be maddeningly useless. He'll reel off lifetimes of predictions for strangers, but with us he's almost totally blocked. It's as if the more he cares about someone, the less he can see. Emotion clouds his vision."

"Doesn't it all of us," came a voice from behind us, and we turned to see Enoch standing there. "And on that tip, I hope you aren't distracting the American too much, Emma dear. It's hard to keep a lookout for hollowgast when there's a young lady's tongue in your ear."

"Don't be disgusting!" Emma said.

"I couldn't ignore the Feeling if I wanted to," I said, though I did wish I could ignore the icky feeling that Enoch was jealous of me.

"So, tell me about your secret meeting," Enoch said. "Did the Gypsies really protect us because of some dusty old alliance none of us have heard of?"

"The leader and his wife have a peculiar son," said Emma. "They hoped we could help him."

"That's madness," said Enoch. "They nearly let themselves be filleted alive by those soldiers for the sake of one boy? Talk about emotion clouding vision! I figured they wanted to enslave us for our abilities, or at the very least sell us at auction—but then I'm always overestimating people."

"Oh, go find a dead animal to play with," said Emma.

"I'll never understand ninety-nine percent of humanity," said Enoch, and he went away shaking his head.

"Sometimes I think that boy is part machine," Emma said. "Flesh on the outside, metal on the inside."

I laughed, but secretly I wondered if Enoch was right. *Was* it crazy, what Bekhir had risked for his son? Because if Bekhir was crazy, then certainly I was. How much had I given up for the sake of just one girl? Despite my curiosity, despite my grandfather, despite the debts we owed Miss Peregrine, ultimately I was here—now—for one reason alone: because from the day I met Emma I'd known I wanted to be part of any world she belonged to. Did that make me crazy? Or was my heart too easily conquered?

Maybe I could use a little metal on the inside, I thought. If I'd kept my heart better armored, where would I be now?

Easy—I'd be at home, medicating myself into a monotone. Drowning my sorrows in video games. Working shifts at Smart Aid. Dying inside, day by day, from regret.

You coward. You weak, pathetic child. You threw your chance away.

But I hadn't. In reaching toward Emma, I'd risked everything—was risking it again, every day—but in doing so I had grasped and pulled myself into a world once unimaginable to me, where I lived among people who were more alive than anyone I'd known, did things I'd never dreamed I could do, survived things I'd never dreamed I could survive. All because I'd let myself feel something for one peculiar girl.

Despite all the trouble and danger we found ourselves in, and despite the fact that this strange new world had started to crumble the moment I'd discovered it, I was profoundly glad I was here. Despite everything, this peculiar life was what I'd always wanted. Strange, I thought, how you can be living your dreams and your nightmares at the very same time.

"What is it?" Emma said. "You're staring at me."

"I wanted to thank you," I said.

She wrinkled her nose and squinted like I'd said something funny. "Thank me for what?" she said.

"You give me strength I didn't know I had," I said. "You make me better."

She blushed. "I don't know what to say."

Emma, bright soul. I need your fire—the one inside you.

"You don't have to say anything," I said. And then I was seized with the sudden urge to kiss her, and I did.

*   *   *

Though we were dead tired, the Gypsies were in a buoyant mood and seemed determined to keep the party going, and after a few cups of hot, sweet, highly caffeinated something and a few more songs, they'd won us over. They were natural storytellers and beautiful singers; innately charming people who treated us like long-lost cousins. We stayed up half the night trading stories. The young guy who'd thrown his voice like a bear did a ventriloquist act that was so good I almost believed his dummies had come alive. He seemed to have a little crush on Emma and delivered the whole routine to her, smiling encouragingly, but she pretended not to notice and made a point of holding my hand.

Later they told us the story of how, during the First World War, the British army had taken all their horses, and for a while they'd had none to pull their wagons. They had been left stranded in the forest—this very forest—when one day a herd of long-horned goats wandered into their camp. They looked wild but were tame enough to eat out of your hand, so someone got the idea to hitch one to a wagon, and these goats turned out to be nearly as strong as the horses they'd lost. So the Gypsies got unstuck, and until the end of the war their wagons were pulled by these peculiarly strong goats, which is how they became known throughout Wales as Goat People. As proof they passed around a photo of Bekhir's uncle riding a goat-pulled wagon. We knew without anyone having to say it that this was the lost herd of peculiar goats Addison had talked about. After the war, the army gave back the Gypsies' horses, and the goats, no longer needed, disappeared again into the forest.

Finally, campfires dwindling, they laid out sleeping rolls for us and sang a lullaby in a lilting foreign language, and I felt pleasantly like a child. The ventriloquist came to say good night to Emma. She shooed him away, but not before he left a calling card. On the back was an address in Cardiff where he picked up mail every few months, whenever the Gypsies stopped through. On the front was his photo, with dummies, and a little note written to Emma. She showed it to me and snickered, but I felt bad for the guy. He was guilty only of liking her, same as me.

To Emma,

Yours for a smile

G. M. S. etc.

I curled up with Emma in a sleeping roll at the forest's edge. Just as we were drifting off, I heard footsteps in the grass nearby, and opened my eyes to see no one at all. It was Millard, back again after having spent the evening talking with the Gypsy boy.

"He wants to come with us," said Millard.

"Who?" Emma mumbled groggily. "Where?"

"The boy. With us."

"And what did you say?"

"I told him it was a bad idea. But I didn't say no, precisely."

"You know we can't take on anyone else," Emma said. "He'll slow us down."

"I know, I know," said Millard. "But he's disappearing very rapidly, and he's frightened. Soon he'll be entirely invisible, and he's afraid he'll fall behind their group one day and the Gypsies won't notice and he'll be lost forever in the woods among the wolves and spiders."

Emma groaned and rolled over to face Millard. He wasn't going to let us sleep until this was decided. "I know he'll be disappointed," she said. "But it's really impossible. I'm sorry, Mill."

"Fair enough," Millard said heavily. "I'll give him the news."

He rose and slipped away.

Emma sighed, and for a while she tossed and turned, restless.

"You did the right thing," I whispered. "It isn't easy being the one everybody looks to."

She said nothing, but snuggled into the hollow of my chest. Gradually we drifted off, the whispers of breeze-blown branches and the breathing of horses gentling us to sleep.

* * *

It was a night of thin sleep and bad dreams, spent much as I'd spent the previous day: being chased by packs of nightmare dogs. By morning I was worn out. My limbs felt heavy as wood, my head cottony. I might've felt better if I hadn't slept at all.

Bekhir woke us at dawn. "Rise and shine, *syndrigasti*!" he shouted, tossing out hunks of brick-hard bread. "There'll be time for sleeping when you're dead!"

Enoch knocked his bread against a rock and it clacked like wood. "We'll be dead soon enough, with breakfast like this!"

Bekhir roughed Enoch's hair, grinning. "Ahh, come on. Where's your peculiar spirit this morning?"

"In the wash," said Enoch, covering his head with the sleeping roll.

Bekhir gave us ten minutes to prepare for the ride to town. He was making good on his promise and would have us there before the morning's first train. I got up, stumbled to a bucket of water, splashed some on my face, brushed my teeth with my finger. Oh, how I missed my toothbrush. How I longed for my minty floss, my ocean-breeze-scented deodorant stick. What I wouldn't have given, just then, to find a Smart Aid store.

My kingdom for a pack of fresh underwear!

As I raked bits of hay from my hair with my fingers and bit into a loaf of inedible bread, the Gypsies and their children watched us with mournful faces. It was as if they knew, somehow, that the previous night's fun had been a last hurrah, and now we were being led off to the gallows. I tried to cheer one of them up. "It's okay," I said to a towheaded little boy who seemed on the verge of tears. "We're going to be fine."

He looked at me as if I were a talking ghost, his eyes wide and uncertain.

Eight horses were rounded up, and eight Gypsy riders—one for each of us. Horses would get us to town much faster than a caravan of wagons could. They were also terrifying to me.

I'd never ridden a horse. I was probably the only marginally rich kid in America who hadn't. It wasn't because I didn't think horses were beautiful, majestic creatures, the pinnacle of animal creation, etc., etc.—it's just that I didn't believe any animal had the slightest interest in being mounted or ridden by a human being. Besides, horses were very large, with rippling muscles and big, grinding teeth, and they looked at me as if they knew I was afraid and were hoping for an opportunity to kick my head in. Not to mention the lack of a seatbelt on a horse—no secondary restraint systems of any kind—and yet horses could go nearly as fast as cars but were much bouncier. So the whole endeavor just seemed inadvisable.

I said none of this, of course. I shut up and set my jaw and hoped I'd live at least long enough to die in a more interesting way than by falling off a horse.

From the first *giddyap!* we were at full gallop. I abandoned my dignity right away and bear-hugged the Gypsy man on the saddle in front of me who held the reins—so quickly that I didn't have a chance to wave goodbye to the Gypsies who had gathered to see us off. Which was just as well: goodbyes had never been my strong suit anyway, and lately my life had felt like an unbroken series of them. Goodbye, goodbye, goodbye.

We rode. My thighs went numb from squeezing the horse. Bekhir led the pack, his peculiar boy riding with him in the saddle. The boy rode with his back straight and arms at his sides, confident and unafraid, such a contrast from last night. He was in his element here, among the Gypsies. He didn't need us. *These* were his people.

Eventually we slowed to a trot and I found the courage to unbury my face from the rider's jacket and take in the changing landscape. The forest had flattened into fields. We were descending into a valley, in the middle of which was a town that, from here, looked no bigger than a postage stamp, overwhelmed by green on all sides. Tracing toward it from the north was a long ellipsis of puffy white dots: the smoky breath of a train.

Bekhir stopped the horses just shy of the town gates. "This is as far as we go," he said. "We're not much welcome in towns. You don't want the sort of attention we'd draw."

It was hard to imagine anyone objecting to these kindly people. Then again, similar prejudices were among the reasons peculiars had withdrawn from society. Such was the way the sad world turned.

The children and I dismounted. I stood behind the others, hoping no one would notice my trembling legs. Just as we were about to go, Bekhir's boy sprang down from his father's horse and cried, "Wait! Take me with you!"

"I thought you were going to talk to him," Emma said to Millard.

"I *did*," Millard replied.

The boy pulled a knapsack from the saddlebag and slung it over his shoulder. He was packed and ready to go. "I can cook," he said, "and chop wood, and ride a horse, and tie all sorts of knots!"

"Someone give him a merit badge," said Enoch.

"I'm afraid it's impossible," Emma said to him gently.

"But I'm like you—and becoming more so all the time!" The boy began to unbuckle his pants. "Look what's happening to me!"

Before anyone could stop him, he'd sent his pants to his ankles. The girls gasped and looked away. Hugh shouted, "Keep your trousers on, you depraved lunatic!"

But there was nothing to see—he was invisible from the midsection down. Morbid curiosity compelled me to peek at the underside of his visible half, which earned me a crystal-clear view of the inner workings of his bowels.

"Look how much I've disappeared since yesterday," Radi said, his voice panicky. "Soon I'll be gone altogether!"

The Gypsy men gawked and murmured. Even their horses

seemed disturbed, shying away from what seemed to be a disembodied child.

"I'll be winged!" said Enoch. "He's only half there."

"Oh, you poor thing," said Bronwyn. "Can't we keep him?"

"We aren't some traveling circus you can join whenever the notion takes you," said Enoch. "We're on a dangerous mission to save our ymbryne, and in no position to play babysitter to a clueless new peculiar!"

The boy's eyes grew wide and began to water, and he let his knapsack slide off his shoulder and fall to the road.

Emma took Enoch aside. "That was too harsh," she said. "Now tell him you're sorry."

"I won't. This is a ridiculous waste of our precious and dwindling time."

"These people saved our lives!"

"Our lives wouldn't have *needed* saving if they hadn't stuck us in that blessed cage!"

Emma gave up on Enoch and turned to the boy. "If circumstances were different, we'd welcome you with open arms. But as it stands, our entire civilization and way of life are in danger of being snuffed out. So it's rather bad timing, you see."

"It isn't fair," the boy moped. "Why couldn't I have started disappearing ages ago? Why did it have to happen *now*?"

"Every peculiar's ability manifests in its own time," said Millard. "Some in infancy; others not until they're quite old. I once heard of a man who didn't realize he could levitate objects with his mind until he was ninety-two years of age."

"I was lighter than air from the minute I was born," Olive said proudly. "I popped out of me mum and floated straight up to the hospital ceiling! Only thing that stopped me from rolling out the window and into the clouds was the umbilical cord. They say the doctor fainted from the shock!"

"You're *still* quite shocking, love," Bronwyn said, giving her a reassuring pat on the back.

Millard, visible thanks to the coat and boots he wore, went to the boy. "What does your father think about all of this?" he said.

"Naturally, we don't want him to go," Bekhir said, "but how can we properly care for our son if we can't even *see* him? He wants to leave—and I wonder if perhaps he'd be better off among his own kind."

"Do you love him?" Millard asked bluntly. "Does he love you?"

Bekhir's brow furrowed. He was a man of traditional sensibilities, and the question made him uncomfortable. But after some hemming and hawing, he growled, "Of course. He's my child."

"Then *you* are his kind," said Millard. "The boy belongs with you, not us."

Bekhir was loath to show emotion in front of his men, but at this I saw his eyes flicker and his jaw tighten. He nodded, looked down at his son, and said, "Come on, then. Pick up your bag and let's go. Your mother'll have tea waiting."

"All right, Papa," the boy said, seeming at once disappointed and relieved.

"You'll be fine," Millard assured the boy. "Better than fine. And when this is all over, I'll look for you. There are more like us out there, and we'll find them one day, together."

"Promise?" the boy said, his eyes full of hope.

"I do," said Millard.

And with that the boy climbed back onto his father's horse, and we turned and walked through the gates into town.

CHAPTER SIX

*T*he town was named Coal. Not Coaltown or Coalville. Just Coal. The stuff was everywhere, piled in gritty drifts by the side doors of houses, wafting up from the chimneys as oily smoke, smeared on the overalls of men walking to work. We hurried past them toward the depot in a tight pack.

"Quickly now," Emma said. "No talking. Eyes down."

It was a well-established rule that we were to avoid unnecessary eye contact with normals, because looks could lead to conversations, and conversations to questions, and peculiar children found questions posed by normal adults difficult to answer in a way that didn't invite still more questions. Of course, if anything was going to invite questions, it was a group of bedraggled-looking children traveling alone during wartime—especially with a big, sharp-taloned bird of prey perched on one of the girls' shoulders—but the townspeople hardly seemed to notice us. They haunted the laundry lines and pub doorways of Coal's twisting lanes, drooping like wilted flowers, eyes flicking toward us and away again. They had other worries.

The train depot was so small I wondered if trains ever bothered stopping there. The only covered portion was the ticket counter, a little hut in the middle of an open-air platform. Inside the hut was a man asleep in a chair, bottle-thick bifocals slipping down his nose.

Emma rapped sharply on the window, startling the clerk awake. "Eight tickets to London!" she said. "We must be there this very afternoon."

The clerk peered at us through the glass. Took off his bifocals and wiped them clean and put them on again, just to make sure he was seeing properly. I'm sure we were a shocking sight: our clothes were mud-splotched, our hair greasy and sticking up at odd angles. We probably stank, too.

"So sorry," the clerk said. "The train is full."

I looked around. Aside from a few people dozing on benches, the depot was empty.

"That's absurd!" said Emma. "Sell us the tickets at once or I shall report you to the rail authority for child discrimination!"

I might've handled the clerk with a softer touch, but Emma had no patience for the self-important authority of petty bureaucrats.

"If there were any such statute," the clerk replied, his nose rising disdainfully, "it would certainly not apply to *you*. There's a war on, you know, and more important things to be hauled about her majesty's countryside than children and animals!" He gave Miss Peregrine a hard look. "Which aren't allowed in any case!"

A train hissed into the station and squealed to a stop. The conductor stuck his head out of one of its windows and shouted, "Eight-thirty to London! All aboard!" The bench-sleepers in the depot roused themselves and began to shuffle across the platform.

A man in a gray suit shoved past us to the window. He pushed money at the clerk, received a ticket in exchange, and hurried off toward the train.

"You said it was full!" Emma said, rapping hard on the glass. "You can't *do* that!"

"That gentleman bought a *first-class* ticket," the clerk said. "Now be gone with you, pestilent little beggars! Go find pockets to pick somewhere else!"

Horace stepped to the ticket window and said, "Beggars, by definition, do not carry large sums of money," and then he reached into his coat pocket and slapped a fat wad of bills down on the counter. "If it's first-class tickets you're selling, then that's what we'll have!"

The clerk sat up straight, gaping at the pile of money. The rest of us gaped too, baffled as to where Horace had gotten it. Riffling through the bills, the clerk said, "Why, this is enough to buy seats to an entire first-class car!"

"Then give us an entire car!" said Horace. "That way you can be sure we'll pick no one's pocket."

The clerk turned red and stammered, "Y-yes sir—sorry, sir—and I hope you won't take my previous comments as anything other than jest . . ."

"Just give us the blasted tickets so we can get on the train!"

"Right away, sir!"

The clerk slid a stack of first-class tickets toward us. "Enjoy your trip!" he said. "And please don't tell anyone I said so, sirs and madams, but if I were you, I'd hide that bird out of sight. The conductors won't like it, first-class tickets or not."

As we strode away from the counter with tickets in hand, Horace's chest puffed out like a peacock's.

"Where on earth did you get all that money?" said Emma.

"I rescued it from Miss Peregrine's dresser drawer before the house burned," Horace replied. "Tailored a special pocket in my coat to keep it safe."

"Horace, you're a genius!" said Bronwyn.

"Would a real genius have given away every cent of our money like that?" said Enoch. "Did we really need an *entire* first-class car?"

"No," said Horace, "but making that man look stupid felt good, didn't it?"

"I suppose it did," Enoch said.

"That's because the true purpose of money is to manipulate others and make them feel lesser than you."

"I'm not entirely sure about that," Emma said.

"Only kidding!" said Horace. "It's to buy clothes, of course."

We were about to board the train when the conductor stopped us. "Let's see your tickets!" he said, and he was reaching for the stack in Horace's hand when he noticed Bronwyn stuffing something into her coat. "What's that you've got there?" the conductor said, rounding on her suspiciously.

"What's what I've got where?" Bronwyn replied, trying to seem casual while holding her coat closed over a wriggling lump.

"In your coat there!" the conductor said. "Don't toy with me, girl."

"It's, ahhh . . ." Bronwyn tried to think fast and failed. "A bird?"

Emma's head fell. Enoch put a hand over his eyes and groaned.

"No pets on the train!" the conductor barked.

"But you don't understand," said Bronwyn. "I've had her ever since I was a child . . . and we *must* get on this train . . . and we paid *so much* for our tickets!"

"Rules are rules!" the conductor said, his patience fraying. "Do *not* toy with me!"

Emma's head bopped up, her face brightening. "A toy!" she said.

"Excuse me?" said the conductor.

"It isn't a *real* bird, conductor sir. We'd never dream of breaking the rules like that. It's my sister's favorite toy, you see, and she thinks you mean to take it away from her." She clasped her hands pitifully, imploring. "You wouldn't take away a child's favorite toy, would you?"

The conductor studied Bronwyn doubtfully. "She looks too old for toys, wouldn't you say?"

Emma leaned in and whispered, "She's a bit *delayed*, you see . . ."

Bronwyn frowned at this but had no choice but to play along. The conductor stepped toward her. "Let's see this toy, then."

Moment of truth. We held our breath as Bronwyn opened her coat, reached inside, and slowly withdrew Miss Peregrine. When I saw the bird, I thought for one terrible moment that she had died. Miss Peregrine had gone completely stiff, and lay in Bronwyn's hand with her eyes closed and legs sticking out rigidly. Then I realized she was just playing along.

"See?" Bronwyn said. "Birdy ain't real. She's stuffed."

"I saw it moving earlier!" the conductor said.

"It's a—ehm—a wind-up model," said Bronwyn. "Watch."

Bronwyn knelt down and set Miss Peregrine on the ground on her side, then reached under her wing and pretended to wind something. A moment later Miss Peregrine's eyes flew open and she began to toddle around, her head swiveling mechanically and legs kicking out as if spring-loaded. Finally she jerked to a stop and toppled over, stiff as a board. Truly an Oscar-worthy performance.

The conductor seemed almost—but not quite—convinced. "Well," he hemmed, "if it's a toy, you won't mind putting it away in your toy chest." He nodded at the trunk, which Bronwyn had set down on the platform.

Bronwyn hesitated. "It isn't a—"

"Yes, fine, that's no bother," said Emma, flipping open the trunk's latches. "Put it away now, sister!"

"But what if there's no *air* in there?" Bronwyn hissed at Emma.

"Then we'll poke some blessed *holes* in the side of it!" Emma hissed back.

Bronwyn picked up Miss Peregrine and set her gently inside the trunk. "Ever so sorry, ma'am," she whispered, lowering and then latching the lid.

The conductor finally took our tickets. "First class!" he said, surprised. "Your car's all the way down front." He pointed to the far end of the platform. "You'd best hurry!"

"*Now* he tells us!" said Emma, and we took off down the platform at a jog.

With a chug of steam and a metallic groan, the train began to move beside us. For now it was just inching along, but with each turn of its wheels it sped up a little more.

We came even with the first-class car. Bronwyn was first to

jump through the open door. She set her trunk down in the aisle and reached out a hand to help Olive on board.

Then, from behind us, a voice shouted, "Stop! Get away from there!"

It wasn't the conductor's voice. This one was deeper, more authoritative.

"I swear," Enoch said, "if *one more person* tries to stop us getting on this train . . ."

A gunshot rang out, and the sudden shock of it made my feet tangle. I stumbled out the doorway and back onto the platform.

"I said *stop!*" the voice bellowed again, and looking over my shoulder I saw a uniformed soldier standing on the platform, his knees bent in firing stance, rifle aimed at us. With a pair of loud cracks he volleyed two more bullets over our heads, just to drive his point home. "Off the train and on your knees!" he said, striding toward us.

I thought of making a run for it, but then I caught a glimpse of the soldier's eyes, and their bulging, pupil-less whites convinced me not to. He was a wight, and I knew he wouldn't think twice about shooting any one of us. Better not to give him an excuse.

Bronwyn and Olive must've been thinking along the same lines, because they got off the train and dropped to their knees alongside the rest of us.

So close, I thought. *We were* so *close*.

The train pulled out of the station without us, our best hope for saving Miss Peregrine steaming away into the distance.

And Miss Peregrine with it, I realized with a queasy jolt. Bronwyn had left her trunk on board the train! Something automatic took hold of me and I leapt up to chase down the train—but then the barrel of a rifle appeared just inches from my face, and I felt all the power drain from my muscles in an instant.

"Not. Another. *Step*," the soldier said.

I sank back to the ground.

We were on our knees, hands up, hearts hammering. The soldier circled us, tense, his rifle aimed and his finger on its trigger. It was the closest, longest look I'd gotten at a wight since Dr. Golan. He had on a standard-issue British army uniform—khaki shirt tucked into wool pants, black boots, helmet—but he wore them awkwardly, the pants crooked and the helmet seated too far back on his head, like a costume he wasn't used to wearing yet. He seemed nervous, too, his head cocking this way and that as he sized us up. He was outnumbered, and though we were just a bunch of unarmed children, we'd been responsible for the death of one wight and two hollowgast in the last three days. He was scared of us, and that, more than anything else, made me scared of him. His fear made him unpredictable.

He pulled a radio from his belt and chattered into it. There was a burst of static, and then a moment later an answer came back. It was all in code; I couldn't understand a word.

He ordered us to our feet. We stood.

"Where are we going?" Olive asked timidly.

"For a walk," he said. "A nice, orderly walk." He had a clipped, vowel-flattened way of speaking that told me he was from somewhere else but faking a British accent, though not particularly well. Wights were supposed to be masters of disguise, but this one was clearly not a star pupil.

"You will not fall out of line," he said, staring down each of us in turn. "You will not run. I have fifteen rounds in my clip—enough to put two holes in each of you. And don't think I don't see your jacket, invisible boy. Make me chase you and I'll slice off your invisible thumbs for souvenirs."

"Yes, sir," said Millard.

"No talking!" the soldier boomed. "Now *march*!"

We marched past the ticket booth, the clerk now gone, then down off the platform, out of the depot, and into the streets. Though the denizens of Coal hadn't given us a second glance when we'd come through town earlier, now their heads swiveled like owls as we trudged by in single file, at gunpoint. The soldier kept us in tight formation, barking at us when anyone strayed too far. I was at the rear, him behind me, and I could hear his ammunition belt clinking as we walked. We were heading back the way we'd come, straight out of town.

I dreamed up a dozen escape plans. We'd scatter. No—he'd shoot at least a few of us. Maybe someone could pretend to faint in the road, then the person behind would trip, and in the confusion—no, he was too disciplined to fall for anything like that. One of us would have to get close enough to take his gun away.

Me. I was closest. Maybe if I walked a little slower, let him catch up, then ran at him . . . but who was I kidding? I was no action hero. I was so scared I could hardly breathe. Anyway, he was ten whole yards behind me, and had his gun aimed right at my back. He'd shoot me the second I turned around, and I'd bleed out in the middle of the road. That was my idea of stupidity, not heroism.

A jeep zoomed up from behind and pulled alongside us, slowing to match our pace. There were two more soldiers in it, and though both wore mirrored sunglasses, I knew what was behind them. The wight in the passenger seat nodded to the one who'd captured us and gave a little salute—*Nice going!*—then turned to us and stared. From that moment he never took his eyes off us or his hands off his rifle.

Now we had escorts, and one rifle-wielding wight had become three. Any hope of escape I'd had was dashed.

We walked and walked, our shoes crunching on the gravel road, the jeep's engine grumbling beside us like a cheap lawnmower. The town receded and a farm sprang up on either side of the tree-lined road, its fields fallow and bare. The soldiers never exchanged a word. There was something robotic about them, as if their brains had been scooped out and replaced with wires. Wights were supposed to be brilliant, but these guys seemed like drones to me. Then I heard a drone in my ear, and looked up to see a bee circle my head and fly away.

Hugh, I thought. *What's he up to?* I looked for him in line, worried he might be planning something that would get us all shot—but I didn't see him.

I did a quick head count. *One-two-three-four-five-six*. In front of me was Emma, then Enoch, Horace, Olive, Millard, and Bronwyn.

Where was Hugh?

I nearly leapt into the air. Hugh wasn't here! That meant he hadn't been rounded up with the rest of us. He was still free! Maybe in the chaos at the depot he'd slipped down into the gap between the train and the platform, or hopped onto the train without the soldier noticing. I wondered if he was following us—wished I could look back at the road behind without giving him away.

I hoped he wasn't, because that might mean he was with Miss Peregrine. Otherwise, how would we ever find her again? And what if she ran out of air, locked in that trunk? And what did they do with suspiciously abandoned baggage in 1940, anyway?

My face flushed hot and my throat tightened. There were too many things to be terrified of, a hundred horror scenarios all vying for attention in my brain.

"Back in line!" the soldier behind me shouted, and I realized that it was me he was talking to—that in my fevered state I'd strayed too far from the center of the road. I hurried back to my place behind Emma, who gave me a pleading look over her shoulder—*Don't make him angry!*—and I promised myself I'd keep it together.

We walked on in edgy silence, tension humming through us like an electric current. I could see it in Emma as she clenched and unclenched her fists; in Enoch as he shook his head and muttered to himself; in Olive's uneven steps. It seemed like just a matter of time before one of us did something desperate and bullets started flying.

Then I heard Bronwyn gasp and I looked up, a horror scenario I hadn't yet imagined taking shape before my eyes. Three massive forms lay ahead of us, one in the road and two more in the field adjacent, just the other side of a shallow ditch. Heaps of black earth, I thought at first, refusing to see.

Then we got closer, and I couldn't pretend they were anything other than what they were: three horses dead in the road.

Olive screamed. Bronwyn instinctively went to comfort her— "Don't look, little magpie!"—and the soldier riding shotgun fired into the air. We dove to the ground and covered our heads.

"Do that again and you'll be lying in the ditch beside them!" he shouted.

As we returned to our feet, Emma angled toward me and breathed the word *Gypsies*, then nodded at the closest horse. I took her meaning: these were their horses. I even recognized the markings on one—white spots on its hind legs—and realized it was the very horse I'd been clinging to just an hour ago.

I felt like I was about to be sick.

It all came together, playing out like a movie in my head. The wights had done this—the same ones who'd raided our camp the night before. The Gypsies had met them along the road after leaving us at the edge of town. There'd been a skirmish, then a chase. The wights had shot the Gypsies' horses right out from under them.

I knew the wights had killed people—killed peculiar children, Miss Avocet had said—but the brutality of shooting these animals seemed to exceed even that evil. An hour ago they'd been some of the most fully alive creatures I'd ever seen—eyes gleaming with intelligence, bodies rippling with muscle, radiating heat—and now, thanks to the intervention of a few pieces of metal, they were nothing but heaps of cold meat. These proud, strong animals, shot down and left in the road like garbage.

I shook with fear, seethed with anger. I was sorry, too, that I'd been so unappreciative of them. What a spoiled, ungrateful ass I was.

Pull it together, I told myself. *Pull yourself together.*

Where were Bekhir and his men now? Where was his son? All I knew was that the wights were going to shoot us. I was sure of it now. These impostors in soldiers' costumes were nothing but animals themselves; more monstrous even than the hollowgast they controlled. The wights, at least, had minds that could reason—but they used that creative faculty to dismantle the world. To make living things into dead things. And for what? So that *they* might live a little longer. So that they might have a little more power over the world around them, and the creatures in it, for whom they cared so little.

Waste. Such a stupid waste.

And now they were going to waste us. Lead us to some killing field where we'd be interrogated and dumped. And if Hugh had been dumb enough to follow us—if the bee flying up and down our line meant he was nearby—then they'd kill him, too.

God help us all.

The fallen horses were well behind us when the soldiers ordered us to turn off the main road and down a narrow farm lane. It was hardly more than a footpath, just a few feet wide, so the soldiers who'd been riding alongside us had to park their jeep and walk, one in front and two behind. On either side of us the fields grew wild, bursting with flowering weeds and humming with late-summer insects.

A beautiful place to die.

After a while, a thatch-roofed shack came into sight at the edge of the fields. *That's where they'll do it*, I thought. *That's where they'll kill us.*

As we got closer, a door opened and a soldier stepped out of the shack. He was dressed differently than the ones around us: instead of a helmet he wore a black-brimmed officer's hat, and instead of a rifle he carried a holstered revolver.

This one was in charge.

He stood in the lane as we approached, rocking on his heels and flashing a pearly grin. "We meet at last!" he called out. "You've given us quite the go-round, but I knew we'd catch you in the end. Only a matter of time!" He had pudgy, boyish features, thin hair that was so blond it was almost white, and he was full of weird, chipper energy, like an overcaffeinated Cub Scout leader. But all I could think when I looked at him was: *Animal. Monster. Murderer.*

"Come in, come in," the officer said, pulling open the shack's door. "Friends of yours are waiting inside."

As his soldiers shoved us past him, I caught a glimpse of the name stitched on his shirt: WHITE. Like the color.

Mister White. A joke, maybe? Nothing about him seemed genuine; that least of all.

We were pushed inside, shouted into a corner. The shack's one room was bare of furniture and crowded with people. Bekhir and his men sat on the floor with their backs to the walls. They'd been treated badly; they were bruised, bleeding, and slouched in attitudes of defeat. A few were missing, including Bekhir's boy. Standing guard were two more soldiers—that made six altogether, including Mr. White and our escorts.

Bekhir caught my eye and nodded gravely. His cheeks were purpled with bruises. *I'm sorry*, he mouthed to me.

Mr. White saw our exchange and skipped over to Bekhir. "Aha! You recognize these children?"

"No," Bekhir said, looking down.

"No?" Mr. White feigned shock. "But you apologized to that one. You must know him, unless you make a habit of apologizing to strangers?"

"They aren't the ones you're looking for," Bekhir said.

"I think they are," said Mr. White. "I think these are the *very* children we've been looking for. And furthermore, I think they spent last night in your camp."

"I told you, I've never seen them before."

Mr. White clucked his tongue like a disapproving schoolmarm. "Gypsy, do you remember what I promised to do if I found out you were lying to me?" He unsheathed a knife from his belt and held it against Bekhir's cheek. "That's right. I promised to cut your lying tongue out and feed it to my dog. And I always keep my promises."

Bekhir met Mr. White's blank stare and stared back, unflinching. The seconds spun out in unbearable silence. My eyes were fixed on the knife. Finally, Mr. White cracked a smile and stood smartly upright again, breaking the spell. "But," he said cheerily, "first things first!" He turned to face the soldiers who had escorted us. "Which of you has their bird?"

The soldiers looked at one another. One shook his head, then another.

"We didn't see it," said the one who'd taken us prisoner at the depot.

Mr. White's smile faltered. He knelt down next to Bekhir. "You told me they had the bird with them," he said.

Bekhir shrugged. "Birds have wings. They come and go."

Mr. White stabbed Bekhir in the thigh. Just like that: quick and emotionless, the blade going in and out. Bekhir howled in surprise and pain and rolled onto his side, gripping his leg as blood began to flow.

Horace fainted and slid to the floor. Olive gasped and covered her eyes.

"That's twice you've lied to me," Mr. White said, wiping the blade clean on a handkerchief.

The rest of us clenched our teeth and held our tongues, but I could see Emma plotting revenge already, clasping her hands together behind her back, getting them nice and warm.

Mr. White dropped the bloody handkerchief on the floor, slid the knife back into its sheath, and stood up to face us. He was almost but not quite smiling, his eyes wide, unibrow raised in a capital M. "Where is your bird?" he asked calmly. The nicer he pretended to be, the more it scared the hell out of me.

"She flew away," Emma said bitterly. "Just like that man told you."

I wished she hadn't said anything; now I was afraid he'd single her out for torment.

Mr. White stepped toward Emma and said, "Her wing was injured. You were seen with her just yesterday. She couldn't be far from here." He cleared his throat. "I'll ask you again."

"She died," I said. "We threw her in a river."

Maybe if I were a bigger pain in his butt than Emma, he'd forget she'd ever spoken.

Mr. White sighed. His right hand glided across his holstered gun, lingered over the handle of his knife, then came to rest on his belt's brass buckle. He lowered his voice, as if what he was about to say were meant for my ears only.

"I see what the trouble is. You believe there's nothing to be gained by being honest with me. That we will kill you regardless of what you do or say. I need you to know this is not the case. However, in the spirit of total honesty, I will say this: you shouldn't have made us chase you. That was a mistake. This could've been so much easier, but now everyone's *angry*, you see, because you've wasted so much of our time."

He flicked a finger toward his soldiers. "These men? They'd like very much to hurt you. I, on the other hand, am able to consider things from your point of view. We *do* seem frightening, I understand that. Our first meeting, on board my submarine, was regrettably uncivil. What's more, your ymbrynes have been poisoning you with misinformation about us for generations. So it's only natural that you'd run. In light of all that, I'm willing to make you what I believe to be a reasonable offer. Show us to the bird right now, and rather than hurting you, we'll send you off to a nice facility where you'll be well looked after. Fed every day, each with your own bed . . . a place no more restrictive than that ridiculous loop you've been hiding in all these years."

Mr. White looked at his men and laughed. "Can you believe they spent the last—what is it, seventy years?—on a tiny island, living the same day over and over? Worse than any prison camp I can think of. It would've been so much easier to cooperate!" He shrugged, looked back at us. "But pride, venal pride, got the better of you. And to think, all this time we could've been working together toward a common good!"

"Working together?" said Emma. "You hunted us! Sent monsters to kill us!"

Damn it, I thought. *Keep quiet.*

Mr. White made a sad puppy-dog face. "Monsters?" he said. "That hurts. That's *me* you're talking about, you know! Me and all my men here, before we evolved. I'll try not to take your slight personally, though. The adolescent phase is rarely attractive, whatever the species." He clapped his hands sharply, which made me jump. "Now then, down to business!"

He raked us with a slow, icy stare, as if scanning our ranks for weakness. Which of us would crack first? Which would actually tell him the truth about where Miss Peregrine was?

Mr. White zeroed in on Horace. He'd recovered from his faint but was still on the floor, crouched and shaking. Mr. White took a decisive step toward him. Horace flinched at the click of his boots.

"Stand up, boy."

Horace didn't move.

"Someone get him up."

A soldier yanked Horace up roughly by his arm. Horace cowered before Mr. White, his eyes on the floor.

"What's your name, boy?"

"Huh-huh-Horace . . ."

"Well, Huh-Horace, you seem like someone with abundant common sense. So I'll let *you* choose."

Horace raised his head slightly. "Choose . . . ?"

Mr. White unsheathed the knife from his belt and pointed it at the Gypsies. "Which of these men to kill first. Unless, of course, you'd like to tell me where your ymbryne is. Then no one has to die."

Horace squeezed his eyes shut, as if he could simply wish himself away from here.

"Or," Mr. White said, "if you'd rather not choose one of them, I'd be happy to choose one of *you*. Would you rather do that?"

"No!"

"Then *tell me*!" Mr. White thundered, his lips snarling back to reveal gleaming teeth.

"Don't tell them anything, *syndrigasti*!" shouted Bekhir—and then one of the soldiers kicked him in the stomach, and he groaned and fell quiet.

Mr. White reached out and grabbed Horace by the chin, trying to force him to look right into his horrible blank eyes. "You'll tell me, won't you? You'll tell me, and I won't hurt you."

"Yes," Horace said, still squeezing his eyes shut—still wishing himself gone, yet still here.

"Yes, *what*?"

Horace drew a shaking breath. "Yes, I'll tell you."

"Don't!" shouted Emma.

Oh God, I thought. *He's going to give her up. He's too weak.*

We should've left him at the menagerie . . .

"Shh," Mr. White hissed in his ear. "Don't listen to them. Now, go ahead, son. Tell me where that bird is."

"She's in the drawer," said Horace.

Mr. White's unibrow knit together. "The drawer. What drawer?"

"Same one she's always been in," said Horace.

He shook Horace by the jaw and shouted, *"What drawer?!"*

Horace started to say something, then closed his mouth. Swallowed hard. Stiffened his back. Then his eyes came open and he looked hard into Mr. White's and said, "Your mother's knickers drawer," and he spat right in Mr. White's face.

Mr. White slammed Horace in the side of the head with the handle of his knife. Olive screamed and several of us flinched in vicarious pain as Horace dropped to the floor like a sack of potatoes, loose change and train tickets spilling out of his pockets.

"What's this?" said Mr. White, bending down to look.

"I caught them trying to catch a train," said the soldier who'd caught us.

"Why are you just telling me this *now*?"

The soldier faltered. "I thought—"

"Never mind," Mr. White said. "Go intercept it. Now."

"Sir?"

Mr. White glanced at the ticket, then at his watch. "The eight-thirty to London makes a long stop at Porthmadog. If you're quick, it'll be waiting for you there. Search it from front to back—starting with first class."

The soldier saluted him and ran outside.

Mr. White turned to the other soldiers. "Search the rest of them," he said. "Let's see if they're carrying anything else of interest. If they resist, shoot them."

While two soldiers with rifles covered us, a third went from peculiar to peculiar, rooting through our pockets. Most of us had nothing but crumbs and lint, but the soldier found an ivory comb on Bronwyn—"Please, it belonged to my mother!" she begged, but he only laughed and said, "She might've taught you how to use it, mannish girl!"

Enoch was carrying a small bag of worm-packed grave dirt, which the soldier opened, sniffed, and dropped in disgust. In my pocket he found my dead cell phone. Emma saw it clatter to the floor and looked at me strangely, wondering why I still had it. Horace lay unmoving on the floor, either knocked out or playing possum. Then it was Emma's turn, but she wasn't having it. When the soldier came toward her, she snarled, "Lay a hand on me and I'll burn it off!"

"Please, hold your fire!" he said, and broke out laughing. "Sorry, couldn't resist."

"I'm not joking," Emma said, and she took her hands out from behind her back. They were glowing red, and even from three feet away I could feel the heat they gave off.

The soldier jumped out of her reach. "Hot touch and a temper to match!" he said. "I like that in a woman. But burn me and Clark there'll spackle the wall with your brainy bits."

The soldier he'd indicated pressed the barrel of his rifle to Emma's head. Emma squeezed her eyes shut, her chest rising and falling fast. Then she lowered her hands and folded them behind her back. She was positively vibrating with anger.

So was I.

"Careful, now," the soldier warned her. "No sudden moves."

My fists clenched as I watched him slide his hands up and down her legs, then run his fingers under the neckline of her dress, all with unnecessary slowness and a leering grin. I'd never felt so powerless in all my life, not even when we were trapped in that animal cage.

"She doesn't have anything!" I shouted. "Leave her alone!"

I was ignored.

"I like this one," the soldier said to Mr. White. "I think we should keep her awhile. For . . . science."

Mr. White grimaced. "You are a disgusting specimen, corporal.

But I agree with you—she is fascinating. I've heard about you, you know," he said to Emma. "I'd give anything to do what you can do. If only we could bottle those hands of yours . . ."

Mr. White smiled weirdly before turning back to the soldier. "Finish up," he snapped, "we don't have all day."

"With pleasure," the soldier replied, and then he stood, dragging his hands up Emma's torso as he rose.

What happened next seemed to unfold in slow motion. I could see that this disgusting letch was about to lean in and give Emma a kiss. I could also see that, behind her back, Emma's hands were now lined with flame. I knew where this was going: the second his lips got near her, she was going to reach around and melt his face—even if it meant taking a bullet. She'd reached a breaking point.

So had I.

I tensed, ready to fight. These, I was convinced, were our last moments. But we'd live them on our own terms—and if we were going to die, by God, we'd take a few wights with us along the way.

The soldier slid his hands around Emma's waist. The barrel of another's rifle dug into her forehead. She seemed to be pushing back against it, daring it to fire. Behind her back I saw her hands begin to spread, white-hot flame tracing along each of her fingers.

Here we go—

Then *CRACK!*—the report of a gun, stunning and sharp.

I shut down, blacked out for a second.

When my sight came back, Emma was still standing. Her head still intact. The rifle that had been pressed against it was pointed down now, and the soldier who'd been about to kiss her had pulled away and spun around to face the window.

The gunshot had come from outside.

Every nerve in my body had gone numb, tingling with adrenaline.

"What was that?" said Mr. White, rushing to the window.

I could see through the glass over his shoulder. The soldier who'd gone to intercept the train was standing outside, waist-deep in wildflowers. His back was to us, his rifle aimed at the field.

Mr. White reached through the bars that covered the window and pushed it open. "What the hell are you shooting at?" he shouted. "Why are you still here?"

The soldier didn't move, didn't speak. The field was alive with the whine of insects, and briefly, that's all we could hear.

"Corporal Brown!" bellowed Mr. White.

The man turned slowly, unsteady on his feet. The rifle slipped from his hands and fell into the tall grass. He took a few doddering steps forward.

Mr. White took the revolver from his holster and pointed it out the window at Brown. "Say something, damn you!"

Brown opened his mouth and tried to speak—but where his voice should've been, an eerie droning noise came echoing up from his guts, mimicking the sound that was everywhere in the fields around him.

It was the sound of bees. Hundreds, thousands of them. Next came the bees themselves: just a few at first, drifting through his parted lips. Then some power beyond his own seemed to take hold of him: his shoulders pulled back and his chest pressed forward and his jaws ratcheted wide open, and from his gaping mouth there poured forth such a dense stream of bees that they were like one solid object; a long, fat hose of insects unspooling endlessly from his throat.

Mr. White stumbled back from the window, horrified and baffled.

Out in the field, Brown collapsed in a cloud of stinging insects. As his body fell, another was revealed behind him.

It was a boy.

Hugh.

He stood defiantly, staring through the window. The insects swung around him in a great, whirling sphere. The fields were packed with them—honeybees and hornets, wasps and yellow jackets, stinging things I couldn't know or name —and every last one of them seemed to be at his command.

Mr. White raised his gun and fired. Emptied his clip.

Hugh went down, disappearing in the grass. I didn't know whether he had fallen to the ground or dived to it. Then three other soldiers ran to the window, and while Bronwyn cried "Please, don't kill him!" they raked the field with bullets, filling our ears with the thunder of their guns.

Then there were bees in the room. A dozen, maybe, furious and flinging themselves at the soldiers.

"Shut the window!" Mr. White screamed, swatting the air around him.

A soldier slammed the window closed. They all went to work smacking the bees that had gotten in. While they were busy with that, more and more collected outside—a giant, seething blanket of them pulsing against the other side of the glass—so many that by the time Mr. White and his men had finished killing the bees *inside* the room, the ones outside had nearly shut out the sun.

The soldiers clustered in the middle of the floor, backs together, rifles bristling out like porcupine quills. It was dark and hot, and the alien whine of a million manic bees reverberated through the room like something out of a nightmare.

"Make them leave us alone!" Mr. White shouted, his voice cracking, desperate.

As if anyone but Hugh could do that—if he was still alive.

"I'll make you another offer," said Bekhir, pulling himself to his feet using the window bars, his hobbled silhouette outlined against the dark glass. "Put down your guns or I open this window."

Mr. White spun to face him. "Even a Gypsy wouldn't be stupid enough to do that."

"You think too highly of us," Bekhir said, sliding his fingers toward the handle.

The soldiers raised their rifles.

"Go ahead," said Bekhir. "Shoot."

"Don't, you'll break the glass!" Mr. White shouted. "Grab him!"

Two soldiers threw down their rifles and lunged at Bekhir, but not before he punched his fist through the glass.

The entire window shattered. Bees flushed into the room. Chaos erupted—screams, gunfire, shoving—though I could hardly hear it over the roar of the insects, which seemed to fill not just my ears but every pore of my body.

People were climbing over one another to get out. To my right I saw Bronwyn push Olive to the floor and cover her with her body. Emma shouted "Get down!" and we ducked for cover as bees tumbled over our skin, our hair. I waited to die, for the bees to cover every exposed inch of me in stings that would shut down my nervous system.

Someone kicked open the door. Light blasted in. A dozen boots thundered across the floorboards.

It got quiet. I slowly uncovered my head.

The bees were gone. So were the soldiers.

Then, from outside, a chorus of panicked screams. I jumped up and rushed to the shattered window, where a knot of Gypsies and peculiars were already gathered, peering out.

At first I didn't see the soldiers at all—just a giant, swirling mass of insects, so dense it was opaque, about fifty feet down the footpath.

The screams were coming from inside it.

Then, one by one, the screamers fell silent. When it was all over, the cloud of bees began to spread and scatter, unveiling the bodies of Mr. White and his men. They lay clustered in the low grass, dead or nearly so.

Twenty seconds later, their killers were gone, their monstrous hum fading as they settled back into the fields. In their wake fell a strange and bucolic calm, as if it were just another summer day, and nothing out of the ordinary had happened.

Emma counted the soldiers' bodies on her fingers. "Six. That's all of them," she said. "It's over."

I put my arms around her, shaking with gratitude and disbelief.

"Which of you are hurt?" said Bronwyn, looking around frantically. Those last moments had been crazy—countless bees, gunfire in the dark. We checked ourselves for holes. Horace was dazed but conscious, a trickle of blood running from his temple. Bekhir's stab wound was deep but would heal. The rest of us were shaken but unhurt—and miraculously, not a single one of us was bee-stung.

"When you broke the window," I said to Bekhir, "how did you know the bees wouldn't attack us?"

"I didn't," he said. "Luckily, your friend's power is strong."

Our friend . . .

Emma pulled away from me suddenly. "Oh my God!" she gasped. "Hugh!"

In all the chaos, we'd forgotten about him. He was probably bleeding to death right now, somewhere in the tall grass. But just as we were about to tear outside and look for him, he appeared in the doorway—bedraggled and grass-stained, but smiling.

"Hugh!" Olive cried, rushing to him. "You're alive!"

"I am!" he said heartily. "Are all of you?"

"Thanks to you we are!" Bronwyn said. "Three cheers for Hugh!"

"You're our man in a pinch, Hugh!" cried Horace.

"Nowhere am I deadlier than in a field of wildflowers," Hugh said, enjoying the attention.

"Sorry about all the times I made fun of your peculiarity," said Enoch. "I suppose it's not so useless."

"Additionally," said Millard, "I'd like to compliment Hugh on his impeccable timing. Really, if you'd arrived just a few seconds later . . ."

Hugh explained how he'd evaded capture at the depot by slipping down between the train and the platform—just like I'd thought.

He'd sent one of his bees trailing after us, which allowed him to follow from a careful distance. "Then it was just a matter of finding the perfect time to strike," he said proudly, as if victory had been assured from the moment he decided to save us.

"And if you hadn't accidentally stumbled across a field packed with bees?" Enoch said.

Hugh dug something from his pocket and held it up: a peculiar chicken egg. "Plan B," he said.

Bekhir hobbled to Hugh and shook his hand. "Young man," he said, "we owe you our lives."

"What about your peculiar boy?" Millard asked Bekhir.

"He managed to escape with two of my men, thank God. We lost three fine animals today, but no people." Bekhir bowed to Hugh, and I thought for a moment he might even take Hugh's hand and kiss it. "You must allow us to repay you!"

Hugh blushed. "There's no need, I assure you—"

"And no time, either," said Emma, pushing Hugh out the door. "We have a train to catch!"

Those of us who hadn't yet realized Miss Peregrine was gone went pale.

"We'll take their jeep," said Millard. "If we're lucky—and if that wight was correct—we might just be able to catch the train during its stopover in Porthmadog."

"I know a shortcut," Bekhir said, and he drew a simple map in the dirt with his shoe.

We thanked the Gyspies. I told Bekhir we were sorry we'd caused them so much trouble, and he unleashed a big, booming laugh and waved us on down the path. "We'll meet again, *syndrigasti*," he said. "I'm certain of it!"

*   *   *

We squeezed into the wights' jeep, eight kids packed like sardines into a vehicle built for three. Because I was the only one who'd driven a car before, I took the wheel. I spent way too long figuring out how to start the damn thing—not with a key, it turned out, but by pushing a button on the floor—and then there was the matter of shifting gears; I'd only driven a manual transmission a few times, and always with my dad coaching me from the passenger seat. Despite all that, after a minute or two we were—bumpily, jerkily, somewhat hesitatingly—on our way.

I stomped the accelerator and drove as fast as the overloaded jeep would take us, while Millard shouted directions and everyone else held on for dear life. We reached the town of Porthmadog twenty minutes later, the train's whistle blowing as we sped down the main street toward the station. We came to a skidding stop by the depot and tumbled out. I didn't even bother to kill the engine. Racing through the station like cheetahs after a gazelle, we leapt on board the last car of the train just as it was pulling out of the station.

We stood doubled over and panting in the aisle while astonished passengers pretended not to stare. Sweating, dirty, and disheveled—we must've been a sight.

"We made it," Emma gasped. "I can't believe we made it."

"I can't believe I drove stick," I said.

The conductor appeared. "You're back," he said with a beleaguered sigh. "I trust you still have your tickets?"

Horace fished them from his pocket in a wad.

"This way to your cabin," said the conductor.

"Our trunk!" Bronwyn said, clutching at the conductor's elbow. "Is it still there?"

The conductor pried his arm away. "I tried taking it to lost and found. Couldn't move the blessed thing an inch."

We ran from car to car until we reached the first-class cabin, where we found Bronwyn's trunk sitting just where she'd left it. She rushed to it and threw open the latches, then the lid.

Miss Peregrine wasn't inside.

I had a mini heart attack.

"My bird!" Bronwyn cried. "Where's my bird?!"

"Calm down, it's right here," said the conductor, and he pointed above our heads. Miss Peregrine was perched on a luggage rack, fast asleep.

Bronwyn stumbled back against the wall, so relieved she nearly fainted. "How did she get up *there*?"

The conductor raised an eyebrow. "It's a *very* lifelike toy." He turned and went to the door, then stopped and said, "By the way, where can I get one? My daughter would just love it."

"I'm afraid she's one of a kind," Bronwyn said, and she took Miss Peregrine down and hugged her to her chest.

*   *   *

After all we'd been through over the past few days—not to mention the past few hours—the luxury of the first-class cabin came as a shock. Our car had plush leather couches, a dining table, and wide picture windows. It looked like a rich man's living room, and we had it all to ourselves.

We took turns washing up in the wood-paneled bathroom, then availed ourselves of the dining menu. "Order anything you like," Enoch said, picking up a telephone that was attached to the arm of a reclining chair. "Hello, do you have goose liver pâté? I should like all of it. Yes, all that you have. And toast triangles."

No one said anything about what had happened. It was too much, too awful, and for now we just wanted to recover and forget. There was so much else to be done, so many more dangers left to reckon with.

We settled in for the journey. Outside, Porthmadog's squat houses shrank away and Miss Wren's mountain came into view, rising grayly above the hills. While the others drifted into conversations, my nose stayed glued to the window, and the endless unfolding *thereness* of 1940 beyond it—1940 being a place that had until recently been merely pocket-sized in my experience, no wider than a tiny island, and a place I could leave any time I wished by passing through the dark belly of Cairnholm's cairn. Since leaving the island, though, it had become a world, a whole world of marshy forests and smoke-wreathed towns and valleys crisscrossed with shining rivers; and of people and things that looked old but weren't yet, like props and extras in some elaborately staged but plotless period movie—all of it flashing by and by and by out my window like a dream without end.

I fell asleep and woke, fell asleep and woke, the train's rhythm hypnotizing me into a hazy state in which it was easy to forget that I was more than just a passive viewer, my window more than just a movie screen; that *out there* was every bit as real as in here. Then, slowly, I remembered how I'd come to be part of this: my grandfather; the island; the children. The pretty, flint-eyed girl next to me, her hand resting atop mine.

"Am I really here?" I asked her.

"Go back to sleep," she said.

"Do you think we'll be all right?"

She kissed me on the tip of my nose.

"Go back to sleep."

CHAPTER SEVEN

*M*ore terrible dreams, all mixed up, fading in and out of one another. Snippets of horrors from recent days: the steel eye of a gun barrel staring me down from close range; a road strewn with fallen horses; a hollowgast's tongues straining toward me across a chasm; that awful, grinning wight and his empty eyes.

Then this: I'm back home again, but I'm a ghost. I drift down my street, through my front door, into my house. I find my father asleep at the kitchen table, a cordless phone clutched to his chest.

I'm not dead, I say, but my words don't make sound.

I find my mother sitting on the edge of her bed, still in nightclothes, staring out the window at a pale afternoon. She's gaunt, wrung out from crying. I reach out to touch her shoulder, but my hand passes right through it.

Then I'm at my own funeral, looking up from my grave at a rectangle of gray sky.

My three uncles peer down, their fat necks bulging from starched white collars.

Uncle Les: *What a pity. Right?*

Uncle Jack: *You really gotta feel for Frank and Maryann right now.*

Uncle Les: *Yeah. What're people gonna think?*

Uncle Bobby: *They'll think the kid had a screw loose. Which he did.*

Uncle Jack: *I knew it, though. That he'd pull something like this one day. He had that look, you know? Just a little . . .*

Uncle Bobby: *Screwy.*

Uncle Les: *That comes from his dad's side of the family, not ours.*

Uncle Jack: *Still. Terrible.*

Uncle Bobby: *Yeah.*

Uncle Jack: . . .

Uncle Les: . . .

Uncle Bobby: *Buffet?*

My uncles shuffle away. Ricky comes along, his green hair extra spiked for the occasion.

Bro. Now that you're dead, can I have your bike?

I try to shout: *I'm not dead!*

I am just far away

I'm sorry

But the words echo back at me, trapped inside my head.

The minister peers down. It's Golan, holding a Bible, dressed in robes. He grins.

We're waiting for you, Jacob.

A shovelful of dirt rains down on me.

We're waiting.

*   *   *

I bolted upright, suddenly awake, my mouth dry as paper. Emma was next to me, hands on my shoulders. "Jacob! Thank God—you gave us a scare!"

"I did?"

"You were having a nightmare," said Millard. He was seated across from us, looking like an empty suit of clothes starched into position. "Talking in your sleep, too."

"I was?"

Emma dabbed sweat from my forehead with one of the first-class napkins. (Real cloth!) "You were," she said. "But it sounded like gobbledygook. I couldn't understand a word."

I looked around self-consciously, but no else seemed to have noticed. The other children were spread throughout the car, catnapping, daydreaming out the window, or playing cards.

I sincerely hoped I was not starting to lose it.

"Do you often have nightmares?" asked Millard. "You should describe them to Horace. He's good at sussing hidden meanings from dreams."

Emma rubbed my arm. "You sure you're all right?"

"I'm fine," I said, and because I don't like being fussed over, I changed the subject. Seeing that Millard had the *Tales of the Peculiar* open in his lap, I said, "Doing some light reading?"

"Studying," he replied. "And to think I once dismissed these as just stories for children. They are, in fact, extraordinarily complex—cunning, even—in the way they conceal secret information about peculiardom. It would take me years, probably, to decode them all."

"But what good is that to us now?" Emma said. "What good are loops if they can be breached by hollowgast? Even the secret ones in that book will be found out eventually."

"Maybe it was just the one loop that was breached," I said hopefully. "Maybe the hollow in Miss Wren's loop was a freak, somehow."

"A peculiar hollow!" said Millard. "That's amusing—but no. He was no accident. I'm certain these 'enhanced' hollows were an integral part of the assault on our loops."

"But how?" said Emma. "What's changed about hollows that they can get into loops now?"

"That's something I've been thinking about a great deal," said Millard. "We don't know a lot about hollows, having never had the chance to examine one in a controlled setting. But it's thought that, like normals, they lack something which you and I and everyone in this train car possesses—some essential peculiarness—which is what allows us to interact with loops; to bind with and be absorbed into them."

"Like a key," I said.

"Something like that," said Millard. "Some believe that, like blood or spinal fluid, our peculiarness has physical substance. Others think it's inside us but insubstantial. A second soul."

"Huh," I said. I liked this idea: that peculiarness wasn't a deficiency, but an abundance; that it wasn't we who lacked something normals had, but they who lacked peculiarness. That we were more, not less.

"I hate all that crackpot stuff," said Emma. "The idea that you could capture the second soul in a jar? Gives me the quivers."

"And yet, over the years, some attempts have been made to do just this," said Millard. "What did that wight soldier say to you, Emma? 'I wish I could bottle what you have,' or something to that effect?"

Emma shuddered. "Don't remind me."

"The theory goes that if somehow our peculiar essence could be distilled and captured—in a bottle, as he said, or more likely a petri dish—then perhaps that essence could also be transferred from one being to another. If this were possible, imagine the black market in peculiar souls that might spring up among the wealthy and unscrupulous. Peculiarities like your spark or Bronwyn's great strength sold to the highest bidder!"

"That's disgusting," I said.

"Most peculiars agree with you," said Millard, "which is why such research was outlawed many years ago."

"As if the wights cared about our laws," said Emma.

"But the whole idea seems crazy," I said. "It couldn't really work, could it?"

"I didn't think so," said Millard. "At least, not until yesterday. Now I'm not so sure."

"Because of the hollow in the menagerie loop?"

"Right. Before yesterday I wasn't even certain I believed in a 'second soul.' To my mind, there was only one compelling argument for its existence: that when a hollowgast consumes enough of us, it transforms into a different sort of creature—one that can travel through time loops."

"It becomes a wight," I said.

"Yes," he said. "But only if it consumes *peculiars*. It can eat as many normals as it likes and it will never turn into a wight. Therefore, we must have something normals lack."

"But that hollow at the menagerie didn't become a wight," said Emma. "It became a hollow that could enter loops."

"Which makes me wonder if the wights have been tinkering with nature," said Millard, "vis-à-vis the transference of peculiar souls."

"I don't even want to think about it," said Emma. "Can we please, *please* talk about something else?"

"But where would they even *get* the souls?" I asked. "And how?"

"That's it, I'm sitting somewhere else," Emma said, and she got up to find another seat.

Millard and I rode in silence for a while. I couldn't stop imagining being strapped to a table while a cabal of evil doctors removed my soul. How would they do it? With a needle? A knife?

To derail this morbid train of thought, I tried changing the subject again. "How did we all get to be peculiar in the first place?" I asked.

"No one's certain," Millard answered. "There are legends, though."

"Like what?"

"Some people believe we're descended from a handful of peculiars who lived a long, long time ago," he said. "They were very powerful—and enormous, like the stone giant we found."

I said, "Why are we so small, then, if we used to be giants?"

"The story goes that over the years, as we multiplied, our power diluted. As we became less powerful, we got smaller, too."

"That's all pretty hard to swallow," I said. "I feel about as powerful as an ant."

"Ants are quite powerful, actually, relative to their size."

"You know what I mean," I said. "The thing I really don't get is, why *me*? I never asked to be this way. Who decided?"

It was a rhetorical question; I wasn't really expecting an answer, but Millard gave me one anyway. "To quote a famous peculiar: 'At the heart of nature's mystery lies another mystery.'"

"Who said that?"

"We know him as Perplexus Anomalous. An invented name, probably, for a great thinker and philosopher. Perplexus was a cartographer, too. He drew the very first edition of the Map of Days, a thousand-something years ago."

I chuckled. "You talk like a teacher sometimes. Has anyone ever told you that?"

"All the time," Millard said. "I would've liked to try my hand at teaching. If I hadn't been born like this."

"You would've been great at it."

"Thank you," he said. Then he went quiet, and in the silence I could feel him dreaming it: scenes from a life that might've been. After a while he said, "I don't want you to think that I don't like being invisible. I do. I love being peculiar, Jacob—it's the very core of who I am. But there are days I wish I could turn it off."

"I know what you mean," I said. But of course I didn't. My peculiarity had its challenges, but at least I could participate in society.

The door to our compartment slid open. Millard quickly flipped up the hood of his jacket to hide his face—or rather, his apparent lack of one.

A young woman stood in the door. She wore a uniform and held a box of goods for sale. "Cigarettes?" she asked. "Chocolate?"

"No, thanks," I said.

She looked at me. "You're an American."

"Afraid so."

She gave me a pitying smile. "Hope you're having a nice trip. You picked an awkward time to visit Britain."

I laughed. "So I've been told."

She went out. Millard shifted his body to watch her go. "Pretty," he said distantly.

It occurred to me that it had probably been a lot of years since he'd seen a girl outside of those few who lived on Cairnholm. But what chance would someone like him have with a normal girl, anyway?

"Don't look at me like that," he said.

It hadn't occurred to me that I'd been looking at him any particular way. "Like what?"

"Like you feel bad for me."

"I don't," I said.

But I did.

Then Millard stood up from his seat, took off his coat, and disappeared. I didn't see him again for a while.

*　　*　　*

The hours rolled on, and the children passed them by telling stories. They told stories about famous peculiars and about Miss Peregrine in the strange, exciting, early days of her loop, and eventually they came around to telling their own stories. Some I had heard before—like how Enoch had raised the dead in his father's funeral parlor, or the way Bronwyn, at the tender age of ten, had snapped her abusive stepfather's neck without quite meaning to—but others were new to me. For as old as they were, the kids didn't often lapse into bouts of nostalgia.

Horace's dreams had started when he was just six, but he didn't realize they were predictive of anything until two years later, when one night he dreamed about the sinking of the *Lusitania* and the next day heard about it on the radio. Hugh, from a young age, had loved honey more than any other food, and at five he'd started eating honeycomb along with it—so ravenously that the first time he accidentally swallowed a bee, he didn't notice until he felt it buzzing around in his stomach. "The bee didn't seem to mind a bit," Hugh said, "so I shrugged and went on eating. Pretty soon I had a whole hive down there." When the bees needed to pollinate, he'd gone to find a field of blooming flowers, and that's where he met Fiona, who was sleeping among them.

Hugh told her story, too. Fiona was a refugee from Ireland, he said, where she'd been growing food for the people in her village during the famine of the 1840s—until she was accused of being a witch and chased out. This is something Hugh had gleaned only after years of subtle, nonverbal communication with Fiona, who didn't speak not because she couldn't, Hugh said, but "because the things she'd witnessed in the famine were so horrific they stole her voice away."

Then it was Emma's turn, but she had no interest in telling her story.

"Why not?" whined Olive. "Come on, tell about when you found out you were peculiar!"

"It's ancient history," Emma muttered, "relevant to nothing. And hadn't we better be thinking about the future instead of the past?"

"Someone's being a grumplepuss," said Olive.

Emma got up and left, heading to the back of the car where no one would bother her. I let a minute or two pass so that she wouldn't feel hounded, then went and sat next to her. She saw me coming and hid behind a newspaper, pretending to read.

"Because I don't care to discuss it," she said from behind the paper. "That's why!"

"I didn't say anything."

"Yes, but you were going to ask, so I saved you the trouble."

"Just to make it fair," I said, "I'll tell you something about me first."

She peeked over the top of the paper, slightly intrigued. "But don't I know everything about you already?"

"Ha," I said. "Not hardly."

"All right, then tell me three things about you I don't know. Dark secrets only, please. Quickly, now!"

I racked my brain for interesting factoids about myself, but I could only think of embarrassing ones. "Okay, one. When I was little, I was really sensitive to seeing violence on TV. I didn't understand that it wasn't real. Even if it was just a cartoon mouse punching a cartoon cat, I would freak out and start crying."

Her newspaper came down some. "Bless your tender soul!" she said. "And now look at you—impaling monstrous creatures right through their leaky eyeballs."

"Two," I said. "I was born on Halloween, and until I was eight years old my parents had me convinced that the candy people gave out when I knocked on their doors was birthday presents."

"Hmm," she said, lowering the paper a little more. "That one was only middlingly dark. You may continue nevertheless."

"Three. When we first met, I was convinced you were about to cut my throat. But scared as I was, there was this tiny voice in my head saying: *If this is the last face you ever see, at least it's a beautiful one.*"

The paper fell to her lap. "Jacob, that's . . ." She looked at the floor, then out the window, then back at me. "What a sweet thing to say."

"It's true," I said, and slid my hand across the seat to hers. "Okay, your turn."

"I'm not trying to hide anything, you know. It's just that those musty stories make me feel ten years old again, and unwanted. That never goes away, no matter how many magical summer days have come between."

That hurt was still with her, raw even all these years later.

"I want to know you," I said. "Who you are, where you come

from. That's all."

She shifted uncomfortably. "I never told you about my parents?"

"All I know I heard from Golan, that night in the icehouse. He said they gave you away to a traveling circus?"

"No, not quite." She slid down in her seat, her voice falling to a whisper. "I suppose it's better for you to know the truth than rumors and speculation. So, here goes.

"I started manifesting when I was just ten. Kept setting my bed on fire in my sleep, until my parents took away all my sheets and made me lie on a bare metal cot in a bare room with nothing flammable at all in it. They thought I was a pyromaniac and a liar, and the fact that I myself never seemed to get burned was as good as proof. But I *couldn't* be burned, something even I didn't know at first. I was ten: I didn't know fig about anything! It's a very scary thing, manifesting without understanding what's happening to you, though it's a fright nearly all peculiar children experience because so few of us are born to peculiar parents."

"I can imagine," I said.

"One day, as far as anyone knew, I was as common as rice pudding, and the next I felt a curious itch in the palms of my hands. They grew red and swollen, then hot—so hot that I ran to the grocer's and buried them in a case of frozen cod! When the fish began to thaw and stink, the grocer chased me home again, where he demanded that my mother pay for all I'd ruined. My hands were burning up by this time; the ice had only made it worse! Finally, they caught fire, and I was sure I'd gone stark raving mad."

"What did your parents think?" I asked.

"My mother, who was a deeply superstitious person, ran out of the house and never came back. She thought I was a demon, arrived straight from Hell via her womb. The old man took a different approach. He beat me and locked me in my room, and when I tried to burn through the door he tied me down with asbestos sheets. Kept me like that for days, feeding me once in a while by hand, since he didn't trust me enough to untie me. Which was a good thing for him, 'cause the minute he did I would've burned him black."

"I wish you had," I said.

"That's sweet of you. But it wouldn't have done any good. My parents were horrible people—but if they hadn't been, and if I'd stayed with them much longer, there's no question the hollows would've found me. I owe my life to two people: my younger sister, Julia, who freed me late one night so that I could finally run away; and Miss Peregrine, who discovered me a month later, working as a fire-eater at a traveling circus." Emma smiled wistfully. "The day I met her, that's what I call my birthday. The day I met my true mum."

My heart melted a little. "Thank you for telling me," I said. Hearing Emma's story made me feel closer to her, and less alone in my own confusion. Every peculiar had struggled through a period of painful uncertainty. Every peculiar had been tried. The glaring difference between us was that my parents still loved me—and despite the problems I'd had with them, I loved them, too, in my own quiet way. The thought that I was hurting them now was a constant ache.

What did I owe them? How could it be reckoned against the debt I owed Miss Peregrine, or my obligation to my grandfather—or the sweet, heavy thing I felt for Emma, which seemed to grow stronger every time I looked at her?

The scales tipped always toward the latter. But eventually, if I lived through this, I would have to face up to the decision I had made and the pain I had caused.

If.

If always propelled my thoughts back to the present, because *if* depended so much on keeping my wits about me. I couldn't properly sense things if I was distracted. *If* demanded my full presence and participation in *now*.

If, as much as it scared me, also kept me sane.

London approached, villages giving way to towns giving way

to unbroken tracts of suburbia. I wondered what was waiting for us there; what new horrors lay ahead.

I glanced at a headline in the newspaper still open in Emma's lap: AIR RAIDS RATTLE CAPITAL. SCORES DEAD.

I closed my eyes and tried to think of nothing at all.

PART

TWO

I f anyone had been watching as the eight-thirty train hissed into the station and ground to a steaming halt, they wouldn't have noticed anything out of the ordinary about it: not about the conductors and porters who wrestled open its latches and threw back its doors; not about the mass of men and women, some in military dress, who streamed out and disappeared into the swarming crowd; not even about the eight weary children who filed heavily from one of its first-class cars and stood blinking in the hazy light of the platform, their backs pressed together in a protective circle, dazed by the cathedral of noise and smoke in which they found themselves.

On an ordinary day, any group of children as lost and forlorn-looking as these would've been approached by some kindly adult and asked what the matter was, or whether they needed help, or where their parents were. But today the platform teemed with hundreds of children, all of whom looked lost and forlorn. So no one paid much attention to the little girl with tumbling brown hair and button shoes, or the fact that her shoes did not quite touch the floor. No one noticed the moon-faced boy in the flat cap, or the honeybee that drifted from his mouth, tested the sooty air, then dove back from whence it came.

No one's gaze lingered on the boy with dark-ringed eyes, or saw the clay man who peeked from his shirt pocket only to be pushed down again by the boy's finger. Likewise the boy who was dressed to the nines in a muddy but finely tailored suit and stove-in top hat, his face drawn and haggard from lack of sleep, for he hadn't allowed *himself any in days, so afraid was he of his dreams.*

No one more than glanced at the big girl in the coat and simple dress, who was built like a stack of bricks and had lashed to her back a steamer trunk nearly as large as herself. None who saw her could have guessed how stupendously heavy the trunk was, or what it held, or why a screen of tiny holes had been punched into one side. Overlooked completely was the young man next to her, so wrapped in scarves and a hooded coat that not an inch of his bare skin could be seen, though it was early September and the weather still warm.

Then there was the American boy, so ordinary-looking he hardly merited notice; so apparently normal that people's eyes skipped over him—even as he studied them, on tiptoe, neck swiveling, his gaze sweeping across the platform like a sentry's. The girl by his side stood with her hands clasped together, concealing a tendril of flame that curled stubbornly around the nail of her pinky, which happened sometimes when she was upset. She tried shaking her finger as one might to extinguish a match, then blowing on it. When that didn't work, she slipped it into her mouth and let a puff of smoke coil from her nose. No one saw that, either.

In fact, no one looked closely enough at the children from the first-class car of the eight-thirty train to notice anything peculiar about them at all. Which was just as well.

CHAPTER EIGHT

*E*mma nudged me.

"So?"

"I need another minute," I said.

Bronwyn had set down her trunk and I was standing on it now, head above the crowd, casting my eyes over a shifting sea of faces. The long platform teemed with children. They squirmed like amoebas under a microscope, row upon row receding into a haze of smoke. Hissing black trains loomed up on either side, anxious to swallow them.

I could feel my friends' eyes on my back, watching me as I scanned the crowd. I was supposed to know whether, somewhere in that great, seething mass, there were monsters who meant to kill us—and I was supposed to know it simply by looking; by assessing some vague feeling in my gut. Usually it was painful and obvious when a hollow was nearby, but in a giant space like this—among hundreds of people—my warning might only be a whisper, the faintest twinge, easy to miss.

"Do the wights know we're coming?" Bronwyn asked, talking low for fear she'd be overheard by a normal—or worse yet, a wight. They had ears everywhere in the city, or so we'd been led to believe.

"We killed every one of them that might've known where we were going," Hugh said proudly. "Or rather, *I* did."

"Which means they'll be looking for us even harder," Millard said. "And they'll want more than the bird now—they'll want revenge."

"Which is why we can't stand here much longer," Emma said,

tapping me on the leg. "Are you almost finished?"

My focus slipped. I lost my place in the crowd. Began again. "One more minute," I said.

Personally, it wasn't wights that concerned me most, but hollows. I'd killed two of them now, and each encounter had nearly been the end of me. My luck, if that's what had been keeping me alive thus far, had to be running out. That's why I was determined never to be surprised by another hollow. I would do everything in my power to sense them from a distance and avoid contact altogether. There was less glory in running away from a fight, sure, but I didn't care about glory. I just wanted to survive.

The real danger, then, wasn't the figures on the platform, but the shadows that lay between and beyond them; the darkness at the margins. That's where I focused my attention. It gave me an out-of-body sort of feeling, to cast my sense out into a crowd this way, prodding distant corners for traces of danger. It wasn't something I could've done a few days ago. My ability to direct it like a spotlight—this was new.

What else, I wondered, was left to discover about myself?

"We're okay," I said, stepping down from the trunk. "No hollows."

"*I* could've told you that," grumbled Enoch. "If there had been, they'd have eaten us by now!"

Emma took me aside. "If we're to have a fighting chance here, you've got to be faster."

It was like asking someone who'd just learned to swim to compete in the Olympics. "I'm doing my best," I said.

Emma nodded. "I know you are." She turned to the others and snapped her fingers for attention. "Let's head for that phone box," she said, pointing to a tall, red phone booth across the platform, just visible through the surging crowd.

"Who are we calling?" Hugh asked.

"The peculiar dog said that all of London's loops had been

raided and their ymbrynes kidnapped," Emma said, "but we can't simply take his word for it, can we?"

"You can *call* a time loop?" I said, flabbergasted. "On the *phone*?"

Millard explained that the Council of Ymbrynes maintained a phone exchange, though it could be used only within the boundaries of the city. "Quite ingenious how it works, given all the time differences," he said. "Just because we live in time loops doesn't mean we're stuck in the Stone Age!"

Emma took my hand and told the others to join hands, too. "It's crucial we stay together," she said. "London is vast, and there's no lost and found here for peculiar children."

We waded into the crowd, hands linked, our snaking line slightly parabolic in the middle where Olive buoyed up like an astronaut walking on the moon.

"You losing weight?" Bronwyn asked her. "You need heavier shoes, little magpie."

"I get feathery when I ain't had proper meals," Olive said.

"Proper meals? We just ate like kings!"

"Not me," said Olive. "They didn't have any meat pies."

"You're awfully picky for a refugee," said Enoch. "Anyway, since Horace wasted all our money, the only way we're getting more food is if we steal it, or find a not-kidnapped ymbryne who'll cook us some."

"We still have money," Horace said defensively, jingling the coins in his pocket. "Though not enough for meat pies. We could perhaps afford a jacket potato."

"If I have another jacket potato, I'll turn *into* a jacket potato," Olive whined.

"That's impossible, dear," said Bronwyn.

"Why? Miss Peregrine can turn into a bird!"

A boy we were passing turned to stare. Bronwyn shushed Olive angrily. Telling our secrets in front of normals was strictly forbidden, even if they were so fantastic-sounding no one would believe them.

We shouldered through one last knot of children to arrive at the phone booth. It was only large enough to hold three, so Emma, Millard, and Horace squeezed inside while the rest of us crowded around the door. Emma worked the phone, Horace fished our last few coins from his pocket, and Millard paged through a chunky phone book that dangled from a cord.

"Are you kidding?" I said, leaning into the booth. "There are ymbrynes in the phone book?"

"The addresses listed are fakes," said Millard, "and the calls won't connect unless you whistle the right passcode." He tore out a listing and handed it to Emma. "Give this one a go. Millicent Thrush."

Horace fed a coin into the slot and Emma dialed the number. Then Millard took the phone, whistled a bird call into the receiver, and handed it back to Emma. She listened for a moment, then frowned. "It just rings," she said. "No one's picking up."

"No bother!" Millard said. "That was just one of many. Let me find another . . ."

Outside the booth, the crowd that had been flowing around us slowed to a stop, bottlenecking somewhere out of sight. The train platform was reaching capacity. There were normal children on every side of us, chattering to one another, shouting, shoving—and one, who stood right next to Olive, was crying bitterly. She had pigtails and puffy red eyes, and she carried a blanket in one hand and a raggedy cardboard suitcase in the other. Pinned to her blouse was a tag with words and numbers stenciled in large print:

115-201
London → *Sheffield*

Olive watched the girl cry until her own eyes began to shimmer with tears. Finally, she couldn't take it anymore and asked what the matter was. The girl looked away, pretending not to have heard.

Olive didn't take the hint. "What's the matter?" she asked again. "Are you crying because you've been sold?" She pointed to the tag on the girl's blouse. "Was that your price?"

The girl tried to scoot away but was blocked by a wall of people.

"I would buy you and set you free," Olive went on, "but I fear we've spent all our money on train tickets and haven't enough even for meat pies, much less a slave. I'm awfully sorry."

The girl spun to face Olive. "I'm not for sale!" she said, stamping her foot.

"Are you certain?"

"Yes!" the girl shouted, and in a fit of frustration she ripped the tag off her blouse and threw it away. "I just don't want to go and live in the stupid country, that's all."

"I didn't want to leave my home, either, but we had to," Olive said. "It got smashed by a bomb."

The girl's face softened. "Mine did, too." She put down her suitcase and held out her hand. "Sorry I got cross. My name is Jessica."

"I'm Olive."

The two little girls shook hands like gentlemen.

"I like your blouse," Olive said.

"Thanks," said Jessica. "And I like your—the—the whatsit on your head."

"My tiara!" Olive reached up to touch it. "It isn't real silver, though."

"That's okay. It's pretty."

Olive smiled as wide as I'd ever seen her smile, and then a loud whistle blew and a booming voice crackled over a loudspeaker. "All children onto the trains!" it said. "Nice and orderly now!"

The crowd began to flow around us again. Here and there, adults herded the children along, and I heard one say, "Don't worry, you'll see your mummies and daddies again soon!"

That's when I realized why there were so many children here. They were being evacuated. Of all the many hundreds of kids in the train station this morning, my friends and I were the only ones arriving. The rest were leaving, being shuttled out of the city for their own safety—and from the look of the winter coats and overstuffed cases some of them carried, maybe for a long time.

"I have to go," Jessica said, and Olive had hardly begun to say goodbye when her new friend was borne away by the crowd toward a waiting train. Just that quickly, Olive made and lost the only normal friend she'd ever had.

Jessica looked back as she was boarding. Her grim expression seemed to say: *What will become of me?*

We watched her go and wondered the same about ourselves.

Inside the phone box, Emma scowled at the receiver. "No one's answering," she said. "All the numbers just ring and ring."

"Last one," said Millard, handing her another ripped-out page. "Cross your fingers."

I was focused on Emma as she dialed, but then a commotion broke out behind me and I turned to see a crimson-faced man waving an umbrella at us. "What are you dallying about for?" he said. "Vacate that phone box and board your train at once!"

"We just got off one," said Hugh. "We ain't about to get on another!"

"And what have you done with your tag numbers?" the man shouted, flecks of spittle flying from his lips. "Produce them at once or by God I'll have you shipped somewhere a great deal less pleasant than Wales!"

"Piss off this instant," said Enoch, "or we'll have *you* shipped straight to Hell!"

The man's face went so purple I thought he'd burst a blood vessel in his neck. Clearly, he wasn't used to being spoken to this way by children.

"I said *get out of that phone box!*" he roared, and raising the umbrella over his head like an executioner's ax, he brought it down on the cable that stretched between the top of the booth and the wall, snapping it in half with a loud *thwack!*

The phone went dead. Emma looked up from the receiver, boiling with quiet rage. "If he wants to use the phone so badly," she said, "then let's give it to him."

As she, Millard, and Horace squeezed out of the booth, Bronwyn grabbed the man's hands and pinned them behind his back. "Stop!" he screamed. "Unhand me!"

"Oh, I'll unhand you," said Bronwyn, and then she picked

him up, stuffed him headfirst into the booth, and barred the door shut with his umbrella. The man screamed and banged on the glass, jumping up and down like a fat fly trapped in a bottle. Although it would've been fun to stick around and laugh at him, the man had drawn too much attention, and now adults were converging on us from all across the station. It was time to go.

We linked hands and raced off toward the turnstiles, leaving behind us a wake of tripped and flailing normals. A train whistle screeched and was echoed inside Bronwyn's trunk, where Miss Peregrine was being tossed around like laundry in the wash. Too light on her feet to run, Olive clung to Bronwyn's neck, trailing behind her like a half-deflated balloon on a string.

Some of the adults were closer to the exit than we were, and rather than running around them, we tried to barrel straight through.

This didn't work.

The first to intercept us was a big woman who smacked Enoch upside the head with her purse, then tackled him. When Emma tried to pull her off, two men grabbed her by the arms and wrestled her to the floor. I was about to jump in and help her when a third man grabbed *my* arms.

"Someone *do* something!" Brownyn cried. We all knew what she meant, but it wasn't clear which of us was free to act. Then a bee whizzed past Enoch's nose and buried its stinger in the haunches of the woman sitting astride him, and she squealed and leapt up.

"Yes!" Enoch shouted. "More bees!"

"They're tired!" Hugh shouted back. "They only just got to sleep after saving you the last time!" But he could see that there was no other way—Emma's arms were pinned, Bronwyn was busy protecting both her trunk and Olive from a trio of angry train conductors, and there were more adults on the way—so Hugh began pounding his chest as if trying to dislodge a piece of stuck food. A moment later he let out a reverberating belch, and ten or so bees flew out of his mouth. They did a few circles overhead, then got their bearings and began stinging every adult in sight.

The men holding Emma dropped her and fled. The one holding me got stung right on the tip of his nose, and he hollered and flapped his arms as if possessed by demons. Soon all the adults were running, trying to defend themselves from tiny, stinging attackers with spastic dance moves, to the delight of all the children still on the platform, who laughed and cheered and threw their arms in the air in imitation of their ridiculous elders.

With everyone thus distracted, we picked ourselves up, bolted for the turnstiles, and ran out into a bustling London afternoon.

*　　*　　*

We became lost in the chaos of the streets. It felt like we'd been plunged into a jar of stirred liquid, racing with particles: gentlemen, ladies, laborers, soldiers, street kids, and beggars all rushing purposefully in every direction, weaving around tiny, sputtering cars and cart vendors crying their wares and buskers blowing horns and buses blowing horns and shuddering to stops to spill more people onto the teeming sidewalks. Containing all this was a canyon of column-fronted buildings that stretched to vanishing down a street half in shadow, the afternoon sun low and muted, reduced by the smokes of London to a murky glow, a lantern winking through fog.

Dizzy from it, I half closed my eyes and let Emma pull me along while with my free hand I reached into my pocket to touch the cold glass of my phone. I found this strangely calming. My phone was a useless relic of the future but an object which retained some power nevertheless—that of a long, thin filament connecting this baffling world to the sane and recognizable one I'd once belonged to; a thing that said to me as I touched it, *You are here and this is real and you are not dreaming and you are still you*, and somehow that made everything around me vibrate a little less quickly.

Enoch had spent his formative years in London and claimed to still know its streets, so he led. We stuck mostly to alleys and back lanes, which made the city seem at first like a maze of gray walls and gutter pipes, its grandness revealed in glimpses as we dashed across wide boulevards and back to the safety of shadows. We made a game of it, laughing, racing one another between alleys. Horace pretended to trip over a curb, then bounced up nimbly and bowed like a dancer, tipping his hat. We laughed like mad, strangely giddy, half in disbelief that we'd made it this far—across the water, through the woods, past snarling hollows and death squads of wights, all the way to London.

We put a good long way between us and the train station and then stopped in an alley by some trash cans to catch our breath. Bronwyn set down her trunk and lifted Miss Peregrine out, and she wobbled drunkenly across the cobblestones. Horace and Millard broke out laughing.

"What's so funny?" said Bronwyn. "It ain't Miss P's fault she's dizzy."

Horace swept his arms out grandly. "Welcome to beautiful London!" he said. "It's ever so much grander than you described it, Enoch. And oh, did you describe it! For seventy-five years: London, London, London! The greatest city on Earth!"

Millard picked up a trash-can lid. "London! The finest refuse available anywhere!"

Horace doffed his hat. "London! Where even the rats wear top hats!"

"Oh, I didn't go on about it *that* much," Enoch said.

"You did!" said Olive. "'Well, that's not how they do things in *London*,' you'd say. Or, 'In London, the food is *much* finer!'"

"Obviously, we're not on a grand tour of the city right now!" Enoch said defensively. "Would you rather walk through alleys or be spotted by wights?"

Horace ignored him. "London: where every day's a holiday . . . for the trash man!"

He broke down laughing, and his laughter was infectious. Soon nearly all of us were giggling—even Enoch. "I suppose I did glamorize it a *bit*," he admitted.

"I don't see what's so amusing about London," Olive said with a frown. "It's dirty and smelly and full of cruel, nasty people who make children cry and I hate it!" She scrunched her face into a scowl and added, "And I'm becoming *quite peckish*!"—which made us all laugh harder.

"Those people in the station *were* nasty," said Millard. "But they got what they deserved! I'll never forget that man's face when Bronwyn stuffed him into the phone box."

"Or that horrible woman when she got stung in the bum by a bee!" said Enoch. "I'd pay money to see that again."

I glanced at Hugh, expecting him to chime in, but his back was to us, his shoulders trembling.

"Hugh?" I said. "You all right?"

He shied away. "No one gives a whit," he said. "Don't bother checking on old Hugh, he's just here to save everyone's hindquarters with no word of thanks from anybody!"

Shamed, we offered him our thanks and apologies.

"Sorry, Hugh."

"Thanks again, Hugh."

"You're our man in a pinch, Hugh."

He turned to face us. "They were my friends, you know."

"We still are!" said Olive.

"Not *you*—my bees! They can only sting once, and then it's lights out, the big hive in the sky. And now I've only Henry left, and he can't fly 'cause he's missing a wing." He put out his hand and slowly opened the fingers, and there in his palm was Henry, waving his only wing at us.

"C'mon, mate," Hugh whispered to it. "Time to go home." He stuck out his tongue, set the bee upon it, and closed his mouth.

Enoch patted him on the shoulder. "I'd bring them back to life for you, but I'm not sure it would work on creatures so small."

"Thanks anyway," Hugh said, and then he cleared his throat and wiped his cheeks roughly, as if annoyed at his tears for exposing him.

"We'll find you more just as soon as we get Miss P fixed up," said Bronwyn.

"Speaking of which," Enoch said to Emma, "did you manage to get through to any ymbrynes on that phone?"

"Not a one," Emma replied, then sat down on an overturned trash can, her shoulders slumping. "I was really hoping we might catch a bit of good luck for once. But no."

"Then it seems the dog was correct," said Horace. "The great loops of London have fallen to our enemies." He bowed his head solemnly. "The worst has come to pass. All our ymbrynes have been kidnapped."

We all bowed our heads, our giddy mood gone.

"In that case," said Enoch, "Millard, you'd better tell us all you know about the punishment loops. If that's where the ymbrynes are, we're going to have to stage a rescue."

"No," said Millard. "No, no, no."

"What do you mean, *no*?" said Emma.

Millard made a strangled noise in his throat and started breathing weirdly. "I mean . . . we can't . . ."

He couldn't seem to get the words out.

"What's wrong with him?" said Bronwyn. "Mill, what's the matter?"

"You'd better explain right now what you mean by 'no,'" Emma said threateningly.

"Because we'll *die*, that's why!" Millard said, his voice breaking.

"But back at the menagerie you made it sound so easy!" I said. "Like we could just waltz into a punishment loop . . ."

Millard was hyperventilating, hysterical—and it scared me. Bronwyn found a crumpled paper bag and told him to breathe into it. When he'd recovered a bit, he answered.

"Getting *into* one is easy enough," he said, speaking slowly, working to control his breaths. "Getting out again is trickier. Getting out *alive*, I should say. Punishment loops are everything the dog said and worse. Rivers of fire . . . bloodthirsty Vikings . . . pestilence so thick you can't breathe . . . and mixed into all that, like some devilish bouillabaisse, bird knows how many wights and hollowgast!"

"Well, that's fantastic!" said Horace, tossing up his hands. "You might've told us earlier, you know—like back at the menagerie, when we were planning all this!"

"Would it have made any difference, Horace?" He took a few more breaths from the bag. "If I'd made it sound more frightening, would you have chosen to simply let Miss Peregrine's humanity expire?"

"Of course not," said Horace. "But you should've told us the truth."

Millard let the bag drop. His strength was returning, and his conviction with it. "I admit I somewhat downplayed the punishment loops' dangers. But I never thought we'd actually have to go into them! Despite all that irritating dog's doomsaying about the state of London, I was certain we'd find at least *one* unraided loop here, its ymbryne still present and accounted for. And for all we know, we may still! How can we be sure they've all been kidnapped? Have we seen their raided loops with our own eyes? What if the ymbrynes' phones were simply . . . disconnected?"

"*All* of them?" Enoch scoffed.

Even Olive, eternally optimistic Olive, shook her head at that.

"Then what do you suggest, Millard?" said Emma. "That we tour London's loops and hope to find someone still at home? And what would you say the odds are that the corrupted, *who are looking for us,* would leave all those loops unguarded?"

"I think we'd have a better chance of surviving the night if we spent it playing Russian roulette," said Enoch.

"All I mean," Millard said, "is that we have no *proof . . .*"

"What more proof do you want?" said Emma. "Pools of blood? A pile of plucked ymbryne feathers? Miss Avocet told us the corrupted assault began here weeks ago. Miss Wren clearly believed that all of London's ymbrynes had been kidnapped—do you know better than Miss Wren, an ymbryne herself? And now we're here, and none of the loops are answering their telephones. So please, tell me why going loop to loop would be anything other than a suicidally dangerous waste of time."

"Wait a minute—that's it!" Millard exclaimed. "What about Miss Wren?"

"What about her?" said Emma.

"Don't you remember what the dog told us? Miss Wren came to London a few days ago, when she heard that her sister ymbrynes had been kidnapped."

"So?"

"What if she's still here?"

"Then she's probably been captured by now!" said Enoch.

"And if she hasn't?" Millard's voice was bright with hope. "She could help Miss Peregrine—and then we wouldn't have to go anywhere *near* the punishment loops!"

"And how would you suggest we find her?" Enoch said shrilly. "Shout her name from the rooftops? This isn't Cairnholm; it's a city of millions!"

"Her pigeons," said Millard.

"Come again?"

"It was Miss Wren's peculiar pigeons who told her where the ymbrynes had been taken. If they knew where all the other ymbrynes went, then they should know where Miss Wren is, too. They belong to her, after all."

"Hah!" said Enoch. "The only thing commoner here than plain-looking middle-aged ladies are flocks of pigeons. And you want to search all of London for *one flock* in particular?"

"It does seem a bit mad," Emma said. "Sorry, Mill, I just don't see how that could work."

"Then it's a lucky thing for you I spent our train ride studying rather than making idle gossip. Someone hand me the *Tales*!"

Bronwyn fished the book from her trunk and gave it to him. Millard dove right in, flipping pages. "There are many answers to be found within," he said, "if you only know what to look for." He stopped at a certain page and stabbed the top with his finger. "Aha!" he said, turning the book to show us what he'd found.

The title of the story was "The Pigeons of St. Paul's."

"I'll be blessed," said Bronwyn. "Could those be the same pigeons we're talking about?"

"If they're written about in the *Tales*, they're almost certainly peculiar pigeons," said Millard, "and how many flocks of peculiar pigeons could there possibly be?"

Olive clapped her hands and cried, "Millard, you're brilliant!"

"Thank you, yes, I was aware."

"Wait, I'm lost," I said. "What's St. Paul's?"

"Even *I* know that," said Olive. "The cathedral!" And she went to the end of the alley and pointed up at a giant domed roof rising in the distance.

"It's the largest and most magnificent cathedral in London," said Millard, "and if my hunch is correct, it's also the nesting place of Miss Wren's pigeons."

"Let's hope they're at home," said Emma. "And that they've got some good news for us. We've had quite a drought of it lately."

*　　*　　*

As we navigated a labyrinth of narrow streets toward the cathedral, a brooding quiet settled over us. For long stretches no one spoke, leaving only the tap of our shoes on pavement and the sounds of the city: airplanes, the ever-present hum of traffic, sirens that warbled and pitch-shifted around us.

The farther we got from the train station, the more evidence we saw of the bombs that had been raining down on London. Building fronts pocked by shrapnel. Shattered windows. Streets that glinted with frosts of powdered glass. The sky was speckled with puffy silver blimps tethered to the ground by long webs of cable. "Barrage balloons," Emma said when she saw me craning my neck toward one. "The German bombers get caught up in their cables at night and crash."

Then we came upon a scene of destruction so bizarre that I had to stop and gape at it—not out of some morbid voyeurism, but because it was impossible for my brain to process without further study. A bomb crater yawned across the whole width of the street like a monstrous mouth with broken pavement for teeth. At one edge, the blast had sheared away the front wall of a building but left what was inside mostly intact. It looked like a doll's house, its interior rooms all exposed to the street: the dining room with its table still set for a meal; family pictures knocked crooked in a hallway but still hanging; a roll of toilet paper unspooled and caught in the breeze, waving in the air like a long, white flag.

"Did they forget to finish building it?" Olive asked.

"No, dummy," said Enoch. "It got hit by a bomb."

For a moment Olive looked as if she might cry, but then her face went hard and she shook her fist at the sky and yelled, "Nasty Hitler! Stop this horrible war and go right away altogether!"

Bronwyn patted her arm. "Shhh. He can't hear you, love."

"It isn't fair," Olive said. "I'm tired of airplanes and bombs and war!"

"We all are," said Enoch. "Even me."

Then I heard Horace scream and I spun around to see him pointing at something in the road. I ran to see what it was, and then I did see and I stopped, frozen, my brain shouting *Run away!* but my legs refusing to listen.

It was a pyramid of heads. They were blackened and caved,

mouths agape, eyes boiled shut, melted and pooled together in the gutter like some hydra-headed horror. Then Emma came to see and gasped and turned away; Bronwyn came and started moaning; Hugh gagged and clapped his hands over his eyes; and then finally Enoch, who seemed not in the least disturbed, calmly nudged one of the heads with his shoe and pointed out that they were only mannequins made of wax, having spilled from the display window of a bombed wig shop. We all felt a little ridiculous but somehow no less horrified, because even though the heads weren't real, they represented something that was, hidden beneath the rubble around us.

"Let's go," Emma said. "This place is nothing but a graveyard."

We walked on. I tried to keep my eyes to the ground, but there was no shutting out all the ghastly things we passed. A scarred ruin belching smoke, the only fireman dispatched to extinguish it slouched in defeat, blistered and weary, his hose run dry. Yet there he stood watching anyway, as if, lacking water, his job now was to bear witness.

A baby in a stroller, left alone in the street, bawling.

Bronwyn slowed, overcome. "Can't we help them somehow?"

"It wouldn't make any difference," said Millard. "These people belong to the past, and the past can't be changed."

Bronwyn nodded sadly. She'd known it was true but had needed to hear it said. We were barely here, ineffectual as ghosts.

A cloud of ash billowed, blotting out fireman and child. We went on, choking in an eddy of windborne wreck dust, powdered concrete blanching our clothes, our faces bone white.

We hurried past the ruined blocks as quickly as we could, then marveled as the streets returned to life around us. Just a short walk from Hell, people were going about their business, striding down sidewalks, living in buildings that still had electricity and windows and walls. Then we rounded a corner and the cathedral's dome revealed itself, proud and imposing despite patches of fire-blackened stone and a few crumbling arches. Like the spirit of the city itself, it would take more than a few bombs to topple St. Paul's.

Our hunt began in a square close to the cathedral, where old men on benches were feeding pigeons. At first it was mayhem: we bounded in, grabbing wildly as the pigeons took off. The old men grumbled, and we withdrew to wait for their return. They did, eventually, pigeons not being the smartest animals on the planet, at which point we all took turns wading casually into the flock and trying to catch them by surprise, reaching down to snatch at them. I thought Olive, who was small and quick, or Hugh, with his peculiar connection to another sort of winged creature, might have some luck, but both were humiliated. Millard didn't fare any better, and they couldn't even *see* him. By the time my turn came, the pigeons must've been sick of us bothering them, because the moment I strolled into the square they all burst into flight and took one big, simultaneous cluster-bomb crap, which sent me flailing toward a water fountain to wash my whole head.

In the end, it was Horace who caught one. He sat down next to the old men, dropping seeds until the birds circled him. Then, leaning slowly forward, he stretched out his arm and, calm as could be, snagged one by its feet.

"Got you!" he cried.

The bird flapped and tried to get away, but Horace held on tight.

He brought it to us. "How can we tell if it's peculiar?" he said, flipping the bird over to inspect its bottom, as if expecting to find a label there.

"Show it to Miss Peregrine," Emma said. "She'll know."

So we opened Bronwyn's trunk, shoved the pigeon inside with Miss Peregrine, and slammed down the lid. The pigeon screeched like it was being torn apart.

I winced and shouted, "Go easy, Miss P!"

When Bronwyn opened the trunk again, a poof of pigeon feathers fluttered into the air, but the pigeon itself was nowhere to be seen.

"Oh, no—she's ate it!" cried Bronwyn.

"No she hasn't," said Emma. "Look beneath her!"

Miss Peregrine lifted up and stepped aside, and there underneath her was the pigeon, alive but dazed.

"Well?" said Enoch. "Is it or isn't it one of Miss Wren's?"

Miss Peregrine nudged the bird with her beak and it flew away. Then she leapt out of the trunk, hobbled into the square, and with one loud squawk scattered the rest of the pigeons. Her message was clear: not only was Horace's pigeon not peculiar, *none* of them were. We'd have to keep looking.

Miss Peregrine hopped toward the cathedral and flapped her wing impatiently. We caught up to her on the cathedral steps. The building loomed above us, soaring bell towers framing its giant dome. An army of soot-stained angels glared down at us from marble reliefs.

"How are we ever going to search this whole place?" I wondered aloud.

"One room at a time," Emma said.

A strange noise stopped us at the door. It sounded like a faraway car alarm, the note pitching up and down in long, slow arcs. But there were no car alarms in 1940, of course. It was an air-raid siren.

Horace cringed. "The Germans are coming!" he cried. "Death

from the skies!"

"We don't know *what* it means," Emma said. "Could be a false alarm, or a test."

But the streets and the square were emptying fast; the old men were folding up their newspapers and vacating their benches.

"*They* don't seem to think it's a test," Horace said.

"Since when are we afraid of a few bombs?" Enoch said. "Quit talking like a Nancy Normal!"

"Need I remind you," said Millard, "these are not the sort of bombs we're accustomed to. Unlike the ones that fall on Cairnholm, we don't know where they're going to land!"

"All the more reason to get what we came for, and quickly!" Emma said, and she led us inside.

*   *   *

The cathedral's interior was massive—it seemed, impossibly, even larger than the outside—and though damaged, a few hardy believers knelt here and there in silent prayer. The altar was buried under a midden of debris. Where a bomb had pierced the roof, sunlight fell down in broad beams. A lone soldier sat on a fallen pillar, gazing at the sky through the broken ceiling.

We wandered, necks craned, bits of concrete and broken tile crunching beneath our feet.

"I don't see anything," Horace complained. "There are enough hiding places here for ten thousand pigeons!"

"Don't look," Hugh said. "*Listen.*"

We stopped, straining to hear the telltale coo of pigeons. But there was only the ceaseless whine of air-raid sirens, and below that a series of dull cracks like rolling thunder. I told myself to stay calm, but my heart thrummed like a drum machine.

Bombs were falling.

"We need to go," I said, panic choking me. "There has to be a shelter nearby. Somewhere safe we can hide."

"But we're so close!" said Bronwyn. "We can't quit now!"

There was another crack, closer this time, and the others started to get nervous, too.

"Maybe Jacob's right," said Horace. "Let's find somewhere safe to hide until the bombing's through. We can search more when it's over."

"Nowhere is truly safe," said Enoch. "Those bombs can penetrate even a deep shelter."

"They can't penetrate a loop," Emma said. "And if there's a tale about this cathedral, there's probably a loop entrance here, too."

"Perhaps," said Millard, "perhaps, perhaps. Hand me the book and I shall investigate."

Bronwyn opened her trunk and handed Millard the book.

"Let me see now," he said, turning its pages until he reached "The Pigeons of St. Paul's."

Bombs are falling and we're reading stories, I thought. *I have entered the realm of the insane.*

"Listen closely!" Millard said. "If there's a loop entrance nearby, this tale may tell us how to find it. It's a short one, luckily."

A bomb fell outside. The floor shook and plaster rained from the ceiling. I clenched my teeth and tried to focus on my breathing.

Unfazed, Millard cleared his throat. "The Pigeons of St. Paul's!" he began, reading in a big, booming voice.

"We know the title already!" said Enoch.

"Read faster, please!" said Bronwyn.

"If you don't stop interrupting me, we'll be here all night," said Millard, and then he continued.

"Once upon a peculiar time, long before there were towers or steeples or any tall buildings at all in the city of London, there was a flock of pigeons who got it into their minds that they wanted a nice, high place to roost, above the bustle and fracas of human society. They knew just how to build it, too, because pigeons are builders by nature, and much more intelligent than we give them credit for being. But the people of ancient London weren't interested in constructing tall things, so one night the pigeons snuck into the bedroom of the most industrious human they could find and whispered into his ear the plans for a magnificent tower.

"In the morning, the man awoke in great excitement. He had dreamed—or so he thought—of a magnificent church with a great, reaching spire that would rise from the city's tallest hill. A few years later, at enormous cost to the humans, it was built. It was a very towering sort of tower and had all manner of nooks and crannies inside it where the pigeons could roost, and they were very satisfied with themselves.

"Then one day Vikings sacked the city and burned the tower to the ground, so the pigeons had to find another architect, whisper in his ear, and wait patiently for a new church tower to be built—this one even grander and taller than the first. And it was built, and it was very grand and very tall. And then it burned, too.

"Things went on in this fashion for hundreds of years, the towers burning and the pigeons whispering plans for still grander and taller towers to successive generations of nocturnally inspired architects. Though these architects never realized the debt they owed the birds, they still regarded them with tenderness, and allowed them to hang about wherever they liked, in the naves and belfries, like the mascots and guardians of the place they truly were."

"This is *not helpful*," Enoch said. "Get to the loop entrance part!"

"I am getting to what I am *getting to*!" Millard snapped. "Eventually, after many church towers had come and gone, the pigeons' plans became so ambitious that it took an exceedingly long time to find a human intelligent enough to carry them out. When they finally did, the man resisted, believing the hill to be cursed, so many churches having burned there in the past. Though he tried to put the idea out of his mind, the pigeons kept returning, night after night, to whisper it in his ear. Still, the man would not act. So they came to him during the day, which they had never done before, and told him in their strange laughing language that he was the only human capable of constructing their tower, and he simply had to do it. But he refused and chased them from his house, shouting, 'Shoo, begone with ye, filthy creatures!'

"The pigeons, insulted and vengeful, hounded the man until he was nearly mad—following him wherever he went, picking at his clothes, pulling his hair, fouling his food with their hind-feathers, tapping on his windows at night so he couldn't sleep—until one day he fell to his knees and cried, 'O pigeons! I will build whatever you ask, so long as you watch over it and preserve it from the fire!'

"The pigeons puzzled over this. Consulting among themselves, they decided that they might've been better guardians of past towers if they hadn't come to enjoy building them so much, and vowed to do everything they could to protect them in the future. So the man built it, a soaring cathedral with two towers and a dome. It was so grand, and both the man and the pigeons were so pleased with what they'd made that they became great friends; the man never went anywhere for the rest of his life without a pigeon close at hand to advise him. Even after he died at a ripe and happy old age, the birds still went to visit him, now and again, in the land below. And to this very day, you'll find the cathedral they built standing on the tallest hill in London, the pigeons watching over it."

Millard closed the book. "The end."

Emma made an exasperated noise. "Yes, but watching over it *from where*?"

"That could not have been less helpful to our present situation," said Enoch, "were it a story about cats on the moon."

"I can't make heads or tails of it," said Bronwyn. "Can anyone?"

I nearly could—felt close to something in that line about "the land below"—but all I could think was, *The pigeons are in Hell?*

Then another bomb fell, shaking the whole building, and from high overhead came a sudden flutter of wingbeats. We looked up to see three frightened pigeons shoot out of some hiding place in the rafters. Miss Peregrine squawked with excitement—as if to say, *That's them!*—and Bronwyn scooped her up and we all went racing after the birds. They flew down the length of the nave, turned sharply, and disappeared through a doorway.

We reached the doorway a few seconds later. To my relief, it didn't lead outside, where we'd never have a hope of catching them, but to a stairwell, down a set of spiral steps.

"Hah!" Enoch said, clapping his pudgy hands. "They've gone and done it now—trapped themselves in the basement!"

We sprinted down the stairs. At the bottom was a large, dimly lit room walled and floored with stone. It was cold and damp and almost completely dark, the electricity having been knocked out, so Emma sparked a flame in her hand and shone it around, until the nature of the space became apparent. Beneath our feet, stretching from wall to wall, were marble slabs chiseled with writing. The one below me read:

BISHOP ELDRIDGE THORNBRUSH, DYED ANNO 1721

"This is no basement," Emma said. "It's a crypt."

A little chill came over me, and I stepped closer to the light and warmth of Emma's flame.

"You mean, there are people buried in the floor?" said Olive, her voice quavering.

"What of it?" said Enoch. "Let's catch a damned pigeon before one of those bombs buries *us* in the floor."

Emma turned in a circle, throwing light on the walls. "They've got to be down here somewhere. There's no way out but that staircase."

Then we heard a wing flap. I tensed. Emma brightened her flame and aimed it toward the sound. Her flickering light fell on a flat-topped tomb that rose a few feet from the floor. Between the tomb and the wall was a gap we couldn't see behind from where we stood; a perfect hiding spot for a bird.

Emma raised a finger to her lips and motioned for us to follow. We crept across the room. Nearing the tomb, we spread out, surrounding it on three sides.

Ready? Emma mouthed.

The others nodded. I gave a thumbs-up. Emma tiptoed forward to peek behind the tomb—and then her face fell. "Nothing!" she said, kicking the floor in frustration.

"I don't understand!" said Enoch. "They were *right here*!"

We all came forward to look. Then Millard said, "Emma! Shine your light on top of the tomb, please!"

She did, and Millard read the tomb's inscription aloud:

HERE LIETH SIR CHRISTOPHER WREN
BUILDER OF THIS CATHEDRAL

"Wren!" Emma exclaimed. "What an odd coincidence!"

"I hardly think it's a coincidence," said Millard. "He must be related to *Miss* Wren. Perhaps he's her father!"

"That's very interesting," said Enoch, "but how does that help us find her, or her pigeons?"

"That is what I am attempting to puzzle out." Millard hummed to himself and paced a little and recited a line from the tale: "the birds still went to visit him, now and again, in the land below."

Then I thought I heard a pigeon coo. "Shh!" I said, and made everyone listen. It came again a few seconds later, from the rear corner of the tomb. I circled around it and knelt down, and that's when I noticed a small hole in the floor at the tomb's base, no bigger than a fist—just large enough for a bird to wriggle through.

"Over here!" I said.

"Well, I'll be stuffed!" said Emma, holding her flame up to the hole. "Perhaps that's 'the land below'?"

"But the hole is so small," said Olive. "How are we supposed to get the birds out of there?"

"We could wait for them to leave," said Horace, and then a bomb fell so close by that my eyes blurred and my teeth rattled.

"No need for that!" said Millard. "Bronwyn, would you please open Sir Wren's tomb?"

"No!" cried Olive. "I don't want to see his rotten old bones!"

"Don't worry, love," Bronwyn said, "Millard knows what he's doing." She planted her hands on the edge of the tomb lid and began to push, and it slid open with a slow, grating rumble.

The smell that came up wasn't what I'd expected—not of death, but mold and old dirt. We gathered around to look inside.

"Well, I'll be stuffed," Emma said.

CHAPTER NINE

*W*here a coffin should've been, there was a ladder, leading down into darkness. We peered into the open tomb.

"There's no *way* I'm climbing down there!" Horace said. But then a trio of bombs shook the building, raining chips of concrete on our heads, and suddenly Horace was pushing past me, grasping for the ladder. "Excuse me, out of my way, best-dressed go first!"

Emma caught him by the sleeve. "I have the light, so *I'll* go first. Then Jacob will follow, in case there are . . . *things* down there."

I flashed a weak smile, my knees going wobbly at the thought.

Enoch said, "You mean things *other than* rats and cholera and whatever sorts of mad trolls live beneath crypts?"

"It doesn't matter *what's* down there," Millard said grimly. "We'll have to face it, and that's that."

"Fine," said Enoch. "But Miss Wren had better be down there, too, because rat bites don't heal quickly."

"Hollowgast bites even less so," said Emma, and then she swung her foot onto the ladder.

"Be careful," I said. "I'll be right above you."

She saluted me with her flaming hand. "Once more into the breach," she said, and began to climb down.

Then it was my turn.

"Do you ever find yourself climbing into an open grave during a bombing raid," I said, "and just wish you'd stayed in bed?"

Enoch kicked my shoe. "Quit stalling."

I grabbed the lip of the tomb and put my foot on the ladder.

Thought briefly of all the pleasant, boring things I might've been doing with my summer, had my life gone differently. Tennis camp. Sailing lessons. Stocking shelves. And then, through some Herculean effort of will, I made myself climb.

The ladder descended into a tunnel. The tunnel dead-ended to one side, and in the other direction disappeared into blackness. The air was cold and suffused with a strange odor, like clothes left to rot in a flooded basement. The rough stone walls beaded and dripped with moisture of mysterious origin.

As Emma and I waited for everyone to climb down, the cold crept into me, degree by degree. The others felt it, too. When Bronwyn reached the bottom, she opened her trunk and handed out the peculiar sheep's wool sweaters we'd been given in the menagerie. I slipped one over my head. It fit me like a sack, the sleeves falling past my fingers and the bottom sagging halfway to my knees, but at least it was warm.

Bronwyn's trunk was empty now and she left it behind. Miss Peregrine rode inside her coat, where she'd practically made a nest for herself. Millard insisted on carrying the *Tales* in his arms, heavy and bulky as it was, because he might need to refer to it at any moment, he said. I think it had become his security blanket, though, and he thought of it as a book of spells which only he knew how to read.

We were an odd bunch.

I shuffled forward to feel for hollows in the dark. This time, I got a new kind of twinge in my gut, ever so faint, as if a hollow had been here and gone, and I was sensing its residue. I didn't mention it, though; there was no reason to alarm everyone unnecessarily.

We walked. The sound of our feet slapping the wet bricks echoed endlessly up and down the passage. There'd be no sneaking up on whatever was waiting for us.

Every so often, from up ahead, we'd hear a flap of wings or a pigeon's warble, and we'd pick up our pace a little. I got the uneasy feeling we were being led toward some nasty surprise. Embedded in the walls were stone slabs like the ones we'd seen in the crypt, but older, the writing mostly worn away. Then we passed a coffin, graveless, on the floor—then a whole stack of them, leaned against a wall like discarded moving boxes.

"What *is* this place?" Hugh whispered.

"Graveyard overflow," said Enoch. "When they need to make room for new customers, they dig up the old ones and stick them down here."

"What a terrible loop entrance," I said. "Imagine walking through here every time you needed in or out!"

"It's not so different from our cairn tunnel," Millard said. "Unpleasant loop entrances serve a purpose—normals tend to avoid them, so we peculiars have them all to ourselves."

So rational. So wise. All I could think was, *There are dead people everywhere and they're all rotted and bony and dead and, oh God . . .*

"Uh-oh," Emma said, and she stopped suddenly, causing me to run into her and everyone else to pile up behind me.

She held her flame to one side, revealing a curved door in the wall. It hung open slightly, but only darkness showed through the crack.

We listened. For a long moment there was no sound but our breath and the distant drip of water. Then we heard a noise, but not the kind we were expecting—not a wing-flap or the scratch of a bird's feet—but something human.

Very softly, someone was crying.

"Hello?" called Emma. "Who's in there?"

"Please don't hurt me," came an echoing voice.

Or was it a pair of voices?

Emma brightened her flame. Bronwyn crept forward and nudged the door with her foot. It swung open to expose a small chamber filled with bones. Femurs, shinbones, skulls—the dismembered fossils of many hundreds of people, heaped up in no apparent order.

I stumbled backward, dizzy with shock.

"Hello?" Emma said. "Who said that? Show yourself!"

At first I couldn't see anything in there but bones, but then I heard a sniffle and followed the sound to the top of the pile, where two pairs of eyes blinked at us from the murky shadows at the rear of the chamber.

"There's no one here," said a small voice.

"Go away," came a second voice. "We're dead."

"No you're not," said Enoch, "and I would know!"

"Come out of there," Emma said gently. "We're not going to hurt you."

Both voices said at once: "Promise?"

"We promise," said Emma.

The bones began to shift. A skull dislodged from the pile and clattered to the floor, where it rolled to a stop at my feet and stared up at me.

Hello, future, I thought.

Then two young boys crawled into the light, on hands and knees atop the bone pile. Their skin was deathly pale and they peeped at us with black-circled eyes that wheeled dizzyingly in their sockets.

"I'm Emma, this is Jacob, and these are our friends," Emma said. "We're peculiar and we're not going to hurt you."

The boys crouched like frightened animals, saying nothing, eyes spinning, seeming to look everywhere and nowhere.

"What's wrong with them?" Olive whispered.

Bronwyn hushed her. "Don't be rude."

"Can you tell me your names?" Emma said, her voice coaxing and gentle.

"I am Joel and Peter," the larger boy said.

"Which are you?" Emma said. "Joel or Peter?"

"I am Peter and Joel," said the smaller boy.

"We don't have time for games," said Enoch. "Are there any birds in there with you? Have you seen any fly past?"

"The pigeons like to hide," said the larger.

"In the attic," said the smaller.

"What attic?" said Emma. "Where?"

"In our house," they said together, and raising their arms they pointed down the dark passage. They seemed to speak cooperatively, and if a sentence was more than a few words long, one would start and the other finish, with no detectable pause between. I also noticed that whenever one was speaking and the other wasn't, the quiet one would mouth the other's words in perfect synchronicity—as if they shared one mind.

"Could you please show us the way to your house?" asked Emma. "Take us to your attic?"

Joel-and-Peter shook their heads and shrank back into the dark.

"What's the matter?" Bronwyn said. "Why don't you want to go?"

"Death and blood!" cried one boy.

"Blood and screaming!" cried the other.

"Screaming and blood and shadows that bite!" they cried together.

"Cheerio!" said Horace, turning on his heels. "I'll see you all back in the crypt. Hope I don't get squashed by a bomb!"

Emma caught Horace by his sleeve. "Oh, no you don't! You're the only one of us who's managed to catch any of those blasted pigeons."

"Didn't you hear them?" Horace said. "That loop is full of shadows that bite—which could only mean one thing. Hollows!"

"It *was* full of them," I said. "But that might have been days ago."

"When was the last time you were inside your house?" Emma asked the boys.

Their loop had been raided, they explained in their strange and broken way, but they'd managed to escape into the catacombs and hide among the bones. How long ago that was, they couldn't say. Two days? Three? They'd lost all track of time down here in the dark.

"Oh, you poor dears!" said Bronwyn. "What terrors you must've endured!"

"You can't stay here forever," said Emma. "You'll age forward if you don't reach another loop soon. We can help you—but first we have to catch a pigeon."

The boys gazed into one another's spinning eyes and seemed to speak without uttering a word. They said in unison, "Follow us."

They slid down from their bone pile and started down the passage.

We followed. I couldn't take my eyes off them; they were fascinatingly odd. They kept their arms linked at all times, and every few steps, they made loud clicking sounds with their tongues.

"What are they doing?" I whispered.

"I believe that's how they see," said Millard. "It's the same way bats see in the dark. The sounds they make reflect off things and then back to them, which forms a picture in their minds."

"We are echolocators," Joel-and-Peter said.

They were also, apparently, very sharp of hearing.

The passage forked, then forked again. At one point I felt a sudden pressure in my ears and had to wiggle them to release it. That's when I knew we'd left 1940 and entered a loop. Finally we came to a dead-end wall with vertical steps cut into it. Joel-and-Peter stood at the base of the wall and pointed to a pinpoint of daylight overhead.

"Our house—" said the elder.

"Is up there," said the younger.

And with that, they retreated into the shadows.

*　　*　　*

The steps were slimed with moss and difficult to climb, and I had to go slowly or risk falling. They ascended the wall to meet a circular, person-sized door in the ceiling, through which shone a single gleam of light. I wedged my fingers into the crack and pushed sideways, and the doors slid open like a camera shutter, revealing a tubular conduit of bricks that rose twenty or thirty feet to a circle of sky. I was at the false bottom of a fake well.

I pulled myself into the well and climbed. Halfway up I had to stop and rest, pushing my back against the opposite side of the shaft. When the burn in my biceps subsided, I climbed the rest of the way, scrambling over the lip of the well to land in some grass.

I was in the courtyard of a shabby-looking house. The sky was an infected shade of yellow, but there was no smoke in it and no sound of engines. We were in some older time, before the war—before cars, even. There was a chill in the air, and errant flakes of snow drifted down and melted on the ground.

Emma came up the well next, then Horace. Emma had decided that only the three of us should explore the house. We didn't know what we would find up here, and if we needed to leave in a hurry, it was better to have a small group that could move fast. None who stayed below argued; Joel-and-Peter's warning of blood and shadows had scared them. Only Horace was unhappy, and kept muttering to himself that he wished he'd never caught that pigeon in the square.

Bronwyn waved to us from below and then pulled closed the circular door at the bottom of the well. The top side was painted to look like the surface of water—dark, dirty water you'd never want to drop a drinking bucket into. Very clever.

The three of us huddled together and looked around. The courtyard and the house were suffering from serious neglect. The grass around the well was tamped down, but everywhere else it grew up in weedy thickets that reached higher than some of the ground-floor windows. A doghouse sat rotting and half collapsed in one corner, and near it a toppled laundry line was gradually being swallowed by brush.

We stood and waited, listening for pigeons. From beyond the house's walls, I could hear the tap of horses' hooves on pavement. No, this definitely wasn't London circa 1940.

Then, in one of the upper-floor windows, I saw a curtain shift. "Up there!" I hissed, pointing at it.

I didn't know if a bird or a person had done it, but it was worth checking out. I started toward a door that led into the house, beckoning the others after me—then tripped over something. It was a body lying on the ground, covered head to ankle with a black tarp. A pair of worn shoes poked from one end, pointing at the sky. Tucked into one cracked sole was a white card, on which had been written in neat script:

Mr. A. F. Crumbley
Lately of the Outer Provinces
Aged forward rather than be taken alive
Kindly requests his remains be deposited in the Thames

"Unlucky bastard," Horace whispered. "He came here from the country, probably after his own loop was raided—only to have the one he'd escaped to raided, as well."

"But why would they leave poor Mr. Crumbley out in the open this way?" whispered Emma.

"Because they had to leave in a hurry," I said.

Emma bent down and reached for the edge of Mr. Crumbley's tarp. I didn't want to look but couldn't help myself, and I half turned away but peeked back through split fingers. I had expected a withered corpse, but Mr. Crumbley looked perfectly intact and surprisingly young, perhaps only forty or fifty years old, his black hair graying just around the temples. His eyes were closed and peaceful, as if he might've just been sleeping. Could he really have aged forward, like the leathery apple I took from Miss Peregrine's loop?

"Hullo, are you dead or asleep?" Emma said. She nudged the man's ear with her boot, and the side of his head caved and crumbled to dust.

Emma gasped and let the tarp fall back. Crumbley had become a desiccated cast of himself, so fragile that a strong wind could blow him apart.

We left poor, crumbling Mr. Crumbley behind and went to the door. I grasped the knob and turned it. The door opened and we stepped through it into a laundry room. There were fresh-looking clothes in a hamper, a washboard hung neatly above a sink. This place had not been abandoned long.

The Feeling was stronger here, but was still only residue. We opened another door and came into a sitting room. My chest tightened. Here was clear evidence of a fight: furniture scattered and overturned, pictures knocked off the mantel, stripes of wallpaper shredded to ribbons.

Then Horace muttered, "Oh, *no*," and I followed his gaze upward, to a dark stain discoloring a roughly circular patch of ceiling. Something awful had happened upstairs.

Emma squeezed her eyes closed. "Just listen," she said. "Listen for the birds and don't think about anything else."

We closed our eyes and listened. A minute passed. Then, finally, the fluttering coo of a pigeon. I opened my eyes to see where it had come from.

The staircase.

We mounted the stairs gently, trying not to creak them under our feet. I could feel my heartbeat in my throat, in my temple. I could handle old, brittle corpses. I wasn't sure if I could take a murder scene.

The second-floor hallway was littered with debris. A door, torn from its hinges, lay splintered. Through the broken doorway was a fallen tower of trunks and dressers; a failed blockade.

In the next room, the white carpet was soaked with blood—the stain that had leaked through the floor to the ceiling below. But whomever it had leaked from was long gone.

The last door in the hall showed no signs of forced entry. I pushed it open warily. My eyes scanned the room: there was a wardrobe, a dresser topped with carefully arranged figurines, lace curtains fluttering in a window. The carpet was clean. Everything undisturbed.

Then my eyes went to the bed, and what was in it, and I stumbled back against the doorjamb. Nestled under clean white covers were two men, seemingly asleep—and between them, two skeletons.

"Aged forward," said Horace, his hands trembling at his throat. "Two of them considerably more than the others."

The men who looked asleep were as dead as Mr. Crumbley downstairs, Horace said, and if we touched them, they would disintegrate in just the same way.

"They gave up," Emma whispered. "They got tired of running and they gave up." She looked at them with a mix of pity and disgust.

She thought they were weak and cowardly—that they'd taken the easy way out. I couldn't help wondering, though, if these peculiars simply knew more than we did about what the wights did with their captives. Maybe we would choose death, too, if we knew.

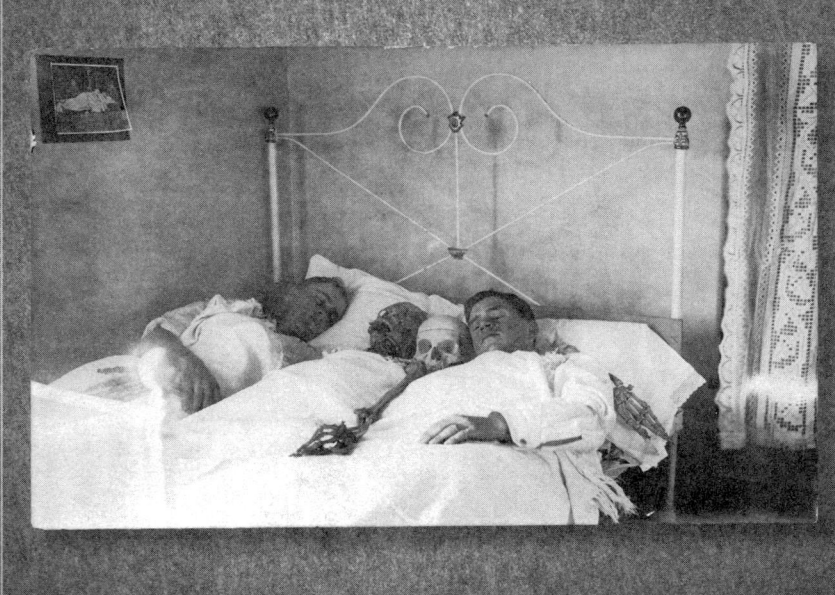

We drifted into the hall. I felt dizzy and sick, and I wanted out of this house—but we couldn't leave yet. There was one last staircase to climb.

At the top, we found a smoke-damaged landing. I imagined peculiars who'd withstood the initial attack on this house gathering here for a last stand. Maybe they'd tried to fight the corrupted with fire—or maybe the corrupted had tried to smoke them out. Either way, it looked like the house had come close to burning down.

Ducking through a low doorway, we entered a narrow, slope-walled attic. Everything here was burned black. Flames had made gaping holes in the roof.

Emma prodded Horace. "It's here somewhere," she said quietly. "Work your magic, bird-catcher."

Horace tiptoed into the middle of the room and sing-songed, "Heeeeere, pigeon, pigeon, pigeon . . ."

Then, from behind us, we heard a wingbeat and a strangled chirp. We turned to see not a pigeon but a girl in a black dress, half hidden in the shadows.

"Is this what you're after?" the girl said, raising one arm into a shaft of sunlight. The pigeon squirmed in her hand, struggling to free itself.

"Yes!" Emma said. "Thank heaven you caught it!" She moved toward the girl with her hands out to take the pigeon, but the girl shouted, "Stop right there!" and snapped her fingers. A charred throw rug flew out from beneath Emma and took her feet with it, sending her crashing to the floor.

I rushed to Emma. "Are you okay?"

"On your knees!" the girl barked at me. "Put your hands on your head!"

"I'm fine," Emma said. "Do as she says. She's telekinetic and clearly unstable."

I knelt down by Emma and laced my fingers behind my head.

Emma did the same. Horace, trembling and silent, sat heavily and placed his palms on the floor.

"We don't mean you any harm," Emma said. "We're only after the pigeon."

"Oh, I know perfectly well what you're after," the girl said with a sneer. "Your kind never gives up, do you?"

"Our *kind*?" I said.

"Lay down your weapons and slide them over!" barked the girl.

"We don't have any," Emma said calmly, trying her best not to upset the girl any further.

"This will go easier for you if you don't assume I'm stupid!" the girl shouted. "You're weak and have no powers of your own, so you rely on guns and things. Now lay them on the floor!"

Emma turned her head and whispered, "She thinks we're wights!"

I almost laughed out loud. "We aren't wights. We're *peculiar*!"

"You aren't the first blank-eyes to come here pigeon-hunting," she said, "nor the first to try impersonating peculiar children. And you wouldn't be the first I've killed, neither! Now put your weapons on the floor before I snap this pigeon's neck—and then yours!"

"But we aren't wights!" I insisted. "Look at our pupils if you don't believe us!"

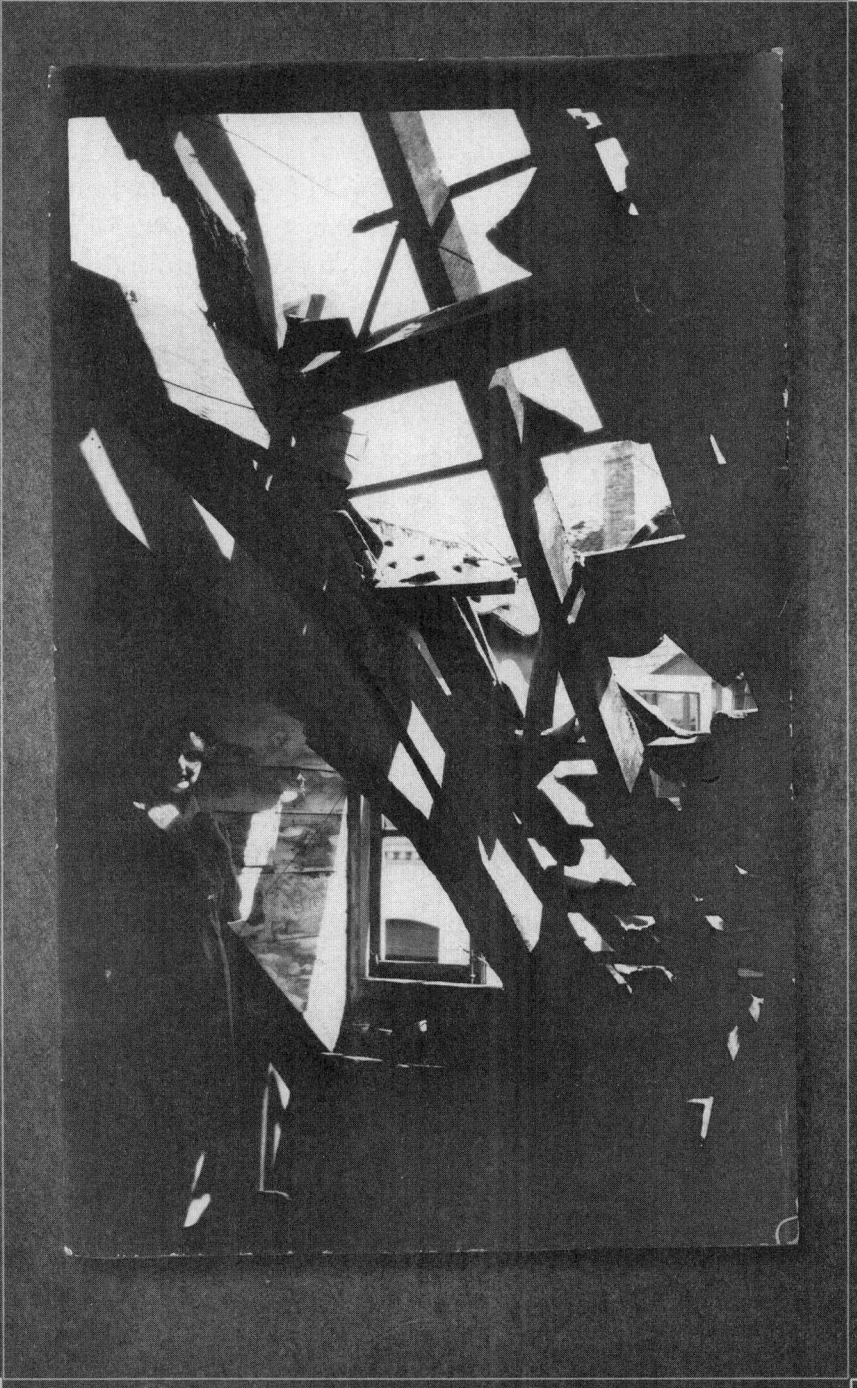

"Your eyes don't mean *nothing*!" the girl said. "False lenses are the oldest trick in the book—and trust me, I know 'em all."

The girl took a step toward us, into the light. Hate smoldered in her eyes. She was tomboyish, except for the dress, with short hair and a muscular jaw. She had the glassy look of someone who hadn't slept in days; who was running now on instinct and adrenaline. Someone in that condition wouldn't be kind to us, nor patient.

"We *are* peculiar, I swear!" Emma said. "Watch—I'll show you!" She lifted one hand from her head and was about to make a flame when a sudden intuition made me grab her wrist.

"If there are hollows close by, they'll sense it," I said. "I think they can feel us kind of like I feel them—but it's much easier for them when we use our powers. It's like setting off an alarm."

"But you're using *your* power," she said, irritated. "And she's using hers!"

"Mine is passive," I said. "I can't turn it off, so it doesn't leave much of a trail. As for her—maybe they already know she's here. Maybe it's not her they want."

"How convenient!" the girl said to me. "And that's supposed to be your power? Sensing shadow creatures?"

"He can see them, too," said Emma. "And kill them."

"You need to invent better lies," the girl said. "No one with half a brain would buy that."

Just as we were talking about it, a new Feeling blossomed painfully inside me. I was no longer sensing the left-behind residue of a hollow, but the active presence of one.

"There's one nearby," I said to Emma. "We need to get out of here."

"Not without the bird," she muttered.

The girl started across the room toward us. "Time to get on with it," she said. "I've given you more than enough chances to prove yourselves. Anyway, I'm beginning to *enjoy* killing you things. After what you did to my friends, I just can't seem to get enough of it!"

She stopped a few feet from us and raised her free hand—about to bring what was left of the roof down on our heads, maybe. If we were going to make a move, it had to be now.

I sprang from my crouched position, threw my arms in front of me, and collided with the girl, knocking her to the floor. She cried out in angry surprise. I rammed my fist into the palm of her free hand so she couldn't snap her fingers again. She let the bird go, and Emma grabbed it.

Then Emma and I were up, rushing toward the open door. Horace was still on the floor in a daze. "Get up and run!" Emma shouted at him.

I was pulling Horace up by his arms when the door slammed in my face and a burned dresser lifted out of the corner and flew across the room. The edge of it connected with my head and I went sprawling, taking Emma down with me.

The girl was in a rage, screaming. I was certain we had only seconds to live. Then Horace stood up and shouted at the top of his lungs:

"*Melina Manon!*"

The girl froze. "What did you say?"

"Your name is Melina Manon," he said. "You were born in Luxembourg in 1899. You came to live with Miss Thrush when you were sixteen years old, and have been here ever since."

Horace had caught her off guard. She frowned, then made an arcing motion with her hand. The dresser that had nearly knocked me unconscious sailed through the air and then stopped, hovering, directly above Horace. If she let it drop, it would crush him. "You've done your homework," said the girl, "but any wight could know my name and birthplace. Unfortunately for you, I no longer find your deceptions interesting."

And yet, she didn't quite seem ready to kill him.

"Your father was a bank clerk," Horace said, speaking quickly. "Your mother was very beautiful but smelled strongly of onions, a lifelong condition she could do nothing to cure."

The dresser wobbled above Horace. The girl stared at him, her brows knit together, hand in the air.

"When you were seven, you badly wanted an Arabian horse," Horace continued. "Your parents couldn't afford such an extravagant animal, so they bought a donkey instead. You named him Habib, which means *beloved*. And loved him you did."

The girl's mouth fell open.

Horace went on.

"You were thirteen when you realized you could manipulate objects using only your mind. You started with small things, paper clips and coins, then larger and larger ones. But you could never pick up Habib with your mind, because your ability did not extend to living creatures. When your family moved houses, you thought it had gone away entirely, because you couldn't move anything at all anymore. But it was simply that you hadn't gotten to know the new house yet. Once you became familiar with it, mapped it in your mind, you could move objects within its walls."

"How could you possibly know all this?" Melina said, gaping at him.

"Because I dreamed about you," said Horace. "That's what *I* can do."

"My God," said the girl, "you *are* peculiar."

And the dresser drifted gently to the floor.

*   *   *

I wobbled to my feet, head throbbing where the dresser had hit me.

"You're bleeding!" Emma said, jumping up to inspect my cut.

"I'm fine, I'm fine," I said, dodging her. The Feeling was shifting inside me, and being touched while it was happening made it harder to interpret; interrupted its development somehow.

"Sorry about your head," Melina Manon said. "I thought I was the only peculiar left!"

"There's a whole gang of us down your well, in the catacomb tunnel," Emma said.

"Really?" Melina's face lit up. "Then there's still hope!"

"There was," said Horace. "But it just flew out the hole in your roof."

"What—you mean Winnifred?" Melina put two fingers in her mouth and whistled. A moment later, the pigeon appeared, flying down through the hole to land on her shoulder.

"Marvelous!" said Horace, clapping his hands. "How'd you do that?"

"Winnie's my chum," Melina said. "Tame as a house cat."

I wiped some blood from my forehead with the back of my hand, then chose to ignore the pain. There wasn't time to be hurt. I said to the girl, "You mentioned that wights have been here, chasing pigeons."

Melina nodded. "Them and their shadow beasts came three nights ago. Surrounded the place, took Miss Thrush and half our wards here, then set fire to the house. I hid on the roof. Since then, wights have come back every day, in little groups, hunting for Winnifred and her friends."

"And you killed them?" Emma asked.

Melina looked down. "That's what I said, ain't it?"

She was too proud to admit she'd lied. It didn't matter.

"Then we're not the only ones hunting for Miss Wren," Emma said.

"That means she's still free," I said.

"Maybe," said Emma. "Maybe."

"We think the pigeon can help us," I said. "We need to find Miss Wren, and we think the bird knows how."

"I never heard of any Miss Wren," said Melina. "I just feed Winnie when she comes into our courtyard. We're friends, she and I. Ain't we, Winnie?"

The bird chirped happily on her shoulder.

Emma moved close to Melina and addressed the pigeon. "Do you know Miss Wren?" she said, enunciating loudly. "Can you help us find her? *Miss Wren?*"

The pigeon leapt off Melina's shoulder and flapped across the room to the door. She warbled and fluttered her wings, then flew back.

This way, it seemed to say.

That was proof enough for me. "We need to take the bird with us," I said.

"Not without me," said Melina. "If Winnie knows how to find this ymbryne, then I'm coming, too."

"Not a good idea," said Horace. "We're on a dangerous mission, you see—"

Emma cut him off. "Give us the bird. We'll come back for you, I promise."

A sudden jolt of pain made me gasp and double over.

Emma rushed to my side. "Jacob! Are you all right?"

I couldn't speak. Instead I hobbled to the window, forced myself upright, and projected my Feeling out toward the cathedral dome, visible over the rooftops just a few blocks away—then down at the street, where horse-drawn wagons rattled past.

Yes, there. I could feel them approaching from a side street, not far away.

Them. Not one hollow, but two.

"We have to go," I said. "*Now.*"

"Please," Horace begged the girl. "We *must* have the pigeon!"

Melina snapped her fingers, and the dresser that had nearly killed me raised up off the floor again. "I can't allow that," she said, narrowing her eyes and flicking them toward the dresser just to make sure we understood one another. "But take me along and you get Winnie in the bargain. Otherwise . . ."

The dresser pirouetted on one wooden leg, then tipped and crashed onto its side.

"Fine then," Emma said through her teeth. "But if you slow us down, we take the bird and leave you behind."

Melina grinned, and with a flick of her hand the door banged open.

"Whatever you say."

*　　*　　*

We flew down the stairs so fast that our feet hardly seemed to touch the ground. In twenty seconds we were back in the courtyard, leaping over dead Mr. Crumbley, diving down the dry well. I went first, kicking in the mirrored door at the bottom rather than wasting time sliding it open. It broke from its hinges and fell in pieces. "Look out below!" I called, then lost my grip on the wet stone steps and fell flailing and tumbling into the dark.

A pair of strong arms caught me—Bronwyn's—and set my feet on the floor. I thanked her, my heart pounding.

"What happened up there?" asked Bronwyn. "Did you catch the pigeon?"

"We got it," I said as Emma and Horace reached the bottom, and a cheer went up among our friends. "That's Melina," I said, pointing up at her, and that was all the time for introductions we had. Melina was still at the top of the steps, fooling with something. "Come on!" I shouted. "What are you doing?"

"Buying us time!" she shouted back, and then she pulled shut and locked a wooden lid that capped the well, closing out the last rays of light. As she climbed down in darkness, I explained about the hollows that were chasing us. In my panicked state, this came out as "*GO NOW RUN HOLLOWS NOW*," which was effective if not terribly articulate, and threw everyone into hysterics.

"How can we run if we can't see?!" Enoch shouted. "Light a flame, Emma!"

She'd been holding off because of my warning back in the attic.

Now seemed like a good time to reinforce that, so I grabbed her arm and said, "Don't! They'll be able to pinpoint us too easily!" Our best hope, I thought, was to lose them in this forking maze of tunnels.

"But we can't just run blindly in the dark!" said Emma.

"Of course," said the younger echolocator.

"We can," said the older.

Melina stumbled toward their voices. "Boys! You're alive! It's me—it's Melina!"

Joel-and-Peter said:

"We thought you were—"

"Dead every last—"

"One of you."

"Everyone link hands!" Melina said. "Let the boys lead the way!"

So I took Melina's hand in the dark and Emma took mine, then she felt for Bronwyn's, and so on until we'd formed a human chain with the blind brothers in the lead. Then Emma gave the word and the boys took off at an easy run, plunging us into the black.

We forked left. Splashed through puddles of standing water. Then from the tunnel behind us came an echoing crash that could only have meant one thing: the hollows had smashed through the well door.

"They're in!" I shouted.

I could almost feel them narrowing their bodies, wriggling down into the shaft. Once they made it to level ground and could run, they'd overtake us in no time. We'd only passed one split in the tunnels—not enough to lose them. Not nearly enough.

Which is why what Millard said next struck me as patently insane: "Stop! Everyone stop!"

The blind boys listened to him. We piled up behind them, tripping and skidding to a halt.

"What the hell is wrong with you?!" I shouted. *"Run!"*

"So sorry," Millard said, "but this just occurred to me—one of us will have to pass through the loop exit before the echolocators or the girl do, or they will cross into the present and we into 1940, and we'll be separated. For them to travel to 1940 with us, one of *us* has to go first and open the way."

"You didn't come from the present?" Melina said, confused.

"From 1940, like he said," Emma replied. "It's raining bombs out there, though. You might want to stay behind."

"Nice try," said Melina, "you ain't getting rid of me that easy. It's got to be worse in the present—wights everywhere! That's why I never left Miss Thrush's loop."

Emma stepped forward and pulled me with her. "Fine! We'll go first!"

I stuck out my free arm, feeling blindly in the dark. "But I can't see a thing!"

The elder echolocator said, "It's just twenty paces ahead there, you—"

"Can't miss it," said the younger.

So we plodded ahead, waving our hands in front of us. I kicked something with my foot and stumbled. My left shoulder scraped the wall.

"Keep it straight!" Emma said, pulling me to the right.

My stomach lurched. I could feel it: the hollows had made it down the well shaft. Now, even if they couldn't sense us, there was a fifty-fifty chance they'd choose the right spur of the tunnel and find us anyway.

The time for sneaking around was over. We had to run.

"Screw it," I said. "Emma, give me a light!"

"Gladly!" She let my hand go and made a flame so large I felt the hair on the right side of my head singe.

I saw the transition point right away. It was just ahead of us, marked by a vertical line painted on the tunnel wall. We took off running for it in a mob.

The moment we passed it, I felt a pressure in my ears. We were back in 1940.

We bolted through the catacombs, Emma's fire casting manic shadows across the walls, the blind boys clicking loudly with their tongues and shouting out "Left!" or "Right!" when we came to splits in the tunnel.

We passed the stack of coffins, the landslide of bones. Finally we returned to the dead end and the ladder to the crypt. I shoved Horace up ahead of me, then Enoch, and then Olive took off her shoes and floated up.

"We're taking too long!" I shouted.

Down the passage I could feel them coming. Could hear their tongues pounding the stone floor, propelling them forward. Could picture their jaws beginning to drip black goo in anticipation of a kill.

Then I saw them. A blur of dark motion in the distance.

I screamed, "Go!" and leapt onto the ladder, the last one to climb it. When I was near the top, Bronwyn reached down her arm and yanked me up the last few rungs, and then I was in the crypt with everyone else.

Groaning loudly, Bronwyn picked up the stone slab that topped Christopher Wren's tomb and dropped it back in place. Not two seconds later, something slammed violently against the underside of it, making the heavy slab leap. It wouldn't hold the hollows for long—not two of them.

They were so close. Alarms blared inside me, my stomach aching like I'd drunk acid. We dashed up the spiral staircase and into the nave. The cathedral was dark now, the only illumination a weird orange glow eking through the stained-glass windows. I thought for a moment it was the last strains of sunset, but then, as we dashed toward the exit, I caught a glimpse of the sky through the broken roof.

Night had fallen. The bombs were falling still, thudding like an irregular heartbeat.

We ran outside.

CHAPTER TEN

*F*rom where we stood, arrested in awe on the cathedral steps, it looked as if the whole city had caught fire. The sky was a panorama of orange flame bright enough to read by. The square where we'd chased pigeons was a smoking hole in the cobblestones. The sirens droned on, a soprano counterpoint to the bombs' relentless bass, their pitch so eerily human it sounded like every soul in London had taken to their rooftops to cry out collective despair. Then awe gave way to fear and the urgency of self-preservation, and we rushed down the debris-strewn steps into the street—past the ruined square, around a double-decker bus that looked like it had been crushed in the fist of an angry giant—running I knew not where, nor cared, so long as it was away from the Feeling that grew stronger and sicker inside me with each passing moment.

I looked back at the telekinetic girl, pulling the blind brothers along by their hands while they clicked with their tongues. I thought of telling her to let the pigeon go so we could follow it—but what use would it be to find Miss Wren now, while hollows were chasing us? We'd reach her only to be slaughtered at her doorstep, and we'd put her life in danger, too. No, we had to lose the hollows first. Or better yet, kill them.

A man in a metal hat stuck his head out of a doorway and shouted, "You are advised to take cover!" then ducked back inside.

Sure, I thought, *but where?* Maybe we could hide in the debris and the chaos around us, and with so much noise and distraction everywhere, the hollows would pass us by. But we were still too close to them, our trail too fresh. I warned my friends not to use their abilities, no matter what, and Emma and I led them zigzagging through the streets, hoping this would make us harder to track.

Still, I could feel them coming. They were out in the open now, out of the cathedral, lurching after us, invisible to all but me. I wondered if even I would be able to see them here, in the dark: shadow creatures in a shadow city.

We ran until my lungs burned. Until Olive couldn't keep up anymore and Bronwyn had to scoop her into her arms. Down long blocks of blacked-out windows staring like lidless eyes. Past a bombed library snowing ash and burning papers. Through a bombed cemetery, long-forgotten Londoners unearthed and flung into trees, grinning in rotted formal wear. A curlicued swing set in a cratered playground. The horrors piled up, incomprehensible, the bombers now and then dropping flares to light it all with the pure, shining white of a thousand camera flashes. As if to say: *Look. Look what we made.*

Nightmares come to life, all of it. Like the hollows themselves. *Don't look don't look don't look . . .*

I envied the blind brothers, navigating a mercifully detail-free topography; the world in wireframe. I wondered, briefly, what their dreams looked like—or if they dreamt at all.

Emma jogged alongside me, her wavy, powder-coated hair flowing behind her. "Everyone's knackered," she said. "We can't keep going like this!"

She was right. Even the fittest of us were flagging now, and soon the hollows would catch up to us and we'd have to face them in the middle of the street. And that would be a bloodbath. We had to find cover.

I steered us toward a row of houses. Because bomber pilots were more likely to target a cheerfully lit house than another smudge in the dark, every house was blacked out—every porch light dark, every window opaque. An empty house would be safest for us, but blacked out like this, there was no way to tell which houses were occupied and which weren't. We'd have to pick one at random.

I stopped us in the road.

"What are you doing?" Emma said, puffing to catch her breath. "Are you mad?"

"Maybe," I said, and then I grabbed Horace, swept my hand toward the row of houses, and said, "Choose."

"What?" he said. "Why me?"

"Because I trust your random guesses more than my own."

"But I never dreamed about this!" he protested.

"Maybe you did and don't remember," I said. "*Choose.*"

Realizing there was no way out of it, he swallowed hard, closed his eyes for a second, then turned and pointed to a house behind us. "That one."

"Why that one?" I asked.

"Because you made me choose!" Horace said angrily.

That would have to do.

*   *   *

The front door was locked. No problem: Bronwyn wrenched off the knob and tossed it into the street, and the door creaked open on its own. We filed into a dark hallway lined with family photos, the faces impossible to make out. Bronwyn closed the door and blocked it with a table she found in the hall.

"Who's there?" came a voice from further inside the house.

Damn. We weren't alone. "You were supposed to pick an *empty* house," I said to Horace.

"I'm going to hit you very hard," Horace muttered.

There was no time to switch houses. We'd have to introduce ourselves to whoever was here and hope they were friendly.

"*Who is there!*" the voice demanded.

"We aren't thieves or Germans or anything like that!" Emma said. "Just here to take cover!"

No response.

"Stay here," Emma told the others, and then she pulled me after her down the hall. "We're coming to say hello!" she called out, loud and friendly. "Don't shoot us, please!"

We walked to the end of the hall and rounded a corner, and there, standing in a doorway, was a girl. She held a wicked-down lantern in one hand and a letter opener in the other, and her hard, black eyes flicked nervously between Emma and me. "There's nothing of value here!" she said. "This house has been looted already."

"I told you, we're not thieves!" Emma said, offended.

"And I told you to leave. If you don't, I'll scream and . . . and my father will come running with his . . . guns and things!"

The girl looked at once childish and prematurely adult. She had her hair in a short bob and wore a little girl's dress with big white buttons trailing down the front, but something in her stony expression made her seem older, world-weary at twelve or thirteen.

"Please don't scream," I said, thinking not about her probably fictitious father but about what other things might come running.

Then a small voice piped up behind her, through the doorway she'd been conspicuously blocking. "Who's there, Sam?"

The girl's face pinched in frustration. "Only some children," she said. "I asked you to keep quiet, Esme."

"Are they nice? I want to meet them!"

"They were just leaving."

"There are lots of us and two of you," Emma said matter-of-factly. "We're staying here for a bit, and that's that. You're not going to scream, either, and we're not going to steal anything."

The girl's eyes flashed with anger, then dulled. She knew she'd lost. "All right," she said, "but try anything and I'll scream *and* bury this in your belly." She brandished the letter opener weakly, then lowered it to her waist.

"Fair enough," I said.

"Sam?" said the little voice. "What's happening now?"

The girl—Sam—stepped reluctantly aside, revealing a bathroom that danced with the flickering light of candles. There was a sink and a toilet and a bathtub, and in the bathtub a little girl of perhaps five. She peeped curiously at us over the rim. "This is my sister, Esme," Sam said.

"Hullo!" said Esme, waggling a rubber duck at us. "Bombs can't get you when you're in the bath, did you know that?"

"I didn't," Emma replied.

"It's her safe place," Sam whispered. "We spend every raid in here."

"Wouldn't you be safer in a shelter?" I said.

"Those are awful places," Sam said.

The others had tired of waiting and began coming down the hall. Bronwyn leaned through the doorway and waved hello.

"Come in!" Esme said, delighted.

"You're too trusting," Sam scolded her. "One day you're going to meet a bad person and then you'll be sorry."

"They aren't bad," said Esme.

"You can't tell just by *looking*."

Then Hugh and Horace pressed their faces through the doorway, curious to see whom we'd met, and Olive scooted between their legs and sat in the middle of the floor, and pretty soon all of us were squeezed into the bathroom together, even Melina and the blind brothers, who stood creepily facing the corner. Seeing so many people, Sam's legs shook and she sat down heavily on the toilet, overwhelmed—but her sister was thrilled, asking everyone's name as they came in.

"Where are your parents?" Bronwyn asked.

"Father's shooting bad people in the war," Esme said proudly. She mimed holding a rifle and shouted, *"Bang!"*

Emma looked at Sam. "You said your father was upstairs," she said flatly.

"You broke into our house," Sam replied.

"True."

"And your mother?" said Bronwyn. "Where is she?"

"A long time dead," Sam said with no apparent feeling. "So when Father went to war they tried shipping us off to family elsewhere—and because Father's sister in Devon is terribly mean and would only take one of us, they tried shipping Esme and me off to different places. But we jumped off the train and came back."

"We won't be split up," Esme declared. "We're *sisters*."

"And you're afraid if you go to a shelter they'll find you?" Emma said. "Send you away?"

Sam nodded. "I won't let that happen."

"It's safe in the tub," said Esme. "Maybe you should get in, too. That way we'd all be safe."

Bronwyn touched her hand to her heart. "Thank you, love, but we'd never fit!"

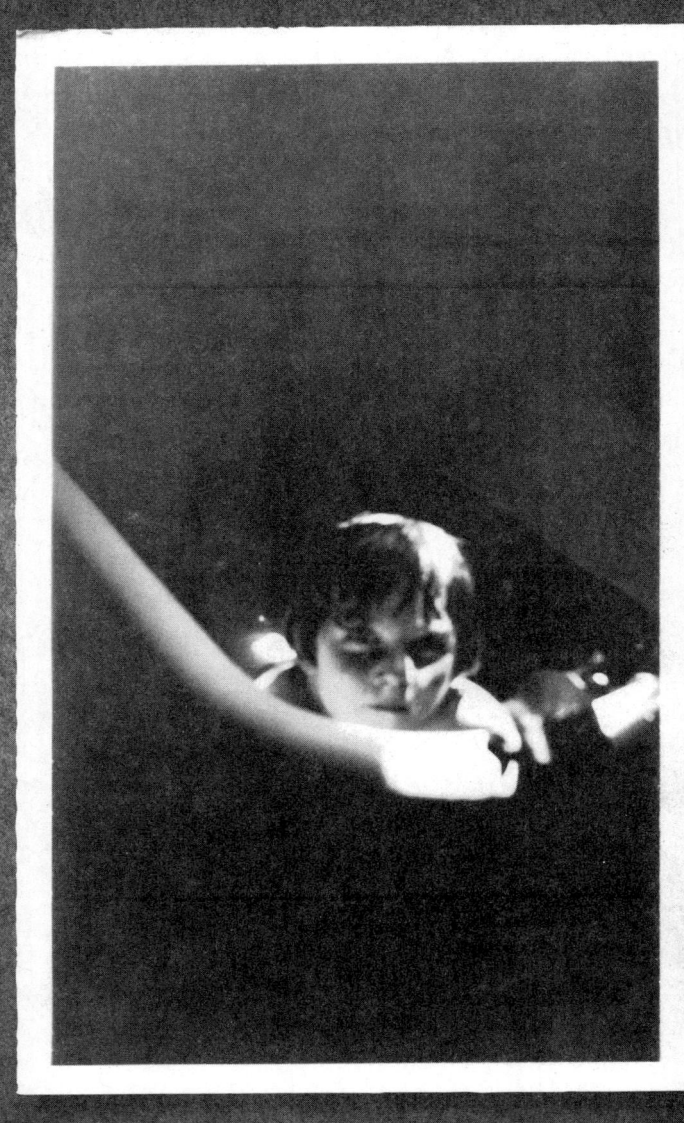

While the others talked, I turned my focus inward, trying to sense the hollows. They weren't running anymore. The Feeling had stabilized, which meant they weren't getting closer or farther away, but were probably sniffing around nearby. I took this as a good sign; if they knew where we were, they'd be coming straight for us. Our trail had gone cold. All we had to do was keep our heads down for a while, and then we could follow the pigeon to Miss Wren.

We huddled on the bathroom floor listening to bombs fall in other parts of the city. Emma found some rubbing alcohol in the medicine cabinet and insisted on cleaning and bandaging the cut on my head. Then Sam began to hum some tune I knew but couldn't quite name, and Esme played with her duck in the tub, and ever so slowly, the Feeling began to diminish. For a scant few minutes, that twinkling bathroom became a world unto itself; a cocoon far away from trouble and war.

But the war outside refused to be ignored for long. Anti-aircraft guns rattled. Shrapnel skittered like claws across the roof. The bombs drew closer until their reports were followed by lower, more ominous sounds—the dull thud of walls collapsing. Olive hugged herself. Horace put his fingers in his ears. The blind boys moaned and rocked on their feet. Miss Peregrine wriggled deep into the folds of Bronwyn's coat and the pigeon trembled in Melina's lap.

"What sort of madness have you led us into?" Melina said.

"I warned you," Emma replied.

The water in Esme's tub rippled with each blast. The little girl clutched her rubber duck and began to cry. Her sobs filled the little room. Sam hummed louder, pausing to whisper, "You're safe, Esme, you're safe in here," between melody lines, but Esme only cried harder. Horace took his fingers out of his ears and tried to distract Esme by making shadow animals on the wall—a crocodile snapping its jaws, a bird flying—but she hardly noticed. Then, the last person I'd expect to care about making a little girl feel better scooted over to the tub.

"Look here," Enoch said, "I have a little man who'd like to ride on your duck, and he'd just about fit, too." From his pocket he took a clay homunculus figure, three inches tall, the last of those he'd made on Cairnholm. Esme's sobs abated as she watched him bend the clay man's legs and sit him on the edge of the tub. Then, with a press of Enoch's thumb against the clay man's tiny chest, he came to life. Esme's face glowed with delight as the clay man sprang to his feet and strolled along the lip of the tub.

"Go on," said Enoch. "Show her what you can do."

The clay man jumped up and clicked his heels, then took an exaggerated bow. Esme laughed and clapped her hands, and when a bomb fell close by a moment later, causing the clay man to lose his balance and fall into the tub, she only laughed harder.

A sudden chill rolled up the back of my neck and prickled my scalp, and then the Feeling came over me so swiftly and sharply that I groaned and doubled over where I sat. The others saw me and knew instantly what it meant.

They were coming. They were coming very quickly.

Of course they were: Enoch had used his power, and I hadn't even thought to stop him. We might as well have sent up a signal flare.

I staggered to my feet, the pain attacking me in debilitating waves. I tried to shout—*Go, run! Run out the back!*—but couldn't force the words. Emma put her hands on my shoulders. "Collect yourself, love, we need you!"

Then something was beating at the front door, each impact echoing through the house. "They're here!" I finally managed to say, but the sound of the door shaking on its hinges had said it for me.

Everyone scrambled to their feet and squeezed into the hall in a panicked knot. Only Sam and Esme stayed put, baffled and cowering. Emma and I had to pry Bronwyn away from the tub. "We can't just *leave* them!" she cried as we dragged her toward the door.

"Yes, we can!" said Emma. "They'll be all right—they aren't

the ones the hollows are after!"

I knew that was true, but I also knew the hollows would tear apart anything in their path, including a couple of normal girls.

Bronwyn struck the wall in anger, leaving a fist-shaped hole. "I'm sorry," she said to the girls, then let Emma push her into the hall.

I hobbled after them, my stomach writhing. "Lock this door and don't open it for anyone!" I shouted, then looked back to catch a last glimpse of Sam's face, framed in the closing door, her eyes big and scared.

I heard a window smash in the front hall. Some suicidal curiosity made me peek around the corner. Squirming through the blackout curtains was a mass of tentacles.

Then Emma took my arm and yanked me away—down another hall—into a kitchen—out the back door—into an ash-dusted garden—down an alley where the others were running in a loose group. Then someone said "Look, look!" and, still running, I swiveled to see a great white bird fluttering high above the street. Enoch said, "Mine—it's a mine!" and what had seemed like gossamer wings resolved suddenly and clearly into a parachute, the fat silver body hanging below it packed with explosives; an angel of death floating serenely toward earth.

The hollows burst outside. I could see them distantly, loping through the garden, tongues waving in the air.

The mine landed by the house with a gentle *clink.*

"*Get down!*" I screamed.

We never had a chance to run for cover. I'd only just hit the ground when there was a blinding flash and a sound like the earth ripping open and a shock wave of searing hot wind that knocked the air from my lungs. Then a black hail of debris whipped hard against my back and I hugged my knees to my chest, making myself as compact as I could.

After that, there was only wind and sirens and a ringing in my ears. I gasped for air and choked on the swirling dust. Pulling the collar of my sweater up over my nose and mouth to filter it, I slowly caught my breath.

I counted my limbs: two arms, two legs.

Good.

I sat up slowly and looked around. I couldn't see much through the dust, but I heard my friends calling out for one another. There was Horace's voice, and Bronwyn's. Hugh's. Millard's.

Where was Emma?

I shouted her name. Tried to get up and fell back again. My legs were intact but shaking; they wouldn't take my weight.

I shouted again. *"Emma!"*

"I'm here!"

My head snapped toward her voice. She materialized through the smoke.

"Jacob! Oh, God. Thank God."

Both of us were shaking. I put my arms around her, running my hands over her body to make sure she was all there.

"Are you all right?" I said.

"Yes. Are you?"

My ears hurt and my lungs ached and my back stung where I'd been pelted by debris, but the pain in my stomach was gone. The moment the blast went off, it was as if someone had flipped a switch inside me, and just like that, the Feeling had vanished.

The hollows had been vaporized.

"I'm okay," I said. "I'm okay."

Aside from scrapes and cuts, so were the rest of us. We staggered together in a cluster and compared injuries. All were minor. "It's some kind of miracle," Emma said, shaking her head in disbelief.

It seemed even more so when we realized that everywhere around us were nails and bits of concrete and knifelike splinters of wood, many of them driven inches into the ground by the blast.

Enoch wobbled to a car parked nearby, its windows smashed,

its frame so pocked with shrapnel that it looked like it had been sprayed by a machine gun. "We should be dead," he marveled, poking his finger into one of the holes. "Why aren't *we* full of holes?"

Hugh said, "Your shirt, mate," then went to Enoch and plucked a crumpled nail from the back of his grit-encrusted sweater.

"And yours," said Enoch, pulling a jagged spike of metal from Hugh's.

Then we all checked our sweaters. Embedded in each were long shards of glass and pieces of metal that should have passed right through our bodies—but hadn't. Our itchy, ill-fitting, peculiar sweaters weren't fireproof or waterproof, as the emu-raffe had guessed. They were *bulletproof*. And they had saved our lives.

"I never dreamed I'd owe my life to such an appalling article of clothing," said Horace, testing the sweater's wool between his fingers. "I wonder if I could make a tuxedo jacket out of it instead."

Then Melina appeared, pigeon on her shoulder, blind brothers at her side. With their sonarlike senses, the brothers had discovered a low wall of reinforced concrete—it had *sounded* hard—and pulled Melina behind it just as the bomb exploded. That left only the two normal girls unaccounted for. But as the dust settled and their house came into view—or what was left of it—any hope of finding them alive seemed to fade. The upper floor had collapsed, pancaking down onto the lower. What remained was a skeletal wreck of exposed beams and smoking rubble.

Bronwyn took off running toward it anyway, shouting the sisters' names. Numbly, I watched her go.

"We could've helped them and we didn't," Emma said miserably. "We left them to die."

"It wouldn't have made the least bit of difference," Millard said. "Their deaths had been written into history. Even if we'd saved their lives today, something else would've taken them tomorrow. Another bomb. A bus crash. They were of the past, and the past always mends itself, no matter how we interfere."

"Which is why you can't go back and kill baby Hitler to stop the war from happening," said Enoch. "History heals itself. Isn't that interesting?"

"No," Emma snapped, "and you're a heartless bastard for talking about killing babies at a time like this. Or ever."

"Baby *Hitler*," said Enoch. "And talking loop theory is better than going into pointless hysterics." He was looking at Bronwyn, who was climbing the rubble, digging in the wreckage, flinging debris this way and that.

She turned and waved her arms at us. "Over here!" she cried.

Enoch shook his head. "Someone please retrieve her. We've got an ymbryne to find."

"Over here!" Bronwyn shouted, louder this time. "I can hear one of them!"

Emma looked at me. "Wait. What did she say?"

And then we were all running to meet her.

*   *   *

We found the little girl beneath a slab of broken ceiling. It had fallen across the bathtub, which was wrecked but had not entirely collapsed. Cowering inside was Esme—wet, filthy, and traumatized—but alive. The tub had protected her, just like her sister promised it would.

Bronwyn lifted the slab enough for Emma to reach in and pull Esme out. She clung to Emma, trembling and weeping. "Where's my sister?" she said. "Where's Sam?"

"Hush, baby, hush," Emma said, rocking her back and forth. "We're going to get you to a hospital. Sam will be along later." That was a lie, of course, and I could see Emma's heart breaking as she told it. That we had survived and the little girl had also were two miracles in one night. To expect a third seemed greedy.

But then a third miracle did happen, or something like one: her sister answered.

"I'm here, Esme!" came a voice from above.

"*Sam!*" the little girl shouted, and we all looked up.

Sam was dangling from a wooden beam in the rafters. The beam was broken and hung down at a forty-five-degree angle. Sam was near the low end, but still too high for any of us to reach.

"Let go!" Emma said. "We'll catch you!"

"I can't!"

Then I looked more closely and saw why she couldn't, and I nearly fainted.

Sam's arms and legs were dangling free. She wasn't hanging *onto* the beam, but *from* it. She'd been impaled through the center of her body. And yet her eyes were open, and she was blinking alertly in our direction.

"I appear to be stuck," she said calmly.

I was sure Sam would die at any moment. She was in shock, so she felt no pain, but pretty soon the adrenaline pumping through her system would dissipate, and she'd fade, and be gone.

"Someone get my sister down!" Esme cried.

Bronwyn went after her. She climbed a crumbling staircase to the ruined ceiling, then reached out to grab onto the beam. She pulled and pulled, and with her great strength was able to angle the beam downward until the broken end was nearly touching the rubble below. This allowed Enoch and Hugh to reach Sam's dangling legs and, very gently, slide her forward until she came free with a soft *ploop!* and landed on her feet.

Sam regarded the hole in her chest dully. It was nearly six inches in diameter and perfectly round, like the beam she'd been impaled on, and yet it didn't seem to concern her much.

Esme broke away from Emma and ran to her sister. "Sam!" she cried, throwing her arms around the injured girl's waist. "Thank Heaven you're all right!"

"I don't think she is!" Olive said. "I don't think she is at all!"

But Sam worried only for Esme, not for herself. Once she'd hugged the stuffing out of her, Sam knelt down and held the little girl at arm's length, scanning for cuts and bruises. "Tell me where it hurts," she said.

"My ears are ringy. I scraped my knees. And I got some dirt in my eye . . ."

Then Esme began to tremble and cry, the shock of what had happened overcoming her again. Sam hugged her close, saying, "There, there . . ."

It made no sense that Sam's body was functioning in any capacity. Stranger still, her wound wasn't even bleeding, and there was no gore or little bits of entrails hanging out of it, like I knew to expect from horror movies. Instead, Sam looked like a paper doll that had been attacked with a giant hole-punch.

Though everyone was dying for an explanation, we had elected to give the girls a moment to themselves, and stared in amazement from a respectful distance.

Enoch, however, paid them no such courtesy. "Excuse me," he said, crowding into their personal space, "but could you please explain how it is that you're alive?"

"It's nothing serious," Sam said. "Although my dress may not survive."

"Nothing serious?!" said Enoch. "I can see clear through you!"

"It does smart a little," she admitted, "but it'll fill in in a day or so. Things like this always do."

Enoch laughed dementedly. *"Things like this?"*

"In the name of all that's peculiar," Millard said quietly. "You know what this means, don't you?"

"She's one of us," I said.

*　　*　　*

We had questions. Lots of questions. As Esme's tears began to fade, we worked up the courage to ask them.

Did Sam realize she was peculiar?

She knew she was different, she said, but had never heard the term *peculiar*.

Had she ever lived in a loop?

She had not ("A what?"), which meant she was just as old as she appeared to be. Twelve, she said.

Had no ymbryne ever come to find her?

"Someone came once," she answered. "There were others like me, but to join them I would've had to leave Esme behind."

"Esme can't . . . *do* anything?" I asked.

"I can count backward from one hundred in a duck voice," Esme volunteered through her sniffles, and then began to demonstrate, quacking: "One hundred, ninety-nine, ninety-eight . . ."

Before she could get any further, Esme was interrupted by a siren, this one high-pitched and moving fast in our direction. An ambulance careened into the alley and raced toward us, its headlights blacked out so that only pinpricks of light shone through. It skidded to a stop nearby, cut its siren, and a driver leapt out.

"Is anyone hurt?" the driver said, rushing over to us. He wore a rumpled gray uniform and a dented metal hat, and though he was full of energy, his face looked haggard, like he hadn't slept in days.

His eyes met the hole in Sam's chest, and he stopped dead in his tracks. "Cor blimey!"

Sam got to her feet. "It's nothing, really!" she said. "I'm fine!" And to demonstrate how fine she was, she passed her fist in and out of the hole a few times and did a jumping jack.

The medic fainted.

"Hm," said Hugh, nudging the fallen man with his foot.

"You'd think these chaps would be made of tougher stuff."

"Since he's clearly unfit for service, I say we borrow his ambulance," Enoch said. "There's no knowing where in the city that pigeon's leading us. If it's far, it could take us all night to reach Miss Wren on foot."

Horace, who'd been sitting on a chunk of wall, sprang to his feet. "That's a fine idea!" he said.

"It's a *reprehensible* idea!" Bronwyn said. "You can't steal an ambulance—injured persons need it!"

"*We're* injured persons," Horace whined. "*We* need it!"

"It's hardly the same thing!"

"Saint Bronwyn!" Enoch said sarcastically. "Are you so concerned with the well-being of normals that you'd risk Miss Peregrine's life to protect a few of theirs? A thousand of them aren't worth one of her! Or one of us, for that matter!"

Bronwyn gasped. "What a thing to say in front of . . ."

Sam stalked toward Enoch with a humorless look on her face. "Look here, boy," she said, "if you imply that my sister's life is worthless again, I will clobber you."

"Calm down, I wasn't referring to your sister. I only meant that . . ."

"I know exactly what you meant. And I'll clobber you if you say it again."

"I'm sorry if I've offended your delicate sensibilities," Enoch said, his voice rising in exasperation, "but you've never had an ymbryne and you've never lived in a loop, and so you couldn't possibly understand that this—right now—is not *real*, strictly speaking. It's the *past*. The life of every normal in this city has already been lived. Their fates are predetermined, no matter how many ambulances we steal! So it doesn't bloody *matter*, you see."

Looking a bit baffled, Sam said nothing, but continued to give Enoch the evil eye.

"Even so," said Bronwyn. "It's not right to make people suffer unnecessarily. We *can't* take the ambulance!"

"That's all well and good, but think of Miss Peregrine!" said Millard. "She can't have more than a day left."

Our group seemed evenly divided between stealing the ambulance or going on foot, so we put it to a vote. I myself was against taking it, but mostly because the roads were so pocked with bomb holes that I didn't know how we'd drive the thing.

Emma took the vote. "Who's for taking the ambulance?" she said.

A few hands shot up.

"And against?"

Suddenly there was a loud pop from the direction of the ambulance, and we all turned to see Miss Peregrine standing by as one of its rear tires hissed air. Miss Peregrine had voted with her beak—by stabbing it into the ambulance's tire. Now *no one* could use it—not us, not injured persons—and there was no point in arguing or delaying any further.

"Well, that simplifies things," said Millard. "We go on foot."

"Miss Peregrine!" Bronwyn cried. "How could you?"

Ignoring Bronwyn's indignation, Miss Peregrine hopped over to Melina, looked up at the pigeon on her shoulder, and screeched. The message was clear: *Let's go already!*

What could we do? Time was wasting.

"Come with us," Emma said to Sam. "If there's any justice in the world, we'll be somewhere safe before the night is through."

"I told you, I won't leave my sister behind," Sam replied. "You're going to one of those places she can't enter, aren't you?"

"I—I don't know," Emma stammered. "It's possible . . ."

"I don't care either way," Sam said coldly. "After what I just saw, I wouldn't so much as cross the road with you."

Emma drew back, going a bit pale. In a small voice she asked, "Why?"

"If even outcasts and downtrodden folk like yourselves can't muster a bit of compassion for others," she said, "then there's no hope for this world." And she turned away and carried Esme toward the ambulance.

Emma reacted as if she'd been slapped, her cheeks going red. She ran after Sam. "We don't all think the way Enoch does! And as for our ymbryne, I'm sure she didn't mean to do what she did!"

Sam spun to face her. "That was no accident! I'm glad my sister's not like all of you. Wish to God *I* wasn't."

She turned away again, and this time Emma didn't follow. With wounded eyes she watched Sam go, then slouched after the others. Somehow the olive branch she'd extended had turned into a snake and bitten her.

Bronwyn peeled off her sweater and set it down on the rubble. "Next time bombs start falling, have your sister wear this," she called to Sam. "It'll keep her safer than any bathtub."

Sam said nothing; didn't even look. She was bending over the ambulance driver, who was sitting up now and mumbling, "I had the queerest dream . . ."

"That was a stupid thing to do," Enoch said to Bronwyn. "Now *you* don't have a sweater."

"Shut your fat gob," Bronwyn replied. "If you'd ever done a nice thing for another person, you might understand."

"I *did* do something nice for another person," Enoch said, "and it nearly got us eaten by hollows!"

We mumbled goodbyes that went unreturned and slipped quietly into the shadows. Melina took the pigeon from her shoulder and tossed it skyward. It flew a short distance before a string she'd tied around its foot snapped taut and it hovered, caught in the air, like a dog straining at its lead. "Miss Wren's this way," Melina said, nodding in the direction the bird was pulling, and we followed the girl and her pigeon friend down the alley.

I was about to assume hollow-watch, my now-customary position near the head of the group, when something made me glance back at the sisters. I turned in time to see Sam lift Esme into the ambulance, then bend forward to plant a kiss on each of her scraped knees. I wondered what would happen to them. Later, Millard would tell me that the fact that none of them had ever heard of Sam—and someone with such a unique peculiarity would've been well known—meant she probably had not survived the war.

The whole episode had really gotten to Emma. I don't know why it was so important for her to prove to a stranger that we were good-hearted, when we knew ourselves to be—but the suggestion that we were anything less than angels walking the earth, that our natures were more complexly shaded, seemed to bother her. "They don't understand," she kept saying.

Then again, I thought, *maybe they do.*

CHAPTER ELEVEN

So it had come to this: everything depended on a pigeon. Whether we would end the night in the womblike safety of an ymbryne's care or half chewed in the churning black of a hollow's guts; whether Miss Peregrine would be saved or we'd wander lost through this hellscape until her clock ran out; whether I would live to see my home or my parents again—it all depended on one scrawny, peculiar pigeon.

I walked at the front of the group, feeling for hollows, but it was really the pigeon who led us, tugging on its leash like a bloodhound after a scent. We turned left when the bird flew left, and right when it jerked right, obedient as sheep even when it meant fumbling down streets cratered with ankle-breaking bomb holes or bristling with the bones of dismembered buildings, their jagged iron spear tips lurking dimly in the wavering fire glow, angled at our throats.

Coming down from the terrifying events of that evening, I'd reached a new low of exhaustion. My head tingled strangely. My feet dragged. The rumble of bombs had quieted and the sirens had finally wound down, and I wondered if all that apocalyptic noise had been keeping me awake. Now the smoky air was alive with subtler sounds: water gushing from broken mains, the whine of a trapped dog, hoarse voices moaning for help. Occasionally fellow travelers would materialize out of the dark, wraithlike figures escaped from some lower world, eyes shining with fear and suspicion, clutching random things in their arms—radios, looted silver, a gilt box, a funerary urn. Dead bearing the dead.

We came to a T in the road and stopped, the pigeon deliberating between left and right. The girl murmured encouragements: "Come on, Winnie. There's a good pigeon. Show us the way."

Enoch leaned in and whispered, "If you don't find Miss Wren, I will personally roast you on a spit."

The bird leapt into the air, urging left.

Melina glowered at Enoch. "You're an ass," she said.

"I get results," he replied.

Eventually we arrived at an underground station. The pigeon led us through its arched entry into a ticket lobby, and I was about to say *We're taking the subway—smart bird*, when I realized the lobby was deserted and the ticket booth shuttered. Though it didn't look like trains would be visiting this station anytime soon, we forged ahead regardless, through an unchained gate, along a hallway lined with peeling notices and chipped white tiles, to a deep staircase where we spiraled down and down into the city's humming, electric-lit belly.

At each landing, we had to step around sleeping people wrapped in blankets: lone sleepers at first, then groups lying like scattered matchsticks, and then, as we reached bottom, an unbroken human tide that swept across the underground platform—hundreds of people squeezed between a wall and the tracks, curled on the floor, sprawled on benches, sunk into folding chairs. Those who weren't sleeping rocked babies in their arms, read paperbacks, played cards, prayed. They weren't waiting for a train; no trains were coming. They were refugees from the bombs, and this was their shelter.

I tried sensing for hollows, but there were too many faces, too many shadows. Luck, if we had any left, would have to sustain us for a while.

Now what?

We needed directions from the pigeon, but it seemed briefly confused—like me, it was probably overwhelmed by the crowd—so we stood and waited, the breaths and snores and mumbles of the sleepers murmuring weirdly around us.

After a minute the pigeon stiffened and flew toward the tracks, then reached the end of its leash and bounced back into Melina's hand like a yo-yo.

We tiptoed around the bodies to the edge of the platform, then hopped down into the pit where the tracks ran. They disappeared into tunnels on either end of the station. I had a sinking feeling that our future lay somewhere inside one of these dark, gaping mouths.

"Oh, I hope we don't have to go mucking about in *there*," said Olive.

"Of course we do," Enoch said. "It isn't a proper holiday until we've plumbed every available sewer."

The pigeon bopped rightward. We started down the tracks.

I hopscotched around an oily puddle and a legion of rats scurried away from my feet, sending Olive into Bronwyn's arms with a shriek. The tunnel yawned before us, black and menacing. It occurred to me that this would be a very bad place to meet a hollowgast. Here there'd be no walls to climb, no houses to shelter in, no tomb lids to close behind us. It was long and straight and lit only by a few red bulbs, glinting feebly at scattered intervals.

I walked faster.

The darkness closed around us.

*   *   *

When I was a kid, I used to play hide-and-seek with my dad. I was always the hider and he the seeker. I was really good at it, primarily because I, unlike most kids of four or five, had the then-peculiar ability to be extremely quiet for long periods of time, and also because I suffered from absolutely no trace of anything resembling claustrophobia: I could wedge myself into the smallest rear-closet crawl space and stay there for twenty or thirty minutes, not making a sound, having the time of my life.

Which is why you'd think I wouldn't have a problem with the

whole dark, enclosed spaces thing. Or why, at the very least, you'd think a tunnel meant to contain trains and tracks and nothing else would be easier for me to handle than one that was essentially an open cemetery, with all manner of Halloweenish things spilling out along it. And yet, the farther into this tunnel we walked, the more I was overcome by clammy, creeping dread—a feeling entirely apart from the one I sensed hollows with; this was simply a *bad feeling*. And so I hurried us through as fast as the slowest of us could go, prodding Melina until she barked at me to back off, a steady drip of adrenaline keeping my deep exhaustion at bay.

After a long walk and several Y-shaped tunnel splits, the pigeon led us to a disused section of track where the ties had warped and rotted and pools of stagnant water spanned the floor. The pressure of trains passing in far-off tunnels pushed the air around like breaths in some great creature's gullet.

Then, way down ahead of us, a pinpoint of light winked into being, small but growing fast. Emma shouted, "Train!" and we split apart and pressed our backs to the walls. I covered my ears, expecting the deafening roar of a train engine at close range, but it never came—all I could hear was a small, high-pitched whine, which I was fairly certain was coming from inside my own head. Just as the light was filling the tunnel, its white glow surrounding us, I felt a sudden pressure in my ears and the light disappeared.

We stumbled away from the walls in a daze. Now the tracks and ties under our feet were new, as if they'd just been laid. The tunnel smelled somewhat less intensely of urine. The bulbs along it had gotten brighter, and instead of giving a steady light, they flickered—because they weren't electric bulbs at all, but gaslamps.

"What just happened?" I said.

"We crossed into a loop," said Emma. "But what was that light? I've never seen anything like that."

"Every loop entrance has its quirks," said Millard.

"Anyone know when we are?" I asked.

"I'd guess the latter half of the nineteenth century," said Millard. "Prior to 1863 there wasn't an underground system in London at all."

Then, from behind us, another light appeared—this one accompanied by a gust of hot wind and a thunderous roar. *"Train!"* Emma shouted again, and this time it really was. We threw ourselves against the walls as it shot past in a cyclone of noise and light and belching smoke. It looked less like a modern subway train than a miniature locomotive. It even had a caboose, where a man with a big black beard and a guttering lantern in his hand gaped at us in surprise as the train strafed away around the next bend.

Hugh's cap had blown off his head and been crushed. He went to pick it up, found it shredded, and threw it down again angrily. "I don't care for this loop," he said. "We've been here all of ten seconds and already it's trying to kill us. Let's do what we have to and get gone."

"I couldn't agree more," said Enoch.

The pigeon guided us on down the track. After ten minutes or so, it stopped, pulling toward what looked like a blank wall. We couldn't understand why, until I looked up and noticed a partially camouflaged door where the wall met the ceiling, twenty feet overhead. Because there seemed no other way to reach it, Olive took off her shoes and floated up to get a closer look. "There's a lock on it," she said. "A combination lock."

There was also a pigeon-sized hole rusted through the door's bottom corner, but that was no help to us—we needed the combination.

"Any idea what it could be?" Emma asked, putting the question out to everyone.

She was met with shrugs and blank looks.

"None," said Millard.

"We'll have to guess," she said.

"Perhaps it's my birthday," said Enoch. "Try three–twelve–

ninety-two."

"Why would anyone know your birthday?" said Hugh.

Enoch frowned. "Just try it."

Olive spun the dial back and forth, then tried the lock. "Sorry, Enoch."

"What about our loop day?" Horace suggested. "Nine–three–forty."

That didn't work, either.

"It's not going to be something easy to guess, like a date," said Millard. "That would defeat the purpose of having a lock."

Olive began to try random combinations. We stood by watching, growing more anxious with each failed attempt. Meanwhile, Miss Peregrine slipped quietly from Bronwyn's coat and hopped over to the pigeon, who was waddling around at the end of its lead, pecking at the ground. When it saw Miss Peregrine, it tried to hop away, but the headmistress followed, making a low, vaguely threatening warble in her throat.

The pigeon flapped its wings and flew up to Melina's shoulder, out of Miss Peregrine's reach. Miss Peregrine stood by Melina's feet, squawking at it. This seemed to make the pigeon extremely nervous.

"Miss P, what are you up to?" said Emma.

"I think she wants something from your bird," I said to Melina.

"If the pigeon knows the way," said Millard, "perhaps it knows the combination, too."

Miss Peregrine turned toward him and squawked, then looked back at the pigeon and squawked louder. The pigeon tried to hide behind Melina's neck.

"Perhaps the pigeon knows the combination but doesn't know how to tell us," said Bronwyn, "but it could tell Miss Peregrine, because both of them speak bird language, and then Miss Peregrine could tell us."

"Make your pigeon talk to our bird," said Enoch.

"Your bird's twice Winnie's size and sharp on three ends," Melina said, backing away a step. "She's scared and I don't blame her."

"There's nothing to be scared of," said Emma. "Miss P would never hurt another bird. It's against the ymbryne code."

Melina's eyes widened, then narrowed. "That bird is an *ymbryne*?"

"She's our headmistress!" said Bronwyn. "Alma LeFay Peregrine."

"Full of surprises, ain't you?" Melina said, then laughed in a way that wasn't exactly friendly. "If you've got an ymbryne right there, what d'you need to find another one for?"

"It's a long story," said Millard. "Suffice to say, our ymbryne needs help that only another ymbryne can give."

"Just put the blasted pigeon on the ground so Miss P can talk to it!" said Enoch.

Finally, reluctantly, Melina agreed. "Come on, Winnie, there's a good girl." She lifted the pigeon from her shoulder and placed it gently at her feet, then pinned its leash under her shoe so it couldn't fly away.

Everyone circled around to watch as Miss Peregrine advanced on the pigeon. It tried to run but was caught short by the leash. Miss Peregrine got right in its face, warbling and clucking. It was like watching an interrogation. The pigeon tucked its head under its wing and began to tremble.

Then Miss Peregrine pecked it on the head.

"Hey!" said Melina. "Stop that!"

The pigeon kept its head tucked and didn't respond, so Miss Peregrine pecked it again, harder.

"That's enough!" Melina said, and lifting her shoe from the leash, she reached down for the pigeon. Before she could get her fingers around it, though, Miss Peregrine severed the leash with a quick slash of her talons, clamped down with her beak on one of the pigeon's twiggy legs, and bounded away, the pigeon screeching and flailing.

Melina freaked out. "Come back here!" she shouted, furious, about to run after the birds when Bronwyn caught her by the arms.

"Wait!" said Bronwyn. "I'm sure Miss P knows what she's doing . . ."

Miss Peregrine stopped a little way down the track, well out of anyone's reach. The pigeon struggled in her beak, and Melina struggled against Bronwyn, both in vain. Miss Peregrine seemed to be waiting for the pigeon to tire out and give up, but then she got impatient and began swinging the pigeon around in the air by its leg.

"Please, Miss P!" Olive shouted. "You'll kill it!"

I was close to rushing over and breaking it up myself, but the birds were a blur of talons and beaks, and no one could get close enough to separate them. We yelled and begged Miss Peregrine to stop.

Finally, she did. The pigeon dropped from her mouth and wobbled on its feet, too stunned to flee. Miss Peregrine warbled at it the way she had earlier, and this time the pigeon chirped in response. Then Miss Peregrine tapped the ground with her beak three times, then ten times, then five.

Three–ten–five. Olive tried the combination. The lock popped open, the door swung inward, and a rope ladder unrolled down the wall to meet the floor.

Miss Peregrine's interrogation had worked. She'd done what she needed to do to help us all, and given that, we might've overlooked her behavior—if not for what happened next. She took the dazed pigeon by its leg again and, seemingly out of spite, flung it hard against the wall.

We reacted with a great collective gasp of horror. I was shocked beyond speaking.

Melina broke away from Bronwyn and ran to pick up the pigeon. It hung limply from her hand, its neck broken.

"Oh my bird, she's killed it!" cried Bronwyn.

"All we went through to catch that thing," said Hugh, "and now look."

"I'm going to stomp your ymbryne's head!" Melina shrieked, crazed with rage.

Bronwyn caught her arms again. "No, you're not! Stop it!"

"Your ymbryne's a savage! If that's how she conducts herself, we're better off with the wights!"

"You take that back!" shouted Hugh.

"I won't!" Melina said.

More harsh words were exchanged. A fistfight was narrowly avoided. Bronwyn held Melina, and Emma and I held Hugh, until the fight went out of them, if not the bitterness.

No one could quite believe what Miss Peregrine had done.

"What's the big fuss?" said Enoch. "It was just a stupid pigeon."

"No, it wasn't," said Emma, scolding Miss Peregrine directly. "That bird was a personal friend of Miss Wren's. It was hundreds of years old. It was written about in the *Tales*. And now it's dead."

"Murdered," said Melina, and she spat on the ground. "That's what it's called when you kill something for no reason."

Miss Peregrine nibbled casually at a mite under her wing, as if she hadn't heard any of this.

"Something wicked's gotten into her," said Olive. "This isn't like Miss Peregrine at all."

"She's changing," said Hugh. "Becoming more animal."

"I hope there's still something human left in her to rescue," Millard said darkly.

So did we all.

We climbed out of the tunnel, each of us lost in our own anxious thoughts.

*　　*　　*

Beyond the door was a passage that led to a flight of steps that led to another passage and another door, which opened onto a room filled with daylight and packed to the rafters with clothes: racks and closets and wardrobes stuffed with them. There were also two wooden privacy screens to change behind, some freestanding mirrors, and a worktable laid out with sewing machines and bolts of raw fabric. It was half boutique, half workshop—and a paradise to Horace, who practically cartwheeled inside, crying, "I'm in Heaven!"

Melina lurked sullenly at the rear, not speaking to anyone.

"What is this place?" I asked.

"It's a disguising room," Millard answered, "designed to help visiting peculiars blend in with this loop's normals." He pointed out a framed illustration demonstrating how clothes of the period were worn.

"When in Rome!" said Horace, bounding toward a rack of clothes.

Emma asked everyone to change. In addition to helping us blend in, new clothes might also throw off any wights who'd been tracking us. "But keep your sweaters on underneath, in case more trouble finds us."

Bronwyn and Olive took some plain-looking dresses behind a screen. I traded my ash-coated, sweat-stained pants and jacket for a mismatched but relatively clean suit. Instantly uncomfortable, I wondered how, for so many centuries, people wore such stiff, formal clothes all the time.

Millard put on a sharp-looking outfit and sat down in front of a mirror. "How do I look?" he said.

"Like an invisible boy wearing clothes," replied Horace.

Millard sighed, lingered in front of the mirror a bit longer, then stripped and disappeared again.

Horace's initial excitement had already waned. "The selection here is atrocious," he complained. "If the clothes aren't moth-eaten, they're patched with clashing fabric! I am *so* weary of looking like a street urchin."

"Street urchins blend," Emma said from behind her changing screen. "Little gents in top hats do not." She emerged wearing shiny red flats and a short-sleeved blue dress that fell just below the knee. "What do you think?" she said, twirling to make the dress billow.

She looked like Dorothy from *The Wizard of Oz*, only cuter. I didn't know how to tell her this in front of everybody, though, so instead I gave her an awkward grin and a thumbs-up.

She laughed. "Like it? Well, that's too bad," she said with a coy smile. "I'd stick out like a sore thumb." Then a pained expression crossed her face, as if she felt guilty for laughing—for having had even a moment of fun, given all that had happened to us and everything yet to be resolved—and she ducked behind the screen again.

I felt it, too: the dread, the weight of the horrors we'd seen, which replayed themselves in an endless, lurid loop in my mind. But you can't feel bad *every second*, I wanted to tell her. Laughing doesn't make bad things worse any more than crying makes them better. It doesn't mean you don't care, or that you've forgotten. It just means you're human. But I didn't know how to say this, either.

When she came out again, she had on a sacklike blouse with ripped sleeves and a broomstick skirt that brushed the top of her feet. (Much more urchin like.) She'd kept the red shoes, though. Emma could never resist a touch of glitter, however small.

"And this?" said Horace, waving a poofy orange wig he'd found. "How's this going to help anyone 'blend in with the normals'?"

"Because it seems we're going to a carnival," said Hugh, looking up at a poster on the wall that advertised one.

"Just a moment!" Horace said, joining Hugh beneath the poster. "I've heard of this place! It's an old tourist loop."

"What's a tourist loop?" I asked.

"Used to be you could find them all across peculiardom," Millard explained, "placed strategically at times and locations of historical import. They made up a sort of Grand Tour that was once considered an essential part of any well-bred peculiar's education. This was many years ago, of course, when it was still relatively safe to travel abroad. I didn't realize there were any left."

Then he got quiet, lost in memories of a better time.

When we'd all finished changing, we left our twentieth-century clothes in a heap and followed Emma through another door, out into an alleyway stacked with trash and empty crates. I recognized the sounds of a carnival in the distance: the arrhythmic wheeze of pipe organs, the dull roar of a crowd. Even through my nerves and exhaustion, I felt a jangle of excitement. Once, this was something peculiars had come from far and wide to see. My parents had never even taken me to Disney World.

Emma gave the usual instructions: "Stay together. Watch Jacob and me for signals. Don't talk to anyone, and look no one in the eye."

"How will we know where to go?" asked Olive.

"We'll have to think like ymbrynes," Emma said. "If you were Miss Wren, where would you be hiding?"

"Anywhere but London?" said Enoch.

"If only someone hadn't *murdered the pigeon*," Bronwyn said, staring bitterly at Miss Peregrine.

The headmistress stood on the cobblestones looking up at us, but no one wanted to touch her. We had to keep her out of sight, though, so Horace went back into the disguising room and fetched a denim sack. Miss Peregrine wasn't enthusiastic about this arrangement, but when it became clear that no one was going to pick her up—least of all Bronwyn, who seemed entirely disgusted with her— she climbed inside and let Horace knot the top closed with a strip of leather.

*　　*　　*

We followed the drunken sound of the carnival through a snarl of cramped lanes, where from wooden carts vendors hawked vegetables and dusty sacks of grain and freshly killed rabbits; where children and thin cats skulked and prowled with hungry eyes, and women with proud, dirty faces squatted in the gutter peeling potatoes, building little mountains with the tossed-away skins. Though we tried very hard to slink by unnoticed, every one of them seemed to turn and stare as we passed: the vendors, the children, the women, the cats, the dead, milk-eyed rabbits swinging by their legs.

Even in my new, period-appropriate clothes, I felt transparently out of place. Blending in was as much about performance as about costume, I realized, and my friends and I carried ourselves with none of the slump-shouldered, shifty-eyed attitude that these people did. In the future, if I wanted to disguise myself as effectively as the wights, I'd have to sharpen my acting skills.

The carnival grew louder as we went, and the smells stronger—overcooked meats, roasting nuts, horse manure, human manure, and the smoke from coal fires all mixing together into something so sickly sweet that it thickened the very air. Finally, we reached a wide square where the carnival was in full, rollicking swing, packed with masses of people and brightly colored tents and more activity than my eyes could take in at once. The whole scene was an assault on my senses. There were acrobats and ropedancers and knife-throwers and fire-eaters and street performers of every type. A quack doctor pitched patent medicines from the back of a wagon: "A rare cordial to fortify the innards against infective parasites, unwholesome damps, and malignant effluvia!" Competing for attention on an adjacent stage was a loudmouthed showman in coattails and a large, prehistoric-looking creature whose gray skin hung from its frame in cascading wrinkles. It took me ten full seconds, as we threaded the crowd past the stage, to recognize it as a bear. It had been shaved and tied to a chair and made to wear a woman's dress, and as its eyes bulged in its head, the showman grinned and pretended to serve it tea, shouting, "Ladies and gentlemen! Presenting the most beautiful lady in all of Wales!"—which earned him a big laugh from the crowd. I half hoped it would break its chains and eat him, right there in front of everyone.

To combat the dizzying effect of all this dreamlike madness, I reached into my pocket to palm the smooth glass of my phone, eyes closed for a moment, and whispered to myself, "I am a time traveler. This is real. I, Jacob Portman, am traveling in time."

This was astonishing enough. More astonishing, perhaps, was the fact that time travel hadn't broken my brain; that by some miracle, I had not yet devolved into a gibbering crazy person ranting on a street corner. The human psyche was much more flexible than I'd imagined, capable of expanding to contain all sorts of contradictions and seeming impossibilities. Lucky for me.

"Olive!" Bronwyn shouted. "Get away from there!" I looked up to see her yank Olive away from a clown who had bent down to talk to her. "I've told you time and again, *never* talk to normals!"

Our group was large enough that keeping it together could be a challenge, especially in a place like this, full of distractions tailor-made to fascinate children. Bronwyn acted as den mother, rounding us up every time one of us strayed to get a closer look at a stall of brightly colored pinwheels or steaming boiled candy. Olive was the most easily distractible, and often seemed to forget that we were in serious danger. It was only possible to keep so many kids in line because they were not actually kids—because there was some older nature inside them, warring against and balancing their childish impulses. With actual children, I'm sure it would've been hopeless.

For a while we wandered aimlessly, looking for anyone who resembled Miss Wren, or anywhere it seemed peculiars were likely to hide. But *everything* here seemed peculiar—this entire loop, with all its chaotic strangeness, was perfect camouflage for peculiars. And yet, even here, people noticed us, their heads turning subtly as we passed. I started to get paranoid. How many of the people around us were spies for the wights—or wights themselves? I was especially wary of the clown, the one Bronwyn had pulled Olive away from. He kept turning up. We must've passed him five times in as many minutes: loitering at the mouth of an alley, staring down from a window, watching us from a tented photo booth, his mussed hair and horrific makeup clashing bizarrely with a backdrop painting of bucolic countryside. He seemed to be everywhere at once.

"It's not good being out in the open like this," I said to Emma. "We can't just circle around forever. People are noticing us. *Clowns.*"

"Clowns?" she said. "Anyway, I agree with you—but it's difficult to know where to start in all this madness."

"We should start at what is always the most peculiar part of *any* carnival," said Enoch, butting between us. "The sideshow." He pointed at a tall, gaudy facade at the edge of the square. "Sideshows and peculiars go together like milk and cookies. Or hollows and wights."

"Usually they do," said Emma, "but the wights know that as well. I'm sure Miss Wren hasn't kept her freedom this long by hiding in such obvious places."

"Have you got a better idea?" said Enoch.

We didn't, and so we shifted direction toward the sideshow. I looked back for the leering clown, but he had melted into the crowd.

At the sideshow, a scruffy carnival barker was shouting through a megaphone, promising glimpses of "the most shocking errors of nature allowed on view by law" for a trivial fee. It was called the Congress of Human Oddities.

"Sounds like dinner parties I've attended," said Horace.

"Some of these 'oddities' might be peculiar," said Millard, "in which case they might know something about Miss Wren. I say it's worth the price of admission."

"We don't have the price of admission," said Horace, pulling a single, lint-flecked coin from his pocket.

"Since when have we ever paid to get into a sideshow?" said Enoch.

We followed Enoch around to the back of the sideshow, where its wall-like facade gave way to a big, flimsy tent. We were scouting for openings to slip through when a flap pulled back and a well-dressed man and woman burst out, the man holding the lady, the lady fanning herself.

"Move aside!" the man barked. "This woman needs air!"

A sign above the flap read: PERFORMERS ONLY.

We slipped inside and were immediately stopped. A plain-looking boy sat on a tufted stool near the entrance, apparently in some official capacity. "You performers?" he said. "Can't come in 'less you're performers."

Feigning offense, Emma said, "Of *course* we're performers," and to demonstrate, she made a tiny flame on the tip of her finger and stubbed it out in her eye.

The boy shrugged, unimpressed. "Go on, then."

We shuffled past him, blinking, our eyes adjusting slowly to the dark. The sideshow was a low-ceilinged maze of canvas—a single, dramatically torchlit aisle that took sharp turns every twenty or thirty feet, so that around each corner we were confronted by a new "abomination of nature." A trickle of spectators, some laughing, others pale and shaking, stumbled past us in the opposite direction.

The first few freaks were standard-issue sideshow fare, and not especially peculiar: an "illustrated" man covered in tattoos; a bearded lady stroking her long chin-whiskers and cackling; a human pincushion who pierced his face with needles and drove nails into his nostrils with a hammer. While I thought this was pretty impressive, my friends, some of whom had traveled Europe in a sideshow with Miss Peregrine, could hardly stifle their yawns.

Under a banner that read THE AMAZING MATCHSTICK MEN, a gentleman with hundreds of matchbooks glued to his suit body-slammed a man similarly clothed in matchsticks, causing flames to erupt across the matchstick man's chest as he flailed in fake terror.

"Amateurs," Emma muttered as she pulled us on to the next attraction.

The oddities got progressively odder. There was a girl in a long, fringed dress who wore a giant python around her body, which wriggled and danced at her command. Emma allowed that this was at least marginally peculiar, since the ability to enchant snakes was something only *syndrigasti* could do. But when Emma mentioned Miss Wren to the girl, she gave us a hard stare and her snake hissed and showed its fangs, and we moved on.

"This is a waste of time," said Enoch. "Miss Peregrine's clock is running out and we're touring a carnival! Why not get some sweets and make a day of it?"

There was only one more freak to see, though, so we continued on. The final stage was empty but for a plain backdrop, a small table with flowers on it, and an easel-propped sign that read: THE WORLD-FAMOUS FOLDING MAN.

A stagehand walked onto the stage lugging a suitcase. He set the case down and left.

A crowd gathered. The suitcase sat there, center stage. People began to shout, "On with the show!" and "Bring out the freak!"

The suitcase jiggled. Then it began to shake, wobbling back and forth until it toppled onto its side. The crowd pressed toward the stage, fixated on the case.

Its latches popped, and very slowly, the case began to open. A pair of white eyes peeped out at the crowd, and then the case opened a little more to reveal a face—that of an adult man, with a neatly trimmed mustache and little round glasses, who had somehow folded himself into a suitcase no larger than my torso.

The crowd burst into applause, which increased as the freak proceeded to unfold himself, limb by limb, and step out of the impossibly small case. He was very tall and as skinny as a beanpole—so alarmingly thin, in fact, that it looked as if his bones were about to break through his skin. He was a human exclamation point, but carried himself with such dignity that I couldn't laugh at him. He studied the hooting crowd dourly before taking a deep bow.

He then took a minute to demonstrate how his limbs could bend in all sorts of exotic ways—his knee twisting so that the top of his foot touched his hip, then his hips folding so that the knee touched his chest—and after more applause and more bows, the show was over.

We lingered as the crowd filtered away. The folding man was leaving the stage when Emma said to him, "You're peculiar, aren't you?"

The man stopped. He turned slowly to look at her with an air of imperious annoyance. "Excuse me?" he said in a thick Russian accent.

"Sorry to corner you this way, but we need to find Miss Wren," Emma said. "We know she's here someplace."

"Peh!" said the man, dismissing her with a noise halfway between laughing and hawking spit.

"It's an emergency!" Bronwyn pleaded.

The folding man crossed his arms in a bony X and said, "I dunno anything what you say," then walked off the stage.

"Now what?" asked Bronwyn.

"We keep looking," said Emma.

"And if we don't find Miss Wren?" said Enoch.

"We *keep looking*," Emma said through her teeth. "Everyone understand?"

Everyone understood perfectly well. We were out of options. If this didn't work—if Miss Wren wasn't here or we couldn't find her soon—then all our efforts would have been for nothing, and Miss Peregrine would be lost just the same as if we'd never come to London at all.

We walked out of the sideshow the way we'd come, dejected, past the now-empty stages, past the plain-looking boy, out of the tent and into the daylight. We were standing outside the exit, unsure what to do next, when the plain-looking boy leaned out through the flap. "Wotsa trouble?" he said. "Show weren't to your liking?"

"It was . . . fine," I said, waving him off.

"Not peculiar enough for you?" he asked.

That got our attention. "What'd you say?" said Emma.

"Wakeling and Rookery," he said, pointing past us toward the far side of the square. "That's where the *real* show is." And then he winked at us and ducked back inside the tent.

"That was mysterious," said Hugh.

"Did he say *peculiar*?" said Bronwyn.

"What's Wakeling and Rookery?" I said.

"A place," said Horace. "Someplace in this loop, maybe."

"Could be the intersection of two streets," said Emma, and she pulled back the tent flap to ask the boy if this was what he meant—but he was already gone.

So we set off through the crowd, toward the far end of the square where he'd pointed, our one last, thin hope pinned to a couple of oddly named streets we weren't even sure existed.

*　　*　　*

There was a point, a few blocks beyond the square, where the noise of the crowd faded and was replaced by an industrial clank and clamor, and the rich funk of roasting meat and animal waste was replaced by a stench far worse and unnameable. Crossing a walled river of Stygian sludge, we entered a district of factories and workhouses, of smokestacks belching black stuff into the sky, and this is where we found Wakeling Street. We walked one way down Wakeling looking for Rookery until it dead-ended at a large open sewer which Enoch said was the River Fleet, then turned and came back the other way. When we'd passed the point along Wakeling where we'd started, the street began to curve and twist, the factories and workhouses shrinking down into squat offices and unassuming buildings with blank faces and no signs, like a neighborhood purpose-built to be anonymous.

The bad feeling I'd been nursing got worse. What if we'd been set up—sent to this deserted part of the city to be ambushed out of view?

The street twisted and straightened again, and then I crashed into Emma, who'd been walking in front of me but had come to a sudden stop.

"What's the matter?" I said.

In lieu of an answer, she just pointed. Up ahead, at a T-shaped intersection, there was a crowd. Though it had been sticky-hot back at the carnival, many of them were bundled in coats and scarves. They were assembled around a particular building, and stood gazing up at it in dumbfounded wonder—just as we were, now. The building itself was nothing special—four stories, the top three just rows of narrow, rounded windows, like an old office building. It was, in fact, nearly identical to all the buildings around it, with one exception: it was totally encased in ice. Ice coated its windows and doors. Icicles hung like fangs from every sill and ledge. Snow spilled from its doorways, collecting in giant heaps on the sidewalk. It looked like a blizzard had struck the building—from the *inside*.

I peered at a snow-blasted street sign: R—KERY STRE—.

"I know this place," said Melina. "It's the peculiar archives, where all our official records are kept."

"How do you know that?" said Emma.

"Miss Thrush was grooming me to be second assistant to the ombudswoman there. The examination's very difficult. I've been studying for twenty-one years."

"Is it supposed to be covered in ice like that?" asked Bronwyn.

"Not that I'm aware," said Melina.

"It's also where the Council of Ymbrynes convene for the annual Nitpicking of the Bylaws," said Millard.

"The Council of Ymbrynes meets *here*?" said Horace. "It's awfully humble. I expected a castle or somesuch."

"It's not meant to stand out," said Melina. "You aren't supposed to notice it at all."

"They're doing a poor job of keeping it hidden, then," said Enoch.

"As I said, it's not usually covered in ice."

"What do you think happened here?" I asked.

"Nothing good," said Millard. "Nothing good at all."

There was no question we'd have to get closer and explore, but that didn't mean we had to rush in like fools. We hung back and watched from a distance. People came and went. Someone tried the door but it was frozen shut. The crowd thinned a bit.

"Tick, tick, tick," said Enoch. "We're wasting time."

We cut through what was left of the crowd and stepped onto the icy sidewalk. The building emanated cold, and we shivered and jammed our hands into our pockets against it. Bronwyn used her strength to pull open the door, and it came straight off, hinges flying— but the hallway it let onto was completely obstructed by ice. It stretched from wall to wall, floor to ceiling, and into the building in a blue and cloudy blur. The same was true of the windows: I wiped the frost from one pane and then another, and through both I could see only ice. It was as if a glacier was being born somewhere in the heart of the place, and its frozen tongues were squeezing out wherever there was an opening.

We tried every way we could think of to get inside. We rounded the building looking for a door or window that wasn't blocked, but every potential entrance was filled with ice. We picked up stones and loose bricks and tried hacking at the ice, but it was almost supernaturally hard—even Bronwyn could dig no more than a few inches into it. Millard scanned the *Tales* for any mention of the building, but there was nothing, no secrets to be found.

Finally, we decided to take a calculated risk. We formed a semicircle around Emma to block her from view, and she heated her hands and placed them against the ice wall that filled the hallway. After a minute they began to sink into the ice, meltwater trickling down to puddle around our feet. But the progress was painfully slow, and after five minutes she'd only gotten up to her elbows.

"At this rate, it'll take the rest of the week just to get down the hall," she said, pulling her arms from the ice.

"Do you think Miss Wren could really be inside?" said Bronwyn.

"She *has* to be," Emma said firmly.

"I find this contagion of optimism positively flabbergasting," said Enoch. "If Miss Wren is in there, then she's frozen solid."

Emma erupted at him. "Doom and gloom! Ruin and ruination! I think you'd be happy if the world came to an end tomorrow, just so you could say *I told you so*!"

Enoch blinked at her, surprised, then said very calmly, "You may choose to live in a world of fantasy if you like, my dear, but I am a realist."

"If you *ever* offered more than simple criticism," Emma said, "if you *ever* gave a single useful suggestion during a crisis, rather than just shrugging your shoulders at the prospect of failure and death, I might be able to tolerate your unrelenting black moods! But as it stands—"

"We've tried everything!" Enoch interjected. "What could I possibly suggest?"

"There's *one* thing we haven't tried," Olive said, piping up from the edge of our group.

"And what's that?" asked Emma.

Olive decided to show rather than tell us. Leaving the sidewalk, she went into the crowd, turned to face the building, and called at the top of her lungs, *"Hello, Miss Wren! If you're in there, please come out! We need your—"*

Before she could finish, Bronwyn had tackled her, and the rest of Olive's sentence was delivered into the big girl's armpit. "Are you *insane*?" Bronwyn said, bringing Olive back to us under her arm. "You're going to get us all found out!"

She set Olive on the sidewalk and was about to chastise her further when tears began streaming down the little girl's face. "What does it matter if we're found out?" Olive said. "If we can't find Miss Wren and we can't save Miss Peregrine, what does it matter if the whole wight army descends on us right now?"

A lady stepped out of the crowd and approached us. She was older, back bent with age, her face partly obscured by the hood of a cloak. "Is she all right?" the lady asked.

"She's fine, thank you," Emma said dismissively.

"I'm *not*!" said Olive. "*Nothing* is right! All we ever wanted was to live in peace on our island, and then bad things came and hurt our headmistress. Now all we want to do is help her—and we can't even do *that*!"

Olive hung her head and began to weep pitifully.

"Well then," said the woman, "it's an awfully good thing you came to see me."

Olive looked up, sniffled, and said, "Why is that?"

And then the woman vanished.

Just like that.

She disappeared right out of her clothes, and her cloak, suddenly empty, collapsed onto the pavement with an airy *whump*. We were all too stunned to speak—until a small bird came hopping out from beneath the folds of the cloak.

I froze, not sure if I should try to catch it.

"Does anyone know what sort of bird that is?" asked Horace.

"I believe that's a wren," said Millard.

The bird flapped its wings, leapt into the air, and flew away, disappearing around the side of the building.

"Don't lose her!" Emma shouted, and we all took off running after it, slipping and sliding on the ice, rounding the corner into the snow-choked alley that ran between the glaciated building and the one next to it.

The bird was gone.

"Drat!" Emma said. "Where'd she go?"

Then a series of odd sounds came up from the ground beneath our feet: metallic clanks, voices, and a noise like water flushing. We kicked the snow away to find a pair of wooden doors set into the bricks, like the entrance to a coal cellar.

The doors were unlatched. We pulled them open. Inside were steps that led down into the dark, covered in quick-melting ice, the

meltwater draining loudly into an unseen gutter.

Emma crouched and called into the darkness. "Hello? Is anyone there?"

"If you're coming," returned a distant voice, "come quickly!"

Emma stood up, surprised. Then shouted: "Who are you?"

We waited for an answer. None came.

"What are we waiting for?" said Olive. "It's Miss Wren!"

"We don't know that," said Millard. "We don't know *what* happened here."

"Well, I'm going to find out," Olive said, and before anyone could stop her she'd gone to the cellar doors and leapt through them, floating gently to the bottom. "I'm still alive!" her voice taunted us from the dark.

And so we were shamed into following her, and climbed down the steps to find a passage tunneled through thick ice. Freezing water dripped from the ceiling and ran down the walls in a steady stream. And it wasn't completely dark, after all—gauzy light glowed from around a turn in the passage ahead.

We heard footsteps approaching. A shadow climbed the wall in front of us. Then a cloaked figure appeared at the turn in the passage, silhouetted in the light.

"Hello, children," the figure said. "I am Balenciaga Wren, and I'm so pleased you're here."

CHAPTER TWELVE

I am Balenciaga Wren.

Hearing those words was like uncorking a bottle under pressure. First came the initial release—gasps, giddy laughter—and then an outpouring of joy: Emma and I jumped and hugged each other; Horace fell to his knees and tossed up his arms in a wordless *hallelujah!* Olive was so excited that she lifted into the air even with her weighted shoes on, stuttering, "We-we-we—we thought we might never—never see another ymbryne ever-ever again!"

This, finally, was Miss Wren. Days ago she'd been nothing more to us than the obscure ymbryne of a little-known loop, but since then she'd achieved mythic stature: she was, as far as we knew, the last free and whole-bodied ymbryne, a living symbol of hope, something we'd all been starving for. And here she was, right in front of us, so human and frail. I recognized her from Addison's photo, only now there was no trace of black left in her silver hair. Deep-set worry lines stacked her brow and held her mouth in parentheses, and her shoulders were hunched as if she were not merely old, but straining under some monumental burden; the weight of all our desperate hope piling down on her.

The ymbryne pulled back the hood of her cloak and said, "I am very glad to meet you, too, dears, but you must come inside at once; it isn't safe out here."

She turned and hobbled away into the passage. We fell into line, waddling behind her through the tunneled ice like a train of ducklings after their mother, feet shuffling and arms held out in awkward balance poses to keep from slipping. Such was the power of an ymbryne over peculiar children: the very presence of one—even one we'd only just met—had an immediate pacifying effect on us.

The floor ramped upward, leading us past silent furnaces bearded with frost, into a large room clogged floor to ceiling and wall to wall with ice except for the tunnel we were in, which had been carved straight through the middle. The ice was thick but clear, and in some places I could see twenty or thirty feet into it with only a slight waver of distortion. The room appeared to be a reception area, with rows of straight-backed chairs facing a massive desk and some filing cabinets, all trapped inside tons of ice. Blue-filtered daylight shone from a row of unreachable windows, beyond which was the street, a smear of indistinct gray.

A hundred hollows could spend a week hacking at that ice and not reach us. If not for the tunnel entrance, this place would make a perfect fortress. Either that or a perfect prison.

On the walls hung dozens of clocks, their stilled hands pointed every which way. (To keep track of the time in different loops, maybe?) Above them, directional signs pointed the way to certain offices:

← UNDERSECRETARY OF TEMPORAL AFFAIRS
← CONSERVATOR OF GRAPHICAL RECORDS
NONSPECIFIC MATTERS OF URGENCY →
DEPT. OF OBFUSCATION AND DEFERMENT →

Through the door to the Temporal Affairs office, I saw a man trapped in the ice. He was frozen in a stooped posture, as if he'd been trying to dislodge his feet as ice overtook the rest of him. He'd been there a long time. I shuddered and looked away.

The tunnel came to an end at a fancy, balustraded staircase that was free of ice but awash in loose papers. A girl stood on one of the lower steps, and she watched our halting, slip-sliding approach without enthusiasm. She had long hair that was parted severely down the middle and fell all the way to her hips, small, round glasses she was constantly adjusting, and thin lips that looked like they'd never once curled into a smile.

"Althea!" Miss Wren said sharply. "You mustn't wander off like that while the passage is open—anything at all might wander in here!"

"Yes, mistress," the girl said, then cocked her head slightly. "Who are they, mistress?"

"These are Miss Peregrine's wards. The ones I was telling you about."

"Have they brought any food with them? Or medicine? Or anything useful at all?" The girl spoke with excruciating slowness, her voice as wooden as her expression.

"No more questions until you've closed up," Miss Wren said. "Quick now!"

"Yes, mistress," the girl said, and with no apparent sense of urgency she ambled away down the tunnel, dragging her hands along the walls as she went.

"Apologies for that," said Miss Wren. "Althea doesn't mean to be obstinate; she's just naturally mulish. But she keeps the wolves at bay, and we badly need her. We'll wait here until she returns."

Miss Wren sat on the bottom step, and as she lowered herself I could almost hear her old bones creaking. I didn't know what she meant by *keeps the wolves at bay*, but there were too many other questions to be asked, so that one would have to wait.

"Miss Wren, how did you know who we are?" asked Emma. "We never said."

"It's an ymbryne's business to know," she replied. "I have watchers in the trees from here to the Irish Sea. And besides, you're famous! There's only one ymbryne whose wards were able to slip the corrupted's grasp complete and entire, and that's Miss Peregrine. But I've no idea how you made it this far without being captured—or how in peculiardom you found me!"

"A boy at the carnival directed us here," said Enoch. He raised a hand level with his chin. "About yea big? Wearing a silly hat?"

"One of our lookouts," said Miss Wren, nodding. "But how did you find *him*?"

"We caught one of your spy pigeons," Emma said proudly, "and she led us to this loop." (She left out the part about Miss Peregrine having killed it.)

"My pigeons!" Miss Wren exclaimed. "But how did you know about them? Much less *catch* one?"

Then Millard stepped forward. He had borrowed Horace's disguising-room overcoat to keep from freezing, and though Miss Wren didn't seem surprised to see a coat hovering in the air, she was astonished when the invisible boy wearing it said, "I deduced your birds' location from the *Tales of the Peculiar*, but we first heard of them in your mountaintop menagerie, from a pretentious dog."

"But *no one* knows the location of my menagerie!"

Miss Wren was now almost too astonished to speak, and since every answer we gave her only sparked more questions, we laid out our whole story for her, as quickly as we could, stretching all the way back to our escape from the island in those tiny, open boats.

"We nearly drowned!" said Olive.

"And got shot, and bombed, and eaten by hollows," said Bronwyn.

"And run over by an underground train," said Enoch.

"And squashed by a dresser," said Horace, scowling at the telekinetic girl.

"We've traveled a long way across dangerous country," Emma said, "all to find someone who could help Miss Peregrine. We were quite hoping that person would be you, Miss Wren."

"Counting on it, really," said Millard.

It took Miss Wren a few moments to find her voice, and when she did, it was gravelly with emotion. "You brave, wonderful children. You're miracles, every one of you, and any ymbryne would be lucky to call you her wards." She dabbed at a tear with the sleeve of her cloak. "I was so sorry to hear about what happened to your Miss Peregrine. I didn't know her well, as I'm a retiring sort of person, but I promise you this: we'll get her back. She and all our sisters!"

Get her back?

That's when I realized Miss Peregrine was still hidden in the sack that Horace was carrying. Miss Wren hadn't seen her yet!

Horace said, "Why, she's right here!" and he put the sack down and untied it.

A moment later, Miss Peregrine came tottering out, dizzy after spending so long in the dark.

"By the Elderfolk!" Miss Wren exclaimed. "But . . . I heard she'd been taken by the wights!"

"She *was* taken," Emma said, "and then we took her back!"

Miss Wren was so excited that she leapt up without her cane, and I had to steady her elbow to keep her from toppling over. "Alma, is that really you?" Miss Wren said breathlessly, and when she had her balance again she rushed over to scoop up Miss Peregrine. "Hullo,

Alma? Is that you in there?"

"It's her!" Emma said. "That's Miss Peregrine!"

Miss Wren held the bird at arm's length, turning her this way and that while Miss Peregrine squirmed. "Hum, hum, hum," Miss Wren said under her breath, her eyes narrowing and lips drawing tight. "Something's not right with your headmistress."

"She got hurt," said Olive. "Hurt on the inside."

"She can't turn human anymore," said Emma.

Miss Wren nodded grimly, as if she'd already figured this out. "How long's it been?"

"Three days," said Emma. "Ever since we stole her back from the wights."

I said, "Your dog told us that if Miss Peregrine didn't change back soon, she'd never be able to."

"Yes," Miss Wren said. "Addison was quite right about that."

"He also said that the sort of help she needed was something only another ymbryne could give her," said Emma.

"That's right, too."

"She's changed," said Bronwyn. "She isn't herself anymore. We need the old Miss P back!"

"We can't let this happen to her!" said Horace.

"So?" said Olive. "Can you turn her human now, please?"

We had surrounded Miss Wren and were pressing in on her, our desperation palpable.

Miss Wren put up her hands in a plea for quiet. "I wish it were that simple," she said, "or so immediate. When an ymbryne remains a bird for too long, she becomes rigid, like a cold muscle. If you try and bend her back to shape too quickly, she'll snap. She's got to be massaged into her true form, delicately; worked and worked like clay. If I work with her through the night, I might have it done by morning."

"If she has that long," said Emma.

"Pray that she does," said Miss Wren.

The long-haired girl returned, walking slowly toward us, dragging her hands along the tunnel walls. Everywhere they touched, layer upon layer of new ice formed. The tunnel behind her had already narrowed to just a few feet wide; soon it would be closed completely, and we'd be sealed in.

Miss Wren waved the girl over. "Althea! Run upstairs ahead of us and have the nurse prepare an examination room. I shall need all my medicinal remedies!"

"When you say remedies, do you mean your solutions, your infusions, or your suspensions?"

"All of them!" Miss Wren shouted. "And quickly—this is an emergency!"

Then I saw the girl notice Miss Peregrine, and her eyes widened a bit—the most I'd seen her react to anything—and she started up the stairs. This time, she was running.

*　　*　　*

I held Miss Wren's arm, steadying her as we climbed the stairs. The building had four stories, and we were heading for the top. Aside from the stairwell, that was the only part of the building still accessible; the other floors were all frozen shut, walls of ice clogging their rooms and hallways. We were, in effect, climbing through the hollowed center of a gigantic ice cube.

I glanced into some of the frozen rooms as we hurried past them. Bulging tongues of ice had broken doors off their hinges, and through their splintered jambs I could see evidence of a raid: kicked-over furniture, drawers torn open, snows of paper on the floor. A machine gun leaned against a desk, its owner frozen in flight. A peculiar slumped in a corner beneath a slash of bullet holes. Like the victims of Pompeii, arrested in ice rather than ash.

It was hard to believe one girl could have been responsible for all this. Apart from ymbrynes, Althea had to be one of the most powerful peculiars I'd ever met. I looked up in time to see her disappear around the landing above us, that endless mane of hair trailing behind her like a blurred afterimage.

I snapped an icicle off the wall. "She really did all this?" I said, turning it in my hand.

"She did indeed," said Miss Wren, puffing beside me. "She is—or was, I should say—apprenticed to the minister of obfuscation and deferment, and was here performing her duties on the day the corrupted raided the building. At the time she knew little of her power other than that her hands radiated unnatural cold. To hear Althea tell it, her ability was the sort of thing that came in useful during hot summer days, but which she'd never thought of as a defense weapon until two hollows began devouring the minister before her very eyes. In mortal fear, she called upon a well of power previously unknown to her, froze the room—and the hollows—and then the entire building, all in the space of a few minutes."

"Minutes!" Emma said. "I don't believe it."

"I rather wish I'd been here to witness it," said Miss Wren, "though if I had, I likely would've been kidnapped along with the other ymbrynes who were present at the time—Miss Nightjar, Miss Finch, and Miss Crow."

"Her ice didn't stop the wights?" I asked.

"It stopped many of them," said Miss Wren. "Several are still with us, I imagine, frozen in the building's recesses. But despite their losses, the wights ultimately got what they came for. Before the entire building froze, they managed to secrete the ymbrynes out through the roof." Miss Wren shook her head bitterly. "I swear on my life, one day I'll personally escort all those that hurt my sisters to Hell."

"All that power she has didn't do any good at all, then," said Enoch.

"Althea wasn't able to save the ymbrynes," Miss Wren said, "but she made this place, and that's blessing enough. Without it we'd have no refuge anywhere. I've been using it as our base of operations for the past few days, bringing back survivors from raided loops as I come across them. This is our fortress, the only safe place for peculiars in all of London."

"And what of *your* efforts, madam?" said Millard. "The dog said you came here to help your sisters. Have you had any luck?"

"No," she said quietly. "My efforts have not been successful."

"Maybe Jacob can help you, Miss Wren," Olive said. "He's very special."

Miss Wren looked sideways at me. "Is that so? And what is your talent, young man?"

"I can see hollows," I said, a little embarrassed. "And sense them."

"And *kill* them, sometimes," added Bronwyn. "If we hadn't found you, Miss Wren, Jacob was going to help us slip past the hollows that guard the punishment loops, so that we could rescue one of the ymbrynes being held there. In fact, maybe he could help *you* . . ."

"That's kind of you," said Miss Wren, "but my sisters are not being held in the punishment loops, or anywhere near London, I'm sure."

"They aren't?" I said.

"No, and they never were. That business about the punishment loops was a ruse concocted to ensnare those ymbrynes whom the corrupted weren't able to capture in their raids. Namely, myself. And it nearly worked. Like a fool, I flew right into their trap—the punishment loops are prisons, after all! I'm lucky to have escaped with only a few scars to show for it."

"Then where were the kidnapped ymbrynes taken?" asked Emma.

"I wouldn't tell you even if I knew, because it's none of your concern," Miss Wren said. "It isn't the duty of peculiar children to worry for the welfare of ymbrynes—it's ours to worry for yours."

"But, Miss Wren, that's hardly fair," Millard began, but she cut him short with a curt "I won't hear anything else about it!" and that was that.

I was shocked by this sudden dismissal, especially considering that if we *hadn't* worried about Miss Peregrine's welfare—and risked our lives to bring her here!—she would've been condemned to spend the rest of her days trapped in the body of a bird. So it did seem like our duty to worry, since the ymbrynes had clearly not done a good enough job worrying to keep their loops from being raided. I didn't like being talked down to that way, and judging from Emma's knitted brow, she didn't, either—but to have said so would've been unthinkably rude, so we finished our climb in awkward silence.

We came to the top of the stairs. Only a few of the doorways on this level were iced over. Miss Wren took Miss Peregrine from Horace and said, "Come on, Alma, let's see what can be done for you."

Althea appeared in an open door, her face flushed, chest heaving. "Your room's all ready, mistress. Everything you asked for."

"Good, good," said Miss Wren.

"If we can do anything to help you," Bronwyn said, "anything at all . . ."

"All I need is time and quiet," Miss Wren replied. "I'll save your ymbryne, young ones. On my life I will." And she turned and took Miss Peregrine into the room with Althea.

Not knowing what else to do with ourselves, we drifted after her and congregated around the door, which had been left open a crack. We took turns peeking inside. In a cozy room dimly lit by oil lamps, Miss Wren sat in a rocking chair holding Miss Peregrine in her lap. Althea stood mixing vials of liquid at a lab table. Every so often she'd lift a vial and swirl it, then walk to Miss Peregrine and pass it under her beak—much the way smelling salts are waved under the nose of someone who's fainted. All the while, Miss Wren rocked in the chair and stroked Miss Peregrine's feathers, singing her a soft, lilting lullaby:

"*Eft kaa vangan soorken, eft ka vangan soorken, malaaya . . .*"

"That's the tongue of the old peculiars," Millard whispered. "Come home, come home . . . remember your true self . . . something like that."

Miss Wren heard him and looked up, then waved us away. Althea crossed the room and shut the door.

"Well, then," said Enoch. "I can see we're not wanted here."

After three days of the headmistress depending on us for everything, we had suddenly become extraneous. Though we were grateful to Miss Wren, she'd made us all feel a bit like children who'd been ordered to bed.

"Miss Wren knows her business," came a Russian-accented voice from behind us. "Best leave her to it."

We turned to see the stick-thin folding man from the carnival, standing with his bony arms crossed.

"You!" said Emma.

"We meet again," the folding man said, his voice deep as an ocean trench. "My name is Sergei Andropov, and I am captain of peculiar resistance army. Come, I will show you around."

*   *   *

"I *knew* he was peculiar!" Olive said.

"No, you didn't," said Enoch. "You only *thought* he was."

"I knew you were peculiar the second I saw you," said the folding man. "How you weren't captured long time ago?"

"Because we're *wily*," said Hugh.

"He means lucky," I said.

"But mostly just hungry," said Enoch. "Got any food around here? I could eat an emu-raffe."

At the mere mention of food, my stomach growled like a wild animal. None of us had eaten since our train ride to London, which seemed eons ago.

"Of course," said the folding man. "This way."

We followed him down the hall.

"So tell me about this peculiar army of yours," Emma said.

"We will crush the wights and take back what's ours. Punish

them for kidnapping our ymbrynes." He opened a door off the hall-way and led us through a wrecked office where people lay sleeping on the floor and under desks. As we stepped around them, I recog-nized a few of their faces from the carnival: the plain-looking boy, the frizzy-haired snake-charmer girl.

"They're all peculiar?" I asked.

The folding man nodded. "Rescued from other loops," he said, holding a door open for us.

"And you?" said Millard. "Where did you come from?"

The folding man led us into a vestibule where we could talk with-out disturbing the sleepers, a room dominated by two large wooden doors emblazoned with dozens of bird insignias. "I come from land of frozen desert beyond Icy Waste," he said. "Hundred years ago, when hollows first born, they strike my home first. Everything destroy. All in village killed. Old woman. Baby. All." He made a chopping motion in the air with his hand. "I hide in butter churn, breathe through reed of straw, while own brother killed in same house. After, I come to London to escape the hollows. But they come, too."

"That's awful," said Bronwyn. "I'm so sorry for you."

"One day we take revenge," he said, his face darkening.

"You mentioned that," said Enoch. "How many are in your army, then?"

"Right now six," he said, gesturing to the room we'd just left.

"Six people?!" said Emma. "You mean . . . *them*?"

I didn't know whether to laugh or cry.

"With you, makes seventeen. We growing quick."

"Whoa, whoa, whoa," I said. "We didn't come here to join any army."

He gave me a look that could freeze Hell, then turned and threw open the double doors.

We followed him into a large room dominated by a massive oval table, its wood polished to a mirror shine. "This is Ymbryne Council meeting place," the folding man said.

All around us were portraits of famous old peculiars, not framed but drawn directly onto the walls in oil and charcoal and grease pencil. The one closest to me was a face with wide, staring eyes and an open mouth, inside of which was a real, functioning water fountain. Around its mouth was a motto written in Dutch, which Millard, standing next to me, translated: "From the mouths of our elders comes a fountain of wisdom."

Nearby was another, this one in Latin. "*Ardet nec consomitur*," Melina said. "Burned but not destroyed."

"How fitting," said Enoch.

"I can't believe I'm really here," said Melina. "I've studied this place and dreamed about it for so many years."

"It's just a room," said Enoch.

"Maybe to you. To me, it's the heart of the whole peculiar world."

"A heart that's been ripped out," said someone new, and I looked to see a clown striding toward us—the same one who'd been stalking us at the carnival. "Miss Jackdaw was standing right where you are when she was taken. We found a whole pile of her feathers on the floor." His accent was American. He stopped a few feet from us and stood, chewing, one hand on his hip. "This them?" he asked the folding man, pointing at us with a turkey leg. "We need *soldiers*, not little kids."

"I'm a hundred and twelve!" said Melina.

"Yeah, yeah, I've heard it all before," said the clown. "I could tell you people were peculiar from across the fairgrounds, by the way. You're the most obviously peculiar bunch of peculiars I've ever laid eyes on."

"I told them same thing," said the folding man.

"How they made it all the way here from Wales without being captured is beyond me," said the clown. "In fact, it's suspicious. Sure one of you ain't a wight?"

"How dare you!" said Emma.

"We *were* captured," Hugh said proudly, "but the wights who took us didn't live to tell about it."

"Uh-huh, and I'm the king of Bolivia," the clown said.

"It's true!" Hugh thundered, going red in the face.

The clown tossed up his hands. "Okay, okay, calm down, kid! I'm sure Wren wouldn't have let you in if you weren't legitimate. Come on, let's be friends, have a turkey leg."

He didn't have to offer twice. We were too hungry to stay offended for long.

The clown showed us to a table stacked with food—the same boiled nuts and roasted meats that had tempted us at the carnival. We crowded around the table and stuffed our faces shamelessly. The folding man ate five cherries and a small hunk of bread and then announced he'd never been so full in his life. Bronwyn paced along the wall, chewing her fingers, too consumed by worry to eat.

When we were done, and the table was a battlefield of gnawed bones and grease stains, the clown leaned back in his chair and said, "So, peculiar children, what's your story? Why'd you come here all the way from Wales?"

Emma wiped her mouth and said, "To help our ymbryne."

"And when she's helped?" the clown asked. "What then?"

I'd been busy sopping up turkey gravy with the last of the bread, but now I looked up. The question was so straightforward, so simply put—so obvious—that I couldn't believe none of us had asked it before.

"Don't talk like that," said Horace. "You'll jinx us."

"Wren's a miracle worker," the clown said. "There's nothing to worry about."

"I hope you're right," said Emma.

"Of course I am. So what's your plan? You'll stay and help us fight, obviously, but where will you sleep? Not with me, my room's a single. Exceptions rarely made." He looked at Emma and raised an eyebrow. "Note I said *rarely*."

All of a sudden everyone was looking off at the paintings on the walls or adjusting their collars—except for Emma, whose face was turning a certain shade of green. Maybe we were naturally pessimistic, and our chances of success had seemed so tiny that we'd never bothered to wonder what we'd do if we actually fixed Miss Peregrine—or maybe the crises of the past few days had been so constant and pressing that we'd never had a chance to wonder. Either way, the clown's question had caught us off guard.

What if we really pulled this off? What would we do if Miss Peregrine walked into the room, right now, restored to her old self?

It was Millard who finally gave an answer. "I suppose we would head west again, back where we come from. Miss Peregrine could make another loop for us. One where we'd never be found."

"That's it?" the clown said. "You'll *hide*? What about all the other ymbrynes—the ones who weren't so lucky? What about *mine*?"

"It isn't our job to save the whole world," Horace said.

"We're not *trying* to save the whole world. Just all of peculiar-dom."

"Well, that's not our job, either." Horace sounded weak and defensive, ashamed to have been cornered into saying this.

The clown leaned forward in his chair and glared at us. "Then whose job is it?"

"There's got to be someone else," said Enoch. "People who are better equipped, who've trained for this sort of thing . . ."

"The first thing the corrupted did three weeks ago was attack the Peculiar Home Guard. In less than a day, they were scattered to the four winds. With them gone, and now our ymbrynes, who does the defense of peculiardom fall to, eh? People like you and me, that's who." The clown threw down his turkey leg. "You cowards disgust me. I just lost my appetite."

"They are tired, had long journey," said the folding man. "Give them break."

The clown waved his finger in the air like a schoolmarm. "Uh-uh. Nobody rides for free. I don't care if you're here for an hour or a month, as long as you're here, you've got to be willing to fight. Now, you're a scrawny-looking bunch, but you're peculiar, so I know you've all got hidden talents. Show me what you can do!"

He got up and moved toward Enoch, one arm extended like he was going to search Enoch's pockets for his peculiar ability. "You there," he said. "Do your thing!"

"I'll need a dead person in order to demonstrate," Enoch said. "That could be you, if you so much as lay one finger on me."

The clown rerouted himself toward Emma. "Then how about you, sweetheart," he said, and Emma held a particular finger up and made a flame dance atop it like a birthday candle. The clown laughed and said, "Sense of humor! I like that," and moved on to the blind brothers.

"They're connected in the head," said Melina, putting herself between the clown and the brothers. "They can see with their ears, and always know what the other's thinking."

The clown clapped his hands. "Finally, something useful! They'll be our lookouts—put one in the carnival and keep the other here. If anything goes wrong out there, we'll know right away!"

He pushed past Melina. The brothers shied away from him.

"You can't separate them!" said Melina. "Joel-and-Peter don't like being apart."

"And I don't like being hunted by invisible corpse beasts," said the clown, and he began to pry the older brother from the younger. The boys locked arms and moaned loudly, their tongues clicking and eyes rolling wildly in their heads. I was about to intervene when the brothers came apart and let out a doubled scream so loud and piercing I feared my head would break. The dishes on the table shattered, everyone ducked and clapped their hands over their ears, and I thought I could hear, from the frozen floors below, cracks spidering through the ice.

As the echo faded, Joel-and-Peter clutched each other on the floor, shaking.

"See what you did!" Melina shouted at the clown.

"Good *God*, that's impressive!" the clown said.

With one hand Bronwyn picked the clown up by his neck. "If you continue to harass us," she said calmly, "I'll put your head through the wall."

"Sorry . . . about . . . that," the clown wheezed through his closing windpipe. "Put . . . me . . . down?"

"Go on, Wyn," said Olive. "He said he's sorry."

Reluctantly, Bronwyn set him down. The clown coughed and straightened his costume. "Looks like I misjudged you," he said. "You'll make fine additions to our army."

"I told you, we're not joining your stupid army," I said.

"What's the point of fighting, anyway?" Emma said. "You don't even know where the ymbrynes are."

The folding man unfolded from his chair to tower above us. "Point is," he said, "if corrupted get rest of ymbrynes, they become unstoppable."

"It seems like they're pretty unstoppable already," I said.

"If you think that's unstoppable, you ain't seen nothin' yet," said the clown. "And if you think that while your ymbryne is free they'll ever stop hunting you, you're stupider than you look."

Horace stood up and cleared his throat. "You've just laid out the worst-case scenario," he said. "Of late, I've heard a great many worst-case scenarios presented. But I haven't heard a single argument laid for the *best*-case scenario."

"Oh, this should be rich," said the clown. "Go ahead, fancy boy, let's hear it."

Horace took a deep breath, working up his courage. "The wights wanted the ymbrynes, and now they have them—or most of them, anyway. Say, for the sake of argument, that's all the wights need, and now they can follow through with their devilish plans. And they do: they become superwights, or demigods, or whatever it is they're after. And then they have no more use for ymbrynes, and no more use for peculiar children, and no more use for time loops, so they go away to be demigods elsewhere and leave us alone. And then things not only go back to normal, they're *better* than they were before, because no longer is anyone attempting to eat us or kidnap our ymbrynes. And then maybe, once in a great while, we could take a vacation abroad, like we used to, and see the world a bit, and put our toes in the sand somewhere that isn't cold and gray three hundred days of the year. In which case, what's the use in staying here and fighting? We'd be throwing ourselves onto their swords when everything might turn out just rosy without our intervention."

For a moment no one said anything. Then the clown began to laugh. He laughed and laughed, his cackles bouncing off the walls, until finally he fell out of his chair.

Then Enoch said, "I simply have no words. Wait—no—I do!

Horace, that is the most stunningly naive and cowardly bit of wishful thinking that I've ever heard."

"But it is *possible*," Horace insisted.

"Yes. It's also possible that the moon is made of cheese. It's just not bloody likely."

"I can end argument right now," said the folding man. "You want to know what wights will do with us once free to do anything? Come—I show you."

"Strong stomachs only," said the clown, glancing at Olive.

"If *they* can handle it, I can, too," she said.

"Fair warning," the clown shrugged. "Follow us."

"I wouldn't follow you off a sinking ship," said Melina, who was just getting the shaking blind brothers to their feet again.

"Stay, then," said the clown. "Anyone who'd rather not go down with the ship, follow us."

*   *   *

The injured lay in mismatched beds in a makeshift hospital room, watched over by a nurse with a bulging glass eye. There were three patients, if you could call them that—a man and two women. The man lay on his side, half catatonic, whispering and drooling. One of the women stared blankly at the ceiling, while the other writhed under her sheets, moaning softly, in the grip of some nightmare. Some of the children watched from outside the door, keeping their distance in case whatever these people suffered from was contagious.

"How are they today?" the folding man asked the nurse.

"Getting worse," she replied, buzzing from bed to bed. "I keep them sedated all the time now. Otherwise they just bawl."

They had no obvious wounds. There were no bloody bandages, no limbs wrapped in casts, no bowls brimming with reddish liquid. The room looked more like overflow from a psychiatric ward than a hospital.

"What's the matter with them?" I asked. "They were hurt in the raid?"

"No, brought here by Miss Wren," answered the nurse. "She found them abandoned inside a hospital, which the wights had converted into some sort of medical laboratory. These pitiful creatures were used as guinea pigs in their unspeakable experiments. What you see is the result."

"We found their old records," the clown said. "They were kidnapped years ago by the wights. Long assumed dead."

The nurse took a clipboard from the wall by the whispering man's bed. "This fellow, Benteret, he's supposed to be fluent in a hundred languages, but now he'll only say one word—over and over again."

I crept closer, watching his lips. *Call, call, call*, he was mouthing. *Call, call, call.*

Gibberish. His mind was gone.

"That one there," the nurse said, pointing her clipboard at the moaning girl. "Her chart says she can fly, but I've never seen her so much as lift an inch out of that bed. As for the other one, she's meant to be invisible. But she's plain as day."

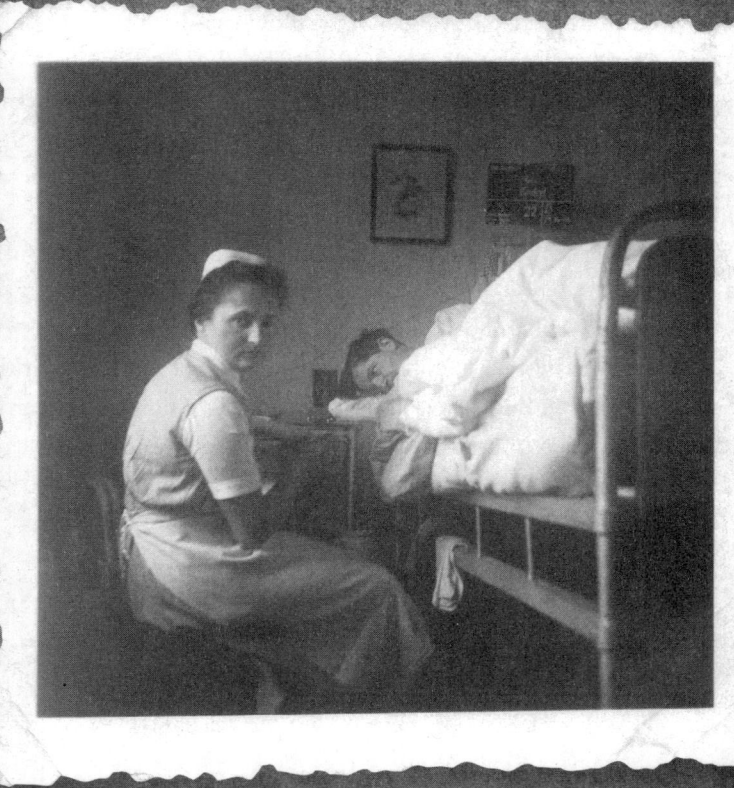

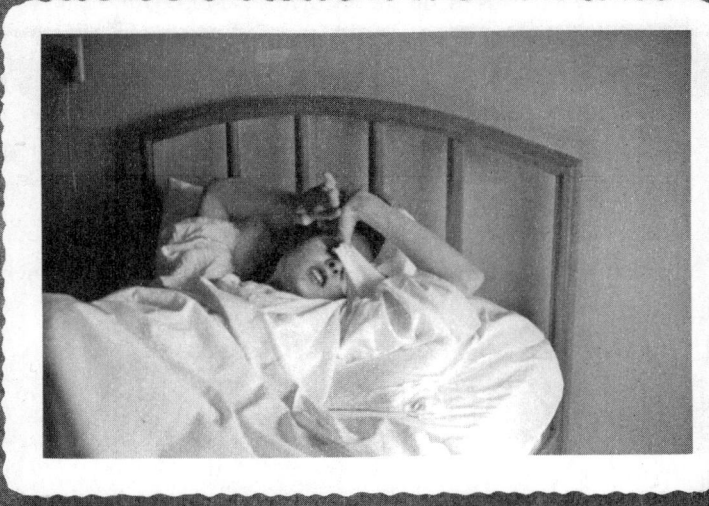

"Were they tortured?" Emma asked.

"Obviously—they were tortured out of their minds!" said the clown. "Tortured until they forgot how to be peculiar!"

"You could torture me all day long," said Millard. "I'd never forget how to be invisible."

"Show them the scars," said the clown to the nurse.

The nurse crossed to the motionless woman and pulled back her sheets. There were thin red scars across her stomach, along the side of her neck, and beneath her chin, each about the length of a cigarette.

"I'd hardly call this evidence of torture," said Millard.

"Then what *would* you call it?" the nurse said angrily.

Ignoring her question, Millard said, "Are there more scars, or is this all she has?"

"Not by a long shot," said the nurse, and she whisked the sheets off to expose the woman's legs, pointing out scars on the back of the woman's knee, her inner thigh, and the bottom of her foot.

Millard bent to examine the foot. "That's odd placement, wouldn't you say?"

"What are you getting at, Mill?" said Emma.

"Hush," said Enoch. "Let him play Sherlock if he wants. I'm rather enjoying this."

"Why don't we cut *him* in ten places?" said the clown. "Then we'll see if he thinks it's torture!"

Millard crossed the room to the whispering man's bed. "May I examine him?"

"I'm sure he won't object," said the nurse.

Millard lifted the man's sheets from his legs. On the bottom of one of his bare feet was a scar identical to the motionless woman's.

The nurse gestured toward the writhing woman. "She's got one too, if that's what you're looking for."

"Enough of this," said the folding man. "If that is not torture, then what?"

"Exploration," said Millard. "These incisions are precise and surgical. Not meant to inflict pain—probably done under anesthetic, even. The wights were *looking* for something."

"And what was that?" Emma asked, though she seemed to dread the answer.

"There's an old saying about a peculiar's foot," said Millard. "Do any of you remember it?"

Horace recited it. "A peculiar's sole is the door to his soul," he said. "It's just something they tell kids, though, to get them to wear shoes when they play outside."

"Maybe it is and maybe it's not," said Millard.

"Don't be ridiculous! You think they were looking for—"

"Their souls. And they found them."

The clown laughed out loud. "What a pile of baloney. Just because they lost their abilities, you think their second souls were removed?"

"Partly. We know the wights have been interested in the second soul for years now."

Then I remembered the conversation Millard and I had had on the train, and I said, "But you told me yourself that the peculiar soul is what allows us to enter loops. So if these people don't have their souls, how are they *here*?"

"Well, they're not *really* here, are they?" said Millard. "By which I mean, their *minds* are certainly elsewhere."

"Now you're grasping at straws," said Emma. "I think you've taken this far enough, Millard."

"Bear with me for just a moment longer," Millard said. He was pacing now, getting excited. "I don't suppose you heard about the time a normal actually *did* enter a loop?"

"No, because everyone knows that's impossible," said Enoch.

"It *nearly* is," said Millard. "It isn't easy and it isn't pretty, but it has been done—once. An illegal experiment conducted by Miss Peregrine's own brother, I believe, in the years before he went mad and formed the splinter group that would become the wights."

"Then why haven't I ever heard about this?" said Enoch.

"Because it was extremely controversial and the results were immediately covered up, so no one would attempt to replicate them. In any event, it turns out that you *can* bring a normal into a loop, but they have to be *forced* through, and only someone with an ymbryne's power can do it. But because normals do not have a second soul, they cannot handle a time loop's inherent paradoxes, and their brains turn to mush. They become drooling, catatonic vegetables from the moment they enter. Not unlike these poor people before us."

There was a moment of quiet while Millard's words registered. Then Emma's hands went to her mouth and she said quietly, "Oh, hell. He's right."

"Well, then," said the clown. "In that case, things are even worse than we thought."

I felt the air go out of the room.

"I'm not sure I follow," said Horace.

"He said the monsters stole their souls!" Olive shouted, and then she ran crying to Bronwyn and buried her face in her coat.

"These peculiars didn't *lose* their abilities," said Millard. "They were stolen from them—extracted, along with their souls, which were then fed to hollowgast. This allowed the hollows to evolve sufficiently to enter loops, a development which enabled their recent assault on peculiardom—and netted the wights even more kidnapped peculiars whose souls they could extract, with which they evolved still more hollows, and so on, in a vicious cycle."

"Then it isn't just the ymbrynes they want," said Emma. "It's us, too—and our souls."

Hugh stood at the foot of the whispering man's bed, his last bee buzzing angrily around him. "All the peculiar children they kidnapped over the years . . . *this* is what they were doing to them? I figured they just became hollowgast food. But this . . . this is *leagues* more evil."

"Who's to say they don't mean to extract the ymbrynes' souls, too?" said Enoch.

That sent a special chill through us. The clown turned to Horace and said, "How's your best-case scenario looking now, fella?"

"Don't tease me," Horace replied. "I bite."

"Everyone out!" ordered the nurse. "Souls or no souls, these people are ill. This is no place to bicker."

We filed sullenly into the hall.

"All right, you've given us the horror show," Emma said to the clown and the folding man, "and we are duly horrified. Now tell us what you want."

"Simple," said the folding man. "We want you to stay and fight with us."

"We just figured we'd show you how much it's in your own best interest to do so," said the clown. He clapped Millard on the back. "But your friend here did a better job of that than we ever could've."

"Stay here and fight for what?" Enoch said. "The ymbrynes aren't even in London—Miss Wren said as much."

"Forget London! London's finished!" the clown said. "The battle's over here. We lost. As soon as Wren has saved every last peculiar she can from these ruined loops, we'll posse up and travel—to other lands, other loops. There must be more survivors out there, peculiars like us, with the fight still burning in them."

"We will build army," said the folding man. "*Real* one."

"As for finding out where the ymbrynes are," said the clown, "no problem. We'll catch a wight and torture it out of him. Make him show us on the Map of Days."

"You have a Map of Days?" said Millard.

"We have two. The peculiar archives is downstairs, you know."

"That is good news indeed," Millard said, his voice charged with excitement.

"Catching a wight is easier said than done," said Emma. "And they lie, of course. Lying is what they do best."

"Then we'll catch two and compare their lies," the clown said. "They come sniffing around here pretty often, so next time we see one—bam! We'll grab him."

"There's no need to wait," said Enoch. "Didn't Miss Wren say there are wights in this very building?"

"Sure," said the clown, "but they're frozen. Dead as door-nails."

"That doesn't mean they can't be interrogated," Enoch said, a grin spreading across his face.

The clown turned to the folding man. "I'm really starting to like these weirdos."

"Then you are with us?" said the folding man. "You stay and fight?"

"I didn't say that," said Emma. "Give us a minute to talk this over."

"What is there to talk over?" said the clown.

"Of course, take all time you need," said the folding man, and he pulled the clown down the hall with him. "Come, I will make coffee."

"All *right*," the clown said reluctantly.

We formed a huddle, just as we had so many times since our troubles began, only this time rather than shouting over one another, we spoke in orderly turns. The gravity of all this had put us in a solemn state of mind.

"I think we should fight," said Hugh. "Now that we know what the wights are doing to us, I couldn't live with myself if we just went back to the way things were, and tried to pretend none of this was happening. To fight is the only honorable thing."

"There's honor in survival, too," said Millard. "Our kind survived the twentieth century by hiding, not fighting—so perhaps all we need is a better way to hide."

Then Bronwyn turned to Emma and said, "I want to know

what *you* think."

"Yeah, I want to know what Emma thinks," said Olive.

"Me too," said Enoch, which took me by surprise.

Emma drew a long breath, then said, "I feel terrible for the other ymbrynes. It's a crime what's happened to them, and the future of our kind may depend on their rescue. But when all is said and done, my allegiance doesn't belong to those other ymbrynes, or to other peculiar children. It belongs to the woman to whom I owe my life—Miss Peregrine, and Miss Peregrine alone." She paused and nodded—as if testing and confirming the soundness of her own words—then continued. "And when, bird willing, she becomes herself again, I'll do whatever she needs me to do. If she says fight, I'll fight. If she wants to hide us away in a loop somewhere, I'll go along with that, too. Either way, my creed has never changed: Miss Peregrine knows best."

The others considered this. Finally Millard said, "Very wisely put, Miss Bloom."

"Miss Peregrine knows best!" cheered Olive.

"Miss Peregrine knows best!" echoed Hugh.

"I don't care what Miss Peregrine says," said Horace. "I'll fight."

Enoch choked back a laugh. "You?"

"Everyone thinks I'm a coward. This is my chance to prove them wrong."

"Don't throw your life away because of a few jokes made at your expense," said Hugh. "Who gives a whit what anyone else thinks?"

"It isn't just that," said Horace. "Remember the vision I had back on Cairnholm? I caught a glimpse of where the ymbrynes are being kept. I couldn't show you on a map, but I'm sure of this—I'll know it when I see it." He tapped his forehead with his index finger. "What I've got up here might just save those chaps a heap of trouble. And save those other ymbrynes, too."

"If some fight and some stay behind," said Bronwyn, "I'll protect whoever stays. Protecting's always been my vocation."

And then Hugh turned to me and said, "What about you, Jacob?" and my mouth went instantly dry.

"Yeah," said Enoch. "What *about* you?"

"Well," I said, "I . . ."

"Let's take a walk," Emma said, hooking her arm around mine. "You and I need to have a chat."

* * *

We walked slowly down the stairs, saying nothing to each other until we'd reached the bottom and the curved wall of ice where Althea had frozen shut the exit tunnel. We sat together and looked into the ice for a long while, at the forms trapped there, blurred and distorted in the darkening light, suspended like ancient eggs in blue amber. We sat, and I could tell from the silence collecting between us that this was going to be a hard conversation—one neither of us wanted to start.

Finally Emma said, "Well?"

I said, "I'm like the others—I want to know what *you* think."

She laughed in the way people do when something's not funny but awkward, and said, "I'm not entirely sure you do."

She was right, but I prodded her to speak anyway. "Come on."

Emma laid a hand on my knee, then retracted it. She fidgeted. My chest tightened.

"I think it's time you went home," she said finally.

I blinked. It took a moment to convince myself she'd really said it. "I don't understand," I mumbled.

"You said yourself you were sent here for a reason," she said quickly, staring into her lap, "and that was to help Miss Peregrine. Now it seems she may be saved. If you owed her any debts, they're paid. You helped us more than you'll ever realize. And now it's time for you to go home." Her words came all in a rush, like they were a painful thing she'd been carrying a long time, and it was a relief to finally be rid of them.

"This *is* my home," I said.

"No, it isn't," she insisted, looking at me now. "Peculiardom is dying, Jacob. It's a lost dream. And even if somehow, by some miracle, we were to take up arms against the corrupted and prevail, we'd be left with a shadow of what we once had; a shattered mess. You *have* a home—one that isn't ruined—and parents who are alive, and who love you, in some measure."

"I told you. I don't want those things. I chose *this*."

"You made a promise, and you've kept it. And now that's over, and it's time for you to go home."

"Quit saying that!" I shouted. "Why are you pushing me away?"

"Because you have a real home and a real family, and if you think any of us would've chosen *this* world over those things— wouldn't have given up our loops and longevity and peculiar powers long ago for even a *taste* of what you have—then you really are living in a fantasy world. It makes me absolutely ill to think you might throw that all away—and for what?"

"For *you*, you idiot! I love you!"

I couldn't believe I'd said it. Neither could Emma—her mouth had fallen open. "No," she said, shaking her head like she could erase my words. "No, that's not going to help anything."

"But it's *true*!" I said. "Why do you think I stayed instead of going home? It wasn't because of my grandfather or some stupid sense of duty—not *really*—or because I hated my parents or didn't appreciate my home and all the nice things we had. I stayed because of you!"

She didn't say anything for a moment, just nodded and then looked away and ran her hands through her hair, revealing a streak of white concrete dust I hadn't noticed before, which made her look suddenly older. "It's my own fault," she said finally. "I should never have kissed you. Perhaps I made you believe something that wasn't true."

That stung me, and I recoiled instinctively, as if to protect myself. "Don't say that to me if you don't mean it," I said. "I may not have a lot of dating experience, but don't treat me like some pathetic loser who's powerless in the face of a pretty girl. You didn't *make* me stay. I stayed because I wanted to—and because what I feel for you is as real as anything I've ever felt." I let that hang in the air between us for a moment, feeling the truth of it. "You feel it too," I said. "I know you do."

"I'm sorry," she said. "I'm sorry, that was cruel, and I shouldn't have said it." Her eyes watered a little and she wiped at them with her hand. She had tried to make herself like stone, but now the facade was falling away. "You're right," she said. "I care about you very much. That's why I can't watch you throw your life away for nothing."

"I *wouldn't* be!"

"Dammit, Jacob, yes you would!" She was so incensed that she inadvertently lit a fire in her hand—which, luckily, she'd since removed from my knee. She clapped her hands together, snuffed the flame, and then stood up. Pointing into the ice, she said, "See that potted plant on the desk in there?"

I saw. Nodded.

"It's green now, preserved by the ice. But inside it's dead. And the moment that ice melts, it'll turn brown and wither into mush." She locked eyes with me. "I'm like that plant."

"You aren't," I said. "You're . . . perfect."

Her face tightened into a expression of forced patience, as if she were explaining something to a thick-headed child. She sat down again, took my hand, and raised it to her smooth cheek. "This?" she said. "Is a lie. It's not really me. If you could see me for what I really am, you wouldn't want me anymore."

"I don't *care* about that stuff—"

"I'm an old woman!" she said. "You think we're alike, but we aren't. This person you say you love? She's really a hag, an old crone hiding in a body of a girl. You're a young man—a *boy*—a baby compared to me. You could never understand what it's like, being this close to death all the time. And you shouldn't. I never want you to. You've still got your whole life to look forward to, Jacob. I've already spent mine. And one day—soon, perhaps—I will die and return to dust."

She said it with such cold finality that I knew she believed it. It hurt her to say these things, just as it hurt me to hear them, but I understood why she was doing it. She was, in her way, trying to save me.

It stung anyway—partly because I knew she was right. If Miss Peregrine recovered, then I would have done what I'd set out to do: solved the mystery of my grandfather; settled my family's debts to Miss Peregrine; lived the extraordinary life I'd always dreamed of— or part of one, anyway. At which point my only remaining obligation was to my parents. As for Emma, I didn't care at all that she was older than me, or different from me, but she'd made up her mind that I should and it seemed there was no convincing her otherwise.

"Maybe when this is all over," she said, "I'll send you a letter, and you'll send one back. And maybe one day you can come see me again."

A letter. I thought of the dusty box of them I'd found in her room, written by my grandfather. Was that all I'd be to her? An old man across the ocean? A memory? And I realized that I was about to follow in my grandfather's footsteps in a way I'd never thought possible. In so many ways, I was living his life. And probably, one day, my guard would relax too much, I'd get old and slow and distracted, and I would die his death. And Emma would continue on without me, without either of us, and one day maybe someone would find *my* letters in her closet, in a box beside my grandfather's, and wonder who we were to her.

"What if you need me?" I said. "What if the hollows come back?"

Tears shimmered in her eyes. "We'll manage somehow," she said. "Look, I can't talk about this anymore. I honestly don't think my heart can take it. Shall we go upstairs and tell the others your decision?"

I clenched my jaw, suddenly irritated by how hard she was pushing me. "I haven't decided anything," I said. "*You* have."

"Jacob, I just told you—"

"Right, you *told* me. But *I* haven't made up my mind yet."

She crossed her arms. "Then I can wait."

"No," I said, and stood up. "I need to be by myself for a while."

And I went up the stairs without her.

CHAPTER THIRTEEN

I moved quietly through the halls. I stood outside the ymbryne meeting room for a while, listening to muffled voices through the door, but I didn't go in. I peeked into the nurse's room and saw her dozing on a stool between the single-souled peculiars. I cracked the door to Miss Wren's room and saw her rocking Miss Peregrine in her lap, gently kneading her fingers into the bird's feathers. I said nothing to anyone.

Wandering through empty halls and ransacked offices, I tried to imagine what home would feel like, if after all this I chose to go back. What I would tell my parents. I'd tell them nothing, most likely. They'd never believe me, anyway. I would say I'd gotten mad, written a letter to my father filled with crazy stories, then caught a boat to the mainland and run away. They'd call it a stress reaction. Chalk it up to some invented disorder and adjust my meds accordingly. Blame Dr. Golan for suggesting I go to Wales. Dr. Golan, whom of course they'd never hear from again. He'd skipped town, they'd say, because he was a fraud, a quack whom we never should've trusted. And I'd go back to being Jacob the poor, traumatized, mentally disturbed rich kid.

It sounded like a prison sentence. And yet, if my best reason for staying in peculiardom didn't want me anymore, I wouldn't debase myself by clinging to her. I had my pride.

How long could I stand Florida, now that I'd had a taste of this peculiar life? I was not nearly as ordinary as I used to be—or if it was true that I'd never been ordinary, now I knew it. I had changed. And that, at least, gave me some hope: that even under ordinary circumstances, I still might find a way to live an extraordinary life.

Yes, it was best to go. It really was best. If this world was dying and there was nothing to be done for it, then what was left for me here? To run and hide until there was no safe place left to go, no loop to sustain my friends' artificial youth. To watch them die. To hold Emma as she crumbled and broke apart in my arms.

That would kill me faster than any hollow could.

So yes, I would go. Salvage what was left of my old life. Goodbye, peculiars. Goodbye, peculiardom.

It was for the best.

I wandered until I came to a place where the rooms were only half frozen, and the ice had risen halfway to the ceiling like water in a sinking ship and then stopped, leaving the tops of desks and the heads of lamps sticking out like faltering swimmers. Beyond the iced windows the sun was sinking. Shadows bloomed across the walls and multiplied in the stairwells, and as the light died it got bluer, painting everything around me a deep-sea cobalt.

It occurred to me that this was probably my last night in peculiardom. My last night with the best friends I'd ever had. My last night with Emma.

Why was I spending it alone? Because I was sad, and Emma had hurt my pride, and I needed to sulk.

Enough of this.

Just as I turned to leave the room, though, I felt it: that old familiar twinge in my gut.

A hollow.

I stopped, waiting for another hit of pain. I needed more information. The intensity of the pain corresponded to the nearness of the hollow and the frequency of the hits with its strength. When two strong hollows had been chasing us, the Feeling had been one long, unbroken spasm, but now it was a long time before I felt another—nearly a minute—and when it came, it was so faint I wasn't even sure I'd felt it.

I crept slowly out of the room and down the hall. As I passed the next doorway, I felt a third twinge: a little stronger now, but still only a whisper.

I tried to open the door carefully and quietly, but it was frozen shut. I had to yank on it, then rattle the door, then kick it, until finally it flew open to reveal a doorway and a room filled with ice that rose to mid-chest height. I approached the ice cautiously and peered across it, and even in the weak light, I saw the hollow right away. It was crouched on the floor, encased in ice up to its ink-black eyeballs. Only the top half of its head was exposed above the ice; the rest of it, the dangerous parts, its open jaws and all its teeth and tongues, were all caught below the surface.

The thing was just barely alive, its heart slowed almost to nothing, beating maybe once per minute. With each feeble pulse I felt a corresponding stitch of pain.

I stood at the mouth of the room and stared at it, fascinated and repulsed. It was unconscious, immobilized, totally vulnerable. It would've been easy to climb onto the ice and drive the point of an icicle into the hollow's skull—and if anyone else had known it was here, I'm sure they would've done just that. But something stopped me. It was no threat to anyone now, this creature. Every hollow I'd come into contact with had left a mark on me. I saw their decaying faces in my dreams. Soon I'd be going home, where I'd no longer be Jacob the hollow-slayer. I didn't want to take this one with me, too. It wasn't my business anymore.

I backed out of the room and closed the door.

*   *   *

When I returned to the meeting hall, it was nearly dark outside and the room was black as night. Because Miss Wren wouldn't allow the gaslamps to be lit for fear they'd be seen from the street, everyone had gathered around a few candles at the big oval table, some in chairs and others perched cross-legged on the table itself, talking in low voices and peering down at something.

At the creak of the heavy doors, everyone turned to look at me. "Miss Wren?" Bronwyn said hopefully, straightening in her chair and squinting.

"It's only Jacob," said another shadowy form.

After a chorus of disappointed sighs, Bronwyn said, "Oh, hullo Jacob," and returned her attention to the table.

As I walked toward them, I locked eyes with Emma. Holding her gaze, I saw something raw and unguarded there—a fear, I imagined, that I had in fact decided to do what she'd urged me to. Then her eyes dulled and she looked down again.

I'd been half hoping Emma had taken pity on me and told the others I was leaving already. But of course she hadn't—I hadn't told *her* yet. She seemed to know, though, just from reading my face as I crossed the room.

It was clear the others had no idea. They were so accustomed to my presence, they'd forgotten it was even under consideration. I steeled myself and asked for everyone's attention.

"Wait a moment," said a heavily accented voice, and in the candlelight I saw the snake girl and her python looking at me. "This boy here was just spewing a lot of rubbish about the place I hail from." She turned to the only chair at the table which was empty and said, "My people call it *Simhaladvipa*—dwelling place of lions."

From the chair Millard replied, "I'm sorry, but it says right here in plain calligraphy: *The Land of Serendip*. The peculiar cartographers who made this were not in the business of making things up!"

Then I got a little closer and saw what it was they were arguing over. It was a Map of Days, though a much larger edition than the one we'd lost at sea. This one stretched practically across the table, and was as thick as a brick stood on end. "I know my own home, and it's called *Simhaladvipa*!" the snake girl insisted, and her python uncoiled from her neck and shot across the table to bang its nose against the Map, indicating a teardrop-shaped island off India's coast. On this map, however, India was called *Malabar*, and the island, which I knew to be Sri Lanka, was overlaid with slinky script that read *Land of Serendip*.

"It's pointless to argue," said Millard. "Some places have as many names as they have occupants to name them. Now please ask your serpent to back away, lest he crinkle the pages."

The snake girl harrumphed and muttered something, and the python slunk away to coil around her neck again. All the while, I couldn't stop staring at the book. The one we'd lost was impressive enough, though I'd seen it opened only once, at night, by the skittish orange firelight of the burning home for peculiar children. This one was of another scale entirely. Not only was it orders of magnitude larger, but it was so ornate that it made the other look like so much leather-bound toilet paper. Colorful maps spilled across its pages, which were made from something stronger than paper, calfskin maybe, and edged with gold. Lush illustrations and legends and blocks of explanatory text stuffed the margins.

Millard noticed me admiring it and said, "Isn't it stunning? Excepting perhaps the *Codex Peculiaris*, this edition of the Map is the finest book in all peculiardom. It took a team of cartographers, artists, and bookmakers a lifetime to create, and it's said that Perplexus Anomalous himself drew some of the maps. I've wanted to see it in person ever since I was a boy. Oh, I am *so* pleased!"

"It's really something," I said, and it was.

"Millard was just showing us some of his favorite parts," said Olive. "I like the pictures best!"

"To take their minds off things," Millard explained, "and make the waiting easier. Here, Jacob, come and help me turn the pages."

Rather than ruin Millard's moment with my sad announcement, I decided it could wait a little while. I wasn't going anywhere until morning, at least, and I wanted to enjoy a few more minutes with my friends unburdened by weightier things. I sidled up next to

Millard and slipped my fingers under the page, which was so large that it took both my hands and his to turn.

We pored over the Map. I was absorbed by it—especially the far-flung and lesser-known parts. Naturally, Europe and its many loops were well-defined, but farther afield things got sketchier. Vast swaths of Africa were simply blank. *Terra incognita*. The same was true of Siberia, although the Map of Days had its own name for Russia's Far East: *The Great Far-Reaching Solitude*.

"Are there loops in these places?" asked Olive, pointing to a void that stretched across much of China. "Are there peculiars there, like us?"

"Certainly there are," Millard said. "Peculiarness is determined by genes, not geography. But large portions of the peculiar world have simply not been explored."

"Why not?"

"I suppose we were too busy surviving."

It occurred to me that the business of surviving precluded a great many things, exploring and falling in love not least among them.

We turned more pages, hunting for blank spots. There were many, and all had fanciful names. *The Mournful Kingdom of Sand. The Land Made in Anger. A High Place Full of Stars.* I mouthed the words silently to myself, appreciating their roundness.

At the margins lurked fearsome places the Map called *Wastes*. The far north of Scandinavia was *The Icy Waste*. The middle of Borneo: *The Stifling Waste*. Much of the Arabian peninsula: *The Pitiless Waste*. The southern tip of Patagonia: *The Cheerless Waste*. Certain places weren't represented at all. New Zealand. Hawaii. Florida, which was just an ingrown nub at America's foot, barely there.

Looking at the Map of Days, even the places that sounded most forbidding evoked in me a strange longing. It reminded me of long-ago afternoons spent with my grandfather studying historic maps in *National Geographic*—maps drawn long before the days of airplanes and satellites, when high-resolution cameras couldn't see into the world's every nook and cranny. When the shape of now-familiar coastlines was guesswork. When the depths and dimensions of icy seas and forbidding jungles were cobbled together from rumors and legends and the wild-eyed ramblings of expeditioners who'd lost half their party exploring them.

While Millard rambled on about the history of the Map, I traced with my finger a vast and trackless desert in Asia. *Where the Winged Creature Ends Not Its Flight.* Here was a whole world yet to be discovered, and I had only just cracked its surface. The thought filled me with regret—but also a shameful kind of relief. I would see my home again, after all, and my parents. And maybe it was childish, this old urge to explore for exploring's sake. There was romance in the unknown, but once a place had been discovered and cataloged and mapped, it was diminished, just another dusty fact in a book, sapped of mystery. So maybe it was better to leave a few spots on the map blank. To let the world keep a little of its magic, rather than forcing it to divulge every last secret.

Maybe it was better, now and then, to wonder.

And then I told them. There was no point in waiting any longer. I just blurted it out: "I'm leaving," I said. "When this is all over, I'm going back home."

There was a moment of shocked silence. Emma met my eyes, finally, and I could see tears standing in them.

Then Bronwyn got up from the table and threw her arms around me. "Brother," she said. "We'll miss you."

"I'll miss you, too," I said. "More than I can say."

"But *why*?" said Olive, floating up to my eye level. "Was I too irritating?"

I put my hand on her head and pushed her back down to the floor. "No, no, it's got nothing to do with you," I said. "You were great, Olive."

Emma stepped forward. "Jacob came here to help us," she said. "But he has to go back to his old life, while it's still there waiting for him."

The children seemed to understand. There was no anger. Most of them seemed genuinely happy for me.

Miss Wren popped her head into the room to give us a quick update—everything was going marvelously, she said. Miss Peregrine was well on her way to recovery. She'd be ready by morning. And then Miss Wren was gone again.

"Thank the gods," said Horace.

"Thank the birds," said Hugh.

"Thank the gods *and* the birds," said Bronwyn. "All the birds in all the trees in all the forests."

"Thank Jacob, too," said Millard. "We never would've made it this far without him."

"We never even would've made it off the *island*," said Bronwyn. "You've done so much for us, Jacob."

They all came and hugged me, each of them, one by one. Then they drifted away and only Emma was left, and she hugged me last—a long, bittersweet embrace that felt too much like goodbye.

"Asking you to leave was the hardest thing I've ever had to do," she said. "I'm glad you came around. I don't think I'd have had the strength to ask again."

"I hate this," I said. "I wish there were a world where we could be together in peace."

"I know," she said. "I know, I know."

"I wish . . . ," I started to say.

"Stop," she said.

I said it anyway. "I wish you could come home with me."

She looked away. "You know what would happen to me if I did."

"I know."

Emma disliked long goodbyes. I could feel her steeling herself, trying to pull her pain inside. "So," she said, businesslike. "Logistics. When Miss Peregrine turns human, she'll lead you back through the carnival, into the underground, and when you pass through the changeover, you'll be back in the present. Think you can manage from there?"

"I think so," I said. "I'll call my parents. Or go to a police station, or something. I'm sure there's a poster of my face in every precinct in Britain by now, knowing my dad." I laughed a little, because if I hadn't, I might've started crying.

"Okay, then," she said.

"Okay, then," I said.

We looked at each other, not quite ready to let go, not sure what else to do. My instinct was to kiss her, but I stopped myself. That wasn't allowed anymore.

"You go," she said. "If you never hear from us again, well, one day you'll be able to tell our story. You can tell your kids about us. Or your grandkids. And we won't entirely be forgotten."

I knew then that, from now on, every word that passed between us would hurt, would be wrapped up with and marked by the pain of this moment, and that I needed to pull away now or it would never stop. So I nodded sadly, hugged her one more time, and retreated to a corner to sleep, because I was very, very tired.

After awhile, the others dragged mattresses and blankets into the room and made a nest around me, and we packed together for warmth against the encroaching chill. But as the others began to bed down, I found myself unable to sleep, despite my exhaustion, and I got up and paced the room for a while, watching the children from a distance.

I'd felt so many things since our journey began—joy, fear, hope, horror—but until now, I'd never once felt alone. Bronwyn had called me brother, but that didn't sound right anymore. I was a second cousin to them at best. Emma was right: I could never understand. They were so old, had seen so much. And I was from another world. Now it was time to go back.

* * *

Eventually, I fell asleep to the sound of ice groaning and cracking in the floors beneath us and the attic above. The building was alive with it.

That night, strange and urgent dreams.

I am home again, doing all the things I used to do. Tearing into a fast-food hamburger—big, brown, and greasy. Riding shotgun in Ricky's Crown Vic, bad radio blaring. At the grocery store with my parents, sliding down long, too-bright aisles, and Emma is there, cooling her hands in the ice at the fish counter, meltwater running everywhere. She doesn't recognize me.

Then I'm at the arcade where I had my twelfth birthday party, firing a plastic gun. Bodies bursting, blood-filled balloons.

Jacob where are you

Then school. Teacher's writing on the board, but the letters don't make sense. Then everyone's on their feet, hurrying outside. Something's wrong. A loud noise rising and falling. Everyone standing still, heads craned to the sky.

Air raid.

Jacob Jacob where are you

Hand on my shoulder. It's an old man. A man without eyes. Come to steal mine. Not a man—a thing—a monster.

Running now. Chasing my old dog. Years ago she'd broken away from me, run off with her leash still attached and got it wrapped around a branch while trying to tree a squirrel. Strangled herself. We spent two weeks wandering the neighborhood calling her name. Found her after three. Old Snuffles.

The siren deafening now. I run and a car pulls alongside and picks me up. My parents are inside, in formal wear. They won't look at me. The doors lock. We're driving and it's stifling hot outside, but the heater is on and the windows are up, and the radio is loud but tuned to the garble between stations.

Mom where are we going

She doesn't answer.

Dad why are we stopping here

Then we're out, walking, and I can breathe again. Pretty green place. Smell of fresh-cut grass. People in black, gathered around a hole in the ground.

A coffin open on a dais. I peer inside. It's empty but for an oily stain slowly spreading across the bottom. Blacking the white satin. *Quick, close the lid!* Black tar bubbles out from the cracks and grooves and drips down into the grass and sinks into the earth.

Jacob where are you say something

The headstone reads: ABRAHAM EZRA PORTMAN. And I'm tumbling into his open grave, darkness spinning up to swallow me, and I keep falling and it's bottomless, and then I'm somewhere underground, alone and wandering through a thousand interconnecting tunnels, and I'm wandering and it's cold, so cold I'm afraid my skin will freeze and my bones will splinter, and everywhere there are yellow eyes watching me from the dark.

I follow his voice. *Yakob, come here. Don't be afraid.*

The tunnel angles upward and there's light at the end, and standing at its mouth, calmly reading a book, is a young man. And he looks just like me, or almost like me, and maybe he is me, I think, but then he speaks, and it's my grandfather's voice. *I have something to show you.*

For a moment I jolted awake in the dark and knew I was dreaming, but I didn't know where I was, only that I was not in bed anymore, not in the meeting hall with the others. I'd gone elsewhere and the room I was in was all black, with ice beneath me, my stomach writhing . . .

Jacob come here where are you

A voice from outside, down the hall—a real voice, not something from a dream.

And then I'm in the dream again, just outside the ropes of a boxing ring, and on the canvas, in the haze and lights, my grandfather faces off against a hollowgast.

They circle each other. My grandfather is young and nimble on his feet, stripped to the waist, a knife in one hand. The hollow is bent and twisted, its tongues waving in the air, open jaws dripping black on the mat. It whips out a tongue and my grandfather dodges it.

Don't fight the pain, that's the key, my grandfather says. *It's telling you something. Welcome it, let it speak to you. The pain says: Hello, I am not other than you; I am of the hollow, but I am you also.*

The hollow whips at him again. My grandfather anticipates it, makes room in advance of the strike. Then the hollow strikes a third time, and my grandfather lashes out with his knife and the tip of the hollow's black tongue falls to the mat, severed and jolting.

They are stupid creatures. Highly suggestible. Speak to them, Yakob. And my grandfather begins to speak, but not in English, nor Polish, nor any language I've heard outside my dreams. It's like some guttural outgassing, the sounds made with something other than a throat or a mouth.

And the creature stops moving, merely swaying where it stands, seemingly hypnotized. Still speaking his frightening gibberish, my grandfather lowers his knife and creeps toward it. The closer he gets, the more docile the creature becomes, finally sinking down to the mat, on its knees. I think it's about to close its eyes and go to sleep when suddenly the hollow breaks free of whatever spell my grandfather has cast over it, and it lashes out with all its tongues and impales my grandfather. As he falls, I leap over the ropes and run toward him, and the hollow slips away. My grandfather is on his back on the mat and I am kneeling by his side, my hand on his face, and he is whispering something to me, blood bubbling on his lips, so I bend closer to hear him. *You are more than me, Yakob,* he says. *You are more than I ever was.*

I can feel his heart slow. Hear it, somehow, until whole seconds elapse between beats. Then tens of seconds. And then . . .

Jacob where are you

I jolted awake again. Now there was light in the room. It was morning, just the blue beginning of it. I was kneeling on the ice in the half-filled room, and my hand wasn't on my grandfather's face but resting atop the trapped hollow's skull, its slow, reptilian brain. Its eyes were open and looking at me, and I was looking right back. *I see you.*

"Jacob! What are you doing? I've been looking for you everywhere!"

It was Emma, frantic, out in the hall. "What are you doing?" she said again. She couldn't see the hollow. Didn't know it was there.

I took my hand away from its head, slid back from it. "I don't know," I said. "I think I was sleepwalking."

"It doesn't matter," she said. "Come quick—Miss Peregrine's about to change!"

*   *   *

Crowded into the little room were all the children and all the freaks from the sideshow, pale and nervous, pressed against the walls and crouched on the floor in a wide berth around the two ymbrynes, like gamblers in a backroom cockfight. Emma and I slipped in among them and huddled in a corner, eyes glued to the unfolding spectacle. The room was a mess: the rocking chair where Miss Wren had sat all night with Miss Peregrine was toppled on its side, the table of vials and beakers pushed roughly against the wall. Althea stood on top of it clutching a net on a pole, ready to wield it.

In the middle of the floor were Miss Wren and Miss Peregrine. Miss Wren was on her knees, and she had Miss Peregrine pinned to the floorboards, her hands in thick falconing gloves, sweating and chanting in Old Peculiar, while Miss Peregrine squawked and flailed with her talons. But no matter how hard Miss Peregrine thrashed, Miss Wren wouldn't let go.

At some point in the night, Miss Wren's gentle massage had turned into something resembling an interspecies pro-wrestling match crossed with an exorcism. The bird half of Miss Peregrine had so thoroughly dominated her nature that it was refusing to be driven away without a fight. Both ymbrynes had sustained minor injuries: Miss Peregrine's feathers were everywhere, and Miss Wren had a long, bloody scratch running down one side of her face. It was a disturbing sight, and many of the children looked on with openmouthed shock. Wild-eyed and savage, the bird Miss Wren was grinding into the floor was one we hardly recognized. It seemed incredible that a fully restored Miss Peregrine of old might result from this violent display, but Althea kept smiling at us and giving us encouraging nods as if to say, *Almost there, just a little more floor-grinding!*

For such a frail old lady, Miss Wren was giving Miss Peregrine a pretty good clobbering. But then the bird jabbed at Miss Wren with her beak and Miss Wren's grasp slipped, and with a big flap of her wings Miss Peregrine nearly escaped from her hands. The children reacted with shouts and gasps. But Miss Wren was quick, and she leapt up and managed to catch Miss Peregrine by her hind leg and thump her down against the floorboards again, which made the children gasp even louder. We weren't used to seeing our ymbryne treated like this, and Bronwyn actually had to stop Hugh from rushing into the fight to protect her.

Both ymbrynes seemed profoundly exhausted now, but Miss Peregrine more so; I could see her strength failing. Her human nature seemed to be winning out over her bird nature.

"Come on, Miss Wren!" Bronwyn cried.

"You can do it, Miss Wren!" called Horace. "Bring her back to us!"

"Please!" said Althea. "We require absolute silence."

After a long time, Miss Peregrine quit struggling and lay on the ground with her wings splayed, gasping for air, feathered chest heaving. Miss Wren took her hands off the bird and sat back on her haunches.

"It's about to happen," she said, "and when it does, I don't want any of you to rush over here grabbing at her. Your ymbryne will likely be very confused, and I want the first face she sees and voice she hears to be mine. I'll need to explain to her what's happened." And then she clasped her hands to her chest and murmured, "Come back to us, Alma. Come on, sister. Come back to us."

Althea stepped down from the table and picked up a sheet, which she unfolded and held up in front of Miss Peregrine to shield her from view. When ymbrynes turned from birds into humans, they were naked; this would give her some privacy.

We waited in breathless suspense while a succession of strange noises came from behind the sheet: an expulsion of air, a sound like someone clapping their hands once, sharply—and then Miss Wren jumped up and took a shaky step backward.

She looked frightened—her mouth was open, and so was Althea's. And then Miss Wren said, "No, this can't be," and Althea stumbled, faint, letting the sheet drop. And there on the floor we saw a human form, but not a woman's.

He was naked, curled into a ball, his back to us. He began to stir, and uncurl, and finally to stand.

"Is that Miss Peregrine?" said Olive. "She came out funny."

Clearly, it was not. The person before us bore no resemblance whatsoever to Miss Peregrine. He was a stunted little man with knobby knees and a balding head and a nose like a used pencil eraser, and he was stark naked and slimed head to toe with sticky, translucent gel. While Miss Wren gaped at him and grasped for something to steady herself against, in shock and anger the others all began to shout, "Who are you? Who are you? What have you done with Miss Peregrine!"

Slowly, slowly, the man raised his hands to his face and rubbed his eyes. Then, for the first time, he opened them.

The pupils were blank and white.

I heard someone scream.

Then, very calmly, the man said, "My name is Caul. And you are all my prisoners now."

*   *   *

"Prisoners!" said the folding man with a laugh. "What he mean, we are prisoners?"

Emma shouted at Miss Wren. "Where's Miss Peregrine? Who's this man, and what have you done with Miss Peregrine?"

Miss Wren seemed to have lost the ability to speak.

As our confusion turned to shock and anger, we barraged the little man with questions. He endured them with a slightly bored expression, standing at the center of the room with his hands folded demurely over his privates.

"If you'd actually permit me to speak, I'll explain everything," he said.

"Where is Miss Peregrine?!" Emma shouted again, trembling with rage.

"Don't worry," Caul said, "she's safely in our custody. We kidnapped her days ago, on your island."

"Then the bird we rescued from the submarine," I said, "that was . . ."

"That was me," Caul said.

"Impossible!" said Miss Wren, finally finding her voice. "Wights can't turn into birds!"

"That is true, as a general rule. But Alma is my sister, you see, and though I wasn't fortunate enough to inherit any of her talents for manipulating time, I do share her most useless trait—the ability to turn into a vicious little bird of prey. I did a rather excellent job impersonating her, don't you think?" And he took a little bow. "Now, may I trouble you for some pants? You have me at a disadvantage."

His request was ignored. Meanwhile, my head was spinning. I remembered Miss Peregrine once mentioning that she'd had two brothers—I'd seen their photo, actually, when they were all in the care of Miss Avocet together. Then I flashed back to the days we'd spent with the bird we had believed was Miss Peregrine; all we'd gone though, everything we'd seen. The caged Miss Peregrine that Golan had thrown into the ocean—that had been the real one, while the one we "rescued" had been her brother. The cruel things Miss Peregrine had done recently made more sense now—that hadn't been Miss Peregrine at all—but I was still left with a million questions.

"All that time," I said. "Why did you stay a bird? Just to watch us?"

"While my lengthy observations of your childish bickering were incontrovertibly fascinating, I was quite hoping you could help me with a piece of unfinished business. When you killed my men in the countryside, I was impressed. You proved yourselves to be quite resourceful. Naturally, my men could've swept in and taken you at any point after that, but I thought it better to let you twist in the wind awhile and see if your ingenuity might not lead us to the one ymbryne who's consistently managed to evade us." With that, he turned to Miss Wren and grinned broadly. "Hello, Balenciaga. So good to see you again."

Miss Wren moaned and fanned herself with her hand.

"You idiots, you cretins, you morons!" the clown shouted. "You led them right to us!"

"And as a nice bonus," said Caul, "we paid a visit to your menagerie, as well! My men came by not long after we left; the stuffed heads of that emu-raffe and boxer dog will look *magnificent* above my mantelpiece."

"You monster!" Miss Wren screeched, and she fell back against the table, legs failing her.

"Oh, my bird!" exclaimed Bronwyn, her eyes wide. "Fiona and Claire!"

"You'll see them again soon," Caul said. "I've got them in safekeeping."

It all began to make a terrible kind of sense. Caul knew he'd be welcomed into Miss Wren's menagerie disguised as Miss Peregrine, and when she wasn't at home to be kidnapped, he'd nudged us after her, toward London. In so many ways, we'd been manipulated from the very beginning—from the moment we chose to leave the island and I chose to go along. Even the tale he'd chosen for Bronwyn to read that first night in the forest, about the stone giant, had been a manipulation. He wanted us to find Miss Wren's loop, and think that it was we who'd cracked its secret.

Those of us who weren't reeling in horror frothed with anger. Several people were shouting that Caul should be killed, and were busily hunting for sharp objects to do the job with, while the few who'd kept their heads were trying to hold them back. All the while, Caul stood calmly, waiting for the furor to die down.

"If I may?" he said. "I wouldn't entertain any ideas about killing me. You *could*, of course; no one can stop you. But it will go much easier for you if I am unharmed when my men arrive." He pretended to check a nonexistent watch on his wrist. "Ah, yes," he said, "they should be here now—yes, just about now—surrounding the building, covering every conceivable point of exit, including the roof. And might I add, there are fifty-six of them and they are armed positively to the teeth. *Beyond* the teeth. Have you ever seen what a mini-gun can do to a child-sized human body?" He looked directly at Olive and said, "It would turn you to cat's meat, darling."

"You're bluffing!" said Enoch. "There's no one out there!"

"I assure you, there is. They've been watching me closely since we left your depressing little island, and I gave my signal to them the moment Balenciaga revealed herself to us. That was over twelve hours ago—more than ample time to muster a fighting force."

"Allow me to verify this," said Miss Wren, and she left to go to the ymbryne meeting room, where the windows were obstructed from ice mostly from the outside, and a few had small telescope tunnels melted through them with mirror attachments that let us look down at the street below.

While we waited for her to return, the clown and the snake girl debated the best ways to torture Caul.

"I say we pull out his toenails first," said the clown. "Then stick hot pokers in his eyes."

"Where I come from," the snake girl said, "the punishment for treason is being covered in honey, bound to an open boat, and floated out into a stagnant pond. The flies eat you alive."

Caul stood cricking his neck from side to side and stretching his arms boredly. "Apologies," he said. "Remaining a bird for so long tends to cramp the muscles."

"You think we're kidding?" said the clown.

"I think you're amateurs," said Caul. "If you found a few young bamboo shoots, I could show you something really wicked. As delightful as that would be, though, I do recommend you melt this ice, because it'll save us all a world of trouble. I say this for your sake, out of genuine concern for your well-being."

"Yeah, right," said Emma. "Where was your concern when you were stealing those peculiars' souls?"

"Ah, yes. Our three pioneers. Their sacrifice was necessary— all for the sake of progress, my dears. What we're trying to do is advance the peculiar species, you see."

"What a joke," she said. "You're nothing but power-hungry sadists!"

"I know you're all quite sheltered and uneducated," said Caul, "but did your ymbrynes not teach you about our people's history? We peculiars used to be like gods roaming the earth! Giants—kings—the world's rightful rulers! But over the centuries and millennia, we've suffered a terrible decline. We mixed with normals to such an extent that the purity of our peculiar blood has been diluted almost to nothing. And now look at us, how degraded we've become! We hide in these temporal backwaters, afraid of the very people we should be ruling, arrested in a state of perpetual childhood by this confederacy of busybodies—these *women*! Don't you see how they've reduced us? Are you not ashamed? Do you have any idea of the power that's rightfully ours? Don't you feel the blood of *giants* in your veins?" He was losing his cool now, going red in the face. "We aren't trying to eradicate peculiardom—we're trying to *save* it!"

"Is that right?" said the clown, and then walked over to Caul and spat right in his face. "Well, you've got a twisted way of going at it."

Caul wiped the spit away with the back of his hand. "I knew it would be pointless to reason with you. The ymbrynes have been feeding you lies and propaganda for a hundred years. Better, I think, to take your souls and start again fresh."

Miss Wren returned. "He speaks the truth," she said. "There must be fifty soldiers out there. All of them armed."

"Oh, oh, oh," moaned Bronwyn, "what are we to *do*?"

"Give up," said Caul. "Go quietly."

"It doesn't matter how many of them there are," Althea said. "They'll never be able to get through all my ice."

The ice! I'd nearly forgotten. We were inside a fortress of ice!

"That's right!" Caul said brightly. "She's absolutely right, they can't get in. So there's a quick and painless way to do this, where you melt the ice voluntarily right now, or there's the long, stubborn, slow, boring, sad way, which is called a siege, where for weeks and months my men stand guard outside while we stay in here, quietly starving to death. Maybe you'll give up when you're desperate and hungry enough. Or maybe you'll start cannibalizing one another. Either way, if my men have to wait that long, they'll torture every last one of you to death when they get in, which inevitably they will. And if we *must* go the slow, boring, sad route, then please, for the sake of the children, bring me some trousers."

"Althea, fetch the man some damned trousers!" said Miss Wren. "But do *not*, under any circumstances, melt this ice!"

"Yes, ma'am," replied Althea, and she went out.

"Now," said Miss Wren, turning to Caul. "Here's what we'll do. You tell your men to allow us safe passage out of here, or we'll kill you. If we have to do it, I assure you we will, and we'll dump your stinking corpse out a hole in the ice a piece at a time. While I'm sure your men won't like that much, we'll have a very long time to devise our next move."

Caul shrugged and said, "Oh, all right."

"Really?" Miss Wren said.

"I thought I could scare you," he said, "but you're right, I'd rather not be killed. So take me to one of these holes in the ice and I'll do as you've asked and shout down to my men."

Althea came back in with some pants and threw them at Caul, and he put them on. Miss Wren appointed Bronwyn, the clown, and the folding man to be Caul's guards, arming them with broken icicles. With their points aimed at his back, we proceeded into the hall. But as we were bottlenecking through the small, dark office that led to the ymbryne meeting room, everything went wrong. Someone tripped over a mattress and went down, and then I heard a scuffle break out in the dark. Emma lit a flame just in time to see Caul dragging Althea away from us by the hair. She kicked and flailed while Caul held a sharpened icicle to her throat and shouted, "Stay back or I drive this through her jugular!"

We followed Caul at a careful distance. He dragged Althea thrashing and kicking into the meeting hall, and then up onto the oval table, where he put her in a choke hold, the icicle held an inch from her eye, and shouted, "*These are my demands!*"

Before he could get any further, though, Althea slapped the icicle from his hand. It flew and landed point-down in the pages of the Map of Days. While his mouth was still forming an O of surprise, Althea's hand latched onto the front of Caul's pants, and the O broadened into a grimace of shock.

"*Now!*" Emma bellowed, and then she and I and Bronwyn rushed toward them through the wooden doors. But as we ran, the distance across that big room seemed to yawn, and in seconds the fight between Althea and Caul had taken another turn: Caul let go of Althea and fell to the table, his arms stretched and grasping for the icicle. Althea fell with him but did not let go—now had both hands wrapped around his thigh—and a coating of ice was spreading quickly across Caul's lower half, paralyzing him from the waist down and freezing Althea's hands to his leg. He got one finger around the icicle, and then his whole hand, and groaning with effort and pain, he wrenched it free from the Map and twisted his upper body until he had the point of it poised above Althea's back. He screamed at her to stop and let him go and melt the ice or he'd plunge it into her.

We were just yards from them now, but Bronwyn caught Emma and me and held us back.

Caul screamed, "Stop! Stop this!" as his face contorted in pain, the ice racing up his chest and over his shoulders. In a few seconds, his arms and hands would be encased, too.

Althea didn't stop.

And then Caul did it—he stabbed the icicle into her back. She tensed in shock, then groaned. Miss Wren ran toward them, screaming Althea's name while the ice that had spread across most of Caul's body began, very quickly, to recede. By the time Miss Wren reached them, he was nearly free of it. But then the ice everywhere was melting, too—fading and retracting just as quickly as Althea's life was—the ice in the attic dripping and raining down through the ceiling just as Althea's own blood ran down her body. She was in Miss Wren's arms now, slack, going.

Bronwyn was on the table, Caul's throat in one hand, his weapon crushed to snow in her other. We could hear the ice in floors below us melting, too, and then it was gone from the windows. We rushed to look out, and could see water flooding from lower windows into the street, where soldiers in gray urban camo were clinging to lampposts and fire hydrants to keep from being washed away by the icy waves.

Then we heard their boots stomping on the stairs below and coming down from the roof above, and moments later they burst in with their guns, shouting. Some of the men wore night-vision headsets and all of them bristled with weapons—compact machine guns, laser-sighted pistols, combat knives. It took three of them to pry Bronwyn away from Caul, who wheezed through his half-crushed windpipe, "Take them away, and don't be gentle!"

Miss Wren was shouting, begging us to comply—"Do as they say or they'll hurt you!"—but she wouldn't let go of Althea's body, so they made an example of her; they tore Althea away and kicked Miss Wren to the ground, and one of the soldiers fired his machine pistol into the ceiling just to scare us. When I saw Emma about to make a fireball with her hands, I grabbed her by the arm and begged her not to—"Don't, please don't, they'll kill you!"—and then a rifle butt slammed into my chest and I fell gasping to the floor. One of the soldiers noosed my hands together behind me.

I heard them counting us, Caul listing our names, making sure even Millard was accounted for—because of course by now, having spent the last three days with us, he knew all of us, knew everything about us.

I was pulled to my feet and we were all pushed out through the doors into the hallway. Stumbling along next to me was Emma, blood in her hair, and I whispered, "Please, just do what they say," and though she didn't acknowledge it, I knew she'd heard me. The look on her face was all rage and fear and shock—and I think pity, too, for all I'd just had snatched away from me.

In the stairwell, the floors and stairs below were a white-water river, a vortex of cascading waves. Up was the only way out. We were shoved up the stairs, through a door and into strong daylight, onto the roof. Everyone wet, frozen, frightened into silence.

All but Emma. "Where are you taking us?" she demanded.

Caul came right to her and grinned in her face while a soldier held her cuffed hands behind her. "A very special place," Caul said, "where not a drop of your peculiar souls will go to waste."

She flinched, and he laughed and turned away, stretching his arms above his head and yawning. From his shoulder blades jutted a weird pair of knobby protrusions, like the stems of aborted wings: the only outward clue that this twisted man bore any relation to an ymbryne.

Voices shouted from the top of another building. More soldiers. They were laying down a collapsible bridge between rooftops.

"What about the dead girl?" one of the soldiers asked.

"Such a pity, such a waste," Caul said, clucking his tongue. "I should have liked to dine on her soul. It's got no taste on its own, the peculiar soul," he said, addressing us. "Its natural consistency is a bit gelatinous and pasty, really, but whipped together with a soupçon of remoulade and spread upon white meat, it's quite palatable."

Then he laughed, very loudly, for a long time.

As they led us away, one by one, over the wide collapsible bridge, I felt a familiar twinge in my gut—faint but strengthening, slow but quickening—the hollowgast, unfrozen now, coming slowly back to life.

*   *   *

Ten soldiers marched us out of the loop at gunpoint, past the carnival tents and sideshows and gaping carnival-goers, down the rats' warren of alleys with their stalls and vendors and ragamuffin kids staring after us, into the disguising room, past the piles of cast-off clothes we'd left behind, and down into the underground. The soldiers prodded us along, barking at us to keep quiet (though no one had said a word in minutes), to keep our heads down and stay in line or be pistol-whipped.

Caul was no longer with us—he had stayed behind with the larger contingent of soldiers to "mop up," which I think meant scouring the loop for hiders and stragglers. The last time we saw him, he was pulling on a pair of modern boots and an army jacket and told us he was absolutely sick of our faces but would see us "on the other side," whatever that meant.

We passed through the changeover, and forward in time again—but not to a version of the tunnels I recognized. The tracks and ties were all metal now, and the lights in the tunnels were different, not red incandescents but flickering fluorescent tubes that glowed a sick-ly green. Then we came out of the tunnel and onto the platform, and I understood why: we were no longer in the nineteenth century, nor even the twentieth. The crowd of sheltering refugees was gone now; the station nearly deserted. The circular staircase we'd come down was gone, too, replaced by an escalator. A scrolling LED screen hung above the platform: TIME TO NEXT TRAIN: 2 MINUTES. On the wall was a poster for a movie I'd seen earlier in the summer, just before my grandfather died.

We'd left 1940 behind. I was back in the present.

A few of the kids took note of this with looks of surprise and fear, as if afraid they would age forward in a matter of minutes, but for most of them I think the shock of our sudden captivity was not about to be trumped by an unexpected trip to the present; they were worried about having their souls extracted, not about developing gray hair and liver spots.

The soldiers corralled us in the middle of the platform to wait for the train. Hard shoes clicked toward us. I risked a look over my shoulder and saw a policeman coming. Behind him, stepping off the escalator, were three more.

"Hey!" Enoch shouted. "Policeman, over here!"

A soldier punched Enoch in the gut, and he doubled over.

"Everything good here?" said the closest policeman.

"They've taken us prisoner!" said Bronwyn. "They aren't really soldiers, they're—"

And then she got a punch to the gut, too, though it didn't seem to hurt her. What stopped her from saying more was the policeman himself, who took off his mirrored sunglasses to reveal stark white eyes. Bronwyn shrank back.

"A bit of advice," the policeman said. "No help is coming to you. We are everywhere. Accept that, and this will all be easier."

Normals were starting to fill the station. The soldiers pressed in on us from all sides, keeping their weapons hidden.

A train hissed into the station, filled with people. Its electric doors whooshed open and a glut of passengers spilled out. The soldiers began pushing us toward the nearest car, the policemen going ahead to scatter what few passengers remained inside. "Find another car!" they barked. "Get out!" The passengers grumbled but complied. But there were more people behind us on the platform, trying to push into the car, and a few of the soldiers who'd been ringing us had to break away to stop them. And then there was just enough confusion—the doors trying to close but the police holding them open until a warning alarm began to sound; the soldiers shoving us forward so hard that Enoch tripped, sending other children tripping over him in a chain reaction—that the folding man, whose wrists were so skinny he'd been able to slip his cuffs, decided to make a break for it, and ran.

A shot rang out, then a second, and the folding man tumbled and splayed onto the ground. The crowd swarmed away in a panic, people screaming and scrambling to escape the gunshots, and what had been merely confusion deteriorated into total chaos.

Then they were shoving us and kicking us onto the train. Beside me, Emma was resisting, making the soldier who was pushing her get close. Then I saw her cuffed hands flare orange, and she reached behind her and grabbed him. The soldier crumpled to the ground, shrieking, a hand-shaped hole melted through his camo. Then the soldier who was pushing *me* raised the butt of his gun and was about to bring it down on Emma's neck when some instinct triggered in me and I drove my shoulder into his back.

He stumbled.

Emma melted through her metal cuffs, which fell away from her hands in a deformed mass of red-hot metal. My soldier turned his gun on me now, howling with rage, but before he could fire, Emma came at him from behind and clapped her hands around his face, her fingers so hot they melted through his cheeks like warm butter. He dropped the gun and collapsed, screaming.

All this happened very quickly, in a matter of seconds.

Then two more soldiers were coming at us. Nearly everyone else was on the train now—all but Bronwyn and the blind brothers, who had never been cuffed and were merely standing by with arms linked. Seeing that we were about to be shot to death, Bronwyn did something I could never have imagined her doing under any other circumstances: she slapped the older brother hard across the face, then took the younger one and wrenched him roughly away from the older.

The moment their connection was severed, they let out a scream so powerful it generated its own wind. It tore through the station like a tornado of pure energy—blowing Emma and me backwards, shattering the soldiers' glasses, eclipsing most of the frequencies my ears could detect so that all I heard was a squeaking, high-pitched *Eeeeeeeee* . . .

I saw all the windows of the train break and the LED screens shiver to knife shards and the glass light tubes along the roof explode, so that we were plunged for a moment into pure blackness, then the hysterical red flashing of emergency lights.

I had fallen onto my back, the wind knocked out of me, my ears ringing. Something was pulling me backwards by the collar, away from the train, and I couldn't quite remember how to work my arms and legs well enough to resist. Beneath the ringing in my ears I could make out frantic voices shouting, "*Go, just go!*"

I felt something cold and wet against the back of my neck, and was dragged into a phone booth. Emma was there, too, folded into a ball in the corner, semiconscious.

"Pull your legs up," I heard a familiar voice say, and from around back of me came trotting a short, furry thing with a pushed-in snout and a jowly mouth.

The dog. Addison.

I pulled my legs into the booth, my wits returning enough to move but not speak.

The last thing I saw, in the hellish red flashing, was Miss Wren being shoved into the train car and the doors snapping closed, and all my friends inside with her, cowering at gunpoint, framed by the shattered windows of the train, surrounded by men with white eyes.

Then the train roared away into the darkness, and was gone.

*   *   *

I startled awake to a tongue licking my face.

The dog.

The door of the phone booth had been pulled closed, and the three of us were crammed inside on the floor.

"You passed out," said the dog.

"They're gone," I said.

"Yes, but we can't stay here. They'll come back for you. We have to go."

"I don't think I can stand up just yet."

The dog had a cut on his nose, and a hunk of one ear was missing. Whatever he'd done to get here, he'd been through hell, too.

I felt a tickle against my leg, but was too tired to look and see what it was. My head was heavy as a boulder.

"Don't go to sleep again," said the dog, and then he turned to Emma and began to lick her face.

The tickle again. This time I shifted my weight and reached for it.

It was my phone. My phone was vibrating. I couldn't believe it. I dug it out of my pocket. The battery was nearly dead, the signal almost nonexistent. The screen read: DAD (177 MISSED CALLS).

If I hadn't been so groggy, I probably wouldn't have answered. At any moment a man with a gun might arrive to finish us off. Not a good time for a conversation with my father. But I wasn't thinking straight, and anytime my phone rang, my old Pavlovian impulse was to pick it up.

I pressed ANSWER. "Hello?"

A choked cry on the other end. Then: "Jacob? Is that you?"

"It's me."

I must've sounded awful. My voice a faint rasp.

"Oh, my God, oh, my God," my father said. He hadn't expected me to answer, maybe had given me up for dead already and was calling now out of some reflexive grief instinct that he couldn't switch off. "I don't—where did you—what happened—where *are* you, son?"

"I'm okay," I said. "I'm alive. In London."

I don't know why I told him that last part. I guess I felt like I owed him some truth.

Then it sounded like he aimed his head away from the receiver to shout to someone else, "It's Jacob! He's in London!" Then back to me: "We thought you were *dead*."

"I know. I mean, I'm not surprised. I'm sorry about leaving the way I did. I hope I didn't scare you too much."

"You scared us to *death*, Jacob." My father sighed, a long, shivering sound that was relief and disbelief and exasperation all at once. "Your mother and I are in London, too. After the police couldn't find you on the island . . . anyway, it doesn't matter, just tell us where you are and we'll come get you!"

Emma began to stir. Her eyes opened and she looked at me, bleary, like she was somewhere deep inside herself and peering out at me through miles of brain and body. Addison said, "Good, very good, now stay with us," and began licking her hand instead.

I said into the phone, "I can't come, Dad. I can't drag you into this."

"Oh, God, I knew it. You're on drugs, aren't you? Look, whoever you've gotten mixed up with, we can help. We don't have to bring the police into it. We just want you back."

Then everything went dark for a second in my head, and when I came to again, I felt such a gut-punch of pain in my belly that I dropped the phone.

Addison jerked his head up to look at me. "What is it?"

That's when I saw a long, black tongue pressing against the outside of the booth's glass. It was quickly joined by a second, then a third.

The hollow. The unfrozen hollowgast. It had followed us.

The dog couldn't see it, but he could read the look on my face easily enough. "It's one of them, isn't it?"

I mouthed, *Yes*, and Addison shrank into a corner.

"Jacob?" My dad's tinny voice from the phone. "Jacob, are you there?"

The tongues began to wrap around the booth, encircling us. I didn't know what to do, only that I had to do *something*, so I shifted my feet under me, planted my hands on the walls, and struggled to my feet.

Then I was face to face with it. Tongues fanned from its gaping, bladed mouth. Its eyes were black and weeping more black and they stared into mine, inches away through the glass. The hollow let out a low, guttural snarl that turned my insides to jelly, and I half wished the beast would just kill me and be done with it so all this pain and terror could end.

The dog barked in Emma's face. "Wake up! We need you, girl! Make your fire!"

But Emma could neither speak nor stand, and we were alone in the underground station but for two women in raincoats who were backing away, holding their noses against the hollow's fetid stench.

And then the booth, the whole booth with all of us in it, swayed one way and then the other, and I heard whatever bolts anchored it to the floor groan and snap. Slowly, the hollow lifted us off the ground—six inches, then a foot, then two—only to slam us back down again, shattering the booth windows, raining glass on us.

Then there was nothing at all between the hollow and me. Not an inch, not a pane of glass. Its tongues wriggled into the booth, snaking around my arm, my waist, then around my neck, squeezing tighter and tighter until I couldn't breathe.

That's when I knew I was dead. And because I was dead, and there was nothing I could do, I stopped fighting. I relaxed every muscle, closed my eyes, and gave in to the hurt bursting inside my belly like fireworks.

Then a strange thing happened: the hurt stopped hurting. The pain shifted and became something else. I entered into it, and it enveloped me, and beneath its roiling surface I discovered something quiet and gentle.

A whisper.

I opened my eyes again. The hollow seemed frozen now, staring at me. I stared back, unafraid. My vision was spotting black from lack of oxygen, but I felt no pain.

The hollow's grip on my neck relaxed. I took my first breath in minutes, calm and deep. And then the whisper I'd found inside me traveled up from my belly and out of my throat and past my lips, making a noise that didn't sound like language, but whose meaning I knew innately.

Back.

Off.

The hollow retracted its tongues. Drew them all back into its bulging mouth and shut its jaws. Bowed its head slightly—a gesture, almost, of submission.

And then it sat down.

Emma and Addison looked up at me from the floor, surprised by the sudden calm. "What just happened?" said the dog.

"There's nothing to be afraid of," I said.

"Is it gone?"

"No, but it won't hurt us now."

He didn't ask how I knew this; just nodded, assured by the tone of my voice.

I opened the booth door and helped Emma to her feet. "Can

you walk?" I asked her. She put an arm around my waist, leaned her weight against mine, and together we took a step. "I'm not leaving you," I said. "Whether you like it or not."

Into my ear she whispered, "I love you, Jacob."

"I love you, too," I whispered back.

I stooped to pick up the phone. "Dad?"

"What was that noise? Who are you with?"

"I'm here. I'm okay."

"No, you're not. Just stay where you are."

"Dad, I have to go. I'm sorry."

"Wait. Don't hang up," he said. "You're confused, Jake."

"No. I'm like Grandpa. I have what Grandpa had."

A pause on the other end. Then: "Please come home."

I took a breath. There was too much to say and no time to say it. This would have to do:

"I hope I'll be able to come home, someday. But there are things I need to do first. I just want you to know I love you and Mom, and I'm not doing any of this to hurt you."

"We love you, too, Jake, and if it's drugs, or whatever it is, we don't care. We'll get you right again. Like I said, you're confused."

"No, Dad. I'm peculiar."

Then I hung up the phone, and speaking a language I didn't know I knew, I ordered the hollow to stand.

Obedient as a shadow, it did.

About the Photography

Like those in the first book, *Miss Peregrine's Home for Peculiar Children*, all the pictures in *Hollow City* are authentic, vintage, found photographs, and with the exception of a handful that have undergone digital postprocessing, they are unaltered. They were painstakingly collected over several years: discovered at flea markets, vintage paper shows, and, more often than not, in the archives of photo collectors much more accomplished than I, who were kind enough to part with some of their most peculiar treasures to help create this book.

The following photos were graciously lent for use by their owners:

PAGE	TITLE	FROM THE COLLECTION OF
8	Jacob in silhouette	Roselyn Leibowitz
8	Emma Bloom	Muriel Moutet
9	Enoch O'Connor	David Bass
10	Claire Densmore	Davis Bass
10	Fiona	John Van Noate
11	Miss Avocet	Erin Waters
212	Girl boarding train	John Van Noate
226	Crying baby	John Van Noate
246	Peculiar brothers	John Van Noate
283	Sam	John Van Noate
300	Millard in the mirror	John Van Noate
309	The lookout	John Van Noate

Acknowledgments

In the acknowledgments of *Miss Peregrine's Home for Peculiar Children*, I thanked my editor, Jason Rekulak, for his "seemingly endless" patience. Now, after a second book that took twice as long to write, I'm afraid I need to thank him for his truly legendary, nay, saintly, patience; verily, he hath the patience of Job! I hope it was worth the wait, and I'll be forever grateful to him for helping me find my way.

Thanks to the team at Quirk Books—Brett, David, Nicole, Moneka, Katherine, Doogie, Eric, John, Mary Ellen, and Blair—for being at once the sanest and most creative people in publishing. Thanks, too, to everyone at Random House Publisher Services, and to my publishers abroad for somehow managing to gracefully translate my oddball, made-up words into other languages (and for occasionally hosting a tall, pale, and slightly confused American author in your country; sorry for the mess I made of your guest room).

Thanks to my agent, Jodi Reamer, for reading many drafts of this book, for always giving notes that made the book better, and for (almost) always using her first-degree black belt for good, not evil.

A hearty thank-you to my photo collector friends, who helped enormously in the creation of this book. Robert E. Jackson, Peter J. Cohen, Steve Bannos, Michael Fairley, Stacy Waldman, John Van Noate, David Bass, Yefim Tovbis, and Fabien Breuvart—I couldn't have done it without you.

Thanks to the teachers who challenged and encouraged me over the years: Donald Rogan, Perry Lentz, P. F. Kluge, Jonathan Tazewell, Kim McMullen, Linda Janoff, Philip Eisner, Wendy Mac-Leod, Doe Mayer, Jed Dannenbaum, Nina Foch, Lewis Hyde, and John Kinsella, among many others.

Thanks most of all to Tahereh, who has brightened my life in uncountable ways. I love you, *azizam*.

A Conversation
with Ransom Riggs

R ansom Riggs grew up in Florida and studied at Kenyon
College and the University of Southern California's School
of Cinema. His first novel, *Miss Peregrine's Home for
Peculiar Children*, was a #1 *New York Times* best seller. He recently
sat down with Quirk Books publisher Jason Rekulak to discuss writing the sequel, *Hollow City*.

When describing how you wrote *Miss Peregrine's Home for Peculiar Children*, you once explained that "the photos came first," and then you shaped the story around the imagery. Was the process different this time around?

Very much so! When I was starting the first book, the slate was blank. I had a pile of strange photographs and some strange ideas, but nothing was set in stone yet. So, a great photograph could lead the way, sparking whole plotlines and inspiring major characters. With *Hollow City*, so much of the story was already in motion that the photos had to play a subtler role. Rather than writing a scene around a photograph, I would go looking for the perfect photograph to fit a scene I knew had to be in the book.

That's interesting. Were there any instances where you had multiple "perfect" photographs but had to choose the most perfect one?

One of the challenges of searching for a photo to fit a scene I'd already written was that there was often no perfect photo. I'd have one in my mind, but it didn't exist—I would have had to stage it like a movie and shoot it myself, which would've been extraordinarily expensive! Usually what happens is, I'll find a photo that's in the neighborhood of the perfect photo, but it's a few houses to the left and the garage is painted the wrong color and the hedges are all wrong. But it's as close as I'm going to get.

So, with that almost-perfect photo in mind, I go back and rewrite the scene a bit to match what I found, tweaking details to align with the specific image. Luckily, where the scene ends up is usually more interesting than where it started, all thanks to the challenge of finding the right picture.

However, there were a few instances where several different photos would've worked for a scene—at least, before I rewrote it to fit one image in particular. An example is the photo of the wights' zeppelins flying over the beach (shown on page 34). Early twentieth-century photos of zeppelins and hot-air balloons are fairly common. I just really happened to like the one I chose, which I thought had a nice foreboding quality. But I could've gone with something like this instead:

Of course, it has French writing on the front of it, and explaining that would've presented a challenge.

Another example: when Addison describes the various indignities suffered by peculiar animals over the years, he shows a photo of a dog pulling a boy in a cart.

Unfortunately, pictures of animals being humiliated by humans are easy to find. I considered but ultimately decided against using this insane photo of a baby riding an eagle, which I'm really happy to have an excuse to share with you here, because it's a picture of a baby riding an eagle.

What was the most challenging aspect of writing *Hollow City*?

The plotting. The ending of *Miss Peregrine* was so open, almost anything could've happened to those kids in their little boats. They were embarking into a world of time loops and infinite possibility, and my temptation as a writer is always to explore everything, every nook and cranny of the world I'm creating, but that's never possible (or advisable). Winnowing those endless possibilities is the hardest part of my job, because it feels like I'm saying no to all these story threads that could be great. But there's only so much time, only so many pages, only so much story I can tell in one book. More's the pity!

You wrote *Miss Peregrine's Home for Peculiar Children* in relative anonymity. Did the blockbuster success of that book—two million copies sold, dozens of translations, a huge movie deal—have an impact on your writing process?

I'd like to think it didn't. I'm probably my own harshest critic, so the judgments of others don't faze me much. I suppose it might be different if I had to, say, read the book aloud in front of an audience of two million people. That would be crazy intimidating. But I still write alone in a quiet room, like I always have, where I can at least pretend that no one's going to read the thing I'm typing besides my wife and my mom.

One of the pleasures of *Hollow City* is that we get to spend more time with the individual peculiars. Do you have a favorite among the children? Are any of the characters especially fun to write?

Each character reflects a slightly exaggerated aspect of my own personality, I think, so whom I enjoy writing about depends on how I'm feeling at the time. Enoch is me when I'm grumpy and petulant. I sometimes have a tendency to deliver mini lectures on obscure subjects people may or may not have any interest in, and I channel that when writing Millard. Emma is always a joy to write because she says exactly what she means, sometimes too forcefully for her own good, which can be cathartic. I aspire to be as noble and loyal as Bronwyn. So, it depends. I love finding new characters along the way, too, like Addison, and seeing where the story takes them.

I was completely floored by Caul's arrival in the finale of *Hollow City*. Were you planning this twist all along? Or did he surprise you, too?

I wish I could say I knew all along, but the idea of having the bird who the kids thought was Miss Peregrine be her evil brother instead came to me about halfway through the writing of the book. When it occurred to me, I clapped my hands and cackled so loud it scared the cat out of the room.

Do you have a favorite photograph in the book?

It's hard to choose a favorite, but I'm partial to the woman in the horned chair smoking a pipe.

The photographs in *Hollow City* depict so many strange and fantastic visions: a house atop a stack of railroad ties, a man snared in a fishing net. Are you ever tempted to research any of their "real" origins?

Yes, and I often do, though I rarely uncover any substantive information. That's a relief, ultimately, because I like having the freedom to make up stories about my photos, and I think knowing the "real" stories—as curious as I am—might take away some of the fun and fantasy.

It's clear that some of these photographers used early forms of trick

photography. I'm thinking particularly of the emu-raffe on page 89 and the invisible boy on page 300. Do you know how these effects were achieved?

I have no idea about the invisible boy. My only guess is that it was some sort of double-exposure applied only to the bottom of the frame, where his feet would be—one photo of him in the chair married to one without him, but just the feet. Then again, maybe he just didn't have any feet! It's Occam's razor: sometimes the simplest answer is the most likely. As for the emu-raffe, my assumption is that it's a really bizarre piece of taxidermy, not a photo manipulation.

Last but not least: We know you're putting the finishing touches on the next book, and we can't wait to see what happens. How about a sneak preview?

Book three picks up right where *Hollow City* left off. Jacob, Emma, and Addison follow their kidnapped friends' quickly vanishing trail to Devils' Acre, the most dangerous loop in peculiardom. It's home to the worst of the worst: peculiar criminals, exiles, addicts, and, at its festering heart, the wights' lair. With the help of a mysterious defector and his ingenious loop-making machine, our peculiar heroes will finally make their stand against the wights. Should they fail, it's not only their lives that hang in the balance, but the future of all peculiars. In other words, fans can expect lots of action, loads of atmosphere, and plenty more peculiar photos:

FEATURING CURIOUS NEW CHARACTERS . . .

... NEW YMBRYNES AND NEW PECULIAR ANIMALS ...

. . . MASKED WEIRDOS AND COWBOYS . . .

. . . AND UNEXPECTED PERILS!

AVAILABLE NOW

THE THIRD NOVEL OF
MISS PEREGRINE'S
PECULIAR CHILDREN

TURN THE PAGE FOR
AN EXCLUSIVE SNEAK PREVIEW!

*T*he monster stood not a tongue's length away, eyes fixed on our throats, shriveled brain crowded with fantasies of murder. Its hunger for us charged the air. Hollows are born lusting after the souls of peculiars, and here we were arrayed before it like a buffet: bite-sized Addison bravely standing his ground at my feet, tail at attention; Emma moored against me for support, still too dazed from the impact to make more than a match flame; our backs laddered against the wrecked phone booth. Beyond our grim circle, the underground station looked like the aftermath of a nightclub bombing. Steam from burst pipes shrieked forth in ghostly curtains. Splintered monitors swung broken-necked from the ceiling. A sea of shattered glass spread all the way to the tracks, flashing in the hysterical strobe of red emergency lights like an acre-wide disco ball. We were boxed in, a wall hard to one side and glass shin-deep on the other, two strides from a creature whose only natural instinct was to disassemble us—and yet it made no move to close the gap. It seemed rooted to the floor, swaying on its heels like a drunk or a sleepwalker, death's head drooping, its tongues a nest of snakes I'd charmed to sleep.

Me. I'd done that. Jacob Portman, boy nothing from Nowhere, Florida. It was not currently murdering us—this horror made of gathered dark and nightmares harvested from sleeping children— because I had asked it not to. Told it in no uncertain terms to unwrap its tongue from around my neck. *Back off*, I'd said. *Stand*, I'd said— in a language made of sounds I hadn't known a human mouth could make—and miraculously it had, eyes challenging me while its body obeyed. Somehow I had tamed the nightmare, cast a spell over it. But sleeping things wake and spells wear off, especially those cast by accident, and beneath its placid surface I could feel the hollow boiling.

Addison nudged my calf with his nose. "More wights will be coming. Will the beast let us pass?"

"Talk to it again," Emma said, her voice woozy and vague. "Tell it to sod off."

I searched for the words, but they'd gotten shy. "I don't know how."

"You did a minute ago," Addison said. "It sounded like there was a demon inside you."

A minute ago, before I'd known I could do it, the words had been right there on my tongue, just waiting to be spoken. Now that I wanted them back, it was like trying to catch fish with bare hands. Every time I touched one, it slipped out of my grasp.

Go away! I shouted.

The words came in English. The hollow didn't move. I stiffened my back, glared into its inkpot eyes, and tried again.

Get out of here! Leave us alone!

English again. The hollow tilted its head like a curious dog but was otherwise a statue.

"Is he gone?" Addison asked.

The others couldn't tell for sure; only I could see it. "Still there," I said. "I don't know what's wrong."

I felt silly and deflated. Had my gift vanished so quickly?

"Never mind," Emma said. "Hollows aren't meant to be reasoned with, anyway." She stuck out a hand and tried to light a flame, but it fizzled. The effort seemed to sap her. I tightened my grip around her waist lest she topple over.

"Save your strength, matchstick," said Addison. "I'm sure we'll need it."

"I'll fight it with cold hands if I have to," said Emma. "All that matters is we find the others before it's too late."

The others. I could see them still, their afterimage fading by the tracks: Horace's fine clothes a mess; Bronwyn's strength no match for the wights' guns; Enoch dizzy from the blast; Hugh using the chaos to pull off Olive's heavy shoes and float her away; Olive caught by the heel and yanked down before she could rise out of reach. All of them weeping in terror, kicked onto the train at gunpoint, gone. Gone with the ymbryne we'd nearly killed ourselves to find, hurtling now through London's guts toward a fate worse than death. *It's already too late,* I thought. It was too late the moment Caul's soldiers stormed Miss Wren's frozen hideout. It was too late the night we mistook Miss Peregrine's wicked brother for our beloved ymbryne. But I swore to myself that we'd find our friends and our ymbryne, no matter the cost, even if there were only bodies to recover—even if it meant adding our own to the pile.

So, then: somewhere in the flashing dark was an escape to the street. A door, a staircase, an escalator, way off against the far wall. But how to reach them?

Get the hell out of our way! I shouted at the hollow, giving it one last try.

English, naturally. The hollow grunted like a cow but didn't move. It was no use. The words were gone.

"Plan B," I said. "It won't listen to me, so we go around it, hope it stays put."

"Go around it where?" said Emma.

To give it a wide berth, we'd have to wade through heaps of glass—but the shards would slice Emma's bare calves and Addison's paws to ribbons. I considered alternatives: I could carry the dog, but that still left Emma. I could find a swordlike piece of glass and stab the thing in the eyes—a technique that had served me well in the past—but if I didn't manage to kill it with the first strike, it would surely snap awake and kill us instead. The only other way around it was through a small, glass-free gap between the hollow and the wall.

It was narrow, though—a foot, maybe a foot and a half wide. A tight squeeze even if we flattened our backs to the wall. I worried that getting so close to the hollow, or worse, touching it by accident, would break the fragile trance holding it in check. Short of growing wings and flying over its head, though, it seemed like our only option.

"Can you walk a little?" I asked Emma. "Or at least hobble?"

She locked her knees and loosened her grip on my waist, testing her weight. "I can limp."

"Then here's what we're going to do: slide past it, backs to the wall, through that gap there. It's not a lot of space, but if we're careful . . . "

Addison saw what I meant and shrank back into the phone booth. "Do you think we should get so close to it?"

"Probably not."

"What if it wakes up while we're . . . ?"

"It won't," I said, faking confidence. "Just don't make any sudden moves—and whatever you do, don't touch it."

"You're our eyes now," Addison said. "Bird preserve us."

I chose a nice long shard from the floor and slid it into my pocket. Shuffling two steps to the wall, we pressed our backs to the cold tiles and began inching toward the hollow. Its eyes moved as we did, locked on me. A few creeping sidesteps later and we were enveloped by a pocket of hollow-stink so foul, it made my eyes water. Addison coughed and Emma cupped a hand over her nose.

"Just a little farther," I said, my voice reedy with forced calm. I took the glass from my pocket, gripping it with the pointed end out, then took another step, and another. We were close enough now that I could've touched the hollow with an outstretched arm. I heard its heart knocking inside its ribs, the beat quickening with each step we took. It was straining against me, fighting with every neuron to wrest my clumsy hands from its controls. *Don't move*, I said, mouthing the words in English. *You're mine. I control you. Don't move.*

I sucked in my chest, lined up and laddered each vertebra

against the wall, then crab-walked into the tight gap between the wall and the hollow.

Don't move, don't move.

Slide, shuffle, slide. I held my breath while the hollow's quickened, wet and wheezing, a vile black mist blooming from its nostrils. The urge to devour us must've been excruciating. So was my urge to run, but I ignored it; that would've been acting like prey, not master.

Don't move. Do not move.

Another few steps, a few more feet, and we'd be past it. Its shoulder a hairsbreadth from my chest.

Don't—

—and then it did. In one swift motion the hollow swiveled its head and pivoted its body to face me.

I went rigid. "Don't move," I said, this time aloud, to the others. Addison buried his face between his paws and Emma froze, her arm squeezing mine like a vise. I steeled myself for what was to come—its tongues, its teeth, the end.

Get back, get back, get back.

English, English, English.

Seconds passed during which, astonishingly, we weren't killed. But for the rising and falling of its chest, the creature seemingly had turned once again to stone.

Experimentally, moving by millimeters, I slid along the wall. The hollow followed me with slight turns of its head—locked onto me like a compass needle, its body in perfect sympathy with mine—but it didn't follow, didn't open its jaws. If whatever spell I'd cast had been broken, we'd already be dead.

The hollow was only watching me. Awaiting instructions I didn't know how to give. "False alarm," I said, and Emma breathed an audible sigh of relief.

We slid out of the gap, peeled ourselves from the wall, and hurried away as fast as Emma could limp. When we'd put a little distance between us and the hollow, I looked back. It had turned all the way around to face me.

Stay, I muttered in English. *Good.*

* * *

We passed through a veil of steam and the escalator came into view, frozen into stairs, its power cut. Around it glowed a halo of weak daylight, a tantalizing envoy from the world above. World of the living, world of now. A world where I had parents. They were here, both of them, in London, breathing this air. A stroll away.

Oh, hi there!

Unthinkable. Still more unthinkable: not five minutes ago, I'd told my father everything. The Cliff's Notes version, anyway: *I'm like Grandpa Portman was. I'm peculiar.* They wouldn't understand, but at least now they knew. It would make my absence feel less like a betrayal. I could still hear my father's voice, begging me to come home, and as we limped toward the light I had to fight a sudden, shameful urge to shake off Emma's arm and run for it—to escape this suffocating dark, to find my parents and beg forgiveness, and then to crawl into their posh hotel bed and sleep.

That was most unthinkable of all. I could never: I loved Emma, and I'd told her so, and I wouldn't leave her behind for anything. And not because I was noble or brave or chivalrous. I'm not any of those things. I was afraid that leaving her behind would rip me in half.

And the others, the others. Our poor, doomed friends. We had to go after them—but how? A train hadn't entered the station since the one that spirited them away, and after the blast and gunshots that had rocked the place, I was sure there'd be no more coming. That left us two options, each one terrible: go after them on foot through the tunnels and hope we didn't meet any more hollows, or climb the escalator and face whatever was waiting for us up there—most likely a wight mop-up crew—then regroup, reassess.

I knew which option I preferred. I'd had enough of the dark, and more than enough of hollows.

"Let's go up," I said, urging Emma toward the stalled escalator. "We'll find somewhere safe to plan our next move while you get your strength back."

"Absolutely not!" she said. "We can't just abandon the others. Never mind how I feel."

"We aren't. But we need to be realistic. We're hurt and defenseless, and the others are probably miles away by now, out of the underground and halfway to somewhere else. How will we even find them?"

"The same way I found you," said Addison. "With my nose. Peculiar folk have an aroma all their own, you see—one which only dogs of my persuasion can sniff out. And you happen to be one powerfully odoriferous group of peculiars. Fear enhances it, I think, and skipping baths . . . "

"Then we go after them!" Emma said.

She pulled me toward the tracks with a surprising burst of strength. I resisted, tug-of-warring our linked arms. "No, no—there's no way the trains are still running, and if we go in there on foot . . . "

"I don't care if it's dangerous. I won't leave them."

"It isn't just dangerous, it's pointless. They're already gone, Emma."

She took back her arm and started hobbling toward the tracks. Stumbled, caught herself. *Say something*, I mouthed to Addison, and he circled around to block her.

"I'm afraid he's right. If we follow on foot, our friends' scent trail will have dissipated long before we're able to find them. Even my profound abilities have limits."

Emma gazed into the tunnel, then back at me, her expression tortured. I held out my hand. "Please, let's go. It doesn't mean we're giving up."

"All right," she said heavily. "All right."

But just as we were starting toward the escalator, someone called out from the dark, back along the tracks.

"Over here!"

The voice was weak but familiar, the accent Russian. It was the folding man. Peering into the dark, I could just make out his crumpled form by the tracks, one arm raised. He'd been shot during the melee, and I assumed the wights had shoved him onto the train with the others. But there he lay, waving to us.

"Sergei!" cried Emma.

"You know him?" Addison said suspiciously.

"He was one of Miss Wren's peculiar refugees," I said, my ears pricking at the wail of distant sirens echoing down from the surface. Trouble was coming—maybe trouble disguised as help—and I worried that our best chance at a clean exit was slipping away. Then again, we couldn't just leave him.

Addison scuttled toward the man, dodging the deepest reefs of glass. Emma let me take her arm again and we shuffled after. Sergei was lying on his side, covered in glass and streaked with blood. The bullet had hit him somewhere vital. His wire-framed spectacles were cracked and he was adjusting them, trying to get a good look at me. "Is miracle, is miracle," he rasped, his voice thin as twice-strained tea. "I heard you speak with monster's tongue. Is miracle."

"It's not," I said, kneeling beside him. "It's gone, I've already lost it."

"If gift inside you, is forever."

Footsteps and voices echoed from the escalator passage. I cleared away glass so I could get my hands under the folding man. "We're taking you with us," I said.

"Leave me," he croaked. "I'll be gone soon enough . . . "

Ignoring him, I slipped my hands beneath his body and lifted. He was ladder-long but light as a feather, and I held him in my arms like a big baby, his skinny legs dangling over my elbow while his head lolled against my shoulder.

Two figures banged down the last few escalator steps and then stood at the bottom, rimmed by pale daylight and peering into the new dark. Emma pointed at the floor and we sank quietly to our knees, hoping they'd miss us—hoping they were just civilians come to catch a train—but then I heard the squelch of a walkie-talkie and they each fired up a flashlight, the beams shining against their bright reflective jackets.

They might've been emergency responders, or wights disguised as such. I wasn't sure until, in synchrony, they peeled off wraparound sunglasses.

Of course.

Our options had just narrowed by half. Now there were only the tracks, the tunnels. We could never outrun them, damaged as we were, but escape was still possible if they didn't see us—and they hadn't yet, amidst the chaos of the ruined station. Their searchlights dueled across the floor. Emma and I backed toward the tracks. If we could just slip into the tunnels unnoticed . . . but Addison, damn him, wasn't moving.

"Come on," I hissed.

"They are ambulance drivers and this man needs help," he said too loudly, and right away the beams of light bounced up from the floor and whipped toward us.

"Stay where you are!" one of the men boomed, unholstering a gun while the other fumbled for his walkie-talkie.

Then two unexpected things happened in quick succession. The first was that, just as I was about to drop the folding man onto the tracks and dive after him with Emma, a thunderous horn blew from inside the tunnel and a single brilliant headlight flashed into view. The rush of stale wind belonged, of course, to a train—running again, somehow, despite the blast. The second thing, announced by a painful twinge in my gut, was that the hollow had come unstuck and was loping in our direction. The instant after I felt it, I saw it, too, plowing at us through a billow of steam, black lips peeled wide, tongues thrashing the air.

We were trapped. If we ran for the stairs we'd be shot and mauled. If we jumped onto the tracks we'd be crushed by the train. And we couldn't escape onto the train because it would be ten seconds at least before it stopped and twelve before the doors opened and ten more before they shut again, and by then we'd be dead three ways. And so I did as I often do when I'm out of ideas—I looked to Emma. I could read in the desperation on her face that she understood the hopelessness of our situation and in the stony set of her jaw that she meant to act anyway. I remembered only as she began to stagger forward, palms out, that she couldn't see the hollow, and I tried to tell her, reach for her, stop her, but I couldn't get the words out and couldn't grab her without dropping the folding man, and then Addison was alongside her, barking at the wight while Emma tried uselessly to make a flame—spark, spark, nothing, like a lighter low on juice.

The wight broke out laughing, pulled back the hammer of his gun, and aimed it at her. The hollowgast ran at me, howling in counterpoint to the squeal of train brakes behind me. That's when I knew the end had come and there was nothing I could do to stop it. At that moment something inside me relaxed, and as it did, the pain I felt whenever a hollow was near faded, too. That pain was like a high-pitched whine, and as it hushed, I discovered hidden beneath it another sound, a murmur at the edge of consciousness.

A word.

I dove for it. Wrapped both arms around it. Wound up and shouted it with all the force of a major league pitcher. *Him*, I said, in a language not my own. It was only one syllable but held volumes of meaning, and the moment it rattled from my throat, the result was instant. The hollow stopped running at me—stopped dead, skidding on its feet—then turned sharply to one side and lashed out a tongue that whipped across the platform and wrapped three times around the wight's leg. Knocked off balance, he fired a shot that caromed off the ceiling, and then he was flipped upside down and hauled thrashing and screaming into the air.

It took my friends a moment to realize what had happened. While they stood gaping and the other wight shouted into his walkie-talkie, I heard train doors whoosh open behind me.

Here was our moment.

"COME ON!" I shouted, and they did, Emma stumble-running and Addison tangling her feet and me trying to wedge the gangly and blood-slick folding man through the narrow doors until we all crashed together across the threshold into the train car.

More gunshots rang out, the wight firing blindly at the hollow.

The doors closed halfway, then popped back open. "Clear the doors, please," came a cheerful prerecorded announcement.

"His feet!" Emma said, pointing at the shoes at the end of the folding man's long legs, the toes of which were poking through the doors. I scrambled to kick his feet clear, and in the interminable seconds before the doors closed again, the dangling wight fired more wild shots until the hollow grew tired of him and flung him against the wall, where he slid to the floor in an unmoving heap.

The other wight scurried for the exit. *Him, too*, I tried to say, but it was too little too late. The doors were closing, and with an awkward jolt the train began to move.

I looked around, grateful that the car we'd tumbled into was empty. What would regular people make of us?

"Are you okay?" I asked Emma. She was sitting up, breathing hard, studying me intensely.

"Thanks to you," she said. "Did you really make the hollow do all that?"

"I think so," I said, not quite believing it myself.

"That's amazing," she said quietly. I couldn't tell if she was frightened or impressed, or both.

"We owe you our lives," said Addison, nuzzling his head sweetly against my arm. "You're a very special boy."

The folding man laughed, and I looked down to see him grinning at me through a mask of pain. "You see?" he said. "I told you. Is miracle." Then his face turned serious. He grabbed my hand and pressed a small square of paper into it. A photograph. "My wife, my child," he said. "Taken by our enemy long ago. If you find others, perhaps . . ."

I glanced at the photo and got a shock. It was a wallet-sized portrait of a woman holding a baby. Sergei had clearly been carrying it with him a long time. Though the people in the photo were pleasant enough, the photo itself—or the negative—had been seriously damaged, perhaps narrowly survived a fire, exposed to such heat that the faces were warped and fragmented. Sergei had never mentioned his family before now; all he'd talked about since we met him was raising an army of peculiars—going loop to loop to recruit able-bodied survivors of the raids and purges. He never told us what he wanted an army *for*: to get them back.

"We'll find them, too," I said.

We both knew this was far-fetched, but it was what he needed to hear.

"Thank you," he said, and relaxed into a spreading pool of blood.

"He doesn't have long," Addison said, moving to lick Sergei's face.

"I might have enough heat to cauterize the wound," said Emma. Scooting toward him, she began rubbing her hands together.

Addison nosed the folding man's shirt near his abdomen. "Here. He's hurt here." Emma put her hands on either side of the spot, and at the sizzle of flesh I stood up, feeling faint.

I looked out the window. We were still pulling out of the station, slowed perhaps by debris on the tracks. The emergency lights' SOS flicker picked details from the dark at random. The body of a dead wight half buried in glass. The crumpled phone booth, scene of my breakthrough. The hollow—I registered its form with a shock— trotting on the platform alongside us, a few cars back, casual as a jogger.

Stop. Stay away, I spat at the window, in English. My head wasn't clear, the hurt and the whine getting in the way again.

We picked up speed and passed into the tunnel. I pressed my face to the glass, angling backward for another glimpse. It was dark, dark—and then, in a burst of light like a camera flash, I saw the hollow as a momentary still image—flying, its feet lifting from the platform, tongues lassoing the rail of the last car.

Miracle. Curse. I hadn't quite worked out the difference.

"Riggs deftly moves between fantasy and reality, prose and photography to create an enchanting and at times positively terrifying story."   —Associated Press

"Got a tweener child with a taste for creepy horror and time-travel stories? Send them *Miss Peregrine's Home for Peculiar Children*."
                                                   —McClatchy Wire Service

"It's an enjoyable, eccentric read, distinguished by well-developed characters, a believable Welsh setting, and some very creepy monsters."   —*Publishers Weekly*

"An original work that defies categorization, this first novel should appeal to readers who like quirky fantasies. Riggs includes many vintage photographs that add a critical touch of the peculiar to his unusual tale."   —*Library Journal*

"His premise is clever, and Jacob and the children are intriguing characters."   —*Booklist*

"Readers will find this book unique and intriguing."
                                                   —*School Library Journal*

"Somewhat reminiscent of Jack Finney's *Time and Again*, Riggs's first novel is enchanting . . . highly recommended."
                                         —*Ellery Queen Mystery Magazine*

"In a time when so much summer entertainment seems to be more of the same, *Miss Peregrine's Home for Peculiar Children* is a pleasant surprise—a story that is fresh and new, engrosses and grips, and provides enough clues so that the ending makes sense and seems thoughtful."   —Popmatters.com

"Brace yourself for the last 70 pages of relentless, squirm-in-your-chair action. I loved every minute of it." —*Cleveland Plain Dealer*

"An unforgettable novel that mixes fiction and photography in a thrilling reading experience." —*Savannah Morning News*

"This is a Book of the Year candidate and right now I'm calling it the front runner. Absolutely magical in every sense of the word, *Miss Peregrine* has a peerless combination of witty, intelligent dialogue and prose, combined with an absolutely beautiful design. . . . *Miss Peregrine's Home for Peculiar Children* is the sharpest thing you'll read all year." —*Shelf Unbound*

MISS
PEREGRINE'S
HOME FOR
PECULIAR
CHILDREN

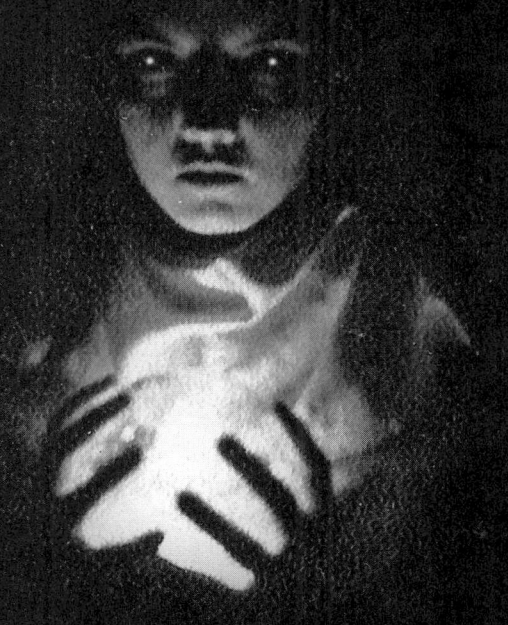

MISS PEREGRINE'S

HOME FOR

PECULIAR CHILDREN

BY RANSOM RIGGS

QUIRK BOOKS
PHILADELPHIA

First paperback edition, Quirk Books, 2013.
Originally published by Quirk Books in 2011.

Library of Congress Cataloging in Publication Number: 2010942876
(hardcover edition)

ISBN: 978-1-59474-603-1

Printed in the United States of America

Typeset in Sabon
Designed by Doogie Horner
Cover photograph courtesy of Yefim Tovbis
Production management by John J. McGurk

Quirk Books
215 Church Street
Philadelphia, PA 19106
quirkbooks.com

50 49 48 47 46 45 44 43 42

SLEEP IS NOT, DEATH IS NOT;
WHO SEEM TO DIE LIVE.
HOUSE YOU WERE BORN IN,
FRIENDS OF YOUR SPRING-TIME,
OLD MAN AND YOUNG MAID,
DAY'S TOIL AND ITS GUERDON,
THEY ARE ALL VANISHING,
FLEEING TO FABLES,
CANNOT BE MOORED.

—*Ralph Waldo Emerson*

PROLOGUE

had just come to accept that my life would be ordinary when extraordinary things began to happen. The first of these came as a terrible shock and, like anything that changes you forever, split my life into halves: Before and After. Like many of the extraordinary things to come, it involved my grandfather, Abraham Portman.

Growing up, Grandpa Portman was the most fascinating person I knew. He had lived in an orphanage, fought in wars, crossed oceans by steamship and deserts on horseback, performed in circuses, knew everything about guns and self-defense and surviving in the wilderness, and spoke at least three languages that weren't English. It all seemed unfathomably exotic to a kid who'd never left Florida, and I begged him to regale me with stories whenever I saw him. He always obliged, telling them like secrets that could be entrusted only to me.

When I was six I decided that my only chance of having a life half as exciting as Grandpa Portman's was to become an explorer. He encouraged me by spending afternoons at my side hunched over maps of the world, plotting imaginary expeditions with trails of red pushpins and telling me about the fantastic places I would discover one day. At home I made my ambitions known by parading around with a cardboard tube held to my eye, shouting, "Land ho!" and "Prepare a landing party!" until my parents shooed me outside. I think they worried that my grandfather would infect me with some incurable dreaminess from which I'd never recover—that these fantasies were somehow inoculating me against more practical ambitions—so one day my mother sat me down and explained that I couldn't become an explorer because everything in the world had already been discovered. I'd been born in the wrong century, and I felt cheated.

I felt even more cheated when I realized that most of Grandpa Portman's best stories couldn't possibly be true. The tallest tales were always about his childhood, like how he was born in Poland but at twelve had been shipped off to a children's home in Wales. When I would ask why he had to leave his parents, his answer was always the same: because the monsters were after him. Poland was simply rotten with them, he said.

"What *kind* of monsters?" I'd ask, wide-eyed. It became a sort of routine. "Awful hunched-over ones with rotting skin and black eyes," he'd say. "And they walked like this!" And he'd shamble after me like an old-time movie monster until I ran away laughing.

Every time he described them he'd toss in some lurid new detail: they stank like putrefying trash; they were invisible except for their shadows; a pack of squirming tentacles lurked inside their mouths and could whip out in an instant and pull you into their powerful jaws. It wasn't long before I had trouble falling asleep, my hyperactive imagination transforming the hiss of tires on wet pavement into labored breathing just outside my window or shadows under the door into twisting gray-black tentacles. I was scared of the monsters but thrilled to imagine my grandfather battling them and surviving to tell the tale.

More fantastic still were his stories about life in the Welsh children's home. It was an enchanted place, he said, designed to keep kids safe from the monsters, on an island where the sun shined every day and nobody ever got sick or died. Everyone lived together in a big house that was protected by a wise old bird—or so the story went. As I got older, though, I began to have doubts.

"What *kind* of bird?" I asked him one afternoon at age seven, eyeing him skeptically across the card table where he was letting me win at Monopoly.

"A big hawk who smoked a pipe," he said.

"You must think I'm pretty dumb, Grandpa."

He thumbed through his dwindling stack of orange and blue money. "I would never think that about you, Yakob." I knew I'd offended him because the Polish accent he could never quite shake had come out of hiding, so that *would* became *vood* and *think* became *sink*. Feeling guilty, I decided to give him the benefit of the doubt.

"But why did the monsters want to hurt you?" I asked.

"Because we weren't like other people. We were peculiar."

"Peculiar how?"

"Oh, all sorts of ways," he said. "There was a girl who could fly, a boy who had bees living inside him, a brother and sister who could lift boulders over their heads."

It was hard to tell if he was being serious. Then again, my grandfather was not known as a teller of jokes. He frowned, reading the doubt on my face.

"Fine, you don't have to take my word for it," he said. "I got pictures!" He pushed back his lawn chair and went into the house, leaving me alone on the screened-in lanai. A minute later he came back holding an old cigar box. I leaned in to look as he drew out four wrinkled and yellowing snapshots.

The first was a blurry picture of what looked like a suit of clothes with no person in them. Either that or the person didn't have a head.

"Sure, he's got a head!" my grandfather said, grinning. "Only you can't see it."

"Why not? Is he invisible?"

"Hey, look at the brain on this one!" He raised his eyebrows as if I'd surprised him with my powers of deduction. "Millard, his name was. Funny kid. Sometimes he'd say, 'Hey Abe, I know what you did today,' and he'd tell you where you'd been, what you had to eat, if you picked your nose when you thought nobody was looking. Sometimes he'd follow you, quiet as a mouse, with no clothes on so you couldn't see him—just watching!" He shook his head. "Of all the things, eh?"

He slipped me another photo. Once I'd had a moment to look at it, he said, "So? What do you see?"

"A little girl?"

"And?"

"She's wearing a crown."

He tapped the bottom of the picture. "What about her feet?"

I held the snapshot closer. The girl's feet weren't touching the ground. But she wasn't jumping—she seemed to be floating in the air. My jaw fell open.

"She's flying!"

"Close," my grandfather said. "She's levitating. Only she couldn't control herself too well, so sometimes we had to tie a rope around her to keep her from floating away!"

My eyes were glued to her haunting, doll-like face. "Is it real?"

"Of course it is," he said gruffly, taking the picture and replacing it with another, this one of a scrawny boy lifting a boulder. "Victor and his sister weren't so smart," he said, "but boy were they strong!"

"He doesn't *look* strong," I said, studying the boy's skinny arms.

"Trust me, he was. I tried to arm-wrestle him once and he just about tore my hand off!"

But the strangest photo was the last one. It was the back of somebody's head, with a face painted on it.

I stared at the last photo as Grandpa Portman explained. "He had two mouths, see? One in the front and one in the back. That's why he got so big and fat!"

"But it's fake," I said. "The face is just painted on."

"Sure, the *paint's* fake. It was for a circus show. But I'm telling you, he had two mouths. You don't believe me?"

I thought about it, looking at the pictures and then at my grandfather, his face so earnest and open. What reason would he have to lie?

"I believe you," I said.

And I really did believe him—for a few years, at least—though mostly because I wanted to, like other kids my age wanted to believe in Santa Claus. We cling to our fairy tales until the price for believing them becomes too high, which for me was the day in second grade when Robbie Jensen pantsed me at lunch in front of a table of girls and announced that I believed in fairies. It was just deserts, I suppose, for repeating my grandfather's stories at school but in those humiliating seconds I foresaw the moniker "fairy boy" trailing me for years and, rightly or not, I resented him for it.

Grandpa Portman picked me up from school that afternoon, as he often did when both my parents were working. I climbed into the passenger seat of his old Pontiac and declared that I didn't believe in his fairy stories anymore.

"What fairy stories?" he said, peering at me over his glasses.

"You know. The stories. About the kids and the monsters."

He seemed confused. "Who said anything about fairies?"

I told him that a made-up story and a fairy tale were the same thing, and that fairy tales were for pants-wetting babies, and that I knew his photos and stories were fakes. I expected him to get mad or put up a fight, but instead he just said, "Okay," and threw the Pontiac into drive. With a stab of his foot on the accelerator we lurched away from the curb. And that was the end of it.

I guess he'd seen it coming—I had to grow out of them eventually—but he dropped the whole thing so quickly it left me feeling like I'd been lied to. I couldn't understand why he'd made up all that stuff, tricked me into believing that extraordinary things were possible when they weren't. It wasn't until a few years later that my dad explained it to me: Grandpa had told him some of the same stories when he was a kid, and they weren't lies, exactly, but exaggerated versions of the truth—because the story of Grandpa Portman's childhood wasn't a fairy tale at all. It was a horror story.

My grandfather was the only member of his family to escape Poland before the Second World War broke out. He was twelve years old when his parents sent him into the arms of strangers, putting their youngest son on a train to Britain with nothing more than a suitcase and the clothes on his back. It was a one-way ticket. He never saw his mother or father again, or his older brothers, his cousins, his aunts and uncles. Each one would be dead before his sixteenth birthday, killed by the monsters he had so narrowly escaped. But these weren't the kind of monsters that had tentacles and rotting skin, the kind a seven-year-old might be able to wrap his mind around—they were monsters with human faces, in crisp uniforms, marching in lockstep, so banal you don't recognize them for what they are until it's too late.

Like the monsters, the enchanted-island story was also a truth in disguise. Compared to the horrors of mainland Europe, the children's home that had taken in my grandfather must've seemed like a paradise, and so in his stories it had become one: a safe haven of endless summers and guardian angels and magical children, who couldn't *really* fly or turn invisible or lift boulders, of course. The peculiarity for which they'd been hunted was simply their Jewishness. They were orphans of war, washed up on that little island in a tide of blood. What made them amazing wasn't that they had miraculous powers; that they had escaped the ghettos and gas chambers was miracle enough.

I stopped asking my grandfather to tell me stories, and I think secretly he was relieved. An air of mystery closed around the details of his early life. I didn't pry. He had been through hell and had a right to his secrets. I felt ashamed for having been jealous of his life, considering the price he'd paid for it, and I tried to feel lucky for the safe and unextraordinary one that I had done nothing to deserve.

Then, a few years later, when I was fifteen, an extraordinary and terrible thing happened, and there was only Before and After.

CHAPTER ONE

I spent the last afternoon of Before constructing a 1/10,000-scale replica of the Empire State Building from boxes of adult diapers. It was a thing of beauty, really, spanning five feet at its base and towering above the cosmetics aisle, with jumbos for the foundation, lites for the observation deck, and meticulously stacked trial sizes for its iconic spire. It was almost perfect, minus one crucial detail.

"You used Neverleak," Shelley said, eyeing my craftsmanship with a skeptical frown. "The sale's on Stay-Tite." Shelley was the store manager, and her slumped shoulders and dour expression were as much a part of her uniform as the blue polo shirts we all had to wear.

"I thought you said Neverleak," I said, because she had.

"Stay-Tite," she insisted, shaking her head regretfully, as if my tower were a crippled racehorse and she the bearer of the pearl-handled pistol. There was a brief but awkward silence in which she continued to shake her head and shift her eyes from me to the tower and back to me again. I stared blankly at her, as if completely failing to grasp what she was passive-aggressively implying.

"Ohhhhhh," I said finally. "You mean you want me to do it over?"

"It's just that you used Neverleak," she repeated.

"No problem. I'll get started right away." With the toe of my regulation black sneaker I nudged a single box from the tower's foundation. In an instant the whole magnificent structure was cascading down around us, sending a tidal wave of diapers crashing across the floor, boxes caroming off the legs of startled customers, skidding as far as the automatic door, which slid open, letting in a rush of August heat.

Shelley's face turned the color of ripe pomegranate. She should've fired me on the spot, but I knew I'd never be so lucky. I'd been trying to get fired from Smart Aid all summer, and it had proved next to impossible. I came in late, repeatedly and with the flimsiest of excuses; made shockingly incorrect change; even misshelved things on purpose, stocking lotions among laxatives and birth control with baby shampoo. Rarely had I worked so hard at anything, and yet no matter how incompetent I pretended to be, Shelley stubbornly kept me on the payroll.

Let me qualify my previous statement: It was next to impossible for *me* to get fired from Smart Aid. Any other employee would've been out the door a dozen minor infractions ago. It was my first lesson in politics. There are three Smart Aids in Englewood, the small, somnolent beach town where I live. There are twenty-seven in Sarasota County, and one hundred and fifteen in all of Florida, spreading across the state like some untreatable rash. The reason I couldn't be fired was that my uncles owned every single one of them. The reason I couldn't quit was that working at Smart Aid as your first job had long been a hallowed family tradition. All my campaign of self-sabotage had earned me was an unwinnable feud with Shelley and the deep and abiding resentment of my coworkers—who, let's face it, were going to resent me anyway, because no matter how many displays I knocked over or customers I short-changed, one day I was going to inherit a sizable chunk of the company, and they were not.

*   *   *

Wading through the diapers, Shelley poked her finger into my chest and was about to say something dour when the PA system interrupted her.

"Jacob, you have a call on line two. Jacob, line two."

She glared at me as I backed away, leaving her pomegranate-faced amid the ruins of my tower.

*   *   *

The employee lounge was a dank, windowless room where I found the pharmacy assistant, Linda, nibbling a crustless sandwich in the vivid glow of the soda machine. She nodded at a phone screwed to the wall.

"Line two's for you. Whoever it is sounds *freaked*."

I picked up the dangling receiver.

"Yakob? Is that you?"

"Hi, Grandpa Portman."

"Yakob, thank God. I need my key. Where's my key?" He sounded upset, out of breath.

"What key?"

"Don't play games," he snapped. "You know what key."

"You probably just misplaced it."

"Your father put you up to this," he said. "Just tell me. He doesn't have to know."

"Nobody put me up to anything." I tried to change the subject. "Did you take your pills this morning?"

"They're coming for me, understand? I don't know how they found me after all these years, but they did. What am I supposed to fight them with, the goddamned butter knife?"

It wasn't the first time I'd heard him talk like this. My grandfather was getting old, and frankly he was starting to lose it. The signs of his mental decline had been subtle at first, like forgetting to buy groceries or calling my mother by my aunt's name. But over the summer his encroaching dementia had taken a cruel twist. The fantastic stories he'd invented about his life during the war—the monsters, the enchanted island—had become completely, oppressively real to him. He'd been especially agitated the last few weeks, and my parents, who feared he was becoming a danger to himself, were seriously considering putting him in a home. For some reason, I was the only one who received these apocalyptic phone calls from him.

As usual, I did my best to calm him down. "You're safe. Everything's fine. I'll bring over a video for us to watch later, how's that sound?"

"No! Stay where you are! It's not safe here!"

"Grandpa, the monsters aren't coming for you. You killed them all in the war, remember?" I turned to face the wall, trying to hide my end of this bizarre conversation from Linda, who shot me curious glances while pretending to read a fashion magazine.

"Not all of them," he said. "No, no, no. I killed a lot, sure, but there are always more." I could hear him banging around his house, opening drawers, slamming things. He was in full meltdown. "You stay away, hear me? I'll be fine—cut out their tongues and stab them in the eyes, that's all you gotta do! If I could just find that goddamned *KEY!*"

The key in question opened a giant locker in Grandpa Portman's garage. Inside was a stockpile of guns and knives sufficient to arm a small militia. He'd spent half his life collecting them, traveling to out-of-state gun shows, going on long hunting trips, and dragging his reluctant family to rifle ranges on sunny Sundays so they could learn to shoot. He loved his guns so much that sometimes he even slept with them. My dad had an old snapshot to prove it: Grandpa Portman napping with pistol in hand.

When I asked my dad why Grandpa was so crazy about guns, he said it sometimes happened to people who used to be soldiers or who had experienced traumatic things. I guess that after everything my grandfather had been through, he never really felt safe anywhere, not even at home. The irony was, now that delusions and paranoia were starting to get the best of him, it was true—he wasn't safe at home, not with all those guns around. That's why my dad had swiped the key.

I repeated the lie that I didn't know where it was. There was more swearing and banging as Grandpa Portman stomped around looking for it.

"Feh!" he said finally. "Let your father have the key if it's so important to him. Let him have my dead body, too!"

I got off the phone as politely as I could and then called my dad.

"Grandpa's flipping out," I told him.

"Has he taken his pills today?"

"He won't tell me. Doesn't sound like it, though."

I heard my dad sigh. "Can you stop by and make sure he's okay? I can't get off work right now." My dad volunteered part-time at the bird rescue, where he helped rehabilitate snowy egrets hit by cars and pelicans that had swallowed fishhooks. He was an amateur ornithologist and a wannabe nature writer—with a stack of unpublished manuscripts to prove it—which are real jobs only if you happen to be married to a woman whose family owns a hundred and fifteen drugstores.

Of course, mine was not the realest of jobs either, and it was easy to ditch whenever I felt like it. I said I would go.

"Thanks, Jake. I promise we'll get all this Grandpa stuff sorted out soon, okay?"

All this Grandpa stuff. "You mean put him in a home," I said. "Make him someone else's problem."

"Mom and I haven't decided yet."

"Of course you have."

"Jacob . . . "

"I can handle him, Dad. Really."

"Maybe now you can. But he's only going to get worse."

"Fine. Whatever."

I hung up and called my friend Ricky for a ride. Ten minutes later I heard the unmistakable throaty honk of his ancient Crown Victoria in the parking lot. On my way out I broke the bad news to Shelley: her tower of Stay-Tite would have to wait until tomorrow.

"Family emergency," I explained.

"Right," she said.

I emerged into the sticky-hot evening to find Ricky smoking on the hood of his battered car. Something about his mud-encrusted boots and the way he let smoke curl from his lips and how the sinking sun lit his green hair reminded me of a punk, redneck James Dean. He was all of those things, a bizarre cross-pollination of subcultures possible only in South Florida.

He saw me and leapt off the hood. "You fired yet?" he shouted across the parking lot.

"Shhhh!" I hissed, running toward him. "They don't know my plan!"

Ricky punched my shoulder in a manner meant to be encouraging but that nearly snapped my rotator cuff. "Don't worry, Special Ed. There's always tomorrow."

He called me Special Ed because I was in a few gifted classes, which were, technically speaking, part of our school's special-education curriculum, a subtlety of nomenclature that Ricky found endlessly amusing. That was our friendship: equal parts irritation and cooperation. The cooperation part was an unofficial brains-for-brawn trade agreement we'd worked out in which I helped him not fail English and he helped me not get killed by the roided-out sociopaths who prowled the halls of our school. That he made my parents deeply uncomfortable was merely a bonus. He was, I suppose, my best friend, which is a less pathetic way of saying he was my only friend.

Ricky kicked the Crown Vic's passenger door, which was how you opened it, and I climbed in. The Vic was amazing, a museum-worthy piece of unintentional folk art. Ricky bought it from the town dump with a jar of quarters—or so he claimed—a pedigree whose odor even the forest of air-freshener trees he'd hung from the mirror couldn't mask. The seats were armored with duct tape so that errant upholstery springs wouldn't find their way up your ass. Best of all was the exterior, a rusted moonscape of holes and dents, the result of a plan to earn extra gas money by allowing drunken partygoers to whack the car with a golf club for a buck a swing. The only rule, which had not been rigorously enforced, was that you couldn't aim at anything made of glass.

The engine rattled to life in a cloud of blue smoke. As we left the parking lot and rolled past strip malls toward Grandpa Portman's house, I began to worry about what we might find when we got there. Worst-case scenarios included my grandfather running naked in the street, wielding a hunting rifle, foaming at the mouth on the front lawn, or lying in wait with a blunt object in hand. Anything was possible, and that this would be Ricky's first impression of a man I'd spoken about with reverence made me especially nervous.

The sky was turning the color of a fresh bruise as we pulled into my grandfather's subdivision, a bewildering labyrinth of interlocking cul-de-sacs known collectively as Circle Village. We stopped at the guard gate to announce ourselves, but the old man in the booth was snoring and the gate was open, as was often the case, so we just drove in. My phone chirped with a text from my dad asking how things were going, and in the short time it took me to respond, Ricky managed to get us completely, stunningly lost. When I said I had no idea where we were, he cursed and pulled a succession of squealing U-turns, spitting arcs of tobacco juice from his window as I scanned the neighborhood for a familiar landmark. It wasn't easy, even though I'd been to visit my grandfather countless times growing up, because each house looked like the next: squat and boxy with minor variations, trimmed with aluminum siding or dark seventies wood, or fronted by plaster colonnades that seemed almost delusionally aspirational. Street signs, half of which had turned a blank and blistered white from sun exposure, were little help. The only real landmarks were bizarre and colorful lawn ornaments, of which Circle Village was a veritable open-air museum.

Finally I recognized a mailbox held aloft by a metal butler that, despite his straight back and snooty expression, appeared to be crying tears of rust. I shouted at Ricky to turn left; the Vic's tires screeched and I was flung against the passenger door. The impact must've jarred something loose in my brain, because suddenly the directions came rushing back to me. "Right at the flamingo orgy! Left at the multiethnic roof Santas! Straight past the pissing cherubs!"

When we passed the cherubs, Ricky slowed to a crawl and peered doubtfully down my grandfather's block. There was not a single porch light on, not a TV glowing behind a window, not a Town Car in a carport. All the neighbors had fled north to escape the punishing summer heat, leaving yard gnomes to drown in lawns gone wild and hurricane shutters shut tight, so that each house looked like a little pastel bomb shelter.

"Last one on the left," I said. Ricky tapped the accelerator and we sputtered down the street. At the fourth or fifth house, we passed an old man watering his lawn. He was bald as an egg and stood in a bathrobe and slippers, spraying the ankle-high grass. The house was dark and shuttered like the rest. I turned to look and he seemed to stare back—though he couldn't have, I realized with a small shock, because his eyes were a perfect milky white. *That's strange*, I thought. *Grandpa Portman never mentioned that one of his neighbors was blind.*

The street ended at a wall of scrub pines and Ricky hung a

sharp left into my grandfather's driveway. He cut the engine, got out, and kicked my door open. Our shoes hushed through the dry grass to the porch.

I rang the bell and waited. A dog barked somewhere, a lonely sound in the muggy evening. When there was no answer I banged on the door, thinking maybe the bell had stopped working. Ricky swatted at the gnats that had begun to clothe us.

"Maybe he stepped out," Ricky said, grinning. "Hot date."

"Go ahead and laugh," I said. "He's got a better shot than we do any night of the week. This place is crawling with eligible widows." I joked only to calm my nerves. The quiet made me anxious.

I fetched the extra key from its hiding place in the bushes. "Wait here."

"Hell I am. Why?"

"Because you're six-five and have green hair and my grandfather doesn't know you and owns lots of guns."

Ricky shrugged and stuck another wad of tobacco in his cheek. He went to stretch himself on a lawn chair as I unlocked the front door and stepped inside.

Even in the fading light I could tell the house was a disaster; it looked like it'd been ransacked by thieves. Bookshelves and cabinets had been emptied, the knickknacks and large-print *Reader's Digest*s that had filled them thrown across the floor. Couch cushions and chairs were overturned. The fridge and freezer doors hung open, their contents melting into sticky puddles on the linoleum.

My heart sank. Grandpa Portman had really, finally lost his mind. I called his name—but heard nothing.

I went from room to room, turning on lights and looking anywhere a paranoid old man might hide from monsters: behind furniture, in the attic crawlspace, under the workbench in the garage. I even looked behind his weapons cabinet, though of course it was locked, the handle ringed by scratches where he'd tried to pick it. Out on the lanai, a gallows of unwatered ferns swung browning in the breeze; while on my knees on the astroturfed floor I peered beneath rattan benches, afraid what I might discover.

I saw a gleam of light from the backyard.

Running through the screen door, I found a flashlight abandoned in the grass, its beam pointed at the woods that edged my grandfather's yard—a scrubby wilderness of sawtoothed palmettos and trash palms that ran for a mile between Circle Village and the next subdivision, Century Woods. According to local legend, the woods were crawling with snakes, raccoons, and wild boars. When I pictured my grandfather out there, lost and raving in nothing but his bathrobe, a black feeling welled up in me. Every other week there was a news story about some geriatric citizen tripping into a retention pond and being devoured by alligators. The worst-case scenario wasn't hard to imagine.

I shouted for Ricky and a moment later he came tearing around the side of the house. Right away he noticed something I hadn't: a long mean-looking slice in the screen door. He let out a low whistle. "That's a helluva cut. Wild pig coulda done it. Or a bobcat maybe. You should see the claws on them things."

A peal of savage barking broke out nearby. We both started then traded a nervous glance. "Or a dog," I said. The sound triggered a chain reaction across the neighborhood, and soon barks were coming from every direction.

"Could be," Ricky said, nodding. "I got a .22 in my trunk. You just wait." And he walked off to retrieve it.

The barks faded and a chorus of night insects rose up in their place, droning and alien. Sweat trickled down my face. It was dark now, but the breeze had died and somehow the air seemed hotter than it had all day.

I picked up the flashlight and stepped toward the trees. My grandfather was out there somewhere, I was sure of it. But where? I was no tracker, and neither was Ricky. And yet something seemed to guide me anyway—a quickening in the chest; a whisper in the viscous air—and suddenly I couldn't wait another second. I tromped into the underbrush like a bloodhound scenting an invisible trail.

It's hard to run in a Florida woods, where every square foot not occupied by trees is bristling with thigh-high palmetto spears and nets of entangling skunk vine, but I did my best, calling my grandfather's name and sweeping my flashlight everywhere. I caught a white glint out of the corner of my eye and made a beeline for it, but upon closer inspection it turned out to be just a bleached and deflated soccer ball I'd lost years before.

I was about to give up and go back for Ricky when I spied a narrow corridor of freshly stomped palmettos not far away. I stepped into it and shone my light around; the leaves were splattered with something dark. My throat went dry. Steeling myself, I began to follow the trail. The farther I went, the more my stomach knotted, as though my body knew what lay ahead and was trying to warn me. And then the trail of the flattened brush widened out, and I saw him.

My grandfather lay facedown in a bed of creeper, his legs sprawled out and one arm twisted beneath him as if he'd fallen from a great height. I thought surely he was dead. His undershirt was soaked with blood, his pants were torn, and one shoe was missing. For a long moment I just stared, the beam of my flashlight shivering across his body. When I could breathe again I said his name, but he didn't move.

I sank to my knees and pressed the flat of my hand against his back. The blood that soaked through was still warm. I could feel him breathing ever so shallowly.

I slid my arms under him and rolled him onto his back. He was alive, though just barely, his eyes glassy, his face sunken and white. Then I saw the gashes across his midsection and nearly fainted. They were wide and deep and clotted with soil, and the ground where he'd lain was muddy from blood. I tried to pull the rags of his shirt over the wounds without looking at them.

I heard Ricky shout from the backyard. "I'M HERE!" I screamed, and maybe I should've said more, like *danger* or *blood,* but I couldn't form the words. All I could think was that grandfathers were supposed to die in beds, in hushed places humming with machines, not in heaps on the sodden reeking ground with ants marching over them, a brass letter opener clutched in one trembling hand.

A letter opener. That was all he'd had to defend himself. I slid it from his fingers and he grasped helplessly at the air, so I took his hand and held it. My nail-bitten fingers twinned with his, pale and webbed with purple veins.

"I have to move you," I told him, sliding one arm under his back and another under his legs. I began to lift, but he moaned and went rigid, so I stopped. I couldn't bear to hurt him. I couldn't leave him either, and there was nothing to do but wait, so I gently brushed loose soil from his arms and face and thinning white hair. That's when I noticed his lips moving.

His voice was barely audible, something less than a whisper. I leaned down and put my ear to his lips. He was mumbling, fading in and out of lucidity, shifting between English and Polish.

"I don't understand," I whispered. I repeated his name until his eyes seemed to focus on me, and then he drew a sharp breath and said, quietly but clearly, "Go to the island, Yakob. Here it's not safe."

It was the old paranoia. I squeezed his hand and assured him we were fine, he was going to be fine. That was twice in one day that I'd lied to him.

I asked him what happened, what animal had hurt him, but he wasn't listening. "Go to the island," he repeated. "You'll be safe there. Promise me."

"I will. I promise." What else could I say?

"I thought I could protect you," he said. "I should've told you a long time ago . . . " I could see the life going out of him.

"Told me what?" I said, choking back tears.

"There's no time," he whispered. Then he raised his head off the ground, trembling with the effort, and breathed into my ear: "Find the bird. In the loop. On the other side of the old man's grave. September third, 1940." I nodded, but he could see that I didn't understand. With his last bit of strength, he added, "Emerson—the letter. Tell them what happened, Yakob."

With that he sank back, spent and fading. I told him I loved him. And then he seemed to disappear into himself, his gaze drifting past me to the sky, bristling now with stars.

A moment later Ricky crashed out of the underbrush. He saw the old man limp in my arms and fell back a step. "Oh man. Oh Jesus. Oh *Jesus*," he said, rubbing his face with his hands, and as he babbled about finding a pulse and calling the cops and did you see anything in the woods, the strangest feeling came over me. I let go of my grandfather's body and stood up, every nerve ending tingling with an instinct I didn't know I had. There was something in the woods, all right— I could feel it.

There was no moon and no movement in the underbrush but our own, and yet somehow I knew just when to raise my flashlight and just where to aim it, and for an instant in that narrow cut of light I saw a face that seemed to have been transplanted directly from the nightmares of my childhood. It stared back with eyes that swam in dark liquid, furrowed trenches of carbon-black flesh loose on its hunched frame, its mouth hinged open grotesquely so that a mass of long eel-like tongues could wriggle out. I shouted something and then it twisted and was gone, shaking the brush and drawing Ricky's attention. He raised his .22 and fired, *pap-pap-pap-pap*, saying, "What was that? What the hell was that?" But he hadn't seen it and I couldn't speak to tell him, frozen in place as I was, my dying flashlight flickering over the blank woods. And then I must've blacked out because he was saying *Jacob, Jake, hey Ed areyouokayorwhat*, and that's the last thing I remember.

CHAPTER TWO

I spent the months following my grandfather's death cycling through a purgatory of beige waiting rooms and anonymous offices, analyzed and interviewed, talked about just out of earshot, nodding when spoken to, repeating myself, the object of a thousand pitying glances and knitted brows. My parents treated me like a breakable heirloom, afraid to fight or fret in front of me lest I shatter.

I was plagued by wake-up-screaming nightmares so bad that I had to wear a mouth guard to keep from grinding my teeth into nubs as I slept. I couldn't close my eyes without seeing it—that tentacle-mouthed horror in the woods. I was convinced it had killed my grandfather and that it would soon return for me. Sometimes a sick panicky feeling would flood over me like it did that night and I'd be sure that nearby, lurking in a stand of dark trees, beyond the next car in a parking lot, behind the garage where I kept my bike, it was waiting.

My solution was to stop leaving the house. For weeks I refused even to venture into the driveway to collect the morning paper. I slept in a tangle of blankets on the laundry room floor, the only part of the house with no windows and also a door that locked from the inside. That's where I spent the day of my grandfather's funeral, sitting on the dryer with my laptop, trying to lose myself in online games.

I blamed myself for what happened. *If only I'd believed him* was my endless refrain. But I hadn't believed him, and neither had anyone else, and now I knew how he must've felt because no one believed me, either. My version of events sounded perfectly rational until I was forced to say the words aloud, and then it sounded insane, particularly on the day I had to say them to the police officer who came to our house. I told him everything that had happened, even about the creature, as he sat nodding across the kitchen table, writing nothing in his spiral notebook. When I finished all he said was, "Great, thanks," and then turned to my parents and asked if I'd "been to see anyone." As if I wouldn't know what that meant. I told him I had another statement to make and then held up my middle finger and walked out.

My parents yelled at me for the first time in weeks. It was kind of a relief, actually—that old sweet sound. I yelled some ugly things back. That they were glad Grandpa Portman was dead. That I was the only one who'd really loved him.

The cop and my parents talked in the driveway for a while, and then the cop drove off only to come back an hour later with a man who introduced himself as a sketch artist. He'd brought a big drawing pad and asked me to describe the creature again, and as I did he sketched it, stopping occasionally to ask for clarifications.

"How many eyes did it have?"

"Two."

"Gotcha," he said, as if monsters were a perfectly normal thing for a police sketch artist to be drawing.

As an attempt to placate me, it was pretty transparent. The biggest giveaway was when he tried to give me the finished sketch.

"Don't you need this for your files or something?" I asked him.

He exchanged raised eyebrows with the cop. "Of course. What was I thinking?"

It was totally insulting.

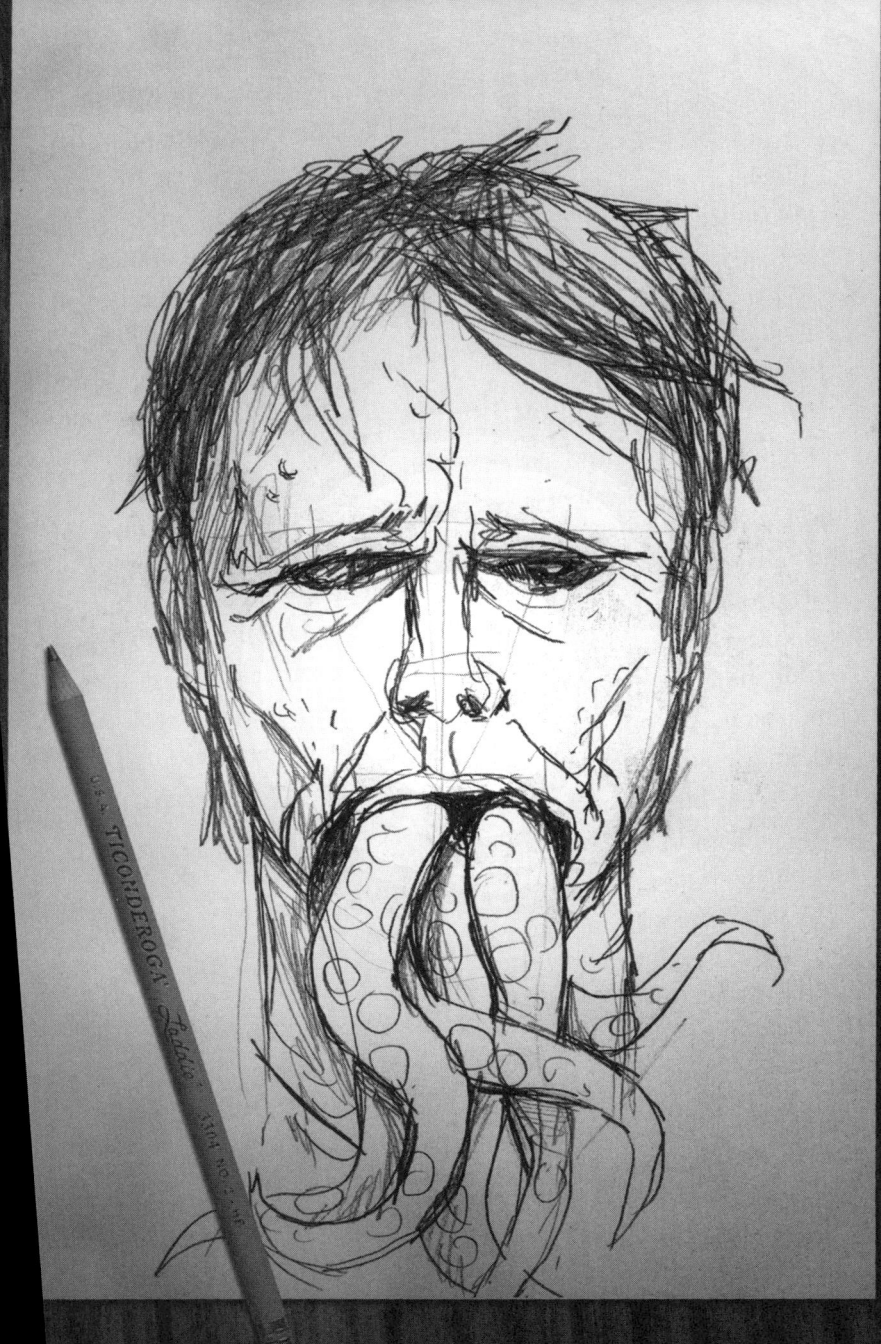

Even my best and only friend Ricky didn't believe me, and he'd been there. He swore up and down that he hadn't seen any creature in the woods that night—even though I'd shined my flashlight right at it—which is just what he told the cops. He'd heard barking, though. We both had. So it wasn't a huge surprise when the police concluded that a pack of feral dogs had killed my grandfather. Apparently they'd been spotted elsewhere and had taken bites out of a woman who'd been walking in Century Woods the week before. All at night, mind you. "Which is exactly when the creatures are hardest to see!" I said. But Ricky just shook his head and muttered something about me needing a "brain-shrinker."

"You mean head-shrinker," I replied, "and thanks a lot. It's great to have such supportive friends." We were sitting on my roof deck watching the sun set over the Gulf, Ricky coiled like a spring in an unreasonably expensive Adirondack chair my parents had brought back from a trip to Amish country, his legs folded beneath him and arms crossed tight, chain-smoking cigarettes with a kind of grim determination. He always seemed vaguely uncomfortable at my house, but I could tell by the way his eyes slid off me whenever he looked in my direction that now it wasn't my parents' wealth that was making him uneasy, but me.

"Whatever, I'm just being straight with you," he said. "Keep talking about monsters and they're gonna put you away. Then you really will be Special Ed."

"Don't call me that."

He flicked away his cigarette and spat a huge glistening wad over the railing.

"Were you just smoking and chewing tobacco at the same time?"

"What are you, my mom?"

"Do I *look* like a truck stop hooker?"

Ricky was a connoisseur of your-mom jokes, but this was apparently more than he could take. He sprang out of the chair and shoved me so hard I almost fell off the roof. I yelled at him to get out, but he was already going.

It was months before I'd see him again. So much for having friends.

*   *   *

Eventually, my parents did take me to a brain-shrinker—a quiet, olive-skinned man named Dr. Golan. I didn't put up a fight. I knew I needed help.

I thought I'd be a tough case, but Dr. Golan made surprisingly quick work of me. The calm, affectless way he explained things was almost hypnotizing, and within two sessions he'd convinced me that the creature had been nothing more than the product of my over-heated imagination; that the trauma of my grandfather's death had made me see something that wasn't really there. It was Grandpa Port-man's stories that had planted the creature in my mind to begin with, Dr. Golan explained, so it only made sense that, kneeling there with his body in my arms and reeling from the worst shock of my young life, I had conjured up my grandfather's own bogeyman.

There was even a name for it: acute stress reaction. "I don't see anything cute about it," my mother said when she heard my shiny new diagnosis. Her joke didn't bother me, though. Almost anything sounded better than *crazy*.

Just because I no longer believed the monsters were real didn't mean I was better, though. I still suffered from nightmares. I was twitchy and paranoid, bad enough at interacting with other people that my parents hired a tutor so that I only had to go to school on days I felt up to it. They also—finally—let me quit Smart Aid. "Feel-ing better" became my new job.

Pretty soon, I was determined to be fired from this one, too. Once the small matter of my temporary madness had been cleared up, Dr. Golan's function seemed mainly to consist of writing prescriptions. Still having nightmares? I've got something for that. Panic attack on the school bus? This should do the trick. Can't sleep? Let's up the dosage. All those pills were making me fat and stupid, and I was still miserable, getting only three or four hours of sleep a night. That's why I started lying to Dr. Golan. I pretended to be fine when anyone who looked at me could see the bags under my eyes and the way I jumped like a nervous cat at sudden noises. One week I faked an entire dream journal, making my dreams sound bland and simple, the way a normal person's should be. One dream was about going to the dentist. In another I was flying. Two nights in a row, I told him, I'd dreamed I was naked in school.

Then he stopped me. "What about the creatures?"

I shrugged. "No sign of them. Guess that means I'm getting better, huh?"

Dr. Golan tapped his pen for a moment and then wrote something down. "I hope you're not just telling me what you think I want to hear."

"Of course not," I said, my gaze skirting the framed degrees on his wall, all attesting to his expertness in various subdisciplines of psychology, including, I'm sure, how to tell when an acutely stressed teenager is lying to you.

"Let's be real for a minute." He set down his pen. "You're telling me you didn't have the dream even *one* night this week?"

I'd always been a terrible liar. Rather than humiliate myself, I copped to it. "Well," I muttered, "maybe one."

The truth was that I'd had the dream *every* night that week. With minor variations, it always went like this: I'm crouched in the corner of my grandfather's bedroom, amber dusk-light retreating from the windows, pointing a pink plastic BB rifle at the door. An enormous glowing vending machine looms where the bed should be, filled not with candy but rows of razor-sharp tactical knives and armor-piercing pistols. My grandfather's there in an old British army uniform, feeding the machine dollar bills, but it takes a lot to buy a gun and we're running out of time. Finally, a .45 spins toward the glass, but before it falls it gets stuck. He swears in Yiddish, kicks the machine, then kneels down and reaches inside to try and grab it, but his arm gets caught. That's when they come, their long black tongues slithering up the windows, looking for a way in. I point the BB gun at them and pull the trigger, but nothing happens. Meanwhile Grandpa Portman is shouting like a crazy person—*find the bird, find the loop, Yakob vai don't you understand you goddamned stupid yutzi*—and then the windows shatter and glass rains in and the black tongues are all over us, and that's generally when I wake up in a puddle of sweat, my heart doing hurdles and my stomach tied in knots.

Even though the dream was always the same and we'd been over it a hundred times, Dr. Golan still made me describe it in every session. It's like he was cross-examining my subconscious, looking for some clue he might have missed the ninety-ninth time around.

"And in the dream, what's your grandfather saying?"

"The same stuff as always," I said. "About the bird and the loop and the grave."

"His last words."

I nodded.

Dr. Golan tented his fingers and pressed them to his chin, the very picture of a thoughtful brain-shrinker. "Any new ideas about what they might mean?"

"Yeah. Jack and shit."

"Come on. You don't mean that."

I wanted to act like I didn't care about the last words, but I did. They'd been eating away at me almost as much as the nightmares. I felt like I owed it to my grandfather not to dismiss the last thing he said to anyone in the world as delusional nonsense, and Dr. Golan was convinced that understanding them might help purge my awful dreams. So I tried.

Some of what Grandpa Portman had said made sense, like the thing about wanting me to go to the island. He was worried that the monsters would come after me, and thought the island was the only place I could escape them, like he had as a kid. After that he'd said, "I should've told you," but because there was no time to tell me whatever it was he should've told me, I wondered if he hadn't done the next best thing and left a trail of bread crumbs leading to someone who *could* tell me—someone who knew his secret. I figured that's what all the cryptic-sounding stuff about the loop and the grave and the letter was.

For a while I thought "the loop" could be a street in Circle Village—a neighborhood that was nothing but looping cul-de-sacs—and that "Emerson" might be a person my grandfather had sent letters to. An old war buddy he'd kept in touch with or something. Maybe this Emerson lived in Circle Village, in one of its loops, by a graveyard, and one of the letters he'd kept was dated September third, 1940, and that was the one I needed to read. I knew it sounded crazy, but crazier things have turned out to be true. So after hitting dead-ends online I went to the Circle Village community center, where the old folks gather to play shuffleboard and discuss their most recent surgeries, to ask where the graveyard was and whether anyone knew a Mr. Emerson. They looked at me like I had a second head growing out of my neck, baffled that a teenaged person was speaking to them. There was no graveyard in Circle Village and no one in the neighborhood named Emerson and no street called Loop Drive or Loop Avenue or Loop anything. It was a complete bust.

Still, Dr. Golan wouldn't let me quit. He suggested I look into Ralph Waldo Emerson, a supposedly famous old poet. "Emerson wrote his fair share of letters," he said. "Maybe that's what your grandfather was referring to." It seemed like a shot in the dark, but, just to get Golan off my back, one afternoon I had my dad drop me at the library so I could check it out. I quickly discovered that Ralph Waldo Emerson had indeed written lots of letters that had been published. For about three minutes I got really excited, like I was close to a breakthrough, and then two things became apparent: first, that Ralph Waldo Emerson had lived and died in the 1800s and therefore could not have written any letters dated September third, 1940, and, second, that his writing was so dense and arcane that it couldn't possibly have held the slightest interest for my grandfather, who wasn't exactly an avid reader. I discovered Emerson's soporific qualities the hard way, by falling asleep with my face in the book, drooling all over an essay called "Self-Reliance" and having the vending-machine dream for the sixth time that week. I woke up screaming and was unceremoniously ejected from the library, cursing Dr. Golan and his stupid theories all the while.

The last straw came a few days later, when my family decided it was time to sell Grandpa Portman's house. Before prospective buyers could be allowed inside, though, the place had to be cleaned out. On the advice of Dr. Golan, who thought it would be good for me to "confront the scene of my trauma," I was enlisted to help my dad and Aunt Susie sort through the detritus. For a while after we got to the house my dad kept taking me aside to make sure I was okay. Surprisingly, I seemed to be, despite the scraps of police tape clinging to the shrubs and the torn screen on the lanai flapping in the breeze; these things—like the rented Dumpster that stood on the curb, waiting to swallow what remained of my grandfather's life—made me sad, not scared.

Once it became clear I wasn't about to suffer a mouth-frothing freak-out, we got down to business. Armed with garbage bags we proceeded grimly through the house, emptying shelves and cabinets and crawl spaces, discovering geometries of dust beneath objects unmoved for years. We built pyramids of things that could be saved or salvaged and pyramids of things destined for the Dumpster. My aunt and father were not sentimental people, and the Dumpster pile was always the largest. I lobbied hard to keep certain things, like the eight-foot stack of water-damaged *National Geographic* magazines teetering in a corner of the garage—how many afternoons had I spent poring over them, imagining myself among the mud men of New Guinea or discovering a cliff-top castle in the kingdom of Bhutan?—but I was always overruled. Neither was I allowed to keep my grandfather's collection of vintage bowling shirts ("They're embarrassing," my dad claimed), his big band and swing 78s ("Someone will pay good money for those"), or the contents of his massive, still-locked weapons cabinet ("You're kidding, right? I hope you're kidding").

I told my dad he was being heartless. My aunt fled the scene, leaving us alone in the study, where we'd been sorting through a mountain of old financial records.

"I'm just being practical. This is what happens when people die, Jacob."

"Yeah? How about when *you* die? Should I burn all your old manuscripts?"

He flushed. I shouldn't have said it; mentioning his half-finished book projects was definitely below the belt. Instead of yelling at me, though, he was quiet. "I brought you along today because I thought you were mature enough to handle it. I guess I was wrong."

"You *are* wrong. You think getting rid of all Grandpa's stuff will make me forget him. But it won't."

He threw up his hands. "You know what? I'm sick of fighting about it. Keep whatever you want." He tossed a sheaf of yellowed papers at my feet. "Here's an itemized schedule of deductions from the year Kennedy was assassinated. Go have it framed!"

I kicked away the papers and walked out, slamming the door behind me, and then waited in the living room for him to come out and apologize. When I heard the shredder roar to life I knew he wasn't going to, so I stomped across the house and locked myself in the bedroom. It smelled of stale air and shoe leather and my grandfather's slightly sour cologne. I leaned against the wall, my eyes following a trail worn into the carpet between the door and the bed, where a rectangle of muted sun caught the edge of a box that poked out from beneath the bedspread. I went over and knelt down and pulled it out. It was the old cigar box, enveloped in dust—as if he'd left it there just for me to find.

Inside were the photos I knew so well: the invisible boy, the levitating girl, the boulder lifter, the man with a face painted on the back of his head. They were brittle and peeling—smaller than I remembered, too—and looking at them now, as an almost adult, it struck me how blatant the fakery was. A little burning and dodging was probably all it took to make the "invisible" boy's head disappear. The giant rock being hoisted by that suspiciously scrawny kid could have easily been made out of plaster or foam. But these observations were too subtle for a six-year-old, especially one who wanted to believe.

Beneath those photos were five more that Grandpa Portman had never shown me. I wondered why, until I looked closer. Three were so obviously manipulated that even a kid would've seen through them: one was a laughable double exposure of a girl "trapped" in a bottle; another showed a "levitating" child, suspended by something hidden in the dark doorway behind her; the third was a dog with a boy's face pasted crudely onto it. As if these weren't bizarre enough, the last two were like something out of David Lynch's nightmares: one was an unhappy young contortionist doing a frightening backbend; in the other a pair of freakish twins were dressed in the weirdest costumes I'd ever seen. Even my grandfather, who'd filled my head with stories of tentacle-tongued monsters, had realized images like these would give any kid bad dreams.

Kneeling there on my grandfather's dusty floor with those photos in my hands, I remembered how betrayed I'd felt the day I realized his stories weren't true. Now the truth seemed obvious: his last words had been just another sleight of hand, and his last act was to infect me with nightmares and paranoid delusions that would take years of therapy and metabolism-wrecking medications to rout out.

I closed the box and brought it into the living room, where my dad and Aunt Susie were emptying a drawer full of coupons, clipped but never used, into a ten-gallon trash bag.

I offered up the box. They didn't ask what was inside.

*   *   *

"So that's it?" Dr. Golan said. "His death was meaningless?"

I'd been lying on the couch watching a fish tank in the corner, its one golden prisoner swimming in lazy circles. "Unless you've got a better idea," I said. "Some big theory about what it all means that you haven't told me. Otherwise . . . "

"What?"

"Otherwise, this is just a waste of time."

He sighed and pinched the bridge of his nose as if trying to dispel a headache. "What your grandfather's last words meant isn't my conclusion to draw," he said. "It's what *you* think that matters."

"That is such psychobabble bullshit," I spat. "It's not what I *think* that matters; it's what's true! But I guess we'll never know, so who cares? Just dope me up and collect the bill."

I wanted him to get mad—to argue, to insist I was wrong—but instead he sat poker faced, drumming the arm of his chair with his pen. "It sounds like you're giving up," he said after a moment. "I'm disappointed. You don't strike me as a quitter."

"Then you don't know me very well," I replied.

I could not have been less in the mood for a party. I'd known I was in for one the moment my parents began dropping unsubtle hints about how boring and uneventful the upcoming weekend was sure to be, when we all knew perfectly well I was turning sixteen. I'd begged them to skip the party this year because, among other reasons, I couldn't think of a single person I wanted to invite, but they worried that I spent too much time alone, clinging to the notion that socializing was therapeutic. So was electroshock, I reminded them. But my mother was loath to pass up even the flimsiest excuse for a celebration—she once invited friends over for our cockatiel's birthday—in part because she loved to show off our house. Wine in hand, she'd herd guests from room to overfurnished room, extolling the genius of the architect and telling war stories about the construction ("It took *months* to get these sconces from Italy").

We'd just come home from my disastrous session with Dr. Golan. I was following my dad into our suspiciously dark living room as he muttered things like "What a shame we didn't plan anything for your birthday" and "Oh well, there's always next year," when all the lights flooded on to reveal streamers, balloons, and a motley assortment of aunts, uncles, cousins I rarely spoke to—anyone my mother could cajole into attending—and Ricky, whom I was surprised to see lingering near the punch bowl, looking comically out of place in a studded leather jacket. Once everyone had finished cheering and I'd finished pretending to be surprised, my mom slipped her arm around me and whispered, "Is this okay?" I was upset and tired and just wanted to play *Warspire III: The Summoning* before going to bed with the TV on. But what were we going to do, send everyone home? I said it was fine, and she smiled as if to thank me.

"Who wants to see the new addition?" she sang out, pouring herself some chardonnay before marching a troupe of relatives up the stairs.

Ricky and I nodded to each other across the room, wordlessly agreeing to tolerate the other's presence for an hour or two. We hadn't spoken since the day he nearly shoved me off the roof, but we both understood the importance of maintaining the illusion of having friends. I was about to go talk to him when my Uncle Bobby grabbed me by the elbow and pulled me into a corner. Bobby was a big barrel-chested guy who drove a big car and lived in a big house and would eventually succumb to a big heart attack from all the foie gras and Monster Thickburgers he'd packed into his colon over the years, leaving everything to my pothead cousins and his tiny quiet wife. He and my uncle Les were copresidents of Smart Aid, and they were always doing this—pulling people into corners for conspiratorial chats, as if plotting a mob hit rather than complimenting the hostess on her guacamole.

"So, your mom tells me you're really turning the corner with, uh . . . on this whole Grandpa thing."

My thing. No one knew what to call it.

"Acute stress reaction," I said.

"What?"

"That's what I had. Have. Whatever."

"That's good. Real good to hear." He waved his hand as if putting all that unpleasantness behind us. "So your mom and I were thinking. How'd you like to come up to Tampa this summer, see how the family business works? Crack heads with me at HQ for a while? Unless you love stocking shelves!" He laughed so loudly that I took an involuntary step backward. "You could even stay at the house, do a little tarpon fishing with me and your cousins on the weekends." He then spent five long minutes describing his new yacht, going into elaborate, almost pornographic detail, as if that alone were enough to close the deal. When he finished, he grinned and stuck out his hand for me to shake. "So whaddaya think, J-dogg?"

I guess it was designed to be an offer I couldn't refuse, but I'd have rather spent the summer in a Siberian labor camp than live with my uncle and his spoiled kids. As for working at Smart Aid HQ, I knew it was a probably inevitable part of my future, but I'd been counting on at least a few more summers of freedom and four years of college before I had to lock myself in a corporate cage. I hesitated, trying to think of a graceful way out. Instead what I said was, "I'm not sure my psychiatrist would think it's such a great idea right now."

His bushy eyebrows came together. Nodding vaguely, he said, "Oh, well, sure, of course. We'll just play it by ear then, pal, how's that sound?" And then he walked off without waiting for an answer, pretending to see someone across the room whose elbow he needed to grab.

My mother announced that it was time to open presents. She always insisted I do this in front of everyone, which was a problem because, as I may have mentioned already, I'm not a good liar. That also means I'm not good at feigning gratitude for regifted CDs of country Christmas music or subscriptions to *Field and Stream*—for years Uncle Les had labored under the baffling delusion that I am "outdoorsy"—but for decorum's sake I forced a smile and held up each unwrapped trinket for all to admire until the pile of presents left on the coffee table had shrunk to just three.

I reached for the smallest one first. Inside was the key to my parents' four-year-old luxury sedan. They were getting a new one, my mom explained, so I was inheriting the old one. My first car! Everyone *oohed* and *aahed*, but I felt my face go hot. It was too much like showing off to accept such a lavish present in front of Ricky, whose car cost less than my monthly allowance at age twelve. It seemed like my parents were always trying to get me to care about money, but I didn't, really. Then again, it's easy to say you don't care about money when you have plenty of it.

The next present was the digital camera I'd begged my parents for all last summer. "Wow," I said, testing its weight in my hand. "This is awesome."

"I'm outlining a new bird book," my dad said. "I was thinking maybe you could take the pictures."

"A new book!" my mom exclaimed. "That's a phenomenal idea, Frank. Speaking of which, whatever happened to that last book you were working on?" Clearly, she'd had a few glasses of wine.

"I'm still ironing out a few things," my dad replied quietly.

"Oh, I *see*." I could hear Uncle Bobby snickering.

"Okay!" I said loudly, reaching for the last present. "This one's from Aunt Susie."

"Actually," my aunt said as I began tearing away the wrapping paper, "it's from your grandfather."

I stopped midtear. The room went dead quiet, people looking at Aunt Susie as if she'd invoked the name of some evil spirit. My dad's jaw tensed and my mom shot back the last of her wine.

"Just open it and you'll see," Aunt Susie said.

I ripped away the rest of the wrapping paper to find an old hard-back book, dog-eared and missing its dust jacket. It was *The Selected Works of Ralph Waldo Emerson*. I stared at it as if trying to read through the cover, unable to comprehend how it had come to occupy my now-trembling hands. No one but Dr. Golan knew about the last words, and he'd promised on several occasions that unless I threatened to guzzle Drano or do a backflip off the Sunshine Skyway bridge, everything we talked about in his office would be held in confidence.

I looked at my aunt, a question on my face that I didn't quite know how to ask. She managed a weak smile and said, "I found it in your grandfather's desk when we were cleaning out the house. He wrote your name in the front. I think he meant for you to have it."

God bless Aunt Susie. She had a heart after all.

"Neat. I didn't know your grandpa was a reader," my mom said, trying to lighten the mood. "That was thoughtful."

"Yes," said my dad through clenched teeth. "Thank you, Susan."

I opened the book. Sure enough, the title page bore an inscription in my grandfather's shaky handwriting.

THE

SELECTED WORKS
OF RALPH WALDO
EMERSON

Edited and with an introduction

BY CLIFTON DURRELL, PH. D.

*To Jacob Magellan Portman,
and the worlds he has
yet to discover —*

ANTHEM BOOKS • NEW YORK

I got up to leave, afraid I might start crying in front of everyone, and something slipped out from between the pages and fell to the floor.

I bent to pick it up. It was a letter.

Emerson. The letter.

I felt the blood drain from my face. My mother leaned toward me and in a tense whisper asked if I needed a drink of water, which was Mom-speak for *keep it together, people are staring.* I said, "I feel a little, uh . . . " and then, with one hand over my stomach, I bolted to my room.

*   *   *

The letter was handwritten on fine, unlined paper in looping script so ornate it was almost calligraphy, the black ink varying in tone like that of an old fountain pen. It read:

Dearest Abe,

I hope this note finds you safe & in the best of health. It's been such a long time since we last received word from you! But I write not to admonish, only to let you know that we still think of you often & pray for your well-being. Our brave, handsome Abe!

As for life on the island, little has changed. But quiet & orderly is the way we prefer things! I wonder if we would recognize you after so many years, though I'm certain you'd recognize us — those few who remain, that is. It would mean a great deal to have a recent picture of you, if you've one to send. I've included a positively ancient snap of myself.

& missed you terribly. Won't you write to her?

With respect & admiration,

Headmistress Alma LeFay Peregrine

As promised, the writer had enclosed an old snapshot.

I held it under the glow of my desk lamp, trying to read some detail in the woman's silhouetted face, but there was none to find. The image was so strange, and yet it was nothing like my grandfather's pictures. There were no tricks here. It was just a woman—a woman smoking a pipe. It looked like Sherlock Holmes's pipe, curved and drooping from her lips. My eyes kept coming back to it.

Was this what my grandfather had meant for me to find? *Yes*, I thought, *it has to be*—not *the* letters of Emerson, but *a* letter, tucked inside Emerson's book. But who was this headmistress, this Peregrine woman? I studied the envelope for a return address but found only a fading postmark that read *Cairnholm Is., Cymru, UK.*

UK—that was Britain. I knew from studying atlases as a kid that *Cymru* meant Wales. *Cairnholm Is* had to be the island Miss Peregrine had mentioned in her letter. Could it have been the same island where my grandfather lived as a boy?

Nine months ago he'd told me to "find the bird." Nine years ago he had sworn that the children's home where he'd lived was protected by one—by "a bird who smoked a pipe." At age seven I'd taken this statement literally, but the headmistress in the picture was smoking a pipe, and her name was Peregrine, a kind of hawk. What if the bird my grandfather wanted me to find was actually the woman who'd rescued him—the headmistress of the children's home? Maybe she was still on the island, after all these years, old as dirt but sustained by a few of her wards, children who'd grown up but never left.

For the first time, my grandfather's last words began to make a strange kind of sense. He wanted me to go to the island and find this woman, his old headmistress. If anyone knew the secrets of his childhood, it would be her. But the envelope's postmark was fifteen years old. Was it possible she was still alive? I did some quick calculations in my head: If she'd been running a children's home in 1939 and was, say, twenty-five at the time, then she'd be in her late nineties today.

So it was possible—there were people older than that in Englewood who still lived by themselves and drove—and even if Miss Peregrine *had* passed away in the time since she'd sent the letter, there might still be people on Cairnholm who could help me, people who had known Grandpa Portman as a kid. People who knew his secrets.

We, she had written. *Those few who remain.*

*   *   *

As you can imagine, convincing my parents to let me spend part of my summer on a tiny island off the coast of Wales was no easy task. They—particularly my mother—had many compelling reasons why this was a wretched idea, including the cost, the fact that I was supposed to spend the summer with Uncle Bobby learning how to run a drug empire, and that I had no one to accompany me, since neither of my parents had any interest in going and I certainly couldn't go alone. I had no effective re-buttals, and my reason for wanting to make the trip—*I think I'm sup-posed to*—wasn't something I could explain without sounding even crazier than they already feared I was. I certainly wasn't going to tell my parents about Grandpa Portman's last words or the letter or the photo—they would've had me committed. The only sane-sounding ar-guments I could come up with were things like, "I want to learn more about our family history" and the never-persuasive "Chad Kramer and Josh Bell are going to Europe this summer. Why can't I?" I brought these up as frequently as possible without seeming desperate (even once resorting to "it's not like you don't have the money," a tactic I instantly regretted), but it looked like it wasn't going to happen.

Then several things happened that helped my case enormously. First, Uncle Bobby got cold feet about my spending the summer with him—because who wants a nutcase living in their house? So my schedule was suddenly wide open. Next, my dad learned that Cairn-holm Island is a super-important bird habitat, and, like, half the world's population of some bird that gives him a total ornithology boner lives there. He started talking a lot about his hypothetical new bird book, and whenever the subject came up I did my best to encourage him and sound interested. But the most important factor was Dr. Golan. After a surprisingly minimal amount of coaxing by me, he shocked us all by not only signing off on the idea but also encouraging my parents to let me go.

"It could be important for him," he told my mother after a session one afternoon. "It's a place that's been so mythologized by his grandfather that visiting could only serve to demystify it. He'll see that it's just as normal and unmagical as anyplace else, and, by extension, his grandfather's fantasies will lose their power. It could be a highly effective way of combating fantasy with reality."

"But I thought he already didn't believe that stuff," my mother said, turning to me. "Do you, Jake?"

"I don't," I assured her.

"Not consciously he doesn't," Dr. Golan said. "But it's his *un*conscious that's causing him problems right now. The dreams, the anxiety."

"And you really think going there could help?" my mother said, narrowing her eyes at him as if readying herself to hear the unvarnished truth. When it came to things I should or should not be doing, Dr. Golan's word was law.

"I do," he replied.

And that was all it took.

*   *   *

After that, things fell into place with astonishing speed. Plane tickets were bought, schedules scheduled, plans laid. My dad and I would go for three weeks in June. I wondered if that was too long, but he claimed he needed at least that much time to make a thorough study of the island's bird colonies. I thought mom would object—three whole weeks!—but the closer our trip got, the more excited for us she seemed. "My two men," she would say, beaming, "off on a big adventure!"

I found her enthusiasm kind of touching, actually—until the afternoon I overheard her talking on the phone to a friend, venting about how relieved she'd be to "have her life back" for three weeks and not have "two needy children to worry about."

I love you too, I wanted to say with as much hurtful sarcasm as I could muster, but she hadn't seen me, and I kept quiet. I did love her, of course, but mostly just because loving your mom is mandatory, not because she was someone I think I'd like very much if I met her walking down the street. Which she wouldn't be, anyway; walking is for poor people.

During the three-week window between the end of school and the start of our trip, I did my best to verify that Ms. Alma LeFay Peregrine still resided among the living, but Internet searches turned up nothing. Assuming she was still alive, I had hoped to get her on the phone and at least warn her that I was coming, but I soon discovered that almost no one on Cairnholm even *had* a phone. I found only one number for the entire island, so that's the one I dialed.

It took nearly a minute to connect, the line hissing and clicking, going quiet, then hissing again, so that I could feel every mile of the vast distance my call was spanning. Finally I heard that strange European ring—*waaap-waaap. . . waaap-waaap*—and a man whom I could only assume was profoundly intoxicated answered the phone.

"Piss hole!" he bellowed. There was an unholy amount of noise in the background, the kind of dull roar you'd expect at the height of a raging frat party. I tried to identify myself, but I don't think he could hear me.

"Piss hole!" he bellowed again. "Who's this now?" But before I could say anything he'd pulled the receiver away from his head to shout at someone. "I said shaddap, ya dozy bastards, I'm on the—"

And then the line went dead. I sat with the receiver to my ear for a long, puzzled moment, then hung up. I didn't bother calling back. If Cairnholm's only phone connected to some den of iniquity called the "piss hole," how did that bode for the rest of the island? Would my first trip to Europe be spent evading drunken maniacs and watching birds evacuate their bowels on rocky beaches? Maybe so. But if it meant that I'd finally be able to put my grandfather's mystery to rest and get on with my unextraordinary life, anything I had to endure would be worth it.

CHAPTER THREE

*F*og closed around us like a blindfold. When the captain announced that we were nearly there, at first I thought he was kidding; all I could see from the ferry's rolling deck was an endless curtain of gray. I clutched the rail and stared into the green waves, contemplating the fish who might soon be enjoying my breakfast, while my father stood shivering beside me in shirtsleeves. It was colder and wetter than I'd ever known June could be. I hoped, for his sake and mine, that the grueling thirty-six hours we'd braved to get this far—three airplanes, two layovers, shift-napping in grubby train stations, and now this interminable gut-churning ferry ride— would pay off. Then my father shouted, "Look!" and I raised my head to see a towering mountain of rock emerge from the blank canvas before us.

It was my grandfather's island. Looming and bleak, folded in mist, guarded by a million screeching birds, it looked like some ancient fortress constructed by giants. As I gazed up at its sheer cliffs, tops disappearing in a reef of ghostly clouds, the idea that this was a magical place didn't seem so ridiculous.

My nausea seemed to vanish. Dad ran around like a kid on Christmas, his eyes glued to the birds wheeling above us. "Jacob, look at that!" he cried, pointing to a cluster of airborne specks. "Manx Shearwaters!"

As we drew nearer the cliffs, I began to notice odd shapes lurking underwater. A passing crewman caught me leaning over the rail to stare at them and said, "Never seen a shipwreck before, eh?"

I turned to him. "Really?"

"This whole area's a nautical graveyard. It's like the old captains used to say—'Twixt Hartland Point and Cairnholm Bay is a sailor's grave by night or day!'"

Just then we passed a wreck that was so near the surface, the outline of its greening carcass so clear, that it looked like it was about to rise out of the water like a zombie from a shallow grave. "See that one?" he said, pointing at it. "Sunk by a U-boat, she was."

"There were U-boats around here?"

"Loads. Whole Irish Sea was rotten with German subs. Wager you'd have half a navy on your hands if you could unsink all the ships they torpedoed." He arched one eyebrow dramatically, then walked off laughing.

I jogged along the deck to the stern, tracking the shipwreck as it disappeared beneath our wake. Then, just as I was starting to wonder if we'd need climbing gear to get onto the island, its steep cliffs sloped down to meet us. We rounded a headland to enter a rocky half-moon bay. In the distance I saw a little harbor bobbing with colorful fishing boats, and beyond it a town set into a green bowl of land. A patchwork of sheep-speckled fields spread across hills that rose away to meet a high ridge, where a wall of clouds stood like a cotton parapet. It was dramatic and beautiful, unlike any place I'd seen. I felt a little thrill of adventure as we chugged into the bay, as if I were sighting land where maps had noted only a sweep of undistinguished blue.

The ferry docked and we humped our bags into the little town. Upon closer inspection I decided it was, like a lot of things, not as pretty up close as it seemed from a distance. Whitewashed cottages, quaint except for the satellite dishes sprouting from their roofs, lined a small grid of muddy gravel streets. Because Cairnholm was too distant and too inconsequential to justify the cost of running power lines from the mainland, foul-smelling diesel generators buzzed on every corner like angry wasps, harmonizing with the growl of tractors, the island's only vehicular traffic. At the edges of town, ancient-looking cottages stood abandoned and roofless, evidence of a shrinking population, children lured away from centuries-old fishing and farming traditions by more glamorous opportunities elsewhere.

We dragged our stuff through town looking for something called the Priest Home, where my dad had booked a room. I pictured an old church converted into a bed and breakfast—nothing fancy, just somewhere to sleep when we weren't watching birds or chasing down leads. We asked a few locals for directions but got only confused looks in return. "They speak English, right?" my dad wondered aloud. Just as my hand was beginning to ache from the weight of my suitcase, we came upon a church. We thought we'd found our accommodations, until we went inside and saw that it had indeed been converted, but into a dingy little museum, not a B&B.

We found the part-time curator in a room hung with old fishing nets and sheep shears. His face lit up when he saw us, then fell when he realized we were only lost.

"I reckon you're after the Priest *Hole*," he said. "It's got the only rooms to let on the island."

He proceeded to give us directions in a lilting accent, which I found enormously entertaining. I loved hearing Welsh people talk, even if half of what they said was incomprehensible to me. My dad thanked the man and turned to go, but he'd been so helpful, I hung back to ask him another question.

"Where can we find the old children's home?"

"The old what?" he said, squinting at me.

For an awful moment I was afraid we'd come to the wrong island or, worse yet, that the home was just another thing my grandfather had invented.

"It was a home for refugee kids?" I said. "During the war? A big house?"

The man chewed his lip and regarded me doubtfully, as if deciding whether to help or to wash his hands of the whole thing. But he took pity on me. "I don't know about any refugees," he said, "but I think I know the place you mean. It's way up the other side of the island, past the bog and through the woods. Though I wouldn't go mucking about up there alone, if I was you. Stray too far from the path and that's the last anyone'll hear of you—nothing but wet grass and sheep patties to keep you from going straight over a cliff."

"That's good to know," my dad said, eyeing me. "Promise me you won't go by yourself."

"All right, all right."

"What's your interest in it, anyhow?" the man said. "It's not exactly on the tourist maps."

"Just a little genealogy project," my father replied, lingering near the door. "My dad spent a few years there as a kid." I could tell he was eager to avoid any mention of psychiatrists or dead grandfathers. He thanked the man again and quickly ushered me out the door.

Following the curator's directions, we retraced our steps until we came to a grim-looking statue carved from black stone, a memorial called the Waiting Woman dedicated to islanders lost at sea. She wore a pitiful expression and stood with arms outstretched in the direction of the harbor, many blocks away, but also toward the Priest Hole, which was directly across the street. Now, I'm no hotel connoisseur, but one glance at the weathered sign told me that our stay was unlikely to be a four-star mints-on-your-pillow-type experience. Printed in giant script at the top was *WINES, ALES, SPIRITS*. Below that, in more modest lettering, *Fine Food*. Handwritten along the bottom, clearly an afterthought, was *Rooms to Let*, though the *s* had been struck out, leaving just the singular *Room*. As we lugged our bags toward the door, my father grumbling about con men and false advertising, I glanced back at the Waiting Woman and wondered if she wasn't just waiting for someone to bring her a drink.

We squeezed our bags through the doorway and stood blinking in the sudden gloom of a low-ceilinged pub. When my eyes had adjusted, I realized that *hole* was a pretty accurate description of the place: tiny leaded windows admitted just enough light to find the beer tap without tripping over tables and chairs on the way. The tables, worn and wobbling, looked like they might be more useful as firewood. The bar was half-filled, at whatever hour of the morning it was, with men in various states of hushed intoxication, heads bowed prayerfully over tumblers of amber liquid.

"You must be after the room," said the man behind the bar, coming out to shake our hands. "I'm Kev and these are the fellas. Say hullo, fellas."

"Hullo," they muttered, nodding at their drinks.

We followed Kev up a narrow staircase to a suite of rooms (plural!) that could charitably be described as basic. There were two bedrooms, the larger of which Dad claimed, and a room that tripled as a kitchen, dining room, and living room, meaning that it contained one table, one moth-eaten sofa, and one hotplate. The bathroom worked "most of the time," according to Kev, "but if it ever gets dicey, there's always Old Reliable." He directed our attention to a portable toilet in the alley out back, conveniently visible from my bedroom window.

"Oh, and you'll need these," he said, fetching a pair of oil lamps from a cabinet. "The generators stop running at ten since petrol's so bloody expensive to ship out, so either you get to bed early or you learn to love candles and kerosene." He grinned. "Hope it ain't too medieval for ya!"

We assured Kev that outhouses and kerosene would be just fine, sounded like fun, in fact—a little adventure, yessir—and then he led us downstairs for the final leg of our tour. "You're welcome to take your meals here," he said, "and I expect you will, on account of there's nowhere else to eat. If you need to make a call, we got a phone box in the corner there. Sometimes there's a bit of a queue for it, though, since we get doodly for mobile reception out here and you're looking at the only land-line on the island. That's right, we got it all—only food, only bed, only phone!" And he leaned back and laughed, long and loud.

The only phone on the island. I looked over at it—it was the kind that had a door you could pull shut for privacy, like the ones you see in old movies—and realized with dawning horror that *this* was the Grecian orgy, *this* was the raging frat party I had been connected to when I called the island a few weeks ago. *This was the piss hole.*

Kev handed my dad the keys to our rooms. "Any questions," he said, "you know where to find me."

"I have a question," I said. "What's a piss—I mean, a priest hole?"

The men at the bar burst into laughter. "Why, it's a hole for priests, of course!" one said, which made the rest of them laugh even harder.

Kev walked over to an uneven patch of floorboards next to the fireplace, where a mangy dog lay sleeping. "Right here," he said, tapping what appeared to be a door in the floor with his shoe. "Ages ago, when just being a Catholic could get you hung from a tree, clergyfolk came here seeking refuge. If Queen Elizabeth's crew of thugs came chasing after, we hid whoever needed hiding in snug little spots like this—priest holes." It struck me the way he said *we*, as if he'd known those long-dead islanders personally.

"Snug indeed!" one of the drinkers said. "Bet they were warm as toast and tight as drums down there!"

"I'd take warm and snug to strung up by priest killers any day," said another.

"Here, here!" the first man said. "To Cairnholm—may she always be our rock of refuge!"

"To Cairnholm!" they chorused, and raised their glasses together.

Jet-lagged and exhausted, we went to sleep early—or rather we went to our beds and lay in them with pillows covering our heads to block out the thumping cacophony that issued through the floorboards, which grew so loud that at one point I thought surely the revelers had invaded my room. Then the clock must've struck ten because all at once the buzzing generators outside sputtered and died, as did the music from downstairs and the streetlight that had been shining through my window. Suddenly I was cocooned in silent, blissful darkness, with only the whisper of distant waves to remind me where I was.

For the first time in months, I fell into a deep, nightmare-free slumber. I dreamed instead about my grandfather as a boy, about his first night here, a stranger in a strange land, under a strange roof, owing his life to people who spoke a strange tongue. When I awoke, sun streaming through my window, I realized it wasn't just my grandfather's life that Miss Peregrine had saved, but mine, too, and my father's. Today, with any luck, I would finally get to thank her.

I went downstairs to find my dad already bellied up to a table, slurping coffee and polishing his fancy binoculars. Just as I sat down, Kev appeared bearing two plates loaded with mystery meat and fried toast. "I didn't know you could fry toast," I remarked, to which Kev replied that there wasn't a food he was aware of that couldn't be improved by frying.

Over breakfast, Dad and I discussed our plan for the day. It was to be a kind of scout, to familiarize ourselves with the island. We'd scope out my dad's bird-watching spots first and then find the children's home. I scarfed my food, anxious to get started.

Well fortified with grease, we left the pub and walked through town, dodging tractors and shouting to each other over the din of generators until the streets gave way to fields and the noise faded behind us. It was a crisp and blustery day—the sun hiding behind giant cloudbanks only to burst out moments later and dapple the hills with spectacular rays of light—and I felt energized and hopeful. We were heading for a rocky beach where my dad had spotted a bunch of birds from the ferry. I wasn't sure how we would reach it, though—the island was slightly bowl shaped, with hills that climbed toward its edges only to drop off at precarious seaside cliffs—but at this particular spot the edge had been rounded off and a path led down to a minor spit of sand along the water.

We picked our way down to the beach, where what seemed to be an entire civilization of birds were flapping and screeching and fishing in tide pools. I watched my father's eyes widen. "Fascinating," he muttered, scraping at some petrified guano with the stubby end of his pen. "I'm going to need some time here. Is that all right?"

I'd seen this look on his face before, and I knew exactly what "some time" meant: hours and hours. "Then I'll go find the house by myself," I said.

"Not alone, you aren't. You promised."

"Then I'll find a person who can take me."

"Who?"

"Kev will know someone."

My dad looked out to sea, where a big rusted lighthouse jutted up from a pile of rocks. "You know what the answer would be if your mom were here," he said.

My parents had differing theories about how much parenting I required. Mom was the enforcer, always hovering, but Dad hung back a little. He thought it was important that I make my own mistakes now and then. Also, letting me go would free him to play with guano all day.

"Okay," he said, "but make sure you leave me the number of whoever you go with."

"Dad, nobody here has phones."

He sighed. "Right. Well, as long as they're reliable."

Kev was out running an errand, and because asking one of his drunken regulars to chaperone me seemed like a bad idea, I went into the nearest shop to ask someone who was at least gainfully employed. The door read *FISHMONGER*. I pushed it open to find myself cowering before a bearded giant in a blood-soaked apron. He left off decapitating fish to glare at me, dripping cleaver in hand, and I vowed never again to discriminate against the intoxicated.

"What the hell for?" he growled when I told him where I wanted to go. "Nothing over there but bogland and barmy weather."

I explained about my grandfather and the children's home. He frowned at me, then leaned over the counter to cast a doubtful glance at my shoes.

"I s'pose Dylan ain't too busy to take you," he said, pointing his cleaver at a kid about my age who was arranging fish in a freezer case, "but you'll be wantin' proper footwear. Wouldn't do to let you go in them trainers—mud'll suck 'em right off!"

"Really?" I said. "Are you sure?"

"Dylan! Fetch our man here a pair of Wellingtons!"

The kid groaned and made a big show of slowly closing the freezer case and cleaning his hands before slouching over to a wall of shelves packed with dry goods.

"Just so happens we've got some good sturdy boots on offer," the fishmonger said. "Buy one get none free!" He burst out laughing and slammed his cleaver on a salmon, its head shooting across the blood-slicked counter to land perfectly in a little guillotine bucket.

I fished the emergency money Dad had given me from my pocket, figuring that a little extortion was a small price to pay to find the woman I'd crossed the Atlantic to meet.

I left the shop wearing a pair of rubber boots so large my sneakers fit inside and so heavy it was difficult to keep up with my begrudging guide.

"So, do you go to school on the island?" I asked Dylan, scurrying to catch up. I was genuinely curious—what was living here like for someone my age?

He muttered the name of a town on the mainland.

"What is that, an hour each way by ferry?"

"Yup."

And that was it. He responded to further attempts at conversation with even fewer syllables—which is to say, none—so finally I just gave up and followed him. On the way out of town we ran into one of his friends, an older boy wearing a blinding yellow tracksuit and fake gold chains. He couldn't have looked more out of place on Cairnholm if he'd been dressed like an astronaut. He gave Dylan a fist-bump and introduced himself as Worm.

"Worm?"

"It's his stage name," Dylan explained.

"We're the sickest rapping duo in Wales," Worm said. "I'm Emcee Worm, and this is the Sturgeon Surgeon, aka Emcee Dirty Dylan, aka Emcee Dirty Bizniss, Cairnholm's number one beat-boxer. Wanna show this Yank how we do, Dirty D?"

Dylan looked annoyed. "Now?"

"Drop some next-level beats, son!"

Dylan rolled his eyes but did as he was asked. At first I thought he was choking on his tongue, except there was a rhythm to his sputtering coughs—*puhh, puh-CHAH, puh-puhhh, puh-CHAH*—over which Worm began to rap.

"I likes to get wrecked up down at the Priest Hole / Your dad's always there 'cause he's on the dole / My rhymes is tight, yeah I make it look easy / Dylan's beats are hot like chicken jalfrezi!"

Dylan stopped. "That don't even make sense," he said. "And it's *your* dad who's on the dole."

"Oh shit, Dirty D let the beat drop!" Worm started beat-boxing while doing a passable robot, his sneakers twisting holes in the gravel. "Take the mic, D!"

Dylan seemed embarrassed but let the rhymes fly anyway. "I met a tight bird and her name was Sharon / She was keen on my tracksuit and the trainers I was wearin' / I showed her the time, like Doctor Who / I thunk up this rhyme while I was in the loo!"

Worm shook his head. "The *loo?*"

"I wasn't ready!"

They turned to me and asked what I thought. Considering that they didn't even like each other's rapping, I wasn't sure what to say.

"I guess I'm more into music with, like, singing and guitars and stuff."

Worm dismissed me with a wave of his hand. "He wouldn't know a dope rhyme if it bit him in the bollocks," he muttered.

Dylan laughed and they exchanged a series of complex, multi-stage handshake-fist-bump-high-fives.

"Can we go now?" I said.

They grumbled and dawdled a while longer, but pretty soon we were on our way, this time with Worm tagging along.

I took up the rear, trying to figure out what I would say to Miss Peregrine when I met her. I was expecting to be introduced to a proper Welsh lady and sip tea in the parlor and make polite small talk until the time seemed right to break the bad news. *I'm Abraham Portman's grandson*, I would say. *I'm sorry to be the one to tell you this, but he's been taken from us.* Then, once she'd finished quietly dabbing away tears, I would ply her with questions.

I followed Dylan and Worm along a path that wound through pastures of grazing sheep before a lung-busting ascent up a ridge. At the top hovered an embankment of rolling, snaking fog so dense it was like stepping into another world. It was truly biblical; a fog I could imagine God, in one of his lesser wraths, cursing the Egyptians with. As we descended the other side it only seemed to thicken. The sun faded to a pale white bloom. Moisture clung to everything, beading on my skin and dampening my clothes. The temperature dropped. I lost Worm and Dylan for a moment and then the path flattened and I came upon them just standing, waiting for me.

"Yank boy!" Dylan called. "This way!"

I followed obediently. We abandoned the path to plow through a field of marshy grass. Sheep stared at us with big leaky eyes, their wool soggy and tails drooping. A small house appeared out of the mist. It was all boarded up.

"You sure this is it?" I said. "It looks empty."

"Empty? No way, there's *loads* of shit in there," Worm replied.

"Go on," said Dylan. "Have a look."

I had a feeling it was a trick but stepped up to the door and knocked anyway. It was unlatched and opened a little at my touch. It was too dark to see inside, so I took a step through—and, to my surprise, *down*—into what looked like a dirt floor but, I quickly realized, was in fact a shin-deep ocean of excrement. This tenantless hovel, so innocent looking from the outside, was really a makeshift sheep stable. Quite literally a shithole.

"Oh my God!" I squealed in disgust.

Peals of laughter exploded from outside. I stumbled backward through the door before the smell could knock me unconscious and found the boys doubled over, holding their stomachs.

"You guys are assholes," I said, stomping the muck off my boots.

"Why?" said Worm. "We *told* you it was full of shit!"

I got in Dylan's face. "Are you gonna show me the house or not?"

"He's serious," said Worm, wiping tears from his eyes.

"Of course I'm serious!"

Dylan's smile faded. "I thought you were taking the piss, mate."

"Taking the what?"

"Joking, like."

"Well, I wasn't."

The boys exchanged an uneasy look. Dylan whispered something to Worm. Worm whispered something back. Finally Dylan turned and pointed up the path. "If you really want to see it," he said, "keep going past the bog and through the woods. It's a big old place. You can't miss it."

"What the hell. You're supposed to go with me!"

Worm looked away and said, "This is as far as we go."

"Why?"

"It just is." And they turned and began to trudge back the way we'd come, receding into the fog.

I weighed my options. I could tuck tail and follow my tormenters back to town, or I could go ahead alone and lie to Dad about it.

After four seconds of intense deliberation, I was on my way.

*   *   *

A vast, lunar bog stretched away into the mist from either side of the path, just brown grass and tea-colored water as far as I could see, featureless but for the occasional mound of piled-up stones. It ended abruptly at a forest of skeletal trees, branches spindling up like the tips of wet paintbrushes, and for a while the path became so lost beneath fallen trunks and carpets of ivy that navigating it was a matter of faith. I wondered how an elderly person like Miss Peregrine would ever be able to negotiate such an obstacle course. *She must get deliveries,* I thought, though the path looked like it hadn't seen a footprint in months, if not years.

I scrambled over a giant trunk slick with moss, and the path took a sharp turn. The trees parted like a curtain and suddenly there it was, cloaked in fog, looming atop a weed-choked hill. The house. I understood at once why the boys had refused to come.

My grandfather had described it a hundred times, but in his stories the house was always a bright, happy place—big and rambling, yes, but full of light and laughter. What stood before me now was no refuge from monsters but a monster itself, staring down from its perch on the hill with vacant hunger. Trees burst forth from broken windows and skins of scabrous vine gnawed at the walls like antibodies attacking a virus—as if nature itself had waged war against it—but the house seemed unkillable, resolutely upright despite the wrongness of its angles and the jagged teeth of sky visible through sections of collapsed roof.

I tried to convince myself that it was possible someone could still live there, run-down as it was. Such things weren't unheard of where I came from—a falling-down wreck on the edge of town, curtains permanently drawn, that would turn out to have been home to some ancient recluse who'd been surviving on ramen and toenail clippings since time immemorial, though no one realizes it until a property appraiser or an overly ambitious census taker barges in to find the poor soul returning to dust in a La-Z-Boy. People get too old to care for a place, their family writes them off for one reason or another—it's sad, but it happens. Which meant, like it or not, that I was going to have to knock.

I gathered what scrawny courage I had and waded through waist-high weeds to the porch, all broken tile and rotting wood, to peek through a cracked window. All I could make out through the smeared glass were the outlines of furniture, so I knocked on the door and stood back to wait in the eerie silence, tracing the shape of Miss Peregrine's letter in my pocket. I'd taken it along in case I needed to prove who I was, but as a minute ticked by, then two, it seemed less and less likely that I would need it.

Climbing down into the yard, I circled the house looking for another way in, taking the measure of the place, but it seemed almost without measure, as though with every corner I turned the house sprouted new balconies and turrets and chimneys. Then I came around back and saw my opportunity: a doorless doorway, bearded with vines, gaping and black; an open mouth waiting to swallow me. Just looking at it made my skin crawl, but I hadn't come halfway around the world just to run away screaming at the sight of a scary house. I thought of all the horrors Grandpa Portman had faced in his life, and felt my resolve harden. If there was anyone to find inside, I would find them. I mounted the crumbling steps and crossed the threshold.

*   *   *

Standing in a tomb-dark hallway just inside the door, I stared frozenly at what looked for all the world like skins hanging from hooks. After a queasy moment in which I imagined some twisted cannibal leaping from the shadows with knife in hand, I realized they were only coats rotted to rags and green with age. I shuddered involuntarily and took a deep breath. I'd only explored ten feet of the house and was already about to foul my underwear. *Keep it together,* I told myself, and then slowly moved forward, heart hammering in my chest.

Each room was a disaster more incredible than the last. Newspapers gathered in drifts. Scattered toys, evidence of children long gone, lay skinned in dust. Creeping mold had turned window-adjacent walls black and furry. Fireplaces were throttled with vines that had descended from the roof and begun to spread across the floors like alien tentacles. The kitchen was a science experiment gone terribly wrong—entire shelves of jarred food had exploded from sixty seasons of freezing and thawing, splattering the wall with evil-looking stains—and fallen plaster lay so thickly over the dining room floor that for a moment I thought it had snowed indoors. At the end of a light-starved corridor I tested my weight on a rickety staircase, my boots leaving fresh tracks in layers of dust. The steps groaned as if woken from a long sleep. If anyone was upstairs, they'd been there a very long time.

Finally I came upon a pair of rooms missing entire walls, into which a little forest of underbrush and stunted trees had grown. I stood in the sudden breeze wondering what could possibly have done that kind of damage, and began to get the feeling that something terrible had happened here. I couldn't square my grandfather's idyllic stories with this nightmare house, nor the idea that he'd found refuge here with the sense of disaster that pervaded it. There was more left to explore, but suddenly it seemed like a waste of time; it was impossible that anyone could still be living here, even the most misanthropic recluse. I left the house feeling like I was further than ever from the truth.

CHAPTER FOUR

Once I'd hopped and tripped and felt my way like a blind man through the woods and fog and reemerged into the world of sun and light, I was surprised to find the sun sinking and the light going red. Somehow the whole day had slipped away. At the pub my dad was waiting for me, a black-as-night beer and his open laptop on the table in front of him. I sat down and swiped his beer before he'd had a chance to even look up from typing.

"Oh, my sweet lord," I sputtered, choking down a mouthful, "what is this? Fermented motor oil?"

"Just about," he said, laughing, and then snatched it back. "It's not like American beer. Not that you'd know what that tastes like, right?"

"Absolutely not," I said with a wink, even though it was true. My dad liked to believe I was as popular and adventuresome as he was at my age—a myth it had always seemed easiest to perpetuate.

I underwent a brief interrogation about how I'd gotten to the house and who had taken me there, and because the easiest kind of lying is when you leave things out of a story rather than make them up, I passed with flying colors. I conveniently forgot to mention that Worm and Dylan had tricked me into wading through sheep excrement and then bailed out a half-mile from our destination. Dad seemed pleased that I'd already managed to meet a couple kids my own age; I guess I also forgot to mention the part about them hating me.

"So how was the house?"

"Trashed."

He winced. "Guess it's been a long time since your Grandpa lived there, huh?"

"Yeah. Or anyone."

He closed the laptop, a sure sign I was about to receive his full attention. "I can see you're disappointed."

"Well, I didn't come thousands of miles looking for a house full of creepy garbage."

"So what're you going to do?"

"Find people to talk to. Someone will know what happened to the kids who used to live there. I figure a few of them must still be alive, on the mainland if not around here. In a nursing home or something."

"Sure. That's an idea." He didn't sound convinced, though. There was an odd pause, and then he said, "So do you feel like you're starting to get a better handle on who your grandpa was, being here?"

I thought about it. "I don't know. I guess so. It's just an island, you know?"

He nodded. "Exactly."

"What about you?"

"Me?" He shrugged. "I gave up trying to understand my father a long time ago."

"That's sad. Weren't you interested?"

"Sure I was. Then, after a while, I wasn't anymore."

I could feel the conversation going in a direction I wasn't entirely comfortable with, but I persisted anyway. "Why not?"

"When someone won't let you in, eventually you stop knocking. Know what I mean?"

He hardly ever talked like this. Maybe it was the beer, or that we were so far from home, or maybe he'd decided I was finally old enough to hear this stuff. Whatever the reason, I didn't want him to stop.

"But he was your dad. How could you just give up?"

"It wasn't me who gave up!" he said a little too loudly, then looked down, embarrassed, and swirled the beer in his glass. "It's just that—the truth is, I think your grandpa didn't know how to be a dad, but he felt like he had to be one anyway, because none of his brothers or sisters survived the war. So he dealt with it by being gone all the time—on hunting trips, business trips, you name it. And even when he *was* around, it was like he wasn't."

"Is this about that one Halloween?"

"What are you talking about?"

"You know—from the picture."

It was an old story, and it went like this: It was Halloween. My dad was four or five years old and had never been trick-or-treating, and Grandpa Portman had promised to take him when he got off work. My grandmother had bought my dad this ridiculous pink bunny costume, and he put it on and sat by the driveway waiting for Grandpa Portman to come home from five o'clock until nightfall, but he never did. Grandma was so mad that she took a picture of my dad crying in the street just so she could show my grandfather what a huge asshole he was. Needless to say, that picture has long been an object of legend among members of my family, and a great embarrassment to my father.

"It was a lot more than just one Halloween," he grumbled. "Really, Jake, you were closer to him than I ever was. I don't know—there was just something unspoken between the two of you."

I didn't know how to respond. Was he jealous of me?

"Why are you telling me this?"

"Because you're my son, and I don't want you to get hurt."

"Hurt how?"

He paused. Outside the clouds shifted, the last rays of daylight throwing our shadows against the wall. I got a sick feeling in my stomach, like when your parents are about to tell you they're splitting up, but you know it before they even open their mouths.

"I never dug too deep with your grandpa because I was afraid of what I'd find," he said finally.

"You mean about the war?"

"No. Your grandpa kept those secrets because they were painful. I understood that. I mean about the traveling, him being gone all the time. What he was really doing. I think—your aunt and I both thought—that there was another woman. Maybe more than one."

I let it hang between us for a moment. My face tingled strangely. "That's crazy, Dad."

"We found a letter once. It was from a woman whose name we didn't know, addressed to your grandfather. *I love you, I miss you, when are you coming back*, that kind of thing. Seedy, lipstick-on-the-collar type stuff. I'll never forget it."

I felt a hot stab of shame, like somehow it was my own crime he was describing. And yet I couldn't quite believe it.

"We tore up the letter and flushed it down the toilet. Never found another one, either. Guess he was more careful after that."

I didn't know what to say. I couldn't look at my father.

"I'm sorry, Jake. This must be hard to hear. I know how much you worshipped him." He reached out to squeeze my shoulder but I shrugged him off, then scraped back my chair and stood up.

"I don't *worship* anyone."

"Okay. I just . . . I didn't want you to be surprised, that's all."

I grabbed my jacket and slung it over my shoulder.

"What are you doing? Dinner's on the way."

"You're wrong about him," I said. "And I'm going to prove it."

He sighed. It was a letting-go kind of sigh. "Okay. I hope you do."

I slammed out of the Priest Hole and started walking, heading nowhere in particular. Sometimes you just need to go through a door.

It was true, of course, what my dad had said: I did worship my grandfather. There were things about him that I needed to be true, and his being an adulterer was not one of them. When I was a kid, Grandpa Portman's fantastic stories meant it was possible to live a magical life. Even after I stopped believing them, there was still something magical about my grandfather. To have endured all the horrors he did, to have seen the worst of humanity and have your life made unrecognizable by it, to come out of all that the honorable and good and brave person I knew him to be—*that* was magical. So I couldn't believe he was a liar and a cheater and a bad father. Because if Grandpa Portman wasn't honorable and good, I wasn't sure anyone could be.

* * *

The museum's doors were open and its lights were on, but no one seemed to be inside. I'd gone there to find the curator, hoping he knew a thing or two about the island's history and people, and could shed some light on the empty house and the whereabouts of its former inhabitants. Figuring he'd just stepped out for a minute—the crowds weren't exactly kicking down his door—I wandered into the sanctuary to kill time checking out museum displays.

The exhibits, such as they were, were arranged in big open-fronted cabinets that lined the walls and stood where pews had once been. For the most part they were unspeakably boring, all about life in a traditional fishing village and the enduring mysteries of animal husbandry, but one exhibit stood out from the rest. It was in a place of honor at the front of the room, in a fancy case that rested atop what had been the altar. It lived behind a rope I stepped over and a little warning sign I didn't bother to read, and its case had polished wooden sides and a Plexiglas top so that you could only see into it from above.

When I looked inside, I think I actually gasped—and for one panicky second thought *monster!*—because I had suddenly and unexpectedly come face-to-face with a blackened corpse. Its shrunken body bore an uncanny resemblance to the creatures that had haunted my dreams, as did the color of its flesh, which was like something that had been spit-roasted over a flame. But when the body failed to come alive and scar my mind forever by breaking the glass and going for my jugular, my initial panic subsided. It was just a museum display, albeit an excessively morbid one.

"I see you've met the old man!" called a voice from behind me, and I turned to see the curator striding in my direction. "You handled it pretty well. I've seen grown men faint dead away!" He grinned and reached out to shake my hand. "Martin Pagett. Don't believe I caught your name the other day."

"Jacob Portman," I said. "Who's this, Wales's most famous murder victim?"

"Ha! Well, he might be that, too, though I never thought of him that way. He's our island's senior-most resident, better known in archaeological circles as Cairnholm Man—though to us he's just the Old Man. More than twenty-seven hundred years old, to be exact, though he was only sixteen when he died. So he's rather a young old man, really."

"Twenty-seven *hundred*?" I said, glancing at the dead boy's face, his delicate features somehow perfectly preserved. "But he looks so . . ."

"That's what happens when you spend your golden years in a place where oxygen and bacteria can't exist, like the underside of our bog. It's a regular fountain of youth down there—provided you're already dead, that is."

"That's where you found him? The bog?"

He laughed. "Not me! Turf cutters did, digging for peat by the big stone cairn out there, back in the seventies. He looked so fresh they thought there might be a killer loose on Cairnholm—till the cops had a look at the Stone Age bow in his hand and the noose of human hair round his neck. They don't make 'em like that anymore."

I shuddered. "Sounds like a human sacrifice or something."

"Exactly. He was done in by a combination of strangulation, drowning, disembowelment, and a blow to the head. Seems rather like overkill, don't you think?"

"I guess so."

Martin roared with laughter. "He guesses so!"

"Okay, yeah, it does."

"Sure it does. But the really fascinating thing, to us modern folk, anyway, is that in all likelihood the boy went to his death willingly. Eagerly, even. His people believed that bogs—and our bog in particular—were entrances to the world of the gods, and so the perfect place to offer up their most precious gift: themselves."

"That's insane."

"I suppose. Though I imagine we're killing ourselves right now in all manner of ways that'll seem insane to people in the future. And as doors to the next world go, a bog ain't a bad choice. It's not quite water and it's not quite land—it's an in-between place." He bent over the case, studying the figure inside. "Isn't he beautiful?"

I looked at the body again, throttled and flayed and drowned and somehow made immortal in the process.

"I don't think so," I said.

Martin straightened, then began to speak in a grandiose tone.

"Come, you, and gaze upon the tar man! Blackly he reposes, tender face the color of soot, withered limbs like veins of coal, feet lumps of driftwood hung with shriveled grapes!" He threw his arms out like a hammy stage actor and began to strut around the case. "Come, you, and bear witness to the cruel art of his wounds! Purled and meandering lines drawn by knives; brain and bone exposed by stones; the rope still digging at his throat. First fruit slashed and dumped—seeker of Heaven—old man arrested in youth—I almost love you!"

He took a theatrical bow as I applauded. "Wow," I said, "did you write that?"

"Guilty!" he replied with a sheepish smile. "I twiddle about with lines of verse now and then, but it's only a hobby. In any case, thank you for indulging me."

I wondered what this odd, well-spoken man was doing on Cairnholm, with his pleated slacks and half-baked poems, looking more like a bank manager than someone who lived on a windswept island with one phone and no paved roads.

"Now, I'd be happy to show you the rest of my collection," he said, escorting me toward the door, "but I'm afraid it's shutting-up time. If you'd like to come back tomorrow, however—"

"Actually, I was hoping you might know something," I said, stopping him before he could shoo me out. "It's about the house I mentioned this morning. I went to see it."

"Well!" he exclaimed. "I thought I'd scared you off it. How's our haunted mansion faring these days? Still standing?"

I assured him that it was, then got right to the point. "The people that lived there—do you have any idea what happened to them?"

"They're dead," he replied. "Happened a long time ago."

I was surprised—though I probably shouldn't have been. Miss Peregrine was old. Old people die. But that didn't mean my search was over. "I'm looking for anyone else who might have lived there, too, not just the headmistress."

"All dead," he repeated. "No one's lived there since the war."

That took me a moment to process. "What do you mean? What war?"

"When we say 'the war' around here, my boy, there's only one that we mean—the second. It was a German air raid that got 'em, if I'm not mistaken."

"No, that can't be right."

He nodded. "In those days, there was an anti-aircraft gun battery at the far tip of the island, past the wood where the house is. It made Cairnholm a legitimate military target. Not that 'legitimate' mattered much to the Germans one way or another, mind you. Anyway, one of the bombs went off track, and, well . . . " He shook his head. "Nasty luck."

"That can't be right," I said again, though I was starting to wonder.

"Why don't you sit down and let me fix you some tea?" he said. "You look a bit off the mark."

"Just feeling a little light-headed . . . "

He led me to a chair in his office and went to make the tea. I tried to collect my thoughts. *Bombed in the war*—that would certainly explain those rooms with blown-out walls. But what about the letter from Miss Peregrine—postmarked Cairnholm—sent just fifteen years ago?

Martin returned, handing me a mug. "There's a nip of Penderyn in it," he said. "Secret recipe, you know. Should get you sorted in no time."

I thanked him and took a sip, realizing too late that the secret ingredient was high-test whiskey. It felt like napalm flushing down my esophagus. "It does have a certain kick," I admitted, my face going red.

He frowned. "Reckon I ought to fetch your father."

"No, no, I'll be fine. But if there's anything else you can tell me about the attack, I'd be grateful."

Martin settled into a chair opposite me. "About that, I'm curious. You say your grandfather lived here. He never mentioned it?"

"I'm curious about that, too," I said. "I guess it must've been after his time. Did it happen late in the war or early?"

"I'm ashamed to admit I don't know. But if you're keen, I can introduce you to someone who does—my Uncle Oggie. He's eighty-three, lived here his whole life. Still sharp as a tack." Martin glanced at his watch. "If we catch him before *Father Ted* comes on the telly, I'm sure he'd be more than happy to tell you anything you like."

* * *

Ten minutes later Martin and I were wedged deep in an overstuffed sofa in Oggie's living room, which was piled high with books and boxes of worn-out shoes and enough lamps to light up Carlsbad Caverns, all but one of them unplugged. Living on a remote island, I was starting to realize, turned people into pack rats. Oggie sat facing us in a threadbare blazer and pajama bottoms, as if he'd been expecting company—just not pants-worthy company—and rocked endlessly in a plastic-covered easy chair as he talked. He seemed happy just to have an audience, and after he'd gone on at length about the weather and Welsh politics and the sorry state of today's youth, Martin was finally able to steer him around to the attack and the children from the home.

"Sure, I remember them," he said. "Odd collection of people. We'd see them in town now and again—the children, sometimes their minder-woman, too—buying milk and medicine and what-have-you. You'd say 'good morning' and they'd look the other way. Kept to themselves, they did, off in that big house. Lot of talk about what might've been going on over there, though no one knew for sure."

"What kind of talk?"

"Lot of rot. Like I said, no one knew. All I can say is they weren't your regular sort of orphan children—not like them Barnardo Home kids they got in other places, who you'll see come into town for parades and things and always have time for a chat. This lot was different. Some of 'em couldn't even speak the King's English. Or any English, for that matter."

"Because they weren't really orphans," I said. "They were refugees from other countries. Poland, Austria, Czechoslovakia . . . "

"Is that what they were, now?" Oggie said, cocking an eyebrow at me. "Funny, I hadn't heard that." He seemed offended, like I'd insulted him by pretending to know more about his island than he did. His chair-rocking got faster, more aggressive. If this was the kind of reception my grandpa and the other kids got on Cairnholm, I thought, no wonder they kept to themselves.

Martin cleared his throat. "So, Uncle, the bombing?"

"Oh, keep your hair on. Yes, yes, the goddamned Jerries. Who could forget them?" He launched into a long-winded description of what life on the island was like under threat of German air raids: the blaring sirens; the panicked scrambles for shelter; the volunteer air-raid warden who ran from house to house at night making sure shades had been drawn and streetlights were put out to rob enemy pilots of easy targets. They prepared as best they could but never really thought they'd get hit, given all the ports and factories on the mainland, all much more important targets than Cairnholm's little gun emplacement. But one night, the bombs began to fall.

"The noise was dreadful," Oggie said. "It was like giants stamping across the island, and it seemed to go on for ages. They gave us a hell of a pounding, though no one in town was killed, thank heaven. Can't say the same for our gunner boys—though they gave as good as they got—nor the poor souls at the orphan home. One bomb was all it took. Gave up their lives for Britain, they did. So wherever they was from, God bless 'em for that."

"Do you remember when it happened?" I asked. "Early in the war or late?"

"I can tell you the exact day," he said. "It was the third of September, 1940."

The air seemed to go out of the room. I flashed to my grandfather's ashen face, his lips just barely moving, uttering those very words. *September third, 1940.*

"Are you—you sure about that? That it was *that day?*"

"I never got to fight," he said. "Too young by a year. That one night was my whole war. So, yes, I'm sure."

I felt numb, disconnected. It was too strange. Was someone playing a joke on me, I wondered—a weird, unfunny joke?

"And there weren't any survivors at all?" Martin asked.

The old man thought for a moment, his gaze drifting up to the ceiling. "Now that you mention it," he said, "I reckon there were. Just one. A young man, not much older than this boy here." His rocking stopped as he remembered it. "Walked into town the morning after with not a scratch upon him. Hardly seemed perturbed at all, considering he'd just seen all his mates go to their reward. It was the queerest thing."

"He was probably in shock," Martin said.

"I shouldn't wonder," replied Oggie. "He spoke only once, to ask my father when the next boat was leaving for the mainland. Said he wanted to take up arms directly and kill the damned monsters who murdered his people."

Oggie's story was nearly as far-fetched as the ones Grandpa Portman used to tell, and yet I had no reason to doubt him.

"I knew him," I said. "He was my grandfather."

They looked at me, astonished. "Well," Oggie said. "I'll be blessed."

I excused myself and stood up. Martin, remarking that I seemed out of sorts, offered to walk me back to the pub, but I declined. I needed to be alone with my thoughts. "Come and see me soon, then," he said, and I promised I would.

I took the long way back, past the swaying lights of the harbor, the air heavy with brine and with chimney smoke from a hundred hearth fires. I walked to the end of a dock and watched the moon rise over the water, imagining my grandfather standing there on that awful morning after, numb with shock, waiting for a boat that would take him away from all the death he'd endured, to war, and more death. There was no escaping the monsters, not even on this island, no bigger on a map than a grain of sand, protected by mountains of fog and sharp rocks and seething tides. Not anywhere. That was the awful truth my grandfather had tried to protect me from.

In the distance, I heard the generators sputter and spin down, and all the lights along the harbor and in house windows behind me surged for a moment before going dark. I imagined how such a thing might look from an airplane's height—the whole island suddenly winking out, as if it had never been there at all. A supernova in miniature.

*   *   *

I walked back by moonlight, feeling small. I found my dad in the pub at the same table where he'd been, a half-eaten plate of beef and gravy congealing into grease before him. "Look who's back," he said as I sat down. "I saved your dinner for you."

"I'm not hungry," I said, and told him what I'd learned about Grandpa Portman.

He seemed more angry than surprised. "I can't believe he never brought this up," he said. "Not one time." I could understand his anger: it was one thing for a grandparent to withhold something like that from a grandchild, quite another for a father to keep it from his son—and for so long.

I tried to steer the conversation in a more positive direction. "It's amazing, isn't it? Everything he went through."

My father nodded. "I don't think we'll ever know the full extent of it."

"Grandpa Portman really knew how to keep a secret, didn't he?"

"Are you kidding? The man was an emotional Fort Knox."

"I wonder if it doesn't explain something, though. Why he acted so distant when you were little." Dad gave me a sharp look, and I knew I needed to make my point quickly or risk overstepping. "He'd already lost his family twice before. Once in Poland and then again here—his adopted family. So when you and Aunt Susie came along . . . "

"Once bombed, twice shy?"

"I'm serious. Don't you think this could mean that maybe he wasn't cheating on Grandma, after all?"

"I don't know, Jake. I guess I don't believe things are ever that simple." He let out a sigh, breath fogging the inside of his beer glass. "I think I know what all this really explains, though. Why you and Grandpa were so close."

"Okay . . ."

"It took him fifty years to get over his fear of having a family. You came along at just the right time."

I didn't know how to respond. How do you say *I'm sorry your father didn't love you enough* to your own dad? I couldn't, so instead I just said goodnight and headed upstairs to bed.

*   *   *

I tossed and turned most of the night. I couldn't stop thinking about the letters—the one my dad and Aunt Susie had found as kids, from this "other woman," and the one I'd found a month ago, from Miss Peregrine. The thought that kept me awake was this: *what if they were the same woman?*

The postmark on Miss Peregrine's letter was fifteen years old, but by all accounts she'd been blown into the stratosphere back in

1940. To my mind, that left two possible explanations: either my grandfather had been corresponding with a dead person—admittedly unlikely—or the person who wrote the letter was not, in fact, Miss Peregrine, but someone who was using her identity to disguise her own.

Why would you disguise your identity in a letter? Because you have something to hide. Because you are the other woman.

What if the only thing I had discovered on this trip was that my grandfather was an adulterous liar? In his last breaths, was he trying to tell me about the death of his adopted family—or admit to some tawdry, decades-long affair? Maybe it was both, and the truth was that by the time he was a young man he'd had his family torn apart so many times he no longer knew how to have one, or to be faithful to one.

It was all just guesswork, though. I didn't know, and there was no one to ask. Anyone who might have had the answer was long dead. In less than twenty-four hours, the whole trip had become pointless.

I fell into an uneasy sleep. At dawn, I woke to the sound of something in my room. Rolling over to see what it was, I bolted upright in bed. A large bird was perched on my dresser, staring me down. It had a sleek head feathered in gray and talons that clacked on the wooden dresser as it sidled back and forth along the edge, as if to get a better look at me. I stared back rigidly, wondering if this could be a dream.

I called out for my dad, and at the sound of my voice the bird launched itself off the dresser. I threw my arm across my face and rolled away, and when I peeked again it was gone, flown out the open window.

My dad stumbled in, bleary-eyed. "What's going on?"

I showed him the talon marks on the dresser and a feather that had landed on the floor. "God, that's weird," he said, turning it over in his hands. "Peregrines almost never come this close to humans."

I thought maybe I'd heard him wrong. "Did you say *peregrines*?"

He held up the feather. "A peregrine falcon," he said. "They're amazing creatures—the fastest birds on earth. They're like shape-shifters, the way they streamline their bodies in the air." The name was just a weird coincidence, but it left me with an uncanny feeling I couldn't shake.

Over breakfast, I began to wonder if I'd given up too easily. Though it was true there was no one left alive whom I could talk to about my grandfather, there was still the house, a lot of it unexplored. If it had ever held answers about my grandfather—in the form of letters, maybe, or a photo album or a diary—they'd probably burned up or rotted away decades ago. But if I left the island without making sure, I knew I'd regret it.

And that is how someone who is unusually susceptible to nightmares, night terrors, the Creeps, the Willies, and Seeing Things That Aren't Really There talks himself into making one last trip to the abandoned, almost-certainly-haunted house where a dozen or more children met their untimely end.

CHAPTER FIVE

*I*t was an almost-too-perfect morning. Leaving the pub felt like stepping into one of those heavily retouched photos that come loaded as wallpaper on new computers: streets of artfully decrepit cottages stretched into the distance, giving way to green fields sewn together by meandering rock walls, the whole scene topped by scudding white clouds. But beyond all that, above the houses and fields and sheep doddering around like little puffs of cotton candy, I could see tongues of dense fog licking over the ridge in the distance, where this world ended and the next one began, cold, damp, and sunless.

I walked over the ridge and straight into a rain shower. True to form, I had forgotten my rubber boots, and the path was a rapidly deepening ribbon of mud. But getting a little wet seemed vastly preferable to climbing that hill twice in one morning, so I bent my head against the spitting rain and trudged onward. Soon I passed the shack, dim outlines of sheep huddled inside against the chill, and then the mist-shrouded bog, silent and ghostly. I thought about the twenty-seven-hundred-year-old resident of Cairnholm's museum and wondered how many more like him these fields held, undiscovered, arrested in death; how many more had given up their lives here, looking for heaven.

By the time I reached the children's home, what had begun as a drizzle was a full-on downpour. There was no time to dally in the house's feral yard and reflect upon its malevolent shape—the way the doorless doorway seemed to swallow me as I dove through it, the way the hall's rain-bloated floorboards gave a little beneath my shoes. I stood wringing water from my shirt and shaking out my hair, and when I was as dry as I was going to get—which was not very—I began to search. For what, I wasn't sure. A box of letters? My grandfather's name scribbled on a wall? It all seemed so unlikely.

I roved around peeling up mats of old newspaper and looking under chairs and tables. I imagined uncovering some horrible scene—a tangle of skeletons dressed in fire-blackened rags—but all I found were rooms that had become more outside than inside, character stripped away by moisture and wind and layers of dirt. The ground floor was hopeless. I went back to the staircase, knowing this time I would have to climb it. The only question was, up or down? One strike against going upstairs was its limited options for quick escape (from squatters or ghouls or whatever else my anxious mind could invent) other than hurling myself from an upper-story window. Downstairs had the same problem, and with the added detractor of being dark, and me without a flashlight. So upstairs it was.

The steps protested my weight with a symphony of shudders and creaks, but they held, and what I discovered upstairs—compared to the bombed-out ground floor, at least—was like a time capsule. Arranged along a hallway striped with peeling wallpaper, the rooms were in surprisingly good shape. Though one or two had been invaded by mold where a broken window had let in the rain, the rest were packed with things that seemed only a layer or two of dust away from new: a mildewed shirt tossed casually over the back of a chair, loose change skimming a nightstand. It was easy to believe that everything was just as the children had left it, as if time had stopped the night they died.

I went from room to room, examining their contents like an archaeologist. There were wooden toys moldering in a box; crayons on a windowsill, their colors dulled by the light of ten thousand afternoons; a dollhouse with dolls inside, lifers in an ornate prison. In a modest library, the creep of moisture had bowed the shelves into crooked smiles. I ran my finger along the balding spines, as if considering pulling one out to read. There were classics like *Peter Pan* and *The Secret Garden*, histories written by authors forgotten by history, textbooks of Latin and Greek. In the corner were corralled a few old desks. This had been their classroom, I realized, and Miss Peregrine, their teacher.

I tried to open a pair of heavy doors, twisting the handle, but they were swelled shut—so I took a running start and rammed them with my shoulder. They flew open with a rasping shriek and I fell face-first into the next room. As I picked myself up and looked around, I realized that it could only have belonged to Miss Peregrine. It was like a room in Sleeping Beauty's castle, with cobwebbed candles mounted in wall sconces, a mirrored vanity table topped with crystal bottles, and a giant oak bed. I pictured the last time she'd been here, scrambling out from under the sheets in the middle of the night to the whine of an air-raid siren, rounding up the children, all groggy and grasping for coats on their way downstairs.

Were you scared? I wondered. *Did you hear the planes coming?*

I began to feel unusual. I imagined I was being watched; that the children were still here, preserved like the bog boy, inside the walls. I could feel them peering at me through cracks and knotholes.

I drifted into the next room. Weak light shone through a window. Petals of powder-blue wallpaper drooped toward a couple of small beds, still clad in dusty sheets. I knew, somehow, that this had been my grandfather's room.

Why did you send me here? What was it you needed me to see?

Then I noticed something beneath one of the beds and knelt down to look. It was an old suitcase.

Was this yours? Is it what you carried onto the train the last time you saw your mother and father, as your first life was slipping away?

I pulled it out and fumbled with its tattered leather straps. It opened easily—but except for a family of dead beetles, it was empty.

I felt empty, too, and strangely heavy, like the planet was spinning too fast, heating up gravity, pulling me toward the floor. Suddenly exhausted, I sat on the bed—*his bed, maybe*—and for reasons I can't quite explain, I stretched out on those filthy sheets and stared at the ceiling.

What did you think about, lying here at night? Did you have nightmares, too?

I began to cry.

When your parents died, did you know it? Could you feel them go?

I cried harder. I didn't want to, but I couldn't stop myself.

I couldn't stop myself, so I thought about all the bad things and I fed it and fed it until I was crying so hard I had to gasp for breath between sobs. I thought about how my great-grandparents had starved to death. I thought about their wasted bodies being fed to incinerators because people they didn't know hated them. I thought about how the children who lived in this house had been burned up and blown apart because a pilot who didn't care pushed a button. I thought about how my grandfather's family had been taken from him, and how because of that my dad grew up feeling like he didn't have a dad, and now I had acute stress and nightmares and was sitting alone in a falling-down house and crying hot, stupid tears all over my shirt. All because of a seventy-year-old hurt that had somehow been passed down to me like some poisonous heirloom, and monsters I couldn't fight because they were all dead, beyond killing or punishing or any kind of reckoning. At least my grandfather had been able to join the army and go fight them. What could I do?

When it was over, my head was pounding. I closed my eyes and pushed my knuckles in to stop them from hurting, if only for a moment, and when I finally released the pressure and opened them again, a miraculous change had come over the room: There was a single ray of sun shining through the window. I got up, went to the cracked glass, and saw that it was both raining and shining outside— a bit of meteorological weirdness whose name no one can seem to agree on. My mom, I kid you not, refers to it as "orphans' tears." Then I remembered what Ricky says about it—"the Devil's beatin' his wife!"—and I laughed and felt a little better.

Then, in the patch of quickly fading sun that fell across the room, I noticed something I hadn't before. It was a trunk—or the edge of one, at least—poking out from under the second bed. I went over and peeled back the bed sheet that hid most of it from view.

It was a big old steamer trunk latched with a giant rusting pad- lock. It couldn't possibly be empty, I thought. You don't lock an empty trunk. *Open me!* it fairly seemed to cry out. *I am full of secrets!*

I grabbed it by the sides and pulled. It didn't move. I pulled again, harder, but it wouldn't give an inch. I wasn't sure if it was just that heavy, or if generations of accumulated moisture and dust had somehow fused it to the floor. I stood up and kicked it a few times, which seemed to jar things loose, and then I managed to move it by pulling on one side at a time, shimmying it forward the way you might move a stove or a fridge, until it had come out all the way from under the bed, leaving a trail of parenthetical scars in the floor. I yanked on the padlock, but despite a thick encrustation of rust it seemed rock solid. I briefly considered searching for a key—it had to be here somewhere—but I could've wasted hours looking, and the lock was so decayed that I wondered if the key would even work any- more. My only option was to break it.

Looking around for something that might do the job, I found a busted chair in one of the other rooms. I pried off a leg and went to town on the lock, raising the leg over my head like an executioner and bringing it down as hard as I could, over and over, until the leg itself finally broke and I was left holding a splintered stump. I scanned the room for something stronger and quickly spotted a loose railing on the bed frame. After a few stomping kicks, it clattered to the floor. I wedged one end through the lock and pulled the other end backward. Nothing happened.

I hung on it with all my weight. The trunk creaked a little, but that was it. I kicked the trunk and pulled on that rail with every bit of my strength, the veins bulging out of my neck, yelling, *Open god damn you, open you stupid trunk!* Finally my frustration and anger had an object: If I couldn't make my dead grandfather give up his secrets, I would damn well pry the secrets out of this old trunk. And then the rail slipped and I crashed to the floor and got the wind knocked out of me.

I lay there and stared at the ceiling, catching my breath. The orphans' tears had ended and now it was just plain old raining outside, harder than ever. I thought about going back to town for a sledgehammer or a hacksaw—but that would only raise questions I didn't feel like answering.

Then I had a brilliant idea. If I could find a way to break the *trunk*, I wouldn't have to worry about the lock at all. And what force would be stronger than me and my admittedly underdeveloped upperbody muscles whaling on the trunk with random tools? *Gravity.* I was, after all, on the second floor of the house, and while I didn't think there was any way I could lift the trunk high enough to get it through a window, the rail along the top of the staircase landing had long ago collapsed. All I had to do was drag the trunk down the hall and push it over. Whether its contents would survive the impact was another issue—but at least I'd find out what was inside.

I hunkered down behind the trunk and began pushing it toward the hall. After a few inches its metal feet dug into the soft floor and it ground stubbornly to a halt. Undeterred, I moved around to the other side, gripped the padlock with both hands and pulled backward. To my great surprise it moved two or three feet in one go. It wasn't a particularly dignified way of working—this squatting, butt-scooting motion I had to repeat over and over, each slide of the trunk accompanied by an ear-splitting metal-on-wood shriek—but before long I'd gotten it out of the room and was dragging it, foot by foot, doorway by doorway, toward the landing. I lost myself in the echoing rhythm of it, working up a manly lather of sweat in the process.

I finally made it to the landing and, with one final indelicate grunt, pulled the trunk onto it after me. It slid easily now, and after a few more shoves I had it teetering precariously on the edge; one last nudge would be enough to send it over. But I wanted to see it shatter—my reward for all this work—so I got up and carefully shuffled toward the edge until I could glimpse the floor of the gloomy chamber below. Then, holding my breath, I gave the trunk a little tap with my foot.

It hesitated for a moment, wobbling there on the edge of oblivion, and then pitched decisively forward and fell, tumbling end over end in beautiful balletic slow-motion. There came a tremendous echoing crash that seemed to rattle the whole house as a plume of dust shot up at me from below and I had to cover my face and retreat down the hall until it cleared. A minute later I came back and peeked again over the landing and saw not the pile of smashed wood that I had so fondly hoped for, but a jagged trunk-shaped hole in the floorboards. It had fallen straight through into the basement.

I raced downstairs and wriggled up to the edge of the buckled floor on my belly like you would a hole in thin ice. Fifteen feet below, through a haze of dust and darkness, I saw what remained of the trunk. It had shattered like a giant egg, its pieces all mixed up in a heap of debris and smashed floorboards. Scattered throughout were little pieces of paper. It looked like I'd found a box of letters, after all! But then, squinting, I could make out shapes on them—faces, bodies—and that's when I realized they weren't letters at all, but photographs. Dozens of them. I got excited—and then just as quickly went cold, because something dreadful occurred to me.

I have to go down there.

*   *   *

The basement was a meandering complex of rooms so lightless I may as well have explored them blindfolded. I descended the creaking stairs and stood at the bottom for a while, hoping my eyes would eventually adjust, but it was the kind of dark there was no adjusting to. I was also hoping I'd get used to the smell—a strange, acrid stink like the supply closet in a chemistry classroom—but no such luck. So I shuffled in, with my shirt collar pulled up over my nose and my hands held out in front of me, and hoped for the best.

I tripped and nearly fell. Something made of glass went skidding away across the floor. The smell only seemed to get worse. I began to imagine things lurking in the dark ahead of me. Forget monsters and ghosts—what if there was another hole in the floor? They'd never find my body.

Then I realized, in a minor stroke of genius, that by dialing up a menu screen on the cellphone I kept in my pocket (despite being ten miles from the nearest bar of reception), I could make a weak flashlight. I held it out, aiming the screen away from me. It barely penetrated the darkness, so I pointed it at the floor. Cracked flagstone and mouse turds. I aimed it to the side; a faint gleam reflected back.

I took a step closer and swept my phone around. Out of the darkness emerged a wall of shelves lined with glass jars. They were all shapes and sizes, mottled with dust and filled with gelatinous-looking things suspended in cloudy fluid. I thought of the kitchen and the exploded jars of fruits and vegetables I'd found there. Maybe the temperature was more stable down here, and that's why these had survived.

But then I got closer still, and looked a little harder, and realized they weren't fruits and vegetables at all, but organs. Brains. Hearts.

Lungs. Eyes. All pickled in some kind of home-brewed formaldehyde, which explained the terrific stench. I gagged and stumbled away from them into the dark, simultaneously grossed out and baffled. What kind of place *was* this? Those jars were something you might expect to find in the basement of a fly-by-night medical school, not a house full of children. If not for all the wonderful things Grandpa Portman had said about this place, I might've wondered if Miss Peregrine had rescued the children just to harvest their organs.

When I'd recovered a little, I looked up to see another gleam ahead of me—not a reflection of my phone, but a weak glimmer of daylight. It had to be coming from the hole I'd made. I soldiered on, breathing through my pulled-up shirt and keeping away from the walls and any other ghastly surprises they might've harbored.

The gleam led me around a corner and into a small room with part of the ceiling caved in. Daylight streamed through the hole onto a mound of splintered floorboards and broken glass from which rose coils of silty dust, pieces of torn carpet plastered here and there like scraps of desiccated meat. Beneath the debris I could hear the scrabble of tiny feet, some rodentine dark-dweller that had survived the implosion of its world. In the midst of it all lay the demolished trunk, photographs scattered around it like confetti.

I picked my way through the wreckage, high-stepping over javelins of wood and planks studded with rusting nails. Kneeling, I began to salvage what I could from the pile. I felt like a rescue worker, plucking faces from the debris, brushing away glass and wood rot. And though part of me wanted to hurry—there was no telling if or when the rest of the floor might collapse on my head—I couldn't stop myself from studying them.

At first glance, they looked like the kind of pictures you'd find in any old family album. There were shots of people cavorting on beaches and smiling on back porches, vistas from around the island, and lots of kids, posing in singles and pairs, informal snapshots and formal portraits taken in front of backdrops, their subjects clutching dead-eyed dolls, like they'd gone to Glamour Shots in some creepy turn-of-the-century shopping mall. But what I found really creepy wasn't the zombie dolls or the children's weird haircuts or how they never, ever seemed to smile, but that the more I studied the pictures, the more familiar they began to seem. They shared a certain night-marish quality with my grandfather's old photos, especially the ones he'd kept hidden in the bottom of his cigar box, as if somehow they'd all come from the same batch.

There was, for instance, a photo of two young women posed before a not-terribly-convincing painted backdrop of the ocean. Not so strange in and of itself; the unsettling thing was *how* they were posed. Both had their backs to the camera. Why would you go to all the trouble and expense of having your picture taken—portraits were pricey back then—and then turn your back on the camera? I half-expected to find another photo in the debris of the same girls facing forward, revealing grinning skulls for faces.

Other pictures seemed manipulated in much the same way as some of my grandfather's had been. One was of a lone girl in a cemetery staring into a reflecting pool—but *two* girls were reflected back. It reminded me of Grandpa Portman's photo of the girl "trapped" in a bottle, only whatever darkroom technique had been used wasn't nearly as fake-looking. Another was of a disconcertingly calm young man whose upper body appeared to be swarming with bees. That would be easy enough to fake, right? Like my grandfather's picture of the boy lifting what was certainly a boulder made from plaster. Fake rock—fake bees.

The hairs on the back of my neck stood up as I remembered something Grandpa Portman had said about a boy he'd known here in the children's home—a boy with bees living inside him. *Some would fly out every time he opened his mouth*, he had said, *but they never stung unless Hugh wanted them to.*

I could think of only one explanation. My grandfather's pictures had come from the trunk that lay smashed before me. I wasn't certain, though, until I found a picture of the freaks: two masked ruffle-collared kids who seemed to be feeding each other a coil of ribbon. I didn't know what they were supposed to be, exactly—besides fuel for nightmares; what were they, sadomasochistic ballerinas?—but there was no doubt in my mind that Grandpa Portman had a picture of these same two boys. I'd seen it in his cigar box just a few months ago.

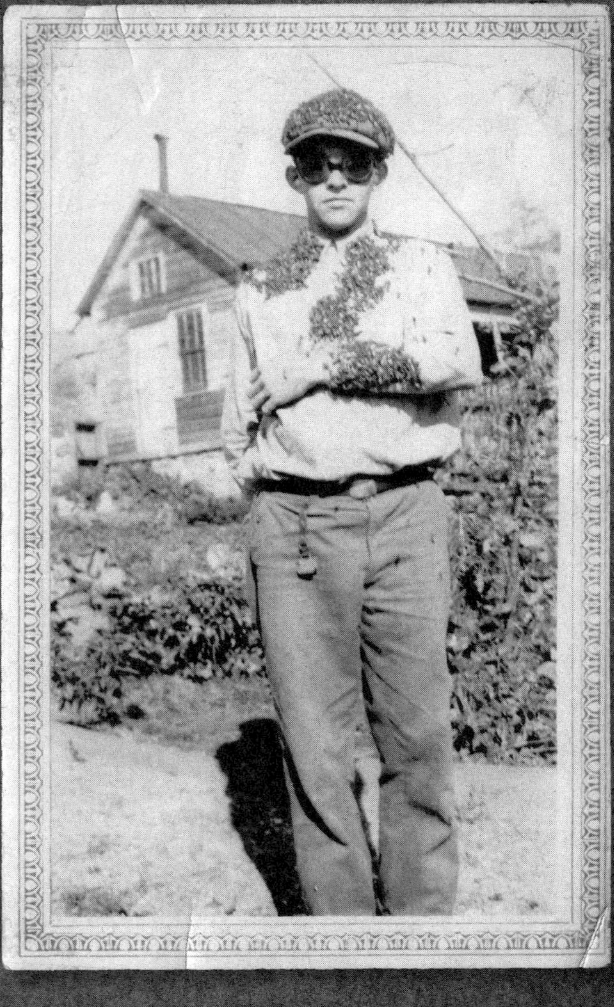

It couldn't have been a coincidence, which meant that the photos my grandfather had shown me—that he'd sworn were of children he'd known in this house—*had really come from this house.* But could that mean, despite the doubts I'd harbored even as an eight-year-old, that the pictures were genuine? What about the fantastic stories that went along with them? That any of them could be true—*literally* true—seemed unthinkable. And yet, standing there in dusty half-light in that dead house that seemed so alive with ghosts, I thought, *maybe* . . .

Suddenly there came a loud crash from somewhere in the house above me, and I startled so badly that all the pictures slipped from my hands.

It's just the house settling, I told myself—*or caving in!* But as I bent down to gather the photos, the crash came again, and in an instant what meager light had shone through the hole in the floor faded away, and I found myself squatting in inky darkness.

I heard footsteps, and then voices. I strained to make out what they were saying, but I couldn't. I didn't dare move, afraid that the slightest motion would set off a noisy avalanche of debris all around me. I knew that my fear was irrational—it was probably just those dumb rapper kids pulling another prank—but my heart was beating a hundred miles an hour, and some deep animal instinct commanded me to be silent.

My legs began to go numb. As quietly as I could, I shifted my weight from one leg to the other to get the blood flowing again. A tiny piece of something came loose from the pile and rolled away, making a sound that seemed huge in the silence. The voices went quiet. Then a floorboard creaked right over my head and a little shower of plaster dust sprinkled down. Whoever was up there, they knew exactly where I was.

I held my breath.

Then, I heard a girl's voice say softly, "Abe? Is that you?"

I thought I'd dreamed it. I waited for the girl to speak again, but for a long moment there was only the sound of rain banking off the roof, like a thousand fingers tapping way off somewhere. Then a lantern glowed to life above me, and I craned my neck to see a half dozen kids kneeling around the craggy jaws of broken floor, peering down.

I recognized them somehow, though I didn't know where from. They seemed like faces from a half-remembered dream. Where had I seen them before—and how did they know my grandfather's name?

Then it clicked. Their clothes, strange even for Wales. Their pale unsmiling faces. The pictures strewn before me, staring up at me just as the children stared down. Suddenly I understood.

I'd seen them in the photographs.

The girl who'd spoken stood up to get a better look at me. In her hands she held a flickering light, which wasn't a lantern or a candle but seemed to be a ball of raw flame, attended by nothing more than her bare skin. I'd seen her picture not five minutes earlier, and in it she looked much the same as she did now, even cradling the same strange light between her hands.

I'm Jacob, I wanted to say. *I've been looking for you.* But my jaw had come unhinged, and all I could do was stare.

The girl's expression soured. I was wretched looking, damp from rain and dust-covered and squatting in a mound of debris. Whatever she and the other children had been expecting to find inside this hole in the floor, I was not it.

A murmur passed among them, and they stood up and quickly scattered. Their sudden movement knocked something loose in me and I found my voice again and shouted for them to wait, but they were already pounding the floorboards toward the door. I tripped through the wreckage and stumbled blindly across the stinking basement to the stairs. But by the time I made it back to the ground floor, where the daylight they'd stolen had somehow returned, they had vanished from the house.

I bolted outside and down the crumbling brick steps into the grass, screaming, "Wait! Stop!" But they were gone. I scanned the yard, the woods, breathing hard, cursing myself.

Something snapped beyond the trees. I wheeled around to look and, through a screen of branches, caught a flash of blurred movement—the hem of a white dress. It was her. I crashed into the woods, sprinting after. She took off running down the path.

I hurdled fallen logs and ducked low branches, chasing her until my lungs burned. She kept trying to lose me, cutting from the path into the trackless forest and back. Finally the woods fell away and we broke into open bogland. I saw my chance. Now she had nowhere to hide—to catch her I had only to pour on the speed—and with me in sneakers and jeans and her in a dress it would be no contest. Just as I started to catch up, though, she made a sudden turn and plunged straight into the bog. I had no choice but to follow.

Running became impossible. The ground couldn't be trusted: It kept giving way, tripping me into knee-deep bog holes that soaked my pants and sucked at my legs. The girl, though, seemed to know just where to step, and she pulled farther and farther away, finally disappearing into the mist so that I had only her footprints to follow.

After she'd lost me, I kept expecting her prints to veer back toward the path, but they plowed ever-deeper into the bog. Then the mist closed behind me and I couldn't see the path anymore, and I began to wonder if I'd ever find my way out. I tried calling to her—*My name is Jacob Portman! I'm Abe's grandson! I won't hurt you!*—but the fog and the mud seemed to swallow my voice.

Her footprints led to a mound of stones. It looked like a big gray igloo, but it was a cairn—one of the Neolithic tombs after which Cairnholm was named.

The cairn was a little taller than me, long and narrow with a rectangular opening in one end, like a door, and it rose from the mud on a tussock of grass. Climbing out of the mire onto the relatively solid ground that ringed it, I saw that the opening was the entrance to a tunnel that burrowed deep inside. Intricate loops and spirals had been carved on either side, ancient hieroglyphs the meaning of which had been lost to the ages. *Here lies bog boy*, I thought. Or, more likely, *Abandon hope, all ye who enter here.*

But enter I did, because that's where the girl's footprints led. Inside, the cairn tunnel was damp and narrow and profoundly dark, so cramped that I could only move forward in a kind of hunchbacked crab-walk. Luckily, enclosed spaces were not one of the many things that scared the hell out of me.

Imagining the girl frightened and trembling somewhere up ahead, I talked to her as I went along, doing my best to reassure her that I meant no harm. My words came slapping back at me in a disorienting echo. Just as my thighs were starting to ache from the bizarre posture I'd been forced to adopt, the tunnel widened into a chamber, pitch black but big enough that I could stand and stretch my arms to either side without touching a wall.

I pulled out my phone and once more pressed it into service as a makeshift flashlight. It didn't take long to size up the place. It was a simple stone-walled chamber about as large as my bedroom—and it was completely empty. There was no girl to be found.

I was standing there trying to figure out how the hell she'd managed to slip by when something occurred to me—something so obvious that I felt like a fool for having taken this long to realize it. There never *was* any girl. I'd imagined her, and the rest of them, too. My brain had conjured them up at the very moment I was looking at their pictures. And the sudden, strange darkness that had preceded their arrival? A blackout.

It was impossible, anyway; those kids had all died a lifetime ago. Even if they hadn't, it was ridiculous to believe they would still look exactly as they had when the photos were taken. Everything had happened so quickly, though, I never had a chance to stop and wonder if I might be chasing a hallucination.

I could already predict Dr. Golan's explanation: *That house is such an emotionally loaded place for you, just being inside was enough to trigger a stress reaction.* Yeah, he was a psychobabble-spewing prick. But that didn't make him wrong.

I turned back, humiliated. Rather than crab-walking, I let go of the last of my dignity and just crawled on my hands and knees toward the gauzy light coming from the mouth of the tunnel. Looking up, I realized I'd seen this view before: in a photograph in Martin's museum of the place where they'd discovered the bog boy. It was baffling to think that people had once believed this foul-smelling wasteland was a gateway to heaven—and believed it with such conviction that a kid my age was willing to give up his life to get there. What a sad, stupid waste.

I decided then that I wanted to go home. I didn't care about the photos in the basement, and I was sick of riddles and mysteries and last words. Indulging my grandfather's obsession with them had made me worse, not better. It was time to let go.

I unfolded myself from the cramped cairn tunnel and stepped outside only to be blinded by light. Shielding my eyes, I squinted through split fingers at a world I hardly recognized. It was the same bog and the same path and the same everything as before, but for the first time since my arrival it was bathed in cheery yellow sunlight, the sky a candy blue, no trace of the twisting fog that, for me, had come to define this part of the island. It was warm, too, more like the dog days of summer than the breezy beginnings of it. *God, the weather changes fast around here*, I thought.

I slogged back to the path, trying to ignore the skin-crawly feeling of bog-mud gooshing into my socks, and headed for town. Strangely, the path wasn't muddy at all—as if it had dried out in just a few minutes—but it had been carpet-bombed with so many grapefruit-size animal turds that I couldn't walk in a straight line. How had I not noticed this earlier? Had I been in some kind of psychotic haze all morning? Was I in one now?

I didn't look up from the turdy checkerboard that stretched out before me until I'd crossed the ridge and was coming back into town, which is when I realized where all the mess had come from. Where this morning a battalion of tractors had plied the gravel paths, hauling carts loaded with fish and peat-bricks up and down from the harbor, now those carts were being pulled by horses and mules. The clip-clop of hooves had replaced the growl of engines.

Missing, too, was the ever-present buzz of diesel generators. Had the island run out of gas in the few hours I'd been gone? And where had the townspeople been hiding all these big animals?

Also, why was everyone *looking* at me? Every person I passed stared at me goggle-eyed, stopping whatever they were doing to rubberneck as I walked by. *I must look as crazy as I feel*, I thought, glancing down to see that I was covered in mud from the waist down and plaster from the waist up, so I ducked my head and walked as fast as I could toward the pub, where at least I could hide in the anonymous gloom until Dad came back for lunch. I decided that when he did, I would tell him straight out that I wanted to go home as soon as possible. If he hesitated, I would admit that I'd been hallucinating, and we'd be on the next ferry, guaranteed.

Inside the Hole were the usual collection of inebriated men bent over foamy pint glasses and the battered tables and dingy decor I'd come to know as my home away from home. But as I headed for the staircase I heard an unfamiliar voice bark, "Where d'ya think yer going?"

I turned, one foot on the bottom step, to see the bartender looking me up and down. Only it wasn't Kev, but a scowling bullet-headed man I didn't recognize. He wore a bartender's apron and had a bushy unibrow and a caterpillar mustache that made his face look striped.

I might've said, *I'm going upstairs to pack my suitcase, and if my dad still won't take me home I'm going to fake a seizure*, but instead I answered, "Just up to my room," which came out sounding more like a question than a statement of fact.

"That so?" he said, clapping down the glass he'd been filling. "This look like a hotel to you?"

Wooden creaks as patrons swiveled around in their stools to get a look at me. I quickly scanned their faces. Not one of them was familiar.

I'm having a psychotic episode, I thought. *Right now. This is what a psychotic episode feels like.* Only it didn't feel like anything. I wasn't seeing lightning bolts or having palm sweats. It was more like the world was going crazy, not me.

I told the bartender that there had obviously been some mistake. "My dad and I have the upstairs rooms," I said. "Look, I've got the key," and I produced it from my pocket as evidence.

"Lemme see that," he said, leaning over the counter to snatch it out of my hand. He held it up to the dingy light, eyeing it like a jeweler. "This ain't our key," he growled, then slipped it into his own pocket. "Now tell me what you really want up there—and this time, don't lie!"

I felt my face go hot. I'd never been called a liar by a nonrelative adult before. "I told you already. We rented those rooms! Just ask Kev if you don't believe me!"

"I don't know no Kev, and I don't fancy bein' fed stories," he said coolly. "There ain't any rooms to let around here, and the only one lives upstairs is me!"

I looked around, expecting someone to crack a smile, to let me in on the joke. But the men's faces were like stone.

"He's American," observed a man sporting a prodigious beard. "Army, could be."

"Bollocks," another one growled. "Look at 'im. He's practically a fetus!"

"His mack, though," the bearded one said, reaching out to pinch the sleeve of my jacket. "You'd have a helluva time finding that in a shop. Army—gotta be."

"Look," I said, "I'm not in the army, and I'm not trying to pull anything on you, I swear! I just want to find my dad, get my stuff, and—"

"American, my arse!" bellowed a fat man. He peeled his considerable girth off a stool to stand between me and the door, toward which I'd been slowly backing. "His accent sounds rubbish to me. I'll wager he's a Jerry spy!"

"I'm not a spy," I said weakly. "Just lost."

"Got that right," he said with a laugh. "I say we get the truth out of 'im the old-fashioned way. With a rope!"

Drunken shouts of assent. I couldn't tell if they were being serious or just "taking the piss," but I didn't much care to stick around and find out. One undiluted instinct coursed through the anxious muddle in my brain: *Run.* It would be a lot easier to figure out what the hell was going on without a roomful of drunks threatening to lynch me. Of course, running away would only convince them of my guilt, but I didn't care.

I tried to step around the fat man.

He made a grab for me, but slow and drunk is no match for fast and scared shitless. I faked left and then dodged around him to the right. He howled with rage as the rest unglued themselves from barstools to lunge at me, but I slipped through their fingers and ran out the door and into the bright afternoon.

*   *   *

I charged down the street, my feet pounding divots into the gravel, the angry voices gradually fading behind me. At the first corner I made a skidding turn to escape their line of sight, cutting through a muddy yard, where squawking chickens dove out of my way, and then an open lot, where a line of women stood waiting to pump water from an old well, their heads turning as I flew past. A thought I had no time to entertain flitted through my head—*Hey, where'd the Waiting Woman go?*—but then I came to a low wall and had to concentrate on vaulting it—*plant the hand, lift the feet, swing over.* I landed in a busy path where I was nearly run down by a speeding cart. The driver yelled something derogatory about my mother as his horse's flank brushed my chest, leaving hoof prints and a wheel track just inches from my toes.

I had no idea what was happening. I understood only two things: that I was quite possibly in the midst of losing my mind, and that I needed to get away from people until I could figure out whether or not I actually was. To that end, I dashed into an alley behind two rows of cottages, where it seemed there would be lots of hiding places, and made for the edge of town. I slowed to a fast walk, hoping that a muddy and bedraggled American boy who was not running would attract somewhat less attention than one who was.

My attempt to act normal was not helped by the fact that every little noise or fleeting movement made me jump. I nodded and waved to a woman hanging laundry, but like everyone else she just stared at me. I walked faster.

I heard a strange noise behind me and ducked into an outhouse. As I waited there, hunkering behind the half-closed door, my eyes scanned the graffitied walls.

Dooleys a buggerloving arsehumper.

Wot, no sugar?

Finally, a dog slinked by, trailed by a litter of yapping puppies. I let out my breath and began to relax a little. Collecting my nerves, I stepped back into the alley.

Something grabbed me by the hair. Before I'd even had a chance to cry out, a hand whipped around from behind and pressed something sharp to my throat.

"Scream and I'll cut you," came a voice.

Keeping the blade to my neck, my assailant pushed me against the outhouse wall and stepped around to face me. To my great surprise, it wasn't one of the men from the pub. It was the girl. She wore a simple white dress and a hard expression, her face strikingly pretty even though she appeared to be giving serious thought to gouging out my windpipe.

"What are you?" she hissed.

"An—uh—I'm an American," I stammered, not quite sure what she was asking. "I'm Jacob."

She pressed the knife harder against my throat, her hand shaking. She was scared—which meant she was dangerous. "What were you doing in the house?" she demanded. "Why are you chasing me?"

"I just wanted to talk to you! Don't kill me!"

She fixed me with a scowl. "Talk to me about what?"

"About the house—about the people who lived there."

"Who sent you here?"

"My grandfather. His name was Abraham Portman."

Her mouth fell open. "That's a lie!" she cried, her eyes flashing. "You think I don't know what you are? I wasn't born yesterday! Open your eyes—let me see your eyes!"

"I am! They are!" I opened my eyes as wide as I could. She stood on tiptoes and stared into them, then stamped her foot and shouted, "No, your *real* eyes! Those fakes don't fool me any more than your ridiculous lie about Abe!"

"It's not a lie—and these *are* my eyes!" She was pushing so hard against my windpipe that it was difficult to breathe. I was glad the knife was dull or she surely would've cut me. "Look, I'm not whatever it is you think I am," I croaked. "I can prove it!"

Her hand relaxed a little. "Then prove it, or I'll water the grass with your blood!"

"I have something right here." I reached into my jacket.

She leapt back and shouted at me to stop, raising her blade so that it hung quivering in the air just between my eyes.

"It's only a letter! Calm down!"

She lowered the blade back to my throat, and I slowly drew Miss Peregrine's letter and photo from my jacket, holding it for her to see. "The letter's part of the reason I came here. My grandfather gave it to me. It's from the Bird. That's what you call your headmistress, isn't it?"

"This doesn't prove anything!" she said, though she'd hardly glanced at it. "And how do you know so bloody much about us?"

"I told you, my grandfather—"

She slapped the letter out of my hands. "I don't want to hear another word of that rubbish!" Apparently, I'd touched a nerve. She went quiet for a moment, face pinched with frustration, as if she were deciding how best to dispose of my body once she'd followed through on her threats. Before she could decide, though, shouts erupted from the other end of the alley. We turned to see the men from the pub running toward us, armed with wooden clubs and farm implements.

"What's this? What've you done?"

"You're not the only person who wants to kill me!"

She took the knife from my throat and held it at my side instead, then grabbed me by the collar. "You are now my prisoner. Do exactly as I say or you'll regret it!"

I made no argument. I didn't know if my chances were any better in the hands of this unbalanced girl than with that slavering mob of club-wielding drunks, but at least with her I figured I had a shot at getting some answers.

She shoved me and I stumbled to snatch the letter and we were off and running down a connecting alley. Halfway to the end she darted to one side and pulled me after her, both of us ducking under a line of sheets and hopping a chicken-wire fence into the yard of a little cottage.

"In here," she whispered and, looking around to make sure we hadn't been seen, pushed me through a door into a cramped hovel that reeked of peat smoke.

There was no one inside save an old dog asleep on a sofa. He opened one eye to look at us, didn't think much of what he saw, and went back to sleep. We darted to a window that looked out on the street and flattened ourselves against the wall next to it. We stood there listening, the girl careful to keep a hand on my arm and her knife at my side.

A minute passed. The men's voices seemed to fade and then return; it was hard to tell where they were. My eyes drifted around the little room. It seemed excessively rustic, even for Cairnholm. Tilting in a corner was a stack of hand-woven baskets. A chair upholstered in burlap stood before a giant coal-fired cooking range cast from iron. Hung on the wall opposite us was a calendar, and though it was too dim to read from where we stood, just looking at it sparked a bizarre thought.

"What year is it?"

The girl told me to shut up.

"I'm serious," I whispered.

She regarded me strangely for a moment. "I don't know what you're playing at, but go have a look for yourself," she said, pushing me toward the calendar.

The top half was a black-and-white photo of a tropical scene, full-bodied girls with enormous bangs and vintage-looking swimsuits smiling on a beach. Printed above the seam was "September 1940." The first and second days of the month had been crossed out.

A detached numbness spread over me. I considered all the strange things I'd seen that morning: the bizarre and sudden change in the weather; the island I thought I'd known, now populated by strangers; how the style of everything around me looked old but the things themselves were new. It could all be explained by the calendar on the wall.

September 3, 1940. But *how*?

And then one of the last things my grandfather said came to me. *On the other side of the old man's grave.* It was something I'd never been able to figure out. There was a time I'd wondered if he'd meant ghosts—that since all the children he'd known here were dead, I'd have to go to the other side of the grave to find them—but that was too poetic. My grandfather was literal minded, not a man who traded in metaphor or suggestion. He'd given me straightforward directions that he simply hadn't had time to explain: "The Old Man," I realized, was what the locals called the bog boy, and his grave was the cairn. And earlier today I had gone inside it and come out someplace else: September third, 1940.

All this occurred to me in the time it took for the room to turn upside down and my knees to go out from under me, and for everything to fade into pulsing, velvety black.

I awoke on the floor with my hands tied to the cooking range. The girl was pacing nervously and appeared to be having an animated conversation with herself. I kept my eyes most of the way shut and listened.

"He *must* be a wight," she was saying. "Why else would he have been snooping around the old house like a burglar?"

"I haven't the slightest idea," someone else said, "but neither, it seems, does he." So she wasn't talking to herself, after all—though from where I was lying, I couldn't see the young man who'd spoken. "You say he didn't even realize he was in a loop?"

"See for yourself," she said, gesturing toward me. "Can you imagine any relative of Abe's being so perfectly clueless?"

"Can you imagine a wight?" said the young man. I turned my head slightly, scanning the room, but still I didn't see him.

"I can imagine a wight *faking* it," the girl replied.

The dog, awake now, trotted over and began to lick my face. I squeezed my eyes shut and tried to ignore it, but the tongue bath he gave me was so slobbery and gross that I finally had to sit up just to rescue myself.

"Well, look who's up!" the girl said. She clapped her hands, giving me a sarcastic round of applause. "That was quite the performance you gave earlier. I particularly enjoyed the fainting. I'm sure the theater lost a fine actor when you chose to devote yourself instead to murder and cannibalism."

I opened my mouth to protest my innocence—and stopped when I noticed a cup floating toward me.

"Have some water," the young man said. "Can't have you dying before we get you back to the headmistress, now can we?"

His voice seemed to come from the empty air. I reached for the cup, and as my pinky brushed an unseen hand, I nearly dropped it.

"He's clumsy," the young man said.

"You're invisible," I replied dumbly.

"Indeed. Millard Nullings, at your service."

"Don't tell him your name!" the girl cried.

"And this is Emma," he continued. "She's a bit paranoid, as I'm sure you've gathered."

Emma glared at him—or at the space I imagined him to occupy—but said nothing. The cup shook in my hand. I began another fumbling attempt to explain myself but was interrupted by angry voices from outside the window.

"Quiet!" Emma hissed. Millard's footsteps moved to the window, and the blinds parted an inch.

"What's happening?" asked Emma.

"They're searching the houses," he replied. "We can't stay here much longer."

"Well, we can't very well go out there!"

"I think perhaps we can," he said. "Just to be certain, though, let me consult my book." The blinds fell closed again and I saw a small leather-bound notebook rise from a table and crack open in midair. Millard hummed as he flipped the pages. A minute later he snapped the book shut.

"As I suspected!" he said. "We have only to wait a minute or so and then we can walk straight out the front door."

"Are you mad?" Emma said. "We'll have every one of those knuckle-draggers on us with brick bats!"

"Not if we're less interesting than what's about to happen," he replied. "I assure you, this is the best opportunity we'll have for hours."

I was untied from the range and led to the door, where we crouched, waiting. Then came a noise from outside even louder than the men's shouting: engines. Dozens, by the sound of it.

"Oh! Millard, that's brilliant!" cried Emma.

He sniffed. "And you said my studies were a waste of time."

Emma put her hand on the doorknob and then turned to me. "Take my arm. Don't run. Act like nothing's the matter." She put away her knife but assured me that if I tried to escape I'd see it again—just before she killed me with it.

"How do I know you won't anyway?"

She thought for a moment. "You don't." And then she pushed open the door.

*　　*　　*

The street outside was thronged with people, not only the men from the pub, whom I spotted immediately just down the block, but grim-faced shopkeepers and women and cart drivers who'd stopped what they were doing to stand in the middle of the road and crane their heads toward the sky. There, not far overhead, a squadron of Nazi fighter planes was roaring by in perfect formation. I'd seen photos of planes like these at Martin's museum, in a display titled "Cairnholm under Siege." How strange it must be, I thought, to find yourself, in the midst of an otherwise unremarkable afternoon, suddenly in the shadow of enemy death machines that could rain fire down upon you at a moment's notice.

We crossed the street as casually as possible, Emma clutching my arm in a death grip. We nearly made it to the alley on the other side before someone finally noticed us. I heard a shout and we turned to see the men start after us.

We ran. The alley was narrow and lined with stables. We'd covered half its length when I heard Millard say, "I'll hang back and trip them up! Meet me behind the pub in precisely five and a half minutes!"

His footsteps fell away behind us, and when we'd reached the end of the alley Emma stopped me. We looked back to see a length of rope uncoil itself and float across the gravel at ankle height. It pulled taut just as the mob reached it, and they went sprawling over it and into the mud, a tangled heap of flailing limbs. Emma let out a cheer, and I was almost certain I could hear Millard laughing.

We ran on. I didn't know why Emma had agreed to meet Millard at the Priest Hole, since it was in the direction of the harbor, not the house. But since I also couldn't explain how Millard had known exactly when those planes were going to fly over, I didn't bother asking. I was even more baffled when, instead of sneaking around the back, any hope of our passing undetected was dashed by Emma pushing me right through the front door.

There was no one inside but the bartender. I turned and hid my face.

"Barman!" Emma said. "When's the tap open round here? I'm thirsty as a bloody mermaid!"

He laughed. "I ain't in the custom of servin' little girls."

"Never mind that!" she cried, slapping her hand on the bar. "Pour me a quadruple dram of your finest cask-strength whiskey. And none of that frightful watered-down piss you generally serve!"

I began to get the feeling she was just messing around—taking the piss, I should say—trying to one-up Millard and his rope-across-the-alley trick.

The bartender leaned across the bar. "So it's the hard stuff yer wantin', is it?" he said, grinning lecherously. "Just don't let your mum and dad hear, or I'll have the priest and constable after me both." He fetched a bottle of something dark and evil looking and began pouring her a tumbler full. "What about your friend, here? Drunk as a deacon already, I suppose?"

I pretended to study the fireplace.

"Shy one, ain't he?" said the barman. "Where's he from?"

"Says he's from the future," Emma replied. "I say he's mad as a box of weasels."

A strange look came over the bartender's face. "Says he's what?" he asked. And then he must've recognized me because he gave a shout, slammed down the whiskey bottle, and began to scramble toward me.

I was poised to run, but before the bartender could even get out from behind the bar Emma had upended the drink he'd poured her, spilling brown liquor everywhere. Then she did something amazing. She held her hand palm-side down just above the alcohol-soaked bar, and a moment later a wall of foot-high flames erupted.

The bartender howled and began beating at the wall of fire with his towel.

"This way, prisoner!" Emma announced, and, hooking my arm, she pulled me toward the fireplace. "Now give me a hand! Pry and lift!"

She knelt and wedged her fingers into a crack that ran along the floor. I jammed my fingers in beside hers, and together we lifted a small section, revealing a hole about the width of my shoulders: the priest hole. As smoke filled the room and the bartender struggled to put out the flames, we lowered ourselves down one after another and disappeared.

The priest hole was little more than a shaft that dropped about four feet to a crawl space. It was pure black down there, but the next thing I knew it was filled with soft orange light. Emma had made a torch of her hand, a tiny ball of flame that seemed to hover just above her palm. I gaped at it, all else forgotten.

"Move it!" she barked, giving me a shove. "There's a door up ahead."

I shuffled forward until the crawl space came to a dead end. Then Emma pushed past me, sat down on her butt, and kicked the wall with both heels. It fell open into daylight.

"*There* you are," I heard Millard say as we crawled into an alley. "Can't resist a spectacle, can you?"

"I don't know what you're talking about," replied Emma, though I could tell she was pleased with herself.

Millard led us to a horse-drawn wagon that seemed to be waiting just for us. We crawled into the back, stowing away beneath a tarpaulin. In what seemed like no time, a man walked up and climbed onto the horse, flicked its reins, and we lurched into juddering motion.

We rode in silence for a while. I could tell from the changing noises around us that we were headed out of town.

I worked up the courage to ask a question. "How'd you know about the wagon? And the planes? Are you psychic or something?"

Emma snickered. "Hardly."

"Because it all happened yesterday," Millard answered, "and the day before that. Isn't that how things go in your loop?"

"My what?"

"He isn't *from* any loop," Emma said, keeping her voice low. "I keep telling you—he's a damned wight."

"I think not. A wight never would've let you take him alive."

"See," I whispered. "I'm not a whatever-you-said. I'm Jacob."

"We'll just see about that. Now keep quiet." And she reached up and peeled back the tarpaulin a little, revealing a blue stripe of shifting sky.

CHAPTER SIX

*W*hen the last cottages had disappeared behind us, we slipped quietly from the wagon and then crossed the ridge on foot in the direction of the forest. Emma walked on one side of me, silent and brooding, never letting go of my arm, while on the other Millard hummed to himself and kicked at stones. I was nervous and baffled and queasily excited all at the same time. Part of me felt like something momentous was about to happen. The other part of me expected to wake up at any moment, to come out of this fever dream or stress episode or whatever it was and wake up with my face in a puddle of drool on the Smart Aid break room table and think, *Well, that was strange,* and then return to the boring old business of being me.

But I didn't wake up. We just kept walking, the girl who could make fire with her hands and the invisible boy and me. We walked through the woods, where the path was as wide and clear as any trail in a national park, then emerged onto a broad expanse of lawn blooming with flowers and striped with neat gardens. We'd reached the house.

I gazed at it in wonder—not because it was awful, but because it was beautiful. There wasn't a shingle out of place or a broken window. Turrets and chimneys that had slumped lazily on the house I remembered now pointed confidently toward the sky. The forest that had seemed to devour its walls stood at a respectful distance.

I was led down a flagstone path and up a set of freshly painted steps to the porch. Emma no longer seemed to regard me as the threat she once did, but before going inside she tied my hands behind me— I think just for the sake of appearances. She was playing the returning hunter, and I was the captured prey. She was about to take me inside when Millard stopped her.

"His shoes are caked with filth," he said. "Can't have him tracking in mud. The Bird'll have an attack." As my captors waited, I stepped out of my shoes one at a time, pressing down on the heels with the opposite foot, wobbling and nearly losing my balance without my arms to steady me. Emma grabbed me before I could fall, then yanked me impatiently through the door.

We proceeded down a hall I remembered being almost impassably clogged with broken furniture, past the staircase, now gleaming with varnish, curious faces peeking at me through the banisters, through the dining room. The snowfall of plaster was gone; in its place was a long wooden table ringed by chairs. It was the same house I'd explored, but everything had been restored to order. Where I remembered patinas of green mold there was wallpaper and wainscoting and cheerful shades of paint. Flowers were arranged in vases. Sagging piles of rotted wood and fabric had rebuilt themselves into fainting couches and armchairs, and sunlight streamed through high windows once so grimy I'd thought they were blacked out.

Finally we came to a small room that looked out onto the back. "Keep hold of him while I inform the headmistress," Emma said to Millard, and I felt his hand grasp my elbow. When she left, it fell away.

"You're not afraid I'll eat your brain or something?" I asked him.

"Not particularly."

I turned to the window and gazed out in wonder. The yard was full of children, almost all of whom I recognized from yellowed photographs. Some lazed under shade trees; others tossed a ball and chased one another past flowerbeds exploding with color. It was exactly the paradise my grandfather had described. This was the enchanted island; these were the magical children. If I was dreaming, I no longer wanted to wake up. Or at least not anytime soon.

Out on the grassy pitch, someone kicked a ball too hard, and it flew up into a giant topiary animal and got stuck. Arranged all in a row were several of these animal bushes—fantastic creatures as tall as the house, standing guard against the woods—including a winged griffin, a rearing centaur, and a mermaid. Chasing after their lost ball, a pair of teenage boys ran to the base of the centaur, followed by a young girl. I instantly recognized her as the "levitating girl" from my grandfather's pictures, only now she wasn't levitating. She walked slowly, every plodding step a chore, anchored to the ground as if by some surplus of gravity.

When she reached the boys she raised her arms and they looped a rope around her waist. She slipped carefully out of her shoes and then bobbed up in the air like a balloon. It was astonishing. She rose until the rope around her waist went taut, then hovered ten feet off the ground, held by the two boys.

The girl said something and the boys nodded and began letting out the rope. She rose slowly up the side of the centaur; when she was level with its chest she reached into the branches for the ball, but it was stuck deep inside. She looked down and shook her head, and the boys reeled her down to the ground, where she stepped back into her weighted shoes and untied the rope.

"Enjoying the show?" asked Millard. I nodded silently. "There are far easier ways to retrieve that ball," he said, "but they know they have an audience."

Outside, a second girl was approaching the centaur. She was in her late teens and wild looking, her hair a nest well on its way to becoming dreadlocks. She bent down, took hold of the topiary's long leafy tail and wrapped it around her arm, then closed her eyes as if concentrating. A moment later I saw the centaur's hand move. I stared through the glass, fixed on that patch of green, thinking it must've been the breeze, but then each of its fingers flexed as if sensation were slowly returning to them. I watched, astonished, as the centaur's huge arm bent at the elbow and reached into its own chest, plucked out the ball, and tossed it back to the cheering kids. As the game resumed, the wild-haired girl dropped the centaur's tail, and it went still once more.

Millard's breath fogged the window by me. I turned to him in amazement. "I don't mean to be rude," I said, "but what *are* you people?"

"We're peculiar," he replied, sounding a bit puzzled. "Aren't you?"

"I don't know. I don't think so."

"That's a shame."

"Why have you let go of him?" a voice behind us demanded, and I turned to see Emma standing in the doorway. "Oh, never mind," she said, coming over to grab the rope. "Come on. The headmistress will see you now."

*   *   *

We walked through the house, past more curious eyes peeping through door cracks and from behind sofas, and into a sunny sitting room, where on an elaborate Persian rug, in a high-backed chair, a distinguished-looking lady sat knitting. She was dressed head to toe in black, her hair pinned in a perfectly round knot atop her head, with lace gloves and a high-collared blouse fastened tightly at her throat—as fastidiously neat as the house itself. I could've guessed who she was even if I hadn't remembered her picture from those I'd found in the smashed trunk. This was Miss Peregrine.

Emma guided me onto the rug and cleared her throat, and the steady rhythm of Miss Peregrine's needles came to a halt.

"Good afternoon," the lady said, looking up. "You must be Jacob."

Emma gaped at her. "How do you know his—"

"My name is Headmistress Peregrine," she said, holding up a finger to silence Emma, "or if you prefer, since you are not currently under my care, Miss Peregrine. Pleased to finally meet you."

Miss Peregrine dangled a gloved hand in my direction and, when I failed to take it, noticed the rope that bound my wrists.

"Miss Bloom!" she cried. "What is the meaning of this? Is that any way to treat a guest? Free him at once!"

"But Headmistress! He's a snoop and a liar and I don't know what else!" Casting a mistrustful glance at me, Emma whispered something in Miss Peregrine's ear.

"Why, Miss Bloom," said Miss Peregrine, letting out a booming laugh. "What undiluted balderdash! If this boy were a wight you'd already be stewing in his soup kettle. Of course he's Abraham Portman's grandson. Just look at him!"

I felt a flush of relief; maybe I wouldn't have to explain myself after all. She'd been expecting me!

Emma began to protest, but Miss Peregrine shut her down with a withering glare. "Oh, all right," Emma sighed, "but don't say I didn't warn you." And with a few tugs at the knot, the rope fell away.

"You'll have to pardon Miss Bloom," said Miss Peregrine as I rubbed at my chafed wrists. "She has a certain flair for the dramatic."

"So I've noticed."

Emma scowled. "If he's who he says he is, then why don't he know the first thing about loops—or even what year he's in? Go on, ask him!"

"Why *doesn't* he know," Miss Peregrine corrected. "And the only person whom I'll be subjecting to questioning is you, tomorrow afternoon, regarding the proper use of grammatical tenses!"

Emma groaned.

"Now, if you don't mind," Miss Peregrine said, "I need to have a word with Mr. Portman in private."

The girl knew it was useless to argue. She sighed and went to the door, but before leaving turned to give me one last look over her shoulder. On her face was an expression I hadn't seen from her before: concern.

"You, too, Mr. Nullings!" Miss Peregrine called out. "Polite persons do not eavesdrop on the conversations of others!"

"I was only lingering to inquire if you should like some tea," said Millard, who I got the feeling was a bit of a suck-up.

"We should not, thank you," Miss Peregrine answered curtly. I heard Millard's bare feet slap away across the floorboards, and the door swung shut behind him.

"I would ask you to sit," said Miss Peregrine, gesturing at a cushy chair behind me, "but you appear to be encrusted with filth." Instead I knelt on the floor, feeling like a pilgrim begging advice from an all-knowing oracle.

"You've been on the island for several days now," Miss Peregrine said. "Why have you dawdled so long before paying us a visit?"

"I didn't know you were here," I said. "How'd you know *I* was?"

"I've been watching you. You've seen me as well, though perhaps you didn't realize it. I had assumed my alternate form." She reached up and pulled a long gray feather from her hair. "It's vastly preferable to assume the shape of a bird when observing humans," she explained.

My jaw dropped. "That was *you* in my room this morning?" I said. "The hawk?"

"The falcon," she corrected. "A peregrine, naturally."

"Then it's true!" I said. "You *are* the Bird!"

"It's a moniker I tolerate but do not encourage," she replied.

"Now, to my question," continued Miss Peregrine. "What on earth were you searching for in that depressing old wreck of a house?"

"You," I replied, and her eyes widened a bit. "I didn't know how to find you. I only figured out yesterday that you were all—"

And then I paused, realizing how strange my next words would sound. "I didn't realize you were dead."

She flashed me a tight smile. "My goodness. Hasn't your grandfather told you *anything* about his old friends?"

"Some things. But for a long time I thought they were fairy tales."

"I see," she replied.

"I hope that doesn't offend you."

"It's a little surprising, that's all. But in general that is how we prefer to be thought of, for it tends to keep away unwanted visitors. These days fewer and fewer people believe in those things—fairies and goblins and all such nonsense—and thus common folk no longer make much of an effort to seek us out. That makes our lives a good bit easier. Ghost stories and scary old houses have served us well, too—though not, apparently, in your case." She smiled. "Lion-heartedness must run in your family."

"Yeah, I guess so," I said with a nervous laugh, though in truth I felt as if I might pass out at any moment.

"In any case, as regards *this* place," she said, gesturing grandly. "As a child you believed your grandfather was 'making it all up,' as they say? Feeding you a great walloping pack of lies. Is that right?"

"Not *lies* exactly, but—"

"Fictions, whoppers, paradiddles—whatever terminology you like. When did you realize Abraham was telling you the truth?"

"Well," I said, staring at the labyrinth of interlocking patterns woven into the carpet, "I guess I'm just realizing it now."

Miss Peregrine, who had been so animated, seemed to fade a little. "Oh my, I see." And then her expression turned grim, as if, in the brief silence between us, she had intuited the terrible thing I'd come to tell her. And yet I still had to find a way to say it aloud.

"I think he wanted to explain everything," I said, "but he waited too long. So he sent me here to find you instead." I pulled the crumpled letter out of my jacket. "This is yours. It's what brought me here."

She smoothed it carefully over the arm of her chair and held it up, moving her lips as she read. "How ungraceful! The way I practically beg him for a reply." She shook her head, wistful for a moment. "We were always so desperate for news of Abe. I asked him once if he should like to worry me to death, the way he insisted on living out in the open like that. He could be so deucedly stubborn!"

She refolded the letter into its envelope, and a dark cloud seemed to pass over her. "He's gone, isn't he?"

I nodded. Haltingly, I told her what had happened—that is, I told her the story the cops had settled on and that, after a great deal of counseling, I, too, had come to believe. To keep from crying, I gave her only the broad strokes: He lived on the rural outskirts of town; we'd just been through a drought and the woods were full of starving, desperate animals; he was in the wrong place at the wrong time. "He shouldn't have been living alone," I explained, "but like you said, he was stubborn."

"I was afraid of this," she said. "I warned him not to leave." She made tight fists around the knitting needles in her lap, as if considering who to stab with them. "And then to make his poor grandson bear the awful news back to us."

I could understand her anger. I'd been through it myself. I tried to comfort her, reciting all the reassuring half-truths my parents and Dr. Golan had spun during my blackest moments last fall: "It was time for him to go. He was lonely. My grandma had been dead a lot of years already, and his mind wasn't sharp anymore. He was always forgetting things, getting mixed up. That's why he was out in the woods in the first place."

Miss Peregrine nodded sadly. "He let himself grow old."

"He was lucky in a way. It wasn't long and drawn-out. No months in a hospital hooked up to machines." That was ridiculous, of course—his death had been needless, obscene—but I think it made us both feel a little better to say it.

Setting aside her needlework, Miss Peregrine rose and hobbled to the window. Her gait was rigid and awkward, as if one of her legs were shorter than the other.

She looked out at the yard, at the kids playing. "The children mustn't hear of this," she said. "Not yet, at least. It would only upset them."

"Okay. Whatever you think."

She stood quietly at the glass for a while, her shoulders trembling. When she finally turned to face me again, she was composed and businesslike. "Well, Mr. Portman," she said briskly, "I think you've been adequately interrogated. You must have questions of your own."

"Only about a thousand."

She pulled a watch from her pocket and consulted it. "We have some time before supper-hour. I hope that will prove sufficient to enlighten you."

Miss Peregrine paused and cocked her head. Abruptly, she strode to the sitting room door and threw it open to find Emma crouched on the other side, her face red and streaked with tears. She'd heard everything.

"Miss Bloom! Have you been eavesdropping?"

Emma struggled to her feet, letting out a sob.

"Polite persons do not listen to conversations that are not meant for—" but Emma was already running from the room, and Miss Peregrine cut herself short with a frustrated sigh. "That was most unfortunate. I'm afraid she's quite sensitive as regards your grandfather."

"I noticed," I said. "Why? Were they . . . ?"

"When Abraham left to fight in the war, he took all our hearts with him, but Miss Bloom's especially. Yes, they were admirers, paramours, sweethearts."

I began to understand why Emma had been so reluctant to believe me; it would mean, in all likelihood, that I was here to deliver bad news about my grandfather.

Miss Peregrine clapped her hands as if breaking a spell. "Ah, well," she said, "it can't be helped."

I followed her out of the room to the staircase. Miss Peregrine climbed it with grim resolve, holding the banister with both hands to pull herself up one step at a time, refusing any help. When we reached the landing, she led me down the hall to the library. It looked like a real classroom now, with desks arranged in a row and a chalkboard in one corner and books dusted and organized on the shelves. Miss Peregrine pointed to a desk and said, "Sit," so I squeezed into it. She took her place at the front of the room and faced me.

"Allow me to give you a brief primer. I think you'll find the answers to most of your questions contained herein."

"Okay."

"The composition of the human species is infinitely more diverse than most humans suspect," she began. "The real taxonomy of Homo sapiens is a secret known to only a few, of whom you will now be one. At base, it is a simple dichotomy: there are the *coerlfolc*, the teeming mass of common people who make up humanity's great bulk, and there is the hidden branch—the crypto-sapiens, if you will—who are called *syndrigast*, or "peculiar spirits" in the venerable language of my ancestors. As you have no doubt surmised, we here are of the latter type."

I bobbed my head as if I understood, though she'd already lost me. Hoping to slow her down a little, I asked a question.

"But why don't people know about you? Are you the only ones?"

"There are peculiars all over the world," she said, "though our numbers are much diminished from what they once were. Those who remain live in hiding, as we do." She lapsed into a soft regretful voice. "There was a time when we could mix openly with common folk. In some corners of the world we were regarded as shamans and mystics, consulted in times of trouble. A few cultures have retained this harmonious relationship with our people, though only in places where both modernity and the major religions have failed to gain a foothold, such as the black-magic island of Ambrym in the New Hebrides. But the larger world turned against us long ago. The Muslims drove us out. The Christians burned us as witches. Even the pagans of Wales and Ireland eventually decided that we were all malevolent faeries and shape-shifting ghosts."

"So why didn't you just—I don't know—make your own country somewhere? Go and live by yourselves?"

"If only it had been that simple," she said. "Peculiar traits often skip a generation, or ten. Peculiar children are not always, or even usually, born to peculiar parents, and peculiar parents do not always, or even usually, bear peculiar children. Can you imagine, in a world so afraid of otherness, why this would be a danger to all peculiar-kind?"

"Because normal parents would be freaked out if their kids started to, like, throw fire?"

"Exactly, Mr. Portman. The peculiar offspring of common parents are often abused and neglected in the most horrific ways. It wasn't so many centuries ago that the parents of peculiar children simply assumed that their 'real' sons or daughters had been made off with and replaced with changelings—that is, enchanted and malevolent, not to mention entirely fictitious, lookalikes—which in darker times was considered a license to abandon the poor children, if not kill them outright."

"That's awful."

"Extremely. Something had to be done, so people like myself created places where young peculiars could live apart from common folk—physically and temporally isolated enclaves like this one, of which I am enormously proud."

"People like yourself?"

"We peculiars are blessed with skills that common people lack, as infinite in combination and variety as others are in the pigmentation of their skin or the appearance of their facial features. That said, some skills are common, like reading thoughts, and others are rare, such as the way I can manipulate time."

"Time? I thought you turned into a bird."

"To be sure, and therein lies the key to my skill. Only birds can manipulate time. Therefore, all time manipulators must be able to take the form of a bird."

She said this so seriously, so matter-of-factly, that it took me a moment to process. "Birds . . . are time travelers?" I felt a goofy smile spread across my face.

Miss Peregrine nodded soberly. "Most, however, slip back and forth only occasionally, by accident. We who can manipulate time fields consciously—and not only for ourselves, but for others—are known as *ymbrynes*. We create temporal loops in which peculiar folk can live indefinitely."

"A loop," I repeated, remembering my grandfather's command: *find the bird, in the loop*. "Is that what this place is?"

"Yes. Though you may better know it as the third of September, 1940."

I leaned toward her over the little desk. "What do you mean? It's only the one day? It repeats?"

"Over and over, though our experience of it is continuous. Otherwise we would have no memory of the last, oh, seventy years that we've resided here."

"That's amazing," I said.

"Of course, we were here on Cairnholm a decade or more *before* the third of September, 1940—physically isolated, thanks to the island's unique geography—but it wasn't until that date that we also needed temporal isolation."

"Why's that?"

"Because otherwise we all would've been killed."

"By the bomb."

"Assuredly so."

I gazed at the surface of the desk. It was all starting to make sense—though just barely. "Are there other loops besides this one?"

"Many," she said, "and nearly all the ymbrynes who mother over them are friends of mine. Let me see: There's Miss Gannett in Ireland, in June of 1770; Miss Nightjar in Swansea on April 3, 1901; Miss Avocet and Miss Bunting together in Derbyshire on Saint Swithin's Day of 1867; Miss Treecreeper I don't remember where exactly—oh, and dear Miss Finch. Somewhere I have a lovely photograph of her."

Miss Peregrine wrestled a massive photo album down from a shelf and set it before me on the desk. She leaned over my shoulder as she turned the stiff pages, looking for a certain picture but pausing to linger over others, her voice tinged with dreamy nostalgia. As they flicked by I recognized photos from the smashed trunk in the basement and from my grandfather's cigar box. Miss Peregrine had collected them all. It was strange to think that she'd shown these same pictures to my grandfather all those years ago, when he was my age—maybe right here in this room, at this desk—and now she was showing them to me, as if somehow I'd stepped into his past.

Finally she came to a photo of an ethereal-looking woman with a plump little bird perched on her hand, and said, "This is Miss Finch and her auntie, Miss Finch." The woman and the bird seemed to be communicating.

"How could you tell them apart?" I asked.

"The elder Miss Finch preferred to stay a finch most all of the time. Which was just as well, really. She never was much of a conversationalist."

Miss Peregrine turned a few more pages, this time landing on a group portrait of women and children gathered humorlessly around a paper moon.

"Ah, yes! I'd nearly forgotten about this one." She slipped the photo out of its album sleeve and held it up reverently. "The lady in front there, that's Miss Avocet. She's as close to royalty as we peculiars have. They tried for fifty years to elect her leader of the Council of Ymbrynes, but she would never give up teaching at the academy she and Miss Bunting founded. Today there's not an ymbryne worth her wings who didn't pass under Miss Avocet's tutelage at one time, myself included! In fact, if you look closely you might recognize that little girl in the glasses."

I squinted. The face she pointed to was dark and slightly blurred. "Is that you?"

"I was one of the youngest Miss Avocet ever took on," she said proudly.

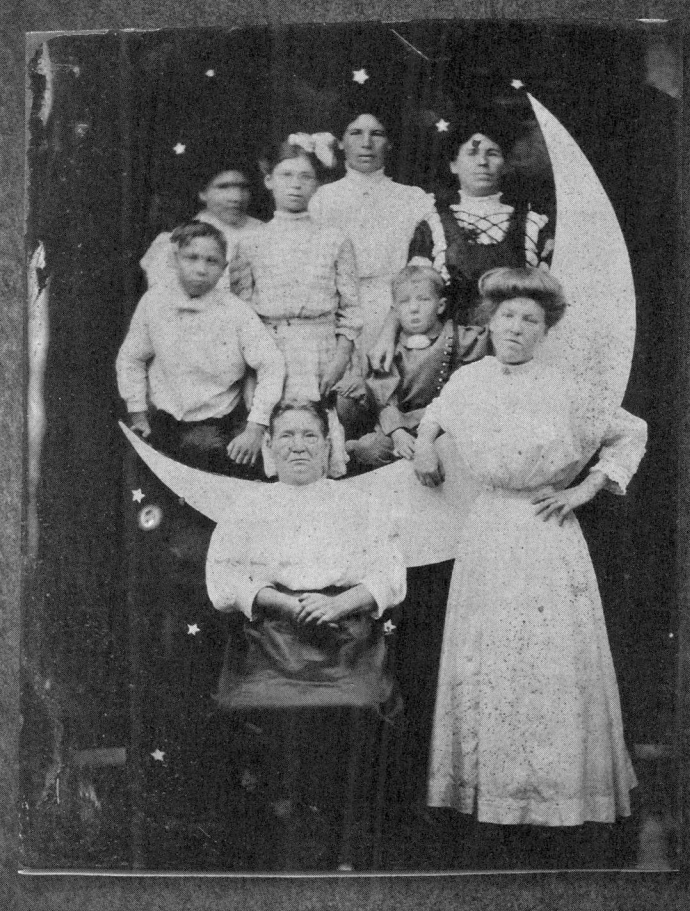

"What about the boys in the picture?" I said. "They look even younger than you."

Miss Peregrine's expression darkened. "You're referring to my misguided brothers. Rather than split us up, they came along to the academy with me. Mollycoddled like a pair of little princes, they were. I dare say it's what turned them rotten."

"They weren't ymbrynes?"

"Oh, *no*," she huffed. "Only *women* are born ymbrynes, and thank heaven for that! Males lack the seriousness of temperament required of persons with such grave responsibilities. We ymbrynes must scour the countryside for young peculiars in need, steer clear of those who would do us harm, and keep our wards fed, clothed, hidden, and steeped in the lore of our people. And as if that weren't enough, we must also ensure that our loops reset each day like clockwork."

"What happens if they don't?"

She raised a fluttering hand to her brow and staggered back, pantomiming horror. "Catastrophe, cataclysm, disaster! I dare not even think of it. Fortunately, the mechanism by which loops are reset is a simple one: One of us must cross through the entryway every so often. This keeps it pliable, you see. The ingress point is a bit like a hole in fresh dough; if you don't poke a finger into it now and then the thing may just close up on its own. And if there's no ingress or egress—no valve through which may be vented the various pressures that accrue naturally in a closed temporal system—" She made a little *poof!* gesture with her hands, as if miming the explosion of a firecracker. "Well, the whole thing becomes unstable."

She bent over the album again and riffled through its pages. "Speaking of which, I may have a picture of—yes, here it is. An ingress point if ever there was one!" She pulled another picture from its sleeve. "This is Miss Finch and one of her wards in the magnificent entryway to Miss Finch's loop, in a rarely used portion of the London Underground. When it resets, the tunnel fills with the most terrific glow. I've always thought our own rather modest by comparison," she said with a hint of envy.

"Just to make sure I understand," I said. "If today is September third, 1940, then tomorrow is . . . *also* September third?"

"Well, for a few of the loop's twenty-four hours it's September second, but, yes, it's the third."

"So tomorrow never comes."

"In a manner of speaking."

Outside, a distant clap of what sounded like thunder echoed, and the darkening window rattled in its frame. Miss Peregrine looked up and again drew out her watch.

"I'm afraid that's all the time I have at the moment. I do hope you'll stay for supper."

I said that I would; that my father might be wondering where I was hardly crossed my mind. I squeezed out from behind the desk and began following her to the door, but then another question occurred to me, one that had been nagging at me for a long time.

"Was my grandfather really running from the Nazis when he came here?"

"He was," she said. "A number of children came to us during those awful years leading up to the war. There was so much upheaval." She looked pained, as if the memory was still fresh. "I found Abraham at a camp for displaced persons on the mainland. He was a poor, tortured boy, but so strong. I knew at once that he belonged with us."

I felt relieved; at least that part of his life was as I had understood it to be. There was one more thing I wanted to ask, though, and I didn't quite know how to put it.

"Was he—my grandfather—was he like . . . "

"Like us?"

I nodded.

She smiled strangely. "He was like you, Jacob." And she turned and hobbled toward the stairs.

Miss Peregrine insisted that I wash off the bog mud before sitting down to dinner, and asked Emma to run me a bath. I think she hoped that by talking to me a little, Emma would start to feel better. But she wouldn't even look at me. I watched as she ran cold water into the tub and then warmed it with her bare hands, swirling them around until steam rose.

"That is awesome," I said. But she left without saying a word in response.

Once I'd turned the water thoroughly brown, I toweled off and found a change of clothes hanging from the back of the door—baggy tweed pants, a button-up shirt, and a pair of suspenders that were far too short but that I couldn't figure out how to adjust. I was left with the choice of wearing the pants either around my ankles or hitched up to my bellybutton. I decided the latter was the lesser of evils, so I went downstairs to have what would likely be the strangest meal of my life while dressed like a clown without makeup.

Dinner was a dizzying blur of names and faces, many of them half-remembered from photographs and my grandfather's long-ago descriptions. When I came into the dining room, the kids, who'd been clamoring noisily for seats around the long table, froze and stared at me. I got the feeling they didn't get a lot of dinner guests. Miss Peregrine, already seated at the head of the table, stood up and used the sudden quiet as an opportunity to introduce me.

"For those of you who haven't already had the pleasure of meeting him," she announced, "this is Abraham's grandson, Jacob. He is our honored guest and has come a very long way to be here. I hope you will treat him accordingly." Then she pointed to each person in the room and recited their names, most of which I immediately forgot, as happens when I'm nervous. The introductions were followed by a barrage of questions, which Miss Peregrine batted away with rapid-fire efficiency.

"Is Jacob going to stay with us?"

"Not to my knowledge."

"Where's Abe?"

"Abe is busy in America."

"Why does Jacob got Victor's trousers on?"

"Victor doesn't need them anymore, and Mr. Portman's are being washed."

"What's Abe doing in America?"

At this question I saw Emma, who had been glowering in a corner, rise from her chair and stalk out of the room. The others, apparently used to her volatile moods, paid no attention.

"Never mind what Abe's doing," Miss Peregrine snapped.

"When's he coming back?"

"Never mind that, too. Now let's eat!"

Everyone stampeded to their seats. Thinking I'd found an empty chair, I went to sit and felt a fork jab my thigh. "Excuse me!" cried Millard. But Miss Peregrine made him give it up anyway, sending him out to put on clothes.

"How many times must I tell you," she called after him, "polite persons do not take their supper in the nude!"

Kids with kitchen duty appeared bearing trays of food, all covered with gleaming silver tops so that you couldn't see what was inside, sparking wild speculation about what might be for dinner.

"Otters Wellington!" one boy cried.

"Salted kitten and shrew's liver!" another said, to which the younger children responded with gagging sounds. But when the covers were finally lifted, a feast of kingly proportions was revealed: a roasted goose, its flesh a perfect golden brown; a whole salmon and a whole cod, each outfitted with lemons and fresh dill and pats of melting butter; a bowl of steamed mussels; platters of roasted vegetables; loaves of bread still cooling from the oven; and all manner of jellies and sauces I didn't recognize but that looked delicious. It all glowed invitingly in the flicker of gaslight lamps, a world away from the oily stews of indeterminate origin I'd been choking down at the Priest Hole. I hadn't eaten since breakfast and proceeded to stuff myself silly.

It shouldn't have surprised me that peculiar children have peculiar eating habits, but between forkfuls of food I found myself sneaking glances around the room. Olive the levitating girl had to be belted into a chair screwed to the floor so that she wouldn't float up to the ceiling. So the rest of us wouldn't be plagued by insects, Hugh, the boy who had bees living in his stomach, ate under a large mosquito net at a table for one in the corner. Claire, a doll-like girl with immaculate golden curls, sat next to Miss Peregrine but ate not a morsel.

"Aren't you hungry?" I asked her.

"Claire don't eat with the rest of us," Hugh volunteered, a bee escaping from his mouth. "She's embarrassed."

"I am not!" she said, glaring at him.

"Yeah? Then eat something!"

"No one here is *embarrassed* of their gift," Miss Peregrine said. "Miss Densmore simply prefers to dine alone. Isn't that right, Miss Densmore?"

The girl stared at the empty place before her, clearly wishing that all the attention would vanish.

"Claire has a backmouth," explained Millard, who sat beside me now in a smoking jacket (and nothing else).

"A what?"

"Go on, show him!" someone said. Soon everyone at the table was pressuring Claire to eat something. And finally, just to shut them up, she did.

A leg of goose was set before her. She turned around in her chair, and gripping its arms she bent over backward, dipping the back of her head to the plate. I heard a distinct smacking sound, and when she lifted her head again a giant bite had disappeared from the goose leg. Beneath her golden hair was a set of sharp-toothed jaws. Suddenly, I understood the strange picture of Claire that I'd seen in Miss Peregrine's album, to which the photographer had devoted two panels: one for her daintily pretty face and another for the curls that so thoroughly masked the back of her head.

Claire
has gold
curls

Claire turned forward and crossed her arms, annoyed that she'd let herself be talked into such a humiliating demonstration. She sat in silence while the others peppered me with questions. After Miss Peregrine had dismissed a few more about my grandfather, the children turned to other subjects. They seemed especially interested in what life in the twenty-first century was like.

"What sort of flying motorcars do you have?" asked a pubescent boy named Horace, who wore a dark suit that made him look like an apprentice undertaker.

"None," I said. "Not yet, anyway."

"Have they built cities on the moon?" another boy asked hopefully.

"We left some garbage and a flag there in the sixties, but that's about it."

"Does Britain still rule the world?"

"Uh . . . not exactly."

They seemed disappointed. Sensing an opportunity, Miss Peregrine said, "You see, children? The future isn't so grand after all. Nothing wrong with the good old here and now!" I got the feeling this was something she often tried to impress upon them, with little success. But it got me wondering: Just how long had they been here, in the "good old here and now?"

"Do you mind if I ask how old you all are?" I said.

"I'm eighty-three," said Horace.

Olive raised her hand excitedly. "I'll be seventy-five and a half next week!" I wondered how they kept track of the months and years if the days never changed.

"I'm either one hundred seventeen or one hundred eighteen," said a heavy-lidded boy named Enoch. He looked no more than thirteen. "I lived in another loop before this one," he explained.

"I'm nearly eighty-seven," said Millard with his mouth full of goose drippings, and as he spoke a half-chewed mass quavered in his invisible jaw for all to see. There were groans as people covered their eyes and looked away.

Then it was my turn. I was sixteen, I told them. I saw a few kids' eyes widen. Olive laughed in surprise. It was strange to them that I should be so young, but what was strange to me was how young *they* seemed. I knew plenty of eighty-year-olds in Florida, and these kids acted nothing like them. It was as if the constance of their lives here, the unvarying days—this perpetual deathless summer— had arrested their emotions as well as their bodies, sealing them in their youth like Peter Pan and his Lost Boys.

A sudden boom sounded from outside, the second one this evening, but louder and closer than the first, rattling silverware and plates.

"Hurry up and finish, everyone!" Miss Peregrine sang out, and no sooner had she said it than another concussion jolted the house, throwing a framed picture off the wall behind me.

"What *is* that?" I said.

"It's those damned Jerries again!" growled Olive, thumping her little fist on the table, clearly in imitation of some ill-tempered adult. Then I heard what sounded like a buzzer going off somewhere far away, and suddenly it occurred to me what was happening. This was the night of September third, 1940, and in a little while a bomb was going to fall from the sky and blow a giant hole in the house. The buzzer was an air-raid siren, sounding from the ridge.

"We have to get out of here," I said, panic rising in my throat. "We have to go before the bomb hits!"

"He doesn't know!" giggled Olive. "He thinks we're going to die!"

"It's only the changeover," said Millard with a shrug of his smoking jacket. "No reason to get your knickers in a twist."

"This happens every night?"

Miss Peregrine nodded. "Every single evening," she said. Somehow, though, I was not reassured.

"May we go outside and show Jacob?" said Hugh.

"Yes, may we?" Claire begged, suddenly enthused after twenty minutes of sulking. "The changeover is ever so beautiful!"

Miss Peregrine demurred, pointing out that they hadn't yet finished their dinners, but the children pleaded with her until she relented. "All right, so long as you all wear your masks," she said.

The children burst out of their seats and ran from the room, leaving poor Olive behind until someone took pity and came to unbelt her from her chair. I ran after them through the house into the wood-paneled foyer, where they each grabbed something from a cabinet before bounding out the door. Miss Peregrine gave me one, too, and I stood turning it over in my hands. It looked like a sagging face of black rubber, with wide glass portholes like eyes that were frozen in shock, and a droopy snout that ended in a perforated canister.

"Go ahead," said Miss Peregrine. "Put it on." Then I realized what it was: a gas mask.

I strapped it over my face and followed her out onto the lawn, where the children stood scattered like chess pieces on an unmarked board, anonymous behind their upturned masks, watching billows of black smoke roll across the sky. Treetops burned in the hazy distance. The drone of unseen airplanes seemed to come from everywhere.

Now and then came a muffled blast I could feel in my chest like the thump of a second heart, followed by waves of broiling heat, like someone opening and closing an oven right in front of me. I ducked at each concussion, but the kids never so much as flinched. Instead they sang, their lyrics timed perfectly to the rhythm of the bombs.

> *Run, rabbit, run, rabbit, run, run, RUN!*
> *Bang, bang, BANG goes the farmer's gun*
> *He'll get by without his rabbit pie, so*
> *Run, rabbit, run, rabbit, RUN!*

Bright tracer bullets scored the heavens just as the song ended.

The kids applauded like onlookers at a fireworks display, violent slashes of color reflected in their masks. This nightly assault had become such a regular part of their lives that they'd ceased to think of it as something terrifying—in fact, the photograph I'd seen of it in Miss Peregrine's album had been labeled *Our beautiful display.* And in its own morbid way, I suppose it was.

our beautiful display

It began to drizzle, as if all that flying metal had riven holes in the clouds. The concussions came less frequently. The attack seemed to be ending.

The children started to leave. I thought we were going back inside, but they passed the front door and headed for another part of the yard.

"Where are we going?" I asked two masked kids.

They said nothing, but seeming to sense my anxiety, they took me gently by the hands and led me along with the others. We rounded the house to the back corner, where everyone was gathering around a giant topiary. This one wasn't a mythical creature, though, but a man reposing in the grass, one arm supporting him, the other pointing to the sky. It took a moment before I realized that it was a leafy replica of Michelangelo's fresco of Adam from the Sistine Chapel. Considering that it was made from bushes, it was really impressive. You could almost make out the placid expression on Adam's face, which had two blooming gardenias for eyes.

I saw the wild-haired girl standing nearby. She wore a flower-print dress that had been patched so many times it almost looked like a quilt. I went over to her and, pointing to Adam, said, "Did you make this?"

The girl nodded.

"How?"

She bent down and held one of her palms above the grass. A few seconds later, a hand-shaped section of blades wriggled and stretched and grew until they were brushing the bottom of her palm.

"That," I said, "is crazy." Clearly, I was not at my most articulate.

Someone shushed me. The children were all standing silently with their necks craned, pointing at a section of sky. I looked up but could see only clouds of smoke, the flickering orange of fires reflected against them.

Then I heard a single airplane engine cut through the rest. It was close, and getting closer. Panic flooded me. *This is the night they were killed. Not just the night, but the moment.* Could it be, I wondered, that these children died every evening only to be resurrected by the loop, like some Sisyphean suicide cult, condemned to be blown up and stitched back together for eternity?

Something small and gray parted the clouds and came hurtling toward us. *A rock*, I thought, but rocks don't whistle as they fall.

Run, rabbit, run, rabbit, run. I would've but now there was no time; all I could do was scream and dive to the ground for cover. But there was no cover, so I hit the grass and threw my arms over my head as if somehow that would keep it attached to my body.

I clenched my jaw and shut my eyes and held my breath, but instead of the deafening blast I was bracing for, everything went completely, profoundly quiet. Suddenly there were no growling engines, no whistling bombs, no pops of distant guns. It was as if someone had muted the world.

Was I dead?

I uncovered my head and slowly looked behind me. The wind-bent boughs of trees were frozen in place. The sky was a photograph of arrested flames licking a cloud bank. Drops of rain hung suspended before my eyes. And in the middle of the circle of children, like the object of some arcane ritual, there hovered a bomb, its downward-facing tip seemingly balanced on Adam's outstretched finger.

Then, like a movie that burns in the projector while you're watching it, a bloom of hot and perfect whiteness spread out before me and swallowed everything.

*   *   *

The first thing I heard when I could hear again was laughter. Then the white faded away and I saw that we were all arranged around Adam just as we had been before, but now the bomb was gone and the night was quiet and the only light in the cloudless sky was a full moon. Miss Peregrine appeared above me and held out her hand. I took it, stumbling to my feet in a daze.

"Please accept my apologies," she said. "I should have better prepared you." She couldn't hide her smile, though, and neither could the other kids as they stripped off their masks. I was pretty sure I'd just been hazed.

I felt lightheaded and out-of-sorts. "I should probably head home for the night," I said to Miss Peregrine. "My dad'll worry." Then I added quickly, "I *can* go home, right?"

"Of course you can," she replied, and in a loud voice asked for a volunteer to escort me back to the cairn. To my surprise, Emma stepped forward. Miss Peregrine seemed pleased.

"Are you sure about her?" I whispered to the headmistress. "A few hours ago she was ready to slit my throat."

"Miss Bloom may be hot-tempered, but she is one of my most trusted wards," she replied. "And I think you and she may have a few things to discuss away from curious ears."

Five minutes later the two of us were on our way, only this time my hands weren't tied and she wasn't poking a knife in my spine. A few of the younger kids trailed us as far as the edge of the yard. They wanted to know whether I'd be back again tomorrow. I made vague assurances, but I could hardly wrap my mind around what was happening at this moment, much less in the future.

We passed into the dark woods alone. When the house had disappeared behind us, Emma held out an upturned palm, flicked her wrist, and a petite ball of fire flared to life just above her fingers. She held it before her like a waiter carrying a tray, lighting the path and casting our twin shadows across the trees.

"Have I told you yet how cool that is?" I said, trying to break a silence that grew more awkward by the second.

"It isn't cool at all," she replied, swinging the flame close enough that I could feel its radiating heat. I dodged it and fell back a few paces.

"I didn't mean—I meant it's cool that you can *do* that."

"Well, if you'd speak properly I might understand you," she snapped, then stopped walking.

We stood facing each other from a careful distance. "You don't have to be afraid of me," she said.

"Oh yeah? How do I know you don't think I'm some evil creature and this is just a plot to get me alone so you can finally kill me?"

"Don't be stupid," she said. "You came unannounced, a stranger I didn't recognize, and chased after me like a madman. What was I meant to think?"

"Fine, I get it," I said, though I didn't really mean it.

She dropped her eyes and began digging a little hole in the dirt with the tip of her boot. The flame in her hand changed color, fading from orange to a cool indigo. "It's not true, what I said. I did recognize you." She looked up at me. "You look so much like him."

"People tell me that sometimes."

"I'm sorry I said all those terrible things earlier. I didn't want to believe you—that you were who you said. I knew what it would mean."

"It's okay," I replied. "When I was growing up, I wanted so much to meet all of you. Now that it's finally happening . . . " I shook my head. "I'm just sorry it has to be because of this."

And then she rushed at me and threw her arms around my neck, the flame in her hand snuffing out just before she touched me, her skin hot where she'd held it. We stood like that in the darkness for a while, me and this teenaged old woman, this rather beautiful girl who had loved my grandfather when he was the age I am now. There was nothing I could do but put my arms around her, too, so I did, and after a while I guess we were both crying.

I heard her take a deep breath in the dark, and then she broke away. The fire flared back to life in her hand.

"Sorry about that," she said. "I'm not usually so . . . "

"Don't worry about it."

"We should be getting on."

"Lead the way," I said.

We walked through the woods in a comfortable silence. When we came to the bog, she said, "Step only where I step," and I did, planting my feet in her prints. Bog gases flared up in green pyres in the distance, as if in sympathy with Emma's light.

We reached the cairn and ducked inside, shuffling in single file to the rear chamber and then out again to a world shrouded in mist. She guided me back to the path, and when we reached it she laced her fingers through mine and squeezed. We were quiet for a moment. Then she turned and went back, the fog swallowing her so quickly that for a moment I wondered if she'd been there at all.

*   *   *

Returning to town, I half-expected to find horse-drawn wagons roaming the streets. Instead I was welcomed by the hum of generators and the glow of TV screens behind cottage windows. I was home, such as it was.

Kev was manning the bar again and raised a glass in my direction as I came in. None of the men in the pub offered to lynch me. All seemed right with the world.

I went upstairs to find Dad asleep in front of his laptop at our little table. When I shut the door he woke with a start.

"Hi! Hey! You're out late. Or are you? What time is it?"

"I don't know," I said. "Before nine, I think. The generators are still on."

He stretched and rubbed his eyes. "What'd you do today? I was hoping I'd see you for dinner."

"Just explored the old house some more."

"Find anything good?"

"Uh . . . not really," I said, realizing that I probably should've bothered to concoct a more elaborate cover story.

He looked at me strangely. "Where'd you get those?"

"Get what?"

"Your clothes," he said.

I looked down and realized I'd completely forgotten about the tweed-pants-and-suspenders outfit I was wearing. "I found them in the house," I said, because I didn't have time to think of a less weird answer. "Aren't they cool?"

He grimaced. "You put on clothes that you *found*? Jake, that's unsanitary. And what happened to your jeans and jacket?"

I needed to change the subject. "They got super dirty, so I, uh . . . " I trailed off, making a point of noticing the document on his computer screen. "Whoa, is that your book? How's it coming?"

He slapped the laptop shut. "My book isn't the issue right now. What's important is your therapy. I'm not sure that spending your days alone in that old house is really what Dr. Golan had in mind when he green-lighted this trip."

"Wow, I think that was the record," I said.

"What?"

"The longest streak ever of you not mentioning my psychiatrist." I pretended to look at a nonexistent wristwatch. "Four days, five hours, and twenty-six minutes." I sighed. "It was good while it lasted."

"That man has been a great help to you," he said. "God only knows the state you'd be in right now if we hadn't found him."

"You're right, Dad. Dr. Golan did help me. But that doesn't mean he has to control every aspect of my life. I mean, Jesus, you and mom might as well buy me one of those little bracelets that says *What Would Golan Do?* That way I can ask myself before I do anything. Before I take a dump. How would Dr. Golan want me to take this dump? Should I bank it off the side or go straight down the middle? What would be the most psychologically beneficial dump I could take?"

Dad didn't say anything for a few seconds, and when he did his voice was all low and gravelly. He told me I was going birding with him the next day whether I liked it or not. When I replied that he was sadly mistaken, he got up and went downstairs to the pub. I thought he'd be drinking or something, so I went to change out of my clown clothes, but a few minutes later he knocked on my bedroom door and said there was someone on the phone for me.

I figured it was Mom, so I gritted my teeth and followed him downstairs to the phone booth in the far corner of the pub. He handed me the receiver and went to sit at a table. I slid the door closed.

"Hello?"

"I just spoke to your father," a man said. "He sounded a little upset."

It was Dr. Golan.

I wanted to say that he and my dad could both stuff it up their asses, but I knew this situation required some tact. If I pissed Golan off now it would be the end of my trip. I couldn't leave yet, not with so much more to learn about the peculiar children. So I played along and explained what I'd been up to—all except the kids-in-a-time-loop part—and tried to make it sound like I was coming around to the idea that there was nothing special about the island or my grandfather. It was like a mini-session over the phone.

"I hope you're not just telling me what I want to hear," he said. That had become his standard line. "Maybe I should come out there and check on you. I could use a little vacation. How does that sound?"

Please be joking, I prayed.

"I'm okay. Really," I said.

"Relax, Jacob, I'm only kidding, though Lord knows I *could* use some time away from the office. And actually, I believe you. You do sound okay. In fact, just now I told your father that probably the best thing he could do is to give you a little breathing room and let you sort things out on your own."

"Really?"

"You've had your parents and me hovering over you for so long. At a certain point it becomes counterproductive."

"Well, I really appreciate that."

He said something else I couldn't quite hear; there was a lot of noise on his end. "It's hard to hear you," I said. "Are you in a mall or something?"

"The airport," he replied. "Picking up my sister. Anyway, all I said was to enjoy yourself. Explore and don't worry too much. I'll see you soon, all right?"

"Thanks again, Dr. G."

As I hung up the phone, I felt bad for having ragged on him earlier. That was twice now he'd stuck up for me when my own parents wouldn't.

My dad was nursing a beer across the room. I stopped by his table on my way upstairs. "About tomorrow . . . " I said.

"Do what you want, I guess."

"Are you sure?"

He shrugged sullenly. "Doctor's orders."

"I'll be home for dinner. Promise."

He just nodded. I left him in the bar and went up to bed.

Falling asleep, my thoughts drifted to the peculiar children and the first question they'd asked after Miss Peregrine had introduced me: *Is Jacob going to stay with us?* At the time I'd thought, *Of course not.* But why not? If I never went home, what exactly would I be missing? I pictured my cold cavernous house, my friendless town full of bad memories, the utterly unremarkable life that had been mapped out for me. It had never once occurred to me, I realized, to refuse it.

CHAPTER SEVEN

*M*orning brought rain and wind and fog, pessimistic weather that made it hard to believe the previous day had been anything more than a strange and wonderful dream. I wolfed down my breakfast and told my dad I was going out. He looked at me like I was nuts.

"In *this*? To do what?"

"To hang out with—" I started, without thinking. Then, to cover my tracks, I pretended to have a piece of food stuck in my throat. But it was too late; he'd heard me.

"Hang out with who? Not those rapper hoodlums, I hope."

The only way out of this hole was to dig deeper. "No. You've probably never seen them, they live on the other side of, um, the island, and—"

"Really? I didn't think anyone lived over there."

"Yeah, well, just a few people. Like, sheep-tenders and whatnot. Anyway, they're cool—they watch my back while I'm at the house." Friends and safety: two things my dad couldn't possibly object to.

"I want to meet them," he said, trying to look stern. He often put on this face, an imitation of the sensible, no-nonsense dad I think he aspired to be.

"Sure thing. We're meeting up over there, though, so another time."

He nodded and took another bite of his breakfast.

"Be back by dinner," he said.

"Roger Wilco, Dad."

I practically raced to the bog. As I picked my way through its shifting muck, trying to remember the route of semi-invisible grass islands Emma had used to cross it, I worried that all I would find on the other side was more rain and a ruined house. So it was with great relief that I emerged from the cairn to find September third, 1940, just as I'd left it: the day warm and sunny and fogless, the sky a dependable blue, clouds forming shapes that seemed comfortingly familiar. Even better, Emma was there waiting for me, sitting on the edge of the mound casting stones into the bog. "About time!" she cried, jumping to her feet. "Come on, everyone's waiting for you."

"They are?"

"*Ye-es,*" she said with an impatient eye roll, taking my hand and pulling me after her. I sparked with excitement—not only at her touch, but at the thought of the day that lay ahead, full of endless possibility. Though in a million superficial ways it would be identical to the day before—the same breeze would blow and the same tree limbs would fall—my experience of it would be new. So would the peculiar children's. They were the gods of this strange little heaven, and I was their guest.

We dashed across the bog and through the forest as if late for an appointment. When we reached the house, Emma led me around to the backyard, where a small wooden stage had been erected. Kids were bustling in and out of the house, carrying props, buttoning up suit jackets, and zipping into sequined dresses. Warming up was a little orchestra, made up of just an accordion, a battered trombone, and a musical saw that Horace played with a bow.

"What's this?" I asked Emma. "Are you guys putting on a play?"

"You'll see," she said.

"Who's in it?"

"You'll see."

"What's it about?"

She pinched me.

A whistle blew and everyone ran to claim seats in a row of folding chairs that faced the stage. Emma and I sat down just as the curtain opened, revealing a straw boater hat floating atop a gaudy red-and-white striped suit. It was only when I heard a voice did I realize that—of course—it was Millard.

"Ladieeees and gentlemen!" he crowed. "It gives me the utmost pleasure to present to you a performance like no other in history! A show of such unrivaled daring, of such accomplished magicianship, that you simply won't believe your eyes! Good citizens, I give you Miss Peregrine and her Peculiar Children!"

The audience burst into uproarious applause. Millard tipped his hat.

"For our first illusion, I will produce Miss Peregrine herself!" He ducked behind the curtain and emerged a moment later, a folded sheet draped over one arm and a peregrine falcon perched on the other. He nodded to the orchestra, which lurched into a kind of wheezing carnival music.

Emma elbowed me. "Watch this," she whispered.

Millard set the falcon down and held the sheet in front, screening the bird from the audience. He began counting backward. "Three, two, one!"

On "one" I heard the unmistakable flap of wings and then saw Miss Peregrine's head—her *human* head—pop up from behind the sheet to even more uproarious applause. Her hair was mussed and I could only see her from the shoulders up; she seemed to be naked behind the sheet. Apparently, when you change into a bird, your clothes don't go along for the ride. Taking the edges of the sheet, she wrapped it chastely around herself.

"Mr. Portman!" she said, peering down at me from the stage. "I'm so happy you've returned. This is a little exhibition we used to tour around the Continent back in the halcyon days. I thought you might find it instructive." And then she swept offstage in a flourish, heading into the house to retrieve her clothes.

One after another, the peculiar children came out of the audience and took the stage, each with an act of their own. Millard removed his tuxedo so that he was completely invisible and juggled glass bottles. Olive removed her leaden shoes and performed a gravity-defying gymnastics routine on a set of parallel bars. Emma made fire, swallowed it, then blew it out again without burning herself. I applauded until I thought my hands would blister.

When Emma returned to her seat, I turned to her and said, "I don't understand. You performed this for people?"

"Of course," she replied.

"*Normal* people?"

"Of course, normal people. Why would peculiars pay to see things they can do themselves?"

"But wouldn't this, like, blow your cover?"

She chuckled. "Nobody suspected a thing," she said. "People come to sideshows to see stunts and tricks and what-all, and as far as anybody knew that's exactly what we showed them."

"So you were hiding in plain sight."

"Used to be the way most peculiars made a living," she said.

"And no one ever caught on?"

"Once in a while we'd get some knob-head backstage asking nosey questions, which is why there'd always be a strong-arm on hand to toss them out on their bums. Speak of the devil—here she is now!"

Up on stage, a mannish-looking girl was dragging a boulder the size of a small refrigerator out from behind the curtain. "She may not be the sharpest tool in the woodshed," Emma whispered, "but she's got a massive heart and she'd go to the grave for her mates. We're thick as thieves, Bronwyn and me."

Someone had passed around a stack of promotional cards Miss

Peregrine had used to advertise their act. It reached me with Bronwyn's card on top. In her picture she stood barefoot, challenging the camera with an icy stare. Emblazoned across the back was *THE AMAZING STRONG-GIRL OF SWANSEA!*

"Why isn't she lifting a boulder, if that's what she does on stage?" I asked.

"She was in a foul mood because the Bird made her 'dress like a lady' for the picture. She refused to lift so much as a hatbox."

"Looks like she drew the line at wearing shoes, too."

"She generally does."

Bronwyn finished dragging the rock to the middle of the stage, and for an awkward moment she just stared into the crowd, as if someone had told her to pause for dramatic effect. Then she bent down and gripped the rock between her big hands and slowly lifted it above her head. Everyone clapped and hooted, the kids' enthusiasm undimmed though they'd probably seen her do this trick a thousand times. It was almost like being at a pep rally for a school I didn't attend.

Bronwyn yawned and walked off with the boulder tucked under one arm. Then the wild-haired girl took the stage. Her name was Fiona, Emma said. She stood facing the crowd behind a planter filled with dirt, her hands raised above it like a conductor. The orchestra began to play "Flight of the Bumblebee" (as well as they could, anyway), and Fiona pawed the air above the planter, her face contorted in effort and concentration. As the song crescendoed, a row of daisies poked up from the dirt and unfurled toward her hands. It was like one of those fast-motion videos of plants blooming, except she seemed to be reeling the flowers up from their loamy bed by invisible strings. The kids ate it up, jumping out of their seats to cheer her on.

Emma flipped through the stack of postcards to Fiona's. "Her card's my favorite," she said. "We worked for days on her costume."

I looked at it. She was dressed like a beggar girl and stood holding a chicken. "What's she supposed to be?" I asked. "A homeless farmer?"

Emma pinched me. "She's meant to look *natural*, like a savage-type person. Jill of the Jungle, we called her."

"Is she really from the jungle?"

"She's from Ireland."

"Are there a lot of chickens in the jungle?"

She pinched me again. While we'd been whispering, Hugh had joined Fiona on stage. He stood with his mouth open, letting bees fly out to pollinate the flowers that Fiona had grown, like a weird mating ritual.

"What else does Fiona grow besides bushes and flowers?"

"All these vegetables," Emma said, gesturing to the garden beds in the yard. "And trees, sometimes."

"Really? Whole trees?"

She sorted through the postcards again. "Sometimes we'll play Jill and the Beanstalk. Someone will grab hold of one of the saplings at the edge of the woods and we'll see how high Fiona can get it to go while we're riding it." She arrived at the photo she'd been hunting for and tapped it with her finger. "That was the record," she said proudly. "Twenty meters."

"You guys get pretty bored around here, huh?"

She moved to pinch me again but I blocked her hand. I'm no expert on girls, but when one tries to pinch you four times, I'm pretty sure that's flirting.

There were a few more acts after Fiona and Hugh left the stage but by then the kids were getting antsy, and soon we dispersed to spend the rest of the day in summery bliss: lazing in the sun sipping limeade; playing croquet; tending to gardens that, thanks to Fiona, hardly needed tending; discussing our options for lunch. I wanted to ask Miss Peregrine more about my grandfather—a subject I avoided with Emma, who turned morose at any mention of his name—but the headmistress had gone to conduct a lesson in the study for the younger kids. It seemed like I had plenty of time, though, and the languid pace and midday heat sapped my will to do anything more taxing than wander the grounds in dreamy amazement.

After a decadent lunch of goose sandwiches and chocolate pudding, Emma began to agitate for the older kids to go swimming. "Out of the question," Millard groaned, the top button of his pants popping open. "I'm stuffed like a Christmas turkey." We were sprawled on velvet chairs around the sitting room, full to bursting. Bronwyn lay curled with her head between two pillows. "I'd sink straight to the bottom," came her muffled reply.

But Emma persisted. After ten minutes of wheedling she'd roused Hugh, Fiona, and Horace from their naps and challenged Bronwyn, who apparently could not forgo a competition of any kind, to a swimming race. Upon seeing us all trooping out of the house, Millard scolded us for trying to leave him behind.

The best spot for swimming was by the harbor, but getting there meant walking straight through town. "What about those crazy drunks who think I'm a German spy?" I said. "I don't feel like getting chased with clubs today."

"You twit," Emma said. "That was *yesterday*. They won't remember a thing."

"Just hang a towel 'round you so they don't see your, er, future clothes," said Horace. I had on jeans and a T-shirt, my usual outfit, and Horace wore his customary black suit. He seemed to be of the

Miss Peregrine school of dress: morbidly ultraformal, no matter the occasion. His photograph was among those I'd found in the smashed trunk, and in an attempt to "dress up" for it he'd gone completely overboard: top hat, cane, monocle—the works.

"You're right," I said, cocking an eyebrow at Horace. "I wouldn't want anyone to think I was dressed weird."

"If it's my waistcoat you're referring to," he replied haughtily, "yes, I admit I am a follower of fashion." The others snickered. "Go ahead, have a laugh at old Horace's expense! Call me a dandy if you will, but just because the villagers won't remember what you wear doesn't give you license to dress like a vagabond!" And with that he set about straightening his lapels, which only made the kids laugh harder. In a snit, he pointed an accusing finger at my clothes. "As for him, God help us if *that's* all our wardrobes have to look forward to!"

When the laughter had died down, I pulled Emma aside and whispered, "What exactly is it that makes Horace peculiar—aside from his clothes, I mean?"

"He has prophetic dreams. Gets these great nightmares every so often, which have a disturbing tendency to come true."

"How often? A lot?"

"Ask him yourself."

But Horace was in no mood to entertain my questions. So I filed it away for another time.

As we came into town I wrapped a towel around my waist and hung another from my shoulders. Though it wasn't exactly prophecy, Horace was right about one thing: nobody recognized me. Walking down the main path we got a few odd looks, but no one bothered us. We even passed the fat man who'd made such a stink over me in the bar. He was stuffing a pipe outside the tobacconist's shop and blathering on about politics to a woman who was barely listening. I couldn't help staring at him as we passed. He stared back, without even a flicker of recognition.

It was like someone had hit "reset" on the whole town. I kept noticing things I'd seen the day before: the same wagon rushing wildly down the path, its back wheel fishtailing in the gravel; the same women lining up outside the well; a man tarring the bottom of a rowboat, no further along in his task than he'd been twenty-four hours ago. I almost expected to see my doppelgänger sprinting across town pursued by a mob, but I guess things didn't work that way.

"You guys must know a lot about what goes on around here," I said. "Like yesterday, with the planes and that cart."

"It's Millard who knows everything," said Hugh.

"It's true," said Millard. "In fact, I am in the midst of compiling the world's first complete account of one day in the life of a town, as experienced by everyone in it. Every action, every conversation, every sound made by each of the one hundred fifty-nine human and three hundred thirty-two animal residents of Cairnholm, minute by minute, sunup to sundown."

"That's incredible," I said.

"I can't help but agree," he replied. "In just twenty-seven years I've already observed half the animals and nearly all the humans."

My mouth fell open. "Twenty-seven *years*?"

"He spent three years on pigs alone!" Hugh said. "That's all day every day for three years taking notes on *pigs*! Can you imagine? 'This one dropped a load of arse biscuits!' 'That one said *oink-oink* and then went to sleep in its own filth!'"

"Notes are absolutely essential to the process," Millard explained patiently. "But I can understand your jealousy, Hugh. It promises to be a work unprecedented in the history of academic scholarship."

"Oh, don't cock your nose," Emma said. "It'll also be unprecedented in the history of dull things. It'll be the dullest thing ever written!"

Rather than responding, Millard began pointing things out just before they happened. "Mrs. Higgins is about to have a coughing fit," he'd say, and then a woman in the street would cough and hack until she was red in the face, or "Presently, a fisherman will lament the difficulty of plying his trade during wartime," and then a man leaning on a cart filled with nets would turn to another man and say, "There's so many damned U-boats in the water now it ain't even safe for a bloke to go tickle his own lines!"

I was duly impressed, and told him so. "I'm glad *someone* appreciates my work," he replied.

We walked along the bustling harbor until the docks ran out and then followed the rocky shore toward the headlands to a sandy cove. We boys stripped down to our underwear (all except Horace, who would remove only his shoes and tie) while the girls disappeared to change into modest, old-school bathing suits. Then we all swam. Bronwyn and Emma raced each other while the rest of us paddled around; once we'd exhausted ourselves, we climbed onto the sand and napped. When the sun was too hot we fell back into the water, and when the chilly sea made us shiver we crawled out again, and so it went until our shadows began to lengthen across the cove.

We got to talking. They had a million questions for me, and, far away from Miss Peregrine, I could answer them frankly. What was my world like? What did people eat, drink, wear? When would sickness and death be overcome by science? They lived in splendor but were starving for new faces and new stories. I told them whatever I could, racking my brain for nuggets of twentieth-century history from Mrs. Johnston's class—the moon landing! the Berlin Wall! Vietnam!—but they were hardly comprehensive.

It was my time's technology and standard of living that amazed them most. Our houses were air-conditioned. They'd heard of televisions but had never seen one and were shocked to learn that my family had a talking-picture box in almost every room. Air travel was as common and affordable to us as train travel was to them. Our army fought with remote-controlled drones. We carried telephone-computers that fit in our pockets, and even though mine didn't work here (nothing electronic seemed to), I pulled it out just to show them its sleek, mirrored enclosure.

It was edging toward sunset when we finally started back. Emma stuck to me like glue, the back of her hand brushing mine as we walked. Passing an apple tree on the outskirts of town, she stopped to pick one, but even on tiptoes the lowest fruit was out of reach, so I did what any gentleman would do and gave her a boost, wrapping my arms around her waist and trying not to groan as I lifted, her white arm outstretched, wet hair glinting in the sun. When I let her down she gave me a little kiss on the cheek and handed me the apple.

"Here," she said, "you earned it."

"The apple or the kiss?"

She laughed and ran off to catch up with the others. I didn't know what to call it, what was happening between us, but I liked it. It felt silly and fragile and good. I put the apple in my pocket and ran after her.

When we came to the bog and I said I had to go home, she pretended to pout. "At least let me escort you," she said, so we waved goodbye to the others and crossed over to the cairn, me doing my best to memorize the placement of her feet as we went.

When we got there I said, "Come with me to the other side a minute."

"I shouldn't. I've got to get back or the Bird will suspect us."

"Suspect us of what?"

She smiled coyly. "Of . . . something."

"Something."

"She's always on the lookout for something," she said, laughing.

I changed tactics. "Then why don't you come see me tomorrow instead?"

"See you? Over there?"

"Why not? Miss Peregrine won't be around to watch us. You could even meet my dad. We won't tell him who you are, obviously. And then maybe he'll ease up a little about where I'm going and what I'm doing all the time. Me hanging out with a hot girl? That's like his fondest dad-dream wish."

I thought she might smile at the hot girl thing, but instead she turned serious. "The Bird only allows us to go over for a few minutes at a time, just to keep the loop open, you know."

"So tell her that's what you're doing!"

She sighed. "I want to. I do. But it's a bad idea."

"She's got you on a pretty short leash."

"You don't know what you're talking about," she said with a scowl. "And thanks for comparing me to a dog. That was brilliant."

I wondered how we'd gone from flirting to fighting so quickly.

"I didn't mean it like that."

"It's not that I wouldn't like to," she said. "I just can't."

"Okay, I'll make you a deal. Forget coming for the whole day. Just come over for a minute, right now."

"One minute? What can we do in one minute?"

I grinned. "You'd be surprised."

"Tell me!" she said, pushing me.

"Take your picture."

Her smile disappeared. "I'm not exactly at my most fetching," she said doubtfully.

"No, you're great. Really."

"Just one minute? Promise?"

I let her go into the cairn first. When we came out again the world was misty and cold, though thankfully the rain had stopped. I pulled out my phone and was happy to see that my theory was right. On this side of the loop, electronic things worked fine.

"Where's your camera?" she said, shivering. "Let's get this over with!"

I held up the phone and took her picture. She just shook her head, as if nothing about my bizarre world could surprise her anymore. Then she dodged away, and I had to chase her around the cairn, both of us laughing, Emma ducking out of view only to pop up again and vamp for the camera. A minute later I'd taken so many pictures that my phone had nearly run out of memory.

Emma ran to the mouth of the cairn and blew me an air-kiss. "See you tomorrow, future boy!"

I lifted my hand to wave goodbye, and she ducked into the stone tunnel.

*   *   *

I skipped back to town freezing and wet and grinning like an idiot. I was still blocks away from the pub when I heard a strange sound rising above the hum of generators—someone calling my name. Following the voice, I found my father standing in the street in a soggy sweater, breath pluming before him like muffler exhaust on a cold morning.

"Jacob! I've been looking for you!"

"You said be back by dinner, so here I am!"

"Forget dinner. Come with me."

My father never skipped dinner. Something was most definitely amiss.

"What's going on?"

"I'll explain on the way," he said, marching me toward the pub. Then he got a good look at me. "You're all wet!" he exclaimed. "For God's sake, did you lose your *other* jacket, too?"

"I, uh . . . "

"And why is your face red? You look sunburned."

Crap. A whole afternoon at the beach without sunblock. "I'm all hot from running," I said, though the skin on my arms was pimpled from cold. "What's happening? Did someone die, or what?"

"No, no, no," he said. "Well, sort of. Some sheep."

"What's that got to do with us?"

"They think it was kids who did it. Like a vandalism thing."

"They who? The sheep police?"

"The farmers," he said. "They've interrogated everyone under the age of twenty. Naturally, they're pretty interested in where you've been all day."

My stomach sank. I didn't exactly have a watertight cover story, and I raced to think of one as we approached the Priest Hole.

Outside the pub, a small crowd was gathered around a quorum of very pissed-off-looking sheep farmers. One wore muddy coveralls and leaned threateningly on a pitchfork. Another had Worm by the collar. Worm was dressed in neon track pants and a shirt that read *I*

LOVE IT WHEN THEY CALL ME BIG POPPA. He'd been crying, snot bubbling on his upper lip.

A third farmer, rail-thin and wearing a knit cap, pointed at me as we approached. "Here he is!" he called out. "Where you been off to, son?"

Dad patted me on the back. "Tell them," he said confidently.

I tried to sound like I had nothing to hide. "I was exploring the other side of the island. The big house."

Knit Cap looked confused. "Which big house?"

"That wonky old heap in the forest," said Pitchfork. "Only a certified idiot would set foot in there. Place is witched, and a death-trap to boot."

Knit Cap squinted at me. "In the big house with *who*?"

"Nobody," I said, and saw Dad give me a funny look.

"Bollocks! I think you was with this one," said the man holding Worm.

"I never killed any sheep!" cried Worm.

"Shaddap!" the man roared.

"Jake?" said my dad. "What about your friends?"

"Ahh, crap, Dad."

Knit Cap turned and spat. "Why you little liar. I oughta belt you right here in fronta God and everybody."

"You stay away from him," my father said, doing his best Stern Dad voice. Knit Cap swore and took a step toward him, and he and my dad squared off. Before either could throw a punch, a familiar voice said, "Hang on, Dennis, we'll get this sorted," and Martin stepped out of the crowd to wedge himself between them. "Just start by telling us whatever your boy told you," he said to my father.

Dad glared at me. "He said he was going to see friends on the other side."

"*What* friends?" Pitchfork demanded.

I could see this was only going to get uglier unless I did something drastic. Obviously, I couldn't tell them about the children—not that they'd believe me anyway—so instead I took a calculated risk.

"It wasn't anybody," I said, dropping my eyes in feigned shame. "They're imaginary."

"What'd he say?"

"He said his friends were imaginary," my dad repeated, sounding worried.

The farmers exchanged baffled glances.

"See?" Worm said, a flicker of hope on his face. "Kid's a bloody psycho! It *had* to be him!"

"I never touched them," I said, though no one was really listening.

"It weren't the American," said the farmer who had Worm. He gave Worm's shirt a wrench. "This one here, he's got a history. Few years back I watched him kick a lamb down a cliffside. Wouldn't of believed it if I hadn't seen it wi' me own eyes. After he done it I asked him why. To see if it could fly, he says. He's a sickie, all right."

People muttered in disgust. Worm looked uncomfortable but didn't dispute the story.

"Where's his fishmongerin' mate?" said Pitchfork. "If this one was in on it, you can bet the other one was, too." Someone said they'd seen Dylan by the harbor, and a posse was dispatched to collect him.

"What about a wolf—or a wild dog?" my dad said. "My father was killed by dogs."

"Only dogs on Cairnholm are sheepdogs," replied Knit Cap. "And it ain't exactly in a sheepdog's nature to go about killin' sheep."

I wished my father would give it up and leave while the leaving was good, but he was on the case like Sherlock Holmes. "Just how many sheep are we talking about?" he asked.

"Five," replied the fourth farmer, a short, sour-faced man who hadn't spoken until then. "All mine. Killed right in their pen. Poor devils never even had a chance to run."

"Five sheep. How much blood do you think is in five sheep?"

"A right tubful, I shouldn't wonder," said Pitchfork.

"So wouldn't whoever did this be covered in it?"

The farmers looked at one another. They looked at me, and then at Worm. Then they shrugged and scratched their heads. "Reckon it coulda been foxes," said Knit Cap.

"A whole pack of foxes, maybe," said Pitchfork doubtfully, "if the island's even got that many."

"I still say the cuts are too clean," said the one holding Worm. "Had to have been done with a knife."

"I just don't believe it," my dad replied.

"Then come see for yourself," said Knit Cap. So as the crowd began to disperse, a small group of us followed the farmers out to the scene of the crime. We trudged over a low rise, through a nearby field, to a little brown shed with a rectangular animal pen beyond it. We approached tentatively and peeked through the fence slats.

The violence inside was almost cartoonish, like the work of some mad impressionist who painted only in red. The tramped grass was bathed in blood, as were the pen's weathered posts and the stiff white bodies of the sheep themselves, flung about in attitudes of sheepish agony. One had tried to climb the fence and got its spindly legs caught between the slats. It hung before me at an odd angle, clam-shelled open from throat to crotch, as if it had been unzipped.

I had to turn away. Others muttered and shook their heads, and someone let out a low whistle. Worm gagged and began to cry, which was seen as a tacit admission of guilt; the criminal who couldn't face his own crime. He was led away to be locked in Martin's museum—in what used to be the sacristy and was now the island's makeshift jail cell—until he could be remanded to police on the mainland.

We left the farmer to ponder his slain sheep and went back to town, plodding across wet hills in the slate-gray dusk. Back in the room, I knew I was in for a Stern Dad talking-to, so I did my best to disarm him before he could start in on me.

"I lied to you, Dad, and I'm sorry."

"Yeah?" he said sarcastically, trading his wet sweater for a dry one. "That's big of you. Now which lie are we talking about? I can hardly keep track."

"The one about meeting friends. There aren't any other kids on the island. I made it up because I didn't want you to worry about me being alone over there."

"Well, I do worry, even if your doctor tells me not to."

"I know you do."

"So what about these imaginary friends? Does Golan know about this?"

I shook my head. "That was a lie, too. I just had to get those guys off my back."

Dad folded his arms, not sure what to believe. "Really."

"Better to have them think I'm a little eccentric than a sheep killer, right?"

I took a seat at the table. Dad looked down at me for a long moment, and I wasn't sure if he trusted me or not. Then he went to the sink and splashed water on his face. When he'd toweled off and turned around again, he seemed to have decided it was a lot less trouble to trust me.

"You sure we don't need to call Dr. Golan again?" he asked. "Have a nice long talk?"

"If you want to. But I'm okay."

"This is exactly why I didn't want you hanging out with those rapper guys," he said, because he needed to close with something sufficiently parental for it to count as a proper talking-to.

"You were right about them, Dad," I said, though secretly I couldn't believe either of them was capable of it. Worm and Dylan talked tough, but that was all.

Dad sat down across from me. He looked tired. "I'd still like to know how someone manages to get a sunburn on a day like this."

Right. The sunburn. "Guess I'm pretty sensitive," I said.

"You can say that again," he said dryly.

He let me go, and I went to take a shower and thought about Emma. Then I brushed my teeth and thought about Emma and washed my face and thought about Emma. After that I went to my room and took the apple she'd given me out of my pocket and set it on the nightstand, and then, as if to reassure myself she still existed, I got out my phone and looked through the pictures of her I'd taken that afternoon. I was still looking when I heard my father go to bed in the next room, and still looking when the gennies kicked off and my lamp went out, and when there was no light anywhere but her face on my little screen, I lay there in the dark, still looking.

CHAPTER EIGHT

*H*oping to duck another lecture, I got up early and set out before Dad was awake. I slipped a note under his door and went to grab Emma's apple, but it wasn't on my nightstand where I'd left it. A thorough search of the floor uncovered a lot of dust bunnies and one leathery thing the size of a golf ball. I was starting to wonder if someone had swiped it when I realized that the leathery thing *was* the apple. At some point during the night it had gone profoundly bad, spoiling like I've never seen fruit spoil. It looked as though it had spent a year locked in a food dehydrator. When I tried to pick it up it crumbled in my hand like a clump of soil.

Puzzled, I shrugged it off and went out. It was pissing rain but I soon left gray skies behind for the reliable sun of the loop. This time, however, there were no pretty girls waiting for me on the other side of the cairn—or anyone, for that matter. I tried not to be too disappointed, but I was, a little.

As soon as I got to the house I started looking for Emma, but Miss Peregrine intercepted me before I'd even made it past the front hall.

"A word, Mr. Portman," she said, and led me into the privacy of the kitchen, still fragrant from the rich breakfast I'd missed. I felt like I'd been summoned to the principal's office.

Miss Peregrine propped herself against the giant cooking range. "Are you enjoying your time with us?" she said.

I told her I was, very much.

"That's good," she replied, and then her smile vanished. "I understand you had a pleasant afternoon with some of my wards yesterday. And a lively discussion as well."

"It was great. They're all really nice." I was trying to keep things light, but I could tell she was winding me up for something.

"Tell me," she said, "how would you describe the nature of your discussion?"

I tried to remember. "I don't know . . . we talked about lots of things. How things are here. How they are where I'm from."

"Where you're from."

"Right."

"And do you think it's wise to discuss events in the future with children from the past?"

"Children? Is that really how you think of them?" I regretted saying this even as the words were passing my lips.

"It is how they regard *themselves* as well," she said testily. "What would you call them?"

Given her mood, it wasn't a subtlety I was prepared to argue. "Children, I guess."

"Indeed. Now, as I was saying," she said, emphasizing her words with little cleaver-chops of her hand on the range, "do you think it's wise to discuss the future with children from the past?"

I decided to go out on a limb. "No?"

"Ah, but apparently you do! I know this because last night at dinner we were treated by Hugh to a fascinating disquisition on the wonders of twenty-first-century telecommunications technology." Her voice dripped with sarcasm. "Did you know that when you send a letter in the twenty-first century, it can be received almost instantaneously?"

"I think you're talking about e-mail."

"Well, Hugh knew *all* about it."

"I don't understand," I said. "Is that a problem?"

She unleaned herself from the range and took a limping step toward me. Even though she was a full foot shorter than I was, she still managed to be intimidating.

"As an ymbryne, it is my sworn duty to keep those children safe and above all that means keeping them *here*—in the loop—on this island."

"Okay."

"Yours is a world they can never be part of, Mr. Portman. So what's the use in filling their heads with grand talk about the exotic wonders of the future? Now you've got half the children begging for a jet-airplane trip to America and the other half dreaming of the day when they can own a telephone-computer like yours."

"I'm sorry. I didn't realize."

"This is their home. I have tried to make it as fine a place as I could. But the plain fact is they cannot leave, and I'd appreciate it if you didn't make them want to."

"But why can't they?"

She narrowed her eyes at me for a moment and then shook her head. "Forgive me. I continue to underestimate the breadth of your ignorance." Miss Peregrine, who seemed to be constitutionally incapable of idleness, took a saucepan from the stove top and began scouring it with a steel brush. I wondered if she was ignoring my question or simply weighing how best to dumb down the answer.

When the pan was clean she clapped it back on the stove and said, "They cannot linger in your world, Mr. Portman, because in a short time they would grow old and die."

"What do you mean, die?"

"I'm not certain how I can be more direct. They'll die, Jacob." She spoke tersely, as if wishing to put the topic behind us as quickly as possible. "It may appear to you that we've found a way to cheat death, but it's an illusion. If the children loiter too long on your side of the loop, all the many years from which they have abstained will descend upon them at once, in a matter of hours."

I pictured a person shriveling up and crumbling to dust like the apple on my nightstand. "That's awful," I said with a shudder.

"The few instances of it that I've had the misfortune to witness are among the worst memories of my life. And let me assure you, I've lived long enough to see some truly dreadful things."

"Then it's happened before."

"To a young girl under my own care, regrettably, a number of years ago. Her name was Charlotte. It was the first and last time I ever took a trip to visit one of my sister ymbrynes. In that brief time Charlotte managed to evade the older children who were minding her and wander out of the loop. It was 1985 or '86 at that time, I believe. Charlotte was roving blithely about the village by herself when she was discovered by a constable. When she couldn't explain who she was or where she'd come from—not to his liking, anyhow—the poor girl was shipped off to a child welfare agency on the mainland. It was two days before I could reach her, and by that time she'd aged thirty-five years."

"I think I've seen her picture," I said. "A grown woman in little girl's clothes."

Miss Peregrine nodded somberly. "She never was the same after that. Not right in the head."

"What happened to her?"

"She lives with Miss Nightjar now. Miss Nightjar and Miss Thrush take all the hard cases."

"But it's not as if they're confined to the island, is it?" I asked. "Couldn't they still leave *now*, from 1940?"

"Yes, and begin aging again, as normal. But to what end? To be caught up in a ferocious war? To encounter people who fear and misunderstand them? And there are other dangers as well. It's best to stay here."

"What other dangers?"

Her face clouded, as if she regretted having brought it up. "Nothing you need concern yourself with. Not yet, at least."

With that she shooed me outside. I asked again what she meant by "other dangers," but she shut the screen door in my face. "Enjoy the morning," she chirped, forcing a smile. "Go find Miss Bloom, I'm sure she's dying to see you." And she disappeared into the house.

I wandered into the yard, wondering how I was supposed to get the image of that withered apple out of my head. Before long, though I did. It's not that I forgot; it just stopped bothering me. It was the strangest thing.

Resuming my mission to find Emma, I learned from Hugh that she was on a supply run to the village, so I settled under a shade tree to wait. Within five minutes I was half-asleep in the grass, smiling like a dope, wondering serenely what might be on the menu for lunch. It was as if just being here had some kind of narcotic effect on me; like the loop itself was a drug—a mood enhancer and a sedative combined—and if I stayed too long, I'd never want to leave.

If that were true, I thought, it would explain a lot of things, like how people could live the same day over and over for decades without losing their minds. Yes, it was beautiful and life was good, but if every day were exactly alike and if the kids really couldn't leave, as Miss Peregrine had said, then this place wasn't just a heaven but a kind of prison, too. It was just so hypnotizingly pleasant that it might take a person years to notice, and by then it would be too late; leaving would be too dangerous.

So it's not even a decision, really. You stay. It's only later—years later—that you begin to wonder what might've happened if you hadn't.

*　　*　　*

I must've dozed off, because around midmorning I awoke to something nudging my foot. I cracked an eye to discover a little humanoid figure trying to hide inside my shoe, but it had gotten tangled in the laces. It was stiff-limbed and awkward, half a hubcap tall, dressed in army fatigues. I watched it struggle to free itself for a moment and then go rigid, a wind-up toy on its last wind. I untied my shoe to extricate it and then turned it over, looking for the wind-up key, but I couldn't find one. Up close it was a strange, crude-looking thing, its head a stump of rounded clay, its face a smeared thumbprint.

"Bring him here!" someone called from across the yard. A boy sat waving at me from a tree stump at the edge of the woods.

Lacking any pressing engagements, I picked up the clay soldier and walked over. Arranged around the boy was a whole menagerie of wind-up men, staggering around like damaged robots. As I drew near, the one in my hands jerked to life again, squirming as if he were trying to get away. I put it with the others and wiped shed clay on my pants.

"I'm Enoch," the boy said. "You must be him."

"I guess I am," I replied.

"Sorry if he bothered you," he said, herding the one I'd returned back to the others. "They get ideas, see. Ain't properly trained yet. Only made 'em last week." He spoke with a slight cockney accent. Cadaverous black circles ringed his eyes like a raccoon, and his overalls—the same ones he'd worn in pictures I'd seen—were streaked with clay and dirt. Except for his pudgy face, he might've been a chimney sweep out of *Oliver Twist*.

"You made these?" I asked, impressed. "How?"

"They're homunculi," he replied. "Sometimes I put doll heads on 'em, but this time I was in a hurry and didn't bother."

"What's a homunculi?"

"More than one homunculus." He said it like it was something any idiot would know. "Some people think its homunculuses, but I think that sounds daft, don't you?"

"Definitely."

The clay soldier I'd returned began wandering again. With his foot, Enoch nudged it back toward the group. They seemed to be going haywire, colliding with one another like excited atoms. "Fight, you nancies!" he commanded, which is when I realized they weren't simply bumping into one another, but hitting and kicking. The errant clay man wasn't interested in fighting, however, and when he began to totter away once more, Enoch snatched him up and snapped off his legs.

"That's what happens to deserters in my army!" he cried, and tossed the crippled figure into the grass, where it writhed grotesquely as the others fell upon it.

"Do you treat all your toys that way?"

"Why?" he said. "Do you feel sorry for them?"

"I don't know. Should I?"

"No. They wouldn't be alive at all if it wasn't for me."

I laughed, and Enoch scowled at me. "What's so funny?"

"You made a joke."

"You are a bit thick, aren't you?" he said. "Look here." He grabbed one of the soldiers and stripped off its clothes. Then with both hands he cracked it down the middle and removed from its sticky chest a tiny, convulsing heart. The soldier instantly went limp. Enoch held the heart between his thumb and forefinger for me to see.

"It's from a mouse," he explained. "That's what I can do—take the life of one thing and give it to another, either clay like this or something that used to be alive but ain't anymore." He tucked the stilled heart into his overalls. "Soon as I figger out how to train 'em up proper, I'll have a whole army like this. Only they'll be *massive*." And he raised an arm up over his head to show me just how massive.

"What can *you* do?" he said.

"Me? Nothing, really. I mean, nothing special like you."

"Pity," he replied. "Are you going to come live with us anyway?" He didn't say it like he wanted me to, exactly; he just seemed curious.

"I don't know," I said. "I hadn't thought about it." That was a lie, of course. I had thought about it, but mostly in a daydreaming sort of way.

He looked at me suspiciously. "But don't you *want* to?"

"I don't know yet."

Narrowing his eyes, he nodded slowly, as if he'd just figured me out.

Then he leaned in and said under his breath, "Emma told you about Raid the Village, didn't she?"

"Raid the what?"

He looked away. "Oh, it's nothing. Just a game some of us play."

I got the distinct feeling I was being set up. "She didn't tell me," I said.

Enoch scooted toward me on the stump. "I *bet* she didn't," he said. "I bet there's a *lot* of things about this place she wouldn't like you to know."

"Oh yeah? Why?"

"Cause then you'll see it's not as great as everybody wants you to think, and you won't stay."

"What kinds of things?" I asked.

"Can't tell," he said, flashing me a devilish smile. "I could get in big trouble."

"Whatever," I said. "You brought it up."

I stood to go. "Wait!" he cried, grabbing my sleeve.

"Why should I if you're not going to tell me anything?"

He rubbed his chin judiciously. "It's true, I ain't allowed to *say* anything . . . but I reckon I couldn't stop you if you was to go upstairs and have a look in the room at the end of the hall."

"Why?" I said. "What's in there?"

"My friend Victor. He wants to meet you. Go up and have a chat."

"Fine," I said. "I will."

I started toward the house and then heard Enoch whistle. He

mimed running a hand along the top of a door. *The key*, he mouthed.

"What do I need a key for if someone's in there?"

He turned away, pretending not to hear.

*   *   *

I sauntered into the house and up the stairs like I had business there and didn't care who knew it. Reaching the second floor unobserved, I crept to the room at the end of the hall and tried the door. It was locked. I knocked, but there was no answer. Glancing over my shoulder to make sure no one was watching, I ran my hand along the top of the doorframe. Sure enough, I found a key.

I unlocked the door and slipped inside. It was like any other bedroom in the house—there was a dresser, a wardrobe, a vase of flowers on a nightstand. Late-morning sun shone through drawn curtains the color of mustard, throwing such yellow light everywhere that the whole room seemed encased in amber. Only then did I notice a young man lying in the bed, his eyes closed and mouth slightly open, half-hidden behind a lace curtain.

I froze, afraid I'd wake him. I recognized him from Miss Peregrine's album, though I hadn't seen him at meals or around the house, and we'd never been introduced. In the picture he'd been asleep in bed, just as he was now. Had he been quarantined, infected with some sleeping sickness? Was Enoch trying to get me sick, too?

"Hello?" I whispered. "Are you awake?"

He didn't move. I put a hand on his arm and shook him gently. His head lolled to one side.

Then something terrible occurred to me. To test a theory, I held my hand in front of his mouth. I couldn't feel his breath. My finger brushed his lips, which were cold as ice. Shocked, I pulled my hand away.

Then I heard footsteps and spun around to see Bronwyn in the doorway. "You ain't supposed to be in here!" she hissed.

"He's dead," I said.

Bronwyn's eyes went to the boy and her face puckered. "That's Victor."

Suddenly it came to me, where I'd seen his face. He was the boy lifting the boulder in my grandfather's pictures. Victor was Bronwyn's brother. There was no telling how long he might've been dead; as long as the loop kept looping, it could be fifty years and only look like a day.

"What happened to him?" I asked.

"Maybe I'll wake old Victor up," came a voice from behind us, "and you can ask him yourself." It was Enoch. He came in and shut the door.

Bronwyn beamed at him through welling tears. "Would you wake him? Oh *please,* Enoch."

"I shouldn't," he said. "I'm running low on hearts as it is, and it takes a right lot of 'em to rise up a human being, even for just a minute."

Bronwyn crossed to the dead boy and began to smooth his hair with her fingers. "Please," she begged, "it's been *ages* since we talked to Victor."

"Well, I do have some cow hearts pickling in the basement," he said, pretending to consider it. "But I *hate* to use inferior ingredients. Fresh is always better!"

Bronwyn began to cry in earnest. One of her tears fell onto the boy's jacket, and she hurried to wipe it away with her sleeve.

"Don't get so choked," Enoch said, "you know I can't stand it. Anyway, it's cruel, waking Victor. He likes it where he is."

"And where's that?" I said.

"Who knows? But whenever we rouse him for a chat he seems in a dreadful hurry to get back."

"What's cruel is you toying with Bronwyn like that, and tricking me," I said. "And if Victor's dead, why don't you just bury him?"

Bronwyn flashed me a look of utter derision. "Then we'd never get to *see* him," she said.

"That stings, mate," said Enoch. "I only mentioned coming up here because I wanted you to have all the facts, like. I'm on your side."

"Yeah? What are the facts, then? How did Victor die?"

Bronwyn looked up. "He got killed by an—*owww*!" she squealed as Enoch pinched the back of her arm.

"Hush!" he cried. "It ain't for you to tell!"

"This is ridiculous!" I said. "If neither of you will tell me, I'll just go ask Miss Peregrine."

Enoch took a quick stride toward me, eyes wide. "Oh no, you mustn't do that."

"Yeah? Why mustn't I?"

"The Bird don't like us talking about Victor," he said. "It's why she wears black all the time, you know. Anyway, she can't find out we been in here. She'll hang us by our pinky toes!"

As if on cue, we heard the unmistakable sound of Miss Peregrine limping up the stairs. Bronwyn turned white and dashed past me out the door, but before Enoch could escape I blocked his path. "Out of the way!" he hissed.

"Tell me what happened to Victor!"

"I *can't*!"

"Then tell me about Raid the Village."

"I can't tell you that, neither!" He tried to shove past me again, but when he realized he couldn't, he gave up. "All right, just shut the door and I'll whisper it to you!"

I closed it just as Miss Peregrine was reaching the landing. We stood with our ears pressed to the door for a moment, listening for a sign that we'd been spotted. The headmistress's footsteps came halfway down the hall toward us, then stopped. Another door creaked open, then shut.

"She's gone into her room," Enoch whispered.

"So," I said. "Raid the Village."

Looking like he was sorry he'd brought it up, he motioned me away from the door. I followed, leaning down so he could whisper into my ear. "Like I said, it's a game we play. It works just like the name says."

"You mean you actually *raid* the village?"

"Smash it up, chase people round, take what we like, burn things down. It's all a good laugh."

"But that's terrible!"

"We got to practice our skills somehow, don't we? Case we ever need to defend ourselves. Otherwise we'd get rusty. Plus there's rules. We ain't allowed to kill anybody. Just scare 'em up a bit, like. And if someone does get hurt, well, they're back right as rain the next day and don't remember nothing about it."

"Does Emma play, too?"

"Nah. She's like you. Says it's *evil*."

"Well, it is."

He rolled his eyes. "You two deserve each other."

"What's *that* supposed to mean?"

He rose up to his full five-foot-four-inch height and poked a finger into my chest. "It means you better not get all high an' mighty with *me*, mate. Because if we didn't raid the damned village once in a while, most of this lot woulda gone off their heads ages ago." He went to the door and put his hand on the knob and then turned back to face me. "And if you think *we're* wicked, wait'll you see *them*."

"Them *who*? What the hell is everyone talking about?"

He held up one finger to shush me, then went out.

I was alone again. My eyes were drawn to the body on the bed.

What happened to you, Victor?

Maybe he'd gone crazy and killed himself, I thought—gotten so sick of this cheerful but futureless eternity that he'd guzzled rat poison or taken a dive off a cliff. Or maybe it was *them*, those "other dangers" Miss Peregrine had alluded to.

I stepped into the hall and had just started toward the stairs when I heard Miss Peregrine's voice behind a half-closed door. I dove into the nearest room, and stayed hidden until she'd limped past me and down the stairs. Then I noticed a pair of boots at the front of a crisply made bed—Emma's boots. I was in her bedroom.

Along one wall was a chest of drawers and a mirror, on the other a writing desk with a chair tucked underneath. It was the room of a neat girl with nothing to hide, or so it seemed until I found a hatbox just inside the closet. It was tied up with string, and in grease pencil across the front was written:

Private

Correspondence of
Emma Bloom
Do not open

It was like waving red underwear at a bull. I sat down with the box in my lap and untied the string. It was packed with a hundred or more letters, all from my grandfather.

My heart picked up speed. This was exactly the kind of gold mine I'd hoped to find in the old ruined house. Sure, I felt bad about snooping, but if people here insisted on keeping things secret, well, I'd just have to find stuff out for myself.

I wanted to read them all but was afraid someone would walk in on me, so I thumbed through them quickly to get an overview. Many were dated from the early 1940s, during Grandpa Portman's time in the army. A random sampling revealed them to be long and sappy, full of declarations of his love and awkward descriptions of Emma's beauty in my grandfather's then-broken English ("You are pretty like flower, have good smell also, may I pick?"). In one he'd enclosed a picture of himself posing atop a bomb with a cigarette dangling from his lips.

Over time, his letters grew shorter and less frequent. By the 1950s there was maybe one a year. The last was dated April 1963; inside the envelope was no letter, just a few pictures. Two were of Emma, snapshots she'd sent him that he'd sent back. The first was from early on—a jokey pose to answer his—of her peeling potatoes and pretending to smoke one of Miss Peregrine's pipes. The next one was sadder, and I imagined she'd sent it after my grandfather had failed to write for a while. The last photo—the last thing he'd ever sent her, in fact—showed my grandfather at middle age, holding a little girl.

Peeling spuds & dreaming of you. Come home soon. Love, your potato.

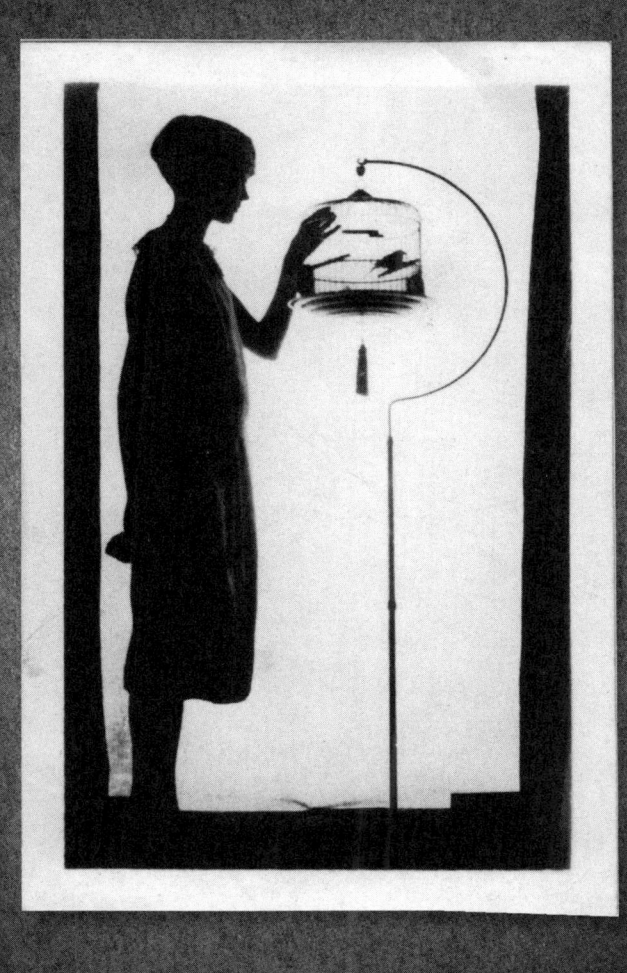

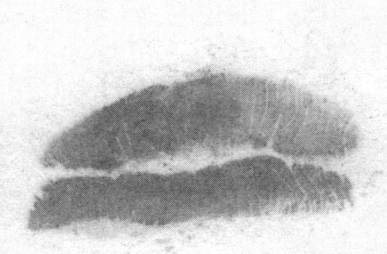

Feeling caged without you.
Won't you write? I worry
so. Kisses, Emma.

THIS IS WHY

I had to stare at the last picture for a minute before I realized who the little girl was. It was my aunt Susie, maybe four years old then. After that, there were no more letters. I wondered how much longer Emma had continued writing to my grandfather without receiving a reply, and what he'd done with her letters. Thrown them out? Stashed them somewhere? Surely, it had to be one of those letters that my father and aunt had found as kids, that made them think their father was a liar and a cheat. How wrong they were.

I heard a throat clear behind me, and turned to see Emma glaring from the doorway. I scrambled to gather the letters, my face flushing, but it was too late. I was caught.

"I'm sorry. I shouldn't be in here."

"I'm bloody well aware of that," she said, "but by all means, don't let me interrupt your reading." She stamped over to her chest of drawers, yanked one out, and threw it clattering to the floor. "While you're at it, why don't you have a look through my knickers, too!"

"I'm really, really sorry," I repeated. "I *never* do things like this."

"Oh, I shouldn't wonder. Too busy peeping in ladies' windows, I suppose!" She towered over me, shaking with anger, while I struggled to fit all the letters back into the box.

"There's a *system*, you know. Just give them here, you're mucking everything up!" She sat down and pushed me aside, emptying the box onto the floor and sorting the letters into piles with the speed of a postal worker. Thinking it best to shut my mouth, I watched meekly while she worked.

When she'd calmed a little, she said, "So you want to know about Abe and me, is that it? Because you could've just asked."

"I didn't want to pry."

"Rather a moot point now, wouldn't you say?"

"I guess."

"So? What is it you want to know?"

I thought about it. I wasn't really sure where to start. "Just . . .

what happened?"

"All right then, we'll skip all the nice bits and go right to the end. It's simple, really. He left. He said he loved me and promised to come back one day. But he never did."

"But he had to go, didn't he? To fight?"

"*Had* to? I don't know. He said he wouldn't be able to live with himself if he sat out the war while his people were being hunted and killed. Said it was his duty. I suppose duty meant more to him than I did. Anyhow, I waited. I waited and worried through that whole bloody war, thinking every letter that came was a death notice. Then, when the war was finally over, he said he couldn't possibly come back. Said he'd go stark raving. Said he'd learned how to defend himself in the army and he damn well didn't need a nanny like the Bird to look after him anymore. He was going to America to make a home for us, and then he'd send for me. So I waited more. I waited so long that if I'd actually gone to be with him I would've been forty years old. By then he'd taken up with some commoner. And that, as they say, was that."

"I'm sorry. I had no idea."

"It's an old story. I don't drag it out much anymore."

"You blame him for being stuck here," I said.

She gave me a sharp look. "Who says I'm stuck?" Then she sighed. "No, I don't blame him. Just miss him is all."

"Still?"

"Every day."

She finished sorting the letters. "There you have it," she said, clapping the lid on them. "The entire history of my love life in a dusty box in the closet." She drew a deep breath and then shut her eyes and pinched the bridge of her nose. For a moment I could almost see the old woman hiding behind her smooth features. My grandfather had trampled her poor, pining heart, and the wound was still raw, even these many years later.

I thought of putting my arm around her, but something stopped me. Here was this beautiful, funny, fascinating girl who, miracle of miracles, really seemed to *like* me. But now I understood that it wasn't me she liked. She was heartbroken for someone else, and I was merely a stand-in for my grandfather. That's enough to give anyone pause, I don't care how horny you are. I know guys who are grossed-out by the idea of dating a *friend's* ex. By that standard, dating your grandfather's ex would practically be incest.

The next thing I knew, Emma's hand was on my arm. Then her head was on my shoulder, and I could feel her chin tracking slowly toward my face. This was kiss-me body language if there ever was such a thing. In a minute our faces would be level and I'd have to choose between locking lips or seriously offending her by pulling away, and I'd already offended her once. It's not that I didn't *want* to—more than anything I did—but the idea of kissing her two feet from a box of obsessively well-preserved love letters from my grandfather made me feel weird and nervous.

Then her cheek was against mine, and I knew it was now or never, so I said the first mood-killing thing that popped into my head.

"Is there something going on between you and Enoch?"

She pulled away instantly, looking at me like I'd suggested we dine on puppies. "What?! No! Where on earth did you get a twisted idea like that?"

"From him. He sounds kind of bitter when he talks about you, and I get the distinct impression he doesn't want me around, like I'm horning in on his game or something."

Her eyes kept getting wider. "First of all, he doesn't have any 'game' to 'horn in' on, I can assure you of that. He's a jealous fool and a liar."

"Is he?"

"Is he which?"

"A liar."

She narrowed her eyes. "Why? What kind of nonsense has he been spouting?"

"Emma, what happened to Victor?"

She looked shocked. Then, shaking her head, she muttered, "Damn that selfish boy."

"There's something no one here is telling me, and I want to know what it is."

"I can't," she said.

"That's all I've been hearing! I can't talk about the future. You can't talk about the past. Miss Peregrine has us all tied up in knots. My grandfather's last wish was for me to come here and find out the truth. Doesn't that mean anything?"

She took my hand and brought it into her lap and looked down at it. She seemed to be searching for the right words. "You're right," she said finally. "There is something."

"Tell me."

"Not here," she whispered. "Tonight."

We arranged to meet late that night, when my dad and Miss Peregrine would be asleep. Emma insisted it was the only way, because the walls had ears and it was impossible to slip off together during the day without arousing suspicion. To complete the illusion that we had nothing to hide, we spent the rest of the afternoon hanging out in the yard in full view of everyone, and when the sun began to set I walked back to the bog alone.

*　　*　　*

It was another rainy evening in the twenty-first century, and by the time I reached the pub I was thankful just to be somewhere dry. I found my dad alone, nursing a beer at a table, so I pulled up a chair and began fabricating stories about my day while toweling off my face with napkins. (Something I was beginning to discover about lying: The more I did it, the easier it got.)

He was hardly even listening. "Huh," he'd say, "that's interesting," and then his gaze would drift off and he'd take another swig of beer.

"What's up with you?" I said. "Are you still pissed at me?"

"No, no, nothing like that." He was about to explain but waved it away. "Ahh, it's stupid."

"Dad. Come on."

"It's just . . . this guy who showed up a couple days ago. Another birder."

"Someone you know?"

He shook his head. "Never seen him before. At first I thought he was just some part-time enthusiast yahoo, but he keeps coming back to the same sites, the same nesting grounds, taking notes. He definitely knows what he's doing. Then today I saw him with a banding cage and a pair of Predators, so I know he's a pro."

"Predators?"

"Binoculars. Real serious glass." He'd wadded up his paper placemat and resmoothed it three times now, a nervous habit. "It's just that I thought I had the scoop on this bird population, you know? I really wanted this book to be something special."

"And then this asshole comes along."

"Jacob."

"I mean, this no-good sonofabitch."

He laughed. "Thank you, son, that'll do."

"It *will* be special," I said reassuringly.

He shrugged. "I dunno. Hope so." But he didn't sound too certain.

I knew exactly what was about to happen. It was part of this pathetic cycle my dad was caught in. He'd get really passionate about some project, talk about it nonstop for months. Then, inevitably, some tiny problem would crop up and throw sand in the gears, and instead of dealing with it he'd let it completely overwhelm him. The next thing you knew, the project would be off and he'd be on to the next one, and the cycle would start again. He got discouraged too easily. It was the reason why he had a dozen unfinished manuscripts locked in his desk, and why the bird store he tried to open with Aunt Susie never got off the ground, and why he had a bachelor's degree in Asian languages but had never been to Asia. He was forty-six years old and still trying to find himself, still trying to prove he didn't need my mother's money.

What he really needed was a pep talk that I didn't feel at all qualified to give, so instead I tried to subtly change the subject. "Where's this interloper staying?" I asked. "I thought we had the only rooms in town."

"I assume he's camping," my dad replied.

"In this weather?"

"It's kind of a hardcore ornithology-geek thing. Roughing it gets you closer to your subjects, both physically and psychologically. Achievement through adversity and all that."

I laughed. "Then why aren't *you* out there?" I said, then immediately wished I hadn't.

"Same reason my book probably won't happen. There's always someone more dedicated than I am."

I shifted awkwardly in my chair. "I didn't mean it like that. What I meant was—"

"Ssh!" My dad stiffened, glancing furtively toward the door. "Look quick but don't make it obvious. He just walked in."

I shielded my face with the menu and peeked over the top. A scruffy-looking bearded guy stood in the doorway, stamping water from his boots. He wore a rain hat and dark glasses and what appeared to be several jackets layered on top of one another, which made him look both fat and vaguely transient.

"I love the homeless Santa Claus thing he's got going," I whispered. "Not an easy look to pull off. Very next-season."

He ignored me. The man bellied up to the bar, and conversations around him quieted a notch or two. Kev asked what he'd like and the man said something and Kev disappeared into the kitchen. He stared straight ahead as he waited, and a minute later Kev came back and handed the guy a doggie bag. He took it, dropped some bills on the bar, and went to the door. Before leaving, he turned to slowly scan the room. Then, after a long moment, he left.

"What'd he order?" my dad shouted when the door had swung shut.

"Coupla steaks," Kev replied. "Said he didn't care how they were cooked, so he got 'em ten-seconds-a-side rare. No complaints."

People began to mutter and speculate, the volume of their conversations rising again.

"Raw steak," I said to my father. "You gotta admit, even for an ornithologist that's a little weird."

"Maybe he's a raw foodist," Dad replied.

"Yeah, right. Or maybe he got tired of feasting on the blood of lambs."

Dad rolled his eyes. "The man obviously has a camp stove. He probably just prefers to cook out in the open."

"In the rain? And why are you defending him, anyway? I thought he was your archnemesis."

"I don't expect you to understand," he said, "but it would be nice if you didn't make fun of me." And he stood up to go to the bar.

*   *   *

A few hours later my dad stumbled upstairs, reeking of alcohol, and flopped into his bed. He was asleep instantly, ripping out monster snores. I grabbed a coat and set out to meet Emma, no sneaking necessary.

The streets were deserted and so quiet you could almost hear the dew fall. Clouds stretched thinly across the sky, with just enough moonlight glowing through to light my way. As I crested the ridge, a prickly feeling crept over me, and I looked around to see a man watching me from a distant outcropping. He had his hands raised to his face and his elbows splayed out like he was looking through binoculars. The first thing I thought was *damn it, I'm caught*, assuming it was one of the sheep farmers out on watch, playing detective. But if so, why wasn't he coming over to confront me? Instead he just stood and watched, and I watched back.

Finally I figured *if I'm caught, I'm caught*, because whether I went back now or kept going, one way or another word of my late-night excursion would circle back to my dad. So I raised my arm in a one-fingered salute and descended into the chilly fog.

Coming out of the cairn, it looked like the clouds had been peeled back and the moon pumped up like a big, yellow balloon, so bright I almost had to squint. A few minutes later Emma came wading through the bog, apologizing and talking a mile a minute.

"Sorry I'm late. It took ages for everyone to get to bed! Then on my way out I stumbled over Hugh and Fiona snogging each other's faces off in the garden. But don't worry. They promised not to tell if I didn't."

She threw her arms around my neck. "I missed you," she said. "Sorry about before."

"I am, too," I said, patting her back awkwardly. "So, let's talk."

She pulled away. "Not here. There's a better place. A special place."

"I don't know . . . "

She took my hand. "Don't be that way. You'll adore it, I promise. And when we get there, I'll tell you everything."

I was pretty certain it was a plot to get me to make out with her, and had I been any older or wiser, or one of those guys for whom make-out sessions with hot girls were so frequent as to be of no consequence, I might've had the emotional and hormonal fortitude to demand that we have our talk right then and there. But I was none of those things. Besides, there was the way she beamed at me, smiling with her whole self, and how a coy gesture like tucking her hair back could make me want to follow her, help her, do anything she asked. I was hopelessly outmatched.

I'll go, but I'm not going to kiss her, I told myself. I repeated it like a mantra as she led me across the bog. *Do not kiss! Do not kiss!* We headed for town but veered off toward the rocky beach that looked out onto the lighthouse, picking our way down the steep path to the sand.

Reaching the water's edge, she told me to wait and ran off to retrieve something. I stood watching the lighthouse beam wheel around and wash over everything—a million seabirds sleeping in the pitted cliffs; giant rocks exposed by the low tide; a rotted skiff drowning in the sand. When Emma came back I saw that she had changed into her swimsuit and was holding a pair of snorkel masks.

"Oh no," I said. "No way."

"You might want to strip to your skivvies," she said, looking doubtfully at my jeans and coat. "Your outfit's all wrong for swimming."

"That's because I'm not *going* swimming! I agreed to sneak out and meet you in the middle of the night, fine, but just to *talk*, not to—"

"We *will* talk," she insisted.

"Underwater. In my boxers."

She kicked sand at me and started to walk away but then turned and came back. "I'm not going to attack you, if that's what you're in a knit about. Don't flatter yourself."

"I'm not."

"Then quit mucking about and take off those silly trousers!" And then she did attack me, wrestling me to the ground and struggling to remove my belt with one hand while rubbing sand in my face with the other.

"Blaggh!" I cried, spitting out sand, "dirty fighter, dirty fighter!" I had no choice but to return the favor with a fistful of my own, and pretty soon things devolved into a no-holds-barred sand fight. When it was over we were both laughing and trying in vain to brush it all out of our hair.

"Well, now you need a bath, so you might as well get in the damned water."

"Okay, *fine*."

The water was shockingly cold at first—not a great situation vis-à-vis wearing only boxer shorts—but I got used to the temperature pretty quickly. We waded out past the rocks where, lashed to a depth marker, was a canoe. We clambered into it and Emma handed me an oar and we both started paddling, headed toward the lighthouse. The night was warm and the sea calm, and for a few minutes I lost myself in the pleasant rhythm of oars slapping water. About a hundred yards from the lighthouse, Emma stopped paddling and stepped overboard. To my amazement, she didn't slip under the waves but stood up, submerged only to her knees.

"Are you on a sandbar or something?" I asked.

"Nope." She reached into the canoe, pulled out a little anchor, and dropped it. It fell about three feet before stopping with a metallic *clang*. A moment later the lighthouse beam swept past and I saw the hull of a ship stretching beneath us on all sides.

"A shipwreck!"

"Come on," she said, "we're nearly there. And bring your mask." She started walking across the wrecked boat's hull.

I stepped out gingerly and followed. To anyone watching from shore, it would've looked like we were walking on water.

"How big is this thing, anyway?" I said.

"Massive. It's an allied warship. Hit a friendly mine and sank right here."

She stopped. "Look away from the lighthouse for a minute," she said. "Let your eyes get used to the dark."

So we stood facing the shore and waited as small waves slapped at our thighs. "All right, now follow me and take a giant breath." She walked over to a dark hole in the ship's hull—a door, from the look of it—then sat down on the edge and plunged in.

This is insane, I thought. And then I strapped on the mask she'd given me and plunged in after her.

I peered into the enveloping blackness between my feet to see Emma pulling herself even farther down by the rungs of a ladder. I grabbed the top of it and followed, descending hand over hand until it stopped at a metal floor, where she was waiting. We seemed to be in some sort of cargo hold, though it was too dark to tell much more than that.

I tapped her elbow and pointed to my mouth. *I need to breathe.* She patted my arm condescendingly and reached for a length of plastic tubing that hung nearby; it was connected to a pipe that ran up the ladder to the surface. She put the tube in her mouth and blew, her cheeks puffing out with the effort, then took a breath from it and passed it to me. I sucked in a welcome lungful of air. We were twenty feet underwater, inside an old shipwreck, and we were breathing.

Emma pointed at a doorway in front of us, little more than a black hole in the murk. I shook my head. *Don't want to.* But she took my hand as though I were a frightened toddler and led me toward it, bringing the tube along.

We drifted through the doorway into total darkness. For a while we just hung there, passing the breathing tube between us. There was no sound but our breaths bubbling up and obscure thuds from deep inside the ship, pieces of the broken hull knocking in the current. If I had shut my eyes it wouldn't have been any darker. We were like astronauts floating in a starless universe.

But then a baffling and magnificent thing happened—one by

one, the stars came out, here and there a green flash in the dark. I thought I was hallucinating. But then more lit up, and still more, until a whole constellation surged around us like a million green twinkling stars, lighting our bodies, reflecting in our masks. Emma held out a hand and flicked her wrist, but rather than producing a ball of fire her hand glowed a scintillating blue. The green stars coalesced around it, flashing and whirling, echoing her movements like a school of fish, which, I realized, is just what they were.

Mesmerized, I lost all track of time. We stayed there for what seemed like hours, though it was probably only a few minutes. Then I felt Emma nudge me, and we retreated through the doorway and up the ladder, and when we broke the surface again the first thing I saw was the great bold stripe of the Milky Way painted across the heavens, and it occurred to me that together the fish and the stars formed a complete system, coincident parts of some ancient and mysterious whole.

We pulled ourselves onto the hull and took off our masks. For a while we just sat like that, half-submerged, thighs touching, speechless.

"What were those?" I said finally.

"We call them flashlight fish."

"I've never seen one before."

"Most people never do," she said. "They hide."

"They're beautiful."

"Yes."

"And peculiar."

Emma smiled. "They are that, too." And then her hand crept onto my knee, and I let it stay there because it felt warm and good in the cool water. I listened for the voice in my head telling me not to kiss her, but it had gone silent.

And then we were kissing. The profoundness of our lips touching and our tongues pressing and my hand cupping her perfect white cheek barred any thoughts of right or wrong or any memory of why

I had followed her there in the first place. We were kissing and kissing and then suddenly it was over. As she pulled away I followed her face with mine. She put a hand on my chest, at once gentle and firm. "I need to breathe, dummy."

I laughed. "Okay."

She took my hands and looked at me, and I looked back. It was almost more intense than kissing, the just looking. And then she said, "You should stay."

"Stay," I repeated.

"Here. With us."

The reality of her words filtered through, and the tingly magic of what had just happened between us numbed out.

"I want to, but I don't think I can."

"Why not?"

I considered the idea. The sun, the feasts, the friends . . . and the sameness, the perfect identical days. You can get sick of anything if you have too much of it, like all the petty luxuries my mother bought and quickly grew bored with.

But Emma. There was Emma. Maybe it wasn't so strange, what we could have. Maybe I could stay for a while and love her and then go home. But no. By the time I wanted to leave, it would be too late. She was a siren. I had to be strong.

"It's him you want, not me. I can't be him for you."

She looked away, stung. "That isn't why you should stay. You belong here, Jacob."

"I don't. I'm not like you."

"Yes, you are," she insisted.

"I'm not. I'm common, just like my grandfather."

Emma shook her head. "Is that really what you think?"

"If I could do something spectacular like you, don't you think I would've noticed by now?"

"I'm not meant to tell you this," she said, "but common people can't pass through time loops."

I considered this for a moment, but couldn't make sense of it. "There's nothing peculiar about me. I'm the most average person you'll ever meet."

"I doubt that very much," she replied. "Abe had a rare and peculiar talent, something almost no one else could do."

And then she met my eyes and said, "He could see the monsters."

CHAPTER NINE

He could see the monsters. The moment she said it, all the horrors I thought I'd put behind me came flooding back. They were real. They were real and they'd killed my grandfather.

"I can see them, too," I told her, whispering it like a secret shame.

Her eyes welled and she embraced me. "I knew there was something peculiar about you," she said. "And I mean that as the highest compliment."

I'd always known I was strange. I never dreamed I was peculiar. But if I could see things almost no one else could, it explained why Ricky hadn't seen anything in the woods the night my grandfather was killed. It explained why everyone thought I was crazy. I wasn't crazy or seeing things or having a stress reaction; the panicky twist in my gut whenever they were close—that and the awful sight of them—that was my gift.

"And you can't see them at all?" I asked her.

"Only their shadows, which is why they hunt mainly at night."

"What's stopping them from coming after you right now?" I asked, then corrected myself. "All of us, I mean."

She turned serious. "They don't know where to find us. That and they can't enter loops. So we're safe on the island—but we can't leave."

"But Victor did."

She nodded sadly. "He said he was going mad here. Said he couldn't stand it any longer. Poor Bronwyn. My Abe left, too, but at least he wasn't murdered by hollows."

I forced myself to look at her. "I'm really sorry to have to tell you this . . . "

"What? Oh no."

"They convinced me it was wild animals. But if what you're saying is true, my grandfather was murdered by them, too. The first and only time I saw one was the night he died."

She hugged her knees to her chest and closed her eyes. I slid my arm around her, and she tilted her head against mine.

"I knew they'd get him eventually," she whispered. "He promised me he'd be safe in America. That he could protect himself. But we're never safe—none of us—not really."

We sat talking on the wrecked ship until the moon got low and the water lapped at our throats and Emma began to shiver. Then we linked hands and waded back to the canoe. Paddling toward the beach, we heard voices calling our names, and then we came around a rock and saw Hugh and Fiona waving at us on the shore. Even from a distance, it was clear something was wrong.

We tied the canoe and ran to meet them. Hugh was out of breath, bees darting around him in a state of agitation. "Something's happened! You've got to come back with us!"

There was no time to argue. Emma pulled her clothes over her swimsuit and I tripped into my pants, all gritty with sand. Hugh regarded me uncertainly. "Not him, though," he said. "This is serious."

"No, Hugh," Emma said. "The Bird was right. He's one of us."

He gaped at her, then at me. "You *told* him?!"

"I had to. He'd practically worked it out for himself, anyway."

Hugh seemed taken aback for a moment but then turned and gave me a resolute handshake. "Then welcome to the family."

I didn't know what to say, so I just said, "Thanks."

On the way to the house, we gleaned sketchy bits of information from Hugh about what had happened, but mostly we just ran. When we stopped in the woods to catch our breath, he said, "It's one of the Bird's ymbryne friends. She winged in an hour ago in a terrible state, yelling blue murder and rousing everyone from their beds. Before we could understand what she was getting at she fainted dead off." He wrung his hands, looking miserable. "Oh, I just *know* something wicked's happened."

"I hope you're wrong," said Emma, and we ran on.

*   *   *

In the hall just outside the sitting room's closed door, children in rumpled nightclothes huddled around a kerosene lantern, trading rumors about what might have happened.

"Perhaps they forgot to reset their loop," said Claire.

"Bet you it was hollows," Enoch said. "Bet they ate the lot of 'em too, right down to their boots!"

Claire and Olive wailed and clapped their little hands over their faces. Horace knelt beside them and said in a comforting voice, "There, there. Don't let Enoch fill your heads with rubbish. Everyone knows hollows like young ones best. That's why they let Miss Peregrine's friend go—she tastes like old coffee grounds!"

Olive peeked out from between her fingers. "What do young ones taste like?"

"Lingonberries," he said matter-of-factly. The girls wailed again.

"Leave them alone!" Hugh shouted, and a squadron of bees sent Horace yelping down the hall.

"What's going on out there?" Miss Peregrine called from inside the sitting room. "Is that Mr. Apiston I hear? Where are Miss Bloom and Mr. Portman?"

Emma cringed and shot Hugh a nervous look. "She knows?"

"When she found out you were gone, she just about went off her chump. Thought you'd been abducted by wights or some barminess. Sorry, Em. I had to tell her."

Emma shook her head, but all we could do was go in and face the music. Fiona gave us a little salute—as if to wish us luck—and we opened the doors.

Inside the sitting room, the only light was a hearth fire that threw our quivering shadows against the wall. Bronwyn hovered anxiously around an old woman who was teetering half-conscious in a chair, mummied up in a blanket. Miss Peregrine sat on an ottoman, feeding the woman spoonfuls of dark liquid.

When Emma saw her face, she froze. "Oh my God," she whispered. "It's Miss Avocet."

Only then did I recognize her, though just barely, from the photograph Miss Peregrine had shown me of herself as a young girl. Miss Avocet had seemed so indomitable then, but now she looked frail and weak.

As we stood watching, Miss Peregrine brought a silver flask to Miss Avocet's lips and tipped it, and for a moment the elder ymbryne seemed to revive, sitting forward with brightening eyes. But then her expression dulled again and she sank back into the chair.

"Miss Bruntley," said Miss Peregrine to Bronwyn, "go and make up the fainting couch for Miss Avocet and then fetch a bottle of coca wine and another flask of brandy."

Bronwyn trooped out, nodding solemnly as they passed. Next Miss Peregrine turned to us and said in a low voice, "I am tremendously disappointed in you, Miss Bloom. Tremendously. And of all the nights to sneak away."

"I'm sorry, Miss. But how was I to know something bad would happen?"

"I should punish you. However, given the circumstances, it hardly seems worth the effort." She raised a hand and smoothed her mentor's white hair. "Miss Avocet would never have left her wards to come here unless something dire had taken place."

The roaring fire made beads of sweat break out on my forehead, but in her chair Miss Avocet lay shivering. Would she die? Was the tragic scene that had played out between my grandfather and me about to play out again, this time between Miss Peregrine and her teacher? I pictured it: me holding my grandfather's body, terrified and confused, never suspecting the truth about him or myself. What was happening now, I decided, was nothing like what had happened to me. Miss Peregrine had always known who she was.

It hardly seemed like the time to bring it up, but I was angry and couldn't help myself. "Miss Peregrine?" I began, and she looked up. "When were you going to tell me?"

She was about to ask *what*, but then her eyes went to Emma, and she seemed to read the answer on her face. For a moment she looked mad, but then she saw my anger, and her own faded. "Soon, lad. Please understand. To have laid the entire truth upon you at our first meeting would have been an awful shock. Your behavior was unpredictable. You might've fled, never to return. I could not take that risk."

"So instead you tried to seduce me with food and fun and girls while keeping all the bad things a secret?"

Emma gasped. "*Seduce*? Oh, please, don't think that of me, Jacob. I couldn't bear it."

"I fear you've badly misjudged us," said Miss Peregrine. "As for seducing you, what you've seen is how we live. There has been no deception, only the withholding of a few facts."

"Well here's a fact for you," I said. "One of those creatures killed my grandfather."

Miss Peregrine stared at the fire for a moment. "I am very sorry to hear that."

"I saw one with my own eyes. When I told people about it,

they tried to convince me I was crazy. But I wasn't, and neither was my grandfather. His whole life he'd been telling me the truth, and I didn't believe him." Shame flooded over me. "If I had, maybe he'd still be alive."

Miss Peregrine saw that I was wobbling and offered me the chair across from Miss Avocet.

I sat, and Emma knelt down beside me. "Abe must've known you were peculiar," she said. "And he must've had a good reason for not telling you."

"He did indeed know," replied Miss Peregrine. "He said as much in a letter."

"I don't understand, then. If it was all true—all his stories—and if he knew I was like him, why did he keep it a secret until the last minute of his life?"

Miss Peregrine spoon-fed more brandy to Miss Avocet, who groaned and sat up a little before settling back into the chair. "I can only imagine that he wanted to protect you," she said. "Ours can be a life of trials and deprivations. Abe's life was doubly so because he was born a Jew in the worst of times. He faced a double genocide, of Jews by the Nazis and of peculiars by the hollowgast. He was tormented by the idea that he was hiding here while his people, both Jews and peculiars, were being slaughtered."

"He used to say he'd gone to war to fight monsters," I said.

"He did," said Emma.

"The war ended the Nazis' rule, but the hollowgast emerged stronger than ever," Miss Peregrine continued. "So, like many peculiars, we remained in hiding. But your grandfather returned a changed man. He'd become a warrior, and he was determined to build a life for himself outside the loop. He refused to hide."

"I begged him not to go to America," Emma said. "We all did."

"Why did he choose America?" I asked.

"It had few hollowgast at that time," Miss Peregrine replied.

"After the war there was a minor exodus of peculiars to America. For a while many were able to pass as common, as your grandfather did. It was his fondest wish to be common, to live a common life. He often mentioned it in his letters. I'm sure that's why he kept the truth from you for so long. He wanted for you what he could never have for himself."

"To be ordinary," I said.

Miss Peregrine nodded. "But he could never escape his peculiarity. His unique skill, coupled with the prowess he'd honed during the war as a hunter of hollows, made him too valuable. He was often pressed into service, asked to help eradicate troublesome pockets of hollows. His nature was such that he rarely refused."

I thought about all the long hunting trips Grandpa Portman used to go on. My family had a picture of him taken during one of these, though I don't know who took it or when since he almost always went alone. But when I was a kid I thought it was the funniest thing because, in the picture, he's wearing a suit. Who brings a suit on a hunting trip?

Now I knew: Someone who's hunting more than just animals.

I was moved by this new idea of my grandfather, not as a paranoiac gun nut or a secretive philanderer or a man who wasn't there for his family, but as a wandering knight who risked his life for others, living out of cars and cheap motels, stalking lethal shadows, coming home shy a few bullets and marked with bruises he could never quite explain and nightmares he couldn't talk about. For his many sacrifices, he received only scorn and suspicion from those he loved. I guess that's why he wrote so many letters to Emma and Miss Peregrine. They understood.

Bronwyn returned with a decanter of coca-wine and another flask of brandy. Miss Peregrine sent her away and set about mixing them together in a teacup. Then she began to pat Miss Avocet gently on her blue-veined cheek.

"Esmerelda," she said, "Esmerelda, you must rouse yourself and drink this tonic I've prepared."

Miss Avocet moaned, and Miss Peregrine raised the teacup to her lips. The old woman took a few sips and, though she sputtered and coughed, most of the purplish liquid disappeared down her throat. For a moment she stared as if about to sink back into her stupor, but then she sat forward, face brightening.

"Oh, my," she said, her voice a dry rasp. "Have I fallen asleep? How indecorous of me." She looked at us in mild surprise, as if we'd appeared out of nowhere. "Alma? Is that you?"

Miss Peregrine kneaded the old woman's bony hands. "Esmerelda, you've come a long way to see us in the dead of night. I'm afraid you've got us all terribly worked up."

"Have I?" Miss Avocet squinted and furrowed her brow, and her eyes seemed to fix on the opposite wall, alive with flickering shadows. Then a haunted expression stole across her face. "Yes," she said, "I've come to warn you, Alma. You must be on your guard. You mustn't allow yourselves to be taken by surprise, as I was."

Miss Peregrine stopped kneading. "By what?"

"They could only have been wights. A pair of them came in the night, disguised as council members. There are no male council members, of course, but it fooled my sleep-dazed wards just long enough for the wights to bind them and drag them away."

Miss Peregrine gasped. "Oh, Esmerelda . . . "

"Miss Bunting and I were awoken by their anguished cries," she explained, "but we found ourselves barricaded inside the house. It took some time to force the doors, but when we did and followed the wights' stink out of the loop, there was a gang of shadow-beasts lying in wait on the other side. They fell upon us, howling." She stopped, choking back tears.

"And the children?"

Miss Avocet shook her head. All the light seemed to have gone out of her eyes. "The children were merely bait," she said.

Emma slid her hand into mine and squeezed, and I saw Miss Peregrine's cheeks glisten in the firelight.

"It was Miss Bunting and myself whom they wanted. I was able to escape, but Miss Bunting was not so fortunate."

"She was killed?"

"No—abducted. Just as Miss Wren and Miss Treecreeper were when their loops were invaded a fortnight ago. They're taking ymbrynes, Alma. It's some sort of coordinated effort. For what purpose, I shudder to imagine."

"Then they'll come for us, too," Miss Peregrine said quietly.

"If they can find you," replied Miss Avocet. "You are better hidden than most, but you must be ready, Alma."

Miss Peregrine nodded. Miss Avocet looked helplessly at her hands, trembling in her lap like a broken-winged bird. Her voice began to hitch. "Oh, my dear children. Pray for them. They are all alone now." And she turned away and wept.

Miss Peregrine pulled the blanket around the old woman's shoulders and rose. We followed her out, leaving Miss Avocet to her grief.

We found the children huddled around the sitting-room door. If they hadn't heard everything Miss Avocet had said, they'd heard enough, and it showed on their anxious faces.

"Poor Miss Avocet," Claire whimpered, her bottom lip trembling.

"Poor Miss Avocet's children," said Olive.

"Are they coming for us now, Miss?" asked Horace.

"We'll need weapons!" cried Millard.

"Battle-axes!" said Enoch.

"Bombs!" said Hugh.

"Stop that at once!" Miss Peregrine shouted, raising her hands for quiet. "We must all remain calm. Yes, what happened to Miss Avocet was tragic—profoundly so—but it was a tragedy that need not be repeated here. However, we must be on watch. Henceforth, you will travel beyond the house only with my consent, and then only in pairs. Should you observe a person unknown to you, even if they appear to be peculiar, come immediately and inform me. We'll discuss these and other precautionary measures in the morning. Until then, to bed with you! This is no hour for a meeting."

"But Miss—" Enoch began.

"To bed!"

The children scurried off to their rooms. "As for you, Mr. Portman, I'm not terribly comfortable with you traveling alone. I think perhaps you should stay, at least until things calm a bit."

"I can't just disappear. My dad will flip out."

She frowned. "In that case, you must at least spend the night. I insist upon it."

"I will, but only if you'll tell me everything you know about the creatures that killed my grandfather."

She tilted her head, studying me with something like amusement.

"Very well, Mr. Portman, I won't argue with your need to know. Install yourself on the divan for the evening and we'll discuss it first thing."

"It has to be now." I'd waited ten years to hear the truth, and I couldn't wait another minute. "Please."

"At times, young man, you tread a precariously thin line between being charmingly headstrong and insufferably pigheaded." She turned to Emma. "Miss Bloom, would you fetch my flask of coca-wine? It seems I won't be sleeping tonight, and I shall have to indulge if I am to keep awake."

*   *   *

The study was too close to the children's bedrooms for a late-night talk, so the headmistress and I adjourned to a little greenhouse that edged the woods. We sat on overturned planters among climbing roses, a kerosene lantern on the grass between us, dawn not yet broken beyond the glass walls. Miss Peregrine drew a pipe from her pocket, and bent to light it in the lamp flame. She drew a few thoughtful puffs, sending up wreaths of blue smoke, then began.

"In ancient times people mistook us for gods," she said, "but we peculiars are no less mortal than common folk. Time loops merely delay the inevitable, and the price we pay for using them is hefty—an irrevocable divorce from the ongoing present. As you know, long-term loop dwellers can but dip their toes into the present lest they wither and die. This has been the arrangement since time immemorial."

She took another puff, then continued.

"Some years ago, around the turn of the last century, a splinter faction emerged among our people—a coterie of disaffected peculiars with dangerous ideas. They believed they had discovered a method by which the function of time loops could be perverted to confer upon the user a kind of immortality; not merely the suspension of aging, but the reversal of it. They spoke of eternal youth enjoyed outside the confines of loops, of jumping back and forth from future to past with impunity, suffering none of the ill effects that have always prevented such recklessness—in other words, of mastering time without being mastered by death. The whole notion was mad—absolute bunkum—a refutation of the empirical laws that govern everything!"

She exhaled sharply, then paused for a moment to collect herself.

"In any case. My two brothers, technically brilliant but rather lacking in sense, were taken with the idea. They even had the audacity to request my assistance in making it a reality. You're talking about making yourselves into gods, I said. It can't be done. And even if it can, it shouldn't. But they would not be deterred. Having grown up among Miss Avocet's ymbrynes-in-training, they knew more about our unique art than most peculiar males—just enough, I'm afraid, to be dangerous. Despite warnings, even threats, from the Council, in the summer of 1908 my brothers and several hundred members of this renegade faction—a number of powerful ymbrynes among them, traitors every one—ventured into the Siberian tundra to conduct their hateful experiment. For the site they chose a nameless old loop unused for centuries. We expected them to return within a week, tails between their legs, humbled by the immutable nature of nature. Instead, their comeuppance was far more dramatic: a catastrophic explosion that rattled windows as far as the Azores. Anyone within three hundred miles surely thought it was the end of the world. We assumed they'd all been killed, that obscene world-cracking bang their last collective utterance."

"But they survived," I guessed.

"In a manner of speaking. Others might call the state of being they subsequently assumed a kind of living damnation. Weeks later there began a series of attacks upon peculiars by awful creatures who, apart from their shadows, could not be seen except by peculiars like yourself—our very first clashes with the hollowgast. It was some time before we realized that these tentacle-mawed abominations were in fact our wayward brothers, crawled from the smoking crater left behind by their experiment. Rather than becoming gods, they had transformed themselves into devils."

"What went wrong?"

"That is still a matter of debate. One theory is that they reverse-aged themselves to a time before even their souls had been conceived, which is why we call them *hollowgast*—because their hearts, their souls, are empty. In a cruel twist of irony, they achieved the immortality they'd been seeking. It's believed that the hollows can live thousands of years, but it is a life of constant physical torment, of humiliating debasement—feeding on stray animals, living in isolation—and of insatiable hunger for the flesh of their former kin, because our blood is their only hope for salvation. If a hollow gorges itself on enough peculiars, it becomes a wight."

"That word again," I said. "When we first met, Emma accused me of being one."

"I might have thought the same thing, if I hadn't observed you beforehand."

"What are they?"

"If being a hollow is a living hell—and it most certainly is—then being a wight is akin to purgatory. Wights are almost common. They have no peculiar abilities. But because they can pass for human, they live in servitude to their hollow brethren, acting as scouts and spies and procurers of flesh. It's a hierarchy of the damned that aims someday to turn all hollows into wights and all peculiars into corpses."

"But what's stopping them?" I said. "If they used to be peculiar, don't they know all your hiding places?"

"Fortunately, they don't appear to retain any memory of their former lives. And though wights aren't as strong or as frightening as hollows, they're often just as dangerous. Unlike hollows, they're ruled by more than instinct, and are often able to blend into the general population. It can be difficult to distinguish them from common folk, though there are certain indicators. Their eyes, for instance. Curiously, wights lack pupils."

I broke out in goosebumps, remembering the white-eyed neighbor I'd seen watering his overgrown lawn the night my grandfather was killed. "I think I've seen one. I thought he was just an old blind man."

"Then you are more observant than most," she said. "Wights are adept at passing unnoticed. They tend to adopt personas invisible to society: the gray-suited man on the train; the indigent begging for spare coins; just faces in the crowd. Though some have been known to risk exposure by placing themselves in more prominent positions—physicians, politicians, clergymen—in order to interact with a greater number of people, or to have some measure of power over them, so that they can more easily discover peculiars who might be hiding among common folk—as Abe was."

Miss Peregrine reached for a photo album she'd brought from the house and began to flip through it. "These have been reproduced and distributed to peculiars everywhere, rather like wanted posters. Look here," she said, pointing to a picture of two girls astride a fake reindeer, a chilling blank-eyed Santa Claus peeping out through its antlers. "This wight was discovered working in an American department store at Christmas. He was able to interact with a great many children in a remarkably short time—touching them, interrogating them—screening for signs of peculiarity."

She turned the page to reveal a photo of a sadistic-looking dentist. "This wight worked as an oral surgeon. It wouldn't surprise me to learn that the skull he's posing with belonged to one of his peculiar victims."

She flipped the page again, this time to a picture of a little girl cowering before a looming shadow. "This is Marcie. She left us thirty years ago to live with a common family in the countryside. I pleaded with her to stay, but she was determined. Not long after, she was snatched by a wight as she waited for the school bus. A camera was found at the scene with this undeveloped picture inside."

"Who took it?"

"The wight himself. They are fond of dramatic gestures, and invariably leave behind some taunting memento."

I studied the pictures, a small, familiar dread turning inside me.

When I couldn't bear to look at the pictures anymore, I shut the album.

"I tell you all this because to know it is your birthright," Miss Peregrine said, "but also because I need your help. You are the only one among us who can go outside the loop without arousing suspicion. So long as you're with us, and you insist upon traveling back and forth, I need you to watch for new arrivals to the island and report them to me."

"There was one just the other day," I said, thinking of the birder who had upset my dad.

"Did you see his eyes?" she asked.

"Not really. It was dark, and he was wearing a big hat that hid part of his face."

Miss Peregrine chewed her knuckle, her brow furrowing.

"Why? Do you think he could be one of them?"

"It's impossible to be certain without seeing the eyes," she said, "but the possibility that you were followed to the island concerns me very much."

"What do you mean? By a wight?"

"Perhaps the very one you described seeing on the night of your grandfather's death. It would explain why they chose to spare your life—so that you could lead them to an even richer prize: this place."

"But how could they have known I was peculiar? *I* didn't even know!"

"If they knew about your grandfather, you can be certain they knew about you, as well."

I thought about all the chances they must've had to kill me. All the times I'd felt them nearby in the weeks after Grandpa Portman died. Had they been watching me? Waiting for me to do exactly what I did, and come here?

Feeling overwhelmed, I put my head down on my knees. "I don't suppose you could let me have a sip of that wine," I said.

"Absolutely not."

All of the sudden I felt my chest clench up. "Will I ever be safe anywhere?" I asked her.

Miss Peregrine touched my shoulder. "You're safe here," she said. "And you may live with us as long as you like."

I tried to speak, but all that came out was little stutters. "But I—I can't—my parents."

"They may love you," she whispered, "but they'll never understand."

*　　*　　*

By the time I got back to town, the sun was casting its first long shadows across the streets, all-night drinkers were wheeling around lampposts on their reluctant journeys home, fishermen were trudging soberly to the harbor in great black boots, and my father was just beginning to stir from a heavy sleep. As he rolled out of his bed I was crawling into mine, pulling the covers over my sandy clothes only seconds before he opened the door to check on me.

"Feeling okay?"

I groaned and rolled away from him, and he went out. Late that afternoon I woke to find a sympathetic note and a packet of flu pills on the common room table. I smiled and felt briefly guilty for lying to him. Then I began to worry about him, out there wandering across the headlands with his binoculars and little notebook, possibly in the company of a sheep-murdering madman.

Rubbing the sleep from my eyes and throwing on a rain jacket, I walked a circuit around the village and then around the nearby cliffs and beaches, hoping to see either my father or the strange ornithologist—and get a good look at his eyes—but I didn't find either of them. It was nearing dusk when I finally gave up and returned to the Priest Hole, where I found my father at the bar, tipping back a beer with the regulars. Judging from the empty bottles around him, he'd been there a while.

I sat down next to him and asked if he'd seen the bearded birder. He said he hadn't.

"Well, if you do," I said, "do me a favor and keep your distance, okay?"

He looked at me strangely. "Why?"

"He just rubs me the wrong way. What if he's some nutcase? What if *he's* the one who killed those sheep?"

"Where do you get these bizarre ideas?"

I wanted to tell him. I wanted to explain everything, and for him to tell me he understood and offer some tidbit of parental advice. I wanted, in that moment, for everything to go back to the way it had been before we came here; before I ever found that letter from Miss Peregrine, back when I was just a sort-of-normal messed-up rich kid in the suburbs. Instead, I sat next to my dad for awhile and talked about nothing, and I tried to remember what my life had been like in that unfathomably distant era that was four weeks ago, or imagine what it might be like four weeks from now—but I couldn't. Eventually we ran out of nothing to talk about, and I excused myself and went upstairs to be alone.

CHAPTER TEN

On Tuesday night, most of what I thought I understood about myself had turned out to be wrong. On Sunday morning, my dad and I were supposed to pack our things and go home. I had just a few days to decide what to do. Stay or go—neither option seemed good. How could I possibly stay here and leave behind everything I'd known? But after all I'd learned, how could I go home?

Even worse, there was no one I could talk to about it. Dad was out of the question. Emma made frequent and passionate arguments as to why I should stay, none of which acknowledged the life I would be abandoning (however meager it seemed), or how the sudden inexplicable disappearance of their only child might affect my parents, or the stifling suffocation that Emma herself had admitted feeling inside the loop. She would only say, "With you here, it'll be better."

Miss Peregrine was even less helpful. Her only answer was that she couldn't make such a decision for me, even though I only wanted to talk it through. Still, it was obvious she wanted me to stay; beyond my own safety, my presence in the loop would make everyone else safer. But I didn't relish the idea of spending my life as their watchdog. (I was beginning to suspect my grandfather had felt the same way, and it was part of the reason he'd refused to return after the war.)

Joining the peculiar children would also mean I wouldn't finish high school or go to college or do any of the normal growing-up things people do. Then again, I had to keep reminding myself, I *wasn't* normal; and as long as hollows were hunting me, any life lived outside the loop would almost certainly be cut short. I'd spend the rest of my days living in fear, looking over my shoulder, tormented by nightmares, waiting for them to finally come back and punch my ticket. That sounded a lot worse than missing out on college.

Then I thought: *Isn't there a third option? Couldn't I be like Grandpa Portman, who for fifty years had lived and thrived and fended off hollows outside the loop?* That's when the self-deprecating voice in my head kicked in.

He was military-trained, dummy. A stone-cold badass. He had a walk-in closet full of sawed-off shotguns. The man was Rambo compared to you.

I could sign up for a class at the gun range, the optimistic part of me would think. *Take Karate. Work out.*

Are you joking? You couldn't even protect yourself in high school! You had to bribe that redneck to be your bodyguard. And you'd wet your pants if you so much as pointed a real gun at anyone.

No, I wouldn't.

You're weak. You're a loser. That's why he never told you who you really were. He knew you couldn't handle it.

Shut up. Shut up.

For days I went back and forth like this. Stay or go. I obsessed constantly without resolution. Meanwhile, Dad completely lost steam on his book. The less he worked, the more discouraged he got, and the more discouraged he got, the more time he spent in the bar. I'd never seen him drink that way—six, seven beers a night—and I didn't want to be around him when he was like that. He was dark, and when he wasn't sulking in silence he would tell me things I really didn't want to know.

"One of these days your mother's gonna leave me," he said one night. "If I don't make something happen pretty soon, I really think she might."

I started avoiding him. I'm not sure he even noticed. It became depressingly easy to lie about my comings and goings.

Meanwhile, at the home for peculiar children, Miss Peregrine instituted a near-lockdown. It was like martial law had been declared: The smaller kids couldn't go anywhere without an escort, the older ones traveled in pairs, and Miss Peregrine had to know where everyone was at all times. Just getting permission to go outside was an ordeal.

Sentries were drafted into rotating shifts to watch the front and rear of the house. At all times of the day and most of the night you could see bored faces peeping out of windows. If they spotted someone approaching, they yanked a pull-chain that rang a bell in Miss Peregrine's room, which meant that whenever I arrived she'd be waiting inside the door to interrogate me. What was happening outside the loop? Had I seen anything strange? Was I sure I hadn't been followed?

Not surprisingly, the kids began to go a little nuts. The little ones got rambunctious while the older ones moped, complaining about the new rules in voices just loud enough to be overheard. Dramatic sighs erupted out of thin air, often the only cue that Millard had wandered into a room. Hugh's insects swarmed and stung people until they were banished from the house, after which Hugh spent all his time at the window, his bees screening the other side of the glass.

Olive, claiming she had misplaced her leaden shoes, took to crawling around the ceiling like a fly, dropping grains of rice on people's heads until they looked up and noticed her, at which point she'd burst into laughter so all-consuming that her levitation would falter and she'd have to grab onto a chandelier or curtain rod just to keep from falling. Strangest of all was Enoch, who disappeared into his basement laboratory to perform experimental surgeries on his clay soldiers that would've made Dr. Frankenstein cringe: amputating the limbs from two to make a hideous spider-man of a third, or cramming four chicken hearts into a single chest cavity in an attempt to create a super-clay-man who would never run out of energy. One by one their little gray bodies failed under the strain, and the basement came to resemble a Civil War field hospital.

For her part, Miss Peregrine remained in a constant state of motion, chain-smoking pipes while limping from room to room to check on the children, as if they might disappear the moment they left her sight. Miss Avocet stayed on, emerging from her torpor now and then to wander the halls, calling out forlornly for her poor abandoned wards before slumping into someone's arms to be taken back to bed. There followed a great deal of paranoid speculation about Miss Avocet's tragic ordeal and why hollows would want to kidnap ymbrynes, with theories ranging from the bizarre (to create the biggest time loop in history, large enough to swallow the whole planet) to the ridiculously optimistic (to keep the hollows company; being a horrible soul-eating monster can get pretty lonely).

Eventually, a morbid quiet settled over the house. Two days of confinement had made everyone lethargic. Believing that routine was the best defense against depression, Miss Peregrine tried to keep everyone interested in her daily lessons, in preparing the daily meals, and in keeping the house spic and span. But whenever they weren't under direct orders to do something, the children sank heavily into chairs, stared listlessly out locked windows, paged through dog-eared books they'd read a hundred times before, or slept.

I'd never seen Horace's peculiar talent in action until, one evening, he began to scream. A bunch of us rushed upstairs to the garret where he'd been on sentry duty to find him rigid in a chair, in the grips of what seemed to be a waking nightmare, clawing at the air in horror. At first his screaming was just that, but then he began to babble, yelling about the seas boiling and ash raining from the sky and an endless blanket of smoke smothering the earth. After a few minutes of these apocalyptic pronouncements, he seemed to wear himself out and fell into an uneasy sleep.

The others had seen this happen before—often enough that there were photos of his episodes in Miss Peregrine's album—and they knew what to do. Under the headmistress's direction, they carried him by the arms and legs to bed, and when he woke a few hours later he claimed he couldn't remember the dream and that dreams he couldn't remember rarely came true. The others accepted this because they already had too much else to worry about. I sensed he was holding something back.

When someone goes missing in a town as small as Cairnholm, it doesn't go unnoticed. That's why on Wednesday, when Martin failed to open his museum or stop by the Priest Hole for his customary nightcap, people began to wonder if he was sick, and when Kev's wife went to check on him and found his front door hanging open and his wallet and glasses on the kitchen counter but no one at home, people began to wonder if he was dead. When he still hadn't turned up the next day, a gang of men was dispatched to open sheds and peer beneath overturned boats, searching anywhere a wifeless man who loved whiskey might sleep off a binge. But they'd only just begun when a call came in over the short-band radio: Martin's body had been fished out of the ocean.

I was in the pub with my dad when the fisherman who'd found him came in. It was hardly past noon but he was issued a beer on principle, and within minutes the man was telling his story.

"I was up Gannet's Point reelin' in my nets," he began. "They was heavy as anything, which was odd since all's I generally catch out thataways is just tidy little nothins, shrimps and such. Thought I'd got snagged on a crab trap, so I grab for the gaff and poke around under the boat till it hooks on something." We all scooted closer on our stools, like it was story-time in some morbid kindergarten. "It was Martin all right. Looked like he'd taken a quick trip down a cliffside and got nibbled by sharks. Lord knows what business he had bein' out by them cliffs in the dead of night in just his robe and trolleys."

"He weren't dressed?" Kev asked.

"Dressed for bed, maybe," said the fisherman. "Not for a walk in the wet."

Brief prayers were muttered for Martin's soul, and then people began trading theories. Within minutes the place was a smoke-filled den of tipsy Sherlock Holmeses.

"He coulda been drunk," one man ventured.

"Or if he was out by the cliffs, maybe he seen the sheep killer and was chasin' after," said another.

"What about that squirrely new fella?" the fisherman said. "The one who's camping."

My father straightened on his barstool. "I ran into him," he said. "Two nights ago."

I turned to him in surprise. "You didn't tell me."

"I was going to the chemist, trying to catch him before he closed, and this guy's headed the other way, out of town. In a huge hurry. I bump his shoulder as he passes, just to ruffle him. He stops and stares at me. Trying to be intimidating. I get in his face, tell him I want to know what he's doing here, what he's working on. Because people here talk about themselves, I say."

Kev leaned across the bar. "And?"

"He looks like he's about to take a swing at me, but then just walks off."

A lot of the men had questions—what an ornithologist does, why the guy was camping, and other things I already knew. I had only one question, which I'd been itching to ask. "Did you notice anything strange about him? About his face?"

My father thought for a second. "Yeah, actually. He had on sunglasses."

"At *night*?"

"Weirdest damn thing."

A sick feeling came over me, and I wondered how close my father had come to something far worse than a fistfight. I knew I had to tell Miss Peregrine about this—and soon.

"Ah, bollocks," said Kev. "There ain't been a murder on Cairnholm in a hundred years. Why would anyone want to kill old Martin, anyway? It don't make sense. I'll bet you all a round that when his autopsy comes back, it says he was arseholed right into the next century."

"Could be a tidy spell before that happens," the fisherman said.

"Storm that's rollin' in now, weatherman says it's gonna be a right bomper. Worst we've had all year."

"Weatherman says," Kev scoffed. "I wouldn't trust that silly bugger to know if it's raining *now*."

* * *

The islanders often made gloomy predictions about what Mother Nature had in store for Cairnholm—they were at the mercy of the elements, after all, and pessimistic by default—but this time their worst fears were confirmed. The wind and rain that had pelted the island all week strengthened that night into a vicious band of storms that closed blackly over the sky and whipped the sea into foam. Between rumors about Martin having been murdered and the weather, the town went into lockdown much as the children's home had. People stayed in their houses. Windows were shuttered and doors bolted tight. Boats clattered against their moorings in the heavy chop but none left the harbor; to take one out in such a gale would've been suicidal. And because the mainland police couldn't collect Martin's body until the seas calmed, the townspeople were left with the nettlesome question of what to do with his body. It was finally decided that the fishmonger, who had the island's largest stockpile of ice, would keep him cool in the back of his shop, among salmon and cod and other things. Which, like Martin, had been pulled from the sea.

I was under strict instructions from my father not to leave the Priest Hole, but I was also under instructions to report any strange goings-on to Miss Peregrine—and if a suspicious death didn't qualify, nothing did. So that night I feigned a flulike illness and locked myself in my room, then slipped out the window and climbed down a drainpipe to the ground. No one else was foolish enough to be outside, so I ran straight down the main path without fear of being spotted, the hood of my jacket scrunched tight against the whipping rain.

When I got to the children's home, Miss Peregrine took one look at me and knew something was wrong. "What's happened?" she said, her bloodshot eyes ranging over me.

I told her everything, all the sketchy facts and rumors I'd overheard, and she blanched. She hurried me into the sitting room, where in a panic she gathered all the kids she could find and then stomped off to find a few who had ignored her shouts. The rest were left to stand around, anxious and confused.

Emma and Millard cornered me. "What's she in such a tiff about?" Millard asked.

I quietly told them about Martin. Millard sucked in his breath and Emma crossed her arms, looking worried.

"Is it really that bad?" I said. "I mean, it can't have been hollows. They only hunt peculiars, right?"

Emma groaned. "Do you want to tell him, or shall I?"

"Hollows vastly prefer peculiars over common folk," Millard explained, "but they'll eat just about anything to sustain themselves, so long as it's fresh and meaty."

"It's one of the ways you know there might be a hollow hanging about," said Emma. "The bodies pile up. That's why they're mostly nomads. If they didn't move from place to place so often, they'd be simple to track down."

"How often?" I asked, a shiver tracing my spine. "Do they need to eat, I mean?"

"Oh, pretty often," said Millard. "Arranging the hollows' meals is what wights spend most of their time doing. They look for peculiars when they can, but a gobsmacking portion of their energy and effort is spent tracking down common victims for the hollows, animal and human, and then hiding the mess." His tone was academic, as if discussing the breeding patterns of a mildly interesting species of rodent.

"But don't the wights get caught?" I said. "I mean, if they're helping *murder* people, you'd think—"

"Some do," Emma said. "Wager you've heard of a few, if you follow the news. There was one fellow, they found him with human heads in the icebox and gibletty goodies in a stock pot over a low boil, like he was making Christmas dinner. In your time this wouldn't have been so very long ago."

I remembered—vaguely—a sensationalized late-night TV special about a cannibalistic serial killer from Milwaukee who'd been apprehended in similarly gruesome circumstances.

"You mean . . . Jeffrey Dahmer?"

"I believe that was the gentleman's name, yes," said Millard. "Fascinating case. Seems he never lost his taste for the fresh stuff, though he'd not been a hollow for many years."

"I thought you guys weren't supposed to know about the future," I said.

Emma flashed a canny smile. "The bird only keeps *good* things about the future to herself, but you can bet we hear all the brown-trouser bits."

Then Miss Peregrine returned, pulling Enoch and Horace behind her by their shirtsleeves. Everyone came to attention.

"We've just had word of a new threat," she announced, giving me an appreciative nod. "A man outside our loop has died under suspicious circumstances. We can't be certain of the cause or whether it represents a true threat to our security, but we must conduct ourselves as if it did. Until further notice, no one may leave the house, not even to collect vegetables or bring in a goose for the evening meal."

A collective groan arose, over which Miss Peregrine raised her voice. "This has been a challenging few days for us all. I beg your continued patience."

Hands shot up around the room, but she rebuffed all questions and marched off to secure the doors. I ran after her in a panic. If there really was something dangerous on the island, it might kill me the minute I set foot outside the loop. But if I stayed here, I'd be leaving my father defenseless, not to mention worried sick about me. Somehow, that seemed even worse.

"I need to go," I said, catching up to Miss Peregrine.

She pulled me into an empty room and closed the door. "You will keep your voice down," she commanded, "and you will respect my rules. What I said applies to you as well. No one leaves this house."

"But—"

"Thus far I have allowed you an unprecedented measure of autonomy to come and go as you please, out of respect for your unique position. But you may have already been followed here, and that puts my wards' lives in jeopardy. I will not permit you to endanger them—or yourself—any further."

"Don't you understand?" I said angrily. "Boats aren't running. Those people in town are stuck. My *father* is stuck. If there really is a wight, and it's who I think it is, he and my dad have almost gotten into one fight already. If he just fed a total stranger to a hollow, who do you think he's going after next?"

Her face was like stone. "The welfare of the townspeople is none of my concern," she said. "I won't endanger my wards. Not for anyone."

"It isn't just townspeople. It's my *father.* Do you really think a couple of locked doors will stop me from going?"

"Perhaps not. But if you insist on leaving here, then I insist you never return."

I was so shocked I had to laugh. "But you *need* me," I said.

"Yes, we do," she replied. "We do very much."

*　　*　　*

I stormed upstairs to Emma's room. Inside was a tableau of frustration that might've been straight out of Norman Rockwell, if

Norman Rockwell had painted people doing hard time in jail. Bronwyn stared woodenly out the window. Enoch sat on the floor, whittling a piece of hard clay. Emma was perched on the edge of her bed, elbows on knees, tearing sheets of paper from a notebook and igniting them between her fingers.

"You're back!" she said when I came in.

"I never left," I replied. "Miss Peregrine wouldn't let me." Everyone listened as I explained my dilemma. "I'm banished if I try to leave."

Emma's entire notebook ignited. "She can't do that!" she cried, oblivious to the flames licking her hand.

"She can do what she likes," said Bronwyn. "She's the Bird."

Emma threw down her book and stamped out the fire.

"I just came to tell you I'm going, whether she wants me to or not. I won't be held prisoner, and I won't bury my head in the sand while my own father might be in real danger."

"Then I'm coming with you," Emma said.

"You ain't serious," replied Bronwyn.

"I am."

"What you are is three-quarters stupid," said Enoch. "You'll turn into a wrinkled old prune, and for what? Him?"

"I won't," said Emma. "You've got to be out of the loop for hours and hours before time starts to catch up with you, and it won't take nearly that long, will it, Jacob?"

"It's a bad idea," I said.

"*What's* a bad idea?" said Enoch. "She don't even know what she's risking her life to do."

"Headmistress won't like it," said Bronwyn, stating the obvious. "She'll *kill* us, Em."

Emma stood up and shut the door. "*She* won't kill us," she said, "those *things* will. And if they don't, living like this might just be worse than dying. The Bird's got us cooped up so tight we can hardly breathe, and all because she doesn't have the spleen to face whatever's out there!"

"Or not out there," said Millard, who I hadn't realized was in the room with us.

"But she won't like it," Bronwyn repeated.

Emma took a combative step toward her friend. "How long can you hide under the hem of that woman's skirt?"

"Have you already forgotten what happened to Miss Avocet?" said Millard. "It was only when her wards left the loop that they were killed and Miss Bunting kidnapped. If they'd only stayed put, nothing bad would've happened."

"Nothing bad?" Emma said dubiously. "Yes, it's true that hollows can't go through loops. But wights can, which is just how those kids were tricked into leaving. Should we sit on our bums and wait for them to come through our front door? What if rather than clever disguises, this time they bring guns?"

"That's what I'd do," Enoch said. "Wait till everyone's asleep and then slide down the chimney like Santa Claus and BLAM!" He fired an imaginary pistol at Emma's pillow. "Brains on the wall."

"Thank you for that," Millard said, sighing.

"We've got to hit them before they know we know they're there," said Emma, "while we've still got the element of surprise."

"But we *don't* know they're there!" said Millard.

"We'll find out."

"And how do you propose to do that? Wander around until you see a hollow? What then? 'Excuse me, we were wondering what your intentions might be, vis à vis eating us.'"

"We've got Jacob," said Bronwyn. "He can see them."

I felt my throat tighten, aware that if this hunting party formed, I would be in some way responsible for everyone's safety.

"I've only ever seen *one*," I warned them. "So I wouldn't exactly call myself an expert."

"And if he shouldn't happen to see one?" said Millard. "It could either mean that there are none to be seen or that they're hiding. You'd still be clueless, as you so clearly are now."

Furrowed brows all around. Millard had a point.

"Well, it appears that logic has prevailed yet again," he said. "I'm off to fetch some porridge for supper, if any of you would-be mutineers would like to join me."

The bedsprings creaked as he got up and moved toward the door. But before he could leave, Enoch leapt to his feet and cried, "I've got it!"

Millard stopped. "Got what?"

Enoch turned to me. "The bloke who may or may not have been eaten by a hollow—do you know where they're keeping him?"

"At the fishmonger's."

He rubbed his hands together. "Then I know how we can be sure."

"And how's that?" said Millard.

"We'll ask him."

*   *   *

An expeditionary team was assembled. Joining me would be Emma, who flatly refused to let me go alone, Bronwyn, who was loath to anger Miss Peregrine but insisted that we needed her protection, and Enoch, whose plan we were to carry out. Millard, whose invisibility might have come in handy, would have no part of it, and he had to be bribed just to keep from ratting us out.

"If we all go," Emma reasoned, "the Bird won't be able to banish Jacob. She'll have to banish all four of us."

"But I don't want to be banished!" said Bronwyn.

"She'd never do it, Wyn. That's the point. And if we can make it back before lights-out, she may not even realize we were gone."

I had my doubts about that, but we all agreed it was worth a shot.

It went down like a jailbreak. After dinner, when the house was at its most chaotic and Miss Peregrine at her most distracted, Emma pretended to head for the sitting room and I for the study. We met a few minutes later at the end of the upstairs hallway, where a rectangle of ceiling pulled down to reveal a ladder. Emma climbed it and I followed, pulling it closed after us, and we found ourselves in a tiny, dark attic space. At one end was a vent, easily unscrewed, that led out onto a flat section of roof.

We stepped into the night air to find the others already waiting. Bronwyn gave us each a crushing hug and handed out black rain slickers she'd snagged, which I'd suggested we wear to provide some measure of protection from the storm raging outside the loop. I was about to ask how we were planning to reach the ground when I saw Olive float into view past the edge of the roof.

"Who's keen for a game of parachute?" she said, smiling broadly. She was barefoot and wore a rope knotted around her waist. Curious what she was attached to, I peeked over the roof to see Fiona, rope in hand, hanging out a window and waving up at me. Apparently, we had accomplices.

"You first," Enoch barked.

"Me?" I said, backing nervously away from the edge.

"Grab hold of Olive and jump," Emma said.

"I don't remember this plan involving me shattering my pelvis."

"You won't, dummy, if you just hang on to Olive. It's great fun. We've done it loads of times." She thought for a moment, "Well, one time."

There seemed to be no alternative, so I steeled myself and approached the roof's edge. "Don't be frightened!" Olive said.

"Easy for you to say," I replied. "You can't fall."

She reached out her arms and bear-hugged me and I hugged her back, and she whispered, "Okay, go." I closed my eyes and stepped into the void. Instead of the drop I'd feared, we drifted slowly to the ground like a balloon leaking helium.

"That was fun," Olive said. "Now let go!"

I did, and she went rocketing back up to the roof, saying "*Wheeeee!*" all the way. The others shushed her and then, one after another, they hugged her and floated down to join me. When we were all together we began sneaking toward the moon-capped woods, Fiona and Olive waving behind us. Maybe it was my imagination, but the breeze-blown topiary creatures seemed to wave at us, too, with Adam nodding a somber farewell.

* * *

When we stopped at the bog's edge to catch our breath, Enoch reached into his bulging coat and handed out packages wrapped in cheesecloth. "Take these," he said. "I ain't carryin' em all."

"What are they?" asked Bronwyn, undoing the cloth to reveal a hunk of brownish meat with little tubes shunting out of it. "Ugh, it *stinks*!" she cried, holding it away from her.

"Calm down, it's only a sheep heart," he said, thrusting something of roughly the same dimensions into my hands. It stank of formaldehyde and, even through the cloth, felt unpleasantly moist.

"I'll chuck my guts if I have to carry this," Bronwyn said.

"I'd like to see that," Enoch grumbled, sounding offended. "Stash it in your slicker and let's get on with it."

We followed the hidden ribbon of solid ground through the bog. I'd been over it so many times now, I'd almost forgotten how dangerous it could be, how many lives it had swallowed over the centuries. Stepping onto the cairn mound, I told everyone to button up their coats.

"What if we see someone?" asked Enoch.

"Just act normal," I said. "I'll tell them you're my friends from

America."

"What if we see a wight?" asked Bronwyn.

"Run."

"And if Jacob sees a hollow?"

"In that case," Emma said, "run like the devil's after you."

One by one we ducked into the cairn, disappearing from that calm summer night. All was quiet until we reached the end chamber, and then the air pressure dropped and the temperature fell and the storm screamed into full-throated being. We spun toward the sound, rattled, and for a moment just stood listening as it seethed and howled at the mouth of the tunnel. It sounded like a caged animal that had just been shown its dinner. There was nothing to do but offer ourselves up to it.

We fell to our knees and crawled into what seemed like a black hole, the stars lost behind a mountain of thunderheads, whipping rain and freezing wind rifling through our coats, wires of lightning bleaching us bone white and making the dark that followed seem darker still. Emma tried to make a flame but she looked like a broken cigarette lighter, every sparking flick of her wrist hissing out before it could catch, so we shrugged up our coats and ran bent against the gale and the swollen bog that sucked at our legs, navigating as much by memory as by sight.

In the town, rain drummed on every door and window, but everyone stayed locked and shuttered inside their cottages as we ran unnoticed through the flooding streets, past scattered roof tiles torn away by the wind, past a single rain-blinded sheep lost and crying, past a tipped outhouse disgorging itself into the road, to the fishmonger's shop. The door was locked, but with two thudding kicks Bronwyn flung it in. Drying her hand inside her coat, Emma was finally able to make a flame. As wide-eyed sturgeon stared from glass cases, I led us into the shop, around the counter where Dylan spent his days mumbling curses and scaling fish, through a rust-pocked door.

On the other side was a little icehouse, just a lean-to shed floored with dirt and roofed with tin, its walls made from rough-cut planks, rain weeping through where they had shivered apart like bad teeth. Crowding the room were a dozen rectangular troughs raised on saw-horses and filled with ice.

"Which one's he in?" Enoch asked.

"I don't know," I said.

Emma shone her flame around as we walked among the troughs, trying to guess which might hold more than just the corpses of fish—but they all looked the same, just lidless coffins of ice. We would have to search every one until we found him.

"Not me," Bronwyn said, "I don't want to see him. I don't like dead things."

"Neither do I, but we have to," said Emma. "We're all in this together."

Each of us chose a trough and dug into it like a dog excavating a prized bed of flowers, our cupped hands scooping mounds of ice onto the floor. I'd emptied half of one and was losing feeling in my fingers when I heard Bronwyn shriek. I turned to see her stumble away from a trough, her hands across her mouth.

We crowded around to see what she'd uncovered. Jutting from the ice was a frozen, hairy-knuckled hand. "I daresay you found our man," Enoch said, and through split fingers the rest of us watched as he scraped away more ice, slowly revealing an arm, then a torso, and finally Martin's entire wrecked body.

It was an awful sight. His limbs were twisted in improbable di-rections. His trunk had been scissored open and emptied out, ice fill-ing the cavity where his vitals had been. When his face appeared, there was a collective intake of breath. Half was a purple contusion that hung in strips like a shredded mask. The other was just undam-aged enough to recognize him by: a jaw stippled with beard, a jig-sawed section of cheek and brow, and one green eye, filmed over and gazing emptily. He wore only boxers and ragged scraps of a terrycloth robe. There was no way he'd walked by himself out to the cliffs at night dressed like that. Someone—or something—had dragged him there.

"He's pretty far gone," said Enoch, appraising Martin as a surgeon might assess an all-but-hopeless patient. "I'm telling you now, this might not work."

"We got to try," Bronwyn said, stepping bravely to the trough with the rest of us. "We come all this way, we at least got to try."

Enoch opened his slicker and pulled one of the wrapped hearts from an interior pocket. It looked like a maroon catcher's mitt folded in on itself. "If he wakes up," Enoch said, "he ain't gonna be happy. So just stand back and don't say I didn't warn you."

All of us took a generous step back except Enoch, who bellied up to the trough and plunged his arm into the ice that filled Martin's chest, swirling it around like he was fishing for a can of soda in a cooler. After a moment he seemed to latch onto something, and with his other hand he raised the sheep heart above his head.

A sudden convulsion passed through Enoch's body and the sheep heart started to beat, spraying out a fine mist of bloody pickling solution. Enoch took fast, shallow breaths. He seemed to be channeling something. I studied Martin's body for any hint of movement, but he lay still.

Gradually the heart in Enoch's hand began to slow and shrink, its color fading to a blackish gray, like meat left too long in the freezer. Enoch threw it on the ground and thrust his empty hand at me. I pulled out the heart I'd been keeping in my pocket and gave it to him. He repeated the same process, the heart pumping and sputtering for a while before faltering like the last one. Then he did it a third time, using the heart he'd given to Emma.

Bronwyn's heart was the only one left—Enoch's last chance. His face took on a new intensity as he raised it above Martin's rude coffin, squeezing it like he meant to drive his fingers through. As the heart began to shake and tremble like an overcranked motor, Enoch shouted, "Rise up, dead man. Rise up!"

I saw a flicker of movement. Something had shifted beneath the ice. I leaned as close as I could stand to, watching for any sign of life. For a long moment there was nothing, but then the body wrenched as suddenly and forcefully as if it had been shocked with a thousand volts. Emma screamed, and we all jumped back. When I lowered my arms to look again, Martin's head had turned in my direction, one cataract eye wheeling crazily before fixing, it seemed, on me.

"He sees you!" Enoch cried.

I leaned in. The dead man smelled of turned earth and brine and something worse. Ice fell away from his hand, which rose up to tremble in the air for a moment, afflicted and blue, before coming to rest on my arm. I fought the urge to throw it off.

His lips fell apart and his jaw hinged open. I bent down to hear him, but there was nothing to hear. *Of course there isn't*, I thought, *his lungs have burst*—but then a tiny sound leaked out, and I leaned closer, my ear almost to his freezing lips. I thought, strangely, of the rain gutter by my house, where if you put your head to the bars and wait for a break in traffic, you can just make out the whisper of an underground stream, buried when the town was first built but still flowing, imprisoned in a permanent night.

The others crowded around, but I was the only one who could hear the dead man. The first thing he said was my name.

"Jacob."

Fear shot through me. "Yes."

"I was dead." The words came slowly, dripping like molasses. He corrected himself. "Am dead."

"Tell me what happened," I said. "Can you remember?"

There was a pause. The wind whistled through the gaps in the walls. He said something and I missed it.

"Say it again. Please, Martin."

"He killed me," the dead man whispered.

"Who."

"My old man."

"You mean Oggie? Your uncle?"

"My old man," he said again. "He got big. And strong, so strong."

"Who did, Martin?"

His eye closed, and I feared he was gone for good. I looked at Enoch. He nodded. The heart in his hand was still beating.

Martin's eye flicked beneath its lid. He began to speak again, slowly but evenly, as if reciting something. "For a hundred generations he slept, curled like a fetus in the earth's mysterious womb, digested by roots, fermenting in the dark, summer fruits canned and forgotten in the larder until a farmer's spade bore him out, rough midwife to a strange harvest."

Martin paused, his lips trembling, and in the brief silence Emma looked at me and whispered, "What's he saying?"

"I don't know," I said. "But it sounds like a poem."

He continued, his voice wavering but loud enough now that everyone could hear—"Blackly he reposes, tender face the color of soot, withered limbs like veins of coal, feet lumps of driftwood hung with shriveled grapes"—and finally I recognized the poem. It was the one he'd written about the bog boy.

"Oh Jacob, I took such good careful care of him!" he said. "Dusted the glass and changed the soil and made him a home—like my own big bruised baby. I took such careful care, but—" He began to shake, and a tear ran down his cheek and froze there. "But he killed me."

"Do you mean the bog boy? The Old Man?"

"Send me back," he pleaded. "It hurts." His cold hand kneaded my shoulder, his voice fading again.

I looked to Enoch for help. He tightened his grip on the heart and shook his head. "Quick now, mate," he said.

Then I realized something. Though he was describing the bog boy, it wasn't the bog boy who had killed him. *They only become visible to the rest of us when they're eating*, Miss Peregrine had told me, *which is to say, when it's too late*. Martin had seen a hollowgast—at night, in the rain, as it was tearing him to shreds—and had mistaken it for his most prized exhibit.

The old fear began to pump, coating my insides with heat. I turned to the others. "A hollowgast did this to him," I said. "It's somewhere on the island."

"Ask him where," said Enoch.

"Martin, where. I need to know where you saw it."

"Please. It hurts."

"Where did you see it?"

"He came to my door."

"The old man did?"

His breath hitched strangely. He was hard to look at but I made myself do it, following his eye as it shifted and focused on something behind me.

"No," he said. "*He* did."

And then a light swept over us and a loud voice barked, *"Who's there!"*

Emma closed her hand and the flame hissed out, and we all spun to see a man standing in the doorway, holding a flashlight in one hand and a pistol in the other.

Enoch yanked his arm out of the ice while Emma and Bronwyn closed ranks around the trough to block Martin from view. "We didn't mean to break in," Bronwyn said. "We was just leaving, honest!"

"Stay where you are!" the man shouted. His voice was flat, accentless. I couldn't see his face through the beam of light, but the layered jackets he wore were an instant giveaway. It was the ornithologist.

"Mister, we ain't had nothing to eat all day," Enoch whined, for once sounding like a twelve-year-old. "All we come for was a fish or two, swear!"

"Is that so?" said the man. "Looks like you've picked one out. Let's see what kind." He waved his flashlight back and forth as if to part us with the beam. "Step aside!"

We did, and he swept the light over Martin's body, a landscape of garish ruin. "Goodness, that's an odd-looking fish, isn't it?" he said, entirely unfazed. "Must be a fresh one. He's still moving!" The beam came to rest on Martin's face. His eye rolled back and his lips moved soundlessly, just a reflex as the life Enoch had given him drained away.

"Who are you?" Bronwyn demanded.

"That depends on whom you ask," the man replied, "and it isn't nearly as important as the fact that I know who *you* are." He pointed the flashlight at each of us and spoke as if quoting some secret dossier. "Emma Bloom, a spark, abandoned at a circus when her parents couldn't sell her to one. Bronwyn Bruntley, berserker, taster of blood, didn't know her own strength until the night she snapped her rotten stepfather's neck. Enoch O'Connor, dead-riser, born to a family of undertakers who couldn't understand why their clients kept walking away." I saw each of them shrink away from him. Then he shone the light at me. "And Jacob. Such peculiar company you're keeping these days."

"How do you know my name?"

He cleared his throat, and when he spoke again his voice had changed radically. "Did you forget me so quick?" he said in a New England accent. "But then I'm just a poor old bus driver, guess you wouldn't remember."

It seemed impossible, but somehow this man was doing a dead-on impression of my middle school bus driver, Mr. Barron. A man so despised, so foul tempered, so robotically inflexible that on the last day of eighth grade we defaced his yearbook picture with staples and left it like an effigy behind his seat. I was just remembering what he used to say as I got off the bus every afternoon when the man before me sang it out:

"End of the line, Portman!"

"Mr. Barron?" I asked doubtfully, struggling to see his face through the flashlight beam.

The man laughed and cleared his throat, his accent changing again. "Either him or the yard man," he said in a deep Florida drawl. "Yon trees need a haircut. Give yah good price!" It was the pitch-perfect voice of the man who for years had maintained my family's lawn and cleaned our pool.

"How are you doing that?" I said. "How do you know those people?"

"Because I *am* those people," he said, his accent flat again. He laughed, relishing my baffled horror.

Something occurred to me. Had I ever seen Mr. Barron's eyes? Not really. He was always wearing these giant, old-man sunglasses that wrapped around his face. The yard man wore sunglasses, too, and a wide-brimmed hat. Had I ever given either of them a hard look? How many other roles in my life had this chameleon played?

"What's happening?" Emma said. "Who is this man?"

"Shut up!" he snapped. "You'll get your turn."

"You've been watching me," I said. "You killed those sheep. You killed Martin."

"Who, me?" he said innocently. "*I* didn't kill anyone."

"But you're a wight, aren't you?"

"That's *their* word," he said.

I couldn't understand it. I hadn't seen the yard man since my mother replaced him three years ago, and Mr. Barron had vanished from my life after eighth grade. Had they—he—really been following me?

"How'd you know where to find me?"

"Why, Jacob," he said, his voice changing yet again, "you told me yourself. In confidence, of course." It was a middle-American accent now, soft and educated. He tipped the flashlight up so that its glow spilled onto his face.

The beard I'd seen him wearing the other day was gone. Now there was no mistaking him.

"Dr. Golan," I said, my voice a whisper swallowed by the drumming rain.

I thought back to our telephone conversation a few days ago. The noise in the background—he'd said he was at the airport. But he wasn't picking up his sister. He was coming after me.

I backed against Martin's trough, reeling, numbness spreading through me. "The neighbor," I said. "The old man watering his lawn the night my grandfather died. That was you, too."

He smiled.

"But your eyes," I said.

"Contact lenses," he replied. He popped one out with his thumb, revealing a blank orb. "Amazing what they can fabricate these days. And if I may anticipate a few more of your questions, yes, I am a licensed therapist—the minds of common people have long fascinated me—and no, despite the fact that our sessions were predicated on a lie, I don't think they were a complete waste of time. In fact, I may be able to continue helping you—or, rather, we may be able to help each other."

"Please, Jacob," Emma said, "don't listen to him."

"Don't worry," I said. "I trusted him once. I won't make that mistake again."

Golan continued as though he hadn't heard me. "I can offer you safety, money. I can give you your life back, Jacob. All you have to do is work with us."

"Us?"

"Malthus and me," he said, turning to call over his shoulder. "Come and say hello, Malthus."

A shadow appeared in the doorway behind him, and a moment later we were overcome by a noxious wave of stench. Bronwyn gagged and fell back a step, and I saw Emma's fists clench, as if she were thinking about charging it. I touched her arm and mouthed, *Wait.*

"This is all I'm proposing," Golan continued, trying to sound reasonable. "Help us find more people like you. In return, you'll have nothing to fear from Malthus or his kind. You can live at home. In your free time you'll come with me and see the world, and we'll pay you handsomely. We'll tell your parents you're my research assistant."

"If I agree," I said, "what happens to my friends?"

He made a dismissive gesture with his gun. "They made their choice long ago. What's important is that there's a grand plan in motion, Jacob, and you'll be part of it."

Did I consider it? I suppose I must have, if only for a moment. Dr. Golan was offering me exactly what I'd been looking for: a third option. A future that was neither *stay here forever* nor *leave and die.* But one look at my friends, their faces etched with worry, banished any temptation.

"Well?" said Golan. "What's your answer?"

"I'd die before I did anything to help you."

"Ah," he said, "but you already have helped me." He began to back toward the door. "It's a pity we won't have any more sessions together, Jacob. Though it isn't a total loss, I suppose. The four of you together might be enough to finally shift old Malthus out of the debased form he's been stuck in so long."

"Oh, no," Enoch whimpered, "I don't want to be eaten!"

"Don't cry, it's degrading," snapped Bronwyn. "We'll just have to kill them, that's all."

"Wish I could stay and watch," Golan said from the doorway. "I do love to watch!"

And then he was gone, and we were alone with it. I could hear the creature breathing in the dark, a viscid leaking like faulty pipeworks. We each took a step back, then another, until our shoulders met the wall, and we stood together like condemned prisoners before a firing squad.

"I need a light," I whispered to Emma, who was in such shock that she seemed to have forgotten her own power.

Her hand came ablaze, and among the flickering shadows I saw it, lurking among the troughs. My nightmare. It stooped there, hairless and naked, mottled gray-black skin hanging off its frame in loose folds, its eyes collared in dripping putrefaction, legs bowed and feet clubbed and hands gnarled into useless claws—every part looking withered and wasted like the body of an impossibly old man—save one. Its outsized jaws were its main feature, a bulging enclosure of teeth as tall and sharp as little steak knives that the flesh of its mouth was hopeless to contain, so that its lips were perpetually drawn back in a deranged smile.

And then those awful teeth came unlocked, its mouth reeling open to admit three wiry tongues into the air, each as thick as my wrist. They unspooled across half the room's length, ten feet or more, and then hung there, wriggling, the creature breathing raggedly through a pair of leprous holes in its face as if tasting our scent, considering how best to devour us. That we would be so easy to kill was the only reason we weren't dead already; like a gourmand about to enjoy a fine meal, there was no reason to rush things.

The others couldn't see it in the way I did but recognized its shadow projected on the wall and that of its ropelike tongues. Emma flexed her arm, and her flame burned brighter. "What's it doing?" she whispered. "Why hasn't it come at us?"

"It's playing with us," I said. "It knows we're trapped."

"We ain't any such thing," Bronwyn muttered. "Just gimme one square go at its face. I'll punch its bloody teeth in."

"I wouldn't get anywhere near those teeth if I were you," I said.

The hollow took a few lumbering steps forward to match the ones we'd taken back, its tongues unfurling more and then splitting apart, one coming toward me, another toward Enoch, and the third toward Emma.

"Leave us be!" Emma yelled, lashing out with her hand like a torch. The tongue twisted away from her flame, then inched back like a snake preparing to strike.

"We've got to try for the door!" I yelled. "The hollow's by the third trough from the left, so keep to the right!"

"We'll never make it!" Enoch cried. One of the tongues touched him on the cheek, and he screamed.

"We'll go on three!" Emma shouted. "One—"

And then Bronwyn launched herself toward the creature, howling like a banshee. The creature shrieked and reared up, its bunched skin pulling tight. Just as it was about to lash its trident of tongues at her, she rammed Martin's ice trough with the full weight of her body and levered her arms under it as it tipped and then heaved it and the whole huge thing, full of ice and fish and Martin's body, careened through the air and fell upon the hollow with a terrific crash.

Bronwyn spun and bounded back in our direction. "MOVE!" she cried, and I leapt away as she collided with the wall beside me, kicking a hole through the rotten planks. Enoch, the smallest of us, dove through first, followed by Emma, and before I could protest Bronwyn had grabbed me by the shoulders and tossed me out into the wet night. I landed chest-first in a puddle. The cold was shocking, but I was elated to feel anything other than the hollow's tongue wrapping around my throat.

Emma and Enoch hauled me to my feet, and we took off running. A moment later Emma shouted Bronwyn's name and stopped. We turned, realizing she hadn't come with us.

We called for her and scanned the dark, not quite brave enough to run back, and then Enoch shouted, "There!" and we saw Bronwyn leaning against a corner of the icehouse.

"What's she doing?!" cried Emma. "BRONWYN! RUN!"

It looked as though she was hugging the building. Then she stepped back and took a running start and rammed her shoulder into its corner support, and like a house made of matchsticks the whole thing tumbled in on itself, a cloud of pulverized ice and splintered wood puffing out and blowing down the street in a gust of wind.

We all hollered and cheered as Bronwyn sprinted toward us with a manic grin on her face, then stood in the pelting rain hugging her and laughing. It didn't take long for our moods to darken, though, as the shock of what had just happened set in, and then Emma turned to me and asked the question that must've been on all their minds.

"Jacob, how did that wight know so much about you? And us?"

"You called him doctor," said Enoch.

"He was my psychiatrist."

"Psychiatrist!" Enoch said. "That's just grand! Not only did he betray us to a wight, he's mad to boot!"

"Take it back!" Emma yelled, shoving him hard. He was about

to shove back when I stepped between them.

"Stop!" I said, pushing them apart. I faced Enoch. "You're wrong. I'm not crazy. He let me think I was, though all along he must've known I was peculiar. You're right about one thing, though. I did betray you. I told my grandfather's stories to a stranger."

"It's not your fault," Emma said. "You couldn't have known we were real."

"Of course he could've!" shouted Enoch. "Abe told him everything. Even showed him bloody pictures of us!"

"Golan knew everything but how to find you," I said. "And I led him straight here."

"But he tricked you," said Bronwyn.

"I just want you to know that I'm sorry."

Emma hugged me. "It's all right. We're alive."

"For now," said Enoch. "But that maniac is still out there, and considering how willing he was to feed us all to his pet hollowgast, it's a good bet he's figured out how to get into the loop on his own."

"Oh god, you're right," said Emma.

"Well then," I said, "we'd better get there before he does."

"And before *it* does," Bronwyn added. We turned to see her pointing at the wrecked icehouse, where broken boards had begun to shift in the collapsed pile. "I imagine he'll be coming for us directly, and I'm fresh out of houses to drop on him."

Someone shouted *Run!* but we already were, tearing down the path toward the one place the hollow couldn't reach us—the loop. We raced out of town in the spitting dark, vague blue outlines of cottages giving way to sloping fields, then charged up the ridge, sheets of water streaming over our feet, making the path treacherous.

Enoch slipped and fell. We hauled him up and ran on. As we were about to crest the ridge, Bronwyn's feet went out from under her, too, and she slid down twenty feet before she could stop herself. Emma and I ran back to help, and as we took her arms I turned to look behind us, hoping to catch a glimpse of the creature. But there was only inky, swirling rain. My talent for spotting hollows wasn't much good without light to see them by. But then, as we made it back to the top, chests heaving, a long flash of lightning lit up the night and I turned and saw it. It was off below us a ways but climbing fast, its muscular tongues punching into the mud and propelling it up the ridge like a spider.

"*Go!*" I shouted, and we all bolted down the far side, the four of us sliding on our butts until we hit level ground and could run again.

There was another flash of lightning. It was even closer than before. At this rate there was no way we'd be able to outrun it. Our only hope was to outmaneuver it.

"If it catches us, it'll kill us all," I shouted, "but if we split up, it'll have to choose. I'll lead it around the long way and try to lose it in the bog. The rest of you get to the loop as quick as you can!"

"You're mad!" shouted Emma. "If anyone stays behind it should be me! I can fight it with fire!"

"Not in this rain," I said, "and not if you can't see it!"

"I won't let you kill yourself!" she shouted.

There was no time to argue, so Bronwyn and Enoch ran ahead while Emma and I veered off the path, hoping the creature would follow, and it did. It was close enough now that I didn't need a lightning flash to know where it was; the twist in my gut was enough.

We ran arm in arm, tripping through a field rent with furrows and ditches, falling and catching each other in an epileptic dance. I was scanning the ground for rocks to use as weapons when, out of the darkness ahead, there appeared a structure—a small sagging shack with broken windows and missing doors, which in my panic I failed to recognize.

"We have to hide!" I said between gasping breaths.

Please let this creature be stupid, I prayed as we sprinted toward the house, *please, please let it be stupid.* We made a wide arc, hoping to enter it unseen.

"Wait!" Emma cried as we rounded the back of it. She pulled one of Enoch's cheesecloths from her coat and quickly tied it around a stone plucked from the ground, making a kind of slingshot. She cradled it in her hands until it caught fire and then hurled it away from us. It landed in the boggy distance, glowing weakly in the dark.

"Misdirection," she explained, and we turned and committed ourselves to the shack's concealing gloom.

*   *   *

We slipped through a door that was hanging off its hinges and stepped down into a sea of dark, aromatic muck. As our feet sank with a nauseating squelch, I realized where we were.

"What *is* this?" Emma whispered, and then a sudden exhalation of animal breath made us both jump. The house was crowded with sheep taking shelter from the unfriendly night, just as we were. As our eyes adjusted, we caught the dull gleam of theirs staring back at us—dozens and dozens of them.

"It's what I think it is, isn't it," she said, lifting one foot gingerly.

"Don't think about it," I replied. "Come on, we need to get away from this door."

I took her hand and we pushed into the house, snaking through a maze of skittish animals that shied from our touch. We threaded a narrow hall and came into a room with one high window and a door that was still in its frame and closed against the night, which was more than could be said for the other rooms. Squeezing into the far corner, we knelt down to wait and listen, hidden behind a wall of nervous sheep.

We tried not to sit too deeply in the muck but there was really no helping it. After a minute of staring blindly into the dark, I began to make out shapes in the room. There were crates and boxes stacked in one corner, and along the wall behind us hung rusted tools. I looked for anything that might be sharp enough to serve as a weapon. Seeing something that looked like a pair of giant scissors, I stood up to grab it.

"Planning on shearing some sheep?" said Emma.

"It's better than nothing."

Just as I was taking the shears down from the wall, a noise came from outside the window. The sheep bleated anxiously, and then a long black tongue drifted through the glassless enclosure. I sank back to the floor as quietly as I could. Emma put her hand over her mouth to silence her breathing.

The tongue poked around the room like a periscope, seeming to test the air. Luckily, we'd taken refuge in the most fragrant room on the island. All that sheep aroma must've masked our scent, because after a minute the creature seemed to give up and reeled out the window. We heard its retreating steps.

Emma's hand came away from her mouth and she let out a shuddering breath. "I think it's taking the bait," she whispered.

"I want you to know something," I said. "If we make it through this, I'm staying."

She grabbed my hand. "Do you mean it?"

"I can't go home. Not after all that's happened. Anyway, whatever help I can be, I owe you that and a lot more. You were all perfectly safe until I got here."

"If we make it through this," she said, leaning into me, "then I don't regret one thing."

And then some strange magnet was pulling our heads together, but just as our lips were about to touch, the quiet was shattered by terrified, bleating shrieks from the next room. We pulled apart as the awful noise set the sheep around us into frantic motion, bounding off one another and pushing us into the wall.

The beast was not as dumb as I'd hoped.

We could hear it coming toward us through the house. If there was a time to run it had already passed, so we screwed ourselves into the reeking soil and prayed it would pass us by.

And then I could smell it, even more pungent than the house's other stinks, and I could feel it at the threshold of the room. All the sheep pushed away from the door at once, herding together like a school of fish and pinning us against the wall so hard the breath was pressed out of us. We gripped each other but didn't dare make a sound, and for an unbearably tense moment we heard only the bleating of sheep and the clop of staggering hooves. Then another hoarse scream erupted, sudden and desperate and just as suddenly silenced, broken off by lurid, ripping bone snap. I knew without looking that a sheep had just been torn apart.

Chaos broke out. Panicked animals ricocheted off one another, throwing us against the wall so many times I got dizzy. The hollow let out an ear-splitting screech and began to lift sheep to its slavering jaws one after another, taking a blood-spurting bite from each and then tossing it aside like a gluttonous king gorging at a medieval feast. It did this again and again—killing its way toward us. I was paralyzed with fear. That's why I can't quite explain what happened next.

My every instinct screamed to stay hidden, to dig myself even deeper into the muck, but then one clear thought cut through all the static—*I won't let us die in this shit-house*—and I pushed Emma behind the biggest sheep I could see and bolted for the door.

The door was closed and ten feet away, and a lot of animals stood between it and me, but I plowed through them like a linebacker. I hit the door with my shoulder and it flung open.

I tumbled outside into the rain and screamed "Come get me, you ugly bastard!" I knew I had its attention because it let out a terrifying howl and sheep came flushing out the door past me. I scrambled to my feet and when I was sure it was coming after me and not Emma, I took off toward the bog.

I could feel it behind me. I might've run faster but I was still holding the shears—I couldn't seem to make myself let go—and then the ground went soft beneath me and I knew I'd reached the bog.

Twice the hollow was close enough for its tongues to lash my back, and twice, just as I was certain one was about to lasso my neck and squeeze until my head popped, it stumbled and fell back. The only reason I made it to the cairn with my head still attached was that I knew exactly where to put my feet; thanks to Emma, I could run that route on a moonless night in half a hurricane.

Clambering onto the cairn-mound, I tore around to the stone entrance and dove in. It was black as tar inside but it didn't matter—I only had to reach the chamber to be safe. I scrambled on my hands and knees, because even standing would've cost time I didn't have to waste, and I was halfway to the end and feeling cautiously optimistic about my chances for survival when suddenly I could crawl no more. One of the tongues had caught my ankle.

The hollow had used two of its tongues to grapple onto the capstones around the tunnel's mouth as leverage against the mud, and it covered the entrance with its body like a lid on a jar. The third tongue was reeling me toward it; I was a fish on a hook.

I scrabbled at the ground, but it was all gravel and my fingers slid right through. I flipped onto my back and clawed at the stones with my free hand, but I was sliding too quickly. I tried hacking at the tongue with my shears, but it was too sinewy and tough, a rope of undulating muscle, and my shears too dull. So I squeezed my eyes shut, because I didn't want its gaping jaws to be the last thing I'd ever see, and gripped the shears in front of me with both hands. Time seemed to stretch out, like they say it does in car crashes and train accidents and free-falls from airplanes, and the next thing I felt was a bone-jarring collision as I slammed into the hollow.

All the breath rushed out of me and I heard it scream. We flew out of the tunnel together and rolled down the cairn mound into the bog, and when I opened my eyes again, I saw my shears buried to the hilt in the beast's eye sockets. It howled like ten pigs being gelded, rolling and thrashing in the rain-swollen mud, weeping a black river of itself, viscous fluid pumping over the blades' rusted handle.

I could feel it dying, the life draining out of it, its tongue loosening around my ankle. I could feel the difference in me, too, the panicky clutch in my stomach slowly coming undone. Finally, the creature stiffened and sank from view, slime closing over its head, a slick of dark blood the only sign it had ever been there.

I could feel the bog sucking me down with it. The more I struggled, the more it seemed to want me. What a strange find the two of us would make a thousand years from now, I thought, preserved together in the peat.

I tried to paddle toward solid ground but succeeded only in pushing myself deeper. The muck seemed to climb me, rising up my arms, my chest, collaring my throat like a noose.

I screamed for help—and miraculously, help came, in the form of what I thought at first was a firefly, flashing as it flew toward me. Then I heard Emma call out, and I answered.

A tree branch landed in the water. I grabbed it and Emma pulled, and when I finally came out of the bog I was shaking too hard to stand. Emma sank down beside me and I fell into her arms.

I killed it, I thought. *I really killed it.* All the time I'd spent being afraid, I never dreamed I could actually *kill* one!

It made me feel powerful. Now I could defend myself. I knew I'd never be as strong as my grandfather, but I wasn't a gutless weakling, either. I could *kill* them.

I tested out the words. "It's dead. I *killed* it."

I laughed. Emma hugged me, pressing her cheek against mine. "I know he would've been proud of you," she said.

We kissed, and it was gentle and nice, rain dripping from our noses and running warm into our just-open mouths. Too soon she broke away and whispered, "What you said before—did you mean it?"

"I'll stay," I said. "If Miss Peregrine will let me."

"She will. I'll make certain of it."

"Before we worry about that, we'd better find my psychiatrist and take away his gun."

"Right," she said, her expression hardening. "No time to waste, then."

*   *   *

We left the rain behind and emerged into a landscape of smoke and noise. The loop hadn't yet reset, and the bog was pocked with bomb holes, the sky buzzing with planes, walls of orange flame marching against the distant tree line. I was about to suggest we wait until today became yesterday and all this disappeared before trying to cross to the house when a set of brawny arms clapped around me.

"You're alive!" Bronwyn cried. Enoch and Hugh were with her, and when she pulled away they moved in to shake my hand and look me over.

"I'm sorry I called you a traitor," Enoch said. "I'm glad you're not dead."

"Me, too," I replied.

"All in one piece?" Hugh asked, looking me over.

"Two arms and two legs," I said, kicking out my limbs to demonstrate their wholeness. "And you won't have to worry about that hollow anymore. We killed it."

"Oh, stuff the modesty!" Emma said proudly. "*You* killed it."

"That's brilliant," Hugh said, but neither he nor the other two could muster a smile.

"What's the matter?" I asked. "Wait. Why aren't you three at the house? Where's Miss Peregrine?"

"She's gone," said Bronwyn, her lip trembling. "Miss Avocet, too. He took them."

"Oh God," said Emma. We were too late.

"He come in with a gun," Hugh said, studying the dirt. "Tried to take Claire hostage, but she chomped him with her backmouth, so he grabbed me instead. I tried to fight, but he knocked me upside the skull with his gun." He touched the back of his ear and his fingers came away spotted with blood. "Locked everyone in the basement and said if Headmistress and Miss Avocet didn't change into birds he'd put an extra hole in my head. So they did, and he stuffed 'em both into a cage."

"He had a cage?" Emma said.

Hugh nodded. "Little one, too, so they didn't have room to do nothing, like change back or fly off. I reckoned I was good as shot, but then he pushed me down the basement with the others and run off with the birds."

"That's how we found 'em when we come in," Enoch said bitterly. "Hiding down there like a lot of cowards."

"We wasn't hiding!" Hugh cried. "He locked us in! He would've shot us!"

"Forget that," snapped Emma. "Where'd he run off to? Why didn't you go after him?!"

"We don't know where he went," said Bronwyn. "We was hoping you'd seen him."

"No, we haven't seen him!" Emma said, kicking a cairn stone in frustration.

Hugh drew something out of his shirt. It was a little photograph. "He stuffed this in my pocket before he went. Said if we tried to come after him, this is what would happen."

CAW CAW CAW

Bronwyn snatched the photo from Hugh. "Oh," she gasped. "Is that Miss Raven?"

"I think it's Miss Crow," said Hugh, rubbing his face with his hands.

"That's it, they're good as dead," Enoch moaned. "I knew this day would come!"

"We should never have left the house," Emma said miserably. "Millard was right."

At the far edge of the bog a bomb fell, its muted blast followed by a distant rain of excavated glop.

"Wait a minute," I said. "First of all, we don't know that this is Miss Crow or Miss Raven. It could just as easily be a picture of a regular crow. And if Golan was going to kill Miss Peregrine and Miss Avocet, why would he go to all the trouble of kidnapping them? If he wanted them dead, they'd be dead already." I turned to Emma. "And if we hadn't left, we'd be locked in the basement with everybody else, and there'd still be a hollowgast wandering around!"

"Don't try to make me feel better!" she said. "It's *your* fault this is happening!"

"Ten minutes ago you said you were *glad*!"

"Ten minutes ago Miss Peregrine wasn't kidnapped!"

"Will you stop!" said Hugh. "All that matters now is that the Bird's gone and we've got to get her back!"

"Fine," I said, "so let's think. If you were a wight, where would you take a couple of kidnapped ymbrynes?"

"Depends on what's to be done with 'em," Enoch said. "And that, we don't know."

"You'd have to get them off the island first," Emma said. "So you'd need a boat."

"But *which* island?" asked Hugh. "In the loop or out of it?"

"The outside's getting torn apart by a storm," I said. "Nobody's getting far in a boat over there."

"Then he's got to be on our side," Emma said, beginning to sound hopeful. "So what are we larking about here for? Let's get to the docks!"

"*Maybe* he's at the docks," Enoch said. "That is, if he ain't gone yet. And even if he ain't and we somehow manage to find him in all this dark, and without getting holes ripped through our guts by shrapnel on the way, there's still his gun to worry about. Have you all gone mad? Would you rather have the Bird kidnapped—or shot right in front of us?"

"Fine, then!" Hugh shouted. "Let's just give up and go home then, shall we? Who'd like a nice hot cup of tea before bed? Hell, as long as the Bird ain't around, make it a toddy!" He was crying, wiping angrily at his eyes. "How can you not even *try,* after all she's done for us?"

Before Enoch could answer, we heard a voice calling us from the path. Hugh stepped forward, squinting, and after a moment his face went strange. "It's Fiona," he said. Before that moment I'd never heard Fiona utter so much as a peep. It was impossible to make out what she was saying over the sound of planes and distant concussions, so we took off running across the bog.

When we got to the path, we were breathing hard and Fiona was hoarse from shouting, her eyes as wild as her hair. Immediately she began to pull at us, to drag and push us down the path toward town, yelling so frantically in her thick Irish accent that none of us could understand. Hugh caught her by the shoulders and told her to slow down.

She took a deep breath, shaking like a leaf, then pointed behind her. "Millard followed him!" she said. "He was hiding when the man shut us all in the basement, and when he lit out Millard followed!"

"Where to?" I said.

"He had a boat."

"See!" cried Emma. "The docks!"

"No," said Fiona, "it was *your* boat, Emma. The one you think nobody knows about, that you keep stowed on that wee strand of yours. He launched off with the cage and was just goin' in circles, but then the tide got too rough, so he pulled onto the lighthouse rock, and that's where he still is."

We made for the lighthouse in a dead run. When we reached the cliffs overlooking it, we found the rest of the children in a thick patch of sawgrass near the edge.

"Get down!" Millard hissed.

We dropped to our knees and crawled over to them. They were crouched in a loose huddle behind the grass, taking turns peeking at the lighthouse. They looked shell-shocked—the younger ones especially—as if they hadn't fully grasped the unfolding nightmare. That we'd just survived a nightmare of our own barely registered.

I crawled through the grass to the edge of the cliff and peered out. Past where the shipwreck lay submerged I could see Emma's canoe tied to the rocks. Golan and the ymbrynes were out of sight.

"What's he doing out there?" I said.

"It's anyone's guess," Millard answered. "Waiting for someone to pick him up, or for the tide to settle so he can row out."

"In my little boat?" Emma said doubtfully.

"As I said, we don't know."

Three deafening cracks sounded in quick succession, and we all ducked as the sky flashed orange.

"Do any bombs fall 'round here, Millard?" asked Emma.

"My research concerns only the behavior of humans and animals," he replied. "Not bombs."

"Fat lot of good that does us now," said Enoch.

"Do you have any more boats hidden around here?" I asked Emma.

"I'm afraid not," she said. "We'll just have to swim across."

"Swim across and what?" said Millard. "Get shot to pieces?"

"We'll figure something out," she replied.

Millard sighed. "Oh, lovely. Improvised suicide."

"Well?" Emma looked at each of us. "Does anyone have a better idea?"

"If I had my soldiers . . . " Enoch began.

"They'd fall to bits in the water," said Millard.

Enoch hung his head. The others were quiet.

"Then it's decided," said Emma. "Who's in?"

I raised my hand. So did Bronwyn. "You'll need someone the wight can't see," Millard said. "Take me along, if you must."

"Four's enough," Emma said. "Hope you're all strong swimmers."

There was no time for second thoughts or long goodbyes. The others wished us luck, and we were on our way.

We shed our black coats and loped through the grass, doubled-over like commandos, until we came to the path that led to the beach. We slid down on our behinds, little avalanches of sand pouring around our feet and down our pants.

Suddenly, there was a noise like fifty chainsaws over our heads, and we ducked as a plane roared by, the wind whipping our hair and blowing up a sandstorm. I clenched my teeth, waiting for a bomb blast to tear us apart. None came.

We kept moving. When we hit the beach, Emma gathered us in a tight huddle.

"There's a shipwreck between here and the lighthouse," she said. "Follow me out to it. Stay low in the water. Don't let him see you. When we reach the wreck, we'll look for our man and decide what's next."

"Let's get our ymbrynes back," Bronwyn said.

We crawled down to the surf and slid into the cold water on our bellies. It was easy going at first, but the farther we swam from shore, the more the current tried to push us back. Another plane buzzed overhead, kicking up a stinging spray of water.

We were breathing hard by the time we reached the shipwreck. Clinging to its rusted hull, just our heads poking out of the water, we stared at the lighthouse and the barren little island that anchored it, but saw no sign of my wayward therapist. A full moon hovered low in the sky, breaking through reefs of bomb smoke now and then to shine like the lighthouse's ghostly double.

We pushed ourselves along the wreck until we reached the end, just a fifty-yard swim in open water to the lighthouse rocks.

"Here's what I reckon we should do," Emma said. "He's seen how strong Wyn is, so she's in the most danger. Jacob and I find Golan and get his attention while Wyn sneaks up from behind and gives him a belter over the head. Meantime, Millard makes a grab for the birdcage. Any objections?"

As if in answer, a shot rang out. At first we didn't realize what it was—it didn't sound like the gunshots we'd been hearing, distant and powerful. This was small caliber—a *pop* rather than a *bang*—and it wasn't until we heard a second one, accompanied by a nearby splash, that we knew it was Golan.

"Fall back!" Emma shouted, and we stood out of the water and sprinted across the hull until it dropped out from beneath us, then dove into the open water beyond it. A moment later we all came up in a cluster, panting for air.

"So much for getting the drop on him!" Millard said.

Golan had stopped shooting, but we could see him standing guard by the lighthouse door, gun in hand.

"He may be an evil bastard, but he ain't stupid," Bronwyn said. "He knew we'd come after him."

"Not now we can't!" Emma said, slapping the water. "He'll shoot us to bits!"

Millard stepped up onto the wreck. "He can't shoot what he can't see. I'll go."

"You're not invisible in the ocean, dummy," Emma said, and it was true—a torso-shaped negative space bobbed in the water where he stood.

"More than you are," he replied. "Anyhow, I followed him all the way across the island and he was none the wiser. I think I can manage a few hundred meters more."

It was difficult to argue, since our only remaining options were either giving up or running into a hail of gunfire.

"Fine," Emma said. "If you really think you can make it."

"Someone's got to be the hero," he replied, and walked off across the hull.

"Famous last words," I muttered.

In the smoky distance, I saw Golan in the lighthouse doorway kneel down and take aim, leveling his arm across a railing.

"Look out!" I shouted, but it was too late.

A shot rang out. Millard groaned.

We all clambered onto the wreck and raced toward him. I felt absolutely certain I was about to be shot, and for a moment I thought the splashes of our feet in the water were bullets raining down on us. But then the shooting stopped—*reloading*, I thought—and we had a brief window of time.

Millard was kneeling in the water, dazed, blood running down his torso. For the first time I could see the true shape of his body, painted red.

Emma took him by the arm. "Millard! Are you all right? Say something!"

"I must apologize," he said. "It seems I've gone and gotten myself shot."

"We have to stop the bleeding!" said Emma. "We've got to take him back to shore!"

"Nonsense," Millard said. "That man will never let you get this close to him again. Turn back now, and we'll certainly lose Miss Peregrine."

More shots rang out. I felt a bullet zip past my ear.

"This way!" Emma shouted. "Dive!"

I didn't know what she meant at first—we were a hundred feet from the end of the wreck—but then I saw what she was running toward. It was the black hole in the hull, the door to the cargo hold.

Bronwyn and I lifted Millard and ran after her. Metal slugs clanged into the hull around us. It sounded like someone kicking a trash can.

"Hold your breath," I told Millard, and we came to the hold and dove in feet-first.

We pulled ourselves down the ladder a few rungs and hung there. I tried to keep my eyes open but the saltwater stung too much. I could taste Millard's blood in the water.

Emma handed me the breathing tube, and we passed it among us. I was winded from running, and the single breath it allowed me every few seconds wasn't enough. My lungs hurt, and I began to feel light-headed.

Someone tugged at my shirt. *Come up.* I pulled myself slowly up the ladder, and then Bronwyn, Emma and I broke the surface just enough to breathe and talk while Millard stayed safe a few feet below, the tube all to himself.

We spoke in whispers and kept our eyes on the lighthouse.

"We can't stay here," Emma said. "Millard will bleed to death."

"It could take twenty minutes to get him back to shore," I said. "He could just as easily die on the way."

"I don't know what else to do!"

"The lighthouse is close," Bronwyn said. "We'll take him there."

"Then Golan will make us *all* bleed to death!" I said.

"No, he won't," replied Bronwyn.

"Why not? Are you bullet-proof?"

"Maybe," Bronwyn replied mysteriously, then took a breath and disappeared down the ladder.

"What's she talking about?" I said.

Emma looked worried. "I haven't a clue. But whatever it is, she'd better hurry." I looked down to see what Bronwyn was doing but instead caught a glimpse of Millard on the ladder below us, surrounded by curious flashlight fish. Then I felt the hull vibrate against my feet, and a moment later Bronwyn surfaced holding a rectangular piece of metal about six feet by four, with a riveted round hole in the top. She had wrenched the cargo hold's door from its hinges.

"And what are you going to do with that?" Emma said.

"Go to the lighthouse," she replied. Then she stood up and held the door in front of her.

"Wyn, he'll shoot you!" Emma cried, and then a shot rang out—and caromed right off the door.

"That's amazing!" I said. "It's a shield!"

Emma laughed. "Wyn, you're a genius!"

"Millard can ride my back," she said. "The rest of you, fall in behind."

Emma brought Millard out of the water and hung his arms around Bronwyn's neck. "It's magnificent down there," he said. "Emma, why did you never tell me about the angels?"

"What angels?"

"The lovely green angels who live just below." He was shivering, his voice dreamy. "They kindly offered to take me to heaven."

"No one's going to heaven just yet," Emma said, looking worried. "You just hang on to Bronwyn, all right?"

"Very well," he said vacantly.

Emma stood behind Millard, pressing him into Bronwyn's back so he wouldn't slide off. I stood behind Emma, taking up the rear of our strange little conga line, and we began to plod forward across the wreck toward the lighthouse.

We were a big target, and right away Golan began to empty his gun at us. The sound of his bullets bouncing off the door was deafening—but somehow reassuring—but after about a dozen shots he stopped. I wasn't optimistic enough to think he'd run out of bullets, though.

Reaching the end of the wreck, Bronwyn guided us carefully into open water, always keeping the massive door held out in front of us. Our conga line became a chain of dog-paddlers swimming in a knot behind her. Emma talked to Millard as we paddled, making him answer questions so he wouldn't drift into unconsciousness.

"Millard! Who's the prime minister?"

"Winston Churchill," he said. "Have you gone daft?"

"What's the capital of Burma?"

"Lord, I've no idea. Rangoon."

"Good! When's your birthday?"

"Will you quit shouting and let me bleed in peace!"

It didn't take long to cross the short distance between the wreck and the lighthouse. As Bronwyn shouldered our shield and climbed onto the rocks, Golan fired a few more shots, and their impact threw her off balance. As we cowered behind her, she wobbled and nearly slipped backward off the rocks, which between her weight and the door's would've crushed us all. Emma planted her hands on the small of Bronwyn's back and pushed, and finally both Bronwyn and the door tottered forward onto dry land. We scrambled after her in a pack, shivering in the crisp night air.

Fifty yards across at its widest, the lighthouse rocks were technically a tiny island. At the lighthouse's rusted base were a dozen stone steps leading to an open door, where Golan stood with his pistol aimed squarely in our direction.

I risked a peek through the porthole. He held a small cage in one hand, and inside were two flapping birds mashed so close together I could hardly tell one from the other.

A shot whizzed past and I ducked.

"Come any closer and I'll shoot them both!" Golan shouted,

rattling the cage.

"He's lying," I said. "He needs them."

"You don't know that," said Emma. "He's a madman, after all."

"Well we can't just do *nothing.*"

"Rush him!" Bronwyn said. "He won't know what to do. But if it's going to work we've got to go NOW!"

And before we had a chance to weigh in, Bronwyn was running toward the lighthouse. We had no choice but to follow—she was carrying our protection, after all—and a moment later bullets were clanging against the door and chipping at the rocks around our feet.

It was like hanging from the back of a speeding train. Bronwyn was terrifying: She bellowed like a barbarian, the veins in her neck bulging, with Millard's blood smeared all over her arms and back. I was very glad, in that moment, not to be on the other side of the door.

As we neared the lighthouse, Bronwyn shouted, "Get behind the wall!" Emma and I grabbed Millard and cut left to take cover behind the far side of the lighthouse. As we ran, I saw Bronwyn lift the door above her head and hurl it toward Golan.

There was a thunderous crash quickly followed by a scream, and moments later Bronwyn joined us behind the wall, flushed and panting.

"I think I hit him!" she said excitedly.

"What about the birds?" Emma said. "Did you even think about them?"

"He dropped 'em. They're fine."

"Well, you might've asked us before you went berserk and risked all our lives!" Emma cried.

"Quiet," I hissed. We heard the faint sound of creaking metal. "What *is* that?"

"He's climbing the stairs," Emma replied.

"You'd better get after him," croaked Millard. We looked at him, surprised. He was slumped against the wall.

"Not before we take care of you," I said. "Who knows how to

make a tourniquet?"

Bronwyn reached down and tore the leg of her pants. "I do," she said. "I'll stop his bleeding; you get the wight. I knocked him pretty good, but not good enough. Don't give him a chance to get his wind back."

I turned to Emma. "You up for this?"

"If it means I get to melt that wight's face off," she said, little arcs of flame pulsing between her hands, "then absolutely."

*   *   *

Emma and I clambered over the ship's door, which lay bent on the steps where it had landed, and entered the lighthouse. The building consisted mainly of one narrow and profoundly vertical room—a giant stairwell, essentially—dominated by a skeletal staircase that corkscrewed from the floor to a stone landing, more than a hundred feet up. We could hear Golan's footsteps as he bounded up the stairs, but it was too dark to tell how far he was from the top.

"Can you see him?" I said, peering up the stairwell's dizzying height.

My answer was a gunshot ricocheting off a wall nearby, followed by another that slammed into the floor at my feet. I jumped back, heart hammering.

"Over here!" Emma cried. She grabbed my arm and pulled me farther inside, to the one place Golan's gunshots couldn't reach us—directly under the stairs.

We climbed a few steps, which were already swaying like a boat in bad weather. "These are frightful!" Emma exclaimed, her fingers white-knuckled as they gripped the rail. "Even if we make it to the top without falling, he'll only shoot us!"

"If we can't go up," I said, "maybe we can bring him down." I began to rock back and forth where I stood, yanking on the railing and stomping my feet, sending shockwaves up the stairs. Emma looked at me like I was nuts for a second, but then got the idea and began to stomp and sway along with me. Pretty soon the staircase was rocking like crazy.

"What if the whole thing comes down?" Emma shouted.

"Let's hope it doesn't!"

We shook harder. Screws and bolts began to rain down. The rail was lurching so violently, I could hardly keep hold of it. I heard Golan scream a spectacular array of curses, and then something clattered down the stairs, landing nearby.

The first thing I thought was, *Oh God, what if that was the birdcage*—and I dashed down the stairs past Emma and ran out on the floor to check.

"What are you doing?!" Emma shouted. "He'll shoot you!"

"No, he won't!" I said, holding up Golan's handgun in triumph. It felt warm from all the firing he'd done and heavy in my hand, and I had no idea if it still had bullets or even how, in the near darkness, to check. I tried in vain to remember something useful from the few shooting lessons Grandpa had been allowed to give me, but finally I just ran back up the steps to Emma.

"He's trapped at the top," I said. "We've got to take it slow, try to reason with him, or who knows what he'll do to the birds."

"I'll reason him right over the side," Emma replied through her teeth.

We began to climb. The staircase swayed terribly and was so narrow that we could only proceed in single-file, crouching so our heads wouldn't hit the steps above. I prayed that none of the fasteners we'd shaken loose had secured anything crucial.

We slowed as we neared the top. I didn't dare look down; there were only my feet on the steps, my hand sliding along the shivering rail and my other hand holding the gun. Nothing else existed.

I steeled myself for a surprise attack, but none came. The stairs ended at an opening in the stone landing above our heads, through which I could feel the snapping chill of night air and hear the whistle of wind. I stuck the gun through, followed by my head. I was tense and ready to fight, but I didn't see Golan. On one side of me spun the massive light, housed behind thick glass—this close it was blinding, forcing me to shut my eyes as it swung past—and on the other side was a spindly rail. Beyond that was a void: ten stories of empty air and then rocks and churning sea.

I stepped onto the narrow walkway and turned to give Emma a hand up. We stood with our backs pressed against the lamp's warm housing and our fronts to the wind's chill. "The Bird's close," Emma whispered. "I can feel her."

She flicked her wrist and a ball of angry red flame sprang to life. Something about its color and intensity made it clear that this time she hadn't summoned a light, but a weapon.

"We should split up," I said. "You go around one side and I'll take the other. That way he won't be able to sneak past us."

"I'm scared, Jacob."

"Me, too. But he's hurt, and we have his gun."

She nodded and touched my arm, then turned away.

I circled the lamp slowly, clenching the maybe-loaded gun, and gradually the view around the other side began to peel back.

I found Golan sitting on his haunches with his head down and his back against the railing, the birdcage between his knees. He was bleeding badly from a cut on the bridge of his nose, rivulets of red streaking his face like tears.

Clipped to the bars of the cage was a small red light. Every few seconds it blinked.

I took another step forward, and he raised his head to look at me. His face was a stubble of caked blood, his one white eye shot through with red, spit flecking the corners of his mouth.

He rose unsteadily, the cage in one hand.

"Put it down."

He bent over as if to comply but faked away from me and tried to run. I shouted and gave chase, but as soon as he disappeared around the lamp housing I saw the glow of Emma's fire flare across the concrete. Golan came howling back toward me, his hair smoking and one arm covering his face.

"Stop!" I screamed at him, and he realized he was trapped. He raised the cage, shielding himself, and gave it a vicious shake. The birds screeched and nipped at his hand through the bars.

"Is this what you want?" Golan shouted. "Go ahead, burn me! The birds will burn, too! Shoot me and I'll throw them over the side!"

"Not if I shoot you in the head!"

He laughed. "You couldn't fire a gun if you wanted to. You forget, I'm intimately familiar with your poor, fragile psyche. It'd give you nightmares."

I tried to imagine it: curling my finger around the trigger and squeezing; the recoil and the awful report. What was so hard about that? Why did my hand shake just thinking about it? How many wights had my grandfather killed? Dozens? Hundreds? If he were here instead of me, Golan would be dead already, laid out while he'd been squatting against the rail in a daze. It was an opportunity I'd already wasted; a split-second of gutless indecision that might've cost the ymbrynes their lives.

The giant lamp spun past, blasting us with light, turning us into glowing white cutouts. Golan, who was facing it, grimaced and looked away. *Another wasted opportunity*, I thought.

"Just put it down and come with us," I said. "Nobody else has to get hurt."

"I don't know," Emma said. "If Millard doesn't make it, I might reconsider that."

"You want to kill me?" Golan said. "Fine, get it over with. But you'll only be delaying the inevitable, not to mention making things worse for yourselves. We know how to find you now. More like me are coming, and I can guarantee the collateral damage they do will make what I did to your friend seem downright charitable."

"Get it *over* with?" Emma said, her flame sending a little pulse of sparks skyward. "Who said it would be quick?"

"I told you, I'll kill them," he said, drawing the cage to his chest.

She took a step toward him. "I'm eighty-eight years old," she said. "Do I look like I need a pair of babysitters?" Her expression was steely, unreadable. "I can't tell you how long we've been dying to get out from under that woman's wing. I swear, you'd be doing us a favor."

Golan swiveled his head back and forth, nervously sizing us up. *Is she serious?* For a moment he seemed genuinely frightened, but then he said, "You're full of shit."

Emma rubbed her palms together and pulled them slowly apart, drawing out a noose of flame. "Let's find out."

I wasn't sure how far Emma would take this, but I had to step in before the birds went up in flames or were sent tumbling over the rail.

"Tell us what you want with those ymbrynes, and maybe she'll go easy on you," I said.

"We only want to finish what we started," Golan said. "That's all we've ever wanted."

"You mean the experiment," Emma said. "You tried it once, and look what happened. You turned yourselves into monsters!"

"Yes," he said, "but what an unchallenging life it would be if we always got things right on the first go." He smiled. "This time we'll be harnessing the talents of all the world's best time manipulators, like these two ladies here. We won't fail again. We've had a hundred years to figure out what went wrong. Turns out all we needed was a bigger reaction!"

"A *bigger* reaction?" I said. "Last time you blew up half of Siberia!"

"If you must fail," he said grandly, "fail spectacularly!"

I remembered Horace's prophetic dream of ash clouds and scorched earth, and I realized what he'd been seeing. If the wights and hollows failed again, this time they'd destroy a lot more than five hundred miles of empty forest. And if they succeeded, and turned themselves into the deathless demigods they'd always dreamed of becoming . . . I shuddered to imagine it. Living under them would be a hell all its own.

The light came around and blinded Golan again—I tensed, ready to lunge—but the moment sped by too quickly.

"It doesn't matter," Emma said. "Kidnap all the ymbrynes you want. They'll never help you."

"Yes, they will. They'll do it or we'll kill them one by one. And if that doesn't work, we'll kill *you* one by one, and make them watch."

"You're insane," I told him.

The birds began to panic and screech. Golan shouted over them.

"No! What's *really* insane is how you peculiars hide from the world when you could rule it—succumb to death when you could dominate it—and let the common genetic trash of the human race drive you underground when you could so easily make them your slaves, as they rightly should be!" He drove home every sentence with another shake of the cage. "*That's* insane!"

"Stop it!" Emma shouted.

"So you *do* care!" He shook the cage even harder. Suddenly, the little red light attached to its bars began to glow twice as bright, and Golan whipped his head around and searched the darkness behind him. Then he looked back at Emma and said, "You want them? Here!" and he pulled back and swung the cage at her face.

She cried out and ducked. Like a discus thrower, Golan continued the swing until the cage sailed over her head, then released. It flew out of his hands and over the rail, tumbling end over end into the night.

I cursed and Emma screamed and threw herself against the rail, clawing at the air as the cage fell toward the sea. In that moment of confusion, Golan leapt and knocked me to the ground. He slammed a fist into my stomach and another into my chin.

I was dizzy and couldn't breathe. He grabbed for the gun, and it took every bit of my strength to keep him from snatching it. Because he wanted it so badly, I knew it must've been loaded. I would've thrown it over the rail, but he almost had it and I couldn't let go. Emma was screaming *bastard, you bastard*, and then her hands, gloved in flame, came from behind and seized him around the neck.

I heard Golan's flesh singe like a cold steak on a hot grill. He howled and rolled off me, his thin hair going up in flame, and then his hands were around Emma's throat, as though he didn't mind burning as long as he could choke the life out of her. I jumped to my feet, held the gun in both hands, and pointed it.

I had, just for a moment, a clear shot. I tried to empty my mind and focus on steadying my arm, creating an imaginary line that extended from my shoulder through the sight to my target—a man's head. No, not a man, but a corruption of one. A thing. A force that had arranged the murder of my grandfather and exploded all that I'd humbly called a life, poorly lived though it may have been, and carried me here to this place and this moment, in much the way less corrupt and violent forces had done my living and deciding for me since I was old enough to decide anything. *Relax your hands, breathe in, hold it.* But now I had a chance to force back, a slim nothing of a chance that I could already feel slipping away.

Now squeeze.

The pistol bucked in my hands and its report sounded like the earth breaking open, so tremendous and sudden that I shut my eyes. When I opened them again, everything seemed strangely frozen. Though Golan stood behind Emma with her arms locked in a hold, wrestling her toward the railing, it was as if they'd been cast in bronze. Had the ymbrynes turned human again and worked their magic on us? But then everything came unstuck and Emma wrenched her arms away and Golan began to totter backward, and he stumbled and sat heavily on the rail.

Gaping at me in surprise, he opened his mouth to speak but found he could not. He clapped his hands over the penny-sized hole I'd made in his throat, blood lacing through his fingers and running down his arms, and then the strength went out of him and he fell back, and he was gone.

The moment Golan disappeared from view, he was forgotten. Emma pointed out to sea and shouted, "There, there!" Following her finger and squinting into the distance I could barely pick out the pulse of a red LED bobbing on the waves. Then we were scrambling to the hatch and sprinting down and down the endless seesawing staircase, hopeless that we could reach the cage before it sank but hysterical to try anyway.

We tore outside to find Millard wearing a tourniquet and Bronwyn by his side. He shouted something I didn't quite hear, but it was enough to assure me he was alive. I grabbed Emma's shoulder and said, "The boat!" pointing to where the stolen canoe had been lashed to a rock, but it was too far away, on the wrong side of the lighthouse, and there was no time. Emma pulled me instead toward the open sea, and, running, we dashed ourselves into it.

I hardly felt the cold. All I could think about was reaching the cage before it disappeared beneath the waves. We tore at the water and sputtered and choked as black swells slapped our faces. It was difficult to tell how far away the beacon was, just a single point of light in a surging ocean of dark. It bobbed and fell and came and went, and twice we lost sight of it and had to stop, searching frantically before spotting it again.

The strong current was carrying the cage out to sea, and us with it. If we didn't reach it soon, our muscles would fail and we'd drown.

I kept this morbid thought to myself for as long as I could, but when the beacon disappeared a third time and we looked for it so long we couldn't even be sure what section of the rolling black sea it had disappeared from, I shouted, "We have to go back!"

Emma wouldn't listen. She swam ahead of me, farther out to sea. I grasped at her scissoring feet but she kicked me off.

"It's gone! We aren't going to find them!"

"Shut up, shut up!" she cried, and I could tell from her labored breaths that she was as exhausted as I was. "Just shut up and look!"

I grabbed her and shouted in her face and she kicked at me, and when I wouldn't let go and she couldn't force me to, she began to cry, just wordless howls of despair.

I tried to drag her back toward the lighthouse, but she was like a stone in the water, pulling me down. "You have to swim!" I shouted. "Swim or we'll drown!"

And then I saw it—the faintest blink of red light. It was close, just below the surface. At first I didn't say anything, afraid I'd imagined it, but then it blinked a second time.

Emma whooped and shouted. It looked like the cage had landed on another wreck—how else could it have come to rest so shallowly? —and because it had only just sunk, I told myself it was possible the birds were still alive.

We swam and prepared to dive for the cage, though I didn't know where the breath would come from, we had so little left. Then, strangely, the cage seemed to rise toward us.

"What's happening?" I shouted. "Is that a wreck?"

"Can't be. There are none over here!"

"Then what the hell is *that*?"

It looked like a whale about to surface, long and massive and gray, or some ghost ship rising from its grave, and there erupted a sudden and powerful swell that came up from below and pushed us away. We tried to paddle against it but had no more luck than flotsam caught in a tidal wave, and then it thudded against our feet and we were rising, too, riding its back.

It came out of the water beneath us, hissing and clanking like some giant mechanical monster. We were caught in a sudden rush of foaming surf that raced off it in every direction, thrown hard onto a surface of metal grates. We hooked our fingers through the grates to keep from being washed into the sea. I squinted through the salt spray and saw that the cage had come to rest between what looked like two fins jutting from the monster's back, one smaller and one larger. And then the lighthouse beam swept past, and in its gleam I realized they weren't fins at all but a conning tower and a giant bolted-down gun. This thing we were riding wasn't a monster or a wreck or a whale—

"It's a U-boat!" I shouted. That it had risen right beneath our feet was no coincidence. It had to be what Golan was waiting for.

Emma was already on her feet and sprinting across the rolling deck toward the cage. I scrambled to stand. As I began to run a wave flashed over the deck and knocked us both down.

I heard a shout and looked up to see a man in a gray uniform rise from a hatch in the conning tower and level a gun at us.

Bullets rained down, hammering the deck. The cage was too far away—we'd be torn to pieces before we could reach it—but I could see that Emma was about to try anyway.

I ran and tackled her and we tumbled sideways off the deck and into the water. The black sea closed above us. Bullets peppered the water, leaving trails of bubbles in their wake.

When we surfaced again, she grabbed me and screamed, "Why did you do that? I nearly had them!"

"He was about to kill you!" I said, wrestling away—and then it occurred to me that she hadn't even seen him, she'd been so focused on the cage, so I pointed up at the deck, where the gunner was striding toward it. He picked the cage up and rattled it. Its door hung open, and I thought I saw movement inside—some reason for hope—

and then the lighthouse beam washed over everything. I saw the gunner's face full in the light, his mouth curled into a leering grin, his eyes depthless and blank. He was a wight.

He reached into the cage and pulled out a single sodden bird. From the conning tower, another soldier whistled to him, and he ran back toward the hatch with it.

The sub began to rattle and hiss. The water around us churned as if boiling.

"Swim or it'll suck us down with it!" I shouted to Emma. But she hadn't heard me—her eyes were locked elsewhere, on a patch of dark water near the stern of the boat.

She swam for it. I tried to stop her but she fought me off. Then, over the whine of the sub, I heard it—a high, shrieking call. Miss Peregrine!

We found her bobbing in the waves, struggling to keep her head above water, one wing flapping, the other broken looking. Emma scooped her up. I screamed that we had to go.

We swam away with what little strength we had. Behind us, a whirlpool was opening up, all the water displaced by the sub rushing back to fill the void as it sank. The sea was consuming itself and trying to consume us, too, but we had with us now a screeching winged symbol of victory, or half a victory at least, and she gave us the strength to fight the unnatural current. Then we heard Bronwyn shouting our names, and our brawny friend came crashing through the waves to tow us back to safety.

*　　*　　*

We lay on the rocks beneath the clearing sky, gasping for air and trembling with exhaustion. Millard and Bronwyn had so many questions, but we had no breath to answer them. They had seen Golan's body fall and the submarine rise and sink and Miss Peregrine come out of the water but not Miss Avocet; they understood what they needed to. They hugged us until we stopped shaking, and Bronwyn tucked the headmistress under her shirt for warmth. Once we'd recovered a little, we retrieved Emma's canoe and pushed off toward the shore.

When we got there, the children all waded into the shallows to meet us.

"We heard shooting!"

"What was that strange boat?"

"Where's Miss Peregrine?"

We climbed out of the rowboat, and Bronwyn raised her shirt to reveal the bird nuzzled there. The children crowded around, and Miss Peregrine lifted her beak and crowed at them to show that she was tired but all right. A cheer went up.

"You did it!" Hugh shouted.

Olive danced a little jig and sang, "The Bird, the Bird, the Bird! Emma and Jacob saved the Bird!"

But the celebration was brief. Miss Avocet's absence was quickly noted, as was Millard's alarming condition. His tourniquet was tight, but he'd lost a lot of blood and was weakening. Enoch gave him his coat, Fiona offered her woolen hat.

"We'll take you to see the doctor in town," Emma said to him.

"Nonsense," Millard replied. "The man's never laid eyes on an invisible boy, and he wouldn't know what to do with one if he did. He'd either treat the wrong limb or run away screaming."

"It doesn't matter if he runs away screaming," Emma said. "Once the loop resets he won't remember a thing."

"Look around you. The loop should've reset an hour ago."

Millard was right—the skies were quiet, the battle had ended, but rolling drifts of bomb smoke still mixed with the clouds.

"That's not good," Enoch said, and everyone got quiet.

"In any case," Millard continued, "all the supplies I need are in the house. Just give me a bolt of Laudanum and swab the wound with alcohol. It's only the fleshy part anyway. In three days I'll be right as rain."

"But it's still bleeding," Bronwyn said, pointing out red droplets that dotted the sand beneath him.

"Then tie the damn tourniquet tighter!"

She did, and Millard gasped in a way that made everyone cringe, then fainted into her arms.

"Is he all right?" Claire asked.

"Just blacked out is all," said Enoch. "He ain't as fit as he pretends to be."

"What do we do now?"

"Ask Miss Peregrine!" Olive said.

"Right. Put her down so she can change back," said Enoch. "She can't very well tell us what to do while she's still a bird."

So Bronwyn set her on a dry patch of sand, and we all stood back and waited. Miss Peregrine hopped a few times and flapped her good wing and then swiveled her feathered head around and blinked at us—but that was it. She remained a bird.

"Maybe she wants a little privacy," Emma suggested. "Let's turn our backs."

So we did, forming a ring around her. "It's safe now, Miss P," said Olive. "No one's looking!"

After a minute, Hugh snuck a peek and said, "Nope, still a bird."

"Maybe she's too tired and cold," Claire said, and enough of the others agreed this was plausible that it was decided we would go back to the house, treat Millard with what supplies we had, and hope that with some time to rest, both the headmistress and her loop would return to normal.

CHAPTER ELEVEN

We marched up the steep trail and across the ridge like a company of war-weary veterans, single file, heads down, Bronwyn carrying Millard in her arms and Miss Peregrine riding the nestlike crown of Fiona's hair. The landscape was gouged with smoking craters, fresh-turned earth thrown everywhere as if some giant dog had been digging at it. We all wondered what awaited us back at the house, but no one dared to ask.

We had our answer even before clearing the forest. Enoch's foot kicked something, and he bent down to look. It was half a charred brick.

Panic broke out. The children began to sprint down the path. When they reached the lawn, the younger ones broke out in tears. There was smoke everywhere. The bomb had not come to rest atop Adam's finger, as it usually did, but had split him straight down the middle and exploded. The back corner of the house had been reduced to a slumped and smoking ruin. Small fires burned in the charred shell of two rooms. Where Adam had been was a raw crater deep enough to bury a person upright. It was easy now to picture what this place would one day become: that sad and desecrated wreck I had first discovered weeks ago. The nightmare house.

Miss Peregrine leapt from Fiona's hair and began to race around on the scorched grass, squawking in alarm.

"Headmistress, what happened?" Olive said. "Why hasn't the changeover come?"

Miss Peregrine could only screech in reply. She seemed as confused and frightened as the rest of us.

"Please turn back!" begged Claire, kneeling before her.

Miss Peregrine flapped and jumped and seemed to be straining herself, but still couldn't shift her shape. The children crowded around in concern.

"Something's wrong," Emma said. "If she could turn human, she would've done it by now."

"Perhaps that's why the loop slipped," Enoch suggested. "Remember that old story about Miss Kestrel, when she was thrown from her bicycle in a road accident? She knocked her head and stayed a kestrel for a whole entire week. That's when her loop slipped."

"What's that got to do with Miss Peregrine?"

Enoch sighed. "Maybe she's only injured her head and we just need to wait a week for her to come to her senses."

"A speeding lorry's one thing," Emma said. "Being abused by wights is quite another. There's no knowing what that bastard did to Miss Peregrine before we got to her."

"Wights? As in plural?"

"It was wights who took Miss Avocet," I said.

"How do you know that?" demanded Enoch.

"They were working with Golan, weren't they? And I saw the eyes of the one who shot at us. There's no question."

"Then Miss Avocet's as good as dead," said Hugh. "They'll kill her for sure."

"Maybe not," I replied. "At least not right away."

"If there's one thing I know about wights," said Enoch, "it's that they kill peculiars. It's their nature. It's what they do."

"No, Jacob's right," said Emma. "Before that wight died, he told us why they've been abducting so many ymbrynes. They're going to force them to re-create the reaction that made the hollows in the first place—only bigger. Much bigger."

I heard someone gasp. Everyone else fell silent. I looked around for Miss Peregrine and saw her perched forlornly on the edge of Adam's crater.

"We've got to stop them," Hugh said. "We've got to find out where they're taking the ymbrynes."

"How?" said Enoch. "Follow a submarine?"

Behind me a throat cleared loudly, and we turned to see Horace sitting cross-legged on the ground. "I know where they're going," he said quietly.

"What do you mean, you know?"

"Never mind how he knows, he *knows*," said Emma. "Where are they taking her, Horace?"

He shook his head. "I don't know the name," he said, "but I've seen it."

"Then draw it," I said.

He thought for a moment and then rose stiffly. Looking like a beggar evangelist in his torn black suit, he shuffled to an ash pile that had spilled from the cracked-open house and bent to gather a palm full of soot. Then, in the soft light of the moon, he began to paint on a broken wall with broad strokes.

We gathered around to watch. He made a row of bold vertical stripes topped with thin loops, like bars and razor wire. To one side was a dark forest. There was snow on the ground, rendered in black. And that was all.

When it was done, he staggered back and sat down hard in the grass, a dull distant look in his eyes. Emma took him gently by the shoulder and said, "Horace, what more do you know about this place?"

"It's somewhere cold."

Bronwyn stepped forward to study the marks Horace had made. She held Olive in the crook of her arm, the little girl's head resting sweetly on her shoulder. "Looks like a jail to me," said Bronwyn.

Olive raised her head. "Well?" came her small voice. "When do we go?"

"Go where?" Enoch said, tossing up his hands. "That's just a lot of squiggles!"

"It's *somewhere*," Emma said, turning to face him.

"We can't simply go someplace snowy and look for a prison."

"And we can't very well stay here."

"Why not?"

"Look at the state of this place. Look at the headmistress. We had a damn good run here, but it's over."

Enoch and Emma went back and forth for a while. People took sides. Enoch's argued that they'd been too long out of the world, that they'd get snared in the war or caught by hollows if they left, that it was better to take their chances here, where at least they knew the territory. The others insisted that the war and the hollows had come to *them* now, and they had no choice. The hollows and wights would return for Miss Peregrine, and in ever-greater numbers. And there was Miss Peregrine herself to consider.

"We'll find another ymbryne," Emma suggested. "If anyone will know how to help the headmistress, it'll be one of her friends."

"But what if all the other loops have slipped too?" said Hugh. "What if all the ymbrynes have already been kidnapped?"

"We can't think that way. There must be *some* left."

"Emma's right," Millard said, lying on the ground with a chunk of broken masonry under his head for a pillow. "If the alternative is to wait and just hope—that no more hollows come, that the headmistress gets better—I say that's no alternative at all."

The dissenters were finally shamed into agreement. The house would be abandoned. Belongings would be packed. A few boats would be requisitioned from the harbor and pressed into service, and in the morning everyone would go.

I asked Emma how they were going to navigate. After all, none of the children had been off the island in nearly eighty years, and Miss Peregrine couldn't speak or fly.

"There's a map," she told me, turning her head slowly to look at the smoking house. "If it hasn't burned, that is."

I volunteered to help her find it. Wrapping wet cloths over our faces, we ventured into the house, entering through the collapsed wall. The windows were shattered, the air hung with smoke, but by the bright light of Emma's hand-flame we found our way to the study. All the shelves had fallen like dominoes, but we shoved them aside and searched through the books spilled across the floor, crouching low. As luck would have it, the book was easy to find: it was the largest one in the library. Emma yelped with joy and held it up.

On the way out, we found alcohol and Laudanum and proper bandages for Millard. Once we'd helped clean and dress his wound, we sat down to examine the book. It was more atlas than map, bound in quilted leather dyed a deep burgundy, each page drawn carefully on what looked like parchment. It was very fine and very old, and big enough to fill Emma's lap.

"It's called the Map of Days," she said. "It's got every loop ever known to exist." The page she'd opened to appeared to be a map of Turkey, though no roads were marked and no borders indicated. Instead, the map was scattered with tiny spirals, which I took to be the location of loops. At the center of each was a unique symbol that corresponded to a legend at the bottom of the page, where the symbols reappeared next to a list of numbers separated by dashes. I pointed to one that read *29-3-316 / ?-?-399* and said, "What is this, some kind of code?"

Emma traced it with her finger. "This loop was the twenty-ninth of March, 316 A.D. It existed until sometime in the year 399, though the day and month are unknown."

"What happened in 399?"

She shrugged. "It doesn't say."

I reached across her and turned to a map of Greece, even more clustered with spirals and numbers. "But what's the point of listing all these?" I said. "How would you even get to these ancient loops?"

"By leapfrogging," said Millard. "It's a highly complex and dangerous undertaking, but by leapfrogging from one loop to another—a day fifty years in the past, for instance—then you'll find you have access to a whole range of loops that have ceased to exist in the last fifty years. Should you have the wherewithal to travel to them, within those you'll find still other loops, and so on exponentially."

"That's time travel," I said, astonished. "*Real* time travel."

"I suppose so, yes."

"So this place," I said, pointing to Horace's ash painting on the wall. "We wouldn't just have to figure out *where* it is, but *when*, too?"

"I'm afraid so. And if Miss Avocet is indeed being held by wights, who are notoriously adept at leapfrogging, then it's extremely likely that the place she and the other ymbrynes are being taken is somewhere in the past. That will make them all the more difficult to find, and getting there all the more dangerous. The locations of historical loops are well known to our enemies, who tend to lurk near the entrances."

"Well then," I said, "it's a good thing I'm coming with you."

Emma spun to look at me. "Oh, that's wonderful!" she cried, and hugged me. "Are you certain?"

I told her I was. Tired as they were, the children whistled and clapped. Some embraced me. Even Enoch shook my hand. But when

I looked at Emma again, her smile had faded.

"What's the matter?" I said.

She shifted uncomfortably. "There's something you should know," she said, "and I'm afraid it'll make you not want to come with us."

"It won't," I assured her.

"When we leave here, this loop will close behind us. It's possible you may never be able to return to the time you came from. At least, not easily."

"There's nothing for me there," I said quickly. "Even if I could go back, I'm not sure I'd want to."

"You say that now. I need you to be sure."

I nodded, then stood.

"Where are you going?" she asked.

"For a walk."

I didn't go far, just around the perimeter of the neat yard in a slow shuffle, watching the sky, clear now, a billion stars spread across it. Stars, too, were time travelers. How many of those ancient points of light were the last echoes of suns now dead? How many had been born but their light not yet come this far? If all the suns but ours collapsed tonight, how many lifetimes would it take us to realize that we were alone? I had always known the sky was full of mysteries—but not until now had I realized how full of them the earth was.

I came to the place where the path emerged from the woods. In one direction lay home and everything I knew, unmysterious and ordinary and safe.

Except it *wasn't*. Not really. Not any more. The monsters had murdered Grandpa Portman, and they had come after me. Sooner or later, they would again. Would I come home one day to find my dad bleeding to death on the floor? My mom? In the other direction, the children were gathering in excited little knots, plotting and planning, for the first time any of them could remember, for the future.

I walked back to Emma, still poring over her massive book. Miss Peregrine was perched next to her, tapping with her beak here and there on the map. Emma looked up as I approached.

"I'm sure," I said.

She smiled. "I'm glad."

"There's just one thing I have to do before I go."

*　*　*

I made it back to town just before dawn. The rain had finally eased, and the beginning of a blue day was percolating on the horizon. The main path looked like an arm with the veins stripped out, long slashes where flooding had washed the gravel away.

I walked into the pub and through the empty bar and up to our rooms. The shades were drawn and my father's door was closed, which was a relief because I hadn't yet figured out how to say what I needed to tell him. Instead I sat down with pen and paper and wrote him a letter.

I tried to explain everything. I wrote about the peculiar children and the hollows and how all of Grandpa Portman's stories had turned out to be true. I told him what had happened to Miss Peregrine and Miss Avocet and tried to make him understand why I had to go. I begged him not to worry.

Then I stopped and read over what I'd written. It was no good. He would never believe it. He'd think I'd lost my mind the way Grandpa had, or that I'd run away or been abducted or taken a nose-dive off the cliffs. Either way, I was about to ruin his life. I wadded up the paper and threw it in the trash.

"Jacob?"

I turned to see my father leaning in the doorjamb, bleary-eyed, hair tangled, dressed in a mud-splashed shirt and jeans.

"Hi, Dad."

"I'm going to ask you a simple, straightforward question," he said, "and I'd like a simple, straightforward answer. Where were you last night?" I could tell he was struggling to maintain his composure.

I decided I was done lying. "I'm fine, Dad. I was with my friends."

It was like I'd pulled the pin on a grenade.

"YOUR FRIENDS ARE IMAGINARY!" he shouted. He came toward me, his face turning red. "I wish your mother and I had never let that crackpot therapist talk us into bringing you out here, because it has been an unmitigated *disaster*! You just lied to me for the last time! Now get in your room and start packing. We're on the next ferry!"

"Dad?"

"And when we get home, you're not leaving the house until we find a psychiatrist who's not a complete *jackass*!"

"Dad!"

I wondered for a moment if I would have to run from him. I pictured my dad holding me down, calling for help, loading me onto the ferry with my arms locked in a straightjacket.

"I'm not coming with you," I said.

His eyes narrowed and he cocked his head, as if he hasn't heard properly. I was about to repeat myself when there was a knock at the door.

"Go away!" my dad shouted.

The knock came again, more insistent this time. He stormed over and flung it open, and there at the top of the stairs stood Emma, a tiny ball of blue flame dancing above her hand. Next to her was Olive.

"Hullo," Olive said. "We're here to see Jacob."

He stared at them, baffled. "What is this . . . "

The girls edged past him into the room.

"What are you *doing* here?" I hissed at them.

"We only wanted to introduce ourselves," Emma replied, flashing a big smile at my dad. "We've come to know your son rather well of late, so we thought it only proper that we should pay a friendly call."

"Okay," my father said, his eyes darting between them.

"He's really a fine boy," said Olive. "So brave!"

"And handsome!" Emma added, winking at me. She began to roll the flame between her hands like a toy. My father stared at it, hypnotized.

"Y-yes," he stammered. "He sure is."

"Do you mind if I slip off my shoes?" Olive asked, and without waiting for an answer she did, and promptly floated to the ceiling. "Thanks. That's much more comfortable!"

"These are my friends, Dad. The ones I was telling you about. This is Emma, and that's Olive, on the ceiling."

He staggered back a step. "I'm still sleeping," he said vaguely. "I'm so tired . . . "

A chair lifted off the floor and floated over to him, followed by an expertly wrapped medical bandage bobbing through the air. "Then please, have a seat," Millard said.

"Okay," my dad replied, and he did.

"What are you doing here?" I whispered to Millard. "Shouldn't you be lying down?"

"I was in the neighborhood." He held up a modern-looking pill bottle. "I must say, they make some marvelously effective pain tablets in the future!"

"Dad, this is Millard," I said. "You can't see him because he's invisible."

"Nice to meet you."

"Likewise," said Millard.

I went over to my father and knelt down beside his chair. His head bobbed slightly. "I'm going away, Dad. You might not see me for a while."

"Oh, yeah? Where are you going?"

"On a trip."

"A trip," he repeated. "When will you be back?"

"I don't really know."

He shook his head. "Just like your grandfather." Millard ran tap water into a glass and brought it to him, and Dad reached out and took it, as though floating glasses weren't at all unusual. I guess he really thought he was dreaming. "Well, goodnight," he said and then stood up, steadied himself on the chair, and stumbled back into his bedroom. Stopping at the door, he turned to face me.

"Jake?"

"Yeah, Dad?"

"Be careful, okay?"

I nodded. He closed the door. A moment later I heard him fall into bed.

I sat down and rubbed my face. I didn't know how to feel.

"Did we help?" Olive asked from her perch on the ceiling.

"I'm not sure," I said. "I don't think so. He'll just wake up later thinking he dreamed all of you."

"You could write a letter," Millard suggested. "Tell him anything you like—it's not as if he'll be able to follow us."

"I did write a letter. But it's not *proof*."

"Ah," he replied. "Yes, I see your problem."

"Nice problem to have," said Olive. "Wish *my* mum and dad had loved me enough to worry when I left home."

Emma reached up and squeezed her hand. Then she said, "I might have proof."

She pulled a small wallet from the waistband of her dress and took out a snapshot. She handed it to me. It was a picture of her and my grandfather when my grandfather was young. All her attention was focused on him, but he seemed elsewhere. It was sad and beautiful and encapsulated what little I knew about their relationship.

"It was taken just before Abe left for the war," Emma said. "Your dad'll recognize me, won't he?"

I smiled at her. "You look like you haven't aged a day."

"Marvelous!" said Millard. "There's your proof."

"Do you always keep this with you?" I asked, handing it back to her.

"Yes. But I don't need it anymore." She went to the table and took my pen and began to write on the back of the photo. "What's your father's name?"

"Franklin."

When she finished writing, she gave it to me. I looked at both sides and then fished my letter from the trash, smoothed it, and left it on the table with the photo.

"Ready to go?" I said.

My friends were standing in the doorway, waiting for me.

"Only if you are," Emma replied.

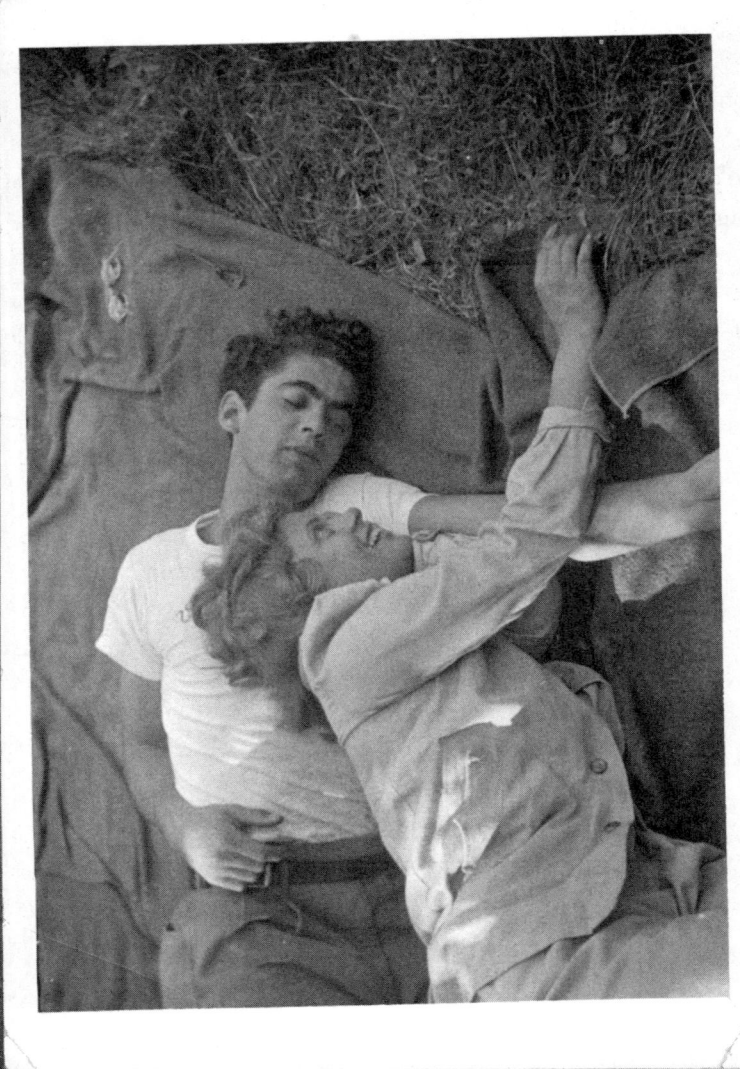

Dear Franklin,

It was a great pleasure meeting you. This is a photograph of your father and me taken when he lived here. I hope it will be sufficient to convince you that I am still among the living, and that Jacob's stories are no fantasy.

Jacob will be traveling with my friends and me for a time. We will keep one another as safe as anyone like us can be. One day, when the danger has passed, he will come back to you. You have my word.

Very sincerely yours,

Emma Bloom

P.S. I understand you may have discovered a letter I sent your father many years ago. It was inappropriate, and I assure you, unsolicited; he did not respond in kind. He was one of the most honorable men I have ever known.

We set out for the ridge. At the spot near the crest where I always stopped to see how far I'd come, this time I kept walking. Sometimes it's better not to look back.

When we reached the cairn, Olive patted the stones like a beloved old pet. "Goodbye, old loop," she said. "You've been such a good loop, and we'll miss you ever so much." Emma squeezed her shoulder, and they both crouched down and went inside.

In the rear chamber, Emma held her flame to the wall and showed me something I'd never noticed before: a long list of dates and initials carved into the rocks. "It's all the other times people have used this loop," she explained. "All the other days the loop's been looped."

Peering at it, I made out a *P.M. 3-2-1853* and a *J.R.R. 1-4-1797* and a barely-legible *X.J. 1580*. Near the bottom were some strange markings I couldn't decipher.

"Runic inscriptions," Emma said. "Quite ancient."

Millard searched through the gravel until he found a sharpened stone, and, using another stone as a hammer, he chipped an inscription of his own below the others. It read *A.P. 3-9-1940*.

"Who's AP?" asked Olive.

"Alma Peregrine," said Millard, and then he sighed. "It should be her carving this, not me."

Olive ran her hand over the rough markings. "Do you think another ymbryne will come along to make a loop here someday?"

"I hope so," he said. "I dearly hope so."

*   *   *

We buried Victor. Bronwyn lifted his whole bed and carried it outside with Victor still in it, and with all the children assembled on the grass she pulled back the sheets and tucked him in, planting one last kiss on his forehead. We boys lifted the corners of his bed like pallbearers and walked him down into the crater that the bomb had made. Then all of us climbed out but Enoch, who took a clay man from his pocket and laid it gently on the boy's chest.

"This is my very best man," he said. "To keep you company." The clay man sat up and Enoch pushed it back down with his thumb. The man rolled over with one arm under his head and seemed to go to sleep.

When the crater had been filled, Fiona dragged some shrubs and vines over the raw soil and began to grow them. By the time the rest of us had finished packing for the journey, Adam was back in his old spot, only now he was marking Victor's grave.

Once the children had said goodbye to their house, some taking chips of brick or flowers from the garden as forget-me-nots, we made one last trip across the island: through the smoking charred woods and the flat bog dug with bomb holes, over the ridge and down through the little town hung with peat smoke, where the townspeople lingered on porches and in doorways, so tired and numb with shock that they hardly seemed to notice the small parade of peculiar-looking children passing them by.

We were quiet but excited. The children hadn't slept, but you wouldn't have known it to look at them. It was September fourth, and for the first time in a very long time, the days were moving again. Some of them claimed they could feel the difference; the air in their lungs was fuller, the race of blood through their veins faster. They felt more vital, more real.

I did, too.

*   *   *

I used to dream about escaping my ordinary life, but my life was never ordinary. I had simply failed to notice how extraordinary it was. Likewise, I never imagined that home might be something I would miss. Yet as we stood loading our boats in the breaking dawn, on a brand new precipice of Before and After, I thought of everything I was about to leave behind—my parents, my town, my once-best-and-only friend—and I realized that leaving wouldn't be like I had imagined, like casting off a weight. Their memory was something tangible and heavy, and I would carry it with me.

And yet my old life was as impossible to return to as the children's bombed house. The doors had been blown off our cages.

Ten peculiar children and one peculiar bird were made to fit in just three stout rowboats, with much being jettisoned and left behind on the dock. When we'd finished, Emma suggested that one of us say something—make a speech to dedicate the journey ahead—but no one seemed ready with words. And so Enoch held up Miss Peregrine's cage and she let out a great screeching cry. We answered with a cry of our own, both a victory yell and a lament, for everything lost and yet to be gained.

Hugh and I rowed the first boat. Enoch sat watching us from the bow, ready to take his turn, while Emma in a sunhat studied the receding island. The sea was a pane of rippled glass spreading endlessly before us. The day was warm, but a cool breeze came off the water, and I could've happily rowed for hours. I wondered how such calm could belong to a world at war.

In the next boat, I saw Bronwyn wave and raise Miss Peregrine's camera to her eye. I smiled back. We'd brought none of the old photo albums with us; maybe this would be the first picture in a brand new one. It was strange to think that one day I might have my own stack of yellowed photos to show skeptical grandchildren—and my own fantastic stories to share.

Then Bronwyn lowered the camera and raised her arm, pointing at something beyond us. In the distance, black against the rising sun, a silent procession of battleships punctuated the horizon.

We rowed faster.

*A*ll the pictures in this book are authentic, vintage found photographs, and with the exception of a few that have undergone minimal postprocessing, they are unaltered. They were lent from the personal archives of ten collectors, people who have spent years and countless hours hunting through giant bins of unsorted snapshots at flea markets and antiques malls and yard sales to find a transcendent few, rescuing images of historical significance and arresting beauty from obscurity—and, most likely, the dump. Their work is an unglamorous labor of love, and I think they are the unsung heroes of the photography world.

ACKNOWLEDGMENTS

I would like to thank:

Everyone at Quirk, especially Jason Rekulak, for his seemingly endless patience and many excellent ideas; Stephen Segal, for his close readings and sharp insights; and Doogie Horner, certainly the most talented book designer/stand-up comic working today.

Mom, to whom I owe everything, obviously.

All my photo collector friends: the very generous Peter Cohen; Leonard Lightfoot, who introduced me around; Roselyn Leibowitz; Jack Mord of the Thanatos Archive; Steve Bannos; John Van Noate; David Bass; Martin Isaac; Muriel Moutet; Julia Lauren; Yefim Tovbis; and especially Robert Jackson, in whose living room I spent many pleasant hours looking at peculiar photographs.

Chris Higgins, whom I consider a leading authority on time travel, for always taking my calls.

Laurie Porter, who took the author photo on the facing page while we were exploring some weird abandoned shacks in the Mojave desert.

A Conversation
with Ransom Riggs

*R*ansom Riggs grew up in Florida but now makes his home in the land of peculiar children—Los Angeles. Along the way he earned degrees from Kenyon College and the University of Southern California's School of Cinema-Television. His first novel, *Miss Peregrine's Home for Peculiar Children*, debuted at #5 on the *New York Times* Best-Seller List. He recently sat down with Quirk Books' creative director Jason Rekulak to discuss its peculiar origins.

Can you tell us how you came to write this book? Which came first: the story or the photographs?

I have no idea where most of my ideas come from, but *Miss Peregrine* has a very specific origin story. A few years ago, I started collecting vintage snapshots—the kind you can find in loose piles at most flea markets for fifty cents or a buck apiece. It was just a casual hobby, nothing serious, but I noticed that among the photos I found, the strangest and most intriguing ones were always of children. I began to wonder who some of these strange-looking children had been—what their stories were—but the photos were old and anonymous and there was no way to know. So I thought: If I can't know their real stories, I'll make them up.

The photographs came first, but I never stopped collecting. Even as I was writing the story I was finding more photographs to work in. Ultimately, the photos and the story influenced each other. Sometimes I'd find a new photo that just demanded to be included in the story, and I'd find a way to work it in; other times I'd look for a certain type of photo to fit a story idea I had. It was a fun, strange, organic writing process, unlike anything I'd attempted before.

Were there any great photographs you just couldn't work into the narrative?

Tons. Some will find their way into future books, whereas others are likely to remain orphans. For instance, I have this great picture of a little boy in suspenders standing in a doorway, and he's dramatically lit and wears this dour expression, and he's strangely *immobile*, despite supposedly being in the act of coming through a doorway. Why is he just *standing* there? He's obviously about to deliver some terrible news—or maybe eat your brain. It looks like a still from a noir film. Unfortunately, I never found a use for it in the story.

Somewhat more tragic is the story of the Santa that got away.

There are many disturbing pictures of department store Santas in the world, but early on in the writing of this book, I found the ultimate creepy Santa—a man with deep, black circles around his eyes, looking as if he'd just come off a three-day bender, and the eyes themselves—blank. I assume the man *has* pupils, which were somehow blurred when the exposure was made, but in this picture they're invisible, his eyes a milky white. It was this photograph, in fact, that gave me the idea to make all the wights' pupils blank. Unfortunately, the fellow who owned it was, understandably, pretty attached to the photo, and it took me over a year to convince him to sell it to me, by which time the book had already gone to press. So the wight-in-disguise department store Santa that appears in chapter 9 is only the *second* scariest department store Santa I've ever seen.

Clowns are almost universally recognized as scary, and though I had a fairly good picture of a strange-looking clown and a little girl, I didn't think the book needed any more photos of people in masks or heavy makeup, or little girls in close proximity to menacing shadows, Santas, and the like, so I passed it over. But there are so many strange things about this picture, I wanted to share it. Just look at the clown's face. Is it just me, or is he terribly scarred?

How many photos did you collect before settling on the final fifty that appear in the book?

In addition to combing through bins of old photos at flea markets and antiques shops, I spent many hours in the homes of a few very patient and generous collectors, searching boxes and folders and albums overflowing with amazing images. Given that most collectors own ten thousand photos at a minimum—and often many more than that—I'd guess that more than one hundred thousand snapshots passed through my hands while creating this book.

You attended film school at the University of Southern California, and you've worked in the film and television industries. How did these experiences inform the creation of *Miss Peregrine*? Many critics have remarked on the book's cinematic qualities.

It's difficult to quantify, because this is my first novel; if I'd written one before film school and another afterward, I'd have a more scientific answer. But I do think that writing screenplays and making films trained me to think in pictures, and sequences of pictures, in a way I didn't before. Perhaps as a result I tend to visualize scenes in a way I wouldn't have five years ago. Sometimes when I'm writing, I imagine that I'm directing the scene—which I am, inasmuch as readers' minds conjure pictures of what they're reading. For instance: *They walked into the room.* That's a wide shot. *Her lip trembled* is a close-up.

The book begins with a passage by Ralph Waldo Emerson (1803– 1882), and of course Jacob receives a book of Emerson's work from his grandfather. Can you discuss how Emerson's philosophy informed this story?

Emerson figured much more heavily into the first draft of *Miss Peregrine*, but his involvement was whittled down quite a bit. Part of that had to do with the story changing direction. In the old version, Jacob met the peculiar children gradually, and it took him several chapters to finally and fully believe they were real. Emerson often speaks about the possibility of fantastic things that exist just out of view, and many of his most famous quotes almost seem to refer directly to the peculiar children. "The power which resides in him is new in nature," he writes in *Self-Reliance* (1841), "and none but he knows what that is which he can do, nor does he know until he has tried." That's certainly true of the children, and of Jacob, too. Then there's this line, from *Nature* (1836): "In the woods, too, a man casts off his years, as the snake his slough, and at what period soever of life is always a child. In the woods is perpetual youth." It's not hard to imagine that Emerson is describing the deep woods surrounding Miss Peregrine's house and its strangely youthful inhabitants.

One of the themes of *Miss Peregrine,* and I think of any novel that involves the discovery of a secret world, is awakening—the protagonist's awakening to an awesome and wonderful and, in some ways, terrible reality he scarcely could've imagined before, but that was right under his nose all along. At the end of *Miss Peregrine*, Jacob writes that his life was never ordinary, but he "had simply failed to notice how extraordinary it was." Noticing the extraordinariness of the world is one of Emerson's major themes. Again, from *Nature*: "If the stars should appear one night in a thousand years, how would men believe and adore, and preserve for many generations the remembrance of the city of God which had been shown!"

Are there other writers whom you find particularly influential or inspiring?

Many, though it's hard to draw a direct line between their work and mine. Reading John Green showed me how ambitious and engaging young adult literature could be—it's so much better than most of the kiddie stuff I read as a teenager. While I'm writing, I like to read books by masters whose technique I can't hope to match, just to keep the bar high. Cormac McCarthy. Tim O'Brien's *The Things They Carried*—his prose has such power and economy. I read a lot of nonfiction while I'm writing, too, to help give the historical bits convincing texture. *The Likes of Us* and *Barnardo Boy* are first-person accounts of what life was like in British orphanages in the first half of the twentieth century, and they were very helpful. And the poems of Seamus Heaney were an inspiration when it came to writing about mucky peat bogs and the strange things they contain.

Would you like to see those mucky peat bogs firsthand? If you could time-travel to any loop in history, where and when would you want to go?

Amazingly, I've never been asked this question! I'm not sure if there are loops in these places (and, anyway, I couldn't get inside them because I'm not peculiar), but I'd love to see New York City in the mid- to late nineteenth century. Or some of Europe's great cities before they were bombed during World War II. A real Roman city—that would be interesting. The opulence and multicultural energy of Venice in its heyday, in the sixteenth or seventeenth century. The Silk Road as traveled by Marco Polo. The list goes on!

We're excited about the forthcoming sequel to *Miss Peregrine's Home for Peculiar Children*. What can you tell us about it?

The first book was about opening a door and discovering a world. In the second book we get to explore that world. But it's no tourist trip—it's a world facing a mortal and existential threat, from both the Axis powers and from the Corrupted: the wights and the hollows. Jacob and his new friends embark upon a death-defying, time-trotting adventure to save their ymbrynes, their way of life, and perhaps the very world, and as they struggle to derail their enemies' disastrous plans, they get themselves into all manner of peculiar and dangerous situations, meet all sorts of curious beings and unusual people, and explore places they never could've imagined. I'm still working out the details, but I can promise you this: It'll be full of surprises!

Until then, I thought I'd share a few photos from Book II to tide everyone over. I don't want to give too much away, but you can expect to see things like . . .

PECULIAR ANIMALS!

FOLDABLE
MEN!

PRISON
BREAKS!

PEOPLE FROM LONG AGO!

AND LOOPS IN EXOTIC LOCALES!

TURN THE PAGE

FOR A PREVIEW OF

HOLLOW CITY

A SECOND NOVEL OF

MISS PEREGRINE'S

PECULIAR CHILDREN

*W*e rowed out through the harbor, past bobbing boats weeping rust from their seams, past silent juries of seabirds roosting atop the barnacled remains of sunken docks, past fishermen who lowered their nets to stare as we slipped by, uncertain whether we were real or imagined; a procession of waterborne ghosts, or ghosts soon to be. We were ten children and one bird in three small and unsteady boats, rowing with quiet intensity straight out to sea, the only safe harbor for miles receding quickly behind us, craggy and magical in the blue-gold light of dawn. Our goal, the rutted coast of mainland Wales, was somewhere before us but only dimly visible, an inky smudge squatting along the far horizon.

We rowed past the old lighthouse, tranquil in the distance, which had just last night been the scene of so many traumas. It was there that, with bombs exploding around us, we had nearly drowned, nearly been torn apart by bullets; that I had taken a gun and pulled its trigger and killed a man, an act still incomprehensible to me; that we had lost Miss Peregrine and got her back again — snatched from the steel jaws of a submarine —though the Miss Peregrine who was returned to us was damaged, in need of help we don't know how to give. She perched now on the stern of our boat, feathered head bowed in something like mourning, watching the sanctuary she'd created slip away, a little more lost with every oar stroke.

Finally we rowed past the breakwater and into the great blank open, and the glassy surface of the harbor gave way to little waves that chopped at the sides of our boats. I heard a plane threading the clouds high above us and let my oars drag, neck craning up, arrested by a vision of our little armada from such a height: this world I had chosen, and everything I had in it, and all our precious, peculiar lives, contained in three splinters of wood adrift upon the vast, unblinking eye of the sea.

Mercy.

*　　*　　*

Our boats slid effortlessly through the waves, three abreast, a stout breeze urging us along and a friendly current bearing us coast-ward. We rowed in shifts, taking turns at the oars to stave off ex-haustion, though I felt so strong and capable that for nearly an hour I refused to give them up. I lost myself in the rhythm of the strokes, my arms tracing long ellipses in the air as if pulling something to-ward me that refused to come. Hugh manned the oars opposite me, and behind him, at the bow, sat Emma, her eyes hidden below the wide brim of a sun hat, head bent toward a map spread across her knees. I watched her as I rowed, and every now and then she'd look up from her map to consult the horizon. Just the sight of her face in the sun like that gave me energy I didn't know I had.

I felt like I could row forever—until Horace, flagging, asked how much ocean stood between us and the mainland.

"Five miles," Emma replied, and as the words left her mouth I could see everyone wilt a little.

Five miles: a journey that would've taken just an hour in the stomach-churning ferry that brought me to Cairnholm weeks ago. A distance easily covered by an engine-powered boat of any size. Roughly one mile less than my out-of-shape uncles ran for charity on odd weekends, and only a bit more than my mother claimed she could manage during rowing-machine classes at her fancy gym. But the ferry between the island and the mainland wouldn't start running for another thirty years, and rowing machines were not loaded down with passengers and luggage, nor did they require constant course corrections just to stay pointed in the right direction. Worse still, the ditch of water we were crossing was treacherous, a notorious ship-swallower: five miles of moody, changeable sea, its floor fanned with greening wrecks and sailors' bones and, lurking somewhere in fathoms-deep darkness, our enemies.

Those of us who worried about such things assumed the wights were nearby, somewhere below us in that German submarine, waiting. If they didn't already know we'd fled the island, they'd find out soon enough. They hadn't gone to such lengths to kidnap Miss Peregrine only to give up after one failed attempt. The warships that inched like centipedes in the distance and British planes that kept watch overhead made it too dangerous for the submarine to surface in broad daylight, but come nightfall, we were easy prey. They would come for us, and take Miss Peregrine, and sink the rest. So we rowed, our only hope that we could reach the mainland before nightfall reached us.

*   *   *

We rowed until our arms ached and our shoulders knotted. We rowed until the morning's cool breeze fell away and the sun blazed down as through a magnifying glass and sweat pooled around our collars, and I realized no one had thought to bring fresh water, and that sunblock in 1940 meant standing in the shade. We rowed until the skin wore away from the ridges of our palms and we were certain we absolutely couldn't row another stroke but then did, and then rowed another and another.

"You're sweating buckets," Emma said. "Let me have a go at

that before you melt away." Her voice startled me out of a daze. I nodded gratefully and let her switch into the oar-seat, but twenty minutes later I asked for it back again. I didn't like the thoughts that crept into my head while my body was at rest: imagined scenes of my father waking up to find me gone from our rooms on Cairnholm, Emma's baffling letter in my place; the panic that would ensue.

I had memory flashes of terrible things I'd witnessed recently. A monster pulling me into its jaws. My former psychiatrist falling to his death. A man buried in a coffin of ice, torn momentarily from the next world to croak into my ear with half a throat. So I rowed despite my exhaustion and a spine that felt like it might never straighten again and hands rubbed raw from friction, and tried to think of exactly nothing, those leaden oars both a life sentence and a life raft.

Bronwyn, seemingly inexhaustible, rowed the third boat all by herself. Olive sat opposite her but was no help; the tiny girl couldn't even pull the oars without pushing herself up into the air, where a stray gust of wind might send her flying away like a kite. So Olive shouted encouragement while Bronwyn did the work of two—or of three or four if you took into account all the suitcases and boxes weighing down their boat, which were stuffed with clothes and food and maps and books and a lot of less practical things, too, like several jars of picked reptile hearts sloshing in Enoch's duffel bag, or the blown-off front doorknob to Miss Peregrine's house, a memento Hugh had found in the grass on our way down to the boats and decided he couldn't live without, or the bulky pillow Horace had rescued from the house's flaming shell—it was his lucky pillow, he said, and the only thing that kept his paralyzing nightmares at bay.

Other items were so precious that the children clung to them even as they rowed. Fiona kept a pot of wormy garden dirt pressed between her knees. Millard had striped his face with a handful of bomb-pulverized brick dust, an odd gesture that seemed part mourning ritual and partly practical: because he was otherwise invisible, it let us know he was there and hadn't fallen overboard. If what they kept and clung to seemed strange to me at first, part of me sympathized, too: it was all they had left of their home. Just because it was lost and they knew it didn't mean they knew how to let it go.

After three hours of rowing like galley slaves, distance had shrunk the island to the size of an open hand. It looked nothing like the foreboding, cliff-ringed fortress I had first seen a few weeks ago, but vulnerable; a fragile shard of rock in danger of being washed away by some rogue wave.

"Look!" shouted Enoch, standing up in his boat to point at it. "It's disappearing!"

A spectral fog had begun to enshroud the island, blanking it from view, and we broke from rowing to watch it fade.

"Farewell, island," Emma called out. "You were so good to us."

Horace set his oar down and waved. "Goodbye, house. I shall miss all your rooms and gardens, but most of all I shall miss my bed."

"So long, loop," Olive sniffled. "Thank you for keeping us safe all those years."

"Good years," said Bronwyn. "The best I've known."

I said a silent goodbye, too, to a place that had changed me forever—and the place that, more than any graveyard, would forever contain the memory, and the mystery, of my grandfather. They were linked inextricably, he and that island, and I wondered, now that they were both gone, if I would ever really understand what had happened to me: what I had become; was becoming. I had come to the island to solve my grandfather's mystery, and in doing so I had discovered my own. Watching Cairnholm disappear felt like watching the only remaining key to that mystery sink beneath the dark waves. And then the island was simply gone, swallowed up by a mountain of fog.

As if it had never existed.

*   *   *

Before long the fog caught up to us. By increments we were blinded, the mainland dimming and the sun fading to a pale white bloom, and we turned circles in the eddying tide until we'd lost all sense of direction. Finally we stopped and put our oars down and waited in the doldrummy quiet, hoping it would pass; there was no use going any further until it did.

"I don't like this," Bronwyn said. "If we wait too long it'll be night, and we'll have worse things to reckon with than just bad weather."

Just then, as if it had heard Bronwyn and decided to put us in our place, the weather turned *really* bad. A strong wind blew up, and within moments our world was transformed. The sea around us whipped into white-capped waves that slapped at our hulls and broke into our boats, sloshing cold water around our feet. Next came rain, hard as little bullets on our skin. Soon we were being tossed around like rubber toys in a bathtub.

"Turn into the waves!" Bronwyn shouted, slicing at the water with her oars. "If they broadside you, you'll flip for sure!" But most of us were too spent to row in calm water, let alone a boiling sea, and the rest were too scared to even reach for the oars, so instead we grabbed for the gunwales and held on for dear life.

A wall of water plowed straight at us. We climbed the massive wave, our boat turning nearly vertical beneath us. Emma clung to me and I clung to the oarlock; behind us Hugh and Enoch held onto similarly immoveable objects. When we crested the wave it felt like we were on a rollercoaster—my stomach dropped into my legs as we flipped a hundred and eighty degrees to race down the far side, and as we made that violent turn, everything in our boat that wasn't nailed down—Emma's map, Hugh's bag, the red roller suitcase I'd lugged with me since Florida—went flying over our heads and into the water.

There was no time to consider the things we'd lost. We couldn't even see the other boats. When we'd resumed an even keel, we peered into the maelstrom and screamed our friends' names. There was a terrible moment of silence, but then we heard voices call back to us, and Millard's boat appeared out of the mist, all four passengers aboard, waving their arms at us.

"Are you all right?" I shouted.

"Over there!" they called. "Look over there!"

I saw that they weren't waving hello, but directing our attention to something in the water—the hull of an overturned boat.

Bronwyn and Olive's boat, I realized with numb horror.

"Oh, my God," Emma said.

"We have to get closer!" Hugh shouted, and for a moment we forgot our exhaustion and grabbed the oars to paddle toward it.

We called their names into the wind. We rowed through a tide of clothes ejected from split-open suitcases, every swirling dress and shirt we passed looking like a drowning child. I was soaked and shivering but hardly knew it.

We met Millard's boat at the overturned hull of Bronwyn's and searched the water with panic.

"Where are they?" Horace said. "Oh, if we've lost them . . ."

"Underneath!" Emma said, pointing at the hull. "Maybe they're trapped underneath it!"

I wrested one of my oars from its lock and banged it against the overturned hull. "It's safe now!" I shouted. "Swim out, we'll rescue you!"

At first there was no response, and for a terrible moment I gave up all hope of finding them. But then came a knock in reply and then a fist smashed through and clawed at the air, making us all jump back in surprise.

"It's Bronwyn!" Emma cried. "They're alive!"

With a few more powerful strikes, Bronwyn knocked a star-shaped hole in the hull and pulled herself out. She was panicked, hysterical, shouting with breath she didn't have to spare. Shouting for Olive, who hadn't been under the hull with her. She was still missing.

I stuck out my oar and Bronwyn grabbed it. Emma and I pulled her through the churning water to our boat just as hers sank and vanished beneath the waves.

"Olive—got to get Olive," Bronwyn sputtered once she'd tumbled into the boat. She was shivering, coughing up seawater. She stood up in the pitching boat and pointed into the rain. "There!" she cried. "See it?"

I shielded my eyes from the stinging rain and looked, but all I could see were waves and fog.

"I don't see anything!"

"She's there!" Bronwyn insisted. "The rope!"

Then I saw what she was pointing at: not a flailing girl in the water but a fat thread of woven hemp trailing up from it, barely visible in all the chaos. A strand of taut brown rope extended up from the water and disappeared into the fog. Olive must've been attached to the other end, unseen.

We paddled to the rope and Bronwyn reeled it down, and after a minute Olive appeared from the clouds of fog above our heads, one end of the rope knotted around her waist. Her shoes had fallen off when her boat flipped, but luckily Bronwyn had the foresight to tie Olive to the anchor line, the other end of which was resting on the seafloor below us. If not for that, she surely would've been lost in the clouds, unrecoverable.

Olive threw her arms around Bronwyn's neck and crowed, "You saved me, you saved me!"

They embraced, and watching them put a lump in my throat.

"We ain't out of danger yet," said Bronwyn. "We still got to reach shore before nightfall, else our troubles have only just begun."

*   *   *

The storm had weakened some and the sea's violent chop died down, but the idea of rowing another stroke, even in a perfectly calm sea, was unimaginable to me now. We hadn't made it even halfway to the mainland and already I was hopelessly exhausted. My hands throbbed. My arms felt as heavy as tree trunks. Not only that, but the endless diagonal rocking was having an unpleasant effect on my stomach—and judging from the color of the faces around me, I wasn't the only one.

"We'll rest awhile," Emma said, trying to sound encouraging. "We'll rest and bail out the boats until the fog clears—"

"Fog like this has a mind of its own," said Enoch from the next boat. "It can go days without breaking. It'll be dark in a few hours, and then we'll have to hope we can last until morning without the wights finding us out here. We'll be utterly defenseless."

"And without water," said Hugh.

"Or food," added Millard.

Olive raised both hands in the air and said, "*I* know where it is!"

Everyone turned to look at her. "Where what is?" said Emma.

"Land. I saw it when I was up at the end of that rope." Olive had gotten above the fog, she explained, and briefly caught a clear view of the mainland.

"Fat lot of good that does," grumbled Enoch. "We've circled back on ourselves a half dozen times since you were dangling up there."

"Then reel me up again."

"Are you certain?" Emma asked her. "It's dangerous. What if a wind catches you or the rope snaps?"

Olive's face went steely. "Reel me up," she said again.

"When she gets like this, there's no arguing," said Emma. "Fetch the rope, Bronwyn."

"You're the bravest little girl I ever knew," Bronwyn said, then set to work. She pulled the anchor out of the water and up into our boat, and with the extra length we lashed the two boats together so they couldn't be separated again. Then we reeled Olive back up through the fog.

There was an odd quiet moment where we were all staring at a rope in the clouds, heads thrown back — waiting for a sign from heaven.

Enoch broke the silence. "Well?" he called, impatient.

"I can see it!" came the reply, Olive's voice barely a squeak over the white noise of waves. "Straight ahead!"

"Good enough for me!" Bronwyn said, and while the rest of us clutched our stomachs and slumped uselessly in our seats, she clambered into the lead boat and took the oars and began to row, guided only by Olive's tiny voice, an unseen angel in the sky.

"Left—more left—not that much!"

And like that we slowly made our way toward land, the fog pursuing us always, its long gray tendrils like the ghostly fingers of some phantom hand, ever trying to draw us back.

As if the island couldn't quite let us go, either.